CW00516521

A few comments from tl have read my first bı

Prior to it being publisl

Ashley Butler
What can I say? I'm already a customer for your book when it comes out, so I'll gladly add this one too. One likes to read what one likes to read and having followed you faithfully day by day for a while now.... yes. Any more is welcome. Doesn't matter if fiction or non-fiction since no one can prove otherwise and why should one bother?

Patsy Milo Woods
Sounds like this is going to be another good read, Paul. Looking forward to more chapters - love it!

Moira Ocean
You are a born grass roots writer. Good luck

Piers Boardman
Think this will be a massive success, can't wait to read it all.

Tiny Pratt
Paul, I honestly don't know what to say, a brilliant story, so down to earth, and brilliantly written.

Beryl Spilsbury
You really are a great writer, Paul. You have the knack of keeping the reader totally enthralled. Please get your book published and I'll be one of the first to buy it.

Julie Clack
I'm up for a copy. Best read in ages! You are a very interesting person.

Sue Price
You know we are all hooked on your books. It takes a lot of time and effort to write a good book. I am a prolific reader but could never compose a book from scratch. Keep going. I hope your stuff is published as you have a guaranteed pension here.

Val Sargeson
Absolutely Brilliant Paul, I just love it can we have more?

Barbara Patterson
Yes Paul, this has good potential. When you mentioned The Sweeney, I immediately thought of John Thaw and Denis Waterman bringing up the rear!

Your way of telling the story is good. You should have been a journalist. Enough to be serious and witty. Keep them coming!

Eileen Davies
I think you'll be on a winner with the Peter Slade stories, I've just caught up with your recent postings and find myself wanting more. I think they'll become just as addictive as your memoirs which I'm now also going to catch up with. Keep going, Paul. x

Kathy Waters Brady
Hi Paul, this story is amazing if your instincts tell you, if it's right then, just go for it. I personally think you tell a wonderful story.

Carol Best
I do read a lot of crime fiction Paul, so found this a good read for me, and I like the fact that you gave an insight into Peter's younger years xx

Amanda O'Donoghue
Love this, is very different than your life story, but so readable and I want to read more. You must get this published.

Ken Coates
I'm a person who does not usually like reading. Up to now I've read all the chapters you've written previously and wait eagerly for the next. lol. The chapter I've just read follows the same pattern. I, who doesn't normally read, would certainly consider purchasing the book as I'm sure many others would too. Best wishes to you in whatever you decide.

Stephen Curtis
Paul this really is exciting to read, as well as being able to associate it with that time, just like yesterday. It's got to be a best seller.

Margaret Shillabeer
This is a great story. Keep posting Paul. You've got us all intrigued.

Molly Malone
This really is a 'grip the arms of the chair' story. Fantastic read!

Jen Brown
An intense read. Chilling words. I am looking forward to the next part.

Barbara Griffiths
A very good read. More so because I can remember these times. Frightening!

Christine Salt
Bloody hell Paul, this is serious stuff. Brilliant and compulsive reading.

Margaret White
This is serious reading Paul, makes me shiver reading it. Don't know where it will all end, but I have an idea, it won't be well.

Lorraine Carpenter
Heavy duty stuff!! Decapitation at its best! Wow!!

Janet Whiteman
I am not sure I will sleep tonight after reading this!

Gill Davies
Omg what a read that was I'm hooked.**Marjorie Parrish Isaacs**
Omg this is so exciting.

About the Author

I was born in Poplar, in the East End of London in March 1951, I was the second of four brothers.

Like thousands of East End families, we were to be no exception when it came to being poor, although we were never at the destitute end of the depravation that many of our neighbours were subjected to.

We lived, with our paternal grandparents, in a privately rented Victorian house with no hot water, or indoor toilet facilities. Our only source of heating was from the coal fire that raged throughout the winter in our tiny living room.

Both of my parents worked, throughout our formative years however this seemed to have no long-lasting negative effect upon either myself or any of my siblings.

I appeared to be bright enough to pass my eleven-plus and win a place at the local grammar school. At the beginning of the third year of my secondary education, I went 'off the rails' choosing to be a long-term truant rather than someone looking to leave school with some academic achievements.

Despite his utter despair at my lack of education, my headmaster, a wise man by the name of Mr. Wilks, decided that I was not beyond hope and duly arranged an interview for me as an apprentice journalist with the daily mirror. Much to Mr. Wilks disappointment I turned down the job offer, deciding instead to follow my ambition of becoming a bookmaker. In August 1966 I started work at the head office of East London's largest independent bookmakers. I stuck with this for some nine years, during which time I learnt so much about life, in particular the shady world of gangsters, crooked fellow employees and how to eat and drink to excess with other peoples' money.

After five years 'out of the game' I re-entered the bookmaking business, having my own betting shop in Hackney E8 and for a brief time, a second one close to Southend-on-Sea. After just two years I was forced out by undesirables, hired by my former employers that simply did not want me as a competitor.

After stints of working for the Post Office and British Rail, I fell into a job as a stock controller for a Barking based Freight Forwarder, these days known as 'Logistics' companies.

Having gained enough knowledge, I confidently formed my own logistics business, taking with me one of my former employer's directors as an equal partner. This was to become a mistake as I became embroiled in a bitter and dangerous battle with that former employer, the consequences of which led to my partner and I splitting.

Now on my own, I built the company from a two-man band into one of the UK's foremost logistic companies. In 1986 I teamed up with one of Singapore's premier shipping companies. This association took me to the far corners of the world and gave me access to some of the largest shipping and forwarding companies. I was then the employer of 76 staff within 7 UK offices and had struck up joint ventures with the Singaporeans in Malaysia, Hong Kong, Thailand, Hamburg, and Rotterdam.

In 1992 the whole business came crashing down, its demise being a combination of our German partners scamming us and our bank pulling the plug on our overdraft.

I negotiated a contract with the world's second-largest logistics company, this lasted for two years and would probably have continued had I not succumbed to the constant demands of my former Singaporean partners to join them in a unique opportunity in Vietnam.

In 1995 I left for Saigon, leaving my wife and two boys at home. I had no idea how long I would be away from home although I did manage to wrangle frequent long-haul flights backwards and forwards.

My time in Vietnam came to a sudden halt in 2010, my world fell apart.

In 2012 I began to write about my experiences during my 15 years in this staunch communist country. I am one of very few that has experienced, first hand, the trials, and tribulations of living and working in such a corrupt and hostile environment. The, yet, unpublished book, is entitled 'The Viet Con.'

A lifelong friend, a published author in his own right, encouraged me to write about my early days in East London. I did as he suggested and then shared my ramblings with my 'friends' on Face Book. This book 'A Life Like no Other' has drawn more positive comments than I ever dreamed possible. This book will be published next.

Whilst writing, I recalled the names and memories of several former classmates, a few of them have become famous, some for all the wrong reasons whilst others have achieved notoriety in certain fields. This book is based loosely on one of those characters.

In signing off, I would like to say that I have offered this book to no less than thirty publishers and agents, I received just three replies. Thanks, but no thanks. For those of you that are reading this book, I sincerely thank you.

Paul Lucas

PETER SLADE

The Special Investigator

Paul Lucas

1 - STOYAN PETROV – The Don

Boyan Petrov, the eldest of five siblings, was born on the 16 th of April 1971. Life began for him in a shabby, run-down maternity hospital in the suburbs of Varna, a Port City, close to the shores of the Black Sea, Bulgaria. Back then, the nearby resorts of Sunny Beach and Golden Sands were just beginning to open-up to foreign tourists, although many wealthy Russians tended to spend their summers there.

Boyan, whose name meant 'warrior or fighter' was the first son of Stoyan Petrov, Stoyan meaning 'he who stands firm' and Todorha 'gift of God'. Todorha Petrov had been Todorha Valov before marriage. Stoyan and Todohra had met in Bulgaria's capital city, Sofia, in 1967 and had married and settled in Varna by 1969. Todorha was just eighteen years old when she married and still only twenty when giving birth to Boyan. Stoyan was twenty-two at the time of his first-born. A daughter and three more sons would be added to the Petrov family, who, like most of their neighbours, lived their day-to-day lives in abject poverty.

Bulgaria was still very much in the grip of Communism and was noted as being one of the world's most corrupt countries. Even today, despite no longer flying the red flag, Bulgaria is the most corrupt country in Europe, with a black market in almost everything. From this low point, some of the most violent and sadistic criminals have emerged, with these underworld figures and gangs apparently controlling every aspect (including the government) of life in this long-time satellite of Moscow.

Boyan was four years older than the next born in his family, this was his sister, Halina, which in Bulgarian meant 'calm'. What this meant for Boyan was that he never really grew up with his brothers, when Chavdar 'leader' came into the world, some six years after him, Boyan was already 'streetwise' and led his own kindergarten gang of a dozen like-minded kids, responsible for a good deal of petty crime in the East Side neighbourhood of Varna, known locally as Vasil Levski. Boyan's gang, whose nickname translated as the 'evil ones' were organised, Boyan had inherited his ability to control others from his father, known on the streets as 'the fixer' his fame for violence, extortion and even murder had spread far beyond the metropolitan limits of Varna.

Every day, except Sunday, the 'evil ones' would be wreaking havoc in and around the twelve miles or so of the pristine Varna Beach, with pickpocketing, bag snatching and card scams being the most prevalent of their daily misdemeanours. In 1977 Varna was the Headquarters of the Bulgarian Navy and often the Black Sea Russian Fleet, with its thousands of sailors, would drop anchor for a spot of R & R in Varna. At evening time, Boyan and his juvenile crew would profit immensely from the easy pickings that drunken sailors would offer up to them. During the day their target would be the thousands of mainly Russian holiday makers that basked in the hot sun, they were never interested in fleecing the locals, they had learnt, even at their tender age, that Foreign Currency was much better to have than their own currency, the 'Lev'.

On Sundays the entire Petrov family would be dressed in their finest attire and, as did almost every other family in the area, they would attend the Sunday service at the local Eastern Orthodox Church, which at the time accounted for 86% of all Bulgaria's churchgoers. It was an open secret that up to 80% of the clergy were, in fact, working for the Secret Police. Stoyan was to use this to his advantage on numerous occasions. To the everyday man in the street, these Sunday morning gatherings were akin to watching a scene from the Godfather movie, as every known criminal would be in attendance. They were not there on 'religious grounds' they would use these prayer meetings to collect debts, exchange information and even handover weapons to those members of the congregation that were unable to settle disputes by peaceful means. The Vicar and his two main assistants at the Petrovs' church were an invaluable source of news. Confessions of rivals were relayed to Stoyan in exchange for large amounts of money. The ill-treatment of parishioners, by the clergy, especially young boys and girls was rife, many of the girls were given over to Stoyan for use in his network of illegal brothels, with some, as young as eleven years old, being sent to other countries to continue their forced sexual activities.

Boyan was just ten years old when his father became the Mayor of Varna. When Stoyan Petrov had become Mayor, he had won the election, not because of his strong political beliefs, but because of his notoriety as a fearsome muscleman. He had become famous and feared due to his vice-like grip on all that is bad in Bulgarian society, only a very few would dare vote against him when he stood for office, most of those disappeared once Stoyan draped the heavy gold chain around his thick-set neck. His father's rise-up the political ladder gave Boyan even more respect out on the streets, he was untouchable. At the age of twelve, he became a pimp, controlling several local prostitutes, whilst also raking in money from the many illegal parking lots that his father had passed down to him.

By 1986 Stoyan was very much within the radar of the polit-bureau in Sofia, he had by then become the 'Don' of Varna and was very much enlarging his network to control the provinces immediately adjacent to Varna. Whilst the communist hierarchy allowed this to continue, on the basis that dealing with one 'mad man' was far better than dealing with several, they were not at all happy with Petrov's intrusion into the very lucrative development of the burgeoning economy in and around Sunny Beach and Golden Sands as, for years, all of the permission needed to build hotels, restaurants, night clubs and associated tourist facilities had to be granted by the 'committee' in Sofia. Stoyan, by virtue of his status as Mayor, had been taking enormous amounts of USD in return for the right of investors, mainly Russian, to build whatever they wished, along the miles and miles of the large, sandy beaches, that year by year, were attracting more and more holiday makers from all over Europe.

Boyan, now aged 15 was the apple of his mother's eye. He had little or no education, however his mother adored him and praised him for having the same group of friends for nearly ten years. She knew that he was involved with the wrong kind of people, but she ignored this as his father always assured her that Boyan would be someone for her to be proud of one day. On the day of Boyan's 16th birthday, April 16th, 1987, his parents put on a lavish party for him, Todorha had no idea as to the level of authority that both her husband and eldest son had achieved. As Stoyan raised his glass, in front of nearly 150 guests, half of whom were well-known underworld figures, a gun was pointed at his head, Todorha instinctively put herself in the line of fire, there was one shot and Todorha fell to the ground, she died instantly.

It had been Bagatur 'hero' Bogdanov that had pulled the trigger, even before he could fire the second shot, he was knocked to the floor, he knew immediately that his days were numbered, it would only be the level of torture that he would be subjected to that would determine exactly how much longer he lived. There was no shortage of volunteers when it came to whom would be Bagatur's executioner. He was removed from the party and taken to a small garage just outside Varna, Stoyan had given the order that no one was to touch him until he, himself, was able to attend. Bagatur was taken away by four of Stoyan's close associates, it did not seem to matter that a high-ranking official, the Chief of Police and some top brass from the navy and army were in attendance, they all understood that the perpetrator of Stoyan's wife death had to be dealt with.

There was a period of ten days between Todorha's slaying and the ending of the mourning, during that time Bagatur had been tied, gagged, and suspended from the overhead pulley in the filthy dirty workshop that had seen its fair share of atrocities during Stoyan's reign of terror. At 11.00am on the 27th, April 1987, Stoyan, his eldest son, Boyan and four gang members entered the workshop, the two guards, that had given Bagatur only water during his time in captivity left, silently, and waited, guns tucked menacingly into their waistband, outside. Stoyan gestured to one of his men to lower the naked killer of his wife to a position where his feet were firmly flat upon the grease-laden garage floor. Stoyan approached Bagatur, putting the tip of his nose against that of his captive and in a calm, almost apologetic voice he asked Bagatur,

'Who was it that gave the order to assassinate me?' Bagatur did not flinch.

'So, you want to be a hero, just like your name, do you?' Let me tell you, if you give up the name of the people that sent you, then you will live, if you do not, then you will die, however you will not die a quick and painless death, as my wife did, you will die slowly, it will take one week to kill you, the choice is yours and yours alone, my friend.'

Bagatur smiling, replied,

'If I were to name all of those that wanted you dead then you would have to stand and listen for one whole day.'

He then spat into Stoyan's face, yet despite the provocation, Stoyan remained calm and unresponsive.

Stoyan took his son's arm and led him through the half gate to the outside and asked him to wait there until he called him back in. Boyan obeyed his father. Stoyan re-entered the workshop, he picked up a pair of plyers from one of the benches, he spoke to two of his comrades, they each started up a fork truck, and drove them so that they were either side of the man that was about to face his first taste of pain, one fork of each truck was lowered onto Bagatur's feet, pinning him firmly to the concrete floor, he screamed in pain, however this scream was to be a whisper in comparison with what came next.

'I will ask you again, hero, who ordered my death?'

To everyone's surprise, Bagatur once again spat into Stoyan's face. Stoyan opened the jaws of the plyers, engaged Bagatur's testicles and closed them shut. The crunching of the condemned man's left testicle was plainly heard. The scream that followed sent a shudder down the spines of the four hard men. Stoyan remained unaffected. Giving the single testicular murderer a minute to compose himself, Stoyan once again touched noses with the man that would not give up his pay masters. Stoyan stared calmly into Bagatur's eyes and asked,

'Do you wish to lose the whole of your manhood?'

Bagatur remained tight-lipped. The second testicle was squeezed and flattened and whilst he still stood upright, Bagatur passed out. One of Stoyan's minders carefully dragged over a small tin bath, which was full of liquid, he picked up one of Bagatur's testicles from the floor, and when the now 'bollock-less' killer came round, the testicle was thrown into the bath, it dissolved immediately.

Bagatur, sensing that he would, bit by bit, suffer the same fate as his once attached manhood, started to murmur, Stoyan stopped him, he then took a small recording device from his pocket and asked Bagatur to start again.

Bagatur did not hesitate, he gave up three men, all known to Stoyan. The five torturers went outside, the two guards returned to watch Bagatur. Boyan got into the imported black Range Rover with his father, two of the gang climbed into the back, the remaining two baddies followed in a 1960s East German-built Trabant. Their massive frames filling the whole of the available space inside. Twenty minutes later the two cars pulled up outside a small hotel, situated on Chinar Street, just north of the City Centre. Stoyan instinctively knew that two of the men fingered by Bagatur would be inside the hotel, after all Stoyan had given this property to them back in 1985, as a reward for many years of loyal service. For a while now, word on the street was that there was a contract out on Stoyan, however as he had scores of enemies, he was unable to know with any certainty exactly whom it was that wished to take over his empire. Boyan was asked to wait in the car, as lookout, whilst Stoyan and his four most trusted men went inside. The young female receptionist was about to ask if she could help when she received a full knuckle of closed fingers firmly against her open mouth, she would not be calling the hunted men to alert them of the pending threat against them.

The hotel consisted of seven floors, with ten rooms to each of them. The eighth floor was configured as a penthouse, with a rooftop garden, this is where Boris Bachev and Dimitar Denev lived. That was apart from when they were in hiding, at those times they hid in separate 'safe houses' on the west side of Varna. Stoyan did not bother with knocking, he managed to cave the door in with one bone-crunching shoulder barge. The two wanted men were stark naked, on their backs, and laid on top of a plush, pure white rug that covered almost all the tiled floor. On top of their middle-aged and rounded bodies were two young females, neither of whom were old enough to have left school. Boris and Dimitar had well and truly been caught with 'their pants down.' The scene froze as Nikolay Nikolov, Stoyan's longest serving and most trusted lieutenant, a man that had been at Stoyan's side ever since they were kids, walked the ten paces over to where all of the action was taking place, he calmly took out his gun, he fired two shots, both to the heads of the poor innocent girls, they each slumped forward, blood pouring from their wounds and onto the two petrified men, who had by now turned their attention away from the girls. Stoyan took the video camera from its tripod and handed it to one of his men.

Stoyan, never a man to be ruffled, sat calmly in the expensive white, leather sofa, he gestured for the two naked former gang members to kneel in front of him, covering their now limp manhood with their hands, the two men flinched as Stoyan reached inside his jacket pocket, taking out the small recorder, not the gun that the blood-soaked men had feared. Stoyan pressed play, the words of Bagatur could be clearly heard, 'Boris Bachev' Dimitar Denev and Petar Paskov.

Stoyan shut off the recorder and looking at the two vulnerable men in front of him, he asked,

'Why?'

Not a word was spoken in reply. At gunpoint Boris and Dimitar were instructed to dress, they were marched out of the penthouse and waited with Stoyan and two of his aides at the lift door. All five men took the lift to the ground floor. The two remaining men piled all the furniture, including the beds, into a huddle and set fire to them. As Nickolay passed the reception, the young girl made the biggest mistake of her life, she raised her head from the floor. Nickolay lifted the flap that gave entry to where the girl lay, he fired one shot, directly into her brain. Stoyan gave him a puzzled look,

'She saw us, boss.'

These were the only words spoken until they were outside in the street.

Nickolay had asked one of the pyrotechnicians to find and bring down the keys to the white Range Rover that had belonged to Boris Bachev. Possession is nine-tenths of the law, even in Bulgaria, the Range Rover would now belong to Nickolay. Boris and Dimitar were now parted, each being put firmly into one of the gangster's favourite modes of transport. The old and broken Trabant, which had been stolen earlier in the day, was simply left behind. Boyan remained quiet in the car that was being driven by his father for the whole twenty-minute journey back to the garage where the tortured Bagartur had suffered the loss of two important pieces of his undercarriage. Upon entering the garage both Bachev and Dimitar were visibly disturbed by what they saw, they tried to protest their innocence, but their pleas were ignored by Stoyan, he simply asked his merry men to secure his two latest captives in place until he once again returned.

Bachev was dragged, against his will, to a long wooden work bench, his right arm was placed into a steel vice which was then tightened until he began to feel extreme discomfort. Nickolay picked up a hammer and lifted a six-inch nail from the floor, and whilst two of his comrades held Bachev's left hand flat on the wooden bench, Nickolay drove the nail through his hand until only the flat end of it was visible. Dimitar, constantly pleading his innocence, was laid on the floor, his hands were secured to one of the wooden uprights that held the bench in place, his feet were tied together and the remainder of the rope was fastened to a towing hook on the back of one of the fork trucks, one of the guards then slowly drove the truck forward, until Dimitar was lifted from the ground, the fork truck stopped and its engine was turned off, just at the point that Dimitar was beginning to feel the pain of being torn apart. Stoyan, Nickolay and two of his men jumped into the newly acquired Range Rover and drove away, leaving young Boyan to oversee the continued incarceration of the three captives.

Fifteen minutes after leaving the garage, the four members of Varna's most feared organised crime family entered the night club on Boulevard Primorski, a long wide, sweeping road that ran the length of Varna's largest and most populated beach. There was to be no resistance from the club owner, a well-known drug importer and former 'enforcer' for Stoyan Petrov, as he, Petar Paskov was sat at the bar, all alone, except for the tall leggy Russian beauty that had been his lover for the past couple of years. Whilst this lack of people was good news for Stoyan, it was absolutely the worst-case scenario for Olga from Moscow as Nickolay brought her down with one shot from a pistol that now sported a silencer on the end of its slim, black barrel. Holding the gun firmly upon Paskov's now sweating temple, he was frog-marched outside and into the waiting Range Rover. It had been so easy for Stoyan to round-up the three men that Bagatur had given up, all that remained was to get to the truth of whom it was that wanted him out of the way.

It was now the hottest part of the day, Nickolay, without warning, pulled up at an ice cream kiosk, got out of the car and bought four ice cream cornets, there was not to be one for their prisoner, Petar Paskov. To an impartial 'onlooker' this would have been an extraordinary thing to do, however in the minds of these members of Varna's Mafia, today was just an ordinary day, no different to many other days in their strange world.

At around 4.15pm, the Range Rover and its five occupants pulled up in front of the rusty corrugated doors that led into the garage. Stoyan, Nickolay and the largest of the thugs manhandled Paskov into the garage whilst the fourth of the muscle men parked the car in a scrapyard that adjoined the building. Paskov was shaken to the core when he saw the three other men, in their various 'pre-torture' positions. Stoyan brought an old wooden chair over and invited Paskov to sit, he did. Moments later he was securely tied to the chair, unable to move either his hands or feet. Taking the hammer and two of the same-sized nails that had been used to pin Bachev to the bench, Stoyan, without words or the slightest emotion, smashed one of the nails straight through the right thigh of one of his most trusted, former associates. The force that Stoyan used to bring the hammer down was such that the nail penetrated not only Paskov's thigh but the thick wooden seat of the chair as well. Looking straight into his former friend's deep blue eyes, Stoyan asked him,

'Was it you that ordered my death?'

Before Paskov could finish his reply, which was going to be,

'Go to hell, you 'bastard.'

The second nail went through his left thigh and came out at least an inch underneath the seat.

It had not gone unnoticed by Stoyan that his 16-year-old son had not in the least been fazed by the events that he had witnessed. The thought 'chip off the old block' had momentarily gone through his head. A large bottle of vodka and a funnel, normally used to pour oil into an engine, were produced. Only Stoyan knew what was going to happen next. He walked over to the suspended Dimitar, one of the guards sidled onto the fork truck. Stoyan forced the funnel into Dimitar's mouth and began to pour the vodka into it, the force with which Stoyan was using to hold the funnel in place prevented the user of underaged girls from ejecting the drink from his mouth. Stoyan withdrew the funnel from Dimitar's mouth and asked,

'Now we are going to do a few stretching exercises, my friend. Only your confession of the involvement in my wife's murder can save you from the pain that no man should have to suffer.'

Dimitar said nothing in reply. Stoyan gave the signal, the fork truck inched forward, Dimitar screamed, sounds of bones and organs being separated inside his body could be heard, Stoyan raised his hand, the fork truck stopped. I will ask you again my friend,

'Did you order my death?'

It was possible at this point, that Dimitar was unable to reply. Stoyan again forced the funnel into Dimitar's mouth and emptied the remaining contents of the vodka bottle into it. This time, just a finger gesture was all that was required to start the fork truck on its journey forward. The first part of Dimitar's body to succumb to this terrible ordeal, was his arms, they came away from the body and hung, limply, underneath the long wooden bench, the remainder of his body fell onto the petrol-laden floor of the garage, leaving a trail of blood and gore until the fork truck came to rest. At this point Dimitar was still alive, Stoyan stepped forward and put one bullet into his head. Nickolay held out his hand and his 'brothers in arms' placed money into it. They had all bet on which part of Dimitar would be the weakest, Nickolay had chosen the arms, he was now five hundred USD richer. It was noticeable that young Boyan did not turn away during any part of the atrocity that he had just witnessed.

It was now 5.00pm and time for everyone to go home for the day, everyone except the two guards, Bagatur, Bachev and Paskov, the latter being just unable to get up from his chair. Turning his head as he exited the half door that led to the forecourt, Stoyan looked back at the three remaining captives, smiled, and said,

'See you all in the morning, we shall have some more fun.'

When they arrived home, there were two armoured vehicles and a car, that Stoyan knew belonged to the Chief of Police, parked just outside the heavily fortified house. The policeman, who had witnessed Todorha's killing, just under two weeks previously, approached Stoyan and out of earshot of anyone else, informed him of the following.

'I know that you have picked up the four men that you believe were responsible for your wife's murder, but believe me, Stoyan, when I tell you that it was not they that ordered the execution, the order to rid Varna of your presence came from a place much higher up the ladder, please let them go and I will make sure that you get the right people.'

The Chief of Police had been on Stoyan's payroll ever since he came to power some six years earlier. During those six-years, he had been able to protect Stoyan from the many accusations that had been levied at his door, this time however, he was telling Stoyan that his hands were tied and that he himself had been 'warned off' by the people that hide in the shadows within the seat of power in Sofia. Stoyan thanked the Chief for the information and together with Boyan, they entered the grounds of the complex they called home. Once inside the sanctuary of his home, Boyan asked his father what he was going to do. Stoyan put one finger to his lips and beckoned Boyan to follow him, together they entered the large summer house, at the back of the garden, that Todorha had built three years since. it was her favourite place, her hideaway. Stoyan also used this building for meetings away from prying ears, he had been convinced for some time that his house had been 'bugged' the summer house was void of any electronics, it was an 'empty shell' where it was impossible to hide bugging devices without them being visible to all. Two chairs and a small table were brought into the pine-clad building, father and son sat down, a bottle of vodka, a beer and two glasses were placed upon the table by a female maid, another female gently put down a thick, leather-clad, diary. Stoyan began,

'My son, I believe my life to be in grave danger, I had hoped that I would not need to have this conversation with you for at least another five years, however time is now of the essence. Within this book are the operations of the business, the monies that have been made, where the money is kept and most importantly, exactly whom you can trust. You must take this book now, apart from me, only Nikolay knows of its existence, Nikolay is the only person you should ever trust. Apart from Nikolay, this book should never be shown to anyone else, I have discussed everything with him, he will guide you until you become 21 years old, you should always listen to him, he is, as you know, more than a brother to me. It was never my wish to involve you in my world, however you have taken your own path towards danger and upon my death, you will take over. I have let it be known that you will succeed me as the Mayor of Varna when I pass. You will be unopposed; however, Nikolay will hold the position until you become a man.'

With tears in his eyes, Boyan responded to his father's words,

'Dad, I have just lost my mum, why do I have to lose you? You must have enough money to get out, retire from the business, please Dad, we can go somewhere else, overseas even.'

With his own tears visibly falling down his sunburnt cheeks, Stoyan looked into his young son's eyes and concluded,

'This is not possible my son, once you are in the kind of business that we now find ourselves in, the only escape is by death, history shows this to be so, there are only a few examples of Mafia bosses retiring to a life of leisure in the Caribbean.'

Boyan understood, he picked up the book, left the summer house and retired to his room.

The next morning, Nikolay arrived at the house at 8.00am, he and Stoyan drank coffee, at 8.30 Boyan joined them and five minutes later they left the house, destination 'torture chamber.' At 9.05, two men and a boy entered the garage, the two guards had been let go by Stoyan's four other close gang members, Boris was half-asleep, slumped over the arm that was held tightly by the vice, a puddle of congealed blood surrounded his nailed down left hand. Paskov was slumped forward on the chair that Stoyan had nailed him to, some seventeen hours previously. Bagatur, still naked, still slightly suspended and ball-less, looked to have succumbed to his painful torture, however one slap of his face by Stoyan was enough to bring him around. Without a single word being spoken, Stoyan walked over to Boris, placed his gun firmly against his temple, and fired. He took ten paces to his left and inflicted the same end-of-life punishment upon Paskov. Petar Paskov fell sideways and then, still tied, and nailed to the wooden chair, assumed the final position of his life. There was an eerie silence in the garage as Stoyan turned his attention to the executor of his beloved Todorha, putting his gun safely back into his waistband, he placed his hand under the chin of Bagatur, lifting his head in order that he could look at him whilst he spoke, he said to his one-time trusted gang member,

'You cannot die such a quick and painless death, as it was you that pulled the trigger and sent my wife to heaven, for you my friend, there awaits a death that no one here will ever forget. I now know that Bagatur, Boris and Dimitar were not responsible for arranging my death, it was the DS (Committee for State Security) that paid you to kill me, and it would have been much better for you if you had done so, to have killed Todorha, albeit by accident, means that you cannot die by a single bullet only.'

Nikolay knew instinctively what would be coming next, he walked over to a large steel toolbox, lifted the heavy lid, and took out a machete, the blade of which was both pristine and as sharp as the tongue of a woman scorned. He handed the machete to Boyan, the 16-year-old did not bat an eyelid, he knew exactly what he had to do. He purposely moved very slowly towards Bagatur, held the machete upright in front of him, as if he were a Samurai Warrior, he then touched Bagatur's left cheek with the pointed end, drawing a small amount of blood, he did the same to his right cheek, Nikolay stepped in and held Bagatur's hand, pulling his arm straight out in front of him, as he did so, and without hesitation, Boyan brought the weapon down with such force that not only did he sever Bagatur's right arm, he also almost severed his right foot, Bagatur passed out, blood was emanating from his two wounds at an alarming rate. Stoyan took the machete from his son and passed it to one of the onlookers, asking that he clean it up and return it to its resting place. As he turned towards the half door, he said,

'Burn them all.'

It took the newspapers four days to report the sadistic killing and burning of the four men, the press named the two men that were now in custody for their executions, neither Stoyan, Nikolay or Boyan were cited as being involved, the two men that were named were members of a rival gang, from another province, a war over drugs had broken out between them and they had taken action, the two men were found dead in their cells whilst awaiting the court hearing.

Just prior to Todorha's murder, Stoyan had been summoned to Sofia to discuss with the 'committee' his ever-increasing foothold on the building and development of the resorts close to Varna. Whilst he knew that he had no choice, other than to go, he was also now aware of the DS involvement in his activities, he had been warned by the Chief of Police to be careful whilst in Sofia. On the 5th of May 1987, Stoyan was driven to Varna Airport by Nikolay, Boyan sat in the back. They were flanked by two cars, each containing four of the gang's most senior members, they trusted no one. Arriving at the doors of the departure lounge, Stoyan, Nikolay and Boyan left the Range Rover, one of the following men got in and drove it away. Boyan carried his father's small suitcase, he would be away for just two nights. After a drink in the airport bar, Boyan and Nikolay watched as Stoyan disappeared through to the departure gate. They then hurried to the large glass windows that overlooked the area where the triple-engine Tupolev 154 was parked prior to its departure. They saw Stoyan climb the aluminium steps and board the aircraft, he would arrive in Sofia one and a half hours after take-off. Stoyan would be met in the VIP lounge of Sofia Airport by a government official that would drive him to his hotel, the following morning he would be taken to the Headquarters of the Bulgarian Communist Party.

When Nikolay, Boyan and the other members of the welcome home party arrived at Varna Airport, three days later, there was no sign of Stoyan. They checked with the airline, they were told that no such person was booked on the flight that had arrived just thirty minutes previously, there were, however, another three flights due in from Sofia that day. They waited, a full six hours elapsed, Stoyan did not arrive. Stoyan had not been able to leave any details of where he was staying or who was meeting him when he arrived in Sofia, he had simply been told that 'everything had been arranged for him.' The next day Boyan endeavoured to contact the Bulgarian Communist Party, he was asked to 'hold' whilst enquiries were made, he was cut off before anyone came back to the phone. This happened several times, Boyan was becoming extremely anxious, he indicated to Nikolay that he would go to Sofia to find his father, Nikolay, charged with protecting Boyan, forbade him from doing so, telling him that he would meet with the Chief of Police in the hope of getting some information. He met with the Chief that evening.

At around lunchtime the following day, the Chief of Police informed Nikolay that, according to the Ministry of the Interior, Stoyan had not arrived on the flight that he was supposed to be on, the official that was due to receive him confirmed that he waited for one hour before realising that his guest had not disembarked from the aircraft. One week later, it was reported that a body had been found, in dense forest, directly under the flight path of the Varna to Sofia route. The body could not be identified due to the amount of it that had been eaten by wildlife. Through his trusted contacts in Sofia, Varna's Chief of Police told Nikolay that the body was without doubt, that of Stoyan, he had been pushed from the plane during the flight, he had been the only business class passenger on board that day.

2 - TANG TAO – The Escapee

Tang Tao had an uneventful birth, being born on the 6th of June 1949, and whilst there would be little of note surrounding his entry into the world, he had the distinction of having been born six years after the Chinese Communist Party became the 'single ruling party' of China. Tang Tao was born in Guangzhou in the province of Canton, the recorded population of this major port city on the yellow river was just 2,567,000, by 2018 this had risen to 14,904,000. Both of Tang Tao's parents had been incarcerated and subsequently died from starvation after being rounded up by the local militia for touting 'anti-subversive propaganda' against the only party that Chinese Citizens could vote for. Tang Tao, at the age of two, had been fortunate enough to have been rescued by his grandparents prior to his own parent's arrest. Tang Tao was taken to Hekou, then a small trading post just a few miles from the Vietnamese border, his grandparents, whilst not poverty-stricken, were by no means opulent, although, with the help of other family members they were able to scrape together enough money to send, at the age of five, the young Tang Tao to school.

The young orphan excelled at school, having a natural ability to learn, albeit the teaching was of a low level and was mainly centred around the brainwashing of children to accept the concept of communism. After school, he would help his grandfather in the tiny lock-up shop that traded tea. The grandfather would 'swap' the tea for a whole host of other products, which he would then sell to the local Chinese community. The trading part of the business took place right on the China-Vietnam border, selected traders from China were allowed to enter Vietnam, at Lao Cai and their Vietnamese counterparts could enter Hekou, the large square where this trade-off took place was half in China and half in Vietnam, making it a kind of a neutral zone. The square was heavily fortified, with armed guards from both Countries surrounding the complex. Tang Tao often dreamed of escaping to Vietnam, he detested the communist way of life, a life that had been bestowed upon him and everyone else by the dictatorship that controlled one of the most oppressed regions of the World. Even at such a tender age, Tang Tao was aware that it was the 'regime' that had taken his parents away from him. In the ensuing years, he would learn all he could about life in Vietnam. Although books were difficult to come by, he would talk to his grandfather's Vietnamese trading partners, they would teach him the Vietnamese language and he would do his best to share his own dialect of Cantonese with them.

By the age of eleven Tang Tao had learnt that North Vietnam was also a staunch communist country, having declared itself independent from French rule shortly after World War 2. He had also heard that Ho Chi Minh (Uncle Ho) had fought the French Army after they tried to take their former colony back and that in 1954 the Geneva Conference had recognised Vietnam as an Independent Country, free from colonial rule. In Geneva it was provisionally agreed that Vietnam be divided into a North and South zone, the North became the Democratic Republic of Vietnam, and the South was known as the State of Vietnam and remained under the control of the French. India, Canada, and Poland were the members of the International Commission responsible for the setting up of 'free elections' however, the South of Vietnam had not signed the Geneva Accord and consequently refused to take part in any elections that involved the communists in the North. In retaliation for the South's refusal to accept the Communist rule of law. The North, led by Uncle Ho and backed by both the Russians and the Chinese, decided to take the South by force. Hostilities commenced in 1955, the United States, fearful of the spread of Communism backed the South, as did Australia, South Korea, and Thailand. Laos and Cambodia, also being Communist regimes, allied themselves to North Vietnam.

Having acquired as much knowledge as he could in respect of what was happening in Vietnam, Tang Tao made his decision to escape from China, his aim was to get to Saigon, which he had read somewhere, was known as 'The Pearl of the Orient.' The war had not really reached the far North of Vietnam, Tang Tao had no idea of what to expect should he manage to venture Southwards, however, he had made up his mind, he informed only his grandfather of his plan, which was, to get to Saigon, some three days away by train, from Hanoi. He had no idea how long it would take him on foot. In December 1960, the eleven-year-old, Tang Tao, with the help of a trader from Haiphong (the major port in the North of Vietnam) entered Vietnam on the back of a rusty old French motorbike, the border guard that let them through having been bribed, bit by bit, over several months. The journey, including stopovers, took forty hours. In Haiphong, Tang Tao boarded a coal ship, the captain of which had assisted many others to escape to the South, he was not a sympathiser, he simply did it for the money. The ship only went as far as Cat Son on the Ben Hai River, as this was the most Southerly point of the 17th Parallel, a fictitious line on the map, drawn up by the Americans. North Vietnamese ships were not able to ply their trade South of this point.

Disembarkation at this port accounted for just one-third of Tang Tao's planned journey.

Armed with just his geographical knowledge of Vietnam, retained entirely in his head, Tang Tao waited until darkness before he made good his escape from the Port, his next obstacle would be the Ben Hai River, across which there was just one foot bridge and this was heavily guarded, with soldiers from two countries on either side. After a walk of about thirty minutes, ahead in the distance Tang Tao could see a dim light and the red-lit ends of several cigarettes. Sliding backwards down the bank, out of sight of the small gathering of Vietcong Soldiers (North Vietnamese Army) he slipped silently into the water, swimming as slowly and calmly as he could, having practised every day for months in the small lake close to his grandparent's house. He was lucky, there were no signs of searchlights and from what he could hear the guards seemed to be drunk. He dived, without a sound, below the surface of the water until he was directly under the bamboo and rope-constructed bridge, he then came up for air, careful not to expel any audible sound. Now with his head above the water line, he swam under the bridge until he was about 100 feet from the riverbank, he then repeated his dive, swam underwater to his left, counting in his head until he reached 95, then, as slowly as he could, he raised his head and turned himself around to face the soldiers of the South Vietnamese Army. Fortunately for him, Tang Tao had managed to emerge from the river without alerting any of the guards, he pulled himself onto the grass-covered verge, twenty seconds later he was hidden by the dense jungle that grew, in abundance, along most of Vietnam's numerous waterways.

Once he was far enough away from discovery by the soldiers, he carefully broke off a dozen large banana leaves and made himself as comfortable as he could, before his intended sleep. He rested with one eye open, wary of the snakes and other reptiles that were sharing the jungle floor with him. He had been blissfully unaware of the fact that fighting between the respective armies of the North and South was becoming more prevalent by the day. He did wonder where his allegiance should lie, he was after all a Chinese Communist, he had escaped to the Communist North of Vietnam, however he dreamed of being in the 'free' South, he would not be changing his mind, he wanted to get to Saigon, in crossing the Ben Hai River he had achieved the second part of his journey, he still had a long way to go.

Having not eaten since leaving the coal ship, some sixteen hours earlier, the young, growing Tang Tao was beginning to feel hungry, he had drank the last of his water before entering the river, he could not simply find a road and thumb a lift, as one, there would be only motorbikes and army vehicles and he could not dare to be recognised as an 'escapee.' His memory had told him that he should head for the coast, he would find many small fishing villages along the way, he had no paperwork at all, there was nothing upon his person that might allude as to whom he was or where he came from, however his Vietnamese was poor, he would have to avoid any chit-chat along the way. For months before he made good his escape, he had planned out a route, this plan was only in his head, he knew that his first aim would be to get to Hue, there were three possible routes, one was via Highway No. 1, but this would be far too dangerous, there were two other roads, one hugged the coastline and the other ran parallel, albeit 10 km inland. Any of these routes, on foot, were around 100 km long and would take him at least 20 hours, without stopping. Tang Tao decided on the coastal road as he figured that he would always know where he was, and that the sea should always be on his left-hand side.

Following the bank of the river, it took him just half an hour to reach the sea, he turned right when there was nowhere else to go and fortunately for him, he saw a white painted post by the side of the clay-covered road that read 'Bai tam Gio Hai – 16 km.' Although he was weak, from lack of sustenance, he was buoyed by the fact that he could probably make it to 'Bai tam' in around three hours or so. The unmade road that he was treading was quiet, whenever he heard the 'pop-pop' of a motorcycle he ducked into the undergrowth, he was however, unable to know when a bicycle or someone on foot was approaching, he encountered his first sighting of a South Vietnamese person at about one hour into his walk. As the three children walked towards him, they mouthed 'xin chao.' Tang Tao knew from his trading friends in the North that this meant 'hello' he replied accordingly. He was to encounter several more locals before, standing on a ridge, he could see 'Bai tam' in the distance, he realised that no one was taking any notice of him, after all a South Chinese looks exactly like a Vietnamese. His main problem now was the language barrier.

Bai tam was a small, quiet, fishing village. There was no harbour, fishing boats, large and small simply rested on the beach, awaiting the next tide. Palm trees lined the white sand, the South China Sea was pristine. Tang Tao approached a small boat, children were gathering the fishing nets in, there was a fire on the beach and two young girls were gutting and cooking fish, as he drew near to them he was offered a piece from a rusty tray, he gladly accepted, he pointed to a large pot of water, one of the girls dipped a metal cup inside, filled it and gave it to the grateful young boy. Several other youngsters gathered around, they were all talking to him at the same time, he just smiled in response. Dusk was nigh, there were no adults, he presumed they were all sleeping after a long day's fishing, he was not being quizzed by anyone as to where he had come from or where he might be going, as night-time fell most of the children slept, right there, on the beach, Tang Tao did likewise.

At 5.00am he was awoken by one of the children and immediately joined the others in pushing several of the boats into the inrushing tide, three elderly men were in the last boat to enter the sea, the last of the boys jumped in, Tang Tao did likewise, they headed out to sea, powered by the smallest and loudest of engines. Once they were away from the shore, the children scooped rice from a large clay bowl and boiled vegetables from another, Tang Tao followed suit. After one hour the engine shut down, the nets were thrown overboard and the local children took to the sea to stretch them out, they then dived downwards, attached steel hooks to the bottom row of the netting and returned to the surface. Tang Tao looked on, slightly worried that he would be asked to perform this task, fortunately he was not. The three elderly men slept, one hour later the boys dived into the sea, gathered up the steel hooks and then helped bring in the fish-laden nets. The fish were landed, the nets were untangled and the whole process began again. Tang Tao helped the others to sort the fish into sizes, there were three separate sections at the rear of the boat, small, medium, and large. Tiny fish were returned to the sea. After four catches they returned to the beach, women from the village greeted them and after examining each individual fish they placed them into large wicker baskets, attached the baskets to bamboo poles and carried them, two at a time across their shoulders. The men sat outside their straw huts and drank rice-wine, passing out shortly after. Tang Tao's evening replicated the one before.

The escapee was long gone before the others were up the next morning. He would continue to follow the coast road, after an hour he arrived at Tan Loi, a much larger village than the one he had just spent two nights at. He had arrived at the Thach Han River, he could see that the bridge was heavily guarded on both sides, people were being asked to show their ID cards, the bridge was around one and a half km in length, to the side of the bridge there was a ferry, there were hundreds of passengers, all carrying goods. Melting into the crowd, he gestured to an elderly lady, volunteering to carry a large bale of material for her, she readily agreed. Lifting the bale onto his shoulder, he turned his head sideways, hiding most of his face and boarded the ferry alongside the old lady, he was not challenged by anyone. Ten minutes later the ferry arrived on the Phu Hoi side of the river. Once off the ferry, he continued to help the elderly lady, she reminded him of his grandmother, momentarily he wished he had not left her. Stopping at her 'almost fallen down shack,' she gave Tang Tao some pork knuckle and a bottle of cloudy water, they nodded their mutual appreciation and the boy from China headed South, deciding to keep walking until darkness began to fall. This plan was thwarted when at 1.30pm he arrived in Bai Bien Thanh Hoi, he had walked just 9 km in two hours. Just away from the beach he spotted a pile of coconuts under a tree, he crawled along the jungle floor, out of sight of the few people that were carrying items to and from the fishing boats that had maybe returned home early from the days fishing. As he took one of the coconuts from the pile, a hand grabbed at his dirty, worn-out shirt-collar, the man that was looking down at him had facial skin that looked as if it had been grafted from a dead Rhino. The man held out his hand as if to say, 'you can have the coconut, but you must pay me for it.' Tang Tao rose, even at eleven years of age he was taller and heavier than the old man, he legged it, coconut tightly within his grasp. He had put just 50 metres between himself and the grim reaper before he was taken completely off his feet by the broom belonging to an old lady, who facially, looked like she had already died. When he opened his eyes, the two elderly people had been joined by four others, they were equally as old, they were all looking down upon him. The old lady handed Tang Tao a tin cup containing water and gestured for him to drink it, he did. Soon he was sat upright on the white sand that surrounded their bamboo and banana leaf house, they brought him a bowl of Pho (soup) which he drank as if he had not eaten for a fortnight. As he sat, wondering what might happen to him, women holding babies stopped at his feet and stared, two pregnant 'mums to be' arrived, they touched his forehead and then disappeared. As dusk arrived around twenty fishing boats came back from their day's toil, the quiet beach came alive to the sound of scores of children and around forty men, for the next two hours Tang Tao was visited by everyone that lived in this small hamlet by the sea.

Waking from the best night's sleep (in a hammock tied to the trunks of two palm trees) that he had had since he had left China, a grey-haired old man sat on the sand beneath Tang Tao. Realising that the young visitor was awake, the man spoke to him, very softly, in Cantonese. Tang Tao was both excited and worried by the fact that here was someone talking to him in his native tongue. He thought that he had been exposed and that the Police would be there at any moment, whereupon he would be hung up by his neck at the nearest tree, he need not have worried as his visitor quickly reassured him that he was in no danger. Tang Tao was to spend the next six months at Bai Bien Thanh Hoi, he worked the fishing boats by day and spent the evenings with both the children and the men as, at his age, he was neither one nor the other. The Cantonese-speaking man, Mr. Lo, acted as his interpreter, whilst also teaching him Vietnamese. Before he left, he would be 90% proficient in his newly adopted tongue.

On June 6th, 1961, Tang Tao was twelve years old, in the Western World he would have been regarded as a boy, in Vietnam he was now a man. The whole village celebrated his birthday, he was humbled by their love and affection. That evening, Mr. Lo informed Tang Tao that, in the early hours of the following morning, he would be taken, by their largest fishing boat to Hue, which, under French rule was once the Capital of Vietnam.

A frightened Tang Tao asked Mr. Lo,

'Have I done something wrong?'

'Of course not, but the war is coming ever closer to this part of Vietnam, you have no papers, if caught you may be treated as an enemy of the North of Vietnam, which would mean your certain death. We think it is time for you to make your journey South.' Mr. Lo, added,

'The village elder will take you to a place in Hue where they can give you a new identity, you will become a South Vietnamese Citizen. Good luck to you, everyone in the village will miss you and you will always be in our hearts.'

At 5.30 the next morning, almost two hundred villagers lined the beach to bid Tang Tao farewell, he continued to sob for ten minutes or so after the fishing boat set sail. Five hours later the boat entered the mouth of the Pho Loi River, this fed into the Perfume River, a major feature of Hue City. They arrived at a small 'floating market' and drew absolutely no attention from any of the hundreds of other fishermen that plied their wares within this vast, Venice like, river city. Le Loi, the village elder, led Tang Tao to a shop in the old quarter of Hue, this area still retained its French flavour, the narrow, cobbled streets and the rows and rows of shops put Tang Tao's young head into a spin, he had never seen anything like this before. They entered a shop that displayed every kind of army artefact that one could imagine, Tang Tao was fascinated by what he saw. After being given some tea, in what Tang Tao believed to have been the World's smallest cup, he and the village elder were taken to the back of the shop. A tin box, containing hundreds of Birth Certificates was placed onto a small table. Mr. Choi, the shop owner, and a good friend of Mr. Le Loi sorted through the pile of documents, some were nearly new in appearance, others were tatty and torn, suddenly Mr. Choi handed one to Le Loi, they both smiled and nodded in agreement, Tang Tao would become, Nguyen (wing) Quang Thanh. The document, which was in good condition, included all the information that a Birth Certificate should contain.

A puzzled Tang Tao asked how Mr. Choi had managed to have all these Birth Certificates, Mr. Choi explained that many boys, from aged ten upwards, volunteered to fight for the freedom of the South and before setting off to war they needed a lot of kit and provisions. The boys would come to the shop, they had little money so Mr. Choi would take their Birth Certificate as collateral, many of them never returned and as they carried no other form of identification they were buried where they fell, without any official naming. Mr. Choi went on to say that once he was certain that the owner of the document would never return, he was able to sell them to the highest bidder, he never asked questions as to why somebody might want a new Birth Certificate. A visible panic appeared on Tang Tao's face, when he said,

'But I have only a little money, I am unable to pay you, Mr. Choi'.

Smiling, Mr. Choi told the newly named Tang Tao not to worry as he was doing this for his old friend, Mr. Lo, who had helped him escape from China many years since. Mr. Choi informed Tang Tao that he must never lose his Birth Certificate as he would need this when applying for his ID card when he became 14 and that he must memorise every detail as he may be asked questions by the police from time to time. Looking at the document, Tang Tao could see that Nguyen Quang Thanh (NQT) would also have been 12 years old, had he been alive. He had been born on the 10th, July 1949, in a coastal town named Nha Trang. Le Loi and NQT left the shop, they walked to the station, Le Loi bought a ticket for Thanh (Tan) as he would now be known and one hour later, he was on his way to Saigon. He would spend 43 hours on the train.

Arriving at Saigon Railway Station, Thanh was taken aback by the sheer volume of people, and whilst he realised that he looked and behaved no differently to anyone else, he did notice that the dialect of most people he could hear, was distinctively different from the local population of almost everywhere else that he had been on his journey so far. The former Tang Tao knew that he had to keep quiet, at least until he reached the address of the contact that Mr. Lo had written down for him. At the railway terminus, there were more buses parked up than he had seen, in total, in the whole of his lifetime back in his home village. He found and boarded the bus that would take him to 'Cho Lon.' When the bus conductor asked for the fare, Thanh showed him the slip of paper, upon which was written the address that he was looking for, the fare was just VND 200, about one old penny in UK money. To his great surprise, and joy, the bus terminated at Binh Tay Market, which was exactly where Ms. Phuong Linh, according to Mr. Lo's note, lived. Her full address was written as, 688 Nganh Muc Trai Cay Chi Bien, Binh Tay Market, District 6, Saigon. The market was huge, with over a thousand small shops. Goods lined the alleyways between the shop fronts, making it nigh impossible to avoid bumping into other people. Arriving at No. 688, Thanh was not sure as to whom he should say he was, should he introduce himself as Tang Tao or Nguyen Quang Thanh, whilst he was deciding what to do, the youngest of four ladies that were sitting at the front of the lock-up shop, took his arm and whispered, are you Tang Tao? He answered yes. The lady, Ms. Linh, led the young illegal immigrant to the end of the alley and sat him down at one of the many street market food stalls. The young boy handed Ms. Linh the envelope that Mr. Lo had asked him to give to her. Opening the envelope, she quickly read the short note written on the back of a food label, nodding as she did so. When the waitress, a girl of a similar age to Thanh came over to take the order, Ms. Linh spoke in fluent Cantonese to her. The relief upon the frightened young runaway's face was immense. Ms. Linh explained to her young ward, that Mr. Lo, a relation, had written to her weeks before and told her to expect his young Nephew, who now wished to live and work in Saigon. She added that, in true Vietnamese tradition, he was now part of her family, however he would have to earn his keep by working long hours, in the hot and sticky environment of Binh Tay Market, he was elated.

That evening, the happy twelve-year-old helped pack away the vast amount of goods that surrounded the front of the shop. He felt that this task was a lot like the work that he had undertaken for his grandfather, albeit Phuong Linh specialised in spices, nuts, dried fruits and other 'non-fresh' foodstuffs, whereas his grandfather exchanged tea for anything he could get his hands on. At 8.00pm, with the market slowly grinding to a halt, Linh closed the roller shutter, climbed through the small door that divided it from the ground and the underside of the counter and ushered her distant relation inside, closing the door behind them. Momentarily there was complete darkness before Linh turned on a small battery-operated lantern, flicking the switch that set the overhead electric fan spinning almost at the same time. In Cantonese, Linh began.

'Well Thanh. Mr. Lo's note has told me of your new identity. Now I must tell you as much as I can about Cho Lon.'

The young boy, not yet a teenager and some 2000 km from his home in China, looked around, all he could see were jars and jars of foodstuffs, he was sat, with his back against the piled-up goods, his left leg was almost in Linh's crutch and his right was perched on a pile of jars containing coffee beans, had sex been on offer it would have been impossible, as there was absolutely no space in which to move.

Ms. Linh continued,

'Here in Cho Lon, you will be safe, as eighty percent of all the people in this area are of Chinese origin, or decent. Cho Lon was once the Capital of the South and is the largest area of Chinese people, anywhere in the world, outside of China. This market is the main wholesale distribution place for almost every type of goods that can be found in Vietnam. When we leave here, we shall go to my place, it is just around the corner, I live with my mama, three brothers, two sisters and four of their children, the marketplace is a much more acceptable place to be. In Cho Lon you do not need to speak Vietnamese, almost everyone talks in Cantonese. You must remember that you are now Thanh, you come from Nha Trang, but you have no family. I will register you with the local police. Every month I will pay them money, they will not bother you. When you are fourteen you will need an ID card, please give me your birth certificate and I will keep it safe until we need it. You will work in the shop, every day. You will run errands, you will fetch and carry goods to and from the street, I will feed you every night, during the day you can eat from the stalls in the market, and I will pay. Every Saturday I will give you some small money, just for your personal things. Any questions, Thanh?'

Through the dim light, Linh could see tears running down the young boy's face,

'You are missing home?'

'Yes, when will I return to see my grandparents and friends in China?'

'Maybe never Thanh. You see, the Vietcong are advancing from the North, every day they are taking more and more land from us. To make your journey back to the North and into China would not be possible, you are safe here, we shall never be the captives of the Communists, you will have a good life here, I have seen the way you looked at Ms. Ha in the coffee shop.'

They both smiled and then crawled out into the now empty market, Ms. Ha, cleaning up the coffee shop for the day, waved at Thanh as he and Ms. Linh walked out into the darkness of the Cho Lon streets.

For the next three and a half years, Thanh worked hard, he made many friends in the market, he and Ms. Ha spent time together, whenever possible, however their relationship was not physical. On the 6th of June 1965, Tang Tao, as he was formerly known, would have been sixteen years old, only in his head was he able to celebrate the fact. On the 10th of July 1965, Thanh became sixteen. At 3.45 in the afternoon three police officers arrived at Phuong Linh's shop, they asked Thanh to go with them. Ms. Linh asked for an explanation, she was told that all sixteen-year-old boys must now join the military, they must fight against the Vietcong, there would be no exemptions. Had Thanh not been registered with the police then he may well have been overlooked for the task that had so far ended in the deaths of almost fifty percent of all conscripted boys under the age of eighteen.

American troops had joined the war in Vietnam in March 1965, most of the young Vietnamese fighters would be trained at South Vietnamese Camps in the jungles surrounding Saigon and once they were deemed to be 'combat-savvy' they would be attached to a fighting unit. In 1966, Thanh was seconded to a joint Vietnam-USA unit, based in Cu Chi, a place that would become famous for the building of the Cu Chi Tunnels. Cu Chi is situated just South of the meandering Saigon River, and Northwest of Cho Lon, it was to be Thanh's 'home' until the end of 1966, he saw very little fighting as the Viet Cong had not penetrated that far South at the time. On his 18th birthday, July 10th, 1967, Thanh was allowed one week's leave, he returned to Cho Lon and his one and only love, Ms. Ha. Thanh achieved two important milestones during his week of 'freedom' firstly, he married Ms. Ha and secondly, he consummated the event, several times, before he returned to his army duties. Upon his return to his unit, he was promoted to the rank of Sergeant, the day after he was transferred to the US Airbase at Bien Hoa, located just North of the Dong Nai River, some 30 km from Cho Lon. The US had gathered intelligence that a major offensive was to be launched by the Viet Cong against the Airbase, many thousands of soldiers from the Army of the South of Vietnam had been seconded to defend the Airbase, the USA's largest outside of America.

On a rare sortie home, Thanh was to find out that his beloved Ha was pregnant, he was overjoyed, however unlike today, he had no idea as to the gender of his first offspring. On the 31st of January 1968, the Viet Cong launched a mortar and rocket fire attack on the base, this would become known forever more as the beginning of the 'Tet Offensive' (Tet = New Year in Vietnam). Thanh had been made a Captain two months earlier, his rank meant that he would be involved in strategic meetings, sometimes held in the offices at the base and sometimes within the many tented command posts. It is recorded that at 2.25am on the morning of February 1st, 1968, Captain Nguyen Quang Thanh, along with seven other officers, two of whom were Americans, met their deaths because of a direct hit, by mortar fire, upon the tent in which they were sat.

3 - YOUNG MICHAEL O'LEARY

Born in the small border town of Pettigo in 1944, the youngest of thirteen children, Michael O'Leary would grow up to become one of Ireland's most notorious men. His father, Patrick, a staunch believer in unprotected sex, was, even by Irish standards, an evil and unforgiving man. Young Michael, not being able to cope with the beatings that his father would hand out to his twelve siblings, four of whom would die before they reached their teenage years, decided, at the age of thirteen, that he would convince his mother, Eileen, to leave the man that had systematically ill-treated her ever since they had first met, some twenty-six years previously.

Pettigo was one of those 'divided' towns, cut in half by the Irish Independence movement of 1922, with one-half of the town being in Ireland and the other half officially located in the newly formed Northern Ireland. The dividing line of the town being the middle of the Termon River, one bridge crossed the river and as time went by, barriers were placed across the middle of the bridge and a Customs Post was established. This division resulted in many families being 'split' against their will and as the tensions rose between the South and the North, many thousands of people were prevented from being able to freely meet with their relatives.

On the first of January 1958, Michael and his mum picked up their previously packed cases and left the run down, freezing cold, terraced house, safe in the knowledge that Patrick would not wake from the drunken state that he had returned home in, after celebrating the arrival of the New Year in his local ale house. Unbeknown to his mum, Michael, the last of her children living at the house that had once been home to twelve other minors, had made several journeys to her relatives and had arranged for her youngest brother, Jimmy Quinn, to collect them on the Irish side of the bridge. True to his word, Jimmy was there, sat at the wheel of an old station wagon. Eileen O'Leary was both surprised and delighted to see her handsome young brother, whom, although he lived just 11 miles away, in Ballymagroarty, County Donegal, she had not seen him for seven long years. The long absence of her brother from her life was mainly due to the beating that she might take from her husband, should he discover that she had crossed the border to fraternize with his sworn enemies, the Catholics. On the twenty-minute journey back to his farmhouse, Jimmy explained to his sister that it would be unsafe for her to stay with him, as firstly, Patrick may well come looking for her, and secondly, he had a few lodgers staying with him and they had not set eyes on a woman for quite a while. Eileen, asking her brother as to where they might go, was told that in the afternoon he would be taking her and Michael to a good friend of his, the racehorse trainer, Sheamus O'Reilly, whose stables were located by the sea, close to Sligo, one of Irelands many racecourse towns, the stables were situated about 40 miles west of Jimmy's farmhouse. Jimmy assured his sister and young nephew that they would be quite safe there.

Jimmy's farmhouse was remote, being about three miles from the town. When they entered the flint-built building, they were greeted by three men, all in their thirties. Each man acknowledged Eileen's arrival however they did not touch hands, or kiss. Michael was very wary of these men and although he was as tall as his mum, he lowered his head deep into her neck, causing the largest of the men to remark,

'Ah, would you look at that, the poor lad is shy.'

Michael in fact, was far from being shy, his instinct told him that these three men were up to no good, he was pleased that he and his mum would be at Uncle Jimmy's cottage for just a few hours.

After a couple of hours, in which time Eileen fried the contents of her brother's fridge, in a frying pan that did not require any additional oil, they bid goodbye to the three 'guests' each of whom turned their faces away when the diminishing light of the winter's afternoon lightened the narrow hallway of the house. In the thirty-year-old station wagon, Eileen sat on the warmness of the engine, covered by some old, World War Two army blankets. Michael, as quiet as a mouse, sat by the door, looking out upon the bleak Irish Countryside, his thoughts consisting of nothing other than how he could exact his revenge upon his evil father, the father that had beaten his mum, day after day, for almost his entire lifetime. For the first time in his thirteen years, Michael realised that his mother, who was only 40 years of age, looked old and frail and maybe only weighed around seven stone. He had long since worked out that his eldest brother would have been twenty-six, had he not succumbed to his father's rage. Despite her poor health, his mother had still managed to produce one child, every year, for thirteen consecutive years, meaning that she had been just fourteen when conceiving her first-born. His father was now fifty-five. Michael did not understand how he had been allowed to do what he had done, these thoughts made him even more determined to make his father pay for all his wrongdoings.

At 4.45pm, in complete darkness, except for one dim light that did its best to brighten up the front porch of the large house at which they had arrived,

Jimmy Quinn asked his sister and nephew to wait in the wagon until he had spoken to Sheamus O'Reilly. Jimmy knocked at the large, imposing black door, a figure stepped out into the cold January evening, shook hands with Jimmy and waved to Eileen and her son to join them. Approaching this enormous-looking man, dressed in tweed trousers, a white shirt and waistcoat, Eileen seemed to courtesy and Michael unintentionally bowed as their eyes met,

'Ah, enough of that my dear, ye are mee guests, not mee servants, so ye are.'

The three newly arrived visitors entered the hallway of the house, Jimmy then remembered that he had to collect the suitcases from the back of the wagon, and despite telling Michael that he could manage, the young lad followed him. As they dragged the cases from the floor of the purple, hand-painted vehicle, Michael tugged at the elbow of his uncle's left arm and said,

'Uncle Jimmy, when I am old enough, I want to repay my father for all that he has done to us, especially for how he has treated my mum.'

Jimmy lightly grasped his nephew's shoulders, looked him in the eyes, and replied,

'Michael, you do not have to worry about that, it is already taken care of.'

At that moment in time, Michael had no clue as to what his Uncle Jimmy meant.

Inside the six-bedroom house, Jimmy and Michael made their way to the kitchen. Michael was momentarily taken aback, the farmhouse table seemed to be larger than the whole of the downstairs of the house where he had lived since birth. Sheamus introduced Michael to Nellie, informing the overawed boy that she was the 'cook and chief bottle washer.' Michael looked around, he could see no bottles in sight, he figured that Nellie must have washed them all and put them outside. Sheamus and his three guests sat at the twelve-seater table, two freshly baked loaves and a slab of butter sat patiently, waiting for someone to consume them. Nellie placed four large dishes in front of her four diners, carried over a large steaming pot and dipped a ladle, a ladle as large as a shovel, into the pot and filled each dish with the 'Irish Stew' the likes of which Michael had only ever read about. Once they had finished the stew and polished off the bread, Nellie took away the dishes and served them all baked jam roll and custard. Jimmy got up from the table, rubbed his stomach, thanked Nellie for such a lovely dinner and then shook the hand of his friend, Sheamus O'Reilly. He then kissed his sister on the forehead and gently punched his nephew on his right arm. Sheamus saw Jimmy to the door, moments later he pulled out of the driveway and onto the narrow, unlit lane that wound around the surrounding countryside for the next five miles. Sheamus beckoned Eileen and Michael to follow him, they obliged. They descended a narrow staircase, walked past several doors until Sheamus stopped and ushered them into a room, lit only by candlelight. A slightly embarrassed Sheamus apologised as they stood in this room, with just one bed, a small chest of drawers, upon which sat a water jug and a bowl. A white ceramic bowl was slightly visible under the middle of the bed.

'I shall move you as soon as an upstairs room becomes available.'

'Now please get some sleep, as we start at 4.00am around here, I bid you goodnight.'

As Sheamus closed the door and was heard to have climbed the stairs, Michael whispered to his mum.

'What does he mean, we start at 4.00am?'

Hugging her youngest son, the only one of the thirteen children that she still had with her, she replied,

'This is a stable-yard Michael, your uncle told me that we have to work and that we should do whatever Mr. Sheamus asks of us.'

Michael did not cross-examine his mum, by 7.00pm they were both fast asleep.

At 3.30am there was a loud bang on their bedroom door, a voice they recognised as being that of Nellie, bellowed,

'Will ye not be getting up then, breakfast is dead on four.'

Eileen was the first out of bed, she found the light switch and turned on the light, it was now darker. She opened the door, the light from the hall lit up the room, she swished her face with water from the bowl and indicated to Michael that he should do the same. At one minute to four, they sat, with ten others, at the massive farmhouse table. Sheamus was conspicuous by his absence. As Nellie served breakfast, the man sat at the head of the table introduced himself.

'I am Ned, the yard boss. You may call me, Ned.'

He then introduced the other nine people, none of whom either Eileen or her son had ever set eyes upon before. There were seven men and two women, no sooner had Ned named them, then Eileen and Michael had already forgot who they were.

'No need to worry my love. Once you have been here a few days you will get to know who's who.'

Breakfast over, Ned asked Michael to follow him. They walked out of the back door and into a force-nine snowstorm.

'You might want to go get your overcoat, lad.'

Back out in the yard, and suitably attired for such a cold and windy day, Ned led Michael to the first of a row of ten stables, each containing a racehorse.

'These are your ten nags, young lad. You clean them out every morning and saddle them up ready for the gallop.'

As Ned started to walk away Michael was ready to cry.

'Just pulling your leg, son. Here, young Joey will show you the ropes.'

Back in the house, Nellie was giving Eileen the grand tour whilst telling her what her duties will be.

'Rosie has just left us, up the duff she is, shipped her off to Shannon because of the shame of it all, poor beggar, could not keep her knickers on, believe she had every man in Sligo, a real pity, she was a real good worker and had only just had her 15th birthday as well. Anyhow, there are six bedrooms, Mr. Sheamus has his own, the other five are each shared by two people, I sleep in the dungeon, where you are, you will only move to a bedroom upstairs when someone leaves or is murdered. Each day you must make the beds, clear out the fires and make new ones, do the washing and the ironing, keep the big bathroom clean, polish all the furniture in the front room, which only Mr. Sheamus is allowed to go into and make sure that the other front room does not become a shit hole as this is shared by everyone else in the house. I take care of all the shopping, cooking, washing up, dealing with the household money and most importantly, keeping Mr. Sheamus satisfied. Anything you need to know, just ask me.'

And so, Eileen and Michael embarked upon a new life, one free of beatings and a lack of food. Sheamus, without a wife, since she had met her death, aged 23, under the hooves of a wild and erratic horse that Sheamus had destroyed on the day that it took his beloved Connie from him, was also without any children. Eileen could not get to grips with one thing that Nellie had said, as keeping Mr. Sheamus 'satisfied' could have had a whole of host of meanings. Did she mean satisfying him by her cooking, her washing up or how she managed the coffers of the house. Looking at Nellie, in her sixties, going on eighty, fat and ugly, boobs almost on her knees, and with a rear that was larger than any of the horses in the yard. Surely, thought Eileen, Mr. Sheamus cannot be servicing this Irish version of Hattie Jacques? Eileen began to worry, would Mr. Sheamus be turning his attention towards her?

One week after taking his sister and nephew to their new beginnings, Jimmy Quinn returned to see how they were getting on. Sheamus confirmed that they were both hard workers and that he had no complaints. After dinner, Jimmy asked Michael to show him some of the horses that he had been charged with looking after and once they were out of earshot, Jimmy told Michael that,

'It was done.'

'What is done?'

'Your father is no more. Three men took him from the house, laid him face down on the bridge, half in the North and half in the South, they shot the backs of both of his kneecaps, stripped him, hot tarred him and then covered him with chicken feathers, you will never hear from him again. I will tell your mum that he was killed in an accident. Please never shed a tear for him, Michael.'

Michael looked at his uncle, smiled and said,

'Don't worry, Uncle Jimmy, you will never see any tears from me, I just wish that I could have done this myself.'

Michael believed that the three men that he had seen at his uncle's house were the people responsible for the demise of his father, he hoped that one day he could thank them.

And so, time, as it invariably does, moved on. Michael, now 14 years of age, had noticed how his mum had changed, she had put on weight and kept herself looking nice. Michael was sure that she now had tits, she worked hard, but she was happy. Two weeks before Christmas, 1958, Michael was moved from the basement, he would now share a room with Sinead, as her previous roommate, Beth, had left, victim of yet another pregnancy. The four other bedrooms were occupied by the eight older 'live in' stable lads and as the youngest, Michael was asked, by Nellie, to 'bunk' with sixteen-year-old Sinead. Michael had suspected for some time that his mum was taking care of Mr. Sheamus, almost every night. The 'boss' would call Eileen to come and stoke the fire, Michael believed that Sheamus was doing most of the stoking. Michael did not fret about this, as for him, if his mum was happy, then so was he.

At first, Michael took little notice of Sinead, he had been used to sharing a bedroom with his brothers and sisters, he had never taken any notice of anyone's anatomy, male or female, but now he was fourteen years old and had the normal urges and thoughts that most red-blooded males of that age have. The first few nights of sharing with his new bunk mate were quite awkward, Michael would wait outside until Sinead undressed and got into her single bed, she would then call him, he would switch off the light, strip down to his underpants and slide nervously into his bed, which was just one small table away from Sinead. They would talk for a while and then sleep soundly, knowing that they would be woken by the heavy-handed Nellie, at 3.30am. In her striped, blanket-like nightdress, that swept the floor as she moved, Sinead did nothing to stir the loins of young Michael, however on the fifth morning of their 'co-habiting' this all changed. Sinead climbed out of bed, opened the bedroom door, and moved silently down the hall to the toilet. Upon her return she had left the bedroom door slightly ajar; a streak of light entered the bedroom at the point where Sinead had shed her nightdress before she was to wash her face, using the bowl of water that was placed on top of the small wooden chest of drawers. She looked over at Michael, his eyes were tightly shut, or at least she thought they were. Michael was able to see Sinead in her full glory. His erection was immediate and the hardest he had ever managed. As he moved his hands down the inside of the bed Sinead was fully aware of the fact that Michael was watching her, she walked slowly over to him, bent over, and kissed him, passionately, on the lips. Almost whispering, she said,

'Let me do that for you, Michael'.

Before he could respond, she had taken his erect knob in her hand, he came even before she had moved her hand to any great degree. Sinead dressed and as she left the room, she barked at the boy whom she had just given his first-ever assisted wank to.

'Come on Michael, yer lazy git, it's time to get up.'

At the breakfast table, with nine men and one female waiting to be fed by Nellie, Ned began to tease Michael, asking him how he was getting on with sharing a room with his 'girlfriend.' A shy Michael, looking down at his empty plate, knew not how to respond. Sinead answered on his behalf,

'Oh, he is doing fine, he is already sharing my bed.'

There were whoops of delight from everyone and when the laughter died down Ned looked at Michael and said,

'Well, you be careful lad, we don't want to be losing Sinead to the pudding club, do we.'

Sinead, being small in height and petit in frame, was responsible for 'riding out' the star horses of the stable, this would normally be done between 4.30 to 8.30 every single morning of the year. Michael, now being shown great favour by Mr. Sheamus, mainly because of *his* affection for Michael's mum, was charged with looking after the horses that Sinead rode. Sheamus had trained some of the best horses that Ireland had to offer, regularly picking up the winner's purse at any of the twenty-six racecourses within the Republic and occasionally sending his top-notch nags to run in England. Sheamus O'Reilly's stable was like many others in the Republic, they trained both flat and jump horses, keeping the stable busy all year round. Up to forty full and part-time staff 'clocked in' every morning and 'clocked out' at various times, each day. The Irish are the leading breeders of thoroughbred bloodstock in the world, however just like any business, there is always a sinister side and in 1961 Michael would begin to become involved in other activities, his involvement would have, far-reaching consequences and rewards that he could never have dreamed of.

On March 2nd, 1959, a big day for Michael on three counts, firstly, before breakfast, he was presented with a large birthday cake, baked exclusively for him by Nellie. Michael was fifteen that day. After breakfast, Mr. Sheamus announced that Michael would accompany the travelling team to the prestigious Cheltenham meeting, taking place in just two days-time. Sinead would go as well. The O'Reilly stable would be running six horses, all but one was looked after by Michael. It was noticeable that when making the announcement of Michael's promotion, his mum was holding Mr. Sheamus' hand, earlier she had been holding something much harder. The third achievement, was, in Michael's opinion the best. As, upon her return from riding out the last of her horses, Sinead tied the steed to one of the yard posts, she then went into the newly cleaned-out stable and stripped off all her riding gear. Michael had been in the yard when Sinead returned to the stable, with its freshly laid straw. Sinead called to him, and he entered the stable. Less than three minutes later, he entered her. There were three reasons why Michael would never forget his 15th birthday, however his first-ever penetration of the girl that he would fall in love with, and whom he came so close to marrying, would never leave his memory.

Cheltenham 1959 would be remembered for many reasons, one of the more notable was the fact that an Irish trained horse 'Roddy Owen' won the Gold Cup, the highlight of every Cheltenham meeting. Michael would remember it for a completely different reason, the corruption. Arriving at the Regency Hotel, just a few minutes, drive from the racecourse Michael was surprised, but pleased, to see that his uncle Jimmy was there, sat at the bar with three others. Hugging Michael, Jimmy introduced two of his three friends, asking Michael if he remembered them. It was only when the biggest of the trio, whom Jimmy had not mentioned by name, announced that he had met Michael's father that the penny dropped, these were the men at the farmhouse on January 1st, 1959, they were almost certainly responsible for his father's death.

'So, young Michael, how many of your nags are going to win?' asked Sean Flynn.

'Oh, I'll be letting you know tomorrow, for sure, for sure.'

With that, Michael headed off to the room that Sheamus had booked for him. Five minutes later he and Sinead were entwined.

Whilst the winning of the Gold Cup by Roddy Owen was notable, the single most memorable event of the three-day Cheltenham Festival was the winning of the Champion Novices Hurdle by 'Bric-a-Brac.' Michael's initial suspicion that something untoward was going on was when he entered Bric-a-Bracs box on the morning of the race. Michael had not travelled over with the horses, this had been left to the specialised team, headed by Ned. Trips across the Irish Sea tended to be fraught, horses had to be attended to by experienced people and Michael was not yet one of them. Looking at Bric-a-Brac in his box, a few hours before he was due to run, Michael concluded that all was not well. He found Sinead and led her to the horse box; he told her that he did not think that the horse was Bric-a-Brac and that somehow the wrong horse had been shipped over. Sinead, smiling, said,

'Oh Michael, sometimes you are so naïve, of course this is not Bric-a-Brac, it's 'Hill House' from the captain's yard.'

Michael was speechless, albeit he managed to say,

'A 'bloody, ringer, 'Sinead?'

This was not the first time, and would not be the last, that the Irish have substituted a bad horse, with a good one. Bric-a-Brac was almost a 'no-hoper' for the Champion Novices Hurdle. In fact, in the early stages of betting, Bric-a-Brac was 33-1 on the course, there were no legal betting shops in 1959, you could only get a bet on with the local 'bookies runner' or go to the racecourse. Hill House was a seasoned runner, having competed in many races, way above the class of the field that he now found himself in. Fifteen minutes before 'the off' the money for Bric-a-Brac started to pour in, his odds were slashed from 33-1 to 25-1 to 20-1 and finally all the way down to 8-1. A ringer could only be possible if the bogus horse looked the same as the real one. Bric-a-Brac and Hill House looked like twins. Bric-a-Brac (alias Hill House) won by ten lengths, the bookies took a beating, the Irish Republican Movement swelled its coffers by tens of thousands of pounds. Some months later, the trainer infamously known as the 'Captain' was banned from racing for ten years. Sheamus O'Reilly was not implicated.

To say there was a party that night would be an understatement. Jimmy's friend Sean Flynn and his associate, Willie McCormack, asked Michael if he was 'up for it' next year. Michael feigned ignorance however he fully understood the meaning of what his uncle's friends were insinuating. Sinead warned Michael not to become involved with 'those' men. Michael assured her that he never would. On their return home to Sligo, Sheamus and Eileen announced that they intended to marry, sometime in the following summer. Michael was so pleased for his mum he had never seen her happier than she was right then. After the excitement of Cheltenham, Michael was finding it hard to resume his duties back in the yard, he loved the buzz of the racecourse, especially the bookmaking side and wondered how he might get himself involved. It would not be long before an opportunity arose. One of the yard's owners was a reputable Irish Bookmaker if there could be such a thing as a 'reputable' bookmaker in the corrupt world of bookmaking. As a respected owner, with five horses in O'Reilly's yard, the bookmaker, Fergus 'Fingers' O'Doyle, was invited to the wedding, which took place in June 1960. Showing 'Fingers' around the yard, Michael made a point of asking him as to how he could make the switch from stable lad to bookie, Fingers asked Michael to look him up the next time he was in Dublin, knowing full well that Michael had little or no opportunity of ever getting to the Fair City.

Michael dreamed of entering the world of bookmaking, after all he could never become a jockey, as his height and weight, even at the age of sixteen, meant that he would never be able to 'don the silks' and although he no longer cleaned out the stables, mainly due to his mum's relationship with Sheamus, his desire was to get away from the constant smell of horse shit, which invaded his nostrils almost all of the time. Sheamus understood that Michael was itching to do something different, he therefore made him Ned's assistant, which meant that he was travelling to various racecourses at least five days of every week. Whilst Michael enjoyed the freedom that his promotion had given him, he missed his beloved Sinead whenever he was away from her. In March 1961, Michael became 17, he had just one more year before he could legally have sex with Sinead. At the Cheltenham Festival meeting, just after his birthday, Michael noticed that 'Fingers' O'Doyle had his bookmaking pitch right next to the rails in the main grandstand. As soon as the last race was over and having seduced Sinead into taking care of his post-race duties, Michael hurried down to the rails. Fingers was busy counting the day's winnings, Michael had never seen so much cash in one place, the sight of so much money, only fuelled his desire to somehow join the ranks of the bookmaking fraternity. Fingers, in a joyful mood after skinning the punters on almost every race that day, was more than receptive to Michael's nagging, asking the young lad to work out a few bets, in his head. Michael, much to the bookie's surprise was spot-on with all his answers.

'There is just one problem my lad, how am I going to clear this with Sheamus?'

'No problem, Mr. O'Doyle, I will get me mum to talk to him.'

Michael turned and left, knowing full well that Sheamus would be joining 'Fingers' for an evening of fun, no doubt fed by an abundance of alcohol.

That evening, with Sheamus out of the way, partying with Fingers and a whole host of other bookmakers in one of Cheltenham's many Irish bars, Michael sat down to dinner with his mum and Sinead and outlined his discussion with the bookie. His mum was not too receptive to Michael's plan and told him that she did not want him to get mixed up in the shady and sometimes dangerous world of bookmaking. To Michael's surprise, Sinead took his side, pointing out to Eileen that Michael did not wish to wait around looking after horses for the foreseeable future, after all there was only Ned's job to be filled and that was not going to happen any day soon. It took some persuading, but by the time they were well into the pudding, Eileen agreed to at least talk to Sheamus. That was the best that Michael could have hoped for. He now had to wait for his mum to approach Sheamus and whatever the result, he would abide by it. Unbeknown to the three diners, 'Fingers' was already having a discussion with Sheamus. Fingers had the need for a young, naïve, but smart kid to join his organisation. Between them, Sheamus and Fingers O'Doyle agreed that they would share Michael's time, at least until he was eighteen, when he would be legally entitled to work in the bookmaking business.

On their return to the stables in Sligo, after firstly talking to his wife, Sheamus called Michael into his office and explained to him that from the first of May, he could work with Mr. O'Doyle for three days of every week.

O'Doyle would be paying him for those three days and the stable would support him for the other four. Sheamus added that all three of them would agree Michael's schedule every Sunday, however he (Sheamus) would always have the ultimate say on where Michael would be on any given day. Michael was of course, in complete agreement with his 'stepfather.' Sinead, who was much wiser than her age suggested, was pleased for Michael, however she urged him not to get involved with some of the more unsavoury gentlemen that Fingers was close to. Eileen was also quick to tell Michael that he was still 'just a boy' and that he should not let all of this go to his head. Michael listened, intently, to all the advice given to him by his 'elders' however no sooner had their words filled his ears, then they were forgotten, well he was just seventeen. Sheamus informed Michael that he could have use of the filthy dirty Ford Poplar 103E, that had nested in one of the barns ever since he had taken it from one of his owners, in payment for training fees, he had no idea if it worked as it had not been started up for over two years. As soon as Sheamus had told him about the car, Michael was opening one of its two doors, the keys were still in the ignition. Half-turning the key, it became evident to the young, excited seventeen-year-old that the old jalopy was not going to start, he opened the boot, took out the starting handle and cranked the engine into life. He then cleaned the windscreen and cleared a path to the stable doors. Michael had no driving license however Ned had let him drive the horse box sometimes. Crunching the gearbox, Michael engaged first gear and drove, stop-start out into the yard, a dozen stable lads gave him a warm round of applause. Sheamus had told Michael that he could drive the car only in the Republic, he could not cross into the North as he might well encounter problems with the Police there. Should he be stopped whilst driving, he should firstly offer a bribe to the Garda and if that did not work then he should tell whoever had stopped him that he was Sheamus O'Reilly's stepson.

At 6.00am, on Monday the first of May 1961, Michael left the yard at Sligo, he had a 140-mile drive in front of him and he would be going alone, his destination was to 'Fingers O'Doyle's' illegal betting office, in the suburbs of Dublin. He had estimated that his drive would take him around four hours, however with the poor road systems and the fact that his newly acquired motor vehicle, at 30 bhp, and with only a 3-speed gear box, which could just about reach a top speed of 52mph, (and that was when going downhill) his four-hour journey time prediction was way wide of the mark. After getting lost several times and being sent the wrong way by some well-meaning pedestrians, it would not be until 2.30pm that Michael knocked on the door of the swanky house, situated at the end of a muddy lane halfway along Acres Road, on the outskirts of Phoenix Park, a fitting location for a bookmaker, as Phoenix Park was then, a world-renowned racecourse.

To Michael's great surprise, the man that answered the door was one of the three men that he had first met at his uncle Jimmy's farmhouse, just outside Ballymagroarty on the Republic side of the border of Pettigo. The man, whom Michael had never been formally introduced to, but was to later find out, was known as Micky McGovern. McGovern was an imposing man, about six foot six, with ginger hair, FA Cup ears and a facial scar that ran the whole length of his rock-like features. Michael had not liked him the first time that he had set eyes upon him, he liked him even less now.

'Ah, young Michael, we expected to see you at 10 o'clock, Fingers left hours ago, he has gone to Roscommon, for the racing, you were to go with him, and he said that if you turned up dead, then you were to go home.'

Ushering Michael into the house, he saw that both the other men present were those that he had first met on January 1st, 1959. One was Sean Flynn, and the other was Willie McCormack. Sean was small, almost jockey material, always joking and quite different from the medium-sized, serious man that was Willie, nicknamed 'knob' for reasons that Michael did not yet understand. Flynn, hugging Michael, said,

'Fingers' asks if you would wait here until he gets back from Roscommon, you will be returning there, with him tomorrow.'

The three men invited Michael to put the kettle on, whilst they all went into another room and locked the door.

Michael was still wearing the kettle when Fingers, his bagman, 'mouse' Magan and the weird looking tic-tac man, 'semaphore' Conway entered the house, all were as drunk as hand carts.

'Michael' a very loud, red-faced Fingers exclaimed.

'Is it your car out front, the one I just hit with me roller? Well, I'm sorry me lad, but ye won't be driving it tomorrow.'

Michael raced outside, the roller was well and truly, embedded into the rear of O'Reilly's Ford Pop.

When he returned to the house, Fingers was slumped, almost unconscious in an armchair and 'mouse' and 'semaphore' had simply disappeared. Searching for the missing pair of misfits, Michael turned the knob belonging to the door into which the three sinister-looking men had retreated some hours since. To his surprise, the door opened, the three men were sat around a large round table, the table was awash with handguns and bullets. Scanning the room, Michael could see rifles, machine guns and other items, enough, he thought, to start a small war. Mickey, Sean, and Willie did not seem at all concerned that Michael had seen the armoury that half-filled the room, on the contrary, Sean asked Michael if he would like one of the weapons, to protect himself on the long and dangerous trips that lie ahead. Sean, wearing gloves, picked up a semi-automatic from the table and handed it to Michael, acting dumb, he thanked

Sean for the offer and placed the gun back onto the table, adding that he must go and take off the kettle, he whistled as he left.

Picking up his small holdall, Michael climbed four flights of stairs and found the room, at the front of the house that Micky had earlier told him was his, whenever he stayed over. Only then did Michael begin to feel hungry, he had not eaten since he had left Sligo, nearly eighteen hours earlier. He descended the same four flights of stairs that three minutes earlier, he had climbed, walked into the kitchen, opened the top door, and froze. He froze, not because of the coldness of the fridge, but because there was a head, eyes wide open, staring back at him. Without closing the door, Michael legged it back upstairs. In his room, he was boiling, he finally took off the kettle. His only thoughts were the words of his mum, telling him that she did not want him to get mixed up in the world of bookmakers, now he knew exactly what she meant. Without further ado Michael picked up his bag and once again descended the stairs, as he reached the end of the long, darkened hall, his heart nearly came out of his chest. Stood in the shadows, creating a silhouette against the backdrop of the dim exterior porch light, was the extra-large frame of Micky McGovern. Once again Michael froze, petrified.

'And where would ye be off to at this late hour young Michael?'

Stuttering, the young lad replied,

'I must go back to Sligo I am not sure if I want to work for Fingers after all.'

Raising the semi-automatic to a level, in line with Michael's thumping heart, Micky calmly asked his shaking captive to turn and go into the room to his left, Michael, in fear of his life, did exactly as he was told. In the room, lit only by a small table lamp, were Fingers, Sean, Willie and, very much to Michael's surprise, his uncle Jimmy.

Jimmy, sat in the shadows, in the comfort of a large chesterfield chair, located in a small, dimly lit alcove, looked straight at his young nephew, and spoke, '

'Sit down Michael, we have a lot to tell you,'

Jimmy, holding a twelve-bore sawn-off shotgun, which he pointed directly at his sister's young son addressed him sternly.

4 - LEON & MONZER ASMAR - Arms Dealers

1945 in Aleppo, Syria, saw the grand opening of the Club d'Alep, the club was housed in one of Aleppo's finest mansions, originally owned by the Ghazale family. Set up to service the wealthy merchants that had been responsible for the enormous riches that Aleppo once enjoyed. The club was run by a democratically elected board, every so often the members of this board would change. In the early days, the club had over 600 members, however the 1950s and 60s saw a steep decline in its fortune, mainly due to the political upheavals at the time. In the 1970's the main reception hall was turned into a mosque. Victor Guerelli had been the first and longest serving President of the club. In 1975, upon his retirement, he handed over to the newly elected, Leon Asmar.

Leon Asmar was just thirty years old when he became the President of the most prestigious members-only club in Syria. He was widely regarded as an upright member of Aleppo's rich and elite, his father, before retiring due to ill health, had been the Governor of the most important of all Syria's Merchant banks and whilst Leon had not exactly followed in his father's footsteps, he was still a member of the Bank's Board of Directors and held many similar posts in a whole range of businesses. This status gave Leon the perfect platform on which to perform his other, less kosher, activities. He had purchased a modern, state-of-the-Art complex in the hills overlooking the playground known as Puerto Banus, Marbella. His yacht, moored in one of the World's most expensive parking lots, had been purchased from Adnan Khashoggi, once the World's leading arms dealer. Leon and his brother, Monzer, would learn a lot from him. Leon's younger brother, Monzer, studied law at school in Rome, however he left the life of luxury that his father provided in Aleppo, choosing to return to Italy after gaining his degree in Criminal Law. In Italy he became involved with a 'family' member of the Sicilian Mafia and took on the job of defending various members of the 'mob.' Interpol's first recording of Monzer's illegal activities took place in Trieste, Italy, in 1970. He was accused of, but never convicted, of masterminding the theft of millions of dollars-worth of art and artefacts from the Vatican. It had been Monzer that had convinced his elder brother to relocate his family and wealth to the Costa-del-Sol.

In July 1976, the brothers were visited, in Marbella, by a government official from Yemen, they were asked to source guns and rifles from Poland, the weapons would be distributed to various terror groups around the middle east. Monzer had already dabbled in the buying and selling on of arms. Leon was nervous about taking this on, he was a successful tobacco smuggler, using his contacts in Afghanistan, Iran, and Turkey to transport his illegal contraband throughout the Middle East and Europe. Monzer was clever, no product would ever enter his homeland of Syria, he was never high on the list of people that might have been suspected of being the 'mastermind' behind this business. When the official from Yemen suggested that Monzer could be appointed as their charge d'attache of Commerce in Warsaw, Leon began to warm to the idea of adding 'Arms Dealer' to his portfolio. A tried and tested way of exporting arms from one Country to another was to be the Syrian's chosen method of transportation, this has worked in the past, especially in cases where Countries have self-imposed trade embargos. Via the cover created for Monzer, he was able to arrange for consignments of Polish two-stroke engines to be shipped from Gdansk to the Port of Felixstowe, the largest East Coast Port in the UK. The documentation would show them to be for use in the assembly, in the UK, of agricultural machinery. The arms would be packed into 'close boarded' crates and addressed to a well-known tractor plant in Essex. The crates would be collected from the Port and delivered to a packing company in Rainham, Essex. Without ever being opened the crates would be placed inside larger crates and 're-addressed' to the Ministry of Agriculture, Hodeidah, Yemen's largest Red Sea Port, which during the 1970s and '80s was also a large Russian Naval Base. The Russians would play a big part in making sure that the arms reached their intended users.

In 1977, having purchased one of those imposing mansions in Sloane Square, London. Leon made his first big mistake, he was arrested, in Copenhagen, for selling Hashish. After a lengthy investigation and subsequent trial, he was acquitted. He continued to Import tobacco and hashish, into the UK, from Lebanon. In 1979 he was arrested in London and convicted, however he served less than two years. In 1981, at the age of thirty-six, he married Raghdaa Farhat, the beautiful seventeen-year-old daughter of a family friend that he was visiting in Beirut. As he already had a wife and children in Marbella, Leon kept Raghdaa at his house in Aleppo, she was his companion at the many functions that he would attend throughout Syria. In 1984 Leon was expelled from the UK on suspicion of tobacco and hashish smuggling, his assets were seized by the authorities.

Monzer Asmar was not as brash as his elder brother, choosing to always keep himself and his name firmly out of the limelight. He still portrayed the role of being an astute and above-board businessman whilst in Aleppo. In

Marbella he was just one of the many 'rich and famous' that had chosen to use their wealth to show off their success. Of course, he was subject to all the usual rumours that surround those people with seamlessly endless amounts of money, however his wife, Milana (meaning Gracious) wore traditional Syrian clothes and his three children enjoyed Spanish State Education. By keeping his life in Spain, 'low-key' Monzer reduced the chances of his family being 'targets' for the kidnapping gangs that had infiltrated the area. Whilst Monzer and his brother now worked 'hand in hand' on many arms deals, especially when tens of millions of dollars were at stake, they each had their own separate lives. Monzer would never deal in hard drugs, he did not like the idea of young kids dying due to overdosing or from taking 'bad gear.' On the other hand, he had absolutely no qualms about supplying guns that would kill one hundred times more children than drugs ever would.

Whilst Monzer did his best to keep his illegal dealings close to his chest, his brother chose to blaze a trail across the Middle East, being portrayed in one famous French magazine as, 'the Syrian merchant that has become one of the most powerful businessmen in the World.' In 1985, the Spanish government accused Leon of selling arms to the hijackers of the 'Achilles Lauro' cruise ship and then flying some of the hijackers, in his private jet, to the safety of Damascus. Investigations by the FBI in 1987, into the Iran-Contra scandal, found that Leon had received GBP 15 million from a USA Government official to sell arms to the Nicaraguan Contras, the money coming from a Swiss Bank Account controlled by a senior US Military man. In 1992, Leon made over forty million USD from the sale of arms to Croatia, Bosnia, and Somalia. In the same year, with the help of a senior Government figure, he fraudulently obtained a Brazilian Passport, with the intention of moving himself and his family to the corrupt South American Country. When a new Government was formed in Brazil, Leon was indicted for 'obtaining fraudulent documents,' he was deported to Spain, where he faced an exact similar charge, in addition he was charged with 'possession of illegal weapons and drug offences,' he spent just over a year in jail, awaiting trial. At his trial he was found 'not guilty' of all charges.'

During this period, Monzer was cutting 'arms deals' with various Governments around the World. By using a 'third parties,' Governments, not able to deal directly with their counterparts, were turning more and more to these 'traders in death.' It was not unusual for Monzer to be selling arms to both sides in any given conflict. In 2006, Iraq listed Monzer as their third 'most wanted' person, claiming that he was supporting the Iraqi insurgency with both money and logistics.

In 2007, the DEA put together a 'sting' their intention was to entrap Leon. The head of the DEA's Special Operations Administration enlisted a 71-year-old Palestinian, formerly a member of the Black September Group, he was given the code name 'Manny' and was released from a prison in the USA. Manny spent nearly a whole year trying to set up a meeting with Leon. Early in 2008, Leon, two Columbian insurgents and Manny, met in Nicosia. The Columbians asked Leon to supply weapons, with which the drug cartels in Columbia could fight the DEA. The group met a further four times, always at different locations, during the final two meetings the informants wore hidden video cameras, Leon was recorded as agreeing to the terms of the deal.

With the deal seemingly going through, Leon was invited to meet the three men again, this time in Istanbul, this is where, he was told, he would be collecting his money, he refused to go, citing that he would not be allowed to enter Turkey, due to a warrant for his arrest being issued ten years previously. When asked, he did agree to meet up in Madrid. Upon his arrival in the Spanish Capital, Special Forces, acting upon information received from the CIA, immediately arrested Leon and charged him with supplying arms to terrorists, money laundering, obtaining air-to-air missiles and conspiring to kill American Citizens. Within two weeks Leon was extradited to the USA, arriving handcuffed and hooded at Houston Airport. In late November 2008 Leon was tried and convicted on eleven charges, he was given eleven, thirty-year sentences. Leon was sixty-three years old when incarcerated. An article in the New York Times suggested that Leon had been unusually lax during his meetings with the fake arms buyers, caused, they wrote, due to his need for money during a period when the demand for arms was at a low ebb, as many World conflicts had ceased. His brother, Monzer, aware of the fall in demand for weapons, had turned his attention to trading in other commodities, his vacation away from arms dealing would lead him into, what many consider to be the most horrendous of all illegal trading.

During the time that his brother had become recognised as the World's leading arms dealer, Monzer had quietly got on with alternative ways of making money and not all of it was illegal. He had several legit businesses in Syria, some of which had the involvement of prominent Ministers within the Bashar Al-Assad Government. These businesses were used as vehicles by Monzer to 'aid and abet' the greyer areas of his organisation.

During his involvement with his brother Leon, in what he had thought to be the biggest arms deal of his career, Monzer, quite by chance, had met with Tayser Malik. Monzer had been invited to a gathering of Syria's elite, this gathering was held in the palatial home of Abu Najib, a first cousin to the Vice President of Syria. Abu Najib was Monzers partner in one of his so-called 'legit' businesses, Syria's largest Freight Forwarding Company (nowadays known as Logistics). Abu introduced Monzer to Malik, a small, wiry man, with a mass of pure white hair and a beard to match. Monzer believed Malik to be about fifty years old, whereas, as Monzer would later find out, he was only thirty-eight. It transpired that Malik had been using Monzers Freight Forwarding Company to Import and Export his illegal cargo throughout the Middle East and its near neighbours, Turkey, Greece, Albania, Bulgaria, and Romania. The company, comically named as, Trust Shipping and Forwarding, ran over six-hundred trucks and forty small cargo planes. Monzer was not really interested in the business itself, however he used it, to his full advantage, to launder money via the vast network of International Agents that the company had appointed since its inception. His brother, Leon had educated him as to just how easy it was to get 'dirty money' into the system, coming out the other side as being perfectly legal. As an example, there was one very lucrative trade route that enabled Monzer to turn his ill-gotten gains into 'proper money.' In any given week, Trust Forwarding would ship around forty of its trailers from the Port of Latakia on Syria's East Coast to Valetta in Malta. The agent in Malta would unload these trailers, reload the cargo onto their own trailers, ship them to Reggio at the Southern tip of Italy, and from there they would be trucked onwards, all over Europe. The receiving agent in Italy, Spain, Germany the UK and almost every other European Country would bill Trust Forwarding for all the services that they provided, the bill however, would be up to three times the normal market rate. Every agent along the route was aware that the goods declared on the paperwork were not necessarily the goods that were in the trucks. Cigarette smuggling accounted for sixty percent of all the illegal cargo. Monzer had four full-time staff working on the financial side of these transactions. Trust Forwarding would pay the overseas agents and those agents would transfer the agreed surplus amounts to Trust Forwarding Inc, in Los Angeles USA. Three Syrians, with USA Nationality, sat in an office in Long Beach, typing out invoices for every one of the shipments. On the face of it, the whole business was quite legal. Each month Trust Forwarding Inc, owned by the husband of Monzers sister, would purchase real estate in the USA, the UK, France, and other countries that were deemed to be a safe bet by Monzer and his team. Until they had met that evening, Malik and Monzer had no idea that they both had a vested interest in the same Syrian Company. From their brief conversation, Monzer was to learn that up to half of the cargo shipping to Malta had been booked by Tayser Malik's company, TM Holdings. Some three months elapsed before they would meet again, in private, to pursue other ways of making money together, however before that meeting took place, Monzer would have to investigate Malik's background. What he discovered worried him.

During the time between their first and second meetings, the latter of which took place in Aleppo in August of 2008, Monzer would discover that Malik ran a small second-hand computer shop in Nassib, a town not known, at that time, to Monzer. Nassib was situated about 10km to the South of Darra City, Darra was close to the border with Jordan and the main road through this City, connected Damascus to Amman in Jordan. Further investigations revealed that Malik used the computer shop as a front, his main, and very lucrative business was running cigarette smuggling between Syria and Jordan. Monzer was puzzled, how could this man, of no real importance or notoriety, be running such a business, right under the noses of Darra's feared political security branch. Soon it was to become clear. Malik's cousin was the head of this powerful and corrupt secret police, he allowed Malik to run his smuggling business, in return for thousands of dollars every week. Malik portrayed the image of a 'small time' smuggler and was often caught, with a sack full of contraband over his shoulder, crossing the border. A small bribe, in USD was all that it took for the border guards to allow him to carry on. Hundreds of Syrians and Jordanians undertook these illegal crossings, every day of the year. Not all carried just cigarettes.

The discussion between Monzer and Malik, in August 2008, threw up many shared passions and ideas. Malik, having used Monzer's freight business to expand his smuggling on an international level, became interested in other routes that were legitimately available to him, via Trust Forwarding. Malik suggested that Monzer should join with him to their mutual advantage. Soon the two men would be running the largest tobacco smuggling operation in the World.

5 - PETER SLADE – The Detective

On the 1st of February 1964, the wife of Inspector Roy Slade, gave birth to their first, and only son, Peter. Roy had worked his way up the ladder, joining the Metropolitan Police, aged eighteen, in 1952. After his training at the Met academy in Hendon, he had been assigned, as a police constable, to Leman Street in Aldgate, London E1. Roy quickly earned promotion to Sergeant and by the time he had reached twenty-nine, he had become the station inspector at Plaistow E13. His role as Inspector meant that he was almost always at his desk, in a back office of the station. He was never promoted beyond the rank of Inspector and retired from the force, on a 'full pay' pension, in 1987. He had given the police force thirty-five years of his life. He and his wife retired to the sedate countryside town of Upminster in Essex.

Young Peter, being the only child in the family, was doted upon. He excelled at school, passing his eleven-plus exams, in 1975. Grammar school was the only option for the studious Peter. He had no problem in securing a place in the well-respected, 'Coopers Grammar School' which had moved from its previous address, in the Mile End area of London E3, to Upminster, in Essex. Peter's father had attended Cooper's in the days when it was a boy's only school. Peter's mother, Violet had been educated at 'Coburn Girls School', the sister school to Coopers. When moving from the East End of London to the leafy lanes of Upminster, in 1971, the two schools had been amalgamated into one.

Peter Slade was as equally clever at Grammar School as he was at Primary. His mother was intent for her only son to go on to university, his father however had already put his name forward for a 'cadet' course with the Met Police, at Hendon. After finishing his sixth grade and obtaining six 'A' and four 'B' passes in his chosen subjects, Peter eagerly awaited the day that his father would take him to, the place that had once been described as the finest police training facility in the World. His first day at Hendon was on Monday 10th August 1981, Peter was seventeen years old. Roy Slade proudly marched his young son into the reception, they were met by Sergeant Malcolm Sergeant, the academies longest serving instructor, and part-time band leader. This sergeant had mentored Slade senior, some twenty-nine years earlier, he should have already retired, however when Mrs. Sergeant had died, suddenly in the scheduled year of his retirement, he was allowed to stay on, in a civilian capacity, although he still wore the uniform, with its three prominent stripes on each of its arms.

It soon became apparent to Segeant Sergeant that he may well have a star in the making. Peter excelled at every task given to him, in the eyes of the long serving 'teacher' Peter was head and shoulders above his father, in fact, he seemed to be way ahead of everyone that he had seen pass through the training school, with one notable exception. In the Met in those days, cadets with potential were brought to the attention of the 'boys in blue' sat, cocooned in their offices at New Scotland Yard (NSY). Peter's exam results at the end of his first year, were exceptional. In Sergeant's opinion, he had taught just one 'trainee' that was more astute than Peter and he had become the youngest ever Commander at NSY. And so, at just nineteen years of age, Peter was 'fast-tracked' into CID work, there would be no 'pounding of the beat' for this young lad. He would not follow his father into the uniformed side of the police. After a further year of training, Peter was assigned a junior role at NSY, under the ultimate charge of Commander Ray Lamb, himself a product of the East End Grammar School system. Ray Lamb was the person that Sergeant believed to have been his number one student. Peter found himself working on the third floor of the most famous police building in the World, the third floor was the home of the 'flying squad' nicknamed, 'the sweeny' in many film and TV programs.

Condemned to desk work, mainly because of his unrivalled investigative intuition, Peter Slade would not actually 'go on a shout' until he was twenty-three, a full four years after joining, what many considered, at the time, to be the most exciting of all the Met's departments. Peter, had achieved the rank of Inspector by 1987, his first-ever exposure to 'crime on the street' was to be as part of the team on the operation known as the 'Pavement Ambush.' Peter's work had led to a team being set-up to lift armed robbers from the scene of a crime, he took part in two such operations, one in 1987, named 'Char' and the other in 1990, codenamed 'Yamoto'. Three armed robbers were shot dead by officers from the flying squad, no police officer was ever named as being the person(s) responsible for the deaths. In 1993, and now a Superintendent, Peter was heading up this specialist unit, their aim was to take down those involved in armed robberies during the actual event. In this episode, bullets from a machine gun, used by robbers for the first time in mainland Britain, narrowly missed Peter, one bullet ricocheted off a car and struck a colleague in the head, he was posthumously awarded the George Medal. The two robbers were apprehended and given life sentences at the Old Bailey.

In 1991, five years prior to his early retirement from the Met, Commander Ray Lamb moved from the Flying Squad to become the head of the Anti-

Terrorist Squad (ATS), or SO13. Commander Lamb had pushed hard to take Supt. Slade with him however his request was met with strong resistance from his Flying Squad successor. Ray Lamb eventually succeeded in securing the services of Peter Slade in 1993. Previously, at the age of twenty-four, Peter Slade had married, his bride was a former WPC whom he had met at NSY, two years previously. Three years after marrying they spawned two children, both girls and had moved to a small village, ten miles, from Upminster. Whilst the Flying Squad had been extremely dangerous and involved working long hours, Peter's move into the world of terrorism would put his life at risk on numerous occasions, and keep him away from home for long periods of time, he was unable to tell his wife any details of what he was up to, and being away from the family home for days on end, inevitably put a great strain upon his marriage.

Retiring in 1996, having held several top jobs in the Met Police, Commander Ray Lamb was to suffer from a media campaign against him in connection with the death of an 'undercover' female officer. It was stated by one prominent national daily newspaper, that Commander Ray Lamb, had used the officer as a 'honey trap' to gain a confession from a totally innocent man, that Lamb had been after for years. The operation ended with the death of the female officer, at the hands of the person that the Commander allegedly lured into the trap. In fact, Ray Lamb had a minimum of involvement in the 'sting' and was exonerated from any connection with the death. He sued the newspaper and was awarded an 'undisclosed' settlement, rumoured to be in the region of £1 million. At the age of forty-five and with twenty-six years continuous service with the Met, Ray Lamb resigned. He left with an 'Exemplary' record and was given a Certificate of Commendation' he did however forfeit a large proportion of his Police Pension. Three months later, Ray was 'headhunted' by one of the World's largest diamond companies, with over twenty thousand employees, and became their Worldwide head of security. He also appeared, for the BBC, as an 'expert advisor' in many of the areas that he had worked on during his time with the Metropolitan Police.

The ATS, originally known as the 'bomb squad' was set up in 1971 specifically to deal with the 'Angry Brigade' however during the 1970's it assisted in the campaign against the IRA, working hand in hand with both the Special Branch and the Security Service (MI5). When Peter Slade joined the ATS in 1993, the unit had just over 200 officers attached to it. When Ray Lamb resigned in 1996 it was widely expected that Peter Slade would take over, however much to everyone's surprise, he turned the job down, preferring to remain 'operational.' Peter enjoyed many successful 'results' whilst working with the Anti-Terrorist Squad, he was also, from time to time, seconded to his previous department, the flying squad, as his sheer knowledge and experience of the UK's most notable individuals and gangs were of invaluable assistance to his former colleagues. At the turn of the new century, Peter was asked to monitor and provide intelligence on a gang that intended to carry out the biggest-ever robbery within the UK, albeit no one was exactly sure as to the location of the crime.

In November 2000, after many months of surveillance, the intended target was known, the gang were seeking to steal the 'Millennium Star,' a flawless 203-carat diamond, weighing in at some 40 grams. The diamond had been on show at the Millennium Dome. On the 7th of November 2000, the gang, using a stolen JCB excavator and armed with a nail gun, ammonia, and smoke bombs, entered the dome, and smashed their way through to the vault. A speedboat was waiting on the Thames, to convey the robbers away from the scene, the plan was to make the short journey from the jetty at the dome, across the Thames arriving at Trinity Buoy Wharf, close to the old East India Docks. From there the criminals would be taken, in a waiting 'black cab' to Southend Airport, from where they would fly to Guernsey before eventually escaping, initially to France and then to the Costa-del-Sol. What they had not planned for, was the fact that Peter Slade had known every detail of their intentions, having gleaned the information from a gang member that had 'done a deal' whereby Superintendent Slade was able to delete all his past misdemeanours, in return for the 'heads-up' on this spectacular robbery attempt. Operation 'Houdini' involved two hundred police officers, forty of which were seconded from SO19. A dummy wall had been built in order that armed officers could hide behind it, part of the team was dressed as cleaners, their guns hidden in black bags and rubbish bins, sixty flying squad personnel were stationed along the promenade of the Thames at Greenwich and twenty more waited on the river. Five men were caught, no one was injured, sentences ranged from twelve to twenty years. Peter Slade received yet another accreditation, to go alongside his, already impressive list of awards.

A few weeks after the failed attempt to steal the 'Millennium Star,' Peter was invited to dinner by his immediate boss, Commander James Reeves, the new head of the Anti-Terrorist Squad.

'Peter' said the Commander, swishing his brandy in two cupped hands,

'What I have to discuss with you now is of the utmost secrecy, my words cannot be heard by anyone else, only the Home Secretary is aware of our meeting tonight.'

Peter had not the slightest inkling of where this conversation was heading.

'As you are aware Peter, the decommissioning of its weapons, by all paramilitary groups, on both sides of the Irish argument, was, according to the Good Friday Agreement, to have been finalised by May of this year. That deadline has passed and the failure of any of the parties concerned to disarm is putting the validity of the agreement in jeopardy. We have been asked to intervene. 'We', and when I say 'we' I mean just you and I, have been asked to set up and attend a meeting with the leaders of all the concerned parties, the meeting will take place in Ireland, at a yet to be agreed venue.'

Peter did not normally do nervous, however on this occasion he was slightly concerned.

'Can I think about it, Sir and let you know?'

'I am afraid not Peter, I cannot compel you to go, however you really have no choice.'

'Then, I'll do it.'

On the 27th, December 2000, Commander James Reeves and the newly promoted Chief Superintendent Peter Slade, boarded a small twelve-seater plane, the plane ultimately belonged to the Ministry of Defence (MOD) but had been 'leased out' five times over, to conceal its exact owners. Its call sign was VIR007, on paper it belonged to the CEO of Virgin Airlines, It, was one of the seventeen small aircraft that MI6 or the Secret Intelligence Services leased from various 'legit' organisations. The pilot, at the behest of all concerned, was a Captain from the commercial side of British Airways, he had flown similar missions previously and was known to be of the utmost trustworthiness. Only half an hour before the flight was scheduled to take off, was the destination divulged to the captain. Once in the air, an amended set of destination grid references flashed onto the onboard computer screen, whilst these were entered into the aircraft's navigation system, they did not reveal the ultimate landing place. Just over an hour after take-off from RAF Brise Norton, VIR007 began its decent, it was to land at a small tarmac strip just outside Ballintra, a town of no real fame, situated about ten miles to the South of the more well-known town of Donegal. The steps of the aircraft were lowered, a tower of a man, dressed in full paramilitary uniform, entered the cabin, and placed black balaclavas, with no eye holes, over the heads of the two men from New Scotland Yard. This was to be of no surprise to the senior policemen as they had been briefed accordingly. Exiting the plane, the soldier was followed by the two suited and booted officers, they were ushered into a Range Rover, at the wheel of which was an immaculately dressed man, possibly in his late sixties or early seventies. He introduced himself as being Sean Flynn, at the time, the name meant nothing to the blinded backseat passengers. Later they would learn all about Sean Flynn and his close associates.

After twenty minutes, or so, of driving, the Range Rover came to a halt. The Commander and his righthand man were helped from the car. Even though they could see nothing, their senses told them that they were in an area of remote isolation. Led by the arm, both men were escorted into a cold and eerie house, the flooring of which was flagstones, they were guided onto hard wooden chairs, these chairs were positioned around a table, they sat, motionless, for a good ten-minutes before anything else happened. A door was opened, they sensed it was a door that led to the outside as a sudden chill descended upon the room. What appeared to be several men joined them at the table, the balaclavas were removed. Six men were introduced, by Sean Flynn to the two guests, four were members of Sinn Fein and the Progressive Unionist Party (PUP), both with links to the Paramilitary Organisation known as the IRA, the other two men were representing the Ulster Volunteer Force (UVF) and its affiliates. The Commander and his Chief Superintendent recognised all six men, although they had never met previously. Three other men, each with blackened faces, and all armed, stood guard over the three doors leading in and out of what was the kitchen of this grey and foreboding farmhouse. The three men, none of whom was introduced or known to the Commander and his Chief Superintendent were, Fergus 'Fingers' Doyle, Willie McCormack, and Mickey McGovern, all three men, together with Sean Flynn, had been given an amnesty under the Belfast Agreement of 1998, all were murderers. Sean Flynn made the tea. Peter Slade struck the first blow as far as the negotiations were concerned, looking at the seated Irishmen, one by one, he asked why they had not been able to decommission their weapons as the Belfast Agreement had outlined just over two and a half years ago. Peter's question was met with a torrent of abuse from all six of the people that were supposed to be there to discuss the one part of the Good Friday Agreement that was still outstanding and thus, making it impossible for the agreement to be fulfilled.

After eight hours of discussions, Commander Reeves, sensing that nothing was about to be achieved, announced that he wished to leave, adding that he would return, should all parties at least agree to be more constructive. Balaclavas were returned to the heads of the men from the Met, the six Irish negotiators left the kitchen, Sean Flynn guided the two sightless coppers to the Range Rover, they were driven back to the small jet, which took off three minutes later, arriving at Biggin Hill in Kent, late in the evening. Having discussed the situation on the plane ride back to the UK, Slade and Reeves had concluded that the IRA would never lay down its weapons and that the UVA would not agree to do likewise unless the IRA did it first. It was a 'stalemate' situation, with no real answer for a solution. Eight parties, in total, had agreed to lay down their arms in return for peace, however after almost two and a half years into that agreement, none of them had done so. In their subsequent report, made personally to the Home Secretary, James Reeves and Peter Slade suggested that if the date for the destruction of arms, by all sides, be delayed, they were certain that given other opportunities to discuss this with six of the most notorious Irishmen ever to exist, then they could achieve a positive result.

Based on this suggestion, the British and Irish Governments agreed to extend the date for the decommissioning of arms until the 30th of June 2001.

The new deadline came and went. Seven of the eight groups that carried, and used arms, did agree to decommission however the IRA stood firm, saying that they would not 'fully decommission' until all the others had. They claimed they had begun to destroy arms but would not officially commit to ridding themselves completely. David Trimble, the leader of the Ulster Unionist Party (UUP) resigned in early July of 2001 in protest, against the IRA's stance on weapons. Commander Reeves and Chief Superintendent Slade were once again asked to conduct a meeting on behalf of the British Government.

On the 25th of July 2001, the two New Scotland Yard negotiators boarded the same jet, the Pilot was the very same Captain as before. The difference between the previous meeting and this one was that there was no sign of balaclavas when the two officers climbed into the Range Rover. They noted that after driving through the small town of Ballymagroarty, they turned right and followed a single-track road for about three miles, they stopped outside 'Flint Cottage' the home of Jimmy Quinn. The tone of the meeting was in stark contrast to that of the previous one, there was to be no tea, this time it would be Irish Whiskey, French Brandy, and Beer. The two members of the IRA, infamous men, and known Worldwide, spoke first. They proclaimed that the IRA and all its factions would start to destroy all its weapons before the second week of August. The meeting ended in less than two hours. As the Irishmen began to file out, the leader of the IRA and one of the most ruthless men ever to walk the green pastures of the Emerald Isle, pulled Peter Slade towards him as he shook his hand and whispered into his ear,

'We are watching you, son.'

Upon hearing these words, Thirty-seven-year-old Peter Slade felt an earthquake-like sensation well up from his feet and enter his head. He had never been frightened before this day.

6 - GENERAL KOS

Albania nestles on the shores of both the Adriatic and Ionian Seas. It shares a border with Greece, North Macedonia, Kosovo, and Montenegro. There is several Sea Routes to and from the South of Italy. Tirana is its Capital. In 2017 the population of Tirana was said to be around 800,000, with Albania as a whole, being home to just under 3 million people. Along with Croatia, Albania gained full membership of NATO in 2009, however its application to become a member of the European Union was rejected.

Officially, the Albanian Mafia or 'Mafia Shqiptare' was founded in 1950. Initially its activities were 'internal,' confined to Tirana and its neighbouring Provinces. One family controlled the day-to-day corruption, which at its beginnings, was centred around extortion, robbery, loan sharking, assault, murder, and bribery. As it grew, extensions of the 'family' were constructed over the entirety of Albania. Fifteen families controlled every aspect of life in Albania. The 'Mafia' ran the country. Anyone that fought against this ruthless regime, simply disappeared. Once the former Communist-run Balkans started to break up, the Albanian Mafia took the opportunity to expand its territory, taking over and wiping out rival gangs in Kosovo, North Macedonia, Czech Republic, Slovakia, Slovenia, and Serbia, amongst others. The Albania Mafia had become 'International.'

The Chinese have reported that the Albanian Mafia has extended its activities into the Country, despite the presence of the once feared and largest organised criminal gang in the World, the Triads. It was reported that the Albanians now transport drugs to every major city in China and is heavily involved in prostitution rackets and people smuggling, both in and out of China.

The US State Department has published a report that says that Albania is now the 'mainstay' of organised crime, worldwide. Drug Trafficking, arms and counterfeit goods being the main points of its illegal activities. It, further claims that four controlling 'clans' lord over twenty 'families' that also operate, human trafficking, prostitution, blackmail, car robberies and money laundering. The Turkish and Italian Mafias within the USA are its main partners. The Albanian

Mafia is said to have strong links with, Government Officials, Police, Customs, Secret Intelligence Organisations and even has some Military connections.

The Israeli Government has confirmed that the Albanian Mafia has infiltrated its banking system, enabling it to 'launder' Billions of USD through the country's Banks.

Some of Australia's most wanted men have 'set up' the 'Albanian Mafia Group' and have established links with almost every level of Australian society. A certain Kosovan Army General, with strong links to Albania, laid down the blueprint for Australia's most feared crime group to Import over six tons of Heroin a year. The General, having set up the operation and appointed the gang members now operates outside of Australia. Law enforcers from the US, the UK and Italy are involved in pursuing him. He lives, openly in a huge, heavily fortified complex that spans the borders of both Albania and Kosovo. Both Governments of these two countries are firmly in the General's pocket. Despite many attempts by foreign powers, he has not been given up. He had begun his criminal activities after his parents had emigrated to Sydney in the early 1980s. At the age of twelve, he was running drugs along the 'Golden Mile' in Sydney's red-light district. He is now the 'kingpin' of Australia's drug market, it is said that there is not one shipment of drugs entering Australia's vast shoreline, that he is not aware of. From his complex, defended by the Kosovan troops that he once commanded, in the hills on both sides of the border, 'General Kos' as he likes to be known as, entertains the heads of the Mexican and Columbian Cartels, the Asian Triads, South African crime lords, the Italian Mafia and the leading Dutch and UK drug gangs. In Australia, the cities of Sydney and Melbourne and the states of Queensland, South & West Australia and Tasmania are serviced by using motorcycle gangs as part of his National Distribution and enforcement network. No one else has, or maybe ever will, try to muscle in on this, extremely violent, network of Albanian enforcers.

In Europe, the Albanians are the most feared crime network, operating in every EU and non-EU country. In 1989, the Belgium Prime Minister was kidnapped. Basri Bajrami, a prominent member of the Albanian Mafia was one of the men behind the plot. A ransom of Euro 30 million was said to have been demanded for the Prime Minister's safe return and whilst officials in Brussels denied that any ransom was ever paid, Paul Vanden Boeynants was released, unharmed, in the Port City of Antwerp. A group of freelance Belgium reporters followed the activities of the Albanian Mafia for around two years, they concluded that the complete secrecy surrounding the 'mob' made it impossible for them to get close to finding out anything of substance, other than that the Albanian Mafia apes itself on the exact same model as that of their Italian counterparts. According to sources in Brussels, the Albanian Mafia has a complete monopoly on activities such as narcotics and arms dealing.

The French Ministry of Home Affairs have stated that, in almost every City in France, the Albanian Mafia has a stranglehold on narcotics, arms distribution, prostitution and people smuggling. They, like their Belgium neighbours, have said that it is impossible to get to the core of the problem and that every single person they have ever interrogated has either died or disappeared.

'Ethnic Albanians' as the German Police refer to them, migrated from Albania, Macedonia, and the former Yugoslavia, mainly due to the war in Kosovo and despite being very small, in number, they now completely control the Heroin and Prostitution rackets in Hamburg and other major German cities. Many 'fake' Albanian banks were formed during the war and the Billions of USD, made from their illegal business, were fed through those banks to purchase arms and weapons for use by the Kosovan Liberation Army (KLA) in Kosovo. The Albanian Mafia is said to use such an extreme level of violence that the German Police have not been able to produce even one witness to testify against them. It is known that one Mafia family in Hamburg has over Euro 300 million in its property portfolio and has firm ties to the Police, the Judiciary and Prosecutors. The 'Wide Awake Firm' a British gang that operates in Germany is in constant battles with the Albanians.

Given the close geographic vicinity between Albania and Italy, which gives access to the rest of the 'borderless' EU, together with its ties to both the Calabrian and Apulia mobs, the Albanians have been able to expand their operations throughout Italy. They have reached agreements with most of the Italian 'families' which allow them to run their drug trafficking and distribution, without hindrance, from the World's most prominent organised gangs. From the coast of Albania, Montenegro, and the southern tip of Bosnia, several 'sea-routes' are used to Import and distribute illegal narcotics, and people, to all points of Western Europe. In the late 1990's the Italian Authorities decided to come down hard on the Sicilian gangs, making it difficult for them to operate as freely as they had done in the past. The Sicilian's answer was to form a close alliance with the Albanians, franchising out to them the lucrative prostitution, drug dealing and gambling that is so rife along the Adriatic Coast. In return, the Italians were able to establish its own base in Albania, they set up their Headquarters in the coastal town of 'Vlore.' Together they formed a partnership in the illegal trade of smuggling Albanian migrants into Italy. It was not long before the Albanians operated in every part of Italy, paying their Italian friends an agreed fee for each of the operations that they undertook.

Other EU Nations have commented on the Albanian problems as follows. The Netherlands have said that Albanian crime groups are the single biggest Importer of cocaine from South America. The Port of Rotterdam, said to be controlled by the Albanian Mafia, is from where Europe-wide distribution is made, human trafficking and property fraud are high on the list of the gang's activities. In 2019 The Dutch Government asked the EU to suspend the 'freedom of movement' under the 'Schengen' agreement, for Albanian nationals, citing the current unrestrictive movement to and from twenty-one EU member states, as the single biggest reason for the ever-growing enlargement of organised crime within the European Union. The Danish national police say that the 'Ethnic Albanian Mafia' smuggle and control more drugs into Denmark than their entire opposing gangs, put together. In Spain, it is thought that the Albanian Mafia has penetrated almost every industrial estate, making it easy to offload trailer cargo without detection, in addition they have infiltrated banks throughout the Costa-del-Sol and Madrid. They are said to be, 'laundering' billions of Euros through legit businesses, such as restaurants, bars, real estate and even opera houses and theatres.

Of all the European Counties, the UK is the most prolific source of income for the Albanians. Whilst the UK is not part of the 'Schengen' agreement, it seems to make little difference to the number of Albanians that now work and reside in the UK. The past fifteen years has seen the setting up of 19,000 car washes, employing over 200,000 people. The Car-Wash Advisory Service (CWAS) reports that only 5% of these businesses are registered with this official body and that a similar percentage are known to Her Majesty's Revenue and Customs (HMRC). It is estimated that over half of all 'car washes' are controlled by Albanians. The Metropolitan Police's 'Vice Squad' estimates that 75% of all the activities in London's Soho district are run by the Albanian Mafia, this alone brings in £25 million of 'untaxed' income. In 2006, it was Albanian Gangsters that carried out the Securitas heist, netting them some £53 million. Together with the Turkish Mafia, the Albanians control 70% of the UK's prostitution service. In 2018, sources from the National Crime Agency (NCA) say that the Albanians have sold more than 500,000 kgs of drugs, in London alone. Scotland is not immune from the influence of the men from the Balkans, the Scottish Crime and Drug Enforcement Agency (SCDEA) say that the Albanian Mafia has muscled in on all aspects of controlled crime in Scotland, riding rough shot over the decade's old local gangs.

In Canada, the Albanians have taken over from the already-established Russian and Italian syndicates, controlling everything in Toronto, Montreal, and Vancouver. Probably the most efficient and frightening of all the Albanian gangs, are those that operate in the USA. By utilising their connections with the EU, the Albanian Mafia in the USA has grown in stature from its humble beginnings of the mid-80s, when burglaries and robberies were its main source of income, to become affiliated with and then taking over from the Cosa

Nostra as America's most fearsome organised crime syndicate, operating under the Iliazi family name.

Investigations into organised crime, in and around New York, undertaken by the FBI, discovered that the headquarters of the gang operated out of Detroit and trafficked drugs throughout Canada, Mexico, the Netherlands, Columbia, Peru and Venezuela and cooperated with over one hundred Mafia gangs that were based in the European Union. To complete their network, the Albanians have managed to set up organised gangs in Central and South America. The state police in Honduras report 'formidable Albanian Mafia activity.' They have set up or taken over several banks in Central America. Prominent politicians in most South American countries have been lured into their network with huge sums of money, the threat of certain death is reward for anyone that dares to betray them. The DEA has estimated that if the entire money generated by the Albanian gangs were to be put together, then they would be the world's 7th largest economy.

2004 saw the arrest of, by the FBI, almost the entire Rudaj Organisation, the single most violent Albanian 'family' operating in the USA. The arrest of Alex Rudaj, the boss, virtually wiped out the gang, this drastically reduced the standing of the 'family' that continued to operate in Albania.

With the weakening of the Rudaj syndicate, General Kos saw the opportunity to take over control of every element of the Rudaj gangs, in Albania, its near neighbours and the USA. Kos was believed to have increased his army of mercenaries and former Kosovan fighters to over three thousand, all of whom lived in the ever-expanding complex, hidden by the forests and hills that abound on the Albanian / Kosovan border. To protect the top people in his organisation, the General allocated a rank to all of those that would control certain territories, although they would all be known as 'Kos.'

At the end of 2018, the FBI listed over one thousand pure Albanians or ethnic Albanians as 'people of interest.' It is estimated that around 10 percent of Albania's population (currently three million) are, in one way or another, associated with gang-type activities, making them, by far, the largest ratio of criminals to non-criminals on the planet.

Many of the more notorious Albanians that crossed swords with General Kos, would meet their deaths at the hands of his merciless gang members, irrespective of where they were at the time -

Zef Mustafa – an associate of the Gambino family. Had his throat cut, by one of the General's men, posing as the barber in a small salon in the Bronx. 'Private' Kos took over the protection rackets, previously controlled by Zef Mustafa.

Xhevdet Lika (Joe) – American-Albanian kingpin, infamous in New York City for his secretive Mafia dealings. Whilst not known outside of the criminal fraternity, Joe and his 'hit crew' would take, for the right money, any contract. It was common knowledge within the underworld that Joe hated Italians and that he would have 'taken out' Paul Castellano or John Gotti, had he been asked to do so. At one time he was asked, by the CIA to assassinate the President. The Italian Mafia gave Joe a wide berth. 'Joe' met his death in a hail of bullets whilst attending his daughter's end-of-year ball in Chicago. 'Major' Kos, the most prolific murderer in the General's regime, became the number one 'hit man' for the Albanians.

Joseph Ardizzone – was an ethnic Albanian from Sicily and the founder and first boss of the Los Angeles crime family. Joseph was lured into a massage parlour in the seedy part of Long Beach and whilst receiving 'oral sex' a machete was buried deep into his back. He was said, to have 'come and gone' at the same time. 'Sergeant' Kos took over the Californian empire that had been lorded over by Ardizzone.

Alfred Shkurti (Aldo Bare) – Before the General's emergence, Shkurti was the boss of the most notorious criminal syndicate in Albania, he ran the Lushnja Gang. The 'Lushnja' were a truly worldwide criminal organisation. Aldo was the only Albanian rival ever to be killed at the General's complex. He and five 'minders' agreed to a 'sit down' in the village of Vlahen, just a few km from the General's fortress. All six men had their drinks spiked, they were taken to the slaughterhouse, cut up and fed to the wild boar the General kept as pets. The rumours of these sadistic killings soon spread, General Kos became the most feared man in the entire Balkan region, his power in Albania became unrivalled. He appointed a man that had been at his side for over thirty years, as the 'Don' in Albania. He was to be known as 'Admiral' Kos, mainly because of the hundreds of sea crossings he had undertaken when escorting both people and drugs, between Albania and Italy.

Lul Berisha – was the leader of the 'Banda e Lul Berishes' clan, based in Durres, Albania. They distributed drugs and arms throughout Europe and controlled many of the routes that connect Europe to the Middle East via Turkey. The entire gang was wiped out in one week of frenetic fighting. 'Admiral' Kos took control of this business.

The Osmani Brothers – were said to control drugs in almost every city in Germany. After twenty-seven of the gang, including two of the brothers, were killed within 48 hours of each other, the two remaining brothers fled to the USA, where six weeks later, 'Major' Kos killed them both.

Kapllan Murat – was Belgium's most famous mobster and was reputed to be the mastermind behind the kidnapping of the Belgium Prime Minister in 1989. He was tortured and mutilated by the newly installed Belgium number one, 'Captain' Kos.

Naser Kelmendi – was the leader of one of the Balkan's most feared Criminal Empires. Interpol named Kelmendi as being the leader of the largest and most violent organisation ever to rule the underworld, the gang spread outwards from Albania to encompass the whole of the Balkans region. The Kelmendi Family were involved in cigarette and drug trafficking as well as controlling much of the money laundering and loan sharking that made their money 'legit.' Their tentacles reached as far as Germany, the UK, and the USA. In their later years they concentrated on the movement and distribution of cocaine and heroin. Naser Kelmendi was kidnapped by a gang led by 'Colonel' Kos during his transfer from prison to court and has never been seen or heard of since. His territory was given over to the General's brother, 'Commodore' Kos, under the watchful eye of the 'Admiral.'

Elvis Kelmendi – Brother of Naser, thought to have been the 'enforcer' within the organisation, twenty- seven gruesome deaths were attributed to him. As an impersonator of the 'King,' Elvis would often dress the same as his idol and sing 'Don't be Cruel' to his victims, before gunning them down. He was blown apart by a hand grenade, whilst performing, 'I'm all shook up' at a small theatre in Damascus. 'Commodore' Kos took the credit for the murder of Elvis and nine innocent music lovers.

Ibrahim Habibovic – was the leader of an Albanian gang that was based in Napoli, Italy. Known as 'Banda e Belo' the clan moved drugs and arms and took part in many other criminal activities throughout Europe, Turkey, and the Middle East. Two men, dressed entirely in black, scaled the walls of Ibrahim's villa one night, cut off his manhood, raped his naked girlfriend, stuffed Koi Carp into their mouths and threw them into a pond. The newly installed, 'Lieutenant' Kos became the General's man in Italy.

Luan Plakici – was known as the 'vice king' of the Albanian Mafia, he operated only in the UK and made a fortune from trafficking women from all parts of the Balkans, the women were promised good jobs in the UK, but were in fact put into prostitution. Although he was born in Albania, Plakici became a British Citizen and was given a British Passport. In all, it was estimated that he made over £70 million in just under three years. Strangely, whilst all of this was going on, Plakici was retained by three London Solicitors as an interpreter, helping with the Asylum applications of many Albanians. He used his expert knowledge of the Immigration system to help with the smuggling of the women into the UK. Luan Plakici was stopped, in his car, as he drove away from one of his many brothels. He was taken to his own house, where one of his hundreds of 'working girls' cut off his genitals with a Stanley knife, then poured acid down his back, before plunging a large kitchen knife into his throat. The girl was then killed by 'Brigadier' Kos, both bodies then enjoyed a sulphuric acid bath, courtesy of the new Albanian UK boss.

General Kos had succeeded in wiping out all opposing Albanian opposition. The ex-Kosovan army general, although now recognised as the most powerful crime boss in Europe, was getting restless. In recent times he had lost several shipments of drugs to rival gangs. He knew that he had a 'mole' within his close circle of gang members but was unable to pinpoint exactly who it might be. Despite never receiving the drugs, he would still have to pay the suppliers. As he tended not to leave his heavily guarded complex, on the Albanian-Kosovan border, he had little to occupy his mind. He used this time to study the innermost workings of all Mafia gangs and other large criminal organisations. What he found was that almost all the criminal organisations that he studied, were heavily into drugs and arms trafficking. With this came the constant battles between rivals, which left a trail of dead and maimed soldiers in its wake. Kos decided to diversify, and he knew exactly what he was going to do. The General would meet with several 'like-minded' gang leaders. The result would be the birth of a money-making racket, the likes of which the world had never seen.

7 - THE TURKISH MAFIA

Organised crime, on a large scale, began in earnest in Turkey in the late 1970s as a direct result of the conflict between the newly established Kurdistan Workers Party (PKK) and the Turkish Government. This gave rise to all kinds of illegal activities. Gangs, using Mafia-like practices and codes of conduct, began to emerge, predominately to supply arms to the PKK and other militant armies that were seeking political autonomy for the Kurdish inhabitants of Turkey, Syria, Iraq, and Iran. A population of over 30 million Kurds lived in the mountainous regions of those four countries.

Initially, there were many gangs operating in Turkey and fighting between them, for ultimate control, was always a problem, that was until the mid-1980s when the 'Gul' family entered the fray. They would not only control organised crime in Turkey but, as satellite communications advanced, they would enlarge their network to become the largest controlling Mafia family in the World. Even larger than the Albanian crime syndicate, led by General Kos.

Osman Gul, the head of the organisation, was born in Cizre, the main town of the Sirnak Province, in 1964. His birthplace was close to the borders with Syria and Iraq, sitting on what is known as the 'Tripoint' of Turkey, Syria, and Iraq. Cizre's main claim to fame, apart from being the home of Turkey's most notorious family, was that the highest-ever temperature in Turkey, of 49c, was recorded there. Osman was one of several brothers, uncles and cousins that ran, what turned out to be Turkey's number-one criminal gang. Their partners in crime, for many years were the PKK, many of whom lived and fought out of the town, that given its geographical position, was amongst the best placed of all the towns that nestled in the foothills of Turkish Kurdistan. The relationship between the Guls and the PKK facilitated the transportation of arms, drugs and other contraband from Pakistan, Syria, Iraq, Iran, and Afghanistan via the almost un-accessible routes that have existed in the mountains of Kurdistan for centuries.

With the competition to supply arms becoming more and more competitive, the Guls supplied the opium derivative (heroin) to the west, using both the Sicilian and Corsican Mafia, the drugs would then be shipped to New York and other US ports, where the American/Italian Mafia would distribute it accordingly. To meet increasing demand, production bases were set up in Afghanistan and Pakistan. Istanbul became the major export point for all heroin leaving Turkey. Production methods for turning opium into heroin have not changed since ancient times. Working 'hand in hand' with the very top Government Officials meant that no shipment of drugs was ever seized by the Turkish Authorities until 2001, by which time a whole new money-making racket was being established.

The Gul family, whose origins were in the Trabzon area of Turkey, with scores of relatives spread along the entire coastal region of the Black Sea, controlled hundreds of villages, and towns. With their close relationship to the PKK, they were able to move vast quantities of drugs, using nomadic tribal people, largely undetected, from Iran, Iraq, and Syria into Turkey, for distribution to all parts of Europe. Whilst the actual movement of the contraband was primitive, as donkeys and camels were used when vehicles were unable to penetrate the inhospitable terrain, the advent of mobile phones and other communication hardware meant that their operations were mainly unaffected by the authorities.

At the age of 20, Osman Gul was apprehended on the road to Mardin, about 150 km from Cizre, he was carrying 11 kgs of hashish, which was packed tightly onto the rear end of his camel. He had not in fact been caught by the police, he had been stopped by a rival gang who did not want him operating on their patch. He was handed over to the local authorities and made to part with everything that he was carrying. Two years later he would get his revenge on the people that 'grassed him up.' Five rivals died in the ambush that he had set up. After several years of smuggling Arms, Tobacco, and Drugs into Turkey, for distribution to the Balkans, he decided that there was a lot more money to be earnt at the very end of the chain. In 1993 he found his way to the UK, claimed Asylum as a 'displaced' person, was detained for five days, and then released into UK society. He had left his older brother, Azad Gul, in charge of operations back in Cizre and via modern communications, he was able to carry on with his illegal smuggling operations. In 1995 Osman was arrested in London and charged with being in possession of a fake passport, he was sentenced to 12 years. For some reason, that was never recorded, after serving four years of his sentence, he was sent back to Turkey to serve the remainder of his time. After just four months in a Turkish jail, he was released. Four days after his release he was apprehended in the town of Golbasi, a medium-sized town, just south of the capital, Ankara. He was said to be carrying several weapons, including machine guns, and a quantity of narcotics, he was 'sprung' whilst on his way to court and turned up in Amsterdam the following year, where the Dutch police arrested him. He served two years in a jail in Rotterdam. Meanwhile, a younger brother, Birusk, had emigrated to and set up business, in North London. Upon his release from jail in Rotterdam, Osman chose to stay in the Netherlands. In March 2002 Osman was arrested at a villa in Eindhoven. His Nephew, Asti, who had been brought over via one of the illegal smuggling routes that Osman had established, was arrested with him. The operation to detain Osman and Asti Gul was undertaken jointly by police and specialist units from the UK, Italy, Belgium, Germany, and the Netherlands. At their trial, uncle and nephew were found guilty of conspiracy to murder, kidnapping and drug smuggling. Osman was described at his trial as being 'Europe's Pablo Escobar.' Osman received 20 years, which was later increased to life. His nephew was given 11 years.

The illegal drug trade in Turkey has played a significant role in its history, the Turkish Government claim that the PKK gains substantial income from the sale of marijuana, opium, and heroin. Whereas the Government itself is said to benefit from the sale of drugs by some USD 40 billion per year. Turkey has long since been the major 'trans-shipment' point for drugs emanating from Pakistan and Afghanistan, from Turkey it is relatively easy to transport them into Bulgaria and Albania, onward distribution into Western Europe became a whole lot easier when Bulgaria was welcomed into the EU in 2007. Estimations of the volume of heroin trans-shipping via Turkey into the EU is said to be between 8 to 12 tons per month. By far the largest drug cartel in Turkish history was the 'Gul' cartel.

In 2004, Osman Gul was declared 'mentally unstable' it was decided that he should never leave prison. Nephew Asti was released in 2007 and remains in the Netherlands. Aram Gul, a cousin to Osman and Birusk had spent his time controlling a large proportion of the drug market in Germany. He was caught and given 15 years back in 2005. In 2013 he was released and lives in one of Hamburg's most salubrious areas. All three men were 'tried in their absence' for various offences, by a court in Istanbul and were each given 15 years, which in Turkey means exactly that. They will only ever serve that sentence should they return to their homeland. Back home in Cizre seventeen related 'Guls' carry on their relationship with the PKK, it is said that the PKK derives over half of its operational money from the cooperation that it formed with the 'Guls of Cizre.'

The 'Gul Clan', just like many other crime gangs in Turkey, have either purchased drugs for their own set-ups in the EU or have acted as 'couriers' for the hundreds of illegal drug operations that single out Turkey as being the most prominent player in the transportation and re-distribution of drugs. The 'Balkan' routes have long been favoured by these gangs their task has been made much easier by the entry of Bulgaria into the EU in 2007. In 2014 it was estimated that 1.5 million trucks, 250,000 coaches and 4 million cars transited from Turkey to Bulgaria and onwards, each year. In the main, just small quantities of heroin are loaded onto a vehicle, 25-50 kgs is the most common amount. These small shipments are difficult to detect, add to this, the fact that it takes a whole day to search a 40-foot trailer, then it is not hard to understand why up to 95% of all shipments remain undetected. 75% of all the heroin smuggled into Europe is transported via the Balkan route.

When NATO and the EU stationed thousands of troops, intelligence officers and specialised narcotics police, inside the Balkans, attempting to stem the flow of illegal drugs, the Gul family and General Kos met for the first time, they were quick to intervene, paying millions of USD to the men charged with stopping their illegal activities, to ensure their operations did not suffer. Pristina in Kosovo is where the largest concentration of these forces can be found and yet this is the very place where the Mafia and their collaborators are at their strongest. The Guls partnered with Hungary's most fearsome crime gang as there are huge storage facilities available for them to store their illegal wares, it is also easy to form 'legit' companies in Hungary, making it easy for drug money to be laundered. The Turks and Albanians have purchased restaurants, bars, fast-food franchises, real estate agencies, travel agencies, vehicle repair shops and International Logistics Companies, in Budapest and the other large towns and cities within Hungary. Many EU transport companies register their vehicles in Budapest, making transport in and out, extremely easy.

The Guls, through their connections Worldwide, have been able to blackmail most of the Turkish Ambassadors around the world. The Ambassadors have leaked classified information and reports to the Gul crime gangs after being subjected to 'honey traps' with the help of escort ladies, some of whom were Foreign Nationals, in return for sex or considerable amounts of money, the diplomats handed over sensitive documents, some of which included the secrets of Foreign Powers. The investigation exposed not only the diplomats, but it also found the names and fortunes of rival gang members, top brass military personnel, Chief of Police Officers, and investigators. A network, of escort workers, was set up to gain knowledge of Turkey's military strength, they seduced eleven Ambassadors and Ministers. Despite their obvious guilt, not one of the 'traitors' were ever taken to task, and they all carried on representing their country. The Gul family were said to have made 'millions' from the sale of the sensitive information to Governments Worldwide.

It is of no coincidence that Germany and the UK are the largest recipients of illegal drugs. The Guls were quick to establish links with the large Kurdish immigrant communities that have formed in the UK and Germany. Criminal gangs within these communities have formed relationships with the Guls and Kurdish gangs back home. They are heavily involved in drug smuggling and contract killing. It is suspected that many murders undertaken by these gangs have been orchestrated in the hills of Kurdistan, with 'hitmen' travelling thousands of miles to 'take out' rivals, returning afterwards to their simple life in the villages and towns of Kurdistan. In London, the two most famous, and feared gangs, are the Tottenham Boys and the Hackney Bombers. Over two hundred gangland killings have been attributed to them since 2001, with hundreds more simply not solved. The Turks in the UK, initially under the control of Birusk Gul, have taken over from the Jamaican Yardies. A 26-year-old asylum seeker, said to be from Kurdistan, was found on the banks of the Regents Canal, his head and hands were found in Cambridge. He had six forms of identity on his body, three of which were known to the UK Social Services, packets of Heroin were stuffed in his mouth, nose, and ears. He was a member of the Tottenham Boys gang. In a revenge attack, two members of the Hackney Bombers were gunned down as they drove through the East End of London in a white convertible BMW. The passenger was hit in the head as the car drove at 60 mph, the car crashed, two men approached and shot the driver seven times, they finished him off by pouring petrol over him and setting the car on fire. The incident took place at 2 pm on a busy Saturday, there were many witnesses, none of whom came forward. In both cases the NCA believed the killers had arrived in the UK, using false documents, and then left again, without detection. Birusk Gul was jailed for 16 years in 1999.

With Birusk incarcerated, rival gangs from both the Albanian and Pakistani communities, in the UK and Germany, fought back, attempting to muscle in, on the ever-growing and lucrative heroin and cocaine trade. In one part of London, the Albanians have formed an alliance with the Pakistanis, together they killed three members of the local Gul gang and were charged, when caught, with eighteen additional counts of attempted murder. The financial return on Heroin and Cocaine, at street level is so great that dealers do not think twice about murdering rivals.

During the time that Birusk Gul was in a UK jail, a new gang, led by one of the most vicious men ever to walk the streets of North London, emerged as the 'Don.' He was, Kagan Kaptan, whose name means 'King or Ruler.' Kagan was part of a convoy of eleven Kurds that had set off from several villages that bordered Turkey, Syria, and Iraq. They had not paid to be smuggled from their homelands, they had all agreed to work in the drug business for their masters, in whichever country they would eventually arrive. The initial part of their journey meant walking, over some of the most hostile terrain in the world. When they reached Mardin, close to the Turkish / Syrian border, they were loaded onto trucks, destined for Mersin, a large Turkish Port, North of the island of Cyprus. From Mersin a small cargo ship conveyed them to Istanbul. This leg of their journey had taken 10 days. Inside the Port of Istanbul, which was almost totally controlled by Kurdish criminal elements, they were hidden under the false floors of container trucks and driven to Sofia in Bulgaria. In Sofia, the stowaways were separated, some days later, three would arrive in Hamburg, Germany, two in Marseilles, South of France, two in Paris and another two found their final stopping point to be Amsterdam. Not one of the nine had encountered any problems whatsoever during the time that they were travelling. The same could not be said for the two poor souls that arrived in Antwerp, Belgium.

Kagan Kaptan and his travelling companion, Adnan Mehmed, a five-foot-two-inch nomad from the Syrian side of the Kurdish mountains, were met in Antwerp by a fellow Kurd, he took them to a small inlet along the Belgium coast, where all three men boarded a dingy that was just big enough for two people. At 10.00 pm, in complete darkness, they gently rowed out into the North Sea before turning on the small outboard motor. The North Sea was rough, it was the middle of November, it was just 2c. The two immigrants had been given waterproof coats however this did not protect them from the 2 to 3, metre waves, that almost capsized the small boat every time the sea swelled around them. One hour out from Belgium the dingy was catapulted from the sea, settling upside down in the choppy waters. Kagan and his tour guide managed to get back to the boat and return it to its upright position. Adnan never made it he would never be found. As dawn broke the next morning, they could see the coastline of the UK. The engine was cut, and without oars, which had been lost during the night, they had to use their hands to motion the dingy forwards, towards the stone-laden beach. They had arrived, just half a mile away from their intended rendezvous point. The courier took a mobile phone, which had been wrapped in plastic and tied with an elastic band, from the inside pocket of his waterproofs and spoke, in Turkish, to a man, who fifteen minutes later would be on the beach to greet them. This man gestured for Kagan to follow him, whilst the captain of the dingy drifted quietly out to sea before firing up the engine. Kagan had arrived on a beach halfway between Felixstowe and Clacton-on-Sea. Of course, Kagan had no idea as to where he was, at that time he was not even aware of the fact that he was safely in the UK, the country that, given the choice, he was most desperate to be in.

Safely ensconced into the passenger seat of a black Range Rover and getting warmer by the minute, Kagan spoke, in Kurdish, for the first time. He asked the driver sat next to him as to exactly where they were going. The driver, introducing himself as Mehmet, replied that they were heading to London, where he would hand Kagan over to his boss. Firstly however, they would stop at a transport café by the side of the busy A12. Mehmet ordered two 'full English' and a pot of tea. Kagan had never seen such food in his life however he cleaned his plate long before his driver did. Ninety minutes later the Range Rover pulled up and parked outside a North London bowling alley. Mehmet asked Kagan to wait until he returned to the car. As soon as Mehmet had entered the lobby of the bowling alley Kagan opened the door and legged it down Green Lanes. Arriving at the junction with Turnpike Lane, he crossed and disappeared down one of the many side-streets that were available to him on both sides of the road. Kagan Kaptan was just 21-years old he had never been outside the sanctuary of the foothills of Kurdistan prior to taking the long journey from his homeland. Now he found himself all alone in one of the world's largest cities, but he was not frightened or worried, his only aim at that time was 'survival.' Kagan was clever, in his village he was the single most educated person. He had handled all the communications that the village elder had received or made, overseas, or to the PKK contacts and whilst his English was not great, it was good enough to get him understood. All he had to do was to stay away from the area that he now found himself in, as to be discovered would mean his certain death.

Kagan had really taken a gamble on whether he would be trafficked to the UK, he could quite as easily have ended up in Germany, France, Belgium, or Holland, had he done so then he would still have somehow made his way to London. He knew the penalty for escaping the clutches of his ruthless countrymen would be death, he had heard stories of how other 'escapees' had been infused with heroin and made to carry out mutilations and murders on anyone that dared to take on his intended boss. Taylan Turgut was the name of the Kurd that Kagan should have been delivered to. He had taken over as the head of the Kurds in North London, in the absence of Birusk Gul. He was ruthless, and said to have 17 murders to his name, but had never been arrested or charged with any crime whatsoever, which was strange, given the fact that he was not registered with any authority in the UK, did not have a National Insurance number, an NHS entitlement or a driving license, even though he drove several 'high end' cars around the streets of London Town. Kagan had done some homework before setting off on his journey, he had the name of a cleric that taught at the Aziziye Mosque in Stoke Newington and as luck would have it, when he came out of the side street and into Lordship Lane, he saw a sign that stated Stoke Newington was just four miles away.

Entering the mosque at 4.30 on Friday afternoon, Kagan needed to find Nur Nazif, once an elder in the village from where he came from. Stepping into the always open doors, he was confronted by an elderly man, sat on a stall in the vast reception area of what was once the Astoria Cinema. Kagan approached the old man, bowed in a prayer-like motion, and simply said, Nur Nazif. The much senior man stood, bowed to Kagan, and gestured for him to follow. Together they crossed the massive prayer hall, strolled down an inner hall, and arrived at a large wooden door. The old man bowed to Kagan and re-traced his steps back to his stall near to the main doors. As Kagan pulled his arm back in readiness to knock, the door opened, and a man brushed passed him. Inside, a man, sat at a large oak desk, beckoned Kagan in. In English, the seated man asked if he could help, Kagan replied,

'I am from the homeland, I come to you with the blessing of Ozturk Ozsoy.'

'And you are?' asked the man now leaning back in his leather-clad chair.

'I am Kagan Kaptan, I have just arrived from the mountains.'

Kagan had no need to ask the name of the man that had now risen and was closing the door to the room, as on his desk was a brass name plate, upon which were written the words, 'Nur Nazif.'

Before he had set out on his perilous journey, the head of the village, Ozturk Ozsoy had informed Kagan that, in London, he should trust only one man, he was now in the company of this man. Before any more words were spoken, Nur Nazif asked Kagan to follow him. Two minutes later they entered a restaurant that was run by the mosque, it served food that Kagan was used to. Nur Nazif did not ask many questions of Kagan, telling him that to tell him too much would leave them both vulnerable, should they fall into the wrong hands, Kagan understood. After they had finished eating Nur Nazif led Kagan upstairs, opened a door to a room that was akin to a London bedsit and said,

'This will be your home until you are able to find somewhere for yourself, you will work in the butchers opposite the restaurant until you are able to find work. In London you should remain quiet, do not frequent any of the kebab shops, barbers, cafes, or restaurants that belong to the Turks, as they are all under the control of the man that you should be working for, Taylan Turgut.'

Kagan looked startled,

'Yes, I know who brought you here, you are owned by this man, he will never stop looking for you, do not give your name to anyone, become someone else, it is the only way that you will survive.' 'Now I must attend prayers, you should only ever talk to me by coming to my office, you cannot be seen talking to me outside of this mosque, God be with you.'

Nur Nazif closed the door to Kagan's new home.

Kagan lay on the bed, exhausted. Putting his hands under the pillow he pulled out some money, an oyster card, and a prayer book. He had no idea what he would do with the oyster card.

Kagan would stay at the mosque for a full two years. During this time, he became 'streetwise' he took the assumed name of Adnan Mehmed, the small man that had drowned during the crossing of the North Sea. He worked his way up the chain of a nearby gang, the Clapton Crew, he was both trusted and liked by his comrades, who believed him to have escaped from Turkey, eventually making his own way across the channel in a truck that he had stowed away in when parked at the 'jungle' near Calais.

One evening, Kagan and four gang members entered the bowling alley that belonged to Taylan Turgut and although Taylan was surrounded by six of his inner circle Kagan approached him and knocked him out with a single punch, the five Clapton Crew members fled before anyone could react. Humiliated, Taylan put a contract out for every member of the 'crew' with the stipulation that 'only the head' of the victim should be brought to him. This one punch was enough to start a seven-year war between two of the most feared of all London's underworld gangs. Innocent shopkeepers were killed, many suffered horrific deaths, their only crime was that they were controlled by one gang or the other. Before this war started, Kagan bid farewell to Nur Nazif and moved on to Southend in Essex, telling not a soul as to his plans. During the 'seven-year' battle between the two rival gangs, 27 gang members and 12 innocents would meet their deaths, nearly 100 others were maimed or seriously injured. Taylan Turgut fled back to and laid low in Turkey, for his own safety, only to be caught for Cocaine smuggling, he received a sentence of 37 years and will be in his 80s, should he survive, until his release date. After the fourteenth member of the two gangs appeared in court, the head of London's 'special branch' was quoted as saying,

'The people of North London are scared, it sounds like a gangster film, but it's real-life.'

At this trial, a video, made by the Clapton Crew, showed a member of the 'Bombers' gang hanging naked, upside down and being slowly castrated with a machete, a female member of the jury passed out when the first testicle hit the floor.

All this violence and the subsequent trials prompted the UK's National Crime Agency to conduct the most extensive (and expensive) investigation ever undertaken on UK soil. What they discovered would leave even the most experienced of officers flabbergasted.

Mohammed, a 21-year-old student of Iranian decent was preparing his dinner at his bedsit above a shop on Green Lanes, Finsbury Park. He heard screams and what he thought sounded like fireworks going off. Looking out of his first-floor window, he saw a man crawling across the pavement below, inching slowly towards another man, who remained motionless. Presuming that both men had been shot, Mohammed called the police. What the young Iranian had witnessed was the 'tail end' of a fight that had begun two miles away at a kebab shop, allegedly controlled by a Turkish gang. At the height of the battle, it had involved over 100 Turks and Kurds, armed with guns, knives, baseball bats and various metal objects. Five men were left dead along Green Lanes and 27 sustained serious injuries, all requiring treatment in hospital. The police surrounded the façade of the kebab shop with a white tent, whilst forensics tried to gather clues. Of the 43 witnesses that the police interviewed, none were willing to make a statement. This prompted the afore mentioned investigation, which was undertaken at the behest of local people, who claimed that it just was not safe to leave their houses, at any time, day, or night.

Two undercover officers were able to shed some light upon the potential suspects however there was no proof to support their claims. What did become clear, several weeks into the investigation, was that the imprisoned Taylan Turgut, recently returned from Turkey, was carrying out 'execution' orders on behalf of Ozturk Ozsoy, the brother-in-law of Osman Gul, who himself was serving life in Rotterdam's most notorious jail. One Kurdish businessman, in a statement to a local newspaper, said,

'That whilst the police always turn-up at the scene of these crimes, no one is ever held to account, the police then just disappear again.' He added,

'What is at stake here is the control of the entire UK heroin trade and that control is fought over on the streets of North London, and it appears that no one can stop it.'

This man later died in a 'hit-and-run' accident, just yards from his clothes shop in Green Lanes. No one was arrested for this 'accident.'

In the 'purge' that followed the battle of Green Lanes, £2 million worth of heroin was seized from 12 shops. One shop owner had his Enfield house raided and 42 kgs of heroin, with a street value of £12 million, together with several handguns' knives and even a rocket launcher, were seized. His shop, like scores of others along the six-mile-long road, was used to supply drugs to users and pushers alike. Most of these shops are open for 24 hours per day however they do not sell any goods, other than drugs. Most local shoppers are discouraged from entering any of these premises, large men control the doors, ensuring that only buyers of illegal substances are allowed in. Failure to pay 'protection money' to the gangs by the 'legit' business owners normally results in a beating, maiming or a shop burning to the ground. The involvement of Interpol in the investigation revealed that, although five members of the Gul family were serving time in various prisons, they were still able to control the heroin market in the UK, Turkey, Germany, Netherlands, Italy, and Spain. The senior policeman heading up the task force said that it was unlikely that the Turks, Kurds, or Albanians would ever be stopped unless they managed to wipe each other out.

Osman Gul, born in Cizre, in the foothills of Kurdistan, had his wealth estimated at £10 Billion, this figure being derived only from the legitimate business that he had set-up over the years, all with money that had come from the sale of drugs, the money was then laundered before being put back into the system. He was by far Turkey's most-wealthiest man.

In Southend-on-Sea, Kagan Kaptan had ditched the alias of, 'Adnan Mehmet' that he was known as back in North London, safe in the knowledge that there was no one, either left alive or not in prison that would know him. When, in 2007, he decided to return to his 'homeland' Kagan was controlling 80% of the drug trade in his adopted town, he left the business under the control of his young brother, Ibrahim and returned to his family, he was not however, going back to once again lead a nomadic existence, he had 'other plans,' plans that would make him a fortune, way and above anything that he was making in the violent and risky world of drug dealing.

8 - NGUYEN QUANG THANH – The Diplomat

On the 6th of June 1968, in the market of Cho Lon, Saigon, a crowd of people gathered around as Ha, the wife of the deceased, former Chinese escapee, Tang Tao, who had become Nguyen Quang Thanh, went into labour, and quickly gave birth to her first and only child. For Ha there was to be no ambulance to take her to hospital when her waters broke in the kitchen of the café where she had worked since the age of 12. There was then, as there is now, no 999 service to call when someone needs medical assistance in Vietnam. The 'old lady' of the market, Ms. Binh, having had several children of her own, knew exactly what to do. There were no clean towels to be had, although hot water was available, some cloth was seconded from the tailors opposite the café. The baby, a boy, was born twenty minutes after his mum had started her labour. The baby's initial clothing was a bright green length of cotton fabric.

Just under five months earlier, Ha's husband, who had assumed the identity of Nguyen Quang Thanh, had been killed by the shells of the Viet Cong. At the time, he was a Captain in the South Vietnamese Army, he was just 18 years old when he met his death. The new-born baby had arrived on the exact same day as his father had, albeit 19 years previously. Ms. Ha, with her baby held tightly in her arms, was helped into a cyclo and taken to the home of Ms. Linh, the market trader that Thanh had lived with after arriving in Saigon six years earlier. The birth of her son would change Ha's life, her income was derived from her work at the café, every day of the week for the past nine years, working fourteen hours each day, she had made coffee, prepared food, served, cleaned tables, carried vegetables through the large market and made everything ready for the following day, before she was able to leave at 8 pm. Ms. Linh, who had treated Thanh as her own son, since arriving in Saigon after fleeing China, had vowed to her adopted son that she would look after Ha and his baby, should anything happen to him. That time had now come, and she was keeping her promise to the young man that had lost his life defending, not his, but someone else's country. Ha, after recovering from the trauma of giving birth, had been given the responsibility of looking after Linh's mother, brothers, sisters, and their children. She would be eternally grateful to Ms. Linh. The market traders would give Ha a wonderful surprise, they laid on a lavish party to celebrate the boy's first birthday and in honour of his father, he was christened as Nguyen Quang Thanh.

As he grew, young Thanh would go to the market with his adopted grandmother, Ms. Linh. He would play with the scores of other children that were taken there every day by their working mums. Most of these children would never attend school, as schooling had to be paid for and most parents were not in any position to part with money that had to be used to buy food for the family. At the age of five, Linh could see that Thanh was different from most of the other children, she saw him as being clever, she discussed with Ha the possibility of sending him to school, however Ha had no money with which to pay for him. Linh, who made reasonable money from her business, told Ha that she would pay the school fees until such time as she, herself could help. Ha only wanted the best for her fatherless son, therefore she agreed. In the summer of 1973, with the war creeping nearer and nearer to Saigon, Thanh attended the small state-run school that ran along the Northern perimeter of Cho Lon market. According to his teacher, Thanh was a model student, studious and polite and never ceasing to talk about the father that he had never met.

With the retirement from her business in February 1974, Ms. Linh handed over the keys to Ha, Linh now ran the house and looked after young Thanh. Soon after taking over the shop, Ha was serving an American soldier, a Sergeant, with some provisions that the cook of his platoon had asked him to get, he had two other soldiers with him, both were privates, neither were older than 17. Ha served the Sergeant, as her staff were just too shy to face 'foreigners,' the Sergeant noticed that Ha had tears in her eyes. He asked her what was wrong, Ha explained that seeing him reminded her of her dead husband, as uniforms always brought back memories to her. Ha was pretty, even though her long hair was tied-back, and she wore bold striped, pyjama-like clothes. Knowing that he might never get the chance again, Sergeant Dwight O'Mara asked Ha if she was free to take coffee with him later that evening. The blushing 26-year-old answered yes, the forty or so onlookers that had gathered around the three servicemen wooed in delight. Ha was to meet the US Airman at 7.30 that evening, the venue was to be one of the open-air coffee shops that lined the street just outside the market.

With her head spinning and her heart racing, Ha entrusted Linh's sister with the running of the shop and left early. She would need to go back to the house, to shower and change, in readiness for her first date with a man since the death of her husband in 1968. Returning to the house, Thanh ran to her and asked why she was home. Thanh was normally fast asleep on the floor whenever his mother returned home from work. Ha felt guilty, she did not want to upset her son, so she decided not to tell him of her pending date. When she went into the bathroom Linh followed her, Ha broke down, sobbing, Linh consoled her and asked what was wrong, Ha explained. Once Ha had calmed down Linh told her that she was not doing anything wrong and that she must take the opportunity to meet with the American. Linh said that there was no need to tell Thanh as this might just be a 'one off' date. Ha felt much better about things, she made herself ready, her son was fast asleep on his bamboo mat when she left the house.

The walk from the house to the coffee shop took Ha less than ten minutes. Sergeant O'Mara was already seated in the open-air pavement area of the café. Standing to greet Ha, who now appeared to be even more pretty than when he had first seen her, less than four hours earlier, Dwight O'Mara offered his hand to Ha, she accepted his gesture, although she turned her head to one side when her hand touched his. From her many years of working in the market, Ha's English was quite good, she had met and chatted with soldiers from the USA, Australia, and New Zealand, however she had always declined the many offers of a date, until now. At first it was quite difficult, with them both speaking at the same time, until O'Mara suggested that Ha tell him all about herself and then he would do likewise. Ms. Ha cried when telling the story of her short life with her deceased husband, although she did not mention the fact that he had escaped from China. Most of her conversation centred around her son, she had decided that O'Mara, or anyone else for that matter, had to know that she already had a child. The sergeant informed Ha that he was 24-years old, he had a fiancé prior to coming to Vietnam, some three years ago, however that relationship had broken down when his intended cheated on him after a year of him being away. He added that he was stationed at the US Airbase at Tan Son Nhat, Saigon's only International Airport and that he was currently on his third 'tour of duty.' Ha looked sad when the uniformed airman told her that he must return to his base immediately after this meeting, her head was telling her that it was not right for her to see him again, however her heart, void of any love or male companionship for so long, was telling her something entirely different. She had seen many girls from the market, go out with US Servicemen, most were 'one-night stands' some even ended up in pregnancy and almost always the girls never saw their lovers again.

When Airman, Sergeant Dwight O'Mara asked Ha to meet him again, in three weeks-time, she found herself saying 'yes,' before he had even finished asking.

For the next three weeks Ha thought of nothing, other than meeting up with the Sergeant again. At 7.30 pm, exactly three weeks to the day after their first encounter, Ha arrived at the coffee shop, O'Mara was sat at the same table, this time they kissed. One hour later they checked into a small hotel, situated less than 100-yards from where their first-ever kiss took place. Ha had of course had sex with her husband, many times, however she had never experienced the sheer exhilaration and pleasure that she derived from that first-ever sexual encounter with Dwight O'Mara. She hoped, beyond hope that she was not going to be just another notch on this man's belt. She would not be disappointed, at least not for a while.

During the remainder of 1974, Sergeant O'Mara would meet up with Ha whenever he was given time off from his duties at the airbase, he even managed to persuade the cook that provisions were required on a more regular basis. It was in December 1974 that O'Mara would first meet with Ha's son, they were both nervous, however unbeknown to Ha, Ms. Linh had prepared Thanh, she had explained to him that his mum was still young and that she was lonely, adding that no one was ever going to replace his dad. After the introductions, Ha and Dwight took young Thanh to the park, they ate noodles from a roadside stall and then had ice cream, which Thanh was rarely given. Later, when they returned to the house, Thanh seemed quite contented, he even hugged Dwight, before stretching out on his bamboo mat, he slept within minutes. Ha was happy that her son seemed to have taken to her boyfriend, everything in her life now seemed to be positive.

Early in 1975 Sergeant O'Mara began to tell Ha of what was happening with the war against the 'commies' from the North. He had been careful not to discuss this with her previously as there were many cases of US Military being 'set-up' by young, pretty, Vietnamese girls. O'Mara presumed that anything he told Ha, she would keep to herself, after all, it was him that had made the first approach to her and not the other way around. He informed Ha that the People's Army of Vietnam (PAVN) and the Viet Cong were getting ever closer to Saigon, having overrun the South Vietnamese Army (SVA) and pushed back their American allies. Ha was alarmed, as were most of Saigon's population, as the city had suffered only slightly from the war that had raged for over ten years, mainly in the Northern and Central areas of South Vietnam. On March 5th, 1975, O'Mara told Ha that in a memo that had circulated his Airbase, both the CIA and the Intelligence Corp were confident that the South would hold out, at least until the middle of 1976, even though the US were withdrawing troops at an ever-increasing rate.

The memo proved to be worthless as just five days later General Dung (PAVN) launched a major offensive in the Central Highlands of South Vietnam, taking the town of Buon Ma Thuot just days later. The SVA retreated, hoping to hold the opposition at bay along the 13th parallel, however the PAVN were far too strong and took the cities of Hue and Da Nang before the end of March. American CIA officers in Vietnam advised their commanders that nothing short of the massive bombing of Hanoi by B52 bombers could halt the progression of the Communists. O'Mara prepared Ha for the worst, informing her that he, along with everyone else at the airbase, would have to take the fight to the enemy. On the 8th of April, the Politburo in Hanoi cabled General Dung, they instructed him to use 'unremitting vigour' in the attack upon Saigon. The South requested an increase in military aid from the USA, the USA were not forthcoming. By the 21st of April, the front line was just 26 miles from the centre of Saigon. At the same time, having committed over 200,000 troops to the Mekong Delta (South of Saigon) the commies were able to take that area, effectively surrounding Saigon from all sides, the situation was dire.

With almost the entire South Vietnamese Army (around 300,000 troops) now defending Saigon, with many units not being under anyone's control, anarchy prevailed. Southern troops were defecting to the North and specialist Communist officers penetrated the army of the South, some even working shoulder-to-shoulder with US platoons. O'Mara sat Ha down and informed her that it was likely that the US would pull its entire operations out of Vietnam before the end of April. He told her that he had made provision to take both her and Thanh out of Vietnam when the time came. There was a major concern that once the Communists entered Saigon a bloodbath would ensue as this had been the case after Hue and Da Nang were taken. Mass graves containing officers, Roman Catholics, intellectuals, businessmen and American collaborators, had been found, many of them had been 'headless. Many captured US personal had suffered the same fate. There was now a mass departure of US staff from Saigon, although many, who had common-law wives and children, refused to leave when ordered, as it was illegal for the US Airforce to move these people onto American soil. Eventually, whilst still illegal, undocumented Vietnamese citizens were flown to Clark Air Base in the Philippines. O'Mara had paved the way for Ha and Thanh to get out of Saigon via this route.

During the first week of April 1975, President Ford announced that the USA would accept 2,500 orphans and that a further 110,000 refugees would also be accepted. The not-so-lucky citizens to be listed as priorities for repatriation would have to sell 'everything' to get an 'under the table' passport and visa that allowed them to enter the USA. Properties were sold at just 25% of their true value, whole families placed newspaper ads in the US, begging to be adopted. American military support was, by now, non-existent. Pilots of the South defected to the North, on the 28th of April, planes piloted by the former South Vietnamese Airforce, bombed Tan Son Nhat Airport, rendering the only remaining runway 'un-operational.' O'Mara, defying orders, made his way to Cho Lon and told Ha to gather up Thanh and make her way to a designated bus stop, from there they could board a 'safe' bus which would take them to

Bien Hoa Air Base. O'Mara then returned, in his jeep to Tan son Nhat. Before leaving he handed Ha two pieces of paper, telling her to show them, firstly to the bus driver and then to Sergeant Reilly at the gatehouse to the base at Bien Hoa. He assured her that he would meet her at Bien Hoa before the departure of the plane that would take them all to the Philippines. He apologised for not being able to take Ms. Linh or any of her family with them.

Two hours later, Ha and Thanh, along with hundreds of others were at the bus stop, a dozen public service buses, driven by US staff, lined the side of the road. US soldiers rushed up and down the line, they all carried clipboards with lists of names, written on sheets of paper, attached to the clipboards. They were seeking out the Vietnamese that carried the authority to board the buses, over half of the people there had no such authority. The noise coming from the crowd was deafening, with screaming, crying, and fighting making it nigh impossible for the American staff to do their job. Eventually, Ha was approached by a Sergeant, she handed him the two pieces of paper that O'Mara had given to her. Studying the paperwork, the Sergeant smiled at Ha and said,

'Dwight O'Mara, right?'

'Yes.'

The Sergeant pushed Ha and Thanh onto the bus, whilst at the same time trying to prevent others from boarding with her. Half an hour later, the bus started to move away from the stop. People were running after the bus, trying to hold on to the mirrors, the open windows and even the wheels, several were injured in their attempt to escape from Saigon. One and a half hours later, the bus joined a long queue of similar buses that were waiting to enter the gates of the Air Base. Hundreds, if not thousands, of people were milling around outside the base, armed US Military Police were doing their best to hold the crowd at bay. The bus was boarded by several US staff as it waited to enter, everyone had to show their paperwork again. A dozen people, without any documents, were taken off the bus and led away from the gates of the base. A further hour elapsed before the bus was safely within the grounds of the massive complex that the US Airforce had made their home for the last eight years. During the segregation of the 'lucky' passengers, they were split into groups of ten and then placed into small open-air tents, Ha was led to one side by a Captain and asked to sit down. With Thanh held tightly to her, as if he had been glued, the captain crouched onto one knee, as his eyes met Ha's, he said,

'I am so sorry Ms. Ha, but Dwight O'Mara was killed earlier today. His jeep was hit by a mortar, whilst driving out of Tan Son Nhat Airport. With no sponsor we are not able to take you to the Philippines, had the boy been Dwight's son, then it would have been different.' I am so sorry Ha, there is nothing that I can do about it.'

The captain turned and left. Ha and Thanh were escorted by two MPs and led outside the gates of the complex.

Ha, crying profusely, was now just one of the people that had gathered outside the heavily armed complex, they all wanted just one thing, to get on a plane and get out of Vietnam. None would be lucky, only those 'invited' people would be leaving. A young Vietnamese woman, also holding a boy of a similar age to Thanh, came over and asked Ha why she had been led back outside the complex, Ha explained, the woman, who introduced herself as Yen, told Ha that exactly the same thing had happened to her, she too was due to leave when she was informed that her boyfriend, and sponsor, had been killed at Tan Son Nhat Airport.

One hundred metres away, a small group of children were playing. Unlike his mum, Thanh was not emotional, after all, he hardly knew Sergeant Dwight O'Mara. Thanh asked if he and Yen's son could go and join the other children, Ha agreed, Yen released her grip on her son, Binh, and both boys ran off. No sooner had they left when three A-37 Dragonflies dropped six Mk81 bombs from above. Their targets had maybe been the line of buses that waited both inside and outside of the base. 357 innocent Vietnamese were killed, Ha and Yen were amongst them. Their boys played on, oblivious to the fact that they were now, both orphans. Thanh and Binh searched for, what seemed like hours, for their respective parents, to no avail. Eventually, after the final cargo plane of that day had successfully taken to the sky, the US Airmen were able to start helping the children, it was a grim task. Searching through the dead and maimed was nobody's idea of fun, but it had to be done. In the eerie silence that had descended on the night of the 28th, April 1975, Thanh heard his name being called, he ran to the US Soldier that appeared to be calling him, his heart raced as he presumed, they had found his mum, unfortunately, it was not to be. The young US Airman informed Thanh that he was to board a C-130E, due to leave Bien Hoa at 4.00am on the 29th of April, the hastily arranged flight was, primarily to take orphaned children out of Vietnam, destination Thailand. Thanh, frightened, beyond reason, managed a slight smile when he learnt that his new playmate, Binh, would be on the same aircraft. At 03.58 on the 29th of April, the aircraft, with six crew and 137 orphans on board, taxied to the end of the runway, but before it could turn it was hit by a 122mm rocket, no one was killed, however the plane was left incapacitated.

There was only one other aircraft capable of flying, that was a C-130 that had landed one hour before. The complex was now under heavy fire from the commies, the crew did their best to hurry the children off the stricken aircraft and on to the other one. 41 of the children did not make it, Thanh and Binh were amongst them. It would later be found that the pilots of the three Dragonflies that had killed the boy's mothers, had in fact recently 'defected' from the South Vietnamese Airforce and joined their former enemies to save their own lives. The Dragonflies were shot down by US fighters before they could return to their base. The C-130, which had managed to load 96 of the stricken youngsters, was in fact the last US Aircraft to take to the skies, within hours, the base and everyone in it would be wiped out by the soldiers of the North.

A group of nine of the children that had not been able to board the last flight out, including Thanh and Binh, escaped through a hole in the airport's perimeter wall and blended into the nearby, dense jungle. Five hours later, the group emerged from the jungle and found themselves by the side of a main road. Thanh was just short of his seventh birthday, but he was clever enough to understand that the soldiers marching along the road were not the same as the ones that he had seen every day on the streets in and around Cho Lon. At first, the nine orphans marched alongside the thousands of Viet Cong troops, heading, as their conversations would reveal, to Saigon. Along the way a few of the children would veer off, back into the jungle or onto another road, whenever they reached a junction. Thanh and Binh remained with the soldiers, who would, at any time, shoot anyone that was not from the North, the boys had no food, or water and the 'enemy' was not sharing theirs.

The following morning, only Thanh and Binh remained from the nine that had escaped through the airport wall, and together with the Viet Cong they entered the Northern suburbs of Saigon. There was some opposition, however the South Vietnamese Army was on its knees. The Americans had managed to evacuate themselves and around 4,000 Vietnamese from the American Embassy and despite continuing thunderstorms, helicopters were still able to land and take out those that had gathered within the sanctuary of its walls. By the time the final helicopter flew away, 420 South Koreans and Vietnamese were left behind. On the 30th of April 1975, South Vietnam was absorbed into the North and became one country, Vietnam. Saigon was renamed as, Ho Chi Minh City and anyone not using the new name, was shot. Thanh had only one objective, to get himself and his friend to Cho Lon and the sanctuary of 'granny Linh's' house. His task was made easier by the fact that the whole City was in turmoil. Looting was rife, the two boys would have to steal food and water to survive. People were being marched out of their properties, at gunpoint. Public transport was at a standstill. Running out of a shop, after stealing some rice and fish, Thanh and Binh were stopped at gunpoint, by a soldier who could not have been much older than twelve, he wore a red strip of fabric around his head, he was, of course a Viet Cong. With his fixed bayonet glistening in the sun, the soldier pinned Binh against the shop wall and forced the blade deep into his chest, as Binh sank to his knees the soldier withdrew his weapon, all the while he held onto Thanh by the top of his trousers. A truck pulled up, it was overfull of children, Thanh was picked up by two Viet Cong and thrown into the pile of bodies that filled the back of the truck. Two other young, victorious Communists, guarded their 'prisoners.' The truck was to make several more stops along the road, before the order was given to take both itself and its cargo of human misery to a park, located along Hai Ba Trung, District 1, Saigon. At the heavily guarded park, Thanh and his fellow captives were unloaded from the truck and lined up in groups, according to their size. From the smallest to the largest, one by one the children were led away to separate areas of the park, eventually being reloaded onto smaller trucks, and driven out, under guard, into the darkness of the night.

Thanh had no idea as to where his destination might be, his thoughts were for his mother and his adopted granny, Linh. He wondered if he would ever see either one of them again. He was still not, for certain, aware of the fate of his mum.

Thirty children, including Thanh, all almost identical in height and size exited the park in the back of a filthy dirty, old, and rusty, Russian truck. The only protection from the elements was a tarpaulin sheet that had been erected atop several bamboo poles. All the children had been given red shorts, matching T-shirts, and red bandanas, they were now the property of the Viet Cong. After a four-hour drive, along roads strewn with dead bodies and hundreds of people, barely alive, pleading for help, all of whom were completely ignored by the guards, the vehicle came to a halt, alongside a clearing in the dense jungle. Lining the boys up by the side of the road, the soldier in charge, who wore nothing to suggest his rank, barked out that each boy was to take a shovel from a large pile nearby and start to dig holes, the holes, explained the soldier, were to be dug to bury the dead traitors. Thanh and three others were dragged to one side, told to take two of the wooden handcarts and start collecting the dead. The remaining captives were told that if holes were not dug when the bodies arrived, then they themselves would be needing a hole. After 100 metres of pushing the empty carts, the four boys came across a pile of six bodies, they loaded one into each of the carts and walked as slow as they could until they reached the 'grave diggers.' The head soldier was incensed, shouting that one body in a cart was not enough, they were told that there must be four bodies each time they return. Calling three of the young guards over, he made two of the boys kneel, the three soldiers stood three metres behind the boys, raised their rifles, and emptied their bullets into the backs of the young men's brains.

'This will make you all obey my orders,' he shouted.

Selecting two more boys from those that were digging graves, he despatched them to collect more dead people. This time the four boys loaded four bodies into each cart, they could hardly push them back, as for one, they were heavy and for two the terrain was full of potholes, fallen trees and pieces of military hardware that had been blown up by the advancing Viet Cong. Some of the grave diggers, having not been fast or strong enough to dig enough holes before the dead bodies returned, were shot. This did not seem to matter to the evil commandant, as more trucks would arrive and more seven, eight and nine-year-old boys would be put to work.

At the end of the day, each boy was given a metal bowl and a spoon and ordered to line up, outside the makeshift kitchen. Each boy received one ladle full of 'soup.' The soup was in fact just water containing leaves, that had no doubt been cut from the trees of the jungle. After their feast, the youngsters were told to sleep. The soldiers would drink, mainly rice-wine and once drunk they would play their favourite game, 'Russian Roulette.' The commandant would select a soldier, who would then walk down the line of children, asleep on the bare jungle floor. The soldier would stick the bayonet of his rifle into the stomach of a random boy, if the boy screamed out, he would be shot. The two boys either side of this unfortunate soul would be summoned to immediately dig a hole and bury him. As time went by, the recipient of the bayonet would learn to remain silent, even when the blade went deep into their body. At least fifty percent of the boys that arrived, were dead within a week.

Nearly all the 'dead bodies' that were collected, were civilians, randomly killed by the red-clad soldiers, who were not really attached to any military unit, they were simply mercenaries, their average age was just fourteen. Thanh imagined that his mother had been thrown into a hand cart and buried in the same manner as he was seeing every day. He was getting weaker and weaker, most of the boys that arrived with him had succumbed to disease, malnutrition or at the hands of his captors. He knew that he must get out or die.

Six weeks after arriving at this hell hole, which, from overheard conversations, he had determined was situated about four miles from the infamous Cu Chi Tunnels, Thanh decided that he must defect. Surviving six weeks under such a ruthless regime was a feat by itself. Thanh, as the longest survivor of the group, was trusted to take the carts every day and show newcomers exactly what they had to do. The following morning, in the middle of a torrential downpour, he and his fellow body retrievers were about one kilometre from the burial site when he told another boy that he had to, take a shit. Thanh disappeared into the jungle he did not return. Punishment for absconding was certain death, usually by beheading. The five boys that retuned, without Thanh, were all shot.

For five days he saw no other sign of life, then, along a trail that had been carved out by local people as an alternative to following any official road, Thanh found himself 'face-to-face' with two men that had simply appeared out of nowhere. At first, he thought he had been caught, however when one of the men offered his hand, pulling a startled Thanh towards him, his thoughts changed. As he focused his weary eyes, Thanh could see two women and five children, hiding in the undergrowth, on the other side of the trail. Thanh was still dressed in the clothing of the Viet Cong and although the men were wary of him, they could see that he was unarmed. The rest of the family stayed hidden, one of the men put his finger to his mouth, to ensure that the young man they had stumbled upon remained quiet. Thanh followed the men, in a few minutes they arrived at a house that had been built entirely from bamboo poles and banana leaves. As they exchanged stories the two women wept as Thanh's tale of woe unfolded. They themselves were lucky to be alive. They were two brothers, their wives and five children, whom the North Vietnamese Army had thrown out of their house and took it for themselves. From the moment the war ended, the triumphant North Vietnamese took hundreds of thousands of houses, land, and businesses from their Southern enemies. Saigon alone saw over 1.5 million people displaced. Thousands of innocent people were tortured and murdered. Anyone found to have been collaborating with the Americans suffered an agonizing death. Officials and Politicians from Hanoi were sent to Ho Chi Minh City to rule, whilst also selecting over half a million people for their 're-education' program, which was basically imprisonment with hard labour. It was said that more people from the South died after the war had ended than had died during the long and brutal conflict.

The elder of the two men had introduced himself to Thanh as being 'Le Long,' whilst his younger, but diminutive brother was known as Hung. They explained to Thanh that their aim was to get to Phan Thiet, a small fishing village, about 240 km from their home in Cu Chi, they had so far covered just 11 km since they had set off eight days ago. Le Long-asked Thanh if he would like to go with them as they had money and would pay to get onto a fishing vessel and away from Vietnam. Thanh, with no other plans at that time, agreed.

For ten long days they trekked through the heat, rain and danger associated with tropical jungles. They lived off the abundance of fruit that grew, naturally, overhead. Occasionally they would catch, kill, and cook a rat, being careful not to create any smoke, which might have given their location away. Whilst the war was officially over, they could still hear pockets of fighting going on in the distance. They were not alone in the jungle, many families, like themselves, run out of their homes by the Viet Cong, were making their way to the coast, in the hope that they could board a ship, leaving the trauma of losing everything, behind them. Many of the fleeing adults had worked, in one capacity or another, for the US during the time of the war, a great many of those worked at the US Embassy in Saigon, all were supposed to have been evacuated by the Americans long before the North marched into Saigon. The US State Department estimated that there were 90,000 Vietnamese staff and their families within their employ, during the time that US troops were 'on the ground' in Vietnam. Of those, 22,294 were officially evacuated by the end of April 1975. Of the remaining 67,706, a report published in 1977, suggested that documents left behind by the retreating US Army, listed 30,000 names of persons that had collaborated with the occupying force. All of these were systematically tortured and killed by the Communists. The US had, effectively, condemned them to death. The remaining 37,000 or so, were never accounted for.

On the 6th of June 1975, the two families and Thanh reached the outskirts of Phan Thiet. It was the day of Thanh's 7th birthday, he told no one, as he himself was not aware of what day it was. The harbour was encircled by armed guards, all wore the red outfits of the Viet Cong. Thanh had discarded his Viet Cong attire when Le Long had given him some of his eldest son's clothes. Le Long and his brother, Hung, were very apprehensive about going any further. As they were dithering, in a darkened side street, three 'red devils' suddenly appeared behind them. They asked Le Long as to where he had come from and to where he was going. Le Long, fearing execution for his family and himself, simply told the truth, they were trying to get out of Vietnam. The oldest of the three guards asked Le Long how much he could pay for all ten of his family to get onto a boat. Le Long and his brother, having previously owned a hotel in District 1 of Saigon, which had also been confiscated by the conquering army, held out USD1,000, which he waved at the soldier. 'Not enough, not enough,' was the reaction. Hung held out another USD1,000, this seemed to do the trick.

'Papers, papers, show me your papers,' barked the soldier, who looked to be no older than 15.

Le Long produced a wad of paperwork from his wife's bag, the soldier sat on the stone floor and studied them for several minutes, then, pointing at Thanh, he asked,

'Where are the papers for this boy?'

'They are lost, we could not find them when we were forced to leave our house.'

Looking up from his place on the floor, the soldier said,

'USD500 more, for the boy,'

Hung produced the money, without flinching. Another of the soldiers handed Le Long some rolled-up papers and told him that,

'The boy' is now Vo Van Hiep, aged nine and born in Haiphong.

By way of explanation, after the war had ended and many thousands of 'chosen' North Vietnamese had been rewarded with houses, land, and businesses, which had been forcibly taken from the people of the South, whereas most of the Viet Cong fighters received nothing. In retaliation, a great many of these 'child fighters' broke away from their units and conducted their own way of being rewarded for their efforts. At Phan Thiet, knowing this to be a place where many fleeing South Vietnamese would try to escape, they formed their own armies and took whatever they could from their much richer Southern Counterparts. Those that intended to leave, without documentation, were given new identities, that of fallen comrades. The identities were not photogenic but, if the age on the paperwork, was within reason, many South Vietnamese became 'people of the North.' Le Long, handed Thanh his new identity, telling him to keep it 'safe and dry.'

Brothers, Le Long and Hung, along with their wives, five children and Thanh, were escorted through the vast crowds that ringed the small fishing harbour. They were loaded onto a small boat, which then headed towards a much larger vessel, anchored about half a mile from the shore. As they approached their 'boat to freedom' Le Long and Hung lamented, as owners of a hotel, just two blocks from the famous Rex Hotel, which had been seconded to house the offices of both the US Army and the International Press, the brothers had been promised a safe way out of Vietnam by the many officers that had rooms at their hotel, however the promise made to them had been broken. They now felt that they were owed a place in the USA, but first they had to get there. One by one they climbed the rope ladder that hung limply over the side of the larger fishing vessel. Hung noted that the water line of the boat was way below where it should have been. The decks were so over-subscribed they had difficulty in finding somewhere to stand, it was almost impossible to sit. A fishing boat, with normally a crew of twelve and a hold that could accommodate 4,000 kgs of fish, was now home to at least 400 refugees, with a total weight of around 16,000 kgs. Within minutes of climbing on board, Le Long and his family heard the noisy diesel engines burst into life and the boat, listing slightly to the port side, chugged slowly away from Phan Thiet.

The intended destination of the boat was to be Thailand or Malaysia; however, the vessel was 'ill-equipped' for fishing, even close to the shoreline, let alone surviving the open seas, with a cargo of fleeing people, weighing in at four times the boats carrying capacity. Even allowing for its poor condition, over-crowding or frequent storms, the biggest threat to it ever making it to another country, was Pirates. The South China Sea was regarded as (and still is) one of the most dangerous areas of Ocean in the World. The first mistake to be made by the captain was, that instead of heading South, towards the Gulf of Thailand, he turned due North, towards China. On the second day out, the fresh water on the vessel had already run out. There was no food at all. The following day they were caught and boarded by Pirates. The Pirates, of North Vietnamese origin, took around eighty women, including the wives of Le Long and Hung. Children were thrown overboard and most of the men were either shot or had their throats cut. Thanh and four others, showing their identification as being from the North, were spared. Had this escape attempt been three days earlier then Thanh would not have been able to show that he was Vo Van Hiep from Haiphong, and he would have met with the same fate as his recently adopted family. This example of the persecution and killing of Vietnamese 'boat people' was typical and lasted well into the early 1990s. Of the estimated 2.1 million people that tried their luck at escaping from their communist captors, between 1975 and 1997, 800,000 safely arrived at Hong Kong, Indonesia, Malaysia, the Philippines, Singapore, and Thailand, before being accepted by the USA, Canada, Italy, Australia, France, West Germany, and the UK. According to the UNHCR, at least 500,000 'boat people' perished at sea. A further 400,000 Hoa Vietnamese, of Chinese descent, fled to China. The rest, around 400,000 were returned to Vietnam, where their fate was often unknown. The USA, Canada and Australia took, by far, the largest proportion of 'boat people.'

Vo Van Hiep, as he now had to be known, was offloaded from the pirate ship in the sanctuary of Ha Long Bay, a concoction of rocks and mountains that rise-up from the seabed. Ha Long Bay is just two days' walk to Hai Phong, the place of his birth, as shown on his new identity papers. Vo Van Hiep, Vo Van Hiep he would continually repeat to himself, decided that Hai Phong was the place for him to be. Hai Phong, the main Port of the North of Vietnam, was not that far from Hanoi, the new capital of the 'unified' Vietnam. Two days later, having stolen and begged his way along the route, Hiep arrived in Hai Phong. He had no idea that fourteen years previously, his father, Tang Tao, had boarded a ship in Haiphong after making his escape from China. Not knowing anything about the place that he was now in, other than the address that was shown on his ID papers, Hiep decided to find out exactly where his alias had come from. After a few hours of asking, walking, and pondering as to what he would say, should he dare to knock on the door of, 171 Phan Dang Luu Street, in the district of Kiet An, he decided just to make it up, as he went along, whatever he was going to say, would be based on the reaction from Mr Vo Van Hiep senior.

At 7pm that evening, the boy that had assumed the identity of the son of the man that he was about to confront, tapped, gingerly, on the door of a house that financially, was way beyond the means of most Vietnamese. A lady, who turned out to be a maid, answered the door.

'Could I see Mr. Vo, please?'

'And who exactly are you?' She asked in reply.

'I am a friend of Hiep.'

The maid became unsteady on her feet and without saying anything else, she ran into the house, calling out, Mr. Vo, Mr. Vo. A few seconds later, a smartly dressed man arrived in the doorway. The boy, formerly known as Nguyen Quang Thanh, played his ace card. He showed the suited gentleman, the papers given to him by the Viet Cong. The man gasped as he digested the contents of the documents, he then beckoned Thanh into his house.

Instructing the maid to bring their visitor both food and drink, Mr. Vo then climbed the stairs and returned a few minutes later with a woman.

'This is my wife, Hien' said Mr. Vo.

He asked the boy to show the papers to her. Vo's wife, Hien perused the papers and then fell to her knees, wailing, in the way that only Vietnamese females can manage. Given their reaction to his arrival and subsequent announcement that their only son was dead, Thanh decided to 'spill the beans.' He proceeded to tell them the whole story of how he has ended up in their house. Mr. Vo asked the maid to show the very tired looking seven-year-old to the bathroom and then prepare one of the guest rooms for their young visitor. Half an hour later, the boy that had lived a whole lifetime in just a few months, was fast asleep, in the most comfortable of beds.

Whilst Mr and Mrs Vo were almost traumatized by the events of the last hour or so, they agreed that they needed to sort out this situation, sooner, rather than later. One year ago, when their son was eight, they were all living happily in the posh part of Hai Phong. Mr. Vo was the principal of one of the city's most respected schools. At this time, the Viet Cong operated a form of conscription, young children, boys, or girls, were the targets. One day, after school, Vo Van Hiep junior was walking back to the family house with two friends when they were all 'snatched' from the street and taken to a training facility close to the banks of the Red River, North of Hanoi. The following day a note was left at the reception of the school. Mr. Vo senior was informed that the 'Vietnamese Freedom Fighters' had taken his son, there was no ransom demand. Based on the information given by the captured boy and the fact that anything could be obtained, for the right amount of money, the local 'peoples committee' in Haiphong, were able to issue authentic copies of all three boys' birth certificates and proof of residence. Mr and Mrs Vo, despite alerting the police and other authorities in Hai Phong and Hanoi, had never heard anything more about their abducted son.

Mrs. Vo tearfully raised the question of whether the story told to them by the boy that was now fast asleep in an upstairs bedroom, was true or not. Could he have just somehow managed to obtain the paperwork, was their son still alive, but brainwashed? A thousand other scenarios entered her mind. Her husband took her hand, looked her straight in the eyes, and said,

'We have to presume that Hiep is gone and may never return, we can look after this boy, he cannot replace our son but as you are unable to give birth to another, we can bring this boy up as if he was our own.'

A weeping, Mrs. Vo agreed with her husband.

Waking at 6am the following morning, the boy was fully prepared to be shown the door and be left with no choice other than to once again, wander aimlessly around Haiphong. At 6.30, the maid asked him to go downstairs, as Mr. Vo wished to talk to him. The seven-year-old was nervous, whilst at the same time, delighted when he was asked to stay at such a grand house. Mr. Vo asked him if he had ever gone to school.

'Yes, in Saigon I studied.'

'I am going to get you to study at my school. I am the headmaster. At school you will be known as Nguyen Quang Thanh, my nephew, you were orphaned when the bombing of Hai Phong took place last year. You will keep the papers of my son, hide them in your room, as one day in the future, you may need them.'

Mr. Vo left the house and during his working day, he registered Thanh for study at his school. No one would challenge him as he was the 'Principal.' Thanh began his schooling in Hai Phong the following week. Mr. Vo soon realised that he was destined for great things, later in life.

Both of his 'adopted' parents were proud of Thanh, he was polite and studied intently, both inside and outside of school. He would mingle with the middle classes of Hai Phong and never felt out of his depth. At the age of eleven, Thanh asked Mr. Vo if he could find out if Ms. Linh was still running her shop and living close to Cho Lon market. Through his connections, Mr. Vo was able to inform Thanh that Ms. Linh had been forced to give up her business to a family from North Vietnam, her house was taken over and given to a Navy Officer, he was unable to tell Thanh if Linh, or any of her family were alive. Thanh was sad, it now seemed that everyone he had ever loved was gone from his life. On the other hand, he was lucky, lucky that he had been given the papers of Vo Van Hiep by the Viet Cong, lucky that he had decided to tell the truth to Mr & Mrs Vo, lucky that he had been given the opportunity to study and live in Hai Phong, but most of all, he was lucky to be alive.

Thanh stayed at the same school until he was seventeen, even though his adopted father had moved on to become the Principal of the Hai Phong Education University. When Thanh gained acceptance to this University, he was to study Politics. He was keen to learn the innermost workings of the Polit-Bureau, he had a plan, he was very much against the Communist way of life, even though he himself was being given a good life. His aim was to become an 'activist' working against the regime, however he could never openly display his true feelings, otherwise he would be monitored, incarcerated, and almost certainly put to death, as thousands upon thousands of like-minded South Vietnamese people had already been. During the time of Thanh's schooling, Mr. Vo had been duplicating every school report, certificate and citation that bore the name of Nguyen Quang Thanh, he had transposed these under the name of his real son, Vo Van Hiep. Thanh would present these when applying for his first job. That job was to be as a junior in the Ministry of Foreign Affairs (MFA), in Hanoi. Thanh, or Hiep as he would now be, was 24 years old when he first sat at his desk at the historic building, situated in the Ba Dinh district of Hanoi.

Within a year, Hiep was seconded into the Department of European Affairs, this was the job that he had set his sights on. For the next five years he would work his way into a position of trust and was graded as A1. This grading would get him onto the short list for an overseas posting. Shortly after he had achieved the required level, he was asked to go to Sofia, Bulgaria. He was to become assistant secretary to the Vietnamese Ambassador he would be just two steps away from becoming the Ambassador himself. On the 30th of March 1999, three months short of his 31st birthday, Vo Van Hiep, junior, flew from Hanoi to Sofia, he was the holder of a diplomatic passport, a document given to just a few Vietnamese people. His adopted parents, both now retired, were as proud of him as they could have been, had he been their real son.

For seven years Hiep alternated between the Embassies of Bucharest, Moscow, Warsaw, East Berlin, and Sofia. He witnessed the gradual decline of the Communist Governments in all the countries that he had been posted to. Vietnam were aware that they needed to look 'outside' of the Iron Curtain, for so long their greatest allies. In 1992 they had declared 'Doi Moi' or 'open door policy' and began to invite other nations to do business with them. Restrictions on Foreigners entering the country were lifted and Vietnam, whilst still a staunch communist-led nation, began to look at Capitalism as being the way forward. Even with all these changes, a great many Vietnamese, especially those from the South, were still risking their lives and paying a great deal of money to leave. Hiep had made it his goal, from the moment he obtained his diplomatic passport, to help the people of his strictly controlled country to escape from the communist regime that was still 'putting to death' those that had worked with the Americans during the long and brutal war.

On the 31st of December 2006 and now the first secretary of the Vietnamese Embassy in Bulgaria, Hiep attended an official function, held at the Grand Palace Hotel, in Sofia. A hotel owned by Boyan Petrov. At midnight, glasses were raised to welcome Bulgaria into the European Union. At 1.00am on the 1st of January 2007, Hiep was introduced, by his ambassador, to Boyan Petrov. That meeting with the Mayor of Varna would change the course of the 39 year old diplomats life.

9 - NIKOLAY NIKOLOV – The Guardian

Ten days after Boyan's father, Stoyan Petrov, had mysteriously fallen to his death from a scheduled flight from Varna to Sofia, the Chief of Police had informed Nikolay Nikolov, Stoyan's righthand man, enforcer, and guardian of his son, that the remains of the feared gang leader were to be returned to Varna. Boyan, as next of kin, would be able to collect the remains from Varna Airport on the 16th of May 1987.

So well-known, respected, and feared was Stoyan, that over 700 people attended his funeral, held in Varna's largest Eastern Orthodox Church. The congregation was made up of a few hundred gangsters, some who had come from as far afield as Italy, Rumania, Albania, Turkey, and Syria, plus officials and high-ranking politicians from Bulgaria, as well as well-known celebrities, and of course, the rather enlarged Petrov family. But, maybe the most surprising of all the mourners, gathered to pay their last respects, was Tommaso Buscetta, a 'made' man within the Sicilian Mafia. Tommaso had chosen to give evidence against his fellow mobsters and had been let free by the judiciary in Palermo. His testimony saw the imprisonment of 338 of his colleagues, the trial that lasted over five years, remains the world's biggest. Tommaso, although now known as Salvatore Lima, had visited Varna on several occasions, staying at one of Stoyan's 'safe houses.' After the burial, which took place in the Petrov family plot, within the church grounds, Nikolay Nikolov approached the man that he knew only as Tommaso Buscetta and thanked him for his attendance. The ex-mafia informant was flanked by eight burly men. Nikolay asked Buscetta what business he had in Varna, other than to mourn the loss of his lifelong friend. Nikolay was quite taken aback by the reply.

'I am here to take over from Stoyan Petrov and by the way, never address me as Tommaso Buscetta, I am Salvatore Lima, from Naples.'

Nikolay instinctively knew that major problems were on the horizon.

As the two 'Dons' parted, Boyan arrived at Nikolay's side, he asked,

'Who is he?'

'Oh, just an old friend of your father's, but not a nice one, so please stay clear of him.'

Nikolay's tone led Boyan to believe that his words were more of an instruction, not just some friendly advice. Boyan carried on,

'You do know that Georgio Yakimov from the polit-bureau is here, don't you?

'Yes, I am aware of that Boyan, and he will be dealt with today.'

Three separate sources had informed Nikolay that it was Georgio Yakimov that had summoned Stoyan to Sofia. Stoyan was to be warned about his ever-expanding criminal activities in and around Varna, however he had met his death before arriving in the capital. It was Boyan's duty to avenge the death of his father, but this could not be done without compelling evidence or a full confession from the suspect. At the wake, held at the town hall, immediately after the funeral. Yakimov was giving a very pretty, young lady, some personal attention. The girl, on Nikolay's payroll, was responding to his charm and soon had her arms wrapped around him. Two hours later, she took his hand and led him to a room on the third floor of the Town Hall, the largest building in Varna. Unbeknown to the eager plump and ugly middle-aged man, he had been followed upstairs. Just as he inserted his manhood into the girl's open mouth, he was stabbed in the neck with a hypodermic needle. The aggressor was Boyan Petrov. Only Nikolay was with him. Boyan had pumped uncut heroin into the body of the third-ranking politician in Bulgaria.

Yakimov had barely hit the floor when the girl dressed, she was given a wad of money and a kiss on the cheek by Nikolay and was gone. Nikolay opened the rear door of the room, walked out onto the steel fire escape, and gestured at some men below. Two minutes later, four of Nikolay's men carried Yakimov down the six flights of stairs and bundled him into a waiting van. Nikolay and Boyan returned to the wake. Not long after, the guests began to leave. Boyan stood beside the large double doors and shook the hand of every single mourner, as they left, disappearing, one by one, into their respective cars. The departure of just one person caused Boyan some discomfort. As he kissed Boyan on each cheek, Salvatore Lima whispered,

'It will never be yours.'

At that moment in time Boyan had no clue as to the meaning of those words.

Nikolay was the last person to shake Boyan's hand, he had watched intently as Buscetta greeted him. Boyan asked Nikolay as to the meaning of the words, whispered to him, just minutes earlier.

'Tomorrow, we will discuss, now I must go to the club as I have some important people to entertain.'

'How about Yakimov?' asked Boyan.

'Also, tomorrow, Boyan. Now go and get some rest, it has been a troublesome day for you.'

Three men appeared from an ante room, situated off the reception area of the town hall.

'These men will be with you from now on Boyan. They will shadow your every move, do you understand?'

Boyan understood. Even at the tender age of sixteen, Boyan knew that he was a 'marked man.'

Nikolay entered the club, part of the Petrov empire, positioned in a prime location, along the many miles of coastline that stretched from Sunny Beach to Golden Sands, on the Western shores of the Black Sea. In this part of Bulgaria, the Petrov's controlled everything, Nikolay was now in charge of this, at least until Boyan, the son of his lifelong, and now deceased friend, Stoyan Petrov, became twenty-one. Retreating to a soundproof office at the rear of the club, Nikolay asked his first Lieutenant, Gregor Levski, to go to the bar and bring back the four men, from Romania, Albania, Turkey, and Greece, that had been sitting, waiting patiently, for his return.

Sat comfortably in Nikolay's office, expensive brandy, poured from the stunning 'cut glass' decanter, in each of their hands, Nikolay began.

'Gentlemen, I have a problem, which means you all share the burden with me. Today I met Tommaso Buscetta, now known as Salvatore Lima. He told me to my face that he was here to take over the Petrov business, if he were able to do this then it would also be probable that he would look to do likewise with your organisations. Today he was surrounded by eight of his loyal Sicilian family, he is on the run from almost every member of the Mafia in Italy and the USA, yet he comes here, boldly proclaiming that he will soon be running things in our homeland.' After a pause and a swig from his glass, Nikolay continued.

'Even though I knew of his presence here only just a few hours ago, I have already been told that he has at least 100 men assembled in and around Varna.'

Victor Bastovoi, head of the largest crime family in Bucharest, was the first of the four visitors to respond.

'Nikolay, we already knew of Buscetta's arrival into the Balkans, he has been in contact with all of us, we were discussing this situation before you called us in.'

Interrupting, General Kos, representing Albania, said,

'Yes, Nikolay, we see him as a threat to all of us, but our loyalties are to you.'

Offering a toast to Nikolay before speaking, Mustafa Gul, a cousin to Osman Gul, Turkey's most prolific criminal, added,

'We are all with you Nikolay, we are aware that Buscetta is building a large stockpile of weapons, that he brings in from Iraq, with the help of Abu Naseeb. We have the means to cut off that supply, but we must all work together on this.'

All four men turned to look at Dimitris Fotopoulos, known to all as 'Dim' he had remained silent throughout. Scanning the four men encircling him, Dim raised his glass and simply said,

'I am with you all, my brothers'.

Nikolay was a shrewd man, he had learnt never to trust anyone, either or all these dangerous men could be 'double-dealing' their allegiance to the Petrov family could all be a front, anything that they might agree with, could easily be shared with Buscetta, alias Salvatore Lima. Turning to Mustafa Gul, Nikolay asked,

'Can you arrange a meeting with Abu Naseeb?'

'Yes, of course, Nikolay,' was the unhesitant reply from Mustafa Gul.

Looking at the uniformed ex-General, Nikolay asked,

'And you, General, are you able to pinpoint exactly where Buscetta has positioned his men?'

'Without a doubt, Nikolay, leave it to me.'

'Victor, my friend, maybe you should invite Buscetta to your palace in Constanta. I am sure that he will bring several of his men with him. Can you arrange that?'

'Of course, I can Nikolay, consider it done.'

Clinking his glass against Dimitris, a man twice the size of Demis Roussos, Nikolay asked him if he could bring 100 of his best fighters across the border into Bulgaria. He would arrange for them to stay in one of his hotels in Burgas, in readiness for whatever might happen.

'No problem, Nikolay, I would consider this as an honour, they will be there within five days.'

'Now gentlemen, kindly excuse me and please return to the bar, the music, the drink, the food, but most importantly the girls.'

The four men shook Nikolay's hand and were gone. Gregor Levski remained. Nikolay, pouring himself another brandy, said,

'Gregor, tomorrow, after we deal with Yakimov, we must devise a plan to see if our four friends are with us or with that bastard Sicilian, now go and join our guests and listen carefully to their conversation.'

'Of course, boss, I will see you in the morning.'

Replied the man that could have been hit by a speeding train and survived.

Nikolay opened a concealed door within the wooden panelled wall and retired for the night.

The following morning, at 8.30, Nikolay, driven by Levski, collected Boyan from his house, the house, now void of both Stoyan and Todorha Petrov, Boyan's parents. They drove for twenty minutes, turning off the main road and onto a narrow track, at the end of which was a massive timber yard. A car containing Boyan's three minders followed closely behind. The yard was once one of Stoyan's legitimate businesses, supplying timber to all manner of customers, now it belonged to Boyan, albeit that Nikolay would oversee the running of this, and every other business that the young boy had been left by his deceased father. Two men stood guard at the heavy, closed wooden gates. No workers had been allowed in, as was always the case when something sinister was about to happen. Nikolay and Levski strode either side of Boyan as they entered the mill through a separate side door. Inside the covered sawmill, on a large wooden bench, tightly chained by both hands and feet, lay Georgio Yakimov. With his head strapped firmly to the bench, Yakimov was unable to raise it, he was therefore unable to see who had entered. What he was able to see, was the large circular saw that was positioned directly above his chest. Walking over to him, Nikolay undid the strap that held Yakimov's head in position, he then beckoned Boyan over. Boyan stood on the other side of the bench. Gregor pushed the green button of the control box and the saw burst into life. It sped at around at 10,000 revs per minute, just nine inches above Yakimov's plump stomach. Turning the terrified Politicians head to face him, Nikolay said,

'Now Georgio, you are going to tell us exactly who it was that ordered the death of Boyan's father.'

'I have no idea, do you know who you are dealing with, I am just two places away from being the President of this Country, if you release me now, I will never tell anyone of what happened here,'

Yakimov's plea was of no consequence to his potential executors.

'Well, if you will not tell us, then the son of the man that you had killed is going to have to treat you a little unkindly,' replied Nikolay, unable to hide the grin that had spread across his face.

Boyan had cut whole trees with this saw, he loved to go to the mill, whenever he could. He had become something of an expert at being able to 'skim the surface' of a log, without cutting right through it. As there were no further words coming from Yakimov's mouth, Boyan pulled down on the handle that moved the spinning saw to within an inch of the belly of the man responsible for his father's early death. Such was Boyan's accuracy and expertise, that he was able to rip a small piece of the expensive suit jacket that Yakimov was still wearing, the machine making a whirring sound as it removed both buttons.

'OK, OK, I will tell you, just turn off the machine,' shouted Yakimov.

Nikolay signalled to Gregor, he pushed the red button, the saw began to slow down, eventually coming to a complete stop. Boyan pushed it back up into its resting position. Nikolay took a barber's cut-throat blade from under the bench and held it tightly upon Yakimov's throat, drawing the slightest trickle of blood as he did so.

'Tell me,' Said Boyan.

Yakimov, visibly trembling, uttered just two words,

'Tommaso Buscetta.'

Gregor pushed the green button, he and Nikolay then walked away. Boyan, showing no emotion, pulled the saw down until the blade was just touching the crutch of Yakimov's trousers, seconds later, a scream, that may well have been heard in Sofia, was the last sound that Georgio Yakimov would ever make. Boyan ran the blade the entire length of his victim's body, it cut through the stomach, chest, and neck as if it were butter. The machine spluttered a little when it met with the chin and skull bone of the 54-year-old, senior member of Bulgaria's ruling party. Yakimov was now cut completely in two. Boyan was smothered, head to toe, in blood, flesh, organs and brain matter. He came out of the mill, not at all perturbed by what he had just done. He crossed the sawdust-laden yard, entered the shower block, stripped off all his clothes, and then washed off the remains of the man that had ordered his father's death. Gregor gathered up the discarded clothes and dropped them onto the fire that continually raged, inside the large steel drum in the yard. One of Boyan's 'minders' brought new clothes from the car, Boyan dressed, shook Nikolay's hand, and climbed into the car that would take him back home. He had avenged his father's death. What Boyan had just carried out, was never ever mentioned. Boyan was never to murder anyone, personally, ever again. Gregor drove Nikolay to the hotel where the four men that had vowed to help him rid Bulgaria of Tommaso Buscetta, were resting.

In the same penthouse room that Nikolay and Stoyan had murdered two innocent girls and abducted two of the men responsible for Stoyan's wife's killing, the meeting with four gang leaders, plus Nikolay and Gregor, was about to take place. Nikolay would do almost all the talking, he was not asking his counterparts from Romania, Albania, Turkey, and Greece to act on his behalf voluntarily, he was instructing them to carry out his orders, without question. Nikolay was almost certain that one, if not more, of those present, were already 'sucking up' to Buscetta and whilst all of them would have felt safe, firstly because of the strength of their own organisations, and secondly from having Buscetta on their side, they would, even if they were double-dealing, have felt almost untouchable. Nikolay feared no one, the Petrov gang, built up over many years by Stoyan and himself, was the single most feared criminal element in the Balkans, they were backed by the Mafia in Italy and the USA, together they had worked on many projects, Nikolay had considered simply informing the Sicilians as to the whereabouts of Buscetta, and just let them deal with the man that had carried out the biggest betrayal in Mafia history. Had he done so he may well have been considered as being weak, instead, in true Mafioso tradition, he asked Palermo for permission to take out Buscetta and his newly created gang members. Permission was granted, but they wanted proof of Buscetta's death.

Addressing Victor Bastovoi, in the privacy of a soundproof room within the penthouse, Nikolay asked that he invite Buscetta to his complex in Constanta, Romania's 'second City' and just 220 km North of Varna, on the Black Sea coast. Bastovoi had been controlling the entire Black Sea area from Constanta up to Odessa, his operation was very similar to the Petrovs, running bars, restaurants, hotels, prostitutes and of course, with the help of corrupt officials, most of the real estate and available land. The one major difference between their respective Modus Operandi was that Bastovoi supplied illegal workers to the more affluent parts of Western Europe, having established overland routes via Hungary. Bastovoi had asked Stoyan, many times, to join with him in this very lucrative business. Now he was asking the same of Nikolay. Nikolay's answer was to say that he should solve the problem of Buscetta first, and then maybe he would have some interest. It was agreed that Bastovoi would invite Buscetta to Constanta to discuss the establishment of an operation in Bulgaria, with a view to taking over the Petrov empire. Nikolay insisted that this meeting should take place within the next week. The two men hugged and kissed each other on each cheek. Levski asked Bastovoi to follow him, they left via an elevator door that was cleverly concealed as a drink cabinet. A few minutes later, Levski returned. Nikolay looked up from his chair and said, Gregor, it is Bastovoi that will betray us. Gregor nodded in agreement.

Nikolay opened a door to the vast living room and Invited General Kos to join them. Kos was immaculately dressed in his formal, white General's uniform, the same one as he had worn the previous day. He always wore this for funerals, of which, he had attended many. He especially enjoyed the ones of people that he had killed personally. Some put that number as high as 100. Kos, a man that so many would like to kill, had set up a heavily fortified complex, on both sides of the Albanian/Kosovan border. Divided by a small mountain range. The General was involved in almost every illegal activity known to man, he probably enjoyed the largest army of gang members, anywhere in the World. Most of his trusted array of killers, torturers, fighters, and guards, were in fact once under his control during the conflict that raged for many years before the eventual break-up of Yugoslavia. Nikolay had, the previous day, asked that Kos gather intelligence on exactly who were the men that Buscetta had recruited and where this ever-expanding group may be hanging out, awaiting their orders. Kos was an extremely intelligent man he required no further input from his host. He stood, clicked the heels of his expensive crocodile boots together, saluted and disappeared into the drink's cabinet. As before, Levski saw him out.

Next to be invited into the room, where no one on the outside could hear a sound, was Mustafa Gul. Mustafa had risen to become the Guls' 'main man' in Turkey, he lorded it over a vast network of arms and drug smuggling that stretched out over the whole of Europe, part of the Middle East, Central and South America, the USA and Canada. Financially, with the money that the Gul clan had accrued, he could have bought out any of the World's largest cartels. Mustafa was a very likeable man, he never personally did violence, although he would not think twice about giving the order to systematically carve up another human being. His facial features resembled a young Omar Sharif, he was a fitness fanatic, playing squash, badminton, and tennis, although his number one passion was for polo. He had taken part in many matches involving members of various Royal Families. All Nikolay was asking Mustafa to do, was to arrange a meeting with a fanatical arms dealer, an Iraqi, known as Abu Naseeb. Abu, outwardly posing as a small-time smuggler back in his homeland, was widely regarded as 'the man' when it came to supplying weapons. He had the ability to sell arms to both sides in any given conflict and at the end of hostilities he was able to buy back the arms of fallen soldiers, at a fraction of what had been paid for them. Nikolay had learnt that Buscetta, through his newly established network, was stockpiling, for use against him and his colleagues, a vast store of weapons, that were being purchased from Abu Naseeb. Mustafa would be the third person to leave the room via the drink cabinet. As he left, he promised Nikolay that he would meet Naseeb within a week. There was now only the Greek, Demis Roussos lookalike to talk to.

Dimitris Fotopoulos had been a long-time friend to the Petrov family. Based in Thessaloniki, a strategic Port on the Aegean Sea, ideal for receiving contraband from Iran and Iraq, shipped overland to the Sea Port of Latakia in Syria. Dimitris' organisation had, for years, arranged the onforwarding of Arms, Drugs, Tobacco, and illegal Medical Supplies from Thessaloniki into Bulgaria. At least 200 Customs officers, along the extensive Greek / Bulgarian border were on the payroll. New roads, funded by money derived from the sales of the cargo, were built. Whole towns and villages grew alongside these roads, there was no Government interference, mainly because the men in power were all being looked after. The nickname of 'Dim' had been attributed to the gang leader on the basis that his knowledge, of anything, was pretty much nil, his speech was flawed and his inability to add two single digits together was quite evident. What he could do, and very well, was to supply fighters, to any given cause, at the drop of a hat. He was also an ace at being able to spot a traitor. He agreed 100% with Nikolay's assumption, that Victor Bastovoi was the one, most likely to be in bed with Buscetta.

Five minutes after Dim had left, Nikolay and Levski were on their way to visit Boyan. Nikolay outlined to young Petrov, the conversations that had taken place earlier, explaining that the sixteen-year-old would not play any part in what was about to happen. Nikolay had made a vow to the late Stoyan, that should he not be around then he, Nikolay, would assume responsibility for his son's upbringing. This had included his continued education. Stoyan and Nikolay had both agreed that Boyan, academically brighter than, either of them, would be better served by pursuing the highest seat of learning that could possibly be open to him. At first Boyan was not receptive to his older and wiser minder, however when Nikolay suggested that he should take a year out, do some travelling and then, when aged 17, attend a finishing school in Paris, with a view to taking a scholarship at Oxford, he warmed to the idea. Asking as to when he might begin his journey, Nikolay answered,

'Tomorrow Boyan, tomorrow.'

The next day, Nikolay drove Boyan to Varna Airport, from there he would fly to Sofia and then onto London. Accompanying Boyan was Pierre Marcel, a man said to be just about the finest bodyguard in the whole of Europe. Pierre had been waiting patiently in Varna, for this day to come. The three 'minders' that had been looking after Boyan were told nothing. Levski was told even less. Only Nikolay, Pierre and Boyan knew of the trip. There would be no one to meet them in London. Pierre had been given £200,000, in cash, which he carried in a large pilot-type bag. Pierre was to pay for everything. Boyan was given just one concession as far as being chaperoned around Europe, he could have his own room at the Savoy in London. Pierre would be in an adjoining room.

Dimitris was the first of the four men from the meeting to contact Nikolay. He informed his Bulgarian counterpart that 108 of his finest fighters were now occupying the first four floors of the 'Empress Hotel' in Burgas, a large town, just south of Sunny Beach, where, leaked information suggested, 50 of Buscetta's men were holed up. A truck, that had entered Bulgaria along one of the roads controlled by the Greeks, had delivered its load, of arms and ammunition, to a warehouse, on the outskirts of Sunny Beach.

The next day, Mustafa Gul contacted Nikolay, telling him that Abu Naseeb had agreed to meet, however he was reluctant to go to Bulgaria. He would agree to meet in Athens, he was able to take a direct flight from Baghdad and meet at a place of Mustafa's choosing. Nikolay confirmed his willingness to cooperate with Abu's request. They would all meet at the Sofitel Airport Hotel, a five-star establishment, within the grounds of Athens Airport.

General Kos, now back in the safety of his heavily fortified complex, told Nikolay, via a satellite phone, that his 'spies' had let him know that Buscetta had, so far, positioned around 50 men in Sunny Beach, a further 40 in Golden Sands and 70 in Central Varna. It had not been possible to pinpoint exactly where Buscetta was, any given time, as he was constantly moving from place to place. There had however, been a suggestion that he was spending a lot of time in Constanta, Romania. Unbeknown to Nikolay, Kos had found out some time ago, that there was a plot to 'overthrow' the Petrov family and take control of the Black Sea area of Bulgaria. Given this knowledge, Kos had placed two of his own 'mercenaries' inside the teams that had been assembled at Buscetta's request. The man behind all of this was none other than Victor Bastovoi. This information from the General confirmed Nikolay's suspicions.

The day prior to leaving for Athens, Bastovoi would be the fourth and last person from the meeting to contact Nikolay. Bastovoi had made the call from the comfort of the expensive chair in his office, the phone was on 'loudspeaker' Buscetta was sat opposite the Romanian when he spoke to Nikolay.

'Hello, my friend, how are things in Varna? Good, I hope. So far, I have not been able to track our friend down, but do not worry, my men are working hard in trying to find him.'

Nikolay sensed that Bastovoi was lying. Given what the General had told him and the fact that both he and Levski were of the same opinion, then Bastovoi was, without doubt, working alongside Buscetta. His days were numbered.

On the morning of Saturday 30th, May 1987, Nikolay Nikolov and Gregor Levski boarded a flight that would take them, firstly to Sofia and from there to Athens in Greece. At 12.30pm they entered the reception of the Sofitel Hotel and were met by Mustafa Gul and his cousin Tony, a name given to him by Mustafa as his birth name was almost unpronounceable. A slightly worried Mustafa approached Nikolay and told him that Abu Naseeb was accompanied by four men, not the customary, single, righthand man. Levski was nervous, he asked,

'Why does he need four others to meet with us?'

'I have no idea' replied Mustafa, adding,

'I have told Naseeb that only one additional man, will be allowed to attend our meeting, he has agreed with this but will still have three others within sight of us, just in case.'

Nikolay, not wanting to waste this journey because of broken protocol, simply said,

'What time have you arranged the 'sit down' for and where will it take place?'

'It will be at 3pm, in the small conference room on the second floor,' said Mustafa.

'OK, just leave it at that. I really do not care how many men Naseeb wishes to invite, so long as you have searched everyone, Mustafa.

'My men will do that before anyone is allowed into the room, Nikolay. You have my word.'

All four men went their own ways.

At 2.55, nine men were frisked outside of the conference room by Mustafa's own security. Once inside, Nikolay, Levski, Mustafa, and Tony sat at the circular table, which could easily accommodate up to ten people. Abu Naseeb sat alone, his four 'bodyguards' stood, menacingly, in each corner of the room. Levski began the conversation.

'Mr. Naseeb, we understand from sources, not in this room today, that you are helping Tommaso Buscetta to arm himself and his fellow Sicilians with an arsenal, so large, that he could take on the entire military of Bulgaria.'

Looking sternly at Nikolay, mainly because he did not want to address Nikolay's number two, he smiled as he said,

'I know of no one of that name.'

Nikolay, sensing a game was being played, spoke for the first time.

'Maybe you know him as Salvatore Lima?' '

'Oh Salvatore, I had no idea that he was someone else.'

There was a sarcastic element to Abu's response.

Nikolay, a man never seemingly ruffled, at least on the outside, replied,

'Well, Mr. Naseeb, whether you are the one supplying Buscetta, or not, it must stop. We can monitor every single shipment that arrives in our area, there will not be one truck, ship or aircraft that is not under our scrutiny. You are playing a dangerous game, my friend. You may think that by having the protection of the biggest grass the Mafia has ever known, you are safe and will sleep like a baby. This is the only warning that you will get. The next time our paths cross, it will be at your burial. Am I clear, Mr. Naseeb?'

Abu banged the table with his fists, his bodyguards reached under their jackets, momentarily it looked as though the meeting was going to conclude with death. Rising to his feet, Abu looked towards Mustafa and said,

'You are a dead man we know that it was you that informed on us.'

Tony began to stir in his chair, Mustafa held him back. Calmly, Mustafa replied,

'I am sorry that you had reason to say those words to me, from this day we are no longer friends, I would ask that you and your men leave now.'

They did. The meeting was over, everyone knew where they stood.

Nikolay and Levski now knew that they had to deal with two men, Victor Bastovoi and Abu Naseeb.

Returning to Varna on Sunday afternoon, Nikolay had decided that a meeting involving the 'made men' within his organisation was required. It was Levski's job to inform all twelve members of the Petrovs' inner circle. Eight direct relatives of Stoyan were on this 'council' all of whom were loyal to

Nikolay. Each had sworn their allegiance to him upon the request of Stoyan, not one of them would ever go against Nikolay. At the meeting the following day, held in the same soundproof room as before, Nikolay and Levski outlined the plans that Tommaso Buscetta was making and the part that Bastovoi and Naseeb were to play in the plot against them. It was decided that all three men and their associates, which could well number over 200, should be taken out, sooner, rather than later. Levski, a master tactician, asked that four of the 'made men' take out Victor Bastovoi, four do likewise to Abu Naseeb and that the remaining four, together with himself should turn their attention to Buscetta and his mini army. Nikolay would confirm everything with General Kos, Mustafa Gul, and Dimitris Fotopoulos, asking for their help, help that he was certainly going to need.

Stephan Petrov, Stoyan's young brother would be responsible for eliminating Abu Naseeb. Ivan Petrov, the son of Stoyan's oldest brother would handle the extinction of Victor Bastovoi, and Teodora Petrov, Stoyan's uncle and oldest member, at 71, of the Petrov clan, would lead the hunt for Buscetta. Levski would be in Teodora's team, his job would be to bring back the head of Tommaso Buscetta.

Acting upon information gathered by Mustafa Gul, two days after getting the instruction from Nikolay, Stephan Petrov and six of his finest men, slipped silently into Turkey and drove for two days until they reached Adana, close to the border with Syria. Their information was that a small convoy of trucks, led by Abu Naseeb, would cross the Syrian border, and enter Turkey, using a track favoured by smugglers for many years. Due to large amounts of cash changing hands, there was never any challenge to be met from the authorities on either side of this border crossing.

Abu Naseeb, for so long, a man that had gone about his dealing in death and destruction in a very low-key manner, had, in recent times, become more of a public figure, in fact, in his stronghold of Al Bukamal, a small town, on the Eastern border of Syria, and just 10 km from Iraq, he was something of a folk hero. He had been selling small arms, armoured vehicles and even tanks, to both Iraq and Iran and had brokered deals with the Saudi Defence Department, that allowed them to buy arms that would not otherwise be available to them. Across the Middle East, Mercenaries, Islamic Fundamentalists, Kurds, and numerous other regimes were fighting with weapons supplied by him and his associates. Naseeb had become a 'marked man' long before he was found to be building a stockpile of arms for Tommaso Buscetta. It seemed ironic, that weapons sold by Naseeb to the Iraqis were now being used by their enemies. Although he was fully aware of the fact that his days were numbered, he never hid away, as General Kos had, he openly plied his trade, he literally would sell to anyone.

At 3.00am, Stephan Petrov and his men drove Eastwards from Adana. Just before daybreak they were in position, hidden by a small mountain range that ran North to South, stretching across both Turkey and Syria. They were on the Turkish side of the border, the convoy would cross just after leaving the town of Kobane, on the Syrian side. Stephan had the use of three vehicles, one was a white Jeep, seconded from the UNHCR, this still bore those letters on its roof. The second vehicle was a Range Rover that bore no registration plates, the third being one of those 'open back' trucks, with a fully operational rocket launcher bolted to the chassis. These motors had been supplied by Mustafa Gul. Stephan had taken delivery of them from a petrol station just outside Nizip, a few kms from where the intended ambush would take place. The vehicles had been concealed in an underground bunker, built at the time that the tanks for the petrol had been installed.

At 5.15am, using his high-powered, expensive binoculars, Stephan spotted a khaki-coloured 4-wheeled drive Jeep. Headlights blazing, speeding along the track from Kobane, it left a trail of thick dust in its wake. Two army wagons, barely visible from being engulfed in the dust cloud, followed. Just as the convoy crossed into Turkey, Stephan gave the signal. A rocket momentarily hovered in mid-air before screeching its way forward. Three seconds later the Jeep exploded, completely blown apart. Two minutes after this Stephan and his crew arrived at the scene. They had no problem in wiping out the four men that were with the two trucks. From what they could see, there had been three men in the Jeep, all had been blown to pieces. Silently, Stephan ran his fingers across his own neck, the gesture was completely understood by his accomplices. Three heads were cut from the torsos of the dead men, that, just a few minutes earlier, had been alive and well. The heads would be returned, along with the borrowed vehicles, to the garage at Nizip. One of Mustafa's men would identify them. The trucks, that once belonged to Abu Naseeb, were boarded, and followed the Bulgarians, until they reached the garage near Nizip.

At the garage, all the vehicles were driven underground. Ten minutes later, a container lorry arrived, the arms contained in the backs of the two trucks that once belonged to Abu Naseeb, were transferred. One of the heads was confirmed as being that of Abu Naseeb, this was thrown into the boot of Stephan's Nissan, the other two heads were dropped into a pen containing several pigs. Two cars and one container truck pulled out from the garage, and onto the highway that connected Nizip with Adana and then Mersin. Stephan and four of his men had a two-day drive back to Bulgaria. The remaining two men accompanied the driver of the container, until they reached the Port of Mersin. The container was then loaded onto a ship that firstly, would navigate the Bosporus Straights, before the container was discharged in the Port of Istanbul. It would then continue, on its journey by road, finally off-loading at

Burgas, where it would be gratefully received by Dimitris Fotopoulos and his men, patiently awaiting further instructions from Nikolay. Dim thought it ironic, that arms purchased by Tommaso Buscetta would be responsible for wiping out his own army.

Even before Stephan Petrov had left to carry out the ambush upon Abu Naseeb, Nikolay had concluded that once Buscetta found out about the death of his arms supplier he would very likely 'go to ground' making it difficult to carry out any operation to eradicate him. Nikolay called General Kos. The General let Nikolay know that he had hatched a plan to lure Buscetta and Bastovoi to his complex. He had told them that he was interested in joining with them in the plan to take control of the Petrovs' empire. Kos had invited both Bucetta and Bastovoi to the wedding of his eldest daughter, a wedding that, in fact, would never take place. The two unsuspecting men agreed to attend. Kos would send his private jet to collect them, excluding the pilot, the plane seated only four persons. With four stopovers, a commercial route would take over 14 hours, the private jet would arrive within two hours of take-off. Nikolay asked Levski to take Teodora and Ivan Petrov with him, as they had been charged with the task of eliminating Buscetta and Bastovoi. The Petrovs' own jet would convey them to the small airfield that belonged to the General. They would have the entire army that was controlled by Kos, at their disposal. Levski and the two Petrovs arrived the day before their intended victims did. There was to be no conversations, the attack would be swift and clinical. It would take place within minutes of Buscetta and Bastovoi's arrival at the airfield. On Sunday morning, the day of the not to be wedding, the small single-engine jet, which once belonged to the most famous of all arms dealers, Adnan Khashoggi, dropped like a stone shortly after clearing the mountains that surrounded the complex of General Kos. It landed safely. On the radio to the control tower, which was in fact a converted shipping container, the pilot asked if it was safe to disembark, he was told,

'Yes, everything is clear.'

The door of the jet was pushed open from the inside, the hydraulics helped it drop, slowly and safely to the ground. A large man, dressed in black and wearing matching shades, eased himself onto the narrow platform at the top of the steps. He looked left, then looked right and moved two steps nearer to the soft grass at the edge of the runway. A second man, who by his appearance and demeanour could have been the first man's twin brother, followed the first man's every move. When both men were officially in Kosovo, two shots were heard, both men fell where they had stood. As they hit the ground, a third shot was heard, the pilot slumped forward in his seat. A uniformed soldier appeared at the side of the plane, he was the first person that Buscetta and Bastovoi had seen. He held aloft a megaphone and invited the two men to disembark. Whilst both men carried guns, they knew there would be no point in drawing them from under there armpits, at least not before they knew whom it was that they were fighting. As they stepped over their fallen bodyguards, a military jeep came to a stop, just a few yards from where the two condemned men stood. In the jeep, was a driver, General Kos, Gregor Levski and Teodora and Ivan Petrov.

'Welcome to my home,' was the greeting from the General, who saluted as he said it.

Levski stood, alighted the jeep from the back seat, reached over, took hold of the AK47 that laid, lifeless in the back of the vehicle, turned and said,

'This is for Stoyan, you Bastards.'

He then pumped the entire contents of the gun into the two men that had threatened to end the reign of the Petrov family. In a carefully 'pre-arranged' finale to this easiest of any murder that Gregor Levski had ever committed, a man, who would have made George Foreman look small, took one almighty swing of the machete that he was holding in his right hand. The force was such that it not only parted Tommaso Buscetta's head from its shoulders, but it also buried the machete deep into the soft ground of the runway. Ivan Petrov placed the head into a polyethene bag and then dropped this into a thick cardboard box. The box was loaded onto the Petrovs' jet and two minutes later the General stood to attention at the edge of the runway and saluted as Levski and the two relatives whizzed by at 140 kmph.

With no losses on their side, and Abu Naseeb, Tommaso Buscetta and Victor Bastovoi all looking for their seats in heaven, there remained only one piece of unfinished business. The destruction of all of those that had either arrived from Sicily or had switched their allegiance from Nikolay, Mustafa, and Dimitris. Whilst it was Teodora Petrov that had the job of wiping out all the men assembled in the hotel in Burgas, a hotel owned by the Petrovs, it was Levski's idea to fit the whole of the first four floors with explosives and as the hotel had accepted no other bookings, all they had to do was to tell the staff to make themselves scarce. At midnight, on the same day as Buscetta and Bastovoi had met their deaths, the hotel was blown to pieces. Those that managed to escape were gunned down by Mustafa's men, armed, ironically, with the weapons that their boss had bought and paid for.

Of the remaining 160 men under Buscetta's control, that had taken up residence in Sunny Beach, Golden Sands and Varna, a few were rounded up and systematically tortured, forcing them to squeal on their potential brothers in arms. One by one, they all disappeared. Either running back to Sicily or by falling foul of the many hit men employed by the Petrovs.

The head of Tommaso Buscetta, alias Salvatore Lima, was placed on the desk of the new boss of the Sicilian Mafia. It later stood atop one of the pillars that supported the gates of Palermo's Town Hall, for several weeks, until it finally disappeared altogether after being pecked by the hungry gulls that swarmed above the most famous of all Mafia strongholds.

For nearly five years afterwards, everything was peaceful and calm in Varna, that was, until Boyan Petrov arrived home, aged 21, with a scholarship in Business Studies, attained at Corpus Christi College, University of Oxford. Boyan was back, to assume control, things would never be the same again.

10 - MICHAEL O'LEARY – The Terrorist

Having come face to face with a severed head, resting peacefully in the freezer compartment of 'Fingers O'Doyle' the bookmaker cum terrorist, that he had longed to work for, Michael O'Leary was now being held in the dimly lit back-room of Fingers' house, which also doubled as an illegal betting office. In the room with Michael were his uncle Jimmy, Fingers, Micky McGovern, Sean Flynn, and Willie McCormack and whilst Michael had toyed with the idea that these men may all be connected, in some way, with the fight to make his place of birth 'one nation', he was now certain of the fact that he had got himself into 'deep shit' as his uncle Jimmy Quinn, was still holding the twelve-bore and it was still aimed at his young nephew. Jimmy spoke softly,

'Michael, it is a great pity that you have seen the head of Inspector Ahearn, the bullet that is lodged in what was once his working brain, is from the gun that now has your fingerprints upon it. It would be a great shame if the head and the gun found their way into the station where Ahearn once worked, do you get my drift young lad?'

Michael, although still only 17 years of age, was worldly-wise, he fully understood the implications of what his uncle had just said to him.

'Well, you go and get some shuteye now and we will talk again in the morning and don't be silly enough to think that you can just run away from this,'

Michael was halfway up the stairs before his former favourite uncle had finished his sermon.

Michael lay on his bed, his head was spinning, his thoughts were ever-changing. Why did he not listen to his mother? She had warned him about the sinister world of bookmaking. When would he be able to see his beloved Sinead? She had given her blessing to his departure from the stables, where they had met and had first consummated their relationship. Why was his uncle Jimmy involved in this criminal world? A world that he had previously only ever read about. Was his mum's new husband, Sheamus O'Reilly, horserace trainer, also involved with these people? Would he ever find out the answer to these questions and more importantly, what was he expected to do for the men assembled in the room directly below him?

The answer to the final thought that had entered Michael's head before he had finally fell off to sleep, was answered as his uncle Jimmy placed a mug of tea and a bacon sandwich upon the kitchen table the following morning. Jimmy sat, dead opposite his frightened young nephew, he looked directly into his deep blue eyes and said,

'Michael, you owe us. We took care of your father we have taken you out of those shitty stables and your life will be different from now on. But for this we need you to do something for 'us.'

Foolishly, Michael envisaged being asked to clean the house, cook the dinner, run a few errands, and wash Fingers' Rolls Royce. He soon realised that he was way 'off the mark' he could feel the contents of his stomach welling up inside of him when Jimmy took hold of the newspaper that was resting on the chair next to him, placing it on the table, directly in front of Michael and pointing at the picture on the front page, Jimmy said,

'We want you to kill this man Michael, when this is done you will have paid us back for the murder of your bastard of a father.'

Jimmy then placed a small holdall on the table,

'And this is the gun that you will kill this bloody traitor with Michael.'

The gun, a semi-automatic was the very gun that Michael had held in his shaking hands the previous evening.

After being mesmerized for a few minutes, as a reaction to what Jimmy had just told him, Michael looked up from the newspaper and said,

'But uncle Jimmy, this man is the Chief Constable of the Garda in Dublin, how am I going to get near enough to be able to shoot him?'

'Ah, you leave all of that to us, Michael, all you must do is pull the trigger. Later Willie will take you into the woods and teach you how to shoot.'

'When is this going to happen, Uncle Jimmy? Asked Michael.

'In five days-time. You will stay here until you are taken to the place, after this you will need to go into hiding for a while, but don't worry Michael, everything will be fine, so it will', replied Jimmy.

Michael, with tears streaming down his face said,

'But I need to see Sinead, can you bring her here?'

'Ah, Michael, I will have to ask the others if this will be possible, I will let you know'. Jimmy stood, patted Michael gently on the back and left the kitchen. Michael climbed the stairs to his room and sobbed his heart out.

Two hours later, Willie McCormack knocked on Michael's door and asked him to be downstairs in five minutes. Once again in the kitchen, Willie asked Michael to pick up the holdall and follow him out of the back door. After walking for half a mile or so, the two men were deep in the woods. Willie set up several bottles on a fallen tree trunk and asked Michael to remove the fully loaded gun from the bag. The first burst of fire took out just one bottle. Willie, without touching the gun, instructed Michael how to reload. This procedure continued for an hour or so, the two men then returned to the house. In the afternoon there was another hour-long session of shooting at empty bottles.

'You need two more days practice, Michael, then you will be fine,' said Willie as they made their way back to the house. In the back-room Jimmy, Sean, Micky, and Fingers awaited their return. Jimmy spoke first,

'We will bring Sinead here Michael, she can spend one night and then be gone, for sure, for sure.'

Sean Flynn, who seemed to be the leader of this gang, spoke, for what Michael believed to have been the very first time.

'On Friday, Martin Keenan will be opening the new Guinness Brewery in West Dublin, this will be an outdoor event, open to the public. This is where you will kill that bastard Michael. I hope you can shoot a lot better by then.'

It was public knowledge that the Chief Constable of Dublin, Martin Keenan, was anti-IRA and as such he had been giving information to the British for some time, his fate had been determined by the high command of one of the world's most feared terrorist organisations. Michael O'Leary was to be the executioner. Sean Flynn invited all five men into the kitchen. On the table was a large map of Dublin. Positioned on the map were five Subbuteo football figures, beside which were written five names, Sean, Willie, Jimmy, Micky, and Fingers. Sean explained to Michael that he would be dropped off by a stolen car, at the gates of the brewery, each of the five thugs would already be in position. He, Michael, would be wearing the long trench coat that hung on the back of the kitchen door. The semi-automatic would be concealed by this coat. You will make your way to the front of the crowd and squeeze in between Willie and Micky, who will already be there. After you have done your job, Michael, you must run and then turn left out of the gates and get into the car that Jimmy will be stood beside. You will be taken to a safe house, and I will send someone to look after you.

'Michael, now for the good news, Sinead will be here tomorrow night, but she must leave the next morning just after you leave for Dublin,' said Jimmy. Willie and Michael left the kitchen, to undertake another round of shooting practice.

Michael thought long and hard as to how he could escape, however he was watched 24/7 by at least two of his captives and even if he was able to tell Sinead of what he was being forced to do, she would not be able to help. Any grassing by her after the deed had been done would mean certain death for her and possibly himself as well. In late afternoon of the following day, June 4th, 1961, Sinead arrived in the back of Fingers' 'roller.' Taking her from the yard of Sheamus O'Reilly had raised little suspicion, as Fingers simply told Michael's mum that he was taking her 'as a surprise' for Michael. Michael had decided to say nothing to Sinead other than Fingers had asked him to go to the UK to look at a couple of horses that he was thinking of buying. This aroused Sinead's suspicions as Michel knew little about horses, other than the fact that they ate at the front and shit at the back, nonetheless, she did not question Michael any further. The couple enjoyed a night of continuous passion, four pissed Irishmen listened intently to the sounds of 'love' that wafted out of the bedroom and into the four ears, that were pressed firmly against the bedroom door.

At 8.30 the following morning, Michael, Fingers, Sean, and Jimmy, climbed into Jimmy's beaten-up old jalopy. Willie and Micky had left one hour before, they had things to arrange. Sinead, still sleeping, was locked into the bedroom, completely shagged out, she had not awoken when Michael had vacated their short-term love nest. The grand opening of the brand-new Guinness facility was scheduled to take place at 10.00am, a few dignitaries had been asked to say a few words, the Mayor of Dublin, a red-faced alcoholic by the name of Paddy Murphy was charged with cutting the rope that would propel a large bottle of the 'black stuff' against the new factory wall. It was not known when Martin Keenan, the boss of the Garda would be making his speech. Jimmy, in his position outside the brewery gates would give the signal to the driver of the stolen Toyota and Michael would be dropped off. At 10.20, Jimmy Quinn blew his nose into a filthy dirty handkerchief. The Toyota parked 200 yards away, moved, at normal speed to within 50 yards of the gates. Michael, balaclava in position, semi-automatic nestling inside the long overcoat, walked into the courtyard and stood between Willie and Micky, nobody challenged him, the crowd had parted without a stir, as if everyone inside were part of the act. As Chief Constable Martin Keenan thanked the previous speaker for his kind words, a hail of bullets burst from the end of the gun. No sooner had the 'traitor' clasped his hands to his chest, then Michael was gone.

Michael came out of the courtyard and into the cobbled street, he turned right, he did not see Jimmy.

A voice called out, 'Michael'.

Michael turned and saw Jimmy, standing by the side of a Ford Cortina. He climbed into the back and lay across the seats. Jimmy ducked into an alleyway, at the other end of which, was parked his old Land Rover. Willie and Micky were just two of the crowd that had run from the yard whilst Michael was still firing. They continued running alongside several others until they were well away from the scene of the crime. Ducking into O'Malley's bar, the bartender asked,

'What will ya be aving lads?'

Fingers and Sean walked to the end of the road, crossed, and were picked up by a small baker's van. It took a full fifteen minutes for the Garda to cordon off the area around the scene of the shooting. Jimmy was the first to arrive back at Fingers' house. He unlocked the door to the room where Sinead was, she asked as to the whereabouts of Michael and was told that he had left for England, with Fingers and that he would be back in a few days or so. A car pulled up outside the house, Jimmy helped Sinead into it, he gave the driver some money, the car pulled out onto the dirt track of a road and was gone. Soon after, a baker's van arrived, Fingers and Sean walked into the hall of the house carrying a tray of freshly baked bread. There would be no suspicion, the baker's van delivered here, twice a week and the two accessories to murder were safely hidden in the back. At O'Malley's bar, the Garda had arrived, the question put to the drinkers inside, was simple.

'Does anyone know who Michael is?'

The men from the Garda had let it be known that three men had met their deaths, at the hands of a man named Michael. They questioned each patron of the pub, individually. When asked, Willie and Micky said that they had been there since 10.00am, O'Malley verified their story. Soon after the roadblocks were lifted, a yellow Ford Cortina arrived at the doors of O'Malley's bar. Willie and Micky, without paying, thanked their host for his hospitality and left. The Cortina took them back to Fingers' house.

All five men sat in the backroom of the house. Bottles of whiskey and brandy were opened, the hand of Jimmy Quinn was shaking so violently that half of his tipple was spilt onto the bare floorboards of the room.

Willie was the first to speak,

'Fuck me, Young Michael has killed three of those fucking scum bags do we know where he is right now?'

'The man will report later tonight', said Jimmy.

Thus far, Sean had not uttered a word. His silence was broken when he asked Jimmy to go with him. The two men went out of the kitchen door and walked into the nearby woods.

'I am sorry Sean, I know I fucked-up, but Michael was going the wrong way, but in the end, everything was OK, was it not?'

'Ah, Jimmy, Jimmy, I have known you for so many years, I knew your bastard of a father before that. You know there is no other way, don't you Jimmy?'

Before Jimmy could muster a word in reply, he lay dead on the ground. Sean had shot him, with a gun sporting a silencer. Sean stood over Jimmy and said,

'All that remains is for you to be buried. Just one word, Jimmy, that is all it took for your life to end this way. You will learn from this Jimmy Quinn.'

Sean returned to the house, entered the backroom, picked up his whiskey glass and gesticulated to Willie and Micky. They knew what had happened. They put on their boots and coats, went out into the woods, and buried their long-time friend. After this, Willie drove Jimmy's battered old Land Rover to the edge of a disused chalk quarry, got out and then physically pushed it, until it plunged over 150 feet and came to a stop in a heavily wooded area below. Micky had followed on his motorbike, they returned to the house. Fingers' job was to start a rumour amongst his bookmaker friends, that Jimmy Quinn was responsible for the three murders that took place at the Guinness factory.

At 11.30pm, Bobby Kelly knocked on the door of the house. Sat with Fingers, Sean, Willie, and Micky he confirmed that Michael had boarded the ferry that would take him from the Port of Larne, in Northern Ireland, to Stranraer on the West coast of Scotland. He would be met by Liam O'Shaughnessy who would then drive him to a safe house in Liverpool. Having been born on the British side of Pettigo, Michael possessed a passport, obtained with the help of Sheamus O'Reilly, the passport showed Michael to be a British subject. Getting him out of the Republic and into NI was not at all taxing for Bobby Kelly and his associates. Bobby asked as to the whereabouts of his good friend, Jimmy Quinn. Sean informed him that Jimmy had gone out earlier, to visit his sister in Sligo. Fingers asked Bobby to keep them informed of Michael's progress, but never to use the telephone and never send anyone else to report. Knocking back the last of his Brandy, Bobby left the house and drove back to his small cottage, situated within the grounds of Naas racecourse.

Within days, Dublin was awash with the rumour that Jimmy Quinn was responsible for the slaying of the three men at the brewery. The Garda, when asked by the press, had concluded that the, as yet unidentified 'man in the street', had mistakenly called out 'Michael' when, in fact, they now believed the murders to have been carried out by Jimmy Quinn, a man suspected of working for the IRA and whom, according to information received, had been a long time 'hit man' for the illegal paramilitary group. It was several weeks before Jimmy's Land Rover was discovered, the Garda concluded that as no body was found and no none seemed to have heard from Jimmy for some time, it stood to reason that he had gone on the run. He was most probably being looked after in a 'safe house' in the North. Jimmy, just like his nephew, Michael, was of British decent.

A week after first reporting the escape of Michael to his fellow conspirators, Bobby Kelly stood next to 'Fingers' Doyle at the Curragh, Ireland's most prestigious racecourse. Fingers was in his bookmaker guise that day. Bobby was asked to meet with Fingers in the car park, forty-five minutes after the last race. Fingers and Bobby sat side-by-side in the sumptuous leather seats that adorned the back of the metallic silver Rolls Royce. Sean Flynn was driving. As they pulled onto the road that would take then to Kildare and to one of the bookies' favourite resting places, Bobby began.

'Michael has been moved from Liverpool to Kilburn, in London. We have placed him with Peter and Maria Fitzpatrick, his story will be that he lost his parents in a road accident in West Belfast, we have given Michael's new parents enough money for six-months, after that Michael will have to fend for himself.'

At the beginning of his life with Peter and Maria, Michael lived the life of a 'holiday maker' going out almost every night to the many Irish pubs that thrived in this part of North London. He made quite a few friends all were quick to make it known to Michael that their sympathy lay with the people of the South. All of this had been carefully planned. Michael was to be what is known as a 'sleeper.' He would be left to pursue his own way in life, however, in the long term he would be converted and asked to carry out tasks for the terror-led organisation, just as he had done, before arriving in England.

In Kilburn, Michael had access to many a pretty, dark-haired Irish beauty. Many of them were the daughters of parents that were 'helped' to relocate to England. Most of these families came from Belfast, in the main they supported the beliefs sought by the people in the South and were only too willing to move over to London, where they enjoyed a much better standard of living. All were expected to 'do their bit' when asked. Michael had one or two steady girlfriends, but what he really wanted, was to be with his beloved Sinead. He asked Peter and Maria if there was a way in which he could see her. He was told that they would ask the right people, to see if this was possible. After a week or so, Michael was to receive the best of news. Sheamus O'Reilly, Michael's mum Eileen, now Mrs. O'Reilly and Sinead McBride would all be attending the four-day racing event at Cheltenham in November. This would be the only safe way for Michael to meet up with Sinead. Michael was both elated and deflated at the same time. On the one hand, he was happy that he would see the love of his life, on the other hand, he must wait for just over five months before he could, once again kiss the mouth, stroke the hair, and get between the legs of the real love of his life. In the meantime, he would make do with Cathy Fitzpatrick, the 18-year-old daughter of his foster parents and Bridget Burns, whom he had met in one of the Irish bars that straddle Kilburn High Road. Cathy was a 'strait-laced' kind of a girl, a staunch catholic, she would not let Michael anywhere near her size 10 knickers, although she had given him oral sex several times, always when her parents were safely out of the house. Bridget was the complete opposite to Cathy. Michael was able to penetrate her any time he wished. He would often follow her to the lady's loo, at the pub, she never wore knickers when out on the town, she was a pushover, good for casual sex, but she was not Sinead.

Michael got himself a job, behind the bar of a newly opened pub, aptly named Michael O'Neil's. Being Irish and always 'up for the craic' he derived great delight from letting the girls know that he was the owner, his dad having bought it for him. This pretence gave him instant access to the delights of many a girl. He would listen, intently, at the stories told by the Irishmen that sat at the bar, some stories were funny, others unbelievable and now and again, just sinister. Three Dubliners sat on stalls at the bar, one rainy Saturday afternoon, talking about 'the murders,' one of them mentioned that Jimmy Quinn was once a mate of his and that Jimmy had been blamed for the deed, but he knew for a fact that it was not Jimmy, it was in fact, Jimmy's nephew, Michael O'Leary that had pulled the trigger. Looking over at eighteen-year-old Michael, the Irishman jokingly said,

'To be sure, it was you, young Michael.'

Michael's whole body shook, spilling the beer from the pint that he was pulling at the time, his confidence and self-assurance drained from him in an instant. He excused himself from further duties and legged it, for two blocks, until he reached home. Inside, he found Peter 'inside' Maria, a belated birthday present, from him to her.

'Peter, I am in big trouble,' gasped a breathless Michael.

'Now would ya be calming down young man,' said an equally breathless Peter, slowly withdrawing from his wife of thirty years.

Maria, very embarrassed, gave Michael a look of death as she hurriedly brushed past him and disappeared upstairs.

'Now would ya be telling me all about it, Michael,' asked the man that was now zipping up his flies.

Michael explained exactly what had taken place in O'Neil's just minutes earlier.

'Oh, they're just messing with you Michael, but just wait here, do not leave the house until I return.'

Peter put on his shoes, collected his jacket from under the stairs, left through the front door and started his car. One hour later, Peter retuned. He instructed Michael to get his things together, they would be leaving in twenty minutes. Without question, or hesitation, Michael climbed the stairs and packed his worldly possessions into two canvas bags, these were once the property of Jimmy Quinn. He walked past the slightly open door of Maria, the kind lady that had looked after him for just under two months, he was about to push the door, to bid her farewell, however he could hear that she was 'busy' playing with herself, no doubt from the frustration of being stopped in her tracks earlier. Michael skipped downstairs into the hall and exited the house through the open street door. Throwing his bags onto the back seat of a Ford Corsair, Michael sat, nervously beside Peter Fitzpatrick, as the car pulled slowly away.

'Where are we going Peter?' asked an anxious Michael.

'We are on our way to Canning Town, East London. You are finished with Kilburn.'

Ninety minutes later they pulled up outside a bay-windowed terraced house, on a street with forty such properties on each side of the road. Peter knocked at the door Michael was stood right beside him. A man, so fat, that it was impossible to see into the long narrow hall, opened the door.

'This is Michael. Michael this is Fatty O'Brien.'

Peter turned, strode the ten paces back to his car, and was gone.

'Would ya be coming in Michael, I have heard so much about ya, I am Ollie O'Brien, but people call me Fatty, would ya be knowing why Michael? The bloody cheek of it, I am just big boned, that's all.'

Michael knew that words were escaping from the fat man's mouth, he just could not hear what they were. His thoughts were only for Sinead and how was he going to be able to meet her now that his cover seemed to have been blown. Showing Michael into the middle room of the house, a room with no natural light, he was introduced to a man that was a complete contradiction to Fatty O'Brien. Stanley McKinley was as thin as O'Brien was fat. He could have escaped under the door, without opening it.

'Would ya be wanting some tea, Michael? Asked Fatty.

'Yes, please Mr. O'Brien, thank you.'

Fatty shut the door. Michael was alone in the room with Stanley, a man, it seemed, that had never eaten a cooked dinner in his life. Stanley spoke, for the first time, he did not have an Irish accent, he was an East Ender, however his words were clear and precise.

'Michael, I hear that you are in a spot of bother, well never mind, I will take care of you, OK?

'Yes, Mr. McKinley, I will not let you down.

'Oh, and no need for the mister business Michael, people call me Slim, and you can no longer be known as Michael, Michael. We have established a new identity for you, tomorrow you will receive the paperwork with the name, Sean Porter. You will be Sean from this day on, have you got that Sean?

'Yes, Mr. McKinley, sorry, Slim. I've got it.'

Slim left the house, Fatty showed Sean to his room, telling him that dinner would be at 7pm, once Mrs. O'Brien gets back from work and cooks it.

The following morning, Fatty informed Sean that he was to have a visitor. Sean's heart rose, thinking that it might be his beloved Sinead, it soon sank again when Fatty told him to expect to see Bobby Kelly, who was over here from Dublin, on official business.

Arriving at the house in Canning Town just after breakfast the following day, Bobby Kelly explained to Michael that the three men he had served in O'Neil's bar, were in fact working for Special Branch. Michael pointed out that they were 'Irish.' Bobby told Michael that Special Branch has agents of many different nationalities, adding that Willie McCormack had been 'lifted' from the streets of Dublin and in return for his freedom, new identity, and re-location, he had spilt the beans on everything that he had been involved in. Bobby carried on. 'Fingers, Sean Flynn, Micky, Sheamus O'Reilly, many others and I are now in hiding. It was lucky for us that we have a man in the Garda that let us know, before we also got detained. You were lucky Michael you were able to get away before you were arrested. I know that you now have a new identity, be careful never to slip up, never discuss your past with anyone, not even your new handler, Slim. Now, I know you will be wondering about your meeting with Sinead, well Michael, it just will not be possible, now that Sheamus and Fingers have been banged up, but I do have some good news for you, Sinead is pregnant. This must be the result of your 'night of passion' back at Fingers' place. I brought her to you that day, Michael. Ah, she is such a lovely girl, that one.'

Michael quickly worked out that as it was now almost the end of September, Sinead must be nearly four months gone.

'I must get to see her Bobby, she is having my child, I cannot let her down, can I?'

Bobby, with a sadness drifting across his face, replied,

'Michael, it will be impossible for you to contact her, they will be watching her, the telephone at O'Reilly's yard will almost certainly be bugged. All of us are in the same boat Michael, we all have families, but we all knew that this day may come and now it has.'

Michael, now weeping, said,

'But I was made to do what I did, they have no proof that it was me that pulled the trigger, I was wearing a balaclava, nobody saw me, I could go back and state my innocence.'

Bobby, looking menacing, said,

'The problem here, Michael, is that they have the gun and only your prints are on it. If they take your prints and match them up, then you are done. You really do not want to go back Michael, as you have murdered three members of the Garda, you might not even make it to your trial. Now I must be going, you should stay here, with Fatty O'Brien. Slim will take care of everything you will need, but now you must think about leading a normal life. I will never refer to you as Michael again, you are now Sean. Take care Sean, it is possible that you will never see me again.'

When Bobby Kelly pulled the front door shut, Sean knew that he was well and truly, fucked. His thoughts were only for Sinead and his mother, back in Sligo. The thought of not being able to see Sinead and his baby would invade Sean's mind for several months. He would have to come up with a plan to see Sinead before she gave birth, which should be at the beginning of March 1962. He later saw, from the racing pages of the morning newspaper, that his mother,

Eileen O'Reilly, had taken over the duties of training the horses at her husband's yard, her name now appeared alongside the horses, whenever the yard had a runner in the UK. 'That's it,' he thought, I will go to Cheltenham in November, they are bound to be there.

Every day, just before noon, Slim would visit Sean. Fatty O'Brien would always leave, he did not wish to know what was being said. One month after his arrival at O'Brien's house, during which time he did nothing, other than to plan his visit to Cheltenham, Slim announced that he had found Sean a job. He was to be a junior clerk at one of the World's foremost Shipping Companies, their Head Office was based just off Fenchurch Street in the City of London. Much to Slim's surprise, Sean did not disagree, he was completely up for it, after all, he needed money to fund his trip to Cheltenham. Slim knew a section manager at the shipping company, there were no questions asked, this was 1961, human resources did not exist, jobs were plentiful, anyone was welcome, even murderers, it appeared. Sean loved his job from the very first day. He would walk the 100 yards or so from O'Brien's house to Barking Road, catch the number 15 bus and alight at Aldgate Bus Terminal, around forty minutes later. He received luncheon vouchers as part of his salary. Within a week, he was almost part of the furniture, making friends with workmates and their friends from other shipping companies. He always told the same story, when asked, of how his parents had been killed in a road accident in Belfast and now he was living with 'Uncle O'Brien' in Canning Town. He was paid, weekly, in cash. Every Friday at 5.30, five or six of his new-found friends would go on a pub crawl around the city. Almost all his gang came from East London. Nights out with them would see his wages disappear before Monday morning, he would borrow from Fatty. Slim was now only visiting once a week, normally on a Wednesday evening.

At the end of his first month at work, Sean found that three of his colleagues, from another department, were going to Cheltenham, for two days, in the second week of November. The trip was being funded by the company. There should have been four people going, however one of them had dropped out as his wife was about to give birth. Seans' manager, a friend of Slims, managed to get him into the fourth slot, everything was paid for, the coach, the hotel, all the food and drink, they were even given a fiver each to bet with. There was just one problem for Sean, he could tell no one, but how would he cover being away from O'Brien's for two nights? His manager knew of his trip, his manager saw Slim on a regular basis, he just had to hope that Slim did not find out before the trip. If he found out afterwards, then Sean did not care, as it would be too late to stop him.

On Monday, the 6th of November 1961, Sean went to work as normal. Arriving at the bus terminus in Aldgate at 8.25am. At 8.35, Sean, along with his three workmates and forty more 'City Slickers' boarded the coach, at the same Terminus. The coach would take them to Cheltenham in Gloucestershire, bringing them back late on Tuesday night. Sean had already purchased a copy of the Sporting Life and was pleased to see that, Eileen O'Reilly still had three runners that afternoon. In the good old fashioned, knees up mother brown days, almost every passenger was three sheets to the wind before they arrived at the racecourse, some four hours later. Sean had rejected most of the offers of free booze, of course he was 'sniped at' by his fellow partygoers, for not also getting pissed, however he had a mission, a mission, unlike any of his travelling companions. Arriving in the coach park, which is a bit like drinking mild and bitter, whilst everyone else is knocking back Champagne, Sean's hardest task was going to be getting himself into the main stand of the racecourse, which was, of course, on the other side of the track. It was 1.00pm, the first race was at 2.00, however, Eileen O'Reilly's first runner was not until 3.05, Sean had time on his side, for now.

His one big advantage was the fact that he had been to Cheltenham previously, his entry point on that occasion, had been as a passenger in one of the horse boxes, carrying two of the runners belonging to his mum's husband, Sheamus O'Reilly. On that occasion, he had entered the gate reserved for 'Trainers and Owners' he could not do that today. It would be impossible for Sean to simply walk across the track and enter the main stand, as for one, he would be seen by thousands of racegoers and would be stopped by one of the stewards, secondly, he had no badge or trainers permit that would allow him admittance. His only option was to leave the course and walk completely around the outside perimeter, this, he figured, would take him a minimum of forty minutes. His workmates were oblivious to the fact that he was no longer in their company, all were either drinking or looking for the best odds on the horse that they were going to bet on. Sean walked back into the coach park, out of the gate and turned left. Five minutes into his walk, a car stopped, it was a Rover 100, known back in the day as 'the poor man's Rolls Royce. The passenger, manually winding down the window, asked in the poshest of voices,

'Where are you going, young man?'

'To the main stand miss. The taxi has dropped me off at the wrong place.'

'Get in lad, we will take you.'

Sean noted that the posh lady was dressed in her finest livery.

At the gate marked, 'Trainers and Owners' a salute was given to the driver as he entered, the driver touched the front of his deerstalker cap, in gratitude. Both occupants of the car put their respective badges around their necks, the lady, adjusting her mink coat against the November chill, asked,

'Where is one's badge, young man?'

'Oh, be Jesus,' I've left it in the taxi, my lady.'

'Here, you can borrow one of ours, everyone here knows us, no one will ask to see my badge. But be sure to return it before you leave.' By the way, we are Lord and Lady Beaverbrook, you will find us in the Royal Box.'

Bowing, Sean thanked them very much, and as he made his way to the stables he thought, that this really had been the 'luck of the Irish'.

Sean's luck was about to continue, for as he turned the corner from the side of the stand, which led directly into the first of over fifty stable yards, he saw little Billy Newman, a slightly uneducated man of about four foot eleven inches. Billy had begun his career as a stable lad to Sheamus O'Reilly, some 25 years previously, he still held that title, however given his slight demeanour, he was allowed to 'ride out' some of the horses in the yard at Sligo. Billy also suffered from acute memory loss, if he saw you at 8.00am he had no idea as to who you were at 10.00. Sticking his head out from the side of the stables, Sean called out, 'Billy' the wee dwarf did not hear. Calling out in a slightly louder tone, Sean managed to draw the attention of the diminutive, wanna-be jockey. Billy turned around. Sean ushered him over and asked,

'Billy, where is Mrs. O'Reilly?'

'Would ya be talking to me, then?' asked the garden gnome.

'Yes Billy, I am talking to you, where is Eileen O'Reilly?'

Sean was now becoming inpatient.

'Who da fuck is Eileen O'Reilly?'

It was 1.30pm, his mother's first runner was not until 3.05, however from experience, Sean knew that his mum would attend the stable of her runner, 'Moonshine Runner' up to one hour before the race was due to be off. Sean decided to go back to the main stand. He went into the bar and bought himself a sandwich and a beer. At 2.15 he returned to the stable block. He did not look out of place, suited, and booted as he was, as many owners, dressed in their Sunday best, would be milling around, wanting to pat their hopefuls on the nose, before they went out and lost them a small fortune.

Sean walked up and down the area where he had spotted the small man that could not remember his boss, let alone him. As he passed the last box, through the top opening of the stable door, he saw the back of his mother. He unbolted the bottom part of the door and walked in. His mum turned and barked out,

'You can't come in here lad.'

'Mum, it's me.'

Eileen managed to say, 'Be Jesus, so it is,' just before she hit the straw-laden stable floor.

Sitting his mum upright, Sean asked her,

'Where is Sinead?'

With tears now streaming down her face, Eileen, now standing and hugging her son, replied,

'Sinead could not come Michael she was not feeling well.'

'Mum, 'you must not call me Michael, I am now Sean Porter, living in London.'

'How is the baby mum, is everything OK?'

'How do you know about the baby?'

'It's a long story, Mum, now you must get this horse ready to race. Where are you staying, Mum?'

Wiping the last of the tears from her face, Eileen replied,

'Same as always.'

'OK, I will be there tonight, I will tell you everything then, and remember Mum, it's Sean.'

As he turned to leave, Billy the dwarf was stood outside, he had not been visible, as he was smaller than half a stable door.

'Ah, there you are, Michael, your Mum is looking for you' said Billy, as Sean brushed past him.

Walking back through the car park, Sean placed the badge under the wiper blades of the Rover 100, turned right and began the long walk back to the 'working man's stand' on the other side of the course.

Arriving back at the bar, where his mates had been when he left, John Duggan asked,

'Where, the fuck did you go Sean? We had a tip in the 3.05 for 'Moonshine Runner' and it pissed home at 8-1 and fuck me, would you believe it, it was trained by a woman?'

Sean felt happy for his Mum. She had trained her first-ever winner at Cheltenham. After the last race, only 31 of the 44 blokes that boarded the coach in London turned up in the car park. They arrived at their hotel 20 minutes later. Sean was sharing a room with John Duggan, he so wanted to tell his best friend of the day's events, perhaps even more than that. He was, of course, unable to do so. He knew that he should never tell anyone. Whilst his mate was sleeping off the effects of an all-day drinking session, Sean ventured down to the small hotel reception and asked the young lady if she knew where the Regency Hotel was situated.

'Oh, it's close by. Just turn left out of the door, take the first right, walk 200 yards down the Bath Road and it's there.'

'Thank you,' said a grateful Sean.

When he reached the Regency, he went into the reception and asked for Eileen O'Reilly. The receptionist picked up the telephone,

'I have a young gentleman asking for you, Mrs. O'Reilly.'

'OK then, I shall send him up.'

Eyeing the good-looking young man up and down, she told him,

It's room 206 on the second floor, and if you don't mind me saying, you look very handsome tonight, young man.'

On another day, at another time, Michael would have had her knickers off in a jiffy. Tonight however, he would spend as much time as he could, with his mum. Arriving at her already open door, Sean stepped inside, Mother and Son hugged, as only this combination of relatives can. Sean spent two hours, meticulously telling his Mum the whole story. At the end, they hugged again.

'Michael, I can call you Michael in private, can I? asked Eileen.

'Better you call me Sean Mum, any slip-up could be costly for us both.'

'I understand son,' said a slightly saddened Eileen.

'Sean', whispered Eileen, 'I am going to write down the address of your Auntie Connie in Sligo, when you get back to London, you should go to the Post Office and arrange a PO Box Number for yourself, we shall correspond in this way. Don't address the envelope to me, but to your Auntie Connie, we can trust her more than anyone else.'

Sean asked his Mum about Sinead,

'She is OK son, but not so great as to be able to travel over here, we left her in charge of everything back home.'

'And Mr. O'Reilly, Mum, asked her son.

'He is still in jail, he is in poor health, I can only see him once every month, but it was a bad thing that he did, when he agreed for you to go and work with Fingers, he knew exactly why they wanted you, now he is paying the price. Now you must go, be careful and write to me as soon as you can. I will keep you informed about Sinead, until we can work out a plan for you to be back together.'

Five days before Christmas, 1961, Sean collected an envelope from his PO Box at a Post Office in Plaistow, East London. He read it, stood outside the shop. His Mum had informed him that Sinead, now seven months pregnant, had got up one morning at 5.00am and had not returned. She had left a brief note on the mantlepiece, it simply read,

'Tell Michael I love him, but I have to think of the safety of our baby.'

There had been no indication of where Sinead was heading. Also, in the letter, Eileen had informed her son of the passing, in prison, of Sheamus O'Reilly, she added that she felt no grief at hearing the news.

For the next few years, Sean Porter, lived his life as a young man, in London. London in the 60s was 'the place' to be. John Duggan moved on from the shipping company to become a manager at the UK's largest European Trucking Company. Soon after, at his friend's insistence, Sean joined him and by 1968 he had become the General Manager of the company, travelling all over Europe, including both Belfast and Dublin. It was in 1968 that Sean met with a young and beautiful Irish nurse. Sean was drinking in the pubs along Whitechapel High Road, the notorious Blind Beggar amongst them. The nurse, Kathleen Green worked in the Royal London Hospital, just across the road from Sean's favourite watering hole. Sean was completely awe-struck by this black-haired, brown-eyed beauty. Her family hailed from Kilburn, what a coincidence Sean had thought. He would later find out, that their meeting was no coincidence at all.

Sean soon learnt, from his frequent trips to North London that Kathleen's family were all 'Republicans' Sean was asked to help the cause. He was introduced to Ireland's largest International Transport Company and soon appointed them as his Irish Agents, ditching his previously reliable partners. At this time, he remained 'off the radar' as far as being, in any way, involved with the terrorist movement that had now made the UK mainland its prime target. To keep up appearances, after they married, Sean and Kathleen moved into a large, eight bedroomed, Victorian house that overlooked Victoria Park, in Hackney. Sean assumed the identity of a doctor. Every morning he would leave the house, carrying, what was, to all intents, a doctor's bag. On the dashboard of his car was a small plastic sign, that read, 'doctor on call.' He would remove this as soon as he left the road on which he lived. He was to maintain this 'double identity' for nearly three years. Then, one night in February 1972, as he left work, he was bundled into a transit van and driven to Wood Green Police Station, where he was held, under Anti-Terrorism laws. In simultaneous raids across East London and Essex, several workmates, including his friend of many years, John Duggan, were held, pending further investigations.

Those investigations would reveal that Kathleen Green was working for the IRA, the Irish Transport Company were being used to bring over arms and explosives. Sean Porter himself would carry those bomb-making materials to various locations. Fatty and Slim were part and parcel of the deceit. Sean Porter, once known as Michael O'Leary, had been a 'sleeper' for over eight years, however whilst he was not a willing party to the murders that occurred in Dublin back in 1961, it was him that had pulled the trigger that had killed three men. In addition, he was almost certainly coerced into performing his part in the deaths of many innocent people on the UK mainland.

Sean Porter received 25 years for his part in the transportation of explosives, with intent to kill, however in a deal brokered by the head of the Anti-Terrorist Squad, in exchange for information, he was given a new identity and a place to live, far away from the repercussions that might otherwise have engulfed him had he chosen to stay. Unbeknown to any police force, Sean wrote to his Auntie Connie, informing his Mum of his new abode, which of course, was fake, however after a series of 'resending' the mail, Sean would get to see the reply, eventually. In one such reply, Sean was to learn that Sinead had given birth to twin boys, they had come into the world on the 2nd of March 1962, the exact same day as their father's birthday. When receiving this news, in 1973, the twins were already 11 years old, their father was 29. Sean had never seen them.

11 - PETER SLADE – Distant Drums

In September 2001, with his time as a mediator in discussions between the warring factions in Ireland and the British Government at an end, Peter Slade stepped out of the Anti-Terrorist Squad and back into a brand-new section of Special Branch, where he had enjoyed unparalleled success. He had risen to the rank of Chief Superintendent during the time that he had 'sat in' on talks to bring the decommissioning of arms to a conclusion. His new role was somewhat secretive, less than a handful of his colleagues knew of the existence of the specially assembled unit of men that operated from a normal 'semi-detached' house in the suburbs of Chelmsford in Essex. The unit, code name 'Jim' thought up by Commander James Reeves, was derived from the shortening of his Christian name and that of his favourite Country and Western singer, Jim Reeves. Peter Slade was the man in charge at Chelmsford, Commander Reeves would meet up with Peter from time to time, but never at the unit's house. Peter's brief was the continuation of investigations into the past activities of all of those that had, and had not, been given an amnesty under the Belfast Agreement. The total number of people listed on the walls of what was once somebody's living room equated to just over 200.

When the IRA and other militant groups had been asked to submit a list of all those known to have carried out atrocities against people in Northern Ireland and the UK mainland, the deal had been that those mentioned on the list would have to reveal, in detail, the exact nature of their crimes. 'Jim' would then attempt to corroborate what had been revealed and if the crimes mentioned could not be tied to the man admitting that crime, then they would need to dig deeper to find out if in fact someone else was involved. It was common knowledge within the Police Force that many terrorists had admitted a crime that they had not performed, simply to deflect the authorities from carrying out any further investigations. It was thought that at least forty guilty men had escaped justice, due to the confessions of others for their crimes. Peter Slade needed to find those that had never been taken to task.

After many frustrating weeks of compiling files on thirty or so of the 'pardoned' terrorists, Peter was summoned, by Commander Reeves, and told that a directive from the Home Office now prevents them from investigating most of the more prominent members of the former paramilitary organisation. Peter was, to say the least, somewhat disappointed by this decision, as he and his team were already on the way to finding some quite disturbing facts surrounding the confessions of some of the household names that had been 'excused' for their past extremist behaviour. On his way back to Chelmsford, Peter came up with an idea that might allow him a route back into investigating some of those that had now been listed as taboo. He and his team would list certain individuals that had been killed, without anyone ever being held responsible for their murders. His team would also, by going back through the archives, try to find out exactly what had happened to other people, those that had simply disappeared, without trace. He could then 'cross reference' these dead, or missing people against those mentioned in the confessions of all those men that had been given an amnesty under the Good Friday agreement. This would not be a simple job, the team would meet with hostility and silence whilst trying to gather information, they would also be putting themselves and their families at risk of threats, kidnapping and even murder, should they get too near to the truth. Peter had also, never forgotten the words, spoken quietly to him, by the most prominent member of the IRA, whilst attending a meeting on the 25th of July. The words, unheard by anyone else, were,

'We are watching you son.'

Peter Slade had replayed this short sentence over and over in his head for the past four months.

At the 25th, July meeting, which took place at a cottage, deep in the remote Countryside near to Ballintra, Ireland, were the six, senior-ranked terrorists that Commander Reeves and Peter Slade had negotiated the final surrender of arms with. All six were now on the home office's 'do not touch list.' The host of that meeting, Sean Flynn, had also been given an amnesty. The intel that was in Peter Slade's hands, named Fergus 'Fingers' Doyle, Willie McCormack, Micky McGovern, Jimmy Quinn, Bobby Kelly and Sheamus O'Reilly as being close associates of Flynn's. All six men, in their statements requesting amnesty, had mentioned being implicit in the murder of Chief Constable Martin Keenan on the 5th of June 1961, although none of them admitted responsibility for the murder itself. A note on Jimmy Quinn's file indicated that his nephew, Michael O'Leary, was, at the time, a recent recruit and that he had been introduced, initially to Sheamus O'Reilly and then to Fergus 'Fingers' Doyle.

Within a week of undertaking the investigation into these men, Peter Slade found that Sheamus O'Reilly had returned to his maker, whilst in prison in December 1961, he was awaiting trial for seventeen separate charges at the time. Jimmy Quinn had 'gone to ground' shortly after the murder of Martin Keenan and two others, and now, forty years later he had not 'resurfaced.' Looking at the ages of these men back in 1961, Sean Flynn was 40, Fingers

O'Doyle 41, Willie McCormack 35, Micky McGovern 32, Bobby Kelly 29, Jimmy Quinn 31. Michael O'Leary was just 17. Peter had personal information on all these men. Such as, where they were born, the names of their parents, brothers and sisters, uncles, aunts, and known criminal associates. He knew where they drank, their bits on the side and a whole lot more. The problem was that most of the info was decades old and no one was likely to cooperate with him and his colleagues, including, as he would find out, his fellow, now retired, officers.

Initially the team concentrated on Jimmy Quinn, as he had not come forward when amnesties were being handed out. The address given for Quinn, Flint Cottage, seemed vaguely familiar to Slade, and so it should have been, as he had visited this address very recently. It was the same cottage where the high-level meeting had taken place just a few months previously. Sean Flynn now claimed to own this property. There was no record of Jimmy Quinn ever selling or disposing of his property to Flynn. Slade handed this query over to his sergeant for further investigation. It did not take them long to establish a link between Quinn and Fergus O'Reilly. They discovered that Eileen O'Leary, Michael's mother, was Quinn's older sister and whilst he had been born in the border town of Pettigo, and could claim British Nationality, he had chosen to live on the Southern side. He was a staunch Republican, who could travel freely between the two countries. Eileen and her son, Michael had left home in January 1958 and whilst their initial movements were not clear, they had ended up at the racing stables of Sheamus O'Reilly, a man, known to be sympathetic towards the IRA. Not long after Eileen and her youngest son had left the violent alcoholic, Patrick O'Leary alone, he was dead. Tarred and feathered and left on a bridge, his body half in NI with the other half in the Republic. The records show that no one was ever taken to task for his murder. Eileen had become Mrs. O'Reilly. Sheamus O'Reilly had died. Quinn had vanished from the face of the earth and Michael O'Leary was known to have been working for the infamous bookmaker, Fergus 'Fingers' O'Doyle at the time of his disappearance from Ireland. Slade was sure that he was on to something.

Investigations into the five men that had all been given amnesties intensified. Flynn, Fingers O'Doyle, McCormack, and McGovern all still lived in Ireland. Slade and his team had little or no jurisdiction there, however in January 2002, Slade learnt that Bobby Kelly was now living in Liverpool, and he was, at the age of seventy, on his last legs. Fifty-five years of chain smoking had left him reliant upon permanent oxygen, he was refusing to go into hospital, choosing to live his final days at home. Slade asked a local Inspector, whom he had known since his days at training school in Hendon, to pay Kelly a visit and ask if he would agree to having a chat with a 'man from the smoke.' Much to both the Inspector's and Slade's surprise, Kelly agreed. Chief Superintendent

Slade and Inspector Phil Neale would visit Kelly, at his home, close to Goodison Park, on the Northern side of the Mersey River.

Two days later, Slade and Neale knocked on the door of the tiny, terraced house that was home to Mr. and Mrs. Kelly, their youngest daughter, Nelly, and five cats. Kelly's house was a throwback to the 1950s, a small, bay-windowed front room, a kitchen, not modernized since the 1930s, was to be found at the end of the narrow, dark green painted hallway. The loo was outside. Upstairs, the two policemen could only imagine, was as grim as the downstairs, but then, they would never find out. Mrs. Kelly, about as Irish as you could get, bowed to the immaculately dressed men as she stood to one side and ushered them into the tiny front room. Bobby sat in an armchair that the local charity shop had refused, twenty years previously. He was as far away from the bay window as he could get, bright light was not his friend. He was 'hooked up' to a home oxygen machine and was wearing a mask that covered both his mouth and nose. CS Slade thought,

'You are not so fucking-clever now, are you Bobby Kelly.'

Kelly's file had shown him to have been a 'link man,' involved in several bombings on the mainland. He had declared most of them under 'admission of guilt' on the amnesty form. To Slade and Neale, he was still a mass-murderer, and they had no sympathy at all for his current illness.

As the two detectives sat, rather reluctantly, side-by-side, on the corduroy sofa that must have been delivered by the dustmen, Mrs. Kelly pushed the door with her foot, walked in, and placed a tray containing, three cups, a tea pot, a bag of sugar and a bottle of milk, onto a side table that was somehow held up by just three legs.

'Would ya be wanting some tea, young men?' she asked.

Purely out of politeness, the two men accepted the gesture. Mrs. Kelly opened the door ever so slightly and called out,

'Nelly, would ya be coming down here and pouring the tea for these lovely gentlemen.'

There were several 'clunks' and then a woman of about 45 years old fell into the room.

Nelly Kelly had been born with defects to all her limbs. Her right leg seemed to stick out at a 45-degree angle, her left leg sported a club foot, upon which, was attached one of those cumbersome 'club boots.' Had she had a club biscuit then she would have had a 'full set.' She had only half of a left arm and the hand of her tea-pouring right arm had been formed the wrong-way-round, meaning that the palm of her hand was underneath where it should have been. As Nelly poured, Mrs. Kelly asked,

'Are both of you lovely gentlemen married?'

The answer, which came simultaneously from both men was,

'Yes, we are, Mrs. Kelly.'

The answer would have been the same, had they both been single.

The tea was poured, albeit most of it ended up in the saucers.

Mrs. Kelly, dragging Nelly by the belt of her 'never been washed' pink nylon dressing gown, purchased from 'Pollards' back in 1965, left the room.

Slade started the conversation, asking Kelly if he knew anything about the disappearance of Jimmy Quinn and his nephew, Michael O'Leary. Stringing together only a few words at a time, before replacing the oxygen mask, Kelly asked,

'If you can look after Mary and Nelly when I'm gone, I will tell you what you want to know.'

Slade was in somewhat of a pickle, he had no remit to do deals with scum such as Bobby Kelly, however he was desperate to unravel forty-year-old questions.

'Bobby, I will do everything that I can, I promise. Please keep your answers short as I can see that it is difficult for you to talk. If you prefer, you can write it all down.'

Gasping for air, Kelly responded,

'Ah, I'm sorry son, I never learnt to read and write, so I did.'

'Never mind, Bobby, just take it slowly.'

The rest of the conversation, which took a full two hours and involved more tea and Nelly parading in one of her Mum's nighties, revealed everything that Slade needed to know. Kelly had said that after the murder of Martin Keenan and two others in Dublin, had been carried out by Michael O'Leary, who was given no choice, Sean Flynn shot Jimmy Quinn in his own back garden, as punishment for revealing Michael's name at the time of the shooting. Flynn had then simply moved into Quinn's cottage and Michael was shipped over, firstly to Liverpool and then onto London. Michael was given a new identity however Kelly swore that he did not know what that was. An Irish girl was coerced into becoming Michael's lover and they married. Michael was caught in London and charged with Importing explosives for use in the bombings. Michael got twenty-five years. Slade had heard enough he could never have imagined that he would get to learn so much. Slade and Neale left Kelly's humble abode at 4.15 in the afternoon, and as they were eating dinner, prior to the Chief Superintendent's train journey back to London, they were to receive the news that Bobby Kelly had passed away.'

'Good fucking-riddance to him,' were Slade's words as he hung up the call.

The next morning Slade gathered his entire team together and explained exactly what Bobby Kelly had told him. He explained that everyone was to put on ice, anything else that they were working on, their priority was to find both Jimmy Quinn, whom Kelly had said was shot in his own back garden, and his nephew, Michael O'Leary, whose last known location was London, we must bear in mind that we need to go back 40 years.

After the meeting with his staff, Slade returned to his office, picked up the phone and called Chief Superintendent Dan Brophy at Police HQ in Dublin. Without revealing the source of his information, Slade asked that CS Brophy, whom he had met twice previously, to find a reason for wanting to excavate the garden of the cottage that, as recently as July of last year, was said to belong to Sean Flynn. Brophy informed the officer, of equal ranking to him, that investigations into the whereabouts of one of the IRAs 'most wanted' had been called to a halt some ten years ago, adding that Flynn was known to the Garda, as well as to almost everyone else in Ireland. The phone call ended with Brophy agreeing 'to see what he could do.'

Dan Brophy took a mobile phone from the locked drawer in his office desk and made a call.

'Hello, Dan' said Sean Flynn,

'it's been a while.'

In reply, Brophy said,

'Yes, Sean. I thought that you should know that someone, high up, across the water, has asked me to dig up your back garden.'

Laughing, Sean Flynn replied,

'Ah that will be no problem, Dan, just send your men here, any time you like.'

'Will they find anything Sean?'

'Oh, yes, I suspect they will, Dan.'

'Can you be away when we come over Sean?'

'Most certainly, just let me know when, will ya.'

Brophy replaced the unregistered mobile back into the drawer and locked it. He picked up the phone on his desk and called Peter Slade.

'Next week, Mr. Slade. We will go digging next week.'

Brophy replaced the phone back into its holder.

One week later, Brophy, five men and a small digger arrived at the ancient flint cottage. Once the home of the long-since missing Jimmy Quinn.

Willie McCormack greeted Brophy on that cold and frosty morning, at the end of February 2002.

'How ya doing, Willie?'

Shaking the senior policeman's hand,

'Ah, I am as well as I can be at 76 years of age, what with the arthritis, the dodgy ticker and me piles.'

And yourself, Chief Superintendent?'

'Yes, I'm tickity-boo, thanks, Willie.'

'Is Sean not around then?

'Oh no, be Jesus. He and Fingers have fucked-off to the races, to be sure, to be sure.

'I'm putting the kettle on, would you and ya lads like some tea?'

I'll put a drop of Ireland's finest in it, to be sure.'

'Thank you, Willie, that would be grand, so it would.'

A few minutes later, the two men left the kitchen, McCormack was carrying a tray with six cups of whiskey-laced tea. Arriving at a spot in the wooded area of Flynn's Garden, Inspector Cook, known to everyone as 'Dud' bade his superior officer 'good morning' and then informed him that an area that was marked by several red flags, was where they would find the body. 'Dud' had dug many holes, in many places, during the seventeen years that he had been a forensic officer, he was rarely wrong. Three hours into the dig, the 'digger' was shut down, by Dud.

'OK, lads, get in, and be careful.'

Four members of the team climbed down the two wooden ladders that had been dropped into the four-foot-deep hole. Painstakingly, they removed clay-like earth with the smallest of trails, it was not long before one of the men would shout,

'I think we've found it guv it looks like a fucking horse.

Looking into the grave, McCormack laughingly said,

'Do ya think it's fucking Shergar?'

McCormack's comical statement may well have had some credibility to it, as Shergar had been 'kidnapped' from his stable by six hooded men, in 1983 and had never been found. In 1999 an ex-member of the IRA made an anonymous telephone call to a national daily newspaper and claimed that the IRA had been responsible for kidnapping the horse, which belonged to the Aga Khan. The caller said that it could be found near to Ballymagroarty, in County Donegal.

'OK, wrap it up lads, unless that nag resembles Jimmy Quinn,'

There was a broad smile upon the face of Chief Superintendent Dan Brophy.

Before he left, Brophy was asked, by McCormack, as to whom it was that wanted to find Jimmy Quinn, after all these years.

'Chief Superintendent Peter Slade, Special Branch, in London,' was Dan's reply.

Back at Dublin Police HQ, Dan Brophy grinned as he explained to Peter Slade what they had found. Slade jokingly asked his Irish counterpart,

'Do you think it was Shergar?'

That seemed to be the end of the line, as far as finding Jimmy Quinn's body was concerned. Only McCormack, Flynn and McGovern knew that when it came to 'laying the horse to rest', it was they, that had exhumed Jimmy's body, dug a bit deeper, put him back and then laid Shergar on top. That secret was taken to the graves of those three, former friends of Jimmy Quinn.

Slade and his team had only one other place to go, and that was in trying to trace the movements of Michael O'Leary after his removal from Dublin to London, via Liverpool, back in 1961. Scrolling back through the archives, one of his team, walked into his guvnor's office and said,

'Eileen O'Reilly, Sir. She was previously Eileen O'Leary. She then became a racehorse trainer in Sligo, after the death of her husband. The good news is, she is still alive, aged 84, and lives in a nursing home in Pettigo, on the British side of the town.'

Slade was ecstatic at that news he asked his colleague to inform the others that 'drinks' were on him after work tomorrow. Slade then asked his secretary to get him the name of a Chief Superintendent in police HQ, in Belfast. Ten minutes later the ace investigator was talking to Eoin Farrell, the head of 'Special Services in Northern Ireland.' A few minutes into their conversation, Slade asked,

'If he could 'come over' and get to meet with Eileen O'Reilly.'

'I will see what I can do, Mr. Slade, leave it with me,' said CS Farrell.

Unbeknown to Slade, CS Eoin Farrell took his mobile from his pocket and made a call. He spoke with Mack McBride, the twin brother of Manson McBride, both aged 40, on that very day, the 2nd of March 2002. They were the sons of Sinead McBride and Michael O'Leary.

Elated at having obtained, what for him was a breakthrough, in tracking down the missing Michael O'Leary, Slade left the office early, he would take his wife, Sandra, out for dinner, as he knew he might be away for a while. Arriving home just after Sandra had returned from the school run, his car, as normal, was the last one on the drive. Sandra and his two children, both girls, Debbie aged 8 and Susan aged 7 were so surprised to see their dad home so unexpectedly. Peter asked Sandra to do the driving when they went out to their favourite Chinese Restaurant, in Epping. Sandra had no problem in driving her husband's large BMW, as she drove an even larger people carrier. Peter would be free to 'have a drink.' The following morning, feeling the worse for wear through drinking too much whiskey, and not feeling as though he wanted to get up and start moving cars, he asked his wife to use his car to take the girls to school. Sandra readily agreed. Peter stayed in bed whilst his wife readied the children for school, they shouted 'bye daddy' as they left the house. The girls climbed into the back of Peter's car. Sandra buckled up and then turned the key in the ignition. The explosion rocked several of the nearby houses. The whole front of Peter Slade's house was demolished. The words that would never go from his head continually resonated,

'We are watching you, son.'

At that moment CS Slade knew exactly who was responsible for wiping out his entire family.

For the next few weeks, he encountered unimaginable grief. His family, friends and work colleagues did their best to console him, he was beginning to sink into a deep depression. He may never have escaped that depression were it not for his boss, Commander James Reeves. The Commander invited Peter to stay with him and his wife at their magnificent country house, just outside Cheshunt in Hertfordshire. Commander Reeves was the only person, outside of Peter himself, that knew of the words spoken to him by one of the IRA's most prominent military leaders. When James Reeves believed that his second in command was sufficiently stable to discuss the happenings of the night of April 23rd, 2002, he told Peter that the man responsible for the death of his wife and children had a 'watertight' alibi, he had been in a public place that morning, and could not, therefore, have been personally responsible for the bombing. The Commander was, however, in complete agreement with his Chief Superintendent that the man, given amnesty by the British Government and who had admitted his part in twenty-seven murders, when submitting his list to the appropriate committee, had been responsible for giving the order to kill Peter Slade. Unfortunately, the wrong people got into the car that morning. Over a glass of the finest Hine Brandy, the Commander told Peter that the order had been given and that the Home Office had sanctioned it, albeit only verbally. The former leader of the IRA was to be eradicated. Peter was told, in no uncertain terms by his boss, that he would play no part in it.

On the night of the 11th of May 2002, eight SAS soldiers, travelling in two 'unmarked' Grand Cherokee Jeeps, entered Ireland near to Killeen. The former, customs posts, that straddled the road, had been unmanned since 1993. It was just past midnight. At 2.00am, in complete silence, the SAS entered the grounds of a mansion that belonged to the man, deemed to be responsible for the murders of Mrs. Sandra Slade and her two daughters. Two dogs, loose in the gardens barked their discontent at the uninvited intruders, both were shot, with a single bullet to their heads. A light came on from inside the house. A curtain was drawn back. The soldier, lying flat on the ground, using a night vision, high-powered rifle, had only a split second to ascertain as to whom the person peeking out of the window was. There was a slight sound from the rifle as it launched just one bullet. Another soldier, lying just inches from his colleague, had trained his 'state-of-the-art' binoculars on the window, he had given the signal to fire, certain that it was the intended target that had looked out into the dark night. Less than two minutes later, all eight of the world's most elite soldiers were safely on their way back to their base in Newry, on the Northern side of these troubled nations. At 4.00am, Peter Slade received a call, on his unregistered mobile phone, he knew not as to whom the caller was, but he understood exactly what the words 'it's done' meant. Two days later, the TV and newspapers, announced that 'a prominent, former member of the IRA, had been found dead at his house, situated on the outskirts of Navan, Ireland.'

Prior to leaving for Belfast, to interview Eileen O'Leary, Slade and his team had come up against a 'wall of silence' whenever Michael O'Leary's name was mentioned. Looking back, they had found few references to the boy that was once the main suspect in the murder of Martin Keenan and two colleagues back in 1961. Whilst Slade knew that O'Leary had received twenty-five years, there were no trial transcripts or records of where he might have served his sentence. Commander Reeves had told Slade that the Home Office were extremely nervous about his investigation, although he was to receive no direct order to stop the search. There was no record of O'Leary entering Northern Ireland during the last 40 years or so. At 10.30am, on the 18th of May 2002, Chief Superintendent Slade and his Chief Inspector, Paul Mayfield, sat in the office of Chief Superintendent Eoin Farrell at Police HQ in Belfast. The following day, all three men arrived at St. Mary's Care Home, on the outskirts of Pettigo. A town split in two by the Irish border. Eileen O'Reilly (nee. O'Leary) at first, claimed to know nothing at all about her son Michael's whereabouts or why he had disappeared, suddenly, in 1961. Then in a surprising about-turn, after the officers had assured her that her son was not in trouble, as he had more than served his time, Eileen showed the detectives the many letters that her son, now known as Sean Porter, had sent to her over the years. The detectives were 'gobsmacked.' They sat for nearly two hours, each of them reading the letters, after which Slade asked Eileen,

'So, Michael never went to prison?'

'Indeed not. He was in Spain for many years and now he comes and goes, back and forth, to Belfast to see the twins, so he does.'

Now the high-ranking officers knew exactly why Michael O'Leary never appeared on any radar, he had become Sean Porter. What they did not know was, who were the twins that Porter was visiting? And where was Porter living now? There surely would be Immigration records of him arriving and leaving NI, under his assumed name. Once outside, Slade made a call to his office and filled them in, asking that they find out all they could about Sean Porter, formerly known as Michael OLeary.

One week later, Eileen O'Reilly died, peacefully in her sleep, in the care home where she had lived in for the past six years, she was 84.

Arriving back in his office in Chelmsford, 36 hours later, Slade was asked to step into the common room by his Chief Inspector. The common room was where they discussed important new developments. CI Paul Mayfield, who had accompanied his boss to Pettigo, had returned to the office the previous day, he had been briefed by the Sergeant on duty and was now stood, at the front of the room, with six pairs of eyes staring, expectantly at him. Paul Mayfield began,

'Michael O'Leary, alias Sean Porter visits his twin sons, in Belfast, three or four times each year. Their mum is Sinead McBride, they met whilst they both lived and worked for Sheamus O'Reilly at his stables in Sligo. The twins were born in 1962, which makes them 40 years old now. They are Mack (the Irish meaning the 'son') and Manson (the 'fierce one') McBride. From what we have been told, Manson certainly lives up to the meaning of his name, as he spends many a weekend banged up after drunken brawls. You may have seen their trucks on the road in the UK as their company, McBride International Transport is the largest trucking company in the whole of Ireland. Sean Porter last entered the Port of Larne on the 2nd of March, which was the day of the twins' 40th birthday. Porter was himself 58 on the very same day. Sinead is now married to Brennan O'Brien, a cousin of Vincent O'Brien, once the most successful and famous of all racehorse trainers. They have two daughters. There is no record of Sean Porter leaving Northern Ireland since his entry into Larne on the 2nd of March.'

CS Slade thanked CI Paul Mayfield and the rest of his team, for their excellent work, in such a short space of time. He then retired to his own office, to think about exactly what they should do next. A few hours later, he picked up the unregistered mobile phone from the top drawer of his desk and called Commander James Reeves. He invited the Commander for dinner, at 6.30pm they sat at a table in a well-respected fish restaurant, on the banks of the river Thames in Wapping, East London. The Chief Superintendent quickly filled his boss in on the events of the last week or so. But when he mentioned the name, McBride, he sensed a distinct change in the Commander's demeanour, who then intervened, saying,

'Peter, you have uncovered something that may cause both of us some problems. You see, the McBride's are already on the radar at Mi5, further investigation might well be treading on the toes of the knobs at Whitehall. I may well have to report your involvement, and if I do, then you will almost certainly be asked to cease. Slade replied,

'And if this conversation never took place, Sir, what do you think might happen?'

James Reeves thought long and hard, before replying,

'Well, Peter, Mi5 know that Sean Porter is the father of the McBride's. Porter seems to have not learnt from his past mistakes. It is believed that the twin brothers are using their transport company to convey all kinds of contraband around Europe, including Arms, Drugs and even People. It is almost certain that their father is the 'middleman' linking the Mafia in Bulgaria and Turkey, a certain General in Albania and the Middle East's most prolific arms dealer. There has been a whisper that Porter is putting together the largest network of drug distribution that the world has ever known. In addition, and hand in hand with his sons, he is almost certainly responsible for 're-arming' the breakaway IRA. Mi5 have infiltrated this network, using a rouge agent, whom I believe is a Syrian. Your intervention, Peter, could well jeopardize the whole operation, which has been live for the past three years, on the other hand, this conversation never took place, did it?'

The two men, colleagues for many years, shook hands. Slade headed for Wapping Underground; James Reeves slid into the back seat of his waiting Mercedes. Both men were oblivious to the fact that they had been photographed, both inside and outside the restaurant. In addition, Commander Reeves had no idea, that his unregistered mobile phone, given to him as 'part of the job' had been monitored since the day that he had received it. Peter Slade had been a lot savvier than his boss, as he had ditched the phone that was handed to him upon his promotion to Chief Superintendent, buying himself a replacement.

As he stood on the platform at Wapping Station and even though he had been one of the UK's best detectives for a good number of years, the Chief Superintendent did not notice the black-suited man that stepped into the same carriage as him. He was equally unaware that the same man was present when changing trains at both Canada Water and Stratford. Slade's home, at the end of the Central Line, in Epping, was still undergoing repair after the car bomb had almost destroyed it, just a few months previously. Only a handful of passengers alighted the train at 11.45pm. The man in black, held back as Slade climbed the stairs, exited the station, and crossed the road towards the 24-hour cab office that the police officer used on a regular basis. As he stepped onto the pavement, 50 yards from the cab office, the man in black gripped Slade's elbow. At that very moment, a white transit van pulled alongside the two men. A side door opened, Slade was half-pulled and half-pushed into it. He was unarmed.

Less than ten minutes later, the van came to a halt. The three men that were keeping him company escorted Slade to a dark red Range Rover, Slade realised that he was in the car park of the Merry Fiddlers, a public house that he considered to be his 'local,' given its proximity to his house. There was of course, no one else about. It had just gone midnight. The Range Rover contained three men, two sat in the front and one in the back. Peter was asked to get in, he obliged, without question. The transit van pulled out onto the unlit road and was gone. The man that Slade was now sat beside held out his hand and introduced himself.

'Good morning, Mr. Slade. I am Julian Pritchard, I work for Mi5.'

The police officer was unresponsive. Inside his head he was kicking himself, for not being aware that he had been followed all the way from Wapping, and maybe even before that, without realising it. Julian Pritchard continued,

'I presume you have a good idea why you have ended up in the car park of a pub in rural Essex, dear boy?'

'Not really, Mr. Pritchard, although I am sure that you are going to explain.'

'Well, Chief Superintendent, we have been fully aware of your movements for some time now, in fact, ever since Commander James Reeves and you brokered the deal with the IRA. Whilst we commend you for your aptitude and service to your country, we must inform you that you are no longer required to investigate the brothers and their father, this matter is being dealt with by us, under the direct orders of the Home Office. Commander Reeves has been relieved of his duties, for divulging, to you, certain information that he was privy to but was not meant to share with any others. I hope you fully understand Mr. Slade?'

'I do, Mr. Pritchard, I do.'

The back door of the Range Rover was opened, by the man in black that had tailed Slade for some time. Peter was escorted to a Ford Mondeo, parked in the darkness, at the far corner of the car park. The Range Rover headed off towards the M11. The darkly dressed man that had tailed him dropped Slade off at the end of his drive. He entered his lounge, poured himself a large Brandy and sat, contemplating his next move.

12 - Mi5

The following morning, Chief Superintendent Peter Slade telephoned his Chief Inspector, Paul Mayfield and informed him of two things. One, he would not be in the office and that the team should be sent home until they are contacted. Two, it looked as though the unit would be asked to investigate other matters or maybe it would be shut down completely, either way, no further investigations were to be carried out in respect of the McBride's or Porter. Slade told his trusted colleague that he would be in touch as soon as he was able to add to the mystery.

Slade then drove to the home of Commander Reeves, he did not call first, as he was now convinced that as Mi5 had a vested interest, it was safe to assume that both his and his Commander's phones would be monitored. Arriving at the electronically controlled gates of his 'guvnor's' house, Slade was relieved to see the large black Mercedes parked on the drive, his relief soon turned to dismay, as behind the Merc was a dark red Range Rover. The sighting of the Range Rover gave him something of a dilemma, should he proceed onto the property, or should he back up and piss-off? As he was chewing this over, the large wrought iron gates opened. Slade drove in and parked alongside the Range Rover. James Reeves chauffeur opened the door and CS Slade stepped into the large, wood-panelled reception area of the six-bedroomed, house. The Commander, still dressed in his tartan pyjamas, with a matching dressing gown, tied around his midriff by a rope, that would surely have held the QE2 in position, ushered Slade into the drawing room. The chauffeur, a man of Eastern European extract, asked,

'Coffee, Sir?'

'Yes, thank you, very much.'

Julian Pritchard, whom Slade had met for the first time, just a few hours earlier, sat in a large leather chesterfield armchair. He did not stand to greet the Chief Superintendent.

The man from Mi5 did not utter a word until the coffee was brought in and served. As soon as the large, double doors, made of solid oak, were pulled shut, and looking directly at Chief Superintendent Slade, Julian Pritchard began.

'Dear Boy, I am not a gambling man, however I would have wagered Commander Reeves splendid abode that you would be here this morning, after all, you no doubt believed your respective telephones would be bugged, would you not?'

James Reeves sensed a discourteous tone to Pritchard's voice, he intervened, saying,

'Whilst you are no doubt the head of Mi5, you have no jurisdiction over the Metropolitan Police, it is understood that your involvement in the investigation takes precedence over our own, however I would take it as a courtesy if you were to taper your obvious obnoxiousness towards Chief Superintendent Slade.'

A totally expressionless Julian Pritchard replied,

'Point taken Commander.'

Having put the Mi5 Chief firmly in his place, the conversation moved on, in a more cordial manner. Pritchard again made the running.

'Gentlemen, I believe that we all understand where we are with this matter. Now, out of pure courtesy and a certain amount of protocol, I will brief you as to where my department is with our investigation, and I would find it immensely pleasing should you choose to do likewise.'

Julian Pritchard, head of Mi5 for the past twelve years, made a sermon-like statement.

'After Sean Porter was released from HM Custody, to enjoy the freedom that was denied to those people that were killed by the explosives that the 'bastard' transported to our shores, we watched him, for three years, mainly for his own protection but also to ensure that we would know should he return to his old ways. In 1975, in a cock up made by my predecessors, Porter disappeared from our radar. We picked him up again, quite by accident, when one of his original minders spotted him on the ferry from Stranraer to Larne and although the spotter had long since left the service of Mi5, he followed him and then reported back that Porter had visited an address on an industrial estate off the Crumlin Road in Belfast. The McBride brothers, who were at the time under suspicion themselves, operated from the address that Porter visited. Further investigations led us to find that the McBride's were in fact Porter's sons. From that point, in 1997, both father and sons have been the subject of intense scrutiny. During the five years since Porter became public enemy number one, we have found out, in conjunction with our counterparts across Europe that he has conducted meetings and cooperated with the likes of the Turkish and Albanian Mafia, a certain, notorious Kosovan General, arms dealers in Syria, Turkey and Jordan, drug cartels and most importantly, to us, the Continuity IRA. I cannot divulge the individuals involved, however the most worrying aspect for us to consider is the arming of the breakaway Irish rebels, those that refuse to disband. They have been stockpiling a sizeable amount, of arms, and the former Michael O'Leary is the link between buyers and sellers, his sons are the purveyors of death. We learnt of your involvement Mr. Slade when you contacted a certain Chief Inspector, Dan Brophy of the Garda in Dublin. You see, Mr. Brophy is playing both sides. He informed Willie McCormack that it was you that had requested Jimmy Quinn to be dug up and as you know, they found only the remains of Shergar. Well, Mr. Slade, they should have carried on digging. It was Flynn that ordered your murder and not whom you had presumed it to have been. Flynn, McCormack, and McGovern are responsible for the loss of your family. Nonetheless, the assassination carried out by the SAS was not a mistake, it was well overdue, Mr. Slade, well overdue.'

After more coffee was delivered by the lurking chauffer, Julian Pritchard continued.

'Mr. Slade, your unit, known as 'Jim', was beginning to infringe upon our own investigation and whilst we take our hat off to you and your team for putting together so much in such a short space of time, we could not allow you to continue for much longer as your mode of investigating is not as covert as our own. This brings me on to why I am here this morning. Commander Reeves has agreed to assist us in our pursuit of Porter, his sons and all the other people that have never been taken to task for their previous criminal deeds. Mr. Reeves will step down as the Commander of Special Branch, he will be succeeded by the current Chief Constable of Essex. You, Mr. Slade were the obvious choice to have taken that position, however we would like you to join with us, as a temporary member of Mi5 as we value your undoubted skills as an investigator. We believe that you know more about this situation than anyone within our existing team. It will be dangerous, you will have to go undercover, but we can give you all the tools and backup that you will require. What do you think Peter? I can call you Peter, can I?'

With no hesitation and no second thoughts, Chief Superintendent Peter Slade simply replied,

'I'm in, Mr. Pritchard, I'm in'

On his way back home, Slade called Chief Inspector Paul Mayfield, who, unlike his colleagues had not taken the day off.

'Can you meet me at Starbucks in Liverpool Street?'

'Yes Sir, what time?'

'3.00pm this afternoon.' Slade hung up.

At 3.00pm, CS Slade was in the queue at the counter of a busy Starbucks when CI Paul Mayfield arrived. They sat, and over coffee Slade informed his Chief Inspector that 'Jim' had to be disbanded, at the behest of the Home Office and that there was nothing that he, or Commander Reeves could do to prevent this. Slade explained that he was to take six months out, as the mental strain of losing his family had taken its toll upon him. Commander Reeves was stepping down and Chief Constable David Skeels, known personally to Paul Mayfield, would assume the role of Commander of Special Branch. Slade went on to say that it had been a pleasure working with someone as dedicated and conscientious as the man sat opposite him and that he would file a recommendation for him to be promoted to Superintendent. The two men stood, shook hands, and went their separate ways. They would never meet again. The next day, Slade, dressed as though he was attending a funeral, entered the building known as Thames House, situated in Millbank, a stone's throw from the houses of Parliament. Thames House, Head Quarters of the most famous Secret Service in the World, Mi5.

After emptying his pockets, walking into a glass pod, like a revolving door and then being frisked by a rather overweight heavy that could not have managed to run further than a couple of steps, if needed, Peter Slade was greeted by a man that was dressed exactly as he was. Black suit, white shirt, black shoes, and a dull blue tie. The 'man' had introduced himself as being, Nigel Smalling. He handed Slade a pass, which was attached to a plastic chain, and invited Slade to follow him. At the lift, Smalling indicated that the first-time visitor to Thames House, should hold the pass against the digital reader, he did as he was asked. There was a series of flashing green lights, seconds later the lift doors opened.

'Would you mind holding your pass against number four,' asked Smalling.

Again, the 'new recruit' obliged. The lift began its journey upwards. Slade's thoughts, as he headed skywards were that there was no such security at New Scotland Yard and even less at the house in Chelmsford. Some days he would see complete strangers just wandering around. They could have been anyone at all. At the fourth floor, the pass was required once more, this time to enter an office that contained four desks and three people.

'I will get your new pass sorted by tomorrow, Mr. Slade. In the meantime, you will have to use the one you have. Your pass will be individually linked to you, no one else will be able to use it.'

Then, without introducing Slade to the three occupants of the room that he now found himself in, Nigel Smalling slinked off down the hall.

As soon as Smalling was out of earshot, the three men rose, as one. The man nearest to Peter was the first to speak.

'Forget about him Mr. Slade, the man's a complete moron. Full of self-importance, but unfortunately you will require his help from time to time.

'I am Archibald Cecil, 'Archie' to everyone in here.'

'This is Pierce Nelson, known to us all as 'column.'

'Finally, may I introduce you to the one real misfit within our office, Roland Ratcliffe, affectionally named 'Rat.'

'In this office, we are all considered as being of equal rank, although we are of course, aware of your background, Chief Superintendent. At this moment, we have only one remit, we are all working on operation 'Cold Harbour' something, we are told, that is very close to your heart'.

Archie continued.

'In the room next door there are two men and two women, collectively we all hold rank over them. They are our coordinators, any legwork, research, or coffee that you may require can be requested from them. At 11.00am we are to meet with our boss, Julian Pritchard and Quentin Proctor, a junior minister from the home office. I understand that you have already met with Mr. Pritchard, he is OK, but he has his nose so far up the Home Secretary's arse that it must be difficult for him to 'shit'.'

Archie opened the adjoining door, using his pass, and requested three coffees and a tea. Slade asked,

'How would you know what I wanted?'

'Well, you use Starbucks quite often, don't you Mr. Slade?'

Replied a smirking Archibald Cecil.

At 11.02am, on Wednesday 31st July 2002, six men, all looking as though they were about to shoot a scene from Men in Black, sat in a conference room on the sixth floor of Thames House. Quentin Proctor, junior home office minister, was the first to address the meeting.

'Gentlemen, we have information from the highest authority in Dublin that a major arms shipment, emanating from Iraq, will be arriving in the City via the Port of Liverpool. We have been given clearance by the authorities to work hand in hand with our counterparts across the Irish Sea, of course this is the last thing that we wish to do, therefore our aim should be to stop the shipment before it crosses into Ireland. In front of each of you, you will find a file containing what intel we have already.' Looking directly at Peter Slade, the junior minister continued.

'Mr. Slade, I would like to welcome you to the party. Our work is of the utmost importance to our Country. I understand that you have a personal interest in bringing about the downfall of those involved, please do not let that interest cloud your judgement. Mr. Pritchard and his team have spent every waking moment for the past two years in trying to nail these 'bastards', so please do your best to work alongside your new colleagues, remembering, at all times, that there is safety in numbers.'

Proctor returned his parker pen to the inside pocket of his jacket, gathered up his paperwork and was gone. Dismissing all but Peter Slade, Julian Pritchard closed the blinds to any prying eyes and addressed his newest recruit.

'Peter, the junior minister is a wanker. He reads from a carefully prepared script. He knows nothing of the world that 'we' live in. I brought you in here to be a 'maverick' to have your own ideas, as you have so successfully had in the past. Share only what you decide with your new colleagues, anything else, please share with me. We have another team, they do not tread the carpets of Thames House, you will find them, one by one, along the way. There are seventeen departments within Mi5, each is trying to bring the others down. You can assume that your office, your home, your phone, and your very movements are monitored 24/7. You can use this knowledge to your advantage. Trust only the first man you met today, Nigel Smalling. Others will tell you that he is basically an idiot, he is not, he just plays the part, and very well, I might add. Smalling will get you anything and everything that you require to enable you to get the job done. He has undertaken more clandestine meetings than any other operator, he will get you into places and people that you and I never knew the existence of. Finally, you can liaise with me through your old Commander, James Reeves. To Mr. Reeves, Smalling, and myself, you will be known as 'Gurney.' Good luck in your new job. Please visit the basement before your leave next Monday. Smalling will be waiting for you.'

Returning to 'his' office and before he could sit down, his three colleagues announced that it was lunchtime.

'Come on, old chap, shake a leg,' said Archie Cecil.

'It is time we showed you the sights of London.'

Before Slade could muster a response or an argument, he found himself walking down Millbank, turning left into Lambeth Road, where 'Column' hailed a black cab. Four minutes later all four men entered the sumptuous reception of the St. James Gentlemen's-Club.

'Good afternoon, gentlemen' was the greeting afforded to all four men by the female Maître d'.

She was buxom and blond. She wore a mini skirt that would have shamed those worn by the Kings Road girls of the 1960s.

'Follow me,' she requested.

All four men entered the restaurant part of the club. Mandy, the Maître d' led them to a circular table in a darkened corner of the room. Pulling each chair out in turn, Archie, Column and Rat obligingly sat.

'Oh, I have not seen you before, have I Sir?' Mandy enquired.

Before the slightly embarrassed man could reply, Mandy pushed the soft fingers of her hand firmly into Slade's groin.

'Oh, my dear, we are going to have to do something about that.'

Taking Slade's hand, she led him back out into the reception and towards a broad wooden staircase, she gestured for Mi5's newest member to climb the stairs and as he did, he was greeted by a girl that was descending. The girl was stunning and looked no older than 16, she wore a black skirt and a white, silk blouse, undone just under her breasts. She took Slade's trembling hand and led him upwards, he could not but notice that her arse was void of any knickers. His hard was attempting to burst through his trousers. At the top of the stairs, the girl opened one of four doors and led Slade inside. Within a minute, he was undressed and inside her. He came as if it was his first time. The teenage seducer guided him from the bed and into the bathroom. The already prepared bath contained a long-padded seat, supported by a stainless-steel frame. The young temptress gently laid her new customer down, the warm water just covering his back. She took some oils from the side of the bath and gently worked it into his manhood. Slade's slightly limp cock stood up like a bollard in the street. Straddling him in the bath, she slowly dropped her pussy down until it was level with his mouth, she invited him to sample the taste of her love box, without hesitation, his tongue slid from his mouth until it touched that part of a woman's fanny that normally sends them into orbit. The girl immediately withdrew from the bath, knelt on the floor, and took the full length of Slade's erection into her mouth. The sensation that rippled through his body at that moment, was like nothing he had ever experienced before and, as it transpired, would never experience again.

Peter Slade asked the girl for her name, she replied,

'That's for me to know and for you to find out.'

She helped him to dress, took his hand and led him to the bottom of the staircase. The Maître d' as if knowing exactly when he would return, led him through the reception doors and into the dining room, where Slade was to receive the most rousing of welcomes from the sixty or so diners that were enjoying an extended lunch.

'Well Peter, how was desert?' asked Rat.

'Unbelievable,' replied a red-faced and out-of-breath Peter Slade.

'Welcome to Mi5.' Said Julian Pritchard, patting Peter on the back as he passed by.

'Does this happen every day?' Peter enquired of Archie.

'No, no, no, my dear boy, this is your inauguration test, which, according to Mandy, you have passed with distinction. Now you must be hungry after your ordeal, we took the liberty of ordering for you.'

The waiter placed in front of Slade, a plate of carefully arranged mashed potato with a large pork sausage, embedded into it, the sausage was standing bolt upright and dripping a white sauce. At 7.30pm, the four men from operation 'cold harbour' called it a day.

Monday, 5th August 2002, would be Peter Slade's first full week in his new job. Having sat with his three new colleagues for the final two days of the previous week, he knew that he would have to 'go it alone' in his quest to find, and bring to book, Sean Porter and possibly, his twin sons. He decided that he would spend at least three days a week away from the office and would only share with his colleagues anything that would not expose him to danger. He had heeded the words of Julian Pritchard, that he should trust only Nigel Smalling. At 5.30pm Slade took the lift to the basement and shook hands with the man that his three new associates had described as being a 'moron.' Over the coming months, the Chief Superintendent would learn if the man in the basement was anything like the title attributed to him by his three new friends on the 4th floor. Smalling handed Slade four items, a new, personalized ID card, a tiny transmitter, a gun, and a box of bullets. Smalling then said to Slade,

'I can arrange a phone for you Mr. Slade, but I guess you will want to source this yourself? If you require, anything else, and I mean anything, please call me on internal number 666 and arrange a meeting time, I am here 12 hours a day, every day. And by the way, how did you get on at the club on your first day?'

Slade smiled and replied,

'Splendidly, Mr. Smalling, splendidly. It was one of the most interesting lunches I have ever had.'

Slade left the building, took a cab to Victoria, and purchased two 'disposable' mobile phones from a kiosk within the station concourse. Arriving at Epping just over an hour later, he climbed into his new BMW and drove to the house of Commander James Reeves.

Ex-Commander James Reeves explained to his former underling, that he had been withdrawn from his post within Special Branch, to collate information from three former police officers that had been seconded, by Julian Pritchard, to investigate the suspected criminal activities of Sean Porter, formerly known as Michael O'Leary, and his twin sons, the McBride brothers. One of the undercover officers under Reeves' care was a Bulgarian, and he was already operational, somewhere in the Balkans. His responsibility is to investigate the proliferation of the Importation of drugs into the UK. The second, whilst having been born in London, is of Syrian extract and had to spend two years in a Mi5 safe house in the city of Aleppo before he could safely be allowed to mingle with his father's fellow countrymen. He now speaks fluent Syriac, an Arab language, spoken mainly in the North of the country. He is investigating the ever-rising problem of 'people smuggling.' The third person, Peter, is of course yourself. I have every faith in your ability to weed out the 'bastard' that is Sean Porter and find the origin of the arms that are now pouring into the UK, eventually ending up with the wrong people in the South of Ireland. I am not at liberty to inform you as to the names of the others, you are fully aware of the reasons behind this, I presume that I do not have to explain, Slade shook his head in reply.

Handing over one of the mobile phones that he had already set up, Slade asked his former boss to set up an account with Cell net, an account that would automatically top up once both phones reached the point of having just £20.00 left in credit. He also handed James Reeves a piece of paper that contained two email addresses, explaining that 'gurney.p' belonged to him and that 'gurney.j' was for him, he just needed to set it up using his own password. Reeves informed Slade that he was entering into a dark and dangerous world, where most of the time he would be without backup and cut off from almost everyone else. The Chief Superintendent acknowledged the Commander's concern, saying,

'At least I have only myself to worry about these days.'

Stood outside the door of the large house in Hertfordshire, the two men shook hands. Slade felt a strong bond between himself and his former Special Branch colleague. As Slade opened the door to his large BMW, James Reeves walked over and softly whispered into the Chief Superintendent's ear,

'Don't trust the man from the Home Office, Peter.'

13 - THE MOLE

Having been seconded from his job at Special Branch, Chief Superintendent Peter Slade had joined a small band of expert undercover agents, whose sole remit was to find and bring down the former terrorist, Sean Porter (aka. Michael O'Leary) and his twin sons, Mack, and Manson McBride. The McBride's had taken their mother's maiden name after fleeing Ireland, for fear of reprisals against them. After years of having no contact with his sons, since their birth in 1962, O'Leary was finally reunited with them, sometime in the late nineties. He had been the subject of grade one surveillance ever since he was spotted on the Larne to Stranraer ferry in 1997, but despite round-the-clock scrutiny by Mi5, he had never been implicated in any wrongdoing. CS Slade was charged with carrying out the investigation into Porter. He knew when joining Mi5, that Porter, was a former supplier of arms and explosives to the Irish cause. He had now been implicated in the continued trade of weapons to the breakaway factions of the Republican Army. What Slade could not understand was why the man that had been given a new identity, had not been taken to task by his, now fellow colleagues.

Slade, for many years the top man in Special Branch operations, had now entered a completely different world. The way that the Secret Service operated was far removed from what he had been used to. He had been told by his new boss, Julian Pritchard, that he could trust only Nigel Smalling, the mysterious man that operated from the basement of Thames House. His old boss at Special Branch, Commander James Reeves had told him not to trust the man from the Home Office. Intel, given to him during his initial briefings was that Porter was running an arms route from Iraq to Ireland, everything had been set up to intercept a current consignment before it left Liverpool for Dublin. At the eleventh-hour Quinten Proctor had given the container number to the team, sitting in wait on the quayside at Liverpool docks. The container was isolated, four members of the SAS were blown to pieces when the container doors were opened. The *actual* container was loaded on board the vessel that safely delivered it to the Port of Dublin the following day. Slade raised his first 'red flag' in respect of the Junior Minister, and he made Commander Reeves aware of his worries, asking that his suspicions be shared with no one else. It had been hoped that by trailing the container to its final-destination at least one person could have been captured in the joint operation between Mi5 and their counterparts on the other side of the Irish Sea. Depending upon whom that one person might have been, a deal could have been struck and other names may have been forthcoming, however it was not to be. Slade had two choices, sit tight, wait until information came in about another shipment, or become more proactive. He decided upon the latter of the choices available to him.

On the 3rd of April 2003, Slade returned to the office, on the 4th floor of Thames House, which he shared with 'Archie' (Archibald Cecil) 'Column' (Pierce Nelson) and 'Rat' (Roland Ratcliff). Slade asked his three colleagues to join him for lunch at the nearby 'Pret-a-Manger' and whilst all three were intrigued by his invitation they did not question him as he had put his finger to his mouth, indicating that they remain silent. At lunch, Slade informed them that he would not be returning to the office for the foreseeable future. He asked that they put together all the information that they had collectively gathered on Sean Porter since he had been 'rediscovered' in 1997. He added that they should not leave out any detail, no matter how insignificant it may seem. He handed 'Archie' a small piece of paper, upon it were written the name and address of Commander Reeves, underneath this he had penned,

'Please deliver what I ask for to this address. '

Collectively, they asked Slade what he was going to do with the information, he replied that he would let them know once he had collated all of it. Shaking their hands before they returned to their desks, Slade quietly said,

'Please do not share this with either Julian Pritchard or Nigel Smalling, as my life may well depend on your silence.'

Slade took the tube to Epping and then drove to the house of James Reeves. He did not enter the house, he simply handed his old boss a slip of paper, it read,

'Please contact me when you receive the delivery. '

Much to his surprise, Slade was to receive a call from the Commander late in the afternoon of the following day. Slade answered the call,

'We have a problem, meet me in the Green Man, Toots Hill at one tomorrow.'

At 1.00pm the following day, the two former Special Branch Investigators sat at a small table in the corner of a bar, where various others had sat for over 300 years. Their meeting was brief, they had both been careful to check that no one was following them. They had previously agreed that they would never meet at each other's houses as they were certain that both had been 'bugged.' Slade asked,

'You got the delivery?'

'I did indeed, but it is not quite what you were expecting.'

Pulling an A5 envelope from his pocket, the Commander extracted a single A4 sheet of paper, that had been carefully folded in two, he handed it to Slade. The Chief Superintendent opened it up to reveal the words,

'All files removed from the basement.'

'Fuck me, so Nigel Smalling is our man,' said Slade.

'It would appear so; however, another person has access to the files, that person is Quinten Proctor.'

'So, what do we do from here, boss?'

'I think you will have to go it alone, Peter. If you remember, you are supposed to deal only with me. I am charged with keeping Julian Pritchard in the loop. I will only pass on what I deem to be necessary.'

With that, James Reeves knocked back the remainder of his single malt and was gone.

Slade, with still half of his pint remaining in its glass, remained seated, instinctively scanning the bar for anyone that looked out of place. Replaying the final words of his Commander, he concluded that he now had another problem, was James Reeves to be trusted? There were six people, closely, involved in what he was investigating, he now had to be wary of all of them all. Somehow, he had to draw them out, knowing that he would be taking a hell of a risk each time he shared information with any of them.

Sat at home, Slade concluded that he would have to work with only limited contact with any of his colleagues. In his study he compiled a comprehensive chronological trail of events, gathered from the limited information that he had gleaned from his meetings with Julian Pritchard, Quinten Proctor, Commander Reeves, Nigel Smalling and the three men that he shared an office with at Thames House. Fixed to the wall of his study, were several cork boards, he pinned 'stick-it' notes, cascading downwards and then up again, in date order.

The first board contained the FAMILY –

Patrick O'Leary (Father) – DECEASED – Murdered

Eileen O'Leary (Mother) – DECEASED – Natural Causes

Sean Porter (formerly Michael O'Leary) Terrorist – Age 58 – Location UNKOWN

Jimmy Quinn (Uncle) – DECEASED – Murdered

Sinead McBride (Girlfriend of Michael O'Leary) – Age 60 – Location BELFAST

Sheamus O'Reilly (Stepfather) – DECEASED – Natural Causes

Mack & Manson McBride (Twin Sons of Sinead McBride & Sean Porter) – Location BELFAST

Kathleen Green (Wife of Porter) – Age 55 – Location UNKNOWN

The second board contained all the historically 'known' associates of Michael O'Leary –

Fergus 'Fingers' O'Doyle – Bookmaker – IRA Member – DECEASED
Sean Flynn – IRA Member – DECEASED
Willie McCormack – IRA Member – DECEASED
Micky McGovern – IRA Enforcer – DECEASED
Bobby Kelly – IRA Member – DECEASED
Ollie 'Fatty' O'Brien – IRA Coordinator – DECEASED
John Duggan – Friend & Business Colleague – LONDON – Age 58 – Location - CANVEY ISLAND

The third and final wallboard listed what little intel Slade had in his hands at the time –
Sean Porter – known to visit his sons on the Crumlin Road, Ind Estate, Belfast - SINCE 1997 – Frequent visits to Bulgaria, Turkey, Albania, Syria, and Jordan. Strong links with the continuity IRA.
Sinead McBride – remarried, to Brennan O'Brien – no criminal record – they have two daughters – has no contact with Porter – sees her sons infrequently, despite all living in Belfast.
Mack McBride – Clean bill of health – Known to the authorities but no criminal record – often visits Bulgaria and Romania.
Manson McBride – String of offences, mainly when drunk – Together with his twin brother, runs the largest transport company on both sides of the Irish border.
Dan Brophy – Chief Inspector, Garda – plays for both sides – in it for the money.
Undercover Officer (Bulgarian) – Name unknown – working in the Balkans.
Undercover Officer (Syrian) – Name unknown - working in Aleppo, Syria.
Commander James Reeves – Go-between – reports to Julian Pritchard only – knows undercover officers. Says NOT to trust Quinten Proctor. But can we trust him?
Julian Pritchard – Boss of Mi5 – says to 'trust' only Nigel Smalling.
Quinten Proctor – Junior Home Office Minister – reports to the Home Secretary.
Archibald Cecil (Archie) – Senior Mi5 man – office bound these days – past retirement age.
Pierce Nelson (Column) – Middle ranking Mi5 man – Typical Civil Servant.
Roland Ratcliffe (Rat) – Youngest of the 4th floor team – Still active in the field.
Nigel Smalling – Main contact at Mi5. Mixed messages as to whether he can be trusted.

Studying the three boards, Slade concluded that Porter certainly had connections with a lot of 'dead' people. He also knew that the man once known as Michael O'Leary had access to an international trucking business and was, therefore, able to move all types of cargo, including himself, into Ireland, the UK and onto Europe in general. He picked up his untraceable mobile phone and called Nigel Smalling. He asked the 'man in the basement' to arrange for him a new identity. The identity would need to be of a man that drove trucks around Europe. He would require an HGV license, an International Permit, a new passport, and a past-history of his driving. He suggested that it would be better if his CV showed that he had worked, in the past, for companies that had gone bust. This way it would be far more difficult for his prospective employers to contact former employers. Slade's final request was to ask Smalling to arrange a three-month 'crash course' at an HGV DVLA driving school. When Smalling told Slade that he would require three passport-size photos, the undercover agent replied,

'I am changing my identity you will have them within six weeks.'

Smalling's response to Slade's request(s) was that he would have to clear it with the 'boss.'

From this, Slade presumed that Smalling himself did not have the authority to sanction his request. He also knew that it sometimes proved fatal to be presumptuous. What he did not know was whether, or not Smalling would ask his boss. On the basis that the man in the basement could not be trusted, Slade made a second call, this time to Commander James Reeves. He repeated the conversation that he had had with Smalling. Reeves asked whether he should pass this on to Julian Pritchard. Slade thought for a moment, and then replied,

'No, I think not. It is Smalling's job to inform his boss, so let's just see if Julian Pritchard shares any of this with you Sir.'

'OK Peter, I will keep quiet. I will not ask as to your intentions as I think I know where you are going with this, good luck.' James Reeves hung up.

Slade now had six weeks or so to burn before he could activate his plan. He spent a lot of this time updating the security of his house. Informing no one, other than his old school chum, Graham Roberts of his requirements. Roberts had become the owner of a private detective and surveillance operation after his father had met his death whilst on the trail of a notorious UK gangster. Slade and his ex, Grammar School's friend, had worked together on the occasions when the Chief Superintendent needed to go outside of Special Branch, normally when certain individuals from within Slade's own team needed watching. Slade's house, in leafy Epping, was fair-sized, and detached. Open fields to the front and rear. Slade's requirements were costly, even with 'mate's rates' and he was given an estimate of twenty-five grand. Roberts was trusted, without question. Slade laid bare the whole story to the friend that he had known since the age of eleven. The man from Mi5 even told of his relationship with Cheryl Smith, the lady next door, who had become widowed not long after his own wife had been blown apart by terrorists. He explained his 'innocent flirting' with Cheryl, whenever she was sat in the kitchen, nattering away with his deceased wife, Sandra. Cheryl had no children, they were both lonely and of the same age, 39. Roberts, sensing that his mate was seeking his approval simply said,

'Just go for it my old friend, you live only the once and from what you have told me, your days could be numbered.'

By the time that Roberts' company had completed the work, which included sophisticated infra-red sensors, a twelve-screen CCTV station and a door leading from his conservatory, directly into Cheryl's side garden, Slade no longer looked like the clean-shaven, short-haired, and smartly dressed agent that was his normal self. He now sported a full-on, unkempt, black beard, long and thick black hair, two studs in his left ear and designer glasses. He was as far removed from being Chief Superintendent Peter Slade, as he could be. On the 4th of June 2003, Slade posted three, passport-size photographs of himself to Nigel Smalling at Mi5 headquarters in London. He would wait ten days before entering the post office on Epping High Street to collect the mail from his PO Box. Sat in his car, Slade opened several envelopes and found that he had now assumed the identity of Stephen Aldridge, aged 39, place of birth, Grays, Essex. On his driving license his address was shown as 20 Manor Road, Grays. He had passed his driving test in August 1985. He also received a new NI Card and a Birth Certificate. There was a copy of his parent's Marriage Certificate, his mum and dad were Tom and Alice, they had married in 1959. The handwritten note informed him that his parents had both passed away. He had no siblings. Any mail that was sent to Manor Road in Grays would be forwarded to his PO Box in Epping. His first day of learning to drive an HGV vehicle would be on Monday 7th July, it would take place in Purfleet, Essex. Just a few miles from his fictitious new home in Grays.

In an effort not to be caught out when he went public with his new details, Stephen Aldridge decided to familiarize himself with his new surroundings, but firstly he would lock his BMW 4x4 away in the garage at Epping and buy himself a less conspicuous vehicle. He paid, after some bargaining with the second-hand dealer on the London Road, West Thurrock, just under two grand, for a 2L dark blue, mid-range, Ford Mondeo. He was told that the five-year-old car, with 11,000 miles shown on the clock was genuine. He felt that he should take the dealer, named 'Deals on Wheels' to task, for 'clocking' however he did not wish to draw attention to himself. He handed over the cash and spent nearly two weeks patrolling the streets of Grays and its immediate area. It did not go unnoticed by the policeman with over twenty-two years of service, that the number of foreigners out on the streets of Grays was considerably more in number than those that he had seen in and around the more rural area of Epping. He did wonder exactly where they all came from.

On the 7th of July, at 8.00am, Peter Slade, now Stephen Aldridge, having never even sat in the passenger seat of an HGV vehicle, now found himself at the wheel of a DAF truck, in a yard close to the quay in Purfleet Docks. His instructor, a Scottish guy by the name of Joe McPherson, introduced himself, informing his new pupil that he could call him Jock. What an original idea thought Aldridge. Jock went through all the things that one should go through before even starting the engine of this tank-like vehicle. Aldridge, having secured a light aircraft Pilots License several years since, found it all so amusing. By the end of the first week, Jock informed him that his handling of the truck was more than adequate and that come next Monday he could move on to hitching up and moving a 40-foot trailer behind him. This would prove to be a much more daunting task for the undercover cop. At the start of his second month behind the wheel, he was allowed out onto the open road and despite some very hairy moments, Jock informed him that, in his opinion, he should put in for his test. Nigel Smalling, whom Aldridge was finding to be extremely helpful, arranged both the theory and practical tests for him. At the end of August, having sailed through the theory part of the examination, Stephen Aldridge would be adding HGV to his license. In mid-September, he received a new license, this one permitted him to drive a whole host of vehicles. The license showed that he had passed his HGV test in 1990. Now that he was in possession of all the documentation that he required, he telephoned Archie Cecil in his office and asked him to find out who it was that represented McBride International Transport in England. The following day Archie texted the details to Slade's official mobile phone.

At weekends, when not entertaining his next-door neighbour, Cheryl Smith, Slade had been busy studying a whole host of European maps. His interests lie in specific routes to and from Bulgaria, Romania, and Turkey. He presumed that he would have to show a certain knowledge of how to get to and come back from those countries. He also studied the much simpler route between the UK, Northern, and Southern Ireland. Having done his homework, at 2.30 in the afternoon, Aldridge knocked on the door of Globe International Transport. They operated from two large warehouses in Motherwell Way, West Thurrock. They were the UK agents for McBride International, Belfast. Tony Head, the owner of Globe Transport and a man not to be messed with, asked the job seeker as to his availability.

'I can start whenever you like.'

'Well, tonight, the trailer outside my window here must be moved to Belgium, and another must be brought back. Do you think you could manage that?' The rather menacing-looking twenty-two stone middle-aged man enquired.

Tony Head called out 'Tommie,' a skinny six-foot bloke appeared from the room next door.

'Tommie, this is Stephen, he will be doing the Zeebrugge run tonight, get the paperwork for him.'

Two minutes later Tommie returned with the paperwork and handed it to their new driver.

Tony Head handed Stephen a bundle of keys and a card with which to purchase diesel, and then said,

'You are on the 11.30pm Ro/Ro from Purfleet, now you can piss off and come back later. We will all be gone when you return so you had better get yourself some food and drink, and do not forget your passport. Your return is booked for 2.30pm tomorrow. When you get back, just put the keys through the letterbox and call me the following morning.'

Stephen Aldridge was astounded that he had been given the keys to a valuable lorry and load just on the basis that he could drive and had an international licence. He got into the Mondeo and drove the two miles to Purfleet, where he parked up and watched as lorries arrived at the terminal. He saw that most drivers got out and handed over their paperwork to a guy through an opening in a window signed, Exports. The drivers hung around for a few minutes, received the paperwork back and then returned to their cabs, drew the curtains, and probably nodded off. This procedure presented no worries to the Chief Superintendent. What was playing on his mind though, was the fact that he was able to walk into a job, without any checking by his employer, and then walk out with the keys to a truck and trailer, worth around a hundred grand, plus a cargo of Tate and Lyle Sugar, the value of which, he had no idea.

At 9.00pm, having first retuned to Epping, with the intention of bidding Cheryl Smith a passionate farewell, which he did manage to achieve. He then told her that he would be in Spain for two or three days. He gathered up his newly issued passport, some food and drink and most importantly, the small handgun that Nigel Smalling had given him upon his first-ever visit to the basement at Thames House. He returned to Motherwell Way, parked the Mondeo, and climbed into the cab of the one-year-old DAF truck. Before he started the engine, he did all the checks that Jock the instructor had asked him to do. He hid the gun behind the sun visor directly in front of him, started up and drove out onto London Road, Purfleet. In a little less than ten minutes he arrived at the Ro/Ro terminal, he lodged his paperwork and was asked to park in row eleven. At 23.05 he was beckoned on board, he drove slowly up the ramp and was stopped, just a few inches from the back of a Ferry master's trailer. The wheels of the truck and trailer were secured by the ship's crew. He noticed that most of the other drivers were leaving their cabs and heading through a door midway into the cargo hold of the ferry, he followed. The ferry was a 'freight only' service, the only passengers were the drivers and maybe a few of their mates. Following a very large, foul-smelling foreign man, he arrived in the restaurant of the ship, it was a restaurant in name only. On a good day, it could maybe have been compared with the canteen of a large factory in Wuhan, China. Having left his food and drink in the fridge of the truck, Stephen Aldridge lined up with the rest of the truckers. He helped himself to two sausages and some chips, ordered a mug of tea and paid at the till, which was manned by a woman of such size and bad looks that she could easily have been used as ballast should there be a need to do so. Aldridge had not booked a bed for the ten-hour crossing, mainly because he did not know that you could do so. He did notice that some drivers were carrying towels and washing gear and within an hour just himself and one other driver remained in the canteen. He made his way back to his truck, climbed in and laid flat out on the bed behind the seats of the cab.

He woke only when the loud banging on his driver's door told him that it was time to get up. Within ten minutes he was driving off the ferry. Every lorry in front of him was corralled into three lanes, each one produced paperwork to the men in the booths. Aldridge showed his, he was not asked for his passport. Not knowing 'where the hell he was going, he reluctantly asked a man stood outside the booth as to where he would find European Cargo Services (ECS), the man laughed as he replied,

'it's just outside the gate.'

As he exited the dock gate, he could see the sign that indicated he was already at the yard of ECS. He pulled into the yard, climbed down from his cab, and walked over to a small portacabin. A window opened as he approached, a large sign on the window read, Imports. He handed the paperwork to a man that wore a 'tank top' the likes of which, he had not seen since the early 70s. Tank Top indicated to Aldridge that he should park the trailer up in slot 'Imp 78.' Now void of any paperwork, the novice HGV driver returned to the cab and panicked when realising that he would have to back the trailer into the allocated slot, then unhitch the trailer from the cab and pull away, hopefully without the trailer in tow. At the fourth attempt the job was done. He returned to the portacabin and was given the paperwork and location of the trailer that he would be taking back to Purfleet. Ten minutes later he was parked in one of the lanes that would, in five hours-time, guide him onto the same ferry that he had arrived on. That night he arrived back in Motherwell Way, parked the truck and trailer, posted the keys and paperwork through the letterbox of Globe Transport, and went home to Epping. The next morning at

7.00am he slipped quietly into Cheryl's bed. At 7.10 he slipped gently into Cheryl's wet fanny.

At 2.00pm, Aldridge walked into Tony Head's office. Tony was on a mobile phone he twice mentioned the name 'Manson' the hairs on the back of Aldridge's neck sprang up. When the call finished, Head put the phone in a drawer and locked it, putting the key in the pocket of his jeans.

Pulling a thick roll of notes from his pocket, Tony Head asked,

'Ah Stephen, I suppose you are here for your dosh?'

'Well, yes, and to ask if there are any more jobs, I suppose.

'Here take this, Head handed his new driver two hundred pounds in ten-pound notes, and then said,

'There is another job, in two days-time, if you want it?'

A wide grin crossed Aldridge's face as he replied,

'Of course, I do, see you on Thursday then.'

For the next six weeks, Aldridge was to duplicate his first-ever venture into international truck driving a further twelve times. Every trip was the same as the one before. Purfleet to Zeebrugge and back. Each load out was of sugar. Each load back was of flour. Aldridge wondered if someone was preparing to bake the world's largest cake. After every trip he was wrapped snugly around Cheryl's legs, he now felt more like a truck driver than an undercover Mi5 agent. He contacted only Commander James Reeves, each time he would tell his former boss that, so far, he had nothing to report, there appeared to be nothing untoward going on as far as Globe Transport and Tony Head were concerned, they agreed it was still early days.

On the morning of Monday, the 1st of December 2003, Tony Head introduced Stephen Aldridge to Brian Murphy, better known in the trucking world as 'Spud.' Spud was of course Irish. His heart missed a beat when shaking his new colleague's hand. Head informed his newest recruit that he would like him to accompany Spud on a trip to Sofia, the capital of Bulgaria. The journey would take just under two days if they shared the driving, whereas with just one man at the wheel it would take a total of at least four. They were to take the trailer load of Irish Moss Peat to an agricultural complex, just South of Sofia. With over ten hours to kill before they were due to leave for the Port at Purfleet, Aldridge drove back to Epping, hopped through the side door of his conservatory, and inserted his key into Cheryl's back door. Soon, he thought, he would be inserting something much more interesting into Cheryl herself. He was slightly disappointed when the key did not open the door. Putting his head close to the glass, he could see that a key was nestling in the other side of the lock. He banged on the door. Cheryl did not appear. He went back through his house and walked onto his neighbour's drive. He rang the bell, knocked on the door and then tapped the glass of the bay window with his key, there was no response. Cheryl's small Toyota was still on the drive, he was now beginning to worry. Stepping back, he rang her mobile number, it rang four or five times and then asked him to leave a message. He was not a man that normally panicked. He remembered Cheryl telling him that she was going to her sisters in York, he did not remember when. He did know that she did not like driving long distances, maybe she had taken the train to York, but why was her car still here? Perhaps she had taken a cab to Epping station, but why had she not informed him. He was worried; however, his priority was to make sure that he was in the truck that was going to take him to a place that had figured, often, in the recent life of Sean Porter.

Sitting himself down in his kitchen, he spread out various maps on the large farmhouse table. He studied every conceivable route that they might take to Sofia, he did not wish to make himself look an idiot, especially in the eyes of an Irishman. Prior to leaving the bungalow, the same recurring thoughts entered his head. He kept thinking of just how easy it had been for him to have obtained a new identity, get an HGV driving course, walk into Tony Head's office and be given a job, on the spot, no checking, and no reference's requested. He was an outsider and whilst he did not believe that he would be trusted to transport any contraband, at least not for now, he could not but help query, in his head, just how quickly this had all fallen into place. Maybe, he thought, that is the difference between working for New Scotland Yard, as opposed to Mi5. There was a nagging doubt as to the loyalty of Nigel Smalling and now he had cause to question the sincerity of his former boss, Commander James Reeves, who so conveniently had moved from the highest position within Special Branch, only to become an underling of Julian Pritchard. For now, he would suppress those thoughts, he was 'in', accepted, or so it seemed, by Tony Head. The situation that he found himself in was a sure-fire route to some of the bastards that he was after, he decided that he just had to go along with it, at least for now. Before leaving home, he made one call, it was to his old friend, the private eye, Graham Roberts. He explained to Roberts that Cheryl Smith had gone missing but believed her to be in York. He asked Roberts to keep an eye on his house whilst he was away and to check the CCTV that he had installed, adding that he would be in touch after his return from the Balkans. At 8.45pm he drove to Motherwell Way and parked up. Spud looking the worse for wear, confessed that he had consumed a few pints of Guinness at the Three Rabbits, which was within walking distance of the parked-up truck. Spud asked Aldridge if he would mind driving the short distance to Purfleet Docks. Aldridge nodded in reply. The truck was a Mercedes, with a much superior specification to that of the DAF, the only other vehicle that Aldridge had thus far driven. After a few embarrassing crunching of the gears, they were on their way. At the dock, Spud jumped out to hand the paperwork to the man in the booth, leaving the large glove compartment fully open. Aldridge could see several delivery notes, headed McBride International Transport. Jackpot, he thought to himself. Once on the ferry, Spud forwent the pleasure of fine dining, informing his co-pilot that he was going to get his head down. As he legged it out of the canteen Spud called out,

'Cabin 17, one deck down, I'll leave the door open.'

Not being able to face the canteen food, or the stench from the adjoining toilets, which seemed to be constantly in the air. Aldridge made his way back to the truck, ate his sandwiches and climbed into the truck's bed. He felt safer there.

One hour before they were due to dock in Zeebrugge, Spud tapped on the door of the truck, Aldridge unlocked it. Spud looked like a different person. He was clean-shaven, had changed his clothing and smelt like an advert for Jean Paul Gaultier. Handing the cabin key to Aldridge, Spud asked him if he would like to take a shower before they berthed. In need of a wash, Aldridge accepted the invitation, returning forty minutes later, refreshed, but still sporting his bushy black beard and long hair. He was now ready for the long drive of some fifteen hundred miles. Thirty minutes into the drive through Belgium, Aldridge asked,

'So how long have you worked for Tony Head?' Spud, laughing, replied,

'Oh, be Jesus, I don't work for him, I work for the McBride's in Belfast. It's eleven years since I delivered my first load for them.'

Aldridge, being careful not to arouse any suspicions by continual questioning, kept his enquires to a minimum.

'So, where do you go on behalf of the McBride's?'

'I literally go everywhere, Stephen.'

'These days I mainly do 'long-haul,' Romania, Bulgaria, Albania and even Turkey. I have no one at home, I am a free man, with a lover in every Country, how about yerself?'

Aldridge thought for a few seconds before answering,

'To be honest Spud, I am new to the international side of things. Until three months ago I had only ever driven in the UK, so I might need your help from time to time.'

'Ah, that's no problem, no problem at all, Stephen.'

'You are from Northern Ireland then?'

'No, no, no, thank God. I am a 'true' Irishman, born and bred on the Southern side of the border, I know many an IRA man, Stephen.'

Spud laughed out loudly after making that statement.

Aldridge felt there had been an edge to Spud's words when mentioning the IRA, for the first time he felt that he should be on his guard. He also realised that he had not brought his handgun.

Not far from the German – Austria border they pulled into a truck stop, ate for the first time in seven hours and then Spud got his head down in the back of the cab. Just before he nodded off, he told Aldridge to head for Graz, then onto Budapest, when he should then wake him up. He would take over the driving.

The drive went like clockwork and forty hours after leaving Zeebrugge they bypassed Sofia City Centre and took the ring road to their destination, a town named Novi Han, situated just off the AI, one of Bulgaria's major trunk roads, which connected Sofia with the Black Sea City of Burgas. The load, twenty-four pallets of Ireland's finest peat, was unloaded within an hour. Spud used the customer's phone to call his boss and was told that he should collect a return load from Istanbul, some 400 miles away, but quite easy to get to from Sofia. Spud jumped up into the driver's seat, despite protests from his co-driver.

'It's OK Stephen, I know where we are going, and I think you will be pleased.'

Half an hour later they pulled into the large car park of a run-down, two-story building, several scantily clad females stood casually outside.

'What is this?

'This is where one of my many girlfriends' live.' Spud grinned as he made this statement.

'But this looks like a brothel, I really do not frequent such places, Spud,'

'Are you Gay then, Stephen?'

One of the few things that ever-made Aldridge angry, was to be called Gay. In a very defensive tone, he looked over at his co-driver and said,

'Well, you just go in by yourself, I will get some shuteye while you are gone and then I will drive all the way to Istanbul.'

Without answering, Spud climbed down from the truck, walked towards the neon-lit entrance of the 'whore house ', and was mobbed by four of the waiting girls. Six hours later, an almost unconscious Stephen Aldridge was woken by Spud's many attempts to climb back into the truck.

'I am well and truly fucked, my friend,' were all the words that passed between them as Aldridge vacated the bed behind the seats and Spud promptly laid himself into the empty space.

At 10.15 the following morning, having driven all night, Aldridge had to wake Spud as he was approaching a complicated interchange and needed some guidance. Spud, slowly raised his head from the pillow and then poked it through the black curtains and said, in a voice that sounded like sandpaper,

'You take the road to Besiktas, just follow the signs, in fact if you can pull over somewhere then I will take over, as I know the way.'

Just after taking the turn off, he pulled up on the dusty hard shoulder and the two men swapped seats. Just before they pulled away, Aldridge looked at Spud and asked,

'Good night, was it?'

Spud, expressionless, replied,

'Do you know Stephen, I went upstairs with four hookers, but I have no idea what happened, all I know is that I have no money left in my pocket.'

Aldridge, with absolutely no sympathy for his driver, simply said,

'Oh well Spud, better luck next time.'

Forty-five minutes later, Spud turned off the main road and entered an Industrial Estate, at the end of which there was a small ferry terminal. They entered a massive warehousing complex, the name of which was, Trust Forwarding, Storage and Distribution. The name meant nothing to Stephen Aldridge at the time. Sometime in the future, he would learn that Trust Forwarding belonged to Monzer Asmar, one of Syria's most wealthy and powerful men.

Spud backed the empty trailer onto one of the many loading bays and then he and Aldridge jumped down and went into the office, an office that Spud had been in many times before. They walked over to a man sat at one of the several desks in the office and Spud handed over the paperwork for the delivery of one empty trailer, the property of McBride International Trucking, Belfast. The man at the desk handed one signed copy of the document back to Spud, they exchanged a few words, in Turkish, and Spud walked away. Aldridge followed closely behind him. Together they walked to the far side of the warehouse and entered another office, this was signed-up as being the despatch department. Spud introduced Stephen Aldridge to the five Turks, they were invited to sit and given tiny cups of strong Turkish coffee. In perfect English, a man that appeared to be the manager handed Spud a wad of papers and said,

'You have one load of towels to take back to Birmingham, please do not thieve more than fifty of them. The curtains of the trailer had been left open this was to allow the trailer to be checked for 'illegals' prior to their departure. Spud checked one side, whilst Aldridge checked the other. Once they were happy that no 'undesirables' were on board, both men pulled the heavy plastic curtains from the front to the back of the trailer and then secured them in place by locking the steel wrenches into the fixings on the trailer. At the rear of the trailer, they fastened the doors, and a warehouse man inserted a steel seal into the holes that only lined up once the doors were perfectly shut. Spud signed a document that stated that the trailer had been examined and checked prior to departure. This would exonerate the warehouse company from any claims arising, should there be a loss of goods or any tampering with the trailer or its contents.'

Spud said his farewells to the many men that he saw on a regular basis and Aldridge drove the truck and trailer out onto the perimeter road of the Industrial Estate. As he approached the main road, where he would turn right and begin the two-thousand-mile journey back to Zeebrugge, two military police vehicles pulled out from a side road and came to a halt directly in front of him. He was forced to brake, sharply. Looking in his mirrors he could see armed, uniformed men, slowly making their way along the side of the trailer, a helicopter hovered above. Spud jumped from the passenger seat, hit the pavement, and legged it; he was not challenged and was soon out of sight. A tear gas grenade was thrown through the half-open window of the driver's door, which was then opened from the outside. Aldridge hung in the air, half in, half out of the cab, the effects of the tear gas blinding him. Two men pulled him completely out, and laid him, face down, upon the slightly damp road, directly in front of the cab. His hands and feet were then secured, as he tilted his head to one side, he could just about see through his gas-impaired eyes, that a rifle was aimed at his head. A large, heavily bearded man came into view, he bent down and placed a polythene bag of white powder directly in front of his captive's face and said,

'So, what is then, Mr. Peter Slade?'

Before he could muster any reply, he received a heavy blow to the side of his head, was bundled into the back of an armoured vehicle and driven away. From his vantage point of a second-floor window of the customs building that overlooked the incident, Alkan Asani called Commander James Reeves and said,

'It's done, Sir.'

Five minutes later, Spud returned to the truck and drove away. Six days after Stephen Aldridge had been taken away, Spud arrived back at Purfleet, where Tony Head shook his hand and simply said,

'Good result Spud.'

Stephen Aldridge had been 'set-up' there was clearly a 'mole' in the camp, but who was it, Smalling, Reeves, or Proctor?

14 - INCARCERATED

Chief Superintendent Peter Slade, currently working undercover for Mi5 and using the assumed name of Stephen Aldridge, lay, face down and unconscious in the back of a Turkish Paramilitary armed response vehicle. He was driven from the industrial estate in Besiktas, a suburb of Istanbul, to a secure unit that was contained within the 'Sisli Chief of Police Station' in central Istanbul. He was revived with smelling salts before being physically lifted from the vehicle and taken inside the building. In the dark and damp basement, he was tied to a chair, he slumped forward on a desk. On the other side of the desk sat a disfigured, uniformed officer. Such was the enormity of the craters upon his face that it looked like the surface of the moon. Slade, whose real identity had been known to his capturers, was still groggy from his earlier experiences. He was immediately slapped in the face by a man whose hands were so large they could easily have scooped up the large pile of excrement that filled the corner of the room. Crater face spoke first.

'I am Captain Ali Reza of the Turkish Military Police, and you are Chief Superintendent Peter Slade, formerly of the world-famous Special Branch of the Metropolitan Police, but more recently working for Mi5. Is that correct Mr. Slade?'

Finding it difficult to hold his head up, Slade replied,

'No, not correct, I am Stephen Aldridge, a lowly truck driver.'

His answer was met by another violent slap to his face.

Speaking in a soft and controlled manner, the captain replied,

'Now, now Mr. Slade, for every lie, you will receive a slap, should you continue to lie then you will receive a much more painful response. Shall we start again?

'I am not who you think I am,' said Slade.

The slap nearly lifted him from his chair.

For the next three days he was starved of food and given water only every eight hours, but still he stuck to his story that he was just a truck driver. On the fourth day he was put into a cell. A man as big as Sonny Liston was laid on the bottom of the bunk bed, his feet dangling over the metal frame. Under the bed, several rats scratched and scurried around.

Slade said,

'Hello' and held out his hand to greet his cellmate. The man rose slowly from the bed and hit Slade squarely on the jaw, within seconds of hitting the floor, he was surrounded by the three largest of the rodents.

Meanwhile, back in Epping, Cheryl had returned from visiting her sister in York. She was sad that Peter was not there to greet her, however she was not unduly worried by his absence. The following day Cheryl let herself into Peter's house on the premise that he may have left a note. Not being able to find any clues as to his whereabouts she rang his mobile phone, Cheryl heard it ringing, it was in his kitchen. Now she was worried. She had no idea that Peter had a second phone or that he had undertaken a long journey as a truck driver. Three days later she drove to Epping Police Station and reported Peter missing. The desk Sergeant knew of the existence of Chief Superintendent Peter Slade, he had known of Slade's fame within Special Branch. He assured Cheryl Smith that he would do some digging and get back to her. Within minutes of her leaving the station, Sergeant Malcolm Jefferies called someone he knew at New Scotland Yard and asked her to make some enquiries. One hour later he heard back from his contact. She told him that CS Slade was working on something that was 'classified' and as such, no one was able to give any information about his whereabouts. The Sergeant, having taken a fancy to the widow Cheryl Smith, decided to call round to see her once his shift had finished. Upon opening her door, Malcolm Jefferies could see that she had been crying, curtailing his intention of flirting with her. She explained her situation and her relationship with the high-ranking police officer. He asked that she let him into Slade's house so that he could look for any clues as to why he had not returned home for nearly ten days. After a quick search he found the paperwork in respect of the purchase of the Ford Mondeo. He rang Essex control room and asked if they could pick the car up on any CCTV during the last fourteen days or so. Having spent many years investigating house burglaries and commercial robberies, the Sergeant conducted a more thorough search of the house. On the landing that led to the bedrooms he moved the large, framed photograph of Slade's wife and two children. Behind the photo he discovered a metal box, about the size of an A4 sheet of paper, embedded into the wall. In a kitchen drawer he found what he thought might be the key. He was correct. One minute later the Sergeant had removed the photo from the wall and opened the box. Michael Miles would have been mortified. Inside he found around £600 in cash, a credit card, Slade's driving license, his passport, and a handwritten note with the names of James Reeves, Julian Pritchard, Nigel Smalling, Archie Cecil, Pierce Nelson, Roland Roberts, and Sean Porter. Only James Reeves meant anything to Sergeant Jefferies.

Back in Sisli Police Station, Slade's cell door had been opened by two guards. They found the dead body of a seventeen stone six-foot six-inch muscle man being feasted upon by several families of rats. Whilst Sonny Liston was fast asleep, Slade had, with one blow from the side of his hand, severed the windpipe of his would-be assailant. Captain Ali Reza was informed. Twenty minutes later Slade was given an injection, bundled into the back of an open-back Jeep, and taken to Metris High-Security Prison, situated in the Esenler District of Istanbul. This prison was known throughout Turkey as being the building that no one would ever like to be incarcerated into. Back in 1988, the inmates had dug out a tunnel of some 200 feet in length, using only canteen spoons. Twenty-nine prisoners escaped, nineteen were returned. Of these eleven were put to death and eight received life sentences. Ten were never captured, at least that was the 'official' version. The following day, Peter Slade, under his assumed name of Stephen Aldridge, appeared in court. The prosecution told that the prisoner had been caught transporting a forbidden substance within Turkey. He was also using fake identification and had killed a fellow prisoner in an unprovoked attack. Stephen Aldridge was unrepresented. The three-man panel of judges sentenced him to life imprisonment, with no right of appeal or remission. The entire hearing was conducted in Turkish and Slade was not offered any translation, other than that of the sentence. When asked if he had anything to say in his defence, he asked that the British Embassy in Ankara should be informed and that someone from there should visit him in prison.

Sergeant Jefferies had been wondering, for several days, as to why Chief Superintendent Peter Slade had not taken his mobile phone, driving license, passport, or credit card with him, especially as Cheryl had told him that Peter travelled a lot. He had been able to find out that Commander James Reeves had stepped down from his role within Special Branch and that Slade had been his 'righthand man' for many years. And whilst it had been difficult to discover, he now knew that Julian Pritchard was the boss of 'undercover' operations within Mi5 and that the 'other' names on the list were in his team. When mentioned, the name of Sean Porter sent most people he asked into silence. He was sure that Slade was very much part of this group, however digging any further might well put him in a dangerous position, as messing with these people was often to the demise of whoever poked their nose in. Three days after tracking down Julian Pritchard, Sergeant Malcolm Jefferies was summoned by the Home Office.

Three weeks after he had been handed a life sentence by the Turkish Court, Peter Slade was taken from his cell and shown into a small interview room. A man that was so obviously a civil servant came in and introduced himself as Basil Cowdrey. He asked Slade as to what he could do for him. The imprisoned

Slade explained the whole scenario. How and why, he was using an assumed name, his rank, and his years at New Scotland Yard. He offered up the names of James Reeves and Julian Pritchard as being people that might help explain his situation to the Turkish authorities. Mr. Cowdrey chose to give Slade the words that members of the UK Foreign Office give to all its citizens that require help.

'You do know that we are unable to interfere with the laws of another country.'

Whilst he was fully aware of the fact that British Embassies and Consulates around the World have no jurisdiction at all in other Countries, Slade did, foolishly believe that some help could be offered to him. Basil Cowdrey pretended to be concerned, he promised Slade that he would check, via his colleagues in London, as to the authenticity of his story and he would then get back to him as soon as he could. At this point, Slade believed that his case would carry, 'top priority' status. As he had been denied any other form of contact with the outside World, he could do nothing, other than to wait for the man in the bowler hat to return.

On Monday 8th March 2004, Sergeant Malcolm Jefferies attended a meeting with Quinten Proctor, a junior Home Office Minister, and a man very much at loggerheads with Julian Pritchard from Mi5. Sergeant Jefferies was accompanied by a Police Solicitor, on the recommendation of his union. The Sergeant was told, in no uncertain terms, that all further investigations into the whereabouts of Chief Superintendent Peter Slade, must cease, forthwith. Any attempts by the Sergeant, acting upon the request of Cheryl Smith, would be met with serious repercussions, his job and pension would be in grave danger should he continue to sniff around Thames House for further information. Proctor stressed to the solicitor that this matter was of great National Importance and to continue with his quest for answers could lead to the death of not only Peter Slade, but to others as well. Before he left the room, Quinten Proctor touched the arm of Sergeant Jefferies and said,

'Please do not worry, Sergeant, we have his back.'

Jefferies returned to Epping, visited Cheryl Smith, and informed her that he had been assured that Peter was being looked after and that it would only be a matter of time before he returned home.

In Istanbul, Slade had been waiting for nearly a whole month, and yet he had heard nothing from Basil Cowdrey. During the second week of April, he received a letter, which had already been opened by the prison authorities, it read,

'Dear Mr. Slade, the Turkish Ministry of Home Affairs has denied us a second visit. However, I can inform you that the word back from London is that neither James Reeves nor Julian Pritchard know of your existence. What

Basil Cowdrey failed to mention was the fact that the message had been relayed by Quinten Proctor. We shall continue to monitor your condition and have been granted a further visit in six-months-time. On behalf of the Foreign and Commonwealth Office, we are sincerely sorry for not being able to assist you any further. Basil Cowdrey.'

Alone in a cell that measured just three metres by three metres Slade was resigned to the fact that not only had he been stitched up by his former boss, Commander James Reeves, he was also facing imprisonment for the rest of his days without anyone fighting his case. Not being allowed visitors, newspapers, or a radio, meant that he was completely cut-off from the outside world. As he lay on the bed of concrete, which lacked either a mattress or pillow, all he could do was 'think.' He had been told, in no uncertain terms, by Julian Pritchard, that if caught, in a Country where UK diplomats had little or no clout, whilst using an assumed name, there would be very little that anyone could do to help him. He knew that being caught in possession of a 'class A' drug, which by itself would normally carry a sentence of death, plus the killing of a fellow inmate, albeit both offences had been manufactured, did not augur well for release any day soon. He resigned himself to having to wait for six months until Basil Cowdrey returned to see him.

Cheryl Smith began to realise that she had more than just an affection for her missing neighbour. She continued to badger Sergeant Jefferies, as he was the only person that seemed to be interested in her plight. Jefferies however, had been 'warned off' by people in high places. He continued to tell Cheryl that he had some leads, but these would take time to follow up and he had to undertake his investigations covertly, as to be found out would almost certainly cost him his job, if not more. In fact, the Sergeant was no longer trying to find the Chief Superintendent and four months after his disappearance he finally informed Cheryl that it looked as if the man that she had feelings for, had simply vanished. He revealed that Peter was seen on CCTV driving his Mondeo along Epping High Road on the last day that he had returned to his house, but there had been no further sightings of him since. Cheryl, at a low ebb, succumbed to Jefferies' constant attention and one evening she found herself in bed with him. Jefferies was married and had three children and six weeks after he and Mrs. Smith had consummated their relationship, he confessed all to his 'bit on the side.' They had become just another couple that had, without any real love for one another, stumbled into a relationship that involved others and would no doubt end in tears for all concerned. Jefferies arranged his life around his work, spending some time with his wife and children and the rest of it with Cheryl Smith. His job gave him the perfect alibi for not being at home that often. Turning his attention to Peter Slade, he started to dig into his past, he was not looking to find him, he simply wanted to know if he had any living relatives and if not, what was going to happen to his sizeable estate. All of this, he kept from his lover.

By the first of August 2004, Slade had been incarcerated for a little over six months. If Basil Cowdrey was true to his word, he could expect a visit at any time. Having been given access to pencils and paper, on the pretence that he could revive his interest in etching, Slade had prepared a full account of his operation on behalf of Mi5, including the names of the people involved, his intention was to hand this account to Basil Cowdrey. From time to time, he would present the guards with drawings of themselves, just to maintain the justification of being allowed to have the materials that he used. At 6.00am on Wednesday 11th August, he was woken by the guards and escorted to a holding room close to the prison gates. He had secreted the written account, intended for the man from the Embassy, into the crack of his backside. At 7.00am, along with two other inmates and four armed guards, he was loaded into a Toyota minivan and driven away. He had not been given any warning and no one had explained what was happening. Five hours later the van arrived at Ayas Prison, geographically situated just outside Ankara. Unbeknown to Slade, at the time of his arrival at Ayas, Basil Cowdrey had presented himself to the front office at Sisli Prison and was told that Stephen Aldridge had been moved. They would not reveal the name of the prison that he had been moved to. Upon arrival at Ayas Prison, Slade was shown to a cell, he would be sharing with one other inmate.

For thirty minutes he sat alone in the cell. His new home had a metal bunk bed and a mattress. He could see that the top bunk was already occupied. The door was opened and a man of about thirty-five, as thin as a rake and wearing Kurdish-type clothing, walked in. Slade already sensed that this prison was a lot more relaxed than the previous one. Having heard all the horrific stories of how brutal life can be in Turkish prisons, Slade had been relieved that he had never suffered any abuse or torture whilst in Sisli. Here in Ayas, he sensed the atmosphere to be even more acceptable.

Saying, 'Hello' to his new cellmate, who in turn offered his hand and replied,

'I am Olan Ocalan, son of Abdullah, the founder of the Kurdish Peoples Working Party (PKK). The Chief Superintendent knew all about the PKK, having studied Middle Eastern History at University.' Could he really believe that the man stood in front of him was the direct descendant of the founding father of the PKK, one of the World's leading terrorist organisations? He knew that he must be very careful, after all, one of his remits was to investigate the supply of drugs into the UK and he was aware that the Turkish PKK derived a lot of their financial support from the sale of such goods. He also knew that the infamous Gul family originated from the hills around Mardin, a stronghold of the PKK. Had he been transferred to this prison and put into a cell with this man in order that he would 'open up' and possibly share his life story? For now, he thought, he must continue to be Stephen Aldridge, truck driver, falsely accused of drug-running and murder. Falling back on his undoubted skills as a highly trained police officer, Slade decided that he would let this man, claiming to be the son of one of the World's most notorious terrorists, make the running. He may well have been simply put there to extract information from him. One way or another, the coming weeks and months would either confirm or deny to him, the exact identity of the man that would now be sleeping on top of him.

Cheryl Smith, fully supporting Sergeant Jefferies in his efforts to locate Peter Slade, allowed him to have the keys to Peter's house. One afternoon, whilst Cheryl was at her Yoga classes, Jefferies found himself rummaging around in Slade's personal belongings. He was not to glean very much from his 'socks and pants' drawer, however he did find an invoice from a solicitor, a solicitor that was very much recommended to police staff. The invoice was for four hundred pounds, for two hours of the briefs time. The breakdown of the charges showed that Slade had sought advice and subsequently had made a will. Jefferies, in his capacity as an investigating officer, contacted the solicitor, a Mr. Joseph Smalling, with the intention of finding out exactly whom it was that Slade would be leaving his, house and money to, in the event of his demise. The following day, Jefferies was sat opposite Joseph Smalling, the meeting was brief. The solicitor pointed out that without a warrant, he was unable to answer any of the policeman's questions. Jefferies had no such warrant as he was acting in an unofficial capacity. Sergeant Jefferies was in dire financial straits, he was both a drinker and a gambler and when his legitimate gambling accounts were closed, he turned to the world of illegal gambling. He currently owed over fifty thousand pounds to some rather unsavoury characters. He was desperate for money and would do almost 'anything' to get his hands on some. He was not to share what he had discovered with Cheryl.

At 6.00pm on the first day of his transfer to Ayas Prison, the man claiming to be Olan Ocalan opened the cell door, from the inside, and said,

'Come, it is dinner time.'

Slade had not heard any key turning in the door and there were no guards in the immediate vicinity of the narrow hallway that contained nine more cells and led directly into the canteen. Slade mimicked everything that his cellmate did. Finally, after collecting their food from the buffet-like service station, they sat together. Soon after, they were joined by two other men.

'This is Peter Slade, also known as Stephen Aldridge. He is the Englishman that I have been telling you about,' said Ocalan.

Slade, hand slightly shaking, lowered his coffee mug to the table. Looking at Slade, Ocalan continued,

'Yes, Mr. Slade. I know who you are, and I can tell you everything that you have been up to in the last year or so.'

Still not ready to divulge his real identity, Slade simply replied,

'But I am Stephen Aldridge.'

'Have it your way Mr. Slade, maybe when we speak further, you may wish to become Chief Superintendent Peter Slade again, it would certainly be safer for you to do so.'

Slade's nerves jangled after hearing Ocalan's statement.

Joseph Smalling watched from the third-floor window of his office in Loughton, Essex, as the uniformed Sergeant Malcolm Jefferies crossed the road and got into his car. He then picked up his mobile phone and called his brother, Nigel. Nigel was at his desk in the basement of Thames House. After explaining the purpose of Jefferies' visit, Nigel suggested that his brother arrange a follow-up appointment for the desperate police Sergeant. Two days later, the solicitor's secretary called Jefferies and asked if he could attend the office the following afternoon, he confirmed that he could. On Friday, the 20th of August 2004, at 4.00pm, Sergeant Malcolm Jefferies walked into the office of Joseph Smalling. He shook hands with the solicitor, who then introduced him to a man sat opposite him, the man was Roland 'Rat' Roberts. Rat stood, moved forward, as if to embrace the police officer and plunged a hypodermic needle, with some force, into his neck. The Sergeant fell, instantly, within seconds he was dead. Rat informed Joseph that the body would be dealt with during nightfall. The solicitor opened a drawer of his desk and handed the Mi5 agent a set of keys. The two men left the office, the secretary had gone one hour earlier. Together they entered the Hollybush public house, drank two beers and then went their separate ways. At 1.00am the following morning, a black transit van parked up at the rear of the solicitor's office. Two men, dressed, head to toe in black, and wearing balaclavas, climbed the steel fire escape stairs, entered Joseph Smalling's office, and carried the deceased body of Sergeant Malcolm Jefferies back down. He was placed into a dark grey body bag and driven to Forest Gate Cemetery, where he was lowered into a 'pre-dug' grave and covered with some of the earth that was piled neatly ten feet above. At 10.00am on Monday 23rd August, the body of a recently deceased cancer victim was buried on top of the unfortunate gambler.

At breakfast the following day, Olan Ocalan took the same seat at the table as he had taken the previous evening. The same two men sat opposite him and Slade. Ocalan began the conversation.

'Mr. Slade I can fully understand your reluctance to talk to me. I may well be an imposter, simply trying to extract information from you. On the other hand,

I may not. You see, I was educated at Cambridge, hence my use of the English language. I studied there under an assumed name, just like yourself. Not knowing that I was who I am, Julian Pritchard seconded me to Mi5, my remit was to infiltrate the drug lords that operate along the mountains of Kurdistan. The Kaptan's and the Gul family now control most of the export of drugs into Europe. It is known to us that your brief is to bring down these two families as they are responsible for almost all the drug-related crime in the UK. When I discussed your situation with my father, we both thought that it would be a great idea for you to join the cause, as we would, with your help, at some time in the future, be able to control the flow of not only drugs, but arms and people too. Our partnership with Mi5 would lead us into relationships with like-minded operations all over Europe. With the help of Mi5 and others we would be able to take down almost all the other players. Drugs, arms, and people will always be trafficked, no matter what. Mi5 figured that by working with just one organisation, everyone would know where they stood. You may be shocked to learn that Governments work hand in hand with terrorists, many governments support us, the displaced Kurdish people, in trying to take back what is rightfully ours. We ourselves could muster the largest 'gang' the World has ever seen. We could wipe out the very violent gangs that heap misery upon millions of people. If there were no longer any gangs to fight with, Europe would return to peaceful times. The PKK has not succumbed to the mighty Turkish Military Forces, the likes of the Albanians, Bulgarians and others would not stand in our way. In the UK alone there are a dozen gangs that emanate from Kurdistan, all are using torture, blackmail, prostitution, and extortion to extract money from their targets. We can stop that. Mr. Slade, you were given a task by Commander James Reeves and Julian Pritchard. Your arrest in Besiktas was not by chance, it was a carefully coordinated operation. Your trial and sentence were preordained and your transfer to this prison was all part of the charade. When you were stopped, with drugs, another Mi5 agent, Alkan Asani made a call to London, everything after that, you already know. The Irishman you got to know as 'Spud' was not part of your detainment, we let him go as we need him to carry on, as one day, he will lead us to the McBride's and Sean Porter'.

After a brief chat with some other inmates, out of Slade's earshot, Ocalan returned. He continued,

'You are wondering which of the people in London will betray you. I can tell you that it will be Quinten Proctor. He is on the payroll of the Guls, and he allows them to operate freely in the UK. He is only fed what Mi5 want him to know. Often, he is excluded from 'closed-door' meetings. This man is as dangerous as Birusk Gul himself. Hopefully, Mr. Proctor will soon be dealt with. In this prison, there are 44 inmates, everyone, except yourself, is a member of the PKK. Even the guards belong to us. We did a deal with the Turks; we guaranteed them that we would not operate along the Black Sea coast. In return they gave us control of five prisons. Three are much like this one, the other two are where we dispose of our enemies. We control seven judges around Turkey, if we did not have this control, then you would have been shot the day after your trial.'

Chief Superintendent Peter Slade, two thousand miles away from the tree-lined street in Epping, on which he lived, took some time to come to terms with what Olan Ocalan, heir to the throne of the PKK, had told him. He concluded that what he had heard could not possibly be just guesswork, this man really had infiltrated the heart of one of the Worlds most renowned secret services, however he himself had still not been told what his part in all of this was going to be. His thoughts turned to the lovely Cheryl Smith, only the second woman that he had ever loved, she must be going through hell, he concluded.

Just before dawn on the 26th of August, two armed men arrived at Slade's cell, they opened the door and simply said to Olan Ocalan,

'Everything is ready.'

Ocalan gestured for his cellmate to follow him. In the tiny courtyard of the small prison stood an army jeep, seconded from the Turkish Army. The vehicle seated four. Six heavily armed men sat, crossed-legged in the open back. Ocalan and Slade climbed into the seats immediately behind the driver and his armed passenger. As they passed through the opened gates of the prison, several other vehicles, all carrying armed PKK personnel, followed. At the first junction, another vehicle with a mounted armed tripod took the lead. Slade could see at least three men, armed with rocket-propelled grenades (RPGs) in the vehicles that followed. Only now did he ask the question,

'Where are we heading Olan?'

Slightly grinning at the man sitting next to him, Ocalan replied,

'We are going to see my father.'

'Your father is where, exactly,' asked Slade.

'He is in the hills, above Mardin. Our journey will take around fifteen hours and could be dangerous, but as you can see Mr. Slade, we are quite prepared for trouble.'

They headed South, towards Mersin, which was about the halfway point. They stopped for two hours and then continued along the road that runs near to the border with Syria, arriving at an unnamed 'tented' village, close to Mardin, just after 9.00pm. Ocalan showed his guest to a tent, he was given coffee and hot food. Ocalan informed Slade that he was leaving the village to visit his father, hiding somewhere in the mountains and that they would both return the following morning.

It had been a whole week since Helen Jefferies had seen or heard from her husband. Their three children, whilst used to being without him for a day or two, were now constantly asking as to their father's whereabouts. Helen contacted the Inspector at Epping Police Station and asked as to when he had last been on duty. The Inspector was slightly surprised by Helen's question as he presumed that she knew that her husband had been selected by the Home Office to go 'undercover' as part of a very important operation that involved some well-known local drug lords. She, of course, denied any knowledge of her husband's part in bringing down some of the richest and most notorious of Epping's criminal inhabitants. The Inspector told her not to worry as it was not unusual for undercover operatives to fly under the radar for a while and that he would personally call her should he hear anything as to when Malcolm might resurface.

On the morning of the 27th of August, Slade could hear the distinctive sound of a helicopter, a minute later he could see it as it came into view above the hills in the far distance. As it drew nearer, he could see that it was once a serving chopper in the Syrian Airforce. Two men sat, legs dangling, in the open door of the flying machine, both held aloft rocket launchers. Two minutes later the chopper touched down. Slade retreated inside his tent to avoid the almost hurricane-like wind that the overhead rotor blades produced. Once the dust had settled, he saw six men alight from the heavily camouflaged helicopter, they were led by Olan Ocalan and a more elderly-looking man. Slade presumed him to be Abdullah Ocalan, leader of the PKK and 'the' most powerful man in this neck of the woods. The two men entered a large tent, bang in the middle of the portable village, at least twenty machine gun-clad soldiers guarded them. A man, carrying a rifle and dressed as though his clothes had never left his body, summoned Slade forward and led him to the largest of all the tents. The man, who most probably had a part as an extra in the film 'Lawrence of Arabia' held open the canvas curtain and ushered Slade in. He then mounted a camel and galloped off to cook Omar Sharif's breakfast.

Olan Ocalan sat on the cold dusty floor of the tent, beside him was the man that Slade presumed was his father. A fire, surrounded by bricks made from dried camel dung, warmed the freezing air of the early morning. Later in the day the temperature would reach 40c, but for now it was cold enough to freeze the undercarriage of anyone that dared to sit for too long. As Slade approached, Abdullah stood, withdrew his scimitar from its protective casing and brought it gently down until it rested upon Slade's shoulder. Slade drew, what he thought might be his last breath, he need not have worried, this act was a centuries-old Kurdish tradition, performed when two men greet each other, for the first time. Abdullah sat back down, as did Slade. Abdullah spoke, in his native language, Olan interpreted and then informed Slade that his father welcomed him to his great land. Slade nodded in appreciation. Olan then set about explaining to his guest, that he and his father had drawn up a plan, a plan that had been agreed by Julian Pritchard. The plan was that Slade would return to his duties of trying to bring down the various gangs and cartels that are operating all over Europe. He would be given the help of the PKK in most European countries. A new identity had already been made for him. He would become Malcolm Jefferies, a recently disposed member of Her Majesty's Police Force. A photographer was waiting outside, to take the photo needed for his passport and driving license, but first he must shave off his beard and cut his hair if he was going to be able to pass himself off as the 'go-between' that would be brokering deals made by gang leaders and their Kurdish suppliers. The three men stood, embraced each other, and exited the tent. Slade was never to see Abdullah Ocalan again.

In mid-afternoon, Slade was summoned, two armed men took him to a waiting jeep. An armoured vehicle, laden with men and arms waited patiently behind. Slade climbed into the rear seat of the jeep. Olan Ocalan appeared, as if by magic, he informed Slade that he was to be taken to the Port of Mersin, some eight hours away, where he would board a container ship, which would arrive some fifteen days later at the port of Tilbury, Essex. At Tilbury the ship would be boarded by UK Customs, with them will be Nigel Smalling, who will interview you in the Captain's Cabin and hand you all the documentation that you will require to live your life as Malcolm Jefferies. Before he was driven off, Olan added,

'I should not have to remind you Mr. Slade, as I am sure you will already understand, that under no circumstances can you contact anyone from your former life. This includes your girlfriend, Cheryl Smith.' Good luck to you Peter.'

The long drive to Mersin was uneventful, the convoy was stopped twice, each time the name of Abdullah Ocalan was mentioned. They incurred no problems. As they approached the dock gates of Mersin Port, the two-armed guards at either side of the gates, stood bolt upright, saluted and lifted the flimsy barrier. Within three minutes Slade was boarding the 'MSC Valetta.' As he approached the deck, some thirty metres above the water line, a man, dressed in the whitest of white uniforms, first saluted and then shook Slade's hand and said,

'Mr. Jefferies, welcome on board, I am Captain Farouk al-Sharaa. I originate from Daraa, Syria. I would show you around, however the sight of seven hundred containers would not be that pleasing to your eye. Come, I will take you to your cabin, it is the second-best room on the ship of course I have the first.' The cabin was everything that Slade would have expected. About three metres by three metres, a single bed along one wall, a small desk, and a bookcase on another. In the corner was a door leading to the world's smallest en-suite. The shower, Slade thought, had been designed for a 'skeleton' crew. It took all of one minute to scan this room before he was shown into the Captain's Cabin. By comparison, this room was almost palatial, with a double bed, king-size wardrobe, a much larger desk, a sofa, two armchairs and a drinks cabinet. The captain dared not to show his guest his bathroom. When he did eventually set eyes upon it, it turned out to be larger than his actual room. The captain, ushering his VIP passenger back into his own room said,

'As it is now 2.00am you may wish to get some sleep, we shall talk in the morning, Mr. Jefferies.'

With that, the captain shut and locked his door.

At 9.00am the following morning, there was a soft knock upon Slade's door. A voice asked,

'Are you ready to see the captain, Sir? Your breakfast will be available in fifteen minutes.'

Slade, through his still closed door replied,

'Yes, I will be there, thank you.'

Washing his face in a sink about the size of an Old Holborn tobacco tin, Slade threw on the only clothes he now possessed and knocked firmly on the captain's door.

'Ah, Mr. Jefferies, please come in, did you sleep well?' Asked Captain Farouk.

For the first time, it dawned upon Slade that the ship was no longer in Port, it was out on the open seas. Sat together at the small table in his room, the captain said,

'Well, Mr. Jefferies, you are faced with fifteen days of sheer boredom. The books in your room are at your disposal, as are the ones in my room, so please feel free to help yourself. There is little else to do, please get started on your breakfast. Should you wish to have anything else, please let me know, all I must do is to pull that rope and my butler will be here.'

Slade smiled and said,

'This will be fine Captain, thank you.'

Between bites of food, Slade quizzed the captain.

'How do you come to speak such good English Captain?

'Well Malcolm, may I call you Malcolm? You may call me Farouk, should you wish to do so. My father was high up in the Syrian Government, as was his father before him. I had been educated at Damascus University, where I studied English Language. In 1995 I moved to London, where I studied International Law. In 1999 I returned to Syria. My father had convinced President Hafez al-Assad to give me the job of assistant to the Foreign Minister of Affairs. Not long after I took up my post, the President died, his son, Bashar, took over and

I was not part of his plans. My father died in mysterious circumstances, and I fled to Turkey. In the beginning the Turkish authorities were good to me, however they soon began to believe that I was a spy, working for the Assad regime. Again, I was forced to flee, it was with the help of Abdullah Ocalan that I was able to do so. Ever since I have tried to help the Kurds in their fight to regain the land, that is historically theirs. Of you, I ask no questions. I have been asked to get you safely to the UK and I will do so. You are welcome to roam the ship, but please be careful. It normally takes many months to get used to life on the ocean. You may take your meals with me, or in your own room, I do not mind which you choose. I am told that someone from Customs will meet you when we arrive at Tilbury. We will call at Athens, Valetta, Marseille, Le Havre and finally Tilbury. Enjoy the voyage.'

On the 12th of September 2004, the 'MSC Valetta' berthed at Tilbury Docks, Essex, England. Even before the first of several hundred containers had been lifted from the ship, Nigel Smalling, posing as a Customs Officer, sat in the cabin of Captain Farouk al-Sharaa and briefed Slade as to his immediate future. During their conversation, which lasted for the best part of two hours, Slade (now Malcolm Jefferies) was handed a mobile phone, a notebook, a photograph album, passport, driving license, NI card, a certified copy of his birth certificate, a debit card and one thousand pounds in cash. In addition, he was given a set of keys and the address of a bungalow, in Maldon, Essex, that they opened the door of.

'There is a car on the drive, you will find its keys in a kitchen drawer, Malcolm. Smalling explained to him that he should only ever use the phone to call the numbers that had already been plumbed into it. Those numbers were his own and that of Julian Pritchard, Alkan Asani and Borislav Topalov. The omission from the phone of the number for James Reeves led Malcolm to ask as to the involvement of his former boss. He was told that the ex-commander would not be involved in this operation as he was busy being the coordinator for two other agents, whom Malcolm may or may not meet during this mission. Guiding Malcolm through the pages of the notebook, the first person of note was none other than Azad Gul, brought over from Cizre in 1999 after his brother, Birusk, was jailed for sixteen years for murder and several other crimes. Azad was referenced as (AG1) and the first page of the photo album showed a picture of him, this was also referenced (AG1). Pages 2,3, 4 etc, named the close associates of Azad Gul and their last known whereabouts. There was a footnote that whilst still in prison, the leader of the gang, the infamous Birusk Gul, was still pulling the strings from his cell. He too would need to be dealt with. Smalling pointed out that all the people mentioned, and shown, were targets, targets to be taken down. Thumbing quickly through the book, that he would study and collate in the coming weeks and months, he found, on the final page, the details and photographs of Abdullah and Olan Ocalan. Looking up at Nigel Smalling, Malcolm said not a word, as the man from the basement already knew the question.

'Yes, them as well.'

They left the ship together, got into Nigel Smalling's car and thirty minutes later they arrived at 19 Acacia Drive, Maldon, Essex.

15 - THE LIST

Malcom Jefferies, previously known as both Peter Slade and Stephen Aldridge turned the key that he had inserted into the lock of the double-glazed door that allowed him access to his new place of residence. He entered the newly decorated hallway of 19 Acacia Drive, located in Maldon, Essex. His new living quarters was in fact, a bungalow. His parents had owned a bungalow. As a child he never really liked it, as it afforded him no escape to an upstairs refuge. Now, on his own, at the age of 40, he had no real reason for wanting to hide away from anyone. He walked from room to room, there were three bedrooms, a living room, a separate dining room, a small study, and a well-equipped kitchen. Adjoining the kitchen was a sizeable conservatory. The garden was of medium size and looked as though it had recently been landscaped. On the kitchen top were several keys, all placed upon yellow 'stick-its' each one indicating which key belonged to which door. Checking the drawers next to the washing machine, he found a set of keys, that he presumed belonged to the Grand Cherokee that was parked on the drive. Under the keys was yet another yellow 'stick-it' written on it were four numbers, 0102 and the words PIN number, which he immediately recognised as being those of his own birthday. A bottle of red wine stood at the end of the worktop; a business card was underneath the bottle. It read,

'Dear Mr. Jefferies, welcome to your new home. Please contact me should you require anything at all.'

The top of the card showed the name of Keith O'Boyle, Estate Agents, High Street, Maldon. The contact person was Johnnie Holden. He presumed that the bungalow had been let by the agents to him and that no doubt Nigel Smalling had made all the arrangements and was paying the rent.

He checked the fridge, there was food and milk. He put the kettle on and made himself tea, laying out the notebook and album upon the large farmhouse table. Then, whilst sipping his tea, he once again thumbed through the notebook. Most of the people listed inside the pages of the book, meant nothing to him. Only Birusk Gul had ever previously come to his attention. By the time he reached the final page he realised that the names of the McBride Brothers and Sean Porter were missing. He checked again they were nowhere to be found. Finishing his tea, he picked up the keys to the front door, took one hundred pounds from the grand that Smalling had given him and returned the rest to the dishwasher. He would have no use for such an item, as firstly he would not be there that often, and secondly, when he was there, he would be dining out or eating takeaways. He left the bungalow, walked past the jeep, and turned right. There were just two other properties to pass before he reached Spital Road. He nodded to an elderly man who was struggling to cut the long, wet grass of his front lawn. Walking the length of Spital Road, he entered the High Street and whilst he did not know whether to turn left or right, he did know that having been to this historic town, on many occasions, with his father, there were a several pubs in which he could get some food. He turned right, this would lead him along the entirety of the High Street, the far end of which contained almost all its Estate Agents. On the other side of the road he saw, Keith Ashton, next to it was Curtis O'Boyle, on his side he had just passed Holdens Estate Agents. He had not brought the card with him, but he was sure that it read, Keith O'Boyle Estate Agents, contact Johnnie Holden. If he was correct, then the card left for him was a combination of all three of these Agents. His first quest was to buy three 'off the shelf' mobile phones. He found a shop selling second-hand / reconditioned phones. He wanted two that simply rang numbers and sent texts and another more sophisticated device. Having agreed a price, he left a deposit and asked the owner to set them up for him, promising to return the next day with the one hundred and ninety-pounds balance. He entered the Ship and Anchor Pub at 4.30pm and ate a full three-course meal.

Returning to Acacia Drive, the elderly man had still not got to grips with cutting his grass. They again exchanged nods and Jefferies let himself into the Bungalow, showered and sat at the desk in the study. In the notebook were the names of twelve gang leaders and their immediate associates. In the UK Azad Gul was the overall boss, (since Birusk Gul had been imprisoned for sixteen years in 1999). Cousin Mustafa Gul flitted between the UK and Germany and close friend, Yusuf Kaya, shown as the gang's enforcer, were all noted as operating from Southend in Essex. They were supplying and cooperating with Bobby Keagan in Liverpool, Jamie Law in Glasgow, and Tony McDonald in Hull. There was a footnote, it read,

'At least three hundred cornermen in London and the Southeast.' According to the intel, the four gangs of Gul, Law, Keagan, and McDonald were responsible for ninety percent of all the drug dealing in the UK mainland. The Gul clan were also present in Rotterdam, Hamburg, Antwerp and Le Havre and each gang leader and his enforcer were listed. The Chief Superintendent soon realised that all these operations, excluding Southend, revolved around major shipping ports. The 'list' also contained the names and details of the leading gangs in Spain, Italy, Austria, Bulgaria, Romania, and Albania, all supposedly supplied by Abdullah and Olan Ocalan, from their stronghold in the mountains of Kurdistan. Jefferies concluded that his task to locate and bring down these people may just be beyond his limitations. His job was to set up deals with these people, let Nigel Smalling know of the details and the PKK were to do the rest. The next day would be the beginning of what could well be, a four-year campaign of deceit and death, and Malcolm Jefferies would be at the heart of it.

Before retiring for the night, Jefferies needed to decide as to where he was going to start on this gargantuan investigation. His decision was to begin at the closest point. Azad Gul and his family, at the nearby seaside resort of Southend-on-Sea.

Over seven months had elapsed since Cheryl Smith had set eyes upon her next-door neighbour and it had been six weeks since Sergeant Malcolm Jefferies had disappeared from her life. Whilst she had been patient, she was no longer receiving any news about either of her lovers from the Metropolitan Police. Having previously worked for the Waltham Forest Gazette for over fifteen years, where her deceased husband had been the editor, Cheryl, still on good terms with the current boss, decided to contact him with a view to them investigating, what she was now convinced was becoming a story of some local interest. Two days after first speaking to Giles Murdoch, the current editor, she sat opposite him in an Indian Restaurant on Loughton High Road. Having given Murdoch everything that she knew, he assured her that he would make his own enquiries and then get back to her.

At 6.00am on the 13th of September 2004, Jefferies started the dark grey Grand Cherokee and drove off, towards Southend. At 7.05 he arrived at Temple Farm Industrial Estate, a complex of warehousing and distribution units, situated on the ever-expanding perimeter of Southend International Airport. According to the notes given to him by Nigel Smalling, the entire estate was owned by Gul Enterprises, a legitimate arm of the family's vast property portfolio. Gul Enterprises owned and operated forty-seven such properties in the UK and Ireland and boasted another sixty complexes within the EU. Parking the jeep close to a portable burger and sandwich bar, he purchased a tea and a hot dog and waited. At 9.15 two top-of-the-range, black Range Rovers pulled up outside the largest of the warehouses on the estate. The large sign, high up above the five roller-shuttered doors showed this business to be 'Gul International Shipping and Forwarding'. Jefferies studied the three photographs that he had taken from the album, looked up at the occupants of the Range Rovers, that were now standing adjacent to one of the loading bays and then looked back at the photographs. He lifted the binoculars that he had found in the driver's door compartment and scanned two of the men more closely. He was as certain as he could be that he had identified one as being Azad Gul, the main man in the UK, the other man that Jefferies identified was Mustafa Gul, the cousin of both Azad and Birusk and currently running the Gul operations in Germany. The six other men from the Range Rovers were not identified by the man from Mi5. Taking the tiny, but powerful digital camera that he had found in the glove compartment. Jefferies took several photographs. Later he would download and forward them to Nigel Smalling.

The warehouse was now becoming busy, trucks and vans were arriving, loading, and unloading their goods. The jeep was now the only car parked up in the vicinity of the burger van. Jefferies felt slightly exposed, the morning breakfast crowd had all disappeared. He started the car and drove forward, towards the warehouse, he then turned left. As he turned, he saw that several cartons, that had been unloaded from a van bearing the Gul logo, had been placed on the ground, at the rear of the two Range Rovers. He made a U-turn at another warehouse entrance, parked up, lent over to his left, and took some further snaps, although he was not sure if they would give any clues as to what was going on. At 11.30am he parked the Cherokee on the drive at the bungalow and walked into Maldon. He parted with the balance he owed and collected three mobile phones from the shop that he had been to the previous day. He then bought some lunch at the M&S on the High Street and walked back home.

Back in his study, Jefferies realised what a task he had undertaken. He had set eyes upon Azad and Mustafa Gul, they were heavily guarded, to go all the way and take them out permanently would mean getting at least six, SAS type soldiers involved. There were also the gangs in Liverpool, Glasgow, and Hull to consider and he could not possibly undertake the surveillance required to keep tabs on them all. He was tempted to call Nigel Smalling and ask for help, but due to the high risk of whether he could trust him or not, he immediately ditched that idea. Using one of his new phones, he decided to call his old school chum, Graham Roberts. Roberts was both surprised and relieved to be hearing from the man, that as a schoolboy had knocked him out in the very first round of the under-thirteen's boxing tournament. It was Roberts' first and last attempt at the Nobel Art of Boxing. Peter Slade, as he was back then, had gone on to win the UK-wide championship. Roberts realised there and then, that he was always going to be second best to the boy that excelled at everything that he took part in. Jefferies asked about the well-being of Cheryl Smith and if he (Roberts) had seen her whilst visiting his house.

'Yes, I have seen Cheryl, she is quite depressed, not knowing where or how you are, has in some part, caused her depression. Should she find out that you have assumed the identity of the man that was, in her eyes, trying to find you, then she may well sink into a situation that she cannot get out of.'

'Well, you cannot, under any circumstances inform her of my return. Just keep your eye on her for me, that is all that I ask.'

'For you Mr. Jefferies, of course.'

Jefferies, as he was now, then updated his friend on all that had happened during his disappearance and all that was planned to happen in the future. Roberts asked,

'Would you like to get, Inside the gang?'

'And how would I do that, pose as a moll, was Jefferies' sarcastic reply.

'No, not all, replied, Philip Marlowe.

'Do you remember Phil Din, from school? The little runt that we used to torment most of the time.'

'Yes, I do.'

'Well, he has an employment agency, specialising in the shipping and transport business, he gets me certain people from time to time. Gul Shipping is bound to want temps, especially drivers, what do you think?

'It's worth a try Mr. Roberts, get me in.'

'OK, and I will give some thought to the other vagabonds up in Liverpool, Glasgow, and Hull.

'Speak soon.' Roberts hung up.

Jefferies, having done his crash IT course when he was Peter Slade, downloaded the photo's that he had taken earlier in the day. He was able to enlarge them and was quickly able to recognise both Azad and Mustafa Gul. He could also see from the last few that he had taken, that several cartons that had been unloaded from the van, were being reloaded into the boots of the two Range Rovers. Had he been a gambling man he would have wagered Mi5's bungalow that the contents of the cartons were drugs. Try as he may, he could not get all twenty-two photos to go through to the man in the basement at the same time. He had to spend a painstaking fifty minutes sending them one by one. Half an hour after receiving the photos, Nigel Smalling called him on the secure phone and said,

'My, my, Malcolm you have hit the jackpot.'

'Two of the men at the rear of the Range Rovers are, 'Ozturk Ozsoy' brother-in-law of Birusk Gul and currently controlling the half of Kurdistan that Abdullah Ocalan does not have, the other man is 'Nur Nazif' he fronts as the leader of the religious Kurds in London and is based at the Aziziye Mosque, in Finsbury Park. He has been on our radar for several years. He 'double deals' with everyone, but strangely, everyone trusts him.

Ozturk Ozsoy and Nur Nazif were two completely new names for the undercover cop to contend with. He now had four main men in his sights. His computer 'pinged.' Nigel had just sent him close-up pictures of the men that he had photographed earlier. His mobile rang, it was Graham Roberts.

'I am going to put round-the-clock surveillance on the Guls, it will be costly, but then you are not paying my bill.'

'Well, things just got a little more complicated, as apart from the Guls, I also managed to take pictures of Ozturk Ozsoy and Nur Nazif.'

'Fuck me Malcolm (Slade had asked Graham to always call him by his new, assumed name) I know of Nur Nazif, having done some surveillance on him for the Anti-Terrorist Team, but I have no idea who Ozturk Ozsoy is.'

'Well, he is the sworn enemy of Abdullah Ocalan, they are both vying for control of, not only the mountains of Kurdistan, but also the entire drug network of the UK and just to complicate matters, both Ozsoy and Ocalan work with the Guls.'

Roberts paused before answering, he then said,

'I have found out that Gul Enterprises own a nine-bed apartment block, overlooking the Thames at Westcliff-on-Sea. I would have a small wager that is where the Guls look after their visitors. I will put two men onto this, please send me the photo's that you have and don't forget to inform your people that I am now on the payroll and will want to be paid at the end of each month. None of my men will know of your existence Malcolm, this way they could never give you up if caught and getting caught by this lot is not something I would like to contemplate.'

'Speak soon Malcolm and take no chances.'

Not being able to progress with the Guls and their associates until Roberts got back to him, Jefferies decided to peruse the intel that he had been given on the other gangs that operated on behalf of Azad Gul. Firstly though, he called Julian Pritchard from the secure phone and informed him that he had had to secure 'outside help' and that he would be forwarding the cost of this to him personally. Pritchard asked as to the name of the person or company that Mi5 would be paying. Jefferies replied,

'I am using G.R. Securities.'

'I know Mr. Roberts very well Malcolm, we go back years.'

Jefferies was surprised by Pritchard's reply, as Roberts had never mentioned his association with the head of Mi5 undercover operations. Pritchard signed off the call by saying,

'Anyhow, welcome back and please remember that a certain member of the Home Office needs to be dealt with.'

'I understand, Sir.' Jefferies hung up.

Pages 5 and 6 of the notebook showed the name of Bobby Keagan, born in 1966, in the Moss Side District, just south of Manchester City Centre. Bobbies' parents had left the troubles of Belfast, only to find, that by the time their son was in his teenage years, Moss Side had become known as 'Gun Chester' as several rival drug gangs had taken up the use of firearms as a way of protecting their territory. By 1982, aged just 16, Bobby had become a fully accepted member of the 'Gooch Close' gang. His duties back then were simply to stand on certain street corners and dish out small wraps of drugs in return for hard cash. By the age of 21 he had become second in command, only Tony 'legs' Adams stood between him and control of one of the four main gangs in Manchester. In 1989 'legs' was taken out by the Cheetham Hill gang and despite claims by others, Bobby Keagan assumed complete control. A truce between the 'Gooch' 'Doddington' and Pepper Hill clans, brokered by Bobby, was quickly broken when a member of the Gooch gang was murdered by the Dodington's. The murder led to a spate of shooting incidents, 81 in total, one of which led to a 15-year-old cyclist being shot down in a hail of bullets. His killers were never taken to task. Early in 2000, Bobby Keagan took complete control of the Manchester and Liverpool drug scene. He moved himself, his wife, three children and their respective parents into a mansion on the Wirral. The records show that the house, purchased for £1.1 million, had been bought by a famous lottery winner. It was signed over to Bobby Keagan six months later. At the age of thirty-eight Keagan had never worked a day in his life and his contributions to the UK Tax Revenue stood at zero. In 2001, he was supplied with cocaine, heroin, arms, and people by Azad Gul. Part of the deal was the guaranteed safety of Keagan, his relatives, and associates. Bobby Keagan appeared to be untouchable.

The next two pages of Nigel Smalling's handwritten notebook revealed that in Glasgow, in 1972, Jamie Law had been sired by 'crack addicts' his mother was just fifteen when she gave birth to her one and only son. His father, a low life from the slums of Laurieston, adjacent to the infamous tenements of the Gorbals, was a dealer who would entice young girls into taking drugs and then use them as prostitutes. By the time he was 29 Law Senior had fathered seven children, three had died and, three were taken into care. Jamie, with the help of his maternal Grandmother, had survived. His mother was found, naked and emaciated on debris. Her death was recorded as an 'overdose.' Jamie's father had absconded when let out of prison to attend the funeral of one of his offspring. Reading this account of the now, 32-year-old Jamie Law, Malcolm could not help but feel a little pity towards his plight. His sympathy was short-lived as he read more of the notes that had been compiled by Nigel Smalling. What he learnt was that at the age of 14, Jamie Law was locked away for his part in the torturing and killing of an eleven-year-old, whose only crime had been the stealing of Jamie's friend's mountain bike. Jamie had been a model inmate at the juvenile prison, however this all changed when he was moved to Glasgow's Barlinnie Prison. Jamie was 18, six foot five inches tall and sixteen stone. His sheer size made most of the other inmates wary of him. Those that did try it on with him, were soon put in their place. Two years after arriving, he was running the distribution of drugs amongst the one thousand plus prisoners. He had been given seven years, for manslaughter, and the judge recommended that he serve the full term. Two months after his twenty-first birthday, he was released. Together with associates that had already been released and others that were let out soon after him, he formed the gang that would forever be known as 'The Law Firm.' With the money that he had amassed from his drug dealings in Barlinnie, he purchased three kilos of uncut cocaine, three years later he was recognised as Scotland's premier drug dealer. In 2001, he met with Azad Gul and was afforded the same deal as Bobby Keagan. 'The Law Firm' also ran the lucrative prostitution business in Glasgow, Edinburgh, Aberdeen, and Perth. When they required weapons, they would normally obtain them from Tony McDonald in Hull.

Reading further into the notebook, that Jefferies was finding so hard to put down, he found that a very lengthy report, the longest in the whole notebook, had been written about Tony McDonald. He read that Tony McDonald had been born to wealthy parents in 1968 and was as far removed from the worlds of Bobby Keagan and Jamie Law as he possibly could be. His father, a doctor, had moved up to Hull, from London, when he had first qualified as a GP. His mother, born in South Cave, just outside Hull was a ward sister in Hull Infirmary. They had met during the doctor's weekly hospital visits. By the time their son was born, they had moved to Walkington, a typical English village, with an idyllic lifestyle, geographically just a few miles from South Cave. McDonald attended Hull's most sought-after private school and then went on to study at Liverpool University. Tony was destined to follow his parents into the world of medicine. However, in the spring of 1989, his 'mapped out' future changed without warning, as, on a 'night out' with three fellow scholars in the area that housed the world-famous 'Cavern Club' the quartet came upon a lifeless-looking body. The body lay between three industrial dustbins, in an alleyway halfway down Matthew Street. McDonald's friends attempted to drag him away, telling him not to get involved. However, with his advanced medical knowledge, the University Graduate sat the distraught man up against the wall and as he did so, three unsavoury characters appeared from the darkness at the 'dead-end' of the alleyway. The trio of his classmates legged it and so did the potential perpetrators of the offence of GBH. Slowly, the bloodied and dazed man started to come around and McDonald was able to help him to his feet. They managed to get to the end of Matthew Street where the young student propped the man, whose name he did not know, up against the window of a cab office. McDonald went inside, a driver got to his feet and went outside, McDonald followed. Together they helped the wounded man into the cab. It was only then that the 'medic to be' realised that his patient had been stabbed in the stomach. Telling the driver to go to the nearest hospital, the driver asked if he knew who the man was? McDonald shook his head. The driver informed him that he was none other than Bobby Keagan. The name meant nothing to Tony McDonald. Half an hour later the injured man was undergoing emergency surgery. Fifteen minutes after that, a blonde, good-looking woman, and an older man entered the room where, the saviour of Bobby Keagan had been waiting, together with two police officers. The officers nodded to the new arrivals. One of them said,

'Good evening, Mr. Keagan, we will need to interview Bobby as soon as the doctors say we can'.

In reply, Keagan Senior said,

'Oh, I am sure that Bobby saw nothing, but stick around if you must.'

With that and having already given an account of his part in the evening's events, McDonald bid Bobby Keagan's father and wife goodnight.

After he had left, Keagan Senior asked the officers as to whom his son's rescuer had been.

'He is Tony McDonald he is from a village near Hull and is attending the University here.'

Two days later Keagan Senior sat in the back of a dark blue Range Rover, outside the steps of Liverpool University, he could not be seen by passers-by due to the darkness of the rear windows. When Joe Keagan recognised his son's good Samaritan, he opened the door and called out,

'Tony, do you have a minute?'

Having not forgotten the face that he had seen just two nights earlier, he approached the car.

'Please get in young man, my son would like to see you.'

Half an hour later, the Range Rover stopped at a set of electronically controlled gates, drove up a steep drive and stopped outside a massive mansion. McDonald had kept a mental note of the route, he was now in the Caldy area of the Wirral and from its vantage point, high above the tree-tops, he could see the banks of the river Dee. Bobby Keagan was resting on a large sofa, he introduced Tony McDonald to his wife, Sandra and to his parents as they passed by, on their way to the kitchen.

'Please sit Tony, would you like some coffee, or maybe something stronger?' asked Bobby.

'Coffee would be great, thanks.'

Tony scanned the room and wondered how could someone that looked only slightly older than himself, have so much?

'How old are you, Tony? Asked the man whose life he had saved.

'Twenty-one.'

'Well, I am just twenty-three and I would not have reached twenty-four if you had not saved my life. In my business there are more people that want me dead than there are who would wish me to be alive.

'How can I reward you?'

'I do not need any reward, Bobby, saving lives is all-important to me, to have saved yours is reward enough.'

'I can buy you a car, get you girls, boys, drugs anything you want Tony, you only need to ask. You see, I am Bobby Keagan, king of the jungle in these parts.'

Three days later, Bobby Keagan sat in a brand-new BMW Coupe, outside Liverpool University. He called out to Tony McDonald as he descended the steps of his place of learning. As Tony approached, Bobby got out and handed Tony the keys.

'Here, it's yours, I do hope you can drive.'

Whilst he did not wish to take such a gift from such a man, his own, beaten-up, fifteen-year-old Ford Cortina, was on its last legs. He took the keys from the Northwest's most celebrated criminal, got in and started up the car that, maybe after ten years of medical practice, he could have afforded. Tony was hooked. He drove Bobby Keagan, the man with whom he would have the closest of associations with, home to the Wirral. The year was 1989, now fifteen years later, Tony McDonald controls almost all the drugs, arms and people smuggling within the Northeast of England. He too, just like Jamie Law and Bobby Keagan has a close affiliation with the Guls. People in the business, refer to Tony McDonald as the 'posh pusher' albeit his dealings go way beyond that of a street corner distributor.

Malcolm Jefferies had not realised that it was 4.00am before he finally put down the most interesting 'notebook' that he had ever read.

At 9.15 he said good morning to Graham Roberts.

'It's your lucky day, Malcom,' said the super sleuth.

'How come?

'Because our puny little mate from school days gone by, has managed to get you a driver's job, through yet another agency, with Gul Enterprises. You are to go and see the haulage manager, Don Rogers, at Southend this afternoon. Are you up for it Malcolm, it could be fraught with, 'danger'

'Malcolm laughed before replying,

'Danger is my middle name I will be there.'

'Oh, and another thing, yesterday my men followed Azad Gul and three of his men, they went to a Garden Centre in Cheshunt and met with Dick White, Bobby Keagan, Jamie Law, and Tony McDonald. Each of them had three minders with them, they all arrived in black Range Rovers, my man said the car park looked like a scene from a gangster movie.'

'Dick White.' We tried for years to nail that 'bastard. I wonder what his part is in all of this? I do know that he never touched drugs. He hated what they did to the kids, keep me updated Graham, and thanks, what would I do without you?

From the secure phone, Jefferies called Nigel Smalling. He explained that he had an 'interview' at the Guls' operation in Southend and asked that Nigel compile him a suitable CV, adding that he would take it with him, but only hand it over if it was asked for. Sat at his study desk, Jefferies began to recall his dealings with Dick White, he remembered that for five years, back in the 80s, Dick White was the UK's most wanted criminal. He had kidnapped a police constable, his panda car and three members of the public, at gunpoint, using his weapon of choice, a sawn-off shotgun. Peter Slade was part of a team that staked out seven separate locations, suspecting Mr. White to be there, on each occasion he managed to get away. He was given the nickname of 'Keyser Soze' by the Flying Squad, a famous fictional character that never seemed to get caught, no matter how good the intel was. So why, Jefferies asked himself, would Dick White be in cahoots with the Guls and their associated drug gangs in the UK? Only time will tell he thought. Changing into clothes that he thought a driver might wear, he arrived at Temple Farm one hour later. He did not dither when he climbed out of the jeep, to do so would be a sure sign to anyone that was watching that he was concerned by whom he might meet. Entering a door, signed 'drivers' to the right of the loading bay, he followed the hand-drawn arrows until he was face-to-face with a woman sat behind a sliding glass door. He noted that this woman must have recently left the circus as the amount of rouge and lipstick on her face gave her a clown-like appearance. Jefferies explained that he had an appointment with Don Rogers. Without removing the fag end from her mouth, she said abruptly,

'Who are you?'

'Malcolm Jefferies' was his reply.

Pointing at a wicker chair, that had obviously seen better days, she said,

'Wait there, he will be out in a minute.'

Twenty minutes later, with no sign of Don Rogers, Jefferies pressed his nose against the glass window, but before he could utter a word, a voice from behind him said,

'Ah, Mr. Jefferies, follow me.'

Sat in an office that looked as though it had just been bombed, Don Rogers asked,

'So, what can you drive Mr. Jefferies?'

'Well, anything up to three and a half tons.'

'I won't beat about the bush Mr. Jefferies, we are looking for someone that can drive a van, most of the work is airport to airport, its long hours and involves nights. It does not suit men with nagging wives or those that like to drink themselves into oblivion every night, however if that is you and you are prepared to work long hours, then you are our man. What do you think?'

Malcolm, remaining very poised, replied,

'So, what is the pay like?'

He was not prepared for Rogers' next words.

'I thought you came to us through an agency, surely they would have told you about the pay?' '

'What I was thinking Mr. Rogers, is that you tell the agency to get stuffed and take me on directly, that way, everyone is a winner.'

Rogers jumped on this straight away, saying, '

'So, what if we paid you 'cash in hand' no tax or other deductions, could you work like that?'

'You bet I could.'

'Well Malcolm, can you start next Monday at 6.00am?

'I sure can Don.'

'See you then, thanks for coming.'

They shook hands and Jefferies made his way back to Maldon.

Feeling 'cock-a-hoop' at landing the job, Jefferies wasted no time in informing Graham Roberts of his successful interview. Whilst Roberts knew that he had no need to remind his friend of the potential dangers, he did so anyway. Jefferies thanked him for the advice. Roberts also advised his friend of the fact that he had now 'put a tail' on Dick White, as he thought it best to know what his involvement was in all of this. And so, on Monday October 10th, 2004, Malcolm Jefferies reported for duty at Gul Enterprises. Don Rogers introduced him to Brian Dear, informing him that Brian would be the person dishing out his instructions every day. After exchanging a few pleasant words, Dear handed Jefferies a whole wad of collection notes and asked him to follow him to one of the many, identical, and 'unmarked' all-white Transit Connect Vans. Each van bore the same personalized number plate, they were all GUL 17. Brian Dear wished his new addition good luck and told him not to worry if people called him Houdini. Sat in the cab, Jefferies thumbed through the collection notes. He fully expected to be going to Heathrow, Gatwick, Stanstead or maybe an International Airport further afield. In fact, neither of those well-known Airports were mentioned on his notes. His first collection was to be from Stapleford Abbotts, a small but fully operational airport, for light aircraft, close to Romford in Essex. Jefferies was aware of this airstrip, having used it for helicopter surveillance several times during his time with special branch. His next collection would be from North Weald, another small airport, close to his home in Epping and known to him. After that he was to go to Little Baddow airstrip, near to Chelmsford, then north to Hunsdon airstrip,

East to Rayne Hall Farm airstrip, near Braintree, then on to Nayland Airfield, and finally head south to Tillingham Airfield, after which he was to return to the warehouse at Southend. He decided not to ask questions at any of his collection points, he would simply observe. He did not wish to jeopardize everything at this early stage.

Arriving at his first collection point, Stapleford Abbotts Aerodrome, Jefferies was guided to a small warehouse, which was named as Gul Aviation (UK) Ltd. He collected three parcels, each the size of a shoebox, he saw no aircraft. At North Weald, a larger unit, also displaying the name of Gul Aviation (UK) Ltd, he loaded four similar-sized packages into the back of his van. There were several light aircraft parked up. At Little Baddow, a much smaller complex, with a grass landing strip, a single-engine plane was just landing when Jefferies arrived. He waited until the aircraft taxied and stopped at the first of a series of large sheds. He watched as three parcels were offloaded from the plane, there were no others. Moments later all three were put into the back of his van. As he got back behind the wheel, the man that had loaded the parcels smiled and said,

'We hope to see you again, Houdini.'

Malcolm drove off, he had been tempted to ask as to the man's comments but decided to let this unfold without his questioning. There were four more collections to do, at Hunsdon, Rayne Hall Farm, Nayland Airfield and Tillingham Aerodrome. From each he collected two parcels, all from small units bearing the name of Gul Aviation (UK) Ltd. Returning to Southend at around 6.15pm, after collecting sixteen parcels from seven airfields, he was met by the waiting Brian Dear. As he pulled up at Guls' warehouse. Dear said,

'You can piss-off now Houdini, we will unload the van.'

Within minutes of arriving, he was driving back to Maldon. His thoughts, on his way back home, were that he did not need to be a senior police officer or a Mi5 agent to work out that what he had done today was not, in any way 'normal.' However, rather than run various scenarios through his inquisitive mind, he would just work for the rest of the week and then discuss his findings with both Nigel Smalling and Graham Roberts.

Back in the sanctuary of the bungalow, Malcolm fired up his newly acquired laptop and searched for 'UK airfields' he was amazed at what he found. He could not believe just how many small to medium-sized airstrips there were in the UK. Many of them had been given operational status during WW2 but had subsequently ceased operations, however there were still over fifty small and medium airfields that were still active in Essex alone. He had visited seven of them today. Further searching would show him how big each airport was, whether it had a 'paved' or 'grass' landing strip, a control tower, customs, a license to accept flights from outside the UK and so on. By Friday of his first week in the job he had collected from forty-four airfields at locations within Essex, Kent, Hertfordshire, Cambridge, and Suffolk, he never collected more than three parcels from any one of them. Discussing this later, with both Nigel Smalling and Graham Roberts they concluded that it was almost certain that the parcels collected by Jefferies contained drugs. Smalling suggested that Jefferies take, wherever possible, photos of any aircraft that were parked up during his collections.

At the beginning of the second week of his collections, Malcolm took with him the small, but powerful camera that he had been given by Nigel Smalling. It was small enough to conceal inside his lunchbox but powerful enough to take close-ups from at least one hundred yards away. He was able to take random photos whilst eating in the van. By the end of the week he had amassed, unnoticed, over forty photos. On the Saturday he downloaded the photos onto his laptop and then edited them, one by one. Some were of no use as they had not focused on any aircraft, however he had nineteen clear views of the type of aircraft he had photographed and its markings. He sent these to Smalling, whose job it was to identify the owners and the people that may have piloted them. Graham Roberts had been given the task of collating all the airstrips that Jefferies had visited and list them in terms of their size, flights in and out each day and whether they were authorised to accept international flights. Whilst waiting for all this information to be processed and relayed back to him, Jefferies carried on with his daily duties. Every day he was collecting from airstrips further afield, it was sometimes midnight before he arrived back at the Guls' warehouse in Southend. He had ceased to take photos until Smalling reported back to him. After a month, the man in the basement informed him that five of the aircraft that he had photographed were registered in the Netherlands, one in Belgium, another in Germany with the rest being listed as UK owned. This was not really a shock, what was significant however, was that all the aircraft belonged to Gul Aviation (UK) Ltd. As it was not policy to discuss matters with non-Mi5 staff, Jefferies would have to relay conversations he had with Smalling to Graham Roberts and vice-versa. Roberts had informed Jefferies that the EU-registered planes had only landed and took off from airstrips with international approval, customs, and specific radar. They believed these 'mother' planes were bringing many parcels in, at least once a week, they were then split into smaller consignments and carried by single-engine, single pilots to the tiny airstrips that were dotted around the UK. Small vans, such as the one that he drove, then collected those parcels and returned them to base. They knew that there were nine major Gul distribution points around the UK. To the three men closest to this operation, it seemed to be an ingenious method of supplying the whole of the UK with drugs, arms and possibly people as well.

Three weeks after her meeting with Giles Murdoch, the local newspaper editor informed Cheryl Smith that he was going to run a story in the coming week's rag. At lunchtime on Thursday Cheryl walked to Mr Patel's Newsagents on Epping High Street intending to purchase a copy of the Waltham Forest Gazette. Although she had not yet entered the shop, she already knew what the headlines on the front page read. On the A-frame outside the shop, boldly displayed on both sides, were the words,

'Top local Detective goes missing. '

Before she had even left the shop, she had read the rest of the front-page story.

Peter Slade, alias Malcolm Jefferies, having walked to Maldon High Street to buy a Sunday paper, required a large brandy upon his return to the bungalow. The most worrying aspect of the reporting of his disappearance was the fact that the front page contained a picture of him, albeit that it was at least ten years old. Fortunately, he had recently grown a beard and had not had his hair cut for a while. Whilst he knew for certain that he had assumed the identity of the now-dead Sergeant, what he did not know, was that Nigel Smalling had arranged the Sergeant's murder, simply to give him that new identity. As soon as Jefferies alerted Smalling of the news, the man that occupied the basement at Thames House ordered the press not to publish anything relating to the disappearance of Peter Slade, citing 'National Security' as being the reason behind his request. This request was not heeded by the press as by Tuesday of the following week, reporters and TV crews constantly staked out Cheryl Smith's house. They reported that Peter Slade had lived next door and that Cheryl had involved her local paper in trying to find him, as he had vanished without explanation. Cheryl had now become suspect number one, as the police were aware of her involvement with Sergeant Jefferies. She was arrested and taken to Police HQ in Chelmsford for questioning. The media were having a field day, reporting all kinds of conspiracy theories in respect of Slade's disappearance. Whilst she remained a suspect, the Police had no real evidence to support any foul play by the pretty, forty-one-year-old widow. She was released on bail, pending further enquiries. Helen Jefferies was visited, at home, by some very unsavoury people. They demanded that she pay them forty-grand, the amount owed to the loan sharks that her husband had borrowed from them. Of course, she did not have that kind of money, they told her to re-mortgage the house. When she enquired, she was to find that her husband had already done that. There was little or no collateral left in the family home. She reported all of this to the Police, they did not want to know. In sheer desperation, Helen Jefferies sat in her ford galaxy, parked in the attached garage, and turned on the engine. Two hours later, she was no longer.

To take away any risk or suspicion from Jefferies, Mi5 had agreed to allow Graham Roberts to expand his surveillance to include long-range photography of the airstrips that were legally able to accept arrivals from other EU countries. The cameras would not only capture the aircraft's signage but the faces of the pilots as well. After two months of keeping his head down and his questions to a minimum, Jefferies felt that he was being accepted as part of the team at Southend. One evening, returning to the warehouse at around 10.00pm, with only Brian Dear about, he asked the overweight haulage manager as to the reason why people kept referring to him as 'Houdini.' Dear's reply was a stark reminder to Jefferies as to the risks that he was taking,

'Well, Malcolm, all of the other airport drivers have disappeared, you have outlasted all of them.'

Whilst he knew that he should now keep quiet, Jefferies could not resist a second question,

'Disappeared where,' he asked.

Without hesitation, Dear responded,

'Well, they all asked too many questions, after which we never saw them again, hence the nickname, 'Houdini.'

Jefferies knew that he would be overstepping the mark by quizzing his boss any further, he turned and said,

'See you in the morning then unless I disappear during the night.' Brian Dear did not respond.

During the final week of November 2004, Graham Roberts informed his old school chum that Dick White held court in the same garden centre in Cheshunt, almost every day of the week. His modus operandi was almost one hundred percent repetitive. He would arrive, chauffer driven, with two heavies in the back of a black Range Rover, the car was registered to, 'Early Doors Ltd' a company with only one shareholder, Dick White. Drawing a short breath, Roberts continued. Every Wednesday, Bobby Keagan, Jamie Law, and Tony McDonald turn up. They always sit under the covered exterior of the coffee shop, rain, or shine. On other days various identified and not so identified people would arrive. Breakfast and lunch were always paid for by the ex-boxer, David Pegg, who nowadays was very much Dick White's main man. We have managed to check the ownership of eleven of the twenty or so of the top-of-the-range, black Range Rovers, that arrive and leave the garden centre, all are registered to 'Early Doors Ltd.' They are all taxed and insured. The legal ownership, we believe, is to avoid any questioning as to how the drivers were able to afford such expensive vehicles. Dick White's company controls the doors of over seven hundred clubs, all over the UK, and is, to all intents 'legit.' We feel that it is almost certain that there is a link between the clubs and the distribution of drugs. We have never witnessed anything change hands at the coffee shop in the garden centre. However, every Wednesday David Pegg accompanies firstly Keagan, then Law and finally McDonald to the car park. Each man hands Pegg a holdall, which he then places into the boot of his own Mitsubishi Shogun. They then return to the café. We have tapped the owner of the garden centre in respect of bugging the place, however he has not been receptive to our requests, citing loss of business or loss of life, should he be found out. The owner seems to be clean, apart from frequent trips to Asia. Our only chance would be to wire the place up at night as the security at the centre is almost non-existent. Of course, your people would have to carry that out Malcolm. Graham Roberts ended by saying that he hoped to have a report from his men on the stakeout at the Guls' apartment block in Westcliffe, early next week. He should also have some good photos of whom was flying the small aircraft in and out of the various airstrips where he had placed his men.

Half an hour later, Jefferies lifted his pint from the bar of the Ship and Anchor on Maldon High Street and found himself a table in the corner of the room. As he sat, awaiting the arrival of yet another pub dinner, he pondered. What he was involved in was far outstretching his resources. Apart from the backup of Nigel Smalling, cocooned in the basement of Thames House, he had no one else from Mi5 to support him. He gave a weekly report to Julian Pritchard, but the man never seemed to be that interested and he certainly had no real input into what should happen next. It seemed that the ever-increasing manpower that was being supplied by Graham Roberts was to continue without query. There was no suggestion from anyone at Mi5 HQ that the cost of employing non-secret-service people was a problem. Jefferies knew that he would be putting that to the test, as soon, he would need to double the amount of surveillance that he currently had. In addition, he had heard nothing from James Reeves, whose number had been omitted from his secure phone and the name of Quinten Proctor had not come up since Olan Ocalan informed him that the Junior Home Office Minister was in the pocket of the Guls. He wondered, whilst swallowing the last of the Cumberland sausages, exactly how much Mr. Proctor knew of his single-handed investigation. He also concluded that Julian Pritchard must be allowing him to use his own 'outsiders' as stakeout men, as to put any of the Thames House pinstripes at his disposal would not be a good thing to do, as any of them could be working with Proctor. Before he knocked back the large single malt that was to wash down his mediocre meal, his mind extended beyond the UK part of the operation. On the list were various members of the Gul family, located in Belgium, Holland, France, and Germany. In addition, he was supposed to deal with both Abdullah and Olan Ocalan. He had no idea why the McBride's and their father, Sean Porter had been excluded from the list. At some stage he would have to touch base with his counterparts, Alkan Asani and Borislav Topalov, both of their numbers were in his secure phone. His task was immense, he desperately needed help, on the other hand he could not trust anyone. He would have to push Graham Roberts' resources to the limit and wondered if he should ask his old Grammar School mate if he had an international division to his company.

16 - THE PLAN

Jefferies continued with the airstrip collections over Christmas 2004. The festivities did not seem to stem the flow of parcels during the holiday period. During the third week of January 2005, and before he was given his collection notes for the day, he was called into the office of Don Rogers. He presumed that he was in trouble, although he could not pinpoint anything that he had done wrong. He half expected to be given the elbow, although he had been told by Brian Dear that he was the longest surviving 'Houdini' they had ever had. Out of politeness, he knocked on the door. Don Rogers called for him to come in, but it was not Don Rogers that was sat behind the desk, it was Azad Gul. Brian Dear sat to his righthand side and Don Rogers to his left. It was important for him to act surprised, he knew exactly who Azad Gul was, however he must have passed the initial test of ignorance, as he was invited to sit opposite the man that was regarded as 'public enemy number one' within the UK.

Azad held out his hand and introduced himself.

A relieved Jefferies said,

'So, you are my boss, I so enjoy working here Sir.'

In a distinct Arab-sounding tone, Gul replied,

'Well, that's good as we are going to promote you, Malcolm. We would like you to service some of our other depots around the UK. This will require you to sometimes stay over, especially if you take on the Liverpool, Hull, and Glasgow deliveries.'

Inwardly, but not audible to the others in the room, Jefferies let out a cheer, reminiscent of the sound made by one hundred thousand England fans as the final whistle blew to bring the 1966 world cup final to a close.

'I have no problem in staying out Sir, I have no mum to go home to.'

'Well, that's done then. You will deal directly with Don from now on.'

Azad again held out his hand as he got up from his chair and exited via a door in the corner of the room, a door that Jefferies had no idea existed until that moment.

As both Jefferies and Dear left the office, Rogers joined them. Rogers walked Jefferies to the rear of the warehouse, where a dozen Luton Transit vans were parked, they all bore the registration plate GUL 18.

'Tomorrow, you will drive one of these Malcolm, now you can piss off home, as tomorrow you will be going to Glasgow, via Liverpool. The van will be loaded, ready for your departure. You will need to leave here by 5.00am otherwise you will not make it to Glasgow before 6.00pm. Are you OK with that?'

'Absolutely, Don. No problem at all.'

'Oh, by the way, I like the new look, suits you.'

'Thanks, shaving was getting on my nerves.'

Whilst he did not outwardly show it, the undercover agent, on the inside, was as 'pleased as punch' with himself. When he arrived back in Maldon, he made a rare telephone call from his secure phone. Julian Pritchard answered,

'Hello, Gurney.'

At first Jefferies thought that he must have the wrong number, then the penny dropped. 'Gurney' was the codename that Pritchard had given to him just over two and a half years ago. This was the first time that it had been used.

'What can I do for you?' asked the Mi5 supremo.

Jefferies began to explain recent events, Pritchard stopped him short and said,

'I think it best to meet face-to-face, but not here at Thames House, too many prying ears and eyes, how about that nice little pub, where we first met?'

'Yes, OK, I know the one you are thinking of. How about Saturday afternoon?'

'Consider it a date and bring Roberts with you.' Pritchard hung up.

The following morning at 4.45, Jefferies parked the Grand Cherokee up and climbed the stairs of the front-loading bay. He entered the only open door and walked the entire length of the massive warehouse and exited through the fire door. Outside, Don Rogers waited, delivery notes in hand.

'Good morning, Malcolm, I knew that you would not let me down.'

Rogers handed the notes and a set of keys to Jefferies and then informed him that the details of the AA and insurance are in the glove compartment and should he encounter any problems, he should only call him. Finally, Rogers reminded him that he must be in Glasgow by 6.00pm, adding that he would see him on Friday. No other Luton vans had been removed from the compound since yesterday and Jefferies could not but wonder why they all bore the same number plates. He resisted the urge to ask.

Before setting off for Gul International Shipping and Forwarding, Gillibrands Road, Skelmersdale, Jefferies opened the Atlas that had been left on the passenger seat and found a handwritten set of instructions on how to get to his first delivery point. It all seemed too easy, get on the M11, A14, M6 and then the M58 and he was there. The warehouse was set halfway between Liverpool and Manchester. The distance was around two hundred and forty miles and with a short break he should be there around 10.00am.

He arrived in Gillibrands Road just after ten but missed the turn-in to the Guls' warehouse. He stopped outside the perimeter fence and took some random photos. When he approached the loading bay, he was directed around to the back of the building. He pulled up and got out of the cab, he could see a man sat on a deck chair in the far corner of the loading bay. It was now snowing, heavily. Jefferies approached the man that obviously thought he was on his holidays at Morecambe Bay, the man stood up and said,

'Are you Houdini from Essex.'

'Yes.'

'OK, then, go inside and get a brew, I will sort out your load. I am Michael Fowler by the way.'

Jefferies handed Michael Fowler the delivery-note and went inside. He was offered a mug of tea, in a mug that had never seen a washing up bowl, he sat with seven or eight scousers, none of whom he could understand. Ten minutes later, Michael Fowler poked his head around the door and said,

'Houdini, it's about time you disappeared.'

Jefferies got to his feet, bid farewell to his new mates, used the filthiest toilet he had ever seen, noting that even the Karsi in Istanbul was cleaner, and climbed back into the still-warm Transit. He opened the Atlas, to find that his route to Glasgow had been mapped out for him. He was to go to Gul Aviation (UK) Ltd, Walkinshaw Road, Glasgow Airport. He was 215 miles away, his journey would take him three and a half hours, under normal driving conditions, however conditions were far from being normal, as it was now snowing a blizzard.

Arriving in Walkinshaw Road at 4.30pm, a whole six hours after he had left Skelmersdale, Jefferies could not help but notice that Gul Aviation was situated within the perimeter fence of Glasgow International Airport. Unfortunately, darkness had already descended upon the area, it was therefore difficult to get any photographic info. He did note the fact that Gul Aviation was utilising two massive aircraft hangers, beside which, was the Glasgow Flying Club. The snow was now thick on the ground. As he did not wish to get marooned for the night, he got out of the van, battled against the fierce wind and snow, and entered the slightly open, huge doors of the aircraft-hanger. Inside, which was as cold as the outside, he saw lights inside a portacabin, situated halfway down the makeshift warehouse. He could not but notice that the huge 40,000 square-foot facility held hardly any goods. He knocked on the door, a man that looked as though he had eaten the whole of the 'Scots porridge oats' factory, opened it.

'Ahhh, ye must be the young Sassenach from Southend.'

'Yes, that's me, Houdini from Essex.'

'I'll get the doors open and ye can bring the wee van inside,'

Jefferies did as he was asked. No sooner had he stopped the engine, when two men appeared from nowhere, one of them drove a forklift to the tail of the van, whilst the other one jumped into the back and began to load cartons onto a pallet, held aloft by the blades of the fork truck. This was the first time that Houdini had seen any of the cargo that he was delivering. Once the twenty-seven parcels had been unloaded, the fork truck took them to a darkened corner of the hanger and soon after returned with five large crates. He guessed that the crates were heavy, as the large man struggled to load them into the van. The body of the Luton visibly sunk towards the rear wheels once all five crates were on board.

'You are to take these back to Essex Sassenach.'

Said the two-ton Scots man.

'Paperwork,' asked Houdini.

'There is nay any, just hand them over to Don, no one else. Where are you staying tonight?

'I'm not, I am going straight back.'

'Then you had better get going before you are snowed in. All flights in and out of here have been suspended. We have not had a night like this for many a day. The big man shook Houdini's hand.

'I am Jocky Stein, by the way. Maybe see you again?'

Jefferies got into the Luton, drove out onto the snow-covered tarmac, found the exit, turned left onto Walkinshaw Road and ten minutes later he was on the M8, which in turn connected him to the M74 and then onto the M6. He arrived at the Carlisle Travelodge just before 9.00pm. With only fast-food available to him, he opted for McDonald's and then checked into the Hotel for the night. Within minutes, he was pleasantly dreaming about Cheryl Smith.

He left Carlisle at 6.30am, but before he set off, he lifted the shutter at the back of the Luton, climbed in and attempted to lift one of the wooden crates that had been spread out evenly, upon the ply-boarded floor. He could just about lift one end of the smallest crate, he knew these crates did not contain drugs, it was more likely that the inside of these well-secured boxes contained arms and he was to return these to the Gul set-up at Southend. It was no longer snowing, however the roads around the Travelodge were icy, he thought it was good to have such a heavy load in the back of the van as it gave more traction to the rear wheels. His journey back was around 350 miles, in a car it could be done in five hours or so, in a Luton van, battling against a fierce headwind, it took him just under eight, stopping just the once for refreshments and a leak.

Pulling up at the back of Guls' warehouse, at just before 2.30pm, Don Rogers, having presumably seen the van on one of the eight CCTV screens that adorned his office wall, was waiting on the loading bay. Jefferies backed onto the bay, a worker opened the unlocked shutter door and he and another man entered the Luton. They loaded the five crates onto a pallet and a fork truck took them inside the warehouse.

'Good trip, Malcolm? Asked Rogers.

'Not bad, apart from the snow, I suppose.'

'Well, you could be seeing a lot more of that bloody Scottish weather in the future. You may as well go home now and no need to come back until next Wednesday, but don't worry, you are being well rewarded.'

As he finished the sentence Rogers handed Jefferies an envelope and said,

'There is a little bit extra, to cover your expenses.'

He took the envelope, walked to the side of the warehouse, and got into the jeep. Before he pulled away, he opened the envelope and counted the wad of twenty-pound notes. He had been given a thousand pounds, a grand, for two days work. Maybe I should resign from Mi5 he thought to himself as he drove along the A127 towards home.

When he awoke on Saturday morning, Jefferies set about making notes that he could refer to at the meeting with Pritchard and Roberts. During the long, lonely drive home from Carlisle, his head had been filled with all kinds of questions, answers, and probabilities. He felt that he should put all that he could, down on paper, for discussion later. Roberts called him at around 10.00am, he had some news in respect of Mustafa Gul's movements. Roberts told Malcolm that there had been news from his men that were staking out the Guls' apartment block. Mustafa Gul had left at 10.15 the previous evening, he was then driven to Stapleford Abbotts Aerodrome where he boarded a six-seater aircraft. Two crates, that had to be lifted on board by two men, accompanied him and the pilot. They managed to get near enough to identify the plane's markings. I have this morning spoken to Rob Liddiard, that ginger haired bully from our school days, believe it or not he is now the Chief Air Traffic Controller at Stansted. I ran the call sign of the plane that Gul took, past him and ten minutes later he confirmed that the aircraft had filed its flight path and destination as being that of Cuxhaven/Nordholtz Airport, a military base that shares its single runway with civil aviation. It is situated on the coast of Germany and is a two-hour drive to Hamburg. The plane loaded two crates at Stapleford Abbotts, they were manifested as, 'ships-spares.' They were not subject to any customs checks and Liddiard reports that no other passengers boarded.

For your information Malcolm, Cuxhaven is close to Bremerhaven, a major ship repairing yard. I thought I had better tell you this before our meeting this afternoon.

'Thanks for the heads-up, Graham, see you later.'

At 2.30pm on Saturday the 29th, January 2005, Jefferies entered the Merry Fiddlers, close to the house that he still owned but had not lived in for three years. Graham Roberts was stood, holding up the bar. Julian Pritchard, whom Malcolm had spotted sat in his Mercedes in the car park of the pub, arrived two minutes later. He had no doubt been staking out the place, looking for uninvited guests.

The three men sat in the far corner of this popular and busy pub. Pritchard invited his underling to give his account of events to date. Glancing down at his extensive notes, Jefferies began.

'Nearly four months ago I was able to secure a driving job at Gul Enterprises. For almost all that time I have been collecting parcels from small provincial airports and taking them back to the Guls set up at Southend. Early on, with Roberts' help, we identified both Azad and Mustafa Gul, both are regular visitors to the warehouse. Mustafa stays at the Guls' apartment block in Westcliffe, when in the UK. Normally, he lives just outside Hamburg. Azad lives with his wife and three children in a heavily secured house in one of Brentwood's most sought-after neighbourhoods. Mustafa's two daughters live with them. We have photographed two men, previously unknown to me, they are Ozturk Ozsoy, from Kurdistan and Nur Nazif, also of Kurdish extraction, currently fronting as the leader of a mosque in Finsbury Park. Parcels, that we presume to have been drugs, have been photographed being loaded into Azad Gul's Range Rover. Through Smalling's comprehensive portfolio, we have identified Bobby Keagan, Jamie Law, and Tony McDonald. We are aware of where all three operate from and reside. In addition to their drug business, we have reason to believe that all three men, plus the Guls, are involved in arms and the art of smuggling illegals into the UK for use in the growing of weed, pickpocketing, and prostitution.'

Dick White, a name that I am sure you will recognise, meets with Keagan, Law, and McDonald on a regular basis at a garden centre in Cheshunt. We do not believe that Mr. White has any direct involvement in the drug business, however we have a tail on him and will inform you of any developments. Apart from their Shipping, Forwarding, Warehousing and apartment business, the Guls also own many small aircraft, we do not yet know the exact number, however the ones that we do know about are all registered to Gul Aviation (UK) Ltd. They range in size from single-engine, two-seaters to twin-engine jets that can carry both passengers and small amounts of freight. Some of the airstrips they use are larger than others. Some have customs on-site, however there is no record of any wrongdoing being attributed to the Guls. This leads us to believe that customs officers and certain individuals within these airstrips are on their payroll.

This week I was 'promoted' I now deliver much larger consignments than I previously collected. Thus far I have delivered to the Guls' shipping business near Liverpool and to Gul Aviation in Glasgow. I believe the deliveries to be drugs. Liverpool, Glasgow, and Hull, which I have not yet visited are the main distribution hubs and are run by the three men that I have mentioned earlier. Roberts monitors the movements of each of them. I brought back from Glasgow a consignment of five heavy wooden crates. It is safe to assume that the crates contained arms and ammo. It is my strong belief that I delivered what I had previously collected, that is the drugs that arrived via the numerous airstrips that the gang utilise. I have learnt from Mr. Roberts today that Mustafa Gul boarded a six-seater jet at Stapleford Abbott just last night and according to our intel, he arrived at Cuxhaven/Nordholzt Airport in Germany about one hour and fifteen minutes later.

Gul took with him two of the crates that I had brought back from Glasgow. At present we have Azad and Mustafa Gul, Bobby Keagan, Jamie Law, Tony McDonald, Dick White, Ozturk Oszoy and Nur Nazif all under surveillance, 24/7. Roberts has allocated four men to monitor each person we are looking at. In total we are utilising thirty-two undercover civilians, the cost of each man is five hundred pounds per twelve-hour shift. This equates to sixteen grand per day, and I bring this to your attention so that you can avoid a heart attack when I submit Roberts' bill for payment. The final pages of Smalling's notebook show Abdullah and Olan Ocalan as being on the 'hit list' whereas I was under the impression that once we had hunted down and taken out the Guls, the Ocalan's would be filling the void left by their fellow countrymen. Am I to assume that this is no longer the case, Sir?

Finally, there is no mention of the McBride Brothers or their father, Sean Porter. It was my belief that those three were an integral part of our investigation, do I not pursue those bastards, Sir?

Looking over at Graham Roberts, Julian Pritchard asked him,

'So, what is your take on all of this?'

'Well Julian,' Jefferies smiled, as protocol dictated that he called Julian, Mr. Pritchard, or Sir, whereas his one-time fellow opening bowler at Grammar School was free to use Christian names.

'Well Julian, you have given my old playmate a massive task, a task that no one could possibly undertake alone. He has done remarkably well to gather all the information that he has outlined to you. If you are unable to provide back up from within your organisation, and I fully understand why you can't, then HM Government is going to have to foot a bill that is far more than anything that you or I have ever worked on before. I believe, from my years of experience, that so far, we have only scratched the surface. Jefferies has been given, not only the UK arm of this vast and dangerous organisation to pursue, but he also has the added burden of infiltrating and bringing down the gangs that operate, ruthlessly, throughout Europe. We could be looking at having to put two hundred, or more, of the finest investigators on the payroll. I will work with and look out for Malcolm for as long as you want me to. I will keep you informed of the cost, as we go along.'

Roberts had finished, Julian Pritchard began.

'Gentlemen, firstly, I must congratulate you both for achieving so much in such a short space of time. I am a little surprised that Dick White seems to be involved. Ozturk Ozsoy and Nur Nazif are known to me. In fact, Ozsoy and Nazif have been under our radar for some time. I use Alkan Asani and Borislav Topalov to watch these two vagabonds. Asani and Topolov were recruited by Mi5 to hunt down and bring to justice, in conjunction with our counterparts in Europe, some of the people that head up the gangs in Turkey, Albania, and Bulgaria. We do have an agreement with the Ocalan's to undertake the eradication of everyone that we finger, however that is an agreement that we could never allow to happen. I hope that answers your question, Malcolm? Asani and Topolov are currently in the UK, watching Ozturk, Nazif and Mustafa Gul, who, as you have confirmed Malcolm, flits between the UK and Germany. Graham, I am not sure if the men that watch the apartments in Westcliffe have told you or not, but Mustafa Gul has three or four 'girlfriends' there. They are all from Asia and all are illegals.'

Asani reports that up to thirty girls work the apartments, earning the Guls tens of thousands of pounds every week. We are not interested in this as an investigation now, however during your investigation, you may well get to the bottom of this and the many other houses of sex that this gang operates. As far as your costs are concerned Graham, it will be a small price to pay if we are to eradicate these people from our society. The cost to the taxpayer for police investigations, deaths, hospitalization, human misery, and social care far exceeds what you may charge us, even allowing for two hundred employees. There are two reasons for not being able to keep this 'in-house' firstly we simply do not have the manpower, without going cap in hand to our colleagues at New Scotland Yard, and secondly, we cannot go to the Home Office, as the traitor in our midst, is of course the Junior Minister, Quinten Proctor.' Ultimately the 'plan' to bring all these unsavoury characters to book, lies with the both of you. Smalling, apart from myself, is the only person within Mi5 to know of this operation, he has carte blanche authority to assist, wherever he can. For anything outside of his remit, he will come to me. Finally, Malcolm, I will put Asani and Topolov in touch with you.

Before I finish up, Malcolm, there is one problem that we may need to deal with in the future. It is the problem of your exposure as being a missing undercover agent. Whilst I can see that you have made every attempt to disguise your features, I think it is fair to say that to anyone who knows you well, you are still recognisable as Peter Slade. Presumably, no one within the Gul organisation has had any reason to query your identity, had they done so then I am sure that you would not be sat here today. Having said that, it will be of no real surprise should you be 'outed' by someone familiar to you. I have personally spoken to the editors of the papers that ran your story and in the interest of national security, they have agreed to put the story on ice, at least for now.

'Goodbye to you both.'

Julian Pritchard picked up his keys and left.

Graham Roberts being fond of a good red wine, tiptoed to the bar and brought back a bottle of the most expensive Malbec and two glasses, he poured two large glasses, sat, and said,

'Now tell me Peter,'

Malcolm looked around the pub, anxiously. In reply, he whispered,

'Please try not to do that Graham, you never know who might be listening.'

Apologetically, the private eye responded with,

'Yes, I am sorry, it's just difficult to think that you are someone else when you are sat with me, it will not happen again.'

'What I was going to ask you Malcolm', was,

'Can you explain the situation with the McBride's, their father and Proctor as I don't seem to be in the loop on this.'

Jefferies explained all that he could about Sean Porter, the fact that he was a terrorist and possibly supplied the Semtex that blew his car apart, with his wife and two daughters, inside. He added that Porter was once, Michael O'Leary, who had fled the UK with his new identity and had not seen his twin boys from their birth in 1962 until he met up with them in 1997. He had originally moved to Spain but ended up in Bulgaria in 1971. Once reunited with his sons, who run a large International Trucking Company from Belfast, he introduced them to similar companies in Bulgaria, Romania, and Turkey and for the last eight years or so they have cooperated with some nasty people in the former iron curtain countries. I was investigating them for transiting arms to Ireland, however, as you know, I got detained in Turkey and was not reintroduced to that investigation once I regained my freedom.

Porter seems to flit freely between Belfast, Dublin and Varna, the latter being his place of residence. I have a strong feeling that all three are involved in the arms, drugs and the people smuggling business. As for Quinten Proctor, I met him at Thames House, he is a typical sweaty palmed Civil Servant, he holds the rank of junior Minister, attached to Mi5. He is the mole within the secret service. I have been 'warned off' as far as pursuing these four people are concerned, so there must be something much bigger going on. Although I cannot imagine what could be bigger than what we are doing right now.'

Graham, replenishing his friend's glass, thanked the man that he had occasionally played truant from school with and began his response.

'We must plan Malcolm. If we are to bring down an organised crime unit, possibly the largest, and most ruthless in Europe, if not the entire world, then we must construct an A to Z of exactly how we are going to achieve our goal. From what you have just told me, somehow, we must trap this Quinten Proctor bloke. I will put somebody on him, I will also get some surveillance on the McBride's and their father. Pritchard need not know, at least for now, but you must agree to stay well-away from it, although I will update you at every opportunity. Now, I have a second house. It's in Poplar, nothing fancy, but its, good for public transport. I inherited it from my Uncle Sam, you might remember him, he always watched us play football and cricket. I use the house if I want to get close to the action. This protects her indoors and the kids from anything sinister. I have firearms and all kinds of surveillance equipment there. We should use that place as our command centre and as you are not required to work on Monday, we should meet there, its number 38 Oban Street, just off Abbotts Road. Never write that down Malcolm, make sure you are not followed, and bring some food and drink with you, it could be a long day.'

Roberts knocked back the last of his vino and left. Jefferies sat, purposely, to observe if anyone had followed his boyhood friend out the door. Nobody immediately left with him. He had parked the jeep at the far end of the car park. Something he had always done, this way he would walk past every other car, noting if anyone was sat inside. If he spotted someone in a parked car, he would not leave until they did. His departure would sometimes be delayed if one of the pub's patrons was shagging one of the barmaids in the back of his car. On this occasion, he saw no sign of life as he passed all the parked cars. He started the jeep and made his way back to Maldon.

At 8.30pm, after consuming Maldon's finest Chinese takeaway, Jefferies hesitantly picked up the secure phone and called one of the numbers already plumbed in by Nigel Smalling.

'Who is this?

'It's Gurney.'

'Ah, I have been expecting your call. Mr. Pritchard advised that I was likely to be contacted, how are you, Gurney? Asked Alkan Asani.

'I am fine thanks, are you still in the UK, I heard that you were here, keeping tabs on a man in a mosque'.

'Yes, Gurney, I am still here.'

'Can we meet then? Preferably on Monday morning.

'Yes, of course. Where and at what time.'

'At Bromley-by-Bow Underground, say 8.00am.'

'That would be perfect. Do you want me to bring Borislav along, Gurney?

'Oh, so he is also still in the UK as well. It would be good to meet him. I will explain our itinerary when we meet.

'OK then, see you on Monday. I will be the one with the Camel.'

Jefferies phoned Graham Roberts and explained what he had set up. Roberts asked as to the trustworthiness of the two additions to their meeting.

'Well, all I can say is that both Pritchard and my old boss, Commander Reeves afford them the highest of recommendations.'

Sat at his study desk, Jefferies had been thumbing the card that had been left for him on the day that he moved into the bungalow. He knew that the card was not altogether kosher, as it combined three of the names of Estate Agents in Maldon High Street, however the names were jumbled, not as they were shown on the shop fronts. Rather timidly he tapped in the number shown for Johnnie Holden. Commander James Reeves answered and said,

'Are you in trouble, Peter?'

Totally surprised, Jefferies replied,

'No, not yet anyway. I had no idea that it would be you at the other end of this call Commander.'

'Well Peter, you should have paid more attention to the words that were written on the 'stick-it' note, and by the way, to you I am James. I am no longer your commander, consider me to be your guardian.'

'Noted. I thought you were no longer part of this melee, James. And by the way, I am Malcolm.

'I have no real input into your investigation Malcolm however I am kept up to speed by Pritchard. In fact, he called me earlier and updated me on your meeting with him and Philip Marlowe. It seems that you are moving on at a rate of knots, well done. By the way, Asani and Topolov report to me. They are working on Ozsoy and Nazif, however Pritchard and I believe that the two investigations can now be pursued as one, this will give you good people to help you in what is fast becoming, possibly the biggest thing ever to cross Mi5's desk.'

There was some light-hearted banter for ten minutes or so, then James Reeves informed Malcolm that he had to go, but that he was there for him, should ever the occasion arise.

At 7.50am on Monday, 31st January 2005, Malcolm Jefferies pulled up in the layby, meant only for buses, outside Bromley-by-Bow underground Station. At 7.54, a small crowd of people exited, two men stood out like nuns in a brothel. Jefferies could spot an undercover man from a mile away and here he was blessed with the sight of two together. Gesturing from his wound-down window, the two men came over, one got into the front passenger seat and the other sat behind him. Before they moved off, Alkan Asani held out his hand, Jefferies accepted it, and the two men shook as though they were lifelong friends.

'I am Alkan Asani, in the back, where he belongs, is Borislav Topolov.' The Bulgarian nodded in acknowledgement.

Having studied his London A to Z, Jefferies pulled onto the A12, reached the roundabout at Bow, and minutes later passed Bromley-by-Bow station, which was now on the opposite side of the road. Five minutes later he parked up in Oban Street, Poplar. He knocked on the door of number 38 by means of a large black lion, that must have hung on the door for at least fifty years. He noticed that the door contained four 'deadbolts' Roberts had previously told him that E14 was no longer the safe haven that it had once been. Roberts opened the door, the three visitors stepped into the narrow hallway, Jefferies did the introductions.

'Please go upstairs, I will bring the tea up with me.'

Whilst he had not seen the downstairs of this 1890s constructed house, with its Victorian bay window and matching masonry, if the upstairs was anything to go by then it must be impressive, thought Jefferies. The two top-floor rooms, which must have seen plenty of action as bedrooms in days gone by, were knocked into one. Ten TV screens were fixed to the largest wall. The perimeter of the room was decked out with worktops, shelving, and cupboards. Computers, screens, printers, walkie-talkies, and other electronic equipment covered almost the entirety of the worktops. There was a large table, with six chairs surrounding it, right bang in the middle of the room. If ever Jefferies had doubted his lifelong friend's prowess as a 'super sleuth' his doubts were now well and truly put to bed. Roberts entered the room, and the tea was handed out. Along the entire length of another wall was a completely blank 'white board' a small pile of different coloured 'stick-its' sat atop one of the printers. In many ways, this was a better-equipped office than the one at Thames House, thought Jefferies.

Like many business meetings, where the attendees are meeting for the very first time, Roberts suggested that each of them provides, a short resume of who they are and where they are, as far as their current task was concerned. Of course, Roberts knew exactly who and where Jefferies was. His suggestion was purely to extract whatever he could from the two foreign-looking men representing Mi5. Asani was invited to speak first.

'I am Alkan Asani, born in Mardin, Turkey in 1960. My parents brought me to the UK, quite legally, when I was nine years old, and I became a British Citizen. In 1980 I joined the Metropolitan Police and being of Turkish origin, I was asked to transfer to drug enforcement in 1997. At the time, my remit was to act as though I was a small-time dealer, doing the street corners of North London. During my growing up years my parents spoke in their native language, which is a mix of standard Turkish and Kurd. I have managed to get close to Kagan Kaptan, the archenemy of the Gul clan. Kaptan works with Ozturk Ozsoy in the mountains of Kurdistan, not far from where I was born. When I was asked, by Mr. Pritchard to return to my homeland to watch Ozsoy, I readily agreed. Ozsoy makes many trips to the UK, almost all of them go unrecorded, with the help of the Guls, he flies in and out without going through passport control. I now have a lot of intel on him and at the request of Mr. Pritchard and Mr. Reeves, I am at your disposal.' There were no questions from either Roberts or Jefferies. They both considered this man to be an unexpected asset to their cause.

Borislav Topalov, explained that he had been born in a small village, just outside the Bulgarian Capital of Sofia. He was now 43, spoke fluent Bulgarian, Turkish and Arabic, his English, by his own admission was the weakest of the four languages that he spoke. Jefferies and Roberts looked at each other when he made that statement, as to them, he was a lot more coherent than a Geordie or a Brummie. He, like Asani had joined the Met Police, and was subsequently seconded to the drug department, where he now works, 'undercover.' He was originally sent to Varna, to follow the exploits of the Petrov gang and then to Istanbul, where most of the heroin is transited through. Recently a General Kos has come to his attention, together with a certain Tayser Malik, he was trying to piece together a worthwhile surveillance on all of them, when he was asked by Mr. Pritchard to help Asani, which meant dropping all of what he was working on, to gather information on Nazif. Jefferies was the first to speak after Topolov had finished, his brief, but revealing resume.

'So, you have intel on General Kos, Boyan Petrov and Tayser Malik, as well as the Gul members within the EU? Asked the impressed Chief Superintendent.

'Yes, I most certainly do.

'Well, my friend, I believe all these people are, in some way connected. Today we shall take the first steps towards finding this out.'

Roberts intervened, asking Jefferies to go through the notes and photographs that had been given to him by Nigel Smalling and as he did so he (Roberts) would make notes upon the vast white board that covered the wall behind him.

'Well, here we go.' said Jefferies.

'And please interject should you have questions or should I miss something out.'

AZAD GUL: Regarded as the Kingpin of the drug distribution business in the UK, he took over from Birusk Gul when he was jailed. Righthand man of Azad Gul is Yusuf Kaya. He is thought to be responsible for at least seventeen gangland murders and numerous other offences. The Guls run many legitimate businesses, but the important ones, as far as our investigation is concerned, are, warehousing, distribution, logistics, aviation, and an employment agency. The illegal side of their business is vast, it includes, people smuggling, drug importation and distribution, extortion, brothels, money laundering, loan sharking, and arms dealing. We are told that the Junior Minister, Quinten Proctor is in their pocket and that many high-ranking police officers are on the payroll. They have formed tight partnerships with violent gangs headed by Bobby Keagan in Liverpool, Jamie Law in Glasgow, and Tony McDonald in Hull. Between them they are said to control ninety percent of the UK drug market. Nazif, fronting as the leader of North London's largest Mosque, takes in and nurtures Kurds that have been smuggled into the UK from the battlefields of Kurdistan, some of them have a connection to General Kos.

Jefferies sipped the dregs of his teacup and looked at Roberts, his queue to make some more.

'A good time for a toilet break.' said Asani.

Ten minutes later, Jefferies resumed.

'Further afield, the Guls have associations with both the Ocalan's and their own family in Turkish Kurdistan. Ozsoy is a recent visitor to the Guls. He is known to bat for both the Guls and the Kaptan's. We know for certain that the drugs arrive at various, small airstrips around the UK, in planes owned and operated by the Guls. Distribution within the UK seems to be from their warehouse in Southend, directly into their set-ups in Liverpool, Glasgow, and Hull. I now have the job of delivering these drugs every week.'

Asani and Topolov looked at each other in amazement.

Roberts intervened,

'Oh yes, Malcolm is very resourceful. By the way, we have surveillance on both Azad Gul and Yusuf Kaya.'

Roberts pointed at the photos of these men, already stuck to the board.

Jefferies carried on.

''The Gul gang control a vast area, the whole of the Southwest, the Home Counties and Greater London.

'I will now move on to BOBBY KEAGAN: He has run the Northwest of the UK for the last four to five years. From Liverpool, he operates North to Cumbria, South to Gloucestershire and East to Leicestershire. He also controls the whole of Wales. He became the main man at the age of 21. His number two is Sammy Yeats, a man in his fifties, he will fight anyone and has the scars to prove it. Suspected of several murders, he likes to dispose of his victims in acid baths. He is a close associate of Dick White, once the UK's 'most wanted' we do not believe that Mr. White is involved in the drug or slavery business, although he does like a gun. He provides protection at most of the UK's nightclubs. Unfortunately for Bobby Keagan, he has no legit businesses that we know of. He would not be able to account for his wealth. The Keagan gang is estimated to have over a thousand children, under the age of fourteen, doing the corners. Both Keagan and Yeats are under 24/7 surveillance.' Roberts stuck mug shots of Keagan and Yeats to the board.

JAMIE LAW was born into the criminal world by default. The son of crack addicts, he has been done for torture, extortion, pimping, murder and thirty-three other offences. He has spent fourteen of his thirty-two years behind bars but has been out for the last six. Was first banged up aged twelve. He is six foot five, a body builder and weighs just under twenty stone. Currently sells drugs obtained from Azad Gul, runs the prostitution scene in all Scotland's major cities, boasts a fully armed gang of over twenty full-time members. Law's number two is Davy McQueen, whose entire family is involved in one way or another with the gang, known as 'The Law Firm.' They run the whole of Scotland and are responsible for eighty percent of the drug-related deaths North of the Border. Jamie Law, with money lent to him by his father-in-law, Jimmy Laidlaw, launders his ill-gotten gains through several car dealerships that he owns throughout the UK. Both Law and McQueen are under our watch, Graham, the mug shots please.

TONY MCDONALD is a real anomaly. He should not really be in this business at all. He saved Bobby Keagan's life whilst studying medicine at Liverpool University. He took a shine to the highlife, enjoyed by Keagan, and set up shop in Hull. He is known as the 'posh pusher' does not do violence, has no record, and is an astute businessman. Half of his family work in private clinics, which he has funded. He also owns Hull's world-renowned sweet factory and several bookies, which is where he cleans his cash. Has no number two, that we are aware of. He also has the same deal with the Guls as Keagan and Law do. The current depravation in Hull is largely due to McDonald's drug dealing. Although we watch him 24/7, we have not been able to pin anything on him. Controls the area to the North-East of the Scottish border, West to Nottingham and as far South as Cambridge and Suffolk. Close-up pictures going up now, please Graham.

DICK WHITE: As you can see from this photo, not a man to be messed with. We do not believe him to be mixed up in the drug business. We watch him and his number two 24/7. He has weekly meetings with Keagan, Law, and McDonald. His legit 'doormen' business seems to stop anyone but our three gang leaders from operating in almost all the UK's night clubs and selected bars. David Pegg, whose photo Graham is adding now, is Dick White's long-time associate, we are following these two as they may just lead us elsewhere. Mr. White is subject to a separate investigation by our friends from the organised crime unit at New Scotland Yard, however in time-honoured tradition we do not share intel with them, and they reciprocate accordingly.

'Now that I have filled you in on the UK side of things, I would like Alkan and you, Borislav, to update us on what you have been doing in Europe since your respective assignments began. But before that, I think we should take a food and drink break.'

After lunch, Alkan Asani, the 45-year-old British Citizen, albeit Turkish by birth, with the rugged and menacing looks that one would expect an unshaven, black-haired, olive-skinned man to look like, began.

'I have been undercover in Europe and the Middle East for just over two years. I was, like Malcolm, plucked from Special Branch by Mr. Pritchard and asked to befriend anyone that had connections with the Gul family in Kurdistan. I returned to my village, near Mardin. I played the part of being a buyer of heroin, just small time and was soon introduced to one of Ozturk Oszoy's people. Whilst Oszoy was beyond my reach, I learnt through some of the hundreds of gang members that he not only sourced for the Guls, but he also had connections to Kagan Kaptan. Once it was known that I had an allegiance with Oszoy and Kagan it was impossible for me to be friendly with the Guls. My attention became focused upon Oszoy and his frequent trips to the UK, often using the Guls' transport system arriving here undetected. The Kaptan's and the Guls share one objective, to wipe each other out, although they also cooperate with each other, when it suits them. In recent times the trade in people smuggling has increased ten-fold, and this has brought to my attention the Irish brothers, the McBride's and their father, Sean Porter, however I have been told to concentrate on the arms and drug side of their criminal activities.

Both Roberts and Jefferies thanked Asani for his input. Roberts added the photograph of Kagan Kaptan, handed to him by Asani, to the board. As one, they all looked at Borislav Topolov. He was 43, clean-shaven, smartly dressed and as thin as a rake. The Bulgarian explained that originally, he had been sent to his native Bulgaria to follow the exploits of the Petrov gang. Unlike Asani he had not infiltrated any gang, he had instead operated at arms-length. As a one-time keen amateur photographer, he had amassed hundreds of photos and where possible he had managed to put a name to them. From Sofia he had followed the heroin trial backwards and had spent some time in Istanbul. He was in Amman when asked to help Asani with the surveillance of Oszoy and Nazif, however before leaving he managed to find out that the Syrian arms and drug dealer, Tayser Malik was having a meeting with a man that ran a whole army from his complex in the hills of Kosovo/Albania, the man was the one-time commander of the Kosovan army, General Kos.

Topolov handed photos of these two men to Roberts, who promptly stuck them to the board. Topolov went on to say that Malik, who now resided permanently in Jordan, had direct access to the poppy fields in Afghanistan and through the intricate transport system that was fully owned by the gangs, he was able to move any contraband as far as Bulgaria, where upon it came under the control of the Petrov's. He finished by saying that he would return to Jordan once his time in the UK was over.

It was now 5.20pm, Asani and Topolov indicated that they should be getting back to their respective surveillance tasks. Roberts and Jefferies thanked them for their time and asked that they return on Saturday, as hopefully Roberts will have organised the board into a sequence of events upon which they could base the future of their joint operation. They all shook hands, Jefferies indicated that he would run them back to the underground station and then he would retreat to Maldon. Roberts asked that he return to Oban Street after the station 'drop-off' as he had arranged to meet someone that may well be of interest to him.

At 5.50pm, Jefferies returned to Roberts' house, a cab was waiting outside. Before Jefferies could re-enter the house, Roberts took his arm and guided him into the cab.

'Abbey Arms, Canning Town,' were Roberts' instructions to the Asian driver.

The driver, looking puzzled, lifted the microphone and asked his Bangladeshi controller as to the geographical location of Canning Town. Roberts, originally from Canning Town, London E16, himself, dropped his guard and in a raised voice, said to the driver,

'Call yourself a fucking cabbie,' we don't want to go to Beirut, it's just Canning Town, over the bridge.'

Turning his head toward his two back seat passengers, the driver replied,

'The bridge' what 'fucking bridge?'

With the words, for fucks sake leaving his mouth, Roberts was out of the cab. Jefferies followed. They got into Roberts' Saab, parked opposite, in the space that cost him the best part of three grand a year and drove the mile or so to the Abbey Arms, on the corner of Barking Road and Balaam Street. The Saab had to be parked 100 yards away, on a yellow line, in a part of London where it was just not advisable to leave an unattended vehicle.

At 6.10pm, Monday January 31st, 2005, the old school friends walked into the saloon bar of one of the East End's oldest pubs.

Growing up, the Abbey Arms and the several pubs along Barking Road had been Graham Roberts' local drinking holes. Jefferies, as Peter Slade, had enjoyed a less common upbringing and had, therefore, never stepped inside this one-time gin palace. The bar was quite busy, mainly because it was one of the few surviving pubs still open for business in 2005. The local immigrant population did not frequent such places. As they made their way past the people that were stood at the bar, Roberts led his partner in the fight against crime, to a small round table at the far end. A floor-to-ceiling oak and stained-glass panel divided the salon bar from the public one. A lone man was sat at the table, Jefferies mind flashed back to that day, in 1980, when several policemen entered his classroom at Coopers Grammar School and took away the, then 16-year-old, Paul Walters. Now, some 25 years later, Jefferies immediately recognised one of the most notorious of his school mates.

'Walters, you old bastard, how long have you been out?

'Well Peter, I have been out, then in, then out and so on. Since my first arrest I have spent only five years outside of HM Custody.'

Jefferies, smiling, replied,

'You got fourteen, didn't you? For the manslaughter of Mr. Cable?'

'Yes, I did, Peter, but I was out in nine. The thing was, I hated Chemistry, but I hated Cable even more.

To be run over several times by your own car is quite funny, don't you think?'

'Well, maybe funny is not the correct word, Paul. Tragic would be more fitting.'

'Anyhow, I have no idea why Roberts has brought me here to meet with you after a 25-year absence, however I am sure that I am going to find out.'

Roberts, having returned from the bar with three pints of what looked like, washing up water, sat in the middle of the two men, one a murderer of his chemistry teacher and now a career criminal, whilst the other was highly regarded as being one of the UK's most prominent policemen. He wondered just how Walters had, with a good education and upbringing, become what he had.

'Firstly Paul, Peter is now Malcolm.'

Walters gulped before he replied,

'Well, I suppose it's better than being Mandy.'

Roberts continued,

'Believe it or not Malcolm, Walters has undertaken some dangerous undercover work for me, that is, whenever he is not on the wrong side of the bars. I feel that he could be useful in our current campaign, after all, look at him, does he look as though he has an ounce of intelligence? The answer is no. I think that because he is intelligent and no one would suspect him of being so, he just might be able to get inside places that you and I can't, what do you think Malcolm?'

Malcolm, holding back full-blown laughter, replied,

'And what exactly do you have in mind for our most inglorious of school mates?'

'I have not yet decided the role he will play, but by the time that you and the others return to the house on Saturday, I will have it all worked out.'

As one, the three, one-time classmates clinked their almost empty glasses together.

Several pints later and after chewing over 'old times' they left the Abbey Arms. Neither of them would ever return.

Paul Walters meandered along the Barking Road until he reached his one room bedsit, above the Chinese takeaway, named, 'Woks up Doc'.

Roberts and Jefferies returned to the Saab, only to find that as all four wheels were missing and the body was resting on house bricks, they might find it difficult to drive home. From his mobile, Roberts called the cab office, ten minutes later the Asian driver from earlier in the evening pulled up.

'So, you do know where Canning Town is after all.'

Cleaning a large blob of wax from his right ear, the Bangladeshi replied,

'Oh, I thought you said, 'Camden Town. '

'Never mind, take us back to Oban Street.'

Five minutes later they passed the turn-off for Oban Street.

'What the fuck are you doing '?

'I am going to Holborn Street, is it, City of London,'

'Stop the 'fucking car ', bellowed the private eye.

The man from Chittagong hit the brakes. Jefferies, not wearing his seat belt and half-asleep, was flung forward, he headbutted the headrest of the passenger seat.

'Bet that woke you up.' Roberts, laughing, said.

Roberts got out of the car, opened the driver's door, and invited the man that could get lost in his own front room, to get out of the car.

Zakir Hasan duly obliged.

Roberts sat in the driver's seat, with its brightly coloured mat of a thousand 'cut in half' golf balls, bowed to the miniature god that was stuck firmly to the dashboard and drove away. Five minutes later he parked up in Leven Road and he and a rather unsteady Malcolm Jefferies walked back to 38 Oban Street.

'You can stay here tonight Malcolm you are in no fit state to be driving.'

Malcolm did not argue with his friend's advice.

The following morning, the two men had a brief discussion about how they should proceed from here. Roberts asked that Jefferies allow him to lay out a chronological plan for the operation that lay ahead. Jefferies agreed, adding that he would update his friend on Friday in respect of what may, or may not be relevant after his deliveries in the next few days.

17 - THE OPERATION

At 4.45am on Wednesday 2nd, February 2005, Jefferies parked his Grand Cherokee right next to Don Rogers Audi A5 and climbed the steps onto the loading bay at the rear of the Guls' warehouse in Southend. As in the previous week, Rogers handed Jefferies the notes and explained that the load may feel a little heavier, as in the back were three large crates, which had to go to Hull. It was still bitterly cold, Malcolm started the engine and sat for a while, waiting for the heat to rise-up from the footwell. Looking at the notes, he could see that he would be delivering to Hull, Birmingham and finally Liverpool. As before, Rogers had left him handwritten instructions, which he would later add to last weeks as they could possibly be used in evidence, one day. Driving the Luton slowly down the exposed side of the warehouse, due to the very icy conditions, he arrived at the front. There was no loading or unloading going on at that time of the morning, however there was an official-looking, black Jaguar, which must just have arrived as a chauffeur was holding the rear door open. Slowing, almost to a stop, he saw a suited and booted man climb out of the back seat, he was shaking hands with Azad Gul. He had met the man only once, that was in the meeting room at Thames House, the man was, without doubt, Junior Home Office Minister, Quinten Proctor.

The journey time to Hull had been calculated by Don Rogers, he had written 'estimated time of arrival' at 9.00am. The route was simple, M11, A1, M18, M62 and A63. Gul Shipping and Forwarding was to be found along Saxon Way, in the Hessle area of the North-East's largest Port. The van pulled into a large square of terraced warehouses, Jefferies could see the Gul property directly in front of him, it was much smaller than the warehouses in Liverpool and Glasgow and as there were two trailers occupying the small loading bays, he stopped, directly facing the offices, which were on the first floor of the building. He did not spot the camera that took his photo as he sat in his cab, waiting for one of the trailers to leave. He also failed to see the large, blue Mercedes van, with its darkened side windows and two occupants, that was parked in the road opposite the entrance to the Industrial Park. Ten minutes after arriving, he reversed onto the loading bay and presented his notes to a man that was keen to receive them. The notes themselves stated that there were three crates, containing 'pumps/ships spares' destined for the 'MV Aluna' drydocked in Bremerhaven. The other eleven parcels were noted as being 'fishing nets and buoys.' Jefferies, of course knew, that the crates contained guns and ammunition and whilst there may well have been 'nets and buoys' in the parcels, he was almost certain that they contained drugs. Spending no longer than fifteen minutes at the warehouse, Jefferies left, and two and a half hours later, he arrived in Skelmersdale, deposited his load of sixteen parcels, drank tea with Michael Fowler and was on his way to Birmingham. Guls' set up in the Coleshill area of Birmingham, adjacent to the M6 motorway, was like that of Hull, albeit the warehouse was three times the size. Here, he met, for the first time a skinny man, with bright ginger hair. He was not unlike Jasper Carrot. Whilst taking the notes from Jefferies, he introduced himself as being Peter Baker, although everyone called him 'Ginger' he commented that he had not seen Malcolm before. The last of the parcels, nine, in total were unloaded and the shutter at the rear of the van was closed. At 3.30pm Jefferies left Coleshill and after stopping at the motorway services, he arrived back in Southend around 6.30pm, parked up, chatted briefly to Brian Dear and then made his way back to Maldon.

It was 7.45pm when he picked up one of the two mobile phones that he never ever took out of the bungalow, he noticed that Graham Roberts had called him several times. The text message read,

'Please call me as soon as you can, we may have a problem.'

Malcolm made himself some tea, sat at the farmhouse table in the kitchen and hit the button.

'Good evening, Malcolm.

'How was it in Hull, Liverpool, and Birmingham?'

'How the fuck, do you know that?'

'Well, my old schoolmate, I have two spies camped out at all the Guls' locations in the UK, however, here lies the potential problem. In Hull, the East Yorkshire Special Ops team are staked out in the empty property next door to the Guls. They are posing as maintenance men, repairing the mess left behind by the previous tenants, they are aware that I have two men operating there and in turn, my men are aware of their presence. You would almost certainly have been photographed today and by now your mugshot will no doubt be doing the rounds at Special Ops HQ in York.'

'Oh, fuck, I cannot afford to be exposed by the local bobbies, they will fuck everything up.'

'Well, I cannot intervene here Malcolm. I have no autonomy to poke my nose in, you are going to have to talk to your chums at Thames House.'

As they were speaking, Sergeant Frankie Laken had uploaded all the day's photos from the camera of the surveillance team in Hull. Every single person, except for the one that the Sergeant had 'pinged' over to his Superintendent, was known to have been 'snapped' previously. Superintendent John Smith, on nights ever since the undercover operation had been active, nearly spat out his single malt when the photo appeared on his screen.

'Fuck me' he said out loud, although he was the only occupant of his office.

Looking again at his screen, he said to himself, '

'It's Peter Slade, 'what the fuck is he doing delivering to one of the Guls' warehouses?'

Pouring himself another of Scotland's only claim to fame in the outside world, except for Irun Bru, he sank back into his fake leather chair and pondered. Peter Slade had been his classmate throughout their time at Coopers Grammar. Peter Slade had gone on to become one of the most noted policemen in the UK. He himself had lingered for many years, initially pounding the beat in the East End of London, attached to Leman Street Station. It had taken him seven years to become the desk Sergeant at East Ham and then the Inspector at Stratford. By the time he had reached the age of 35, with 17 years behind him, he was offered a Superintendent's job at Hull. His wife was from a village near to Hull, and despite the area's decline into total depravation, he took the job. During the last six years he had followed the career of Tony McDonald, public enemy number one, but a man with no criminal record. A year since, he had moved to York to 'head up' the newly formed Special Ops Division, their sole mission was to monitor every person that had any connection, whatsoever, with Tony McDonald. Right now, he was looking at the ugly mush of his fellow schoolboy football striker, Peter Slade.

'But Peter Slade is missing, presumed dead. According to most of the National Newspapers.'

At 8.00am the following morning and having no work to go to, Jefferies called Nigel Smalling from the secure phone and informed him of the previous day's developments.

'Leave it with me, Malcolm.'

At 11.30am, Smalling called back.

'Does the name John Smith mean anything to you?'

Jefferies, laughing, replied,

'I know several John Smiths, Nigel, I don't know if you realise it, but John Smith is quite a common name.'

'Enough of the sarcasm Malcolm, the John Smith in question attended Coopers Grammar School, very much at the same time as you did.'

'Oh, that John Smith. The last I heard about him was that he had become a Sergeant at East Ham. We had a beer to celebrate, not seen him since. Why do you ask Nigel?'

'I ask, dear boy, because last night it was Superintendent John Smith that was looking at your very ugly face on the desktop, in his office at York HQ. This John Smith is now heading up a special ops team that is following Tony McDonald around like a dog following, a bitch, that's in season.'

'Fuck me, so John Smith, who never scored more than six goals in a season is, in charge of something. It can't be the same John Smith, surely,'

'I am afraid that it is, and we must deal with it, otherwise your old partner in crime might just blow our cover, any suggestions?'

'This is John Smith's mobile number. You need to sort this out.'

'How the fuck did you get his mobile number, Nigel?'

'You are forgetting Malcolm, we are Mi5, we can do anything, speak later, no doubt.'

Nigel Smalling hung up and went back to torturing the rats that he caught in the basement every day.

Jefferies dialled the number given to him by the rat torturer.

'John Smith, what can I do for you?'

'It's Peter Slade here.'

'Ah, news travels fast my old friend. So, tell me, why are you delivering contraband for the Guls?'

'It's complicated, John, but I will do my best to explain.'

Replied the man that had once tried to steal John's girlfriend when they were both 14.

Attempting to break the ice, Jefferies asked,

'I wonder whatever happened to that ugly, spotty-faced Angela Gilmore that we used to fight over?'

'I married her,'

Deflecting Smith's answer, Jefferies began to explain what he was involved in, he was careful not to divulge his current identity. At the end of his lengthy explanation, he asked the Superintendent if they could reach a compromise.

'What do you have in mind, Peter?

'Well John, I have two undercover men watching the Guls, in fact I have about twenty in total. What if I withdrew them from Hull and you liaised with Graham Roberts in respect of your intel?'

In a raised voice, John Smith asked,

'What has Graham Roberts got to do with all of this?

At that moment Jefferies knew that John Smith's stakeout men were, as bobbies always were when asked to do a specialist job, total shit. To think that the two men watching the Guls on behalf of Yorkshire's finest were not aware of the two men sat in a blue van, almost dead opposite them, was, if nothing else, laughable.

Jefferies, looking to play his ace card, said,

'You are aware Superintendent, that I hold rank over you, however I would rather us cooperate in a cordial manner than have to go to a higher authority.'

Jefferies had not let on that he was running this op on behalf of Mi5. John Smith was snookered, he knew that Peter Slade could do and get almost anything he wanted, he had the ear of not just his own Chief Constable, but that of almost every other one, throughout the force. There was a pause, then John Smith said,

'OK, for the sake of Cooper's old boy's association, we will do it your way, Peter. However, the intel should be a 'two-way street' understood?

'Of course, I would not have it any other way.'

Jefferies called Julian Pritchard and explained the situation regarding East Yorkshire Special Ops. The following morning an irate John Smith telephoned Jefferies and let go a torrent of abuse. It was of no consequence to Jefferies, as he knew it was coming. John Smith had been summoned to the office of the Chief Constable of Yorkshire and had been ordered to 'stand down' his men from anything to do with Tony McDonald, when he asked as to the reason for this decision, Superintendent John Smith was told that the directive had come from the Secretary of State at the Home Office and that there was nothing that he (the Chief Constable) could do to change it. After leaving the Chief Constable's office, John Smith telephoned Jefferies and asked him what was going on. The undercover detective replied that he could not elaborate on the actual operation, however his own investigation was a matter of state security, and as such, was highly classified. Jefferies asked that his one-time rival for the affections of Angela Gilmore simply accept the decision made by the Home Secretary. John Smith hung up he would never speak with Jefferies again. Calling Graham Roberts, Jefferies asked him to 'reinstate' the watch on the Guls' warehouse in Hull, Roberts laughed and replied,

'I never withdrew our interest Malcolm, as I knew that you would get it sorted.'

'Good man,' replied Malcolm.

For reasons unbeknown to him, on Sunday 6th, Feb 2005, Jefferies found himself driving the Jeep towards his house in Epping. His heart was telling him that it was time to come clean with Cheryl Smith. Roberts, being just too busy to do so, had recruited his brother, Roy, to look after Malcolm's affairs ever since he had returned to the UK after being incarcerated in Turkey. Roy Roberts had introduced himself to Cheryl and had shown her the 'letter of authority' signed by her former lover, a lover that she had not seen since November 2003. As he inched the Jeep ever closer to his house, Cheryl came out of hers and got into her car. Seconds later she drove out, turned left, and headed towards Epping High Road. Jefferies followed, careful to keep his distance. Ten minutes after leaving her house, Cheryl turned into the car park of the Merry Fiddlers and parked close to the exit. Jefferies drove around the back and stopped towards the far end of the car park. Cheryl was still in his view. She got out of her car, a smartly dressed man got out of a car parked almost immediately behind her, they embraced, kissed, and then made their way into the restaurant part of the pub. Jefferies was as deflated as he could be. He had fully intended to knock on Cheryl's door and confess all to her, but now he was glad that she had gone out before he could do so, as to have gone through with his intentions would have put both his operation and Cheryl's safety at risk. The dejected man drove back to Maldon, parked the car on the drive, walked to the Ship and Anchor and got pissed.

The following morning, Alkan Asani and Borislav Topolov were already waiting outside Bromley-by-Bow underground station when Jefferies arrived. The Turk and the Bulgarian offered their good mornings as they settled into the Jeep. Ten minutes later they were sat, mugs of tea and biscuits in front of them, at the large table that stood in the middle of Graham Roberts' upstairs office, at 38 Oban Street, Poplar.

Looking at the surrounding walls, Asani remarked,

'Well, you have been a busy man, Graham.'

'Indeed, I have.'

'Looks like we are in for a busy day,' said Jefferies.

Roberts, seated at the head of the table, which gave him access to both sides of the room, said,

'Yes, we have a lot to get through. I have been in constant contact with the Private Investigator's equivalent of Interpol. It is an organisation that has a membership of over a thousand PIs, many of them former police employees. The HQ is in Berne, Switzerland, and we get to meet up twice every year. It is true to say that as we are not 'bogged down' by the protocol and bureaucratic systems that exist within most police forces, we are able to share information openly and freely, a lot of our data comes from the police itself, anyhow, enough of that. As you can see from looking at the walls, I have put together a comprehensive and detailed resume on everyone that is mentioned in Mi5's dossier. I have obtained intel from, the UK, the EU, and the Balkans/Middle East. If at any time during my presentation you wish to ask anything, then please feel free. I shall begin, UK first.

The Gul Clan: It all began with Osman Gul, born in Cizre, Turkey in 1960. At an early age he would trek the mountains of Kurdistan, bringing cigarettes to the warring factions in his rucksack. It was a small-time business. By the mid-eighties, many members of the family had joined with Osman, and they developed into supplying arms and cigarettes to the PKK, who in turn paid the Gul's in Heroin, which they brought in from Afghanistan. Looking for more and more outlets for the drugs, Osman arrived, illegally, in the UK in 1993 and applied for asylum. Azad Gul was left in charge in Cizre. Not long after arriving in the UK, Osman was caught and tried for Importing and distributing Class A drugs. He received 12 years, however in some 'under the table deal' he was released after four years and sent back to Turkey to serve the remainder of his sentence. To fill the void, Birusk Gul was sent to the UK in 1995, however, he too was caught and incarcerated in 1999. He is due for release in 2007. Meanwhile, Osman somehow managed to leave Turkey in 1998 and headed for Amsterdam, together with his younger cousin, Asti Gul. Both were caught Importing drugs into Holland. Osman received 20 years and Asti eleven. Subsequently, Osman's sentence was increased to life. Last year (2004) he was declared as 'mentally unstable' and will never be released. Asti like Birusk is due to be released in 2007. Azad Gul has taken over the reins in the UK and works with the three people that are now under our scrutiny, i.e., Bobby Keagan, Jamie Law, and Tony McDonald.

Kagan Kaptan: In a journey arranged by Ozturk Oszoy, arrived in the UK, we think, in the year 2002. Nur Nazif was his guardian; his goal was to infiltrate the Taylan Turget gang that had become strong during the time that the Gul's were losing their key members to the UK prison service. Turget managed to flee to Turkey after Kaptan had disposed of most of his gang. In a 'sting' operation in Turkey, administered by Ozsoy, Turget was caught and sentenced to 37 years. Kaptan was now controlling Turget's UK drug market, however with the arrival of Azad Gul, Kaptan appears to be taking a holiday.

Quinten Proctor: Malcolm was told by Mi5 that this Junior Home Office Minister is a mole, offering valuable information to Azad Gul. Malcolm saw with his own eyes, on the 2nd of Feb, Proctor meeting with Gul at the warehouse in Southend. Whatever doubt there was concerning his involvement disappeared with this sighting. Malcolm was asked 'to deal with this problem.' It is not 100% clear whether Proctor should be taken 'dead or alive' our problem is that we are not sanctioned by Julian Pritchard to take any action. Proctor is under observation 24/7.

There was a short break, for tea and buns, before Roberts resumed.

Dick White: Whilst we do not believe White to be directly involved in the drugs or arms business, he does operate on the fringes of our investigation and as such we shall continue, via my surveillance operation, to monitor him closely. If at some stage we can 'offer him up' to Malcolm's former Special Branch colleagues, then so be it. He is well overdue to have his collar felt.

Peter Slade (alias Malcolm Jefferies): Whilst it is not my intention to embarrass my old friend, I think it is important that we all share in his undoubted skills as an undercover operative. I will, for the purpose of avoiding any later confusion, refer to my sidekick as Malcolm. Born in 1964, Malcolm joined the Met Police in 1981 and quickly rose through the ranks. He was involved in the talks that eventually saw the IRA give up their arms, a condition of the Good Friday Agreement. In September 2001 he was promoted to the rank of Chief Superintendent and his boss, Commander James Reeves is known to us all. Covertly he investigated the amnesty given to certain terrorists, he got too close to the truth and on the 11th, May 2002, his car was blown up, outside his front door. Malcolm's wife and two daughters were killed. He managed to track down some notorious terrorists, all of whom had been wrongly 'pardoned' as part of the Good Friday Agreement. Sean Flynn, Fingers Doyle, Willie McCormack, Micky McGovern, and Bobby Kelly were all implicated by Malcolm as having been given a pardon when they should have been imprisoned. Malcolm managed to interview Kelly on the day before he died. Kelly gave up Flynn for the murder of Jimmy Quinn, the uncle of Michael O'Leary, now known as Sean Porter. Kelly added during his chat with Malcolm, that Michael O'Leary was responsible for the murder of Martin Keenan, the then Chief Constable of Dublin. O'Leary fled to London and became part of the IRA, responsible for bringing arms and explosives into England. In a deal manufactured by the Home Office, O'Leary became Sean Porter and was allowed, to head for Spain and then onto Bulgaria. Despite digging up Jimmy Quinn's Garden, his body was never found. Malcolm met with Eileen O'Leary, the mother of Michael, she gave up the fact that her son had changed his identity, she also confirmed that her sons' twin boys, Mack, and Manson McBride were reunited with their father in 1997. During the investigation Malcolm was seconded from New Scotland Yard to Mi5. As of today, at Malcolm's request, we have stakeouts on all the Gul's in the UK, plus Keagan, Law, and McDonald. All of whom we have already discussed. Combining the intel, I have gathered from colleagues across the channel and with the help of you Alkan and you Borislav, we will now move onto the activities of the many gangs that are associated with the Gul's, McBride's, Porter, and Kaptan.

At the end of his assessment of his friend's career, Roberts asked Malcolm if he had missed anything out. Malcolm replied,

'You seem to know more about me than I do myself.'

'We shall break for lunch now.'

After a break of just twenty-five minutes, Roberts continued his lengthy and detailed report, the details of which were neatly laid out on his room-size wallboard.

The Petrov's & Nikolay Nikolov: To give a little history, Stoyan Petrov was born in Varna, Bulgaria in 1949. In 1967 he married Todorha and their son, Boyan was born in 1971. Stoyan was a hard man, many murders were attributed to him and his righthand man, Nikolay Nikolov. Stoyan spread his wings and his organisation panned out way beyond the boundaries of Varna, along the way he became its mayor. He controlled every facet of everyday life along a hundred-mile stretch of the Black Sea Coast. He bought up prime land along the seafronts of Varna, Golden Sands and Sunny Beach and, as Mayor, granted himself permission to build Hotels, Nightclubs, Restaurants, Casinos, and Resorts. He was the first to introduce drugs into the Balkans, initially to service the needs of the many Russians that loved to 'party' along the shores of the Black Sea. In April 1987 Todorha Petrov was gunned down at her son's 16th birthday bash. The enduring repercussions led to many deaths, most of them by extreme torture. Stoyan's fame and notoriety came to the attention of the Commies in Sofia, who of course wanted a piece, if not all, of the action. In May 1987, at the invitation of the top men in Sofia, he was summoned there, to discuss the future. It turned out that Stoyan had no future. He never made it to Sofia, mysteriously falling from an aircraft, enroute from Varna. With Stoyan's son away, being educated at Oxford, Nikolay Nikolov took over the reins. Nikolov had been Stoyan's childhood friend, he was the Petrov's enforcer, although he was never convicted of any crime. On the day of his best friend's (Stoyan) funeral, Nikolov met with Tommaso Buscetta the infamous Sicilian that had turned 'grass' and had squealed on his fellow Mafia members, in exchange for his freedom. Buscetta had made it known, publicly, that he would like to take over the Petrov's empire now that Stoyan had passed. Also, at the funeral were, a certain General Kos, Victor Bastovoi (Romania's Mafia Leader) Mustafa Gul and Dimitris Fotopoulos (the Greek Don). Abu Naseeb, also at the funeral, was regarded as the World's most prolific arms dealer at the time. Initially all these men were to help Nikolov eliminate Buscetta, however the General discovered that Naseeb and Bastovoi were working hand in hand with the most wanted of all Italians. Gregor Levski, now Nikolov's number two, in a carefully organised operation, took out Buscetta, Naseeb and Bastovoi. Boyan Petrov returned to Varna after completing his education at Oxford. Gradually he took over from Nikolov and now runs the organisation as a legit operation. He is Bulgaria's largest property dealer, whilst also being their richest man. At arms-length, he deals in drugs, arms, money laundering and people smuggling. He has no number two, as far as it is known.

Michael O'Leary & the McBride's: Much of O'Leary's, (aka. Sean Porter) past has been covered in Malcolm's investigation. I will only deal with the up-to-date facts that I have obtained from my own sources. The trail goes cold from the moment in 1973 when the now Sean Porter left the UK for Spain. We believe there is little intel on Porter due to the protection afforded to him by Mi6. We know from his more recent visits to Belfast that he now lives mainly in Bulgaria and that he has a strong link to the Petrov's. Porter is now aged 61. His twin sons, Mack and Manson McBride run Ireland's largest international trucking business they are both 43. Since they were all 'reunited' in 1997, the trucking business, having previously only operated to and from the UK mainland, France, Belgium, Netherlands, and Germany, has since added the Balkan countries and Turkey to its portfolio. Porter is a known associate of Boyan Petrov and has criminal links in Romania, Albania, and Turkey. Interpol are following his movements closely. Manson McBride is a frequent visitor to Varna and is always there as a guest of the Petrov's.

Leon & Monzer Asmar: Leon Asmar, born in Aleppo, Syria in 1945. Moved in Syria's highest of societies. Was President of the world-famous Club d'Alep. He was a friend of the Al Hassad. All of this was a good cover for his dealings in drugs and arms. He was as brash as his brother was reserved. Monzer Asmar, born in 1949. Would not deal in drugs but took part in arms deals with his older brother. Monzer also dealt in the illegal tobacco trade. Both brothers sorted a good deal of their ill-gotten gains into the Marbella area of the Costa-del-Sol. Leon also purchased a house in Sloane Square, London. He was arrested and jailed in the UK in 1979 for drug offences. He served two years. Married, with three children, who all live in Marbella. In 1987, without divorcing his first wife, he married a 17-year-old beauty queen from one of Syria's richest families. He came under the radar of the FBI in 1987 after selling arms to Nicaraguan rebels that were used against US advisory troops in the civil war. Said to have made USD 40 million from a single deal. Has links with both Boyan Petrov and General Kos.

Monzer Asmar, keeps a relatively low profile in comparison with his more flamboyant brother. Married to Milana, also has kids and lives mostly in Marbella. Does not like drugs but has dabbled in arms. Big in the tobacco trade. Gets people out of Syria, and into the EU, for a price.

Genera Kos: Possibly the most interesting and powerful man in the whole of our investigation. The 'General' as he likes to be known, emigrated to Australia with his parents in 1982, aged eight. Was known to be 'running drugs' at the age of 12 in the red-light area of Kings Cross, Sydney. Progressed to become the largest Importer/distributor of every kind of drug, known to be sold in Australia. He returned to his native Kosovo in 1995, aged just 21. He had sent a lot of his illegally gained money from Australia back to his homeland, via Albania, to help arm his countrymen in their fight against Serbia and Montenegro. He returned to Kosovo in 1997 and wore the uniform of a fallen General. From then on, he was always known as the 'General'. For three years he fought alongside Kosovans and Albanians in the army known as the KLA. By the end of 1999, the war had almost ended, the General had taken, and kept, a large swathe of land, its boundaries were in both Kosovo and Albania. In the last five years he has built up quite an impressive 'personal' army of over 3500 soldiers, made up of Kosovan, Albanian, Serbian, and Yugoslav fighters. The General has a vast appetite for the learning of what else goes on in the criminal World. He leaves his complex very rarely. He studies the criminal activities of people and gangs everywhere. His knowledge in this field is said to be unbeatable. There is no known illegal organisation that he is not aware of. He still retains his overall control in Australia, even though he never visits. He is said to deal drugs with Mexican and Columbian cartels, the Triads, the Mafia of Italy, and the USA, and controls the supply into the UK, Germany, Netherlands, and the rest of the EU. In addition, he has more than a passing interest in the car washing and kebab business, worldwide, and has recently moved into the people smuggling business. Of all the people in Nigel Smalling's 'notebook' the General is the common link, he knows them all. He is, without doubt, the most dangerous and ruthless name on our list. He can kill almost anyone, without ever leaving his stronghold. Hundreds, if not thousands of people have succumbed to his manic behaviour.

Tayser Malik: Gentlemen, my research into Tayser Malik was, by far, the most interesting. His story is remarkable, if it was not for the fact that his life of crime has led to the death of hundreds of drug addicts and pushers, then you could almost admire him. He was born in the town of Nassib, at the southern end of Syria, in July 1967. By the age of 15, four of his six siblings, plus his parents had met with their deaths. All were connected to the civil unrest that, even to this day, haunts Syria. Aged 14, Malik, took up pickpocketing in the coastal city of Latakia. One day he took a bus to Irbid, a city just over the border, in Jordan. He managed to get a job with a Jordanian by the name of Al Bakhit. His job was to repair old and worn-out electrical items. He was introduced to Tareq Mahmoud, a distributor of drugs, for Amer Deeb, who was based in Amman. Every evening, Malik would smuggle drugs in various radios back to Syria. Salah Mahmoud, Tareq's brother would collect the drugs from Malik and sell them in and around Nassib. Tareq Mahmoud and Bakhit began to 'cut' the drugs, making themselves a 'shitload' of money. Deeb found out and Bakhit and Tareq Mahmoud were picked up by the police that were on Deeb's payroll. They both disappeared. In a letter left by Bakhit to Malik, the young boy inherited everything, the business, a house, a Mercedes and USD 1.5 million, in cash. Malik, at the age of just 15, took his next-door neighbour, Tamara Jamal as his lover, she was 19 years his senior. Deeb was her brother and Nur Jamal, her husband. In a succession of planned deaths, Nur Jamal, Deeb and a Pakistani drugs and arms dealer, Imran Hasni, were all eliminated, by Tamara Jamal.

Tamara Jamal moved to Amman to control her brother's empire. According to sources she had over 1000 employees, 950 of whom worked in the drugs, arms, and tobacco smuggling business. In the meantime, Malik opened an electrical repair shop in his hometown of Nassib. His cousin, Mohamad Malik was installed to look after it. A computer shop in Aleppo, was purchased. This was run by Malik's sister. From Aleppo they sold drugs and cigarettes to the north and west of Syria. Tayser Malik, with heroin supplied by his one-time lover, Tamara Jamal had become Syria's dominate drug baron. With the help of Monzer Asmar's trucking business, he was able to move his contraband into Turkey. Malik was now growing tobacco in Jordan and selling it throughout the Middle East. In 2000 a major problem occurred, this affected the businesses of both Malik and Jamal. The entire poppy growing fields of Afghanistan were 'wiped out' by Mullah Mohammed, the new leader of the Taliban. By the time the Heroin supply dried up, it was estimated the Malik and his ex-girlfriend had made over USD 70 million each. In 2001, General Kos met with Tamara Jamal, soon after, they moved one of the largest arms caches ever to be sold on the open market, from Basra in Iraq to the battlefields of Afghanistan. The arms, all ex-Russian, had been stored by Nur Jamal, prior to his death. The buyers were the Taliban and they paid for the arms, with Heroin, that had been stored before the crops were destroyed. Our latest intel on Malik is that he moves huge quantities of tobacco, using Monzer Asmar's trucking company, Trust Shipping and Forwarding.

To conclude my report, in the UK we are watching Azad and Mustafa Gul, although Mustafa moves to and from the UK and Germany. Bobby Keagan, Jamie Law, Tony McDonald, and Nur Nazif are all under our ever-watchful eye. With Malcolm's approval, we will follow Mack & Manson McBride, however this is to be kept between ourselves, as this monitoring has not been officially sanctioned by Mi5. I can arrange for Sean Porter to be tailed. Currently he is in Varna. Alkan, Borislav, I would ask that you to stake out, Kaptan and Oszoy in Turkey, Boyan Petrov in Varna and Monzer Asmar, who flit between Syria and Spain. You will also need to keep tabs on Tayser Malik and Tamara Jamal, both spend most of their time in Jordan. It is impossible for anyone to follow General Kos, unless of course, either of you can get yourselves embedded into his complex. Handing Asani and Topolov separate sheets of paper, Roberts explained that he had written down the names, locations, and contact details of twelve of his counterparts that are expecting to be called. They can assist you with surveillance.

'We are looking at a costing, in excess, of £1 million per month if we are to keep tabs on all these people. Now I will hand you over to Malcolm, as, after all, it is 'his' operation.

'Thank you, Graham. You are doing a splendid job.'

'As you can all imagine, it would be impossible for me to come up with an 'operational plan' right now. I need to go away and digest everything that Graham has briefed us on.

'Can we meet again, same place, same time, next Saturday?'

Everyone nodded in agreement.

Malcolm returned Asani and Topolov to the station.

When he returned, he asked Graham,

'So, what have you got in mind for our old mate, Paul Walters?

'Malcolm, we need to get him into the Guls' warehouse at Southend.'

'I have spoken to Phil Dinn, and he confirms that he has some vacancies on his books for warehousemen at the Guls. He added that this business has an extremely high turnover of staff, most of whom he never hears from again. Walters has good knowledge of the drug business, having been a small-time pusher for several years. I think it would be best if you could take him with you on your deliveries, as a mate, and then try your luck with Don Rogers in trying to get him a job. This way they might just trust him a little more than if he had come to them via an employment agency. What do you think?'

'It's worth a try, I'll give it a go.'

Before he left Oban Street, he asked Graham to update him on everyone that was being tailed, adding that he would need the report by next Friday for him to prepare his presentation of the operational plan, which he hoped to reveal when they all meet up again the following Saturday.

For the next three days, Jefferies did nothing other than juggle with the operational plan that, hopefully, would see the beginning of the end for all of those involved in the drugs and arms peddling, which was worth billions in the UK alone, whilst also being responsible for thousands of related deaths.

On Wednesday the 10th, Feb 2005, he arrived at Southend, as usual, at just before 5.00am. Paul Walters was in the passenger seat. He was slightly taken aback when he saw that it was Azad Gul that was standing on the loading bay, documents in hand, and not, as had always been the case previously, Don Rogers. In a bold move, Jefferies invited Walters to join them on the loading bay and he then took the opportunity to ask Gul as to whether there were any jobs going.

'Can you drive? Asked the Turk.

'Of course.' replied Paul Walters.

'I will think about it and let Malcolm know.'

Turning to Jefferies, Azad said,

'You have Liverpool, Glasgow and Hull, this week. When you get back, we need to talk, but you will have to make it Friday as I am not here on Thursday.'

Azad returned to the warmth of Don Roger's office. Jefferies, with Walters beside him, pulled out of the yard and headed for his first stop, Liverpool. After Liverpool, he let Walters do the driving to Glasgow.

Whilst enroute to Glasgow and unbeknown to Jefferies, Sergeant Frankie Laken had finally wore-down his boss, Superintendent John Smith. Smith explained the reason as to why he and everyone else had been pulled out of the 'stake out' at McDonald's warehouse in Hull. Laken called Tony McDonald; he had been on the payroll for some time. He informed McDonald that Jefferies was an undercover Mi5 agent. McDonald called Azad Gul. Between them they agreed to let Jefferies and his associate, Paul Walters continue with the delivery to Glasgow. They would not be informing Jamie Law. Gul would drive to Hull in readiness for Jefferies' arrival the following morning.

Staying over at the same Travelodge, near to Carlisle, that he had previously used, Jefferies and Walters set off for Hull early on Thursday morning. Having not fully explained, in-depth, about the suspected contents of the parcels, Jefferies had asked Walters simply to observe, to look at where they were and what they were doing, from a criminal's perspective. Jefferies filled in his co-pilot with as much info as he thought he should know. Walters commented that he knew of the Guls and their position as being the number one UK drug gang, adding that there was no doubt that they had just been delivering the white powder of death. Jefferies was impressed by the astuteness of his one-time classmate, telling him that, if he could keep everything quiet, then he could be quite an asset to the team. Walters grinned with gratitude at his mentor's words.

At 10.15 on the morning of Thursday 11th, February 2005, Jefferies drove the Luton van into yet another of the Guls' warehouses and backed, without waiting, onto one of the two loading bays. Both men got out of the van and walked to the rear. A man on the bay, whom Jefferies had not seen previously, had already opened the roller shutter of the back door.

'The kettle is on in the canteen.'

The two men climbed the seven concrete steps and entered the warehouse. As the door closed behind them, they both received a heavy blow to the back of their heads.

They awoke inside a steel container. Laid on their backs, like Jesus on the cross. Chains, around their hands and feet, secured into the iron rings that are a feature of shipping containers. Duct tape covered their mouths, both men found it difficult to breathe freely through their respective noses. In the dim light, afforded by the slightly open door, stood two men. One, recognisable by Jefferies as being Azad Gul, the other, he did not know.

'This is Tony McDonald. He is not a violent man, but I think that you know that I am, Chief Superintendent Peter Slade. This is your final delivery. You did extremely well to dupe us for so long. We are just lucky that Tony has many friends inside the Yorkshire Police Force.'

Initially, just one thing flashed through Peter Slade's mind, John Smith, the fucking traitor.

Gul and McDonald turned and left the container. The doors were secured, and Slade and Walters were left, spread-eagled upon the floor, in complete darkness. It was no later than 11.00am.

In the conversation between Gul and McDonald, it was agreed that their captives simply be left in the container, without food or water, until they withered and died. Gul then decided that it might be best if the container was sent elsewhere. Gul called over to Jack Bruce, a loyal servant of over five years and asked that he arranged to move the container to Cuxhaven, that night, if possible. Bruce asked no questions. Gul then called his cousin, Mustafa, in Hamburg and advised him that a 'parcel' would be delivered to him the next morning and that Jack Bruce would advise all the details later.

Outside in the road, parked up, was the blue van that belonged to Graham Roberts' local surveillance team. They had clocked the Luton van, reg no: GUL 18 when it had arrived, they had seen Gul leave at 2.00pm and McDonald shortly afterwards. At 5.00pm GUL 18 had still not left. The older of the two lookout men phoned Graham Roberts. He explained the day's events to his paymaster. Roberts had a gut feeling that all was not well. Checking his friend's projected movements, he could see that he was due to deliver to Hull that day. Roberts asked his man to report any movement, in or out between now and 8.00pm.

Joe Cole called Roberts at 8.05pm and told him that GUL 18 was still at the depot, adding that there had not been any untoward movements, in or out since they last spoke. He explained to his boss that the warehouse operated twenty-four hours a day and the staff switchover had taken place, as normal at 6.00pm. Several trucks had arrived and left in the period since they last spoke. Cole confirmed that each vehicle, either arriving or leaving had been photographed. Roberts thanked his lookout man for the info and asked that he send the photos of all the vehicles to him ASAP.

The following morning, one of Mustafa Gul's drivers collected the container from the Port of Cuxhaven and delivered it to the Guls warehouse in Hamburg. It had been declared as an 'empty' container, returning to Hamburg for repairs. It drew no suspicions from the authorities on either side of the North Sea. The container was parked under some trees in the far corner of the Guls complex. Mustafa arrived at noon and asked one of his Kurdish illegals to open it up. As one of the doors was opened, Slade lifted his head slightly off the wooden floor, his eyes took a while to adjust to the light. He recognised the man stood over him as being Mustafa Gul. They had never met however Slade had spent some time studying his photograph, supplied to him by Nigel Smalling. Gul placed the sole of his size eleven boot onto Slade's forehead and said,

'I wonder what Azad wants me to do with you?'

He then turned his attention to Walters, he dripped some water from the bottle that he was holding, directly on to his face, he did not stir. Gul bent down and removed the duct tape, nothing.

'Fuck me, this one is dead, exclaimed Mustafa Gul.

Twenty minutes later, Walters was removed from the container and dumped into the back of a Mercedes van. Sometime in the future, when the 'shit' hit the fan for the Guls, it was discovered that the body of Paul Walters was taken to a kebab processing plant in Dusseldorf, minced and was then served to the unsuspecting patrons of several kebab takeaways. Dusseldorf was and remains a stronghold for the Kurdish illegals and refugees in Germany, with the highest concentration of drug consumption anywhere in Europe.

In Southend, Azad Gul, having taken possession of Slade's keys, was busy searching his Jeep. He could find nothing that associated Slade with Mi5 or the police in general. Then, with his hand fumbling around in the glove compartment, he found a folded A4 piece of paper. Peter Slade, a man of some efficiency had made a mistake. He had, as he always had, placed a copy of his car insurance inside the glove compartment. Whilst the Certificate was not showing any information, other than his name and the make and model of the vehicle, it would prove to be of some use to Gul. He telephoned his wife's sister's husband, a Kurd by the name of Ashti Bashur, he owned a small Insurance Brokers, almost all his clients were Kurds. Gul gave Bashur the Policy Number, ten minutes later he returned Gul's call and told him that the vehicle was part of a block policy, taken out by a government department, listed at Thames House in London. Azad phoned Cousin Mustafa in Hamburg and instructed him to extract Slade's home address, by any means he considered to be viable.

Graham Roberts was becoming more and more concerned about his friend's disappearance. He had spent most of the night scrolling through the hundreds of photos that his team had taken since undertaking the surveillance in Hull. Whilst he could, with the wonders of modern technology, read the container number that had left the Guls' warehouse in Hull at 7.15pm, he could not find the container arriving during the previous six-weeks. He phoned Phil Dinn as he had contacts in the shipping business. He asked Dinn if it were possible to trace a container if he gave him the number.

'Yes, of course it is, provided that it has been manifested on board a ship.'

'Leave it with me, Graham, I will get back to you.'

'Thanks. Be as quick as you can, a life may depend upon it.'

Less than three minutes later, Dinn phoned Roberts back.

'It arrived in Cuxhaven, last night and was collected by Gul Haulage.'

'Phil, I don't know how you did this, but I owe you a pint or two.'

'No prob Graham. It was easy, I just put the container number into my tracking program and out it popped.'

'Well, thanks again. Mr. Slade could well be buying you a lot more than a pint.'

Roberts, becoming totally consumed in his efforts to track down the only boy in his school that could bowl faster than him, at cricket, called Julian Pritchard.

'We may, no, we do, have a problem, Julian.'

'OK, calm down old boy, what has happened?'

Roberts explained all that he knew.

'I am going to make a call to my counterpart in the BND.' (German Intelligence)

Pritchard called, Wolfgang Moller in Berlin and explained. He stressed the urgency of his request to get boots on ground at the Guls' set-up in Hamburg. Moller assured his like-for-like colleague that he would take immediate action. Adding that the Guls are under constant monitoring in Germany already. Moller picked up his internal phone and invited his number two, Dieter Smit, into his office. He asked Smit to get the team 'tooled up' and head for Guls' complex. Smit returned to his own office, took a mobile phone from the locked drawer of his desk, and called Mustafa Gul.

Forty minutes after receiving the call from London, thirty of Germany's elite tactical armed group surrounded Gul warehousing and distribution, at the purpose-built complex on the outskirts of Hamburg. Dieter Smit headed the operation. He instructed the trained negotiator to speak over the megaphone. His message to anyone that was inside the offices and warehouse was to come out, with their hands in the air. Ten minutes after arriving, Dieter Smit entered the container that was said to have held Peter Slade and his associate, Paul Walters. The container was empty and there were no clues as to the fact that anyone had recently been held captive inside it. Mustafa Gul was nowhere to be seen. Smit reported back to his boss, Wolfgang Moller, who in turn informed Julian Pritchard.

18 - REPERCUSSIONS

During his telephone conversation with Wolfgang Moller, Julian Pritchard insisted that the head of the German BND must have a mole in his midst. Moller was adamant that all his men were sound. Pritchard did his best to convince the former Colonel in Germany's armed forces, that almost every Secret Service Organisation in the World has a mole. He asked Moller the following.

'Whom did you inform of the fact that you would be raiding the Guls' place of work?'

'My next in command, Dieter Smit.'

'And would Mr. Smit have shared the details of the operation with anyone else?'

'Our protocol, probably like yours, dictates that the men are assembled and only get to know of the target whilst enroute.'

'Exactly. Don't you see, if Smit never shared the details of the raid, then it must be him that has warned Mustafa Gul of his pending arrival.'

'I understand what you are saying Mr. Pritchard, but Dieter Smit, he has been with me forever.'

'Can I offer you some advice, Mr. Moller?'

'You can, but I may not take it.'

'Then that is your decision, however the life of my best agent is on the line. What would you do in my situation?'

'I see, what do you, suggest?'

'Is Mr. Smit in the office, at this time?'

'No, he is following another lead.'

'Then you should get one of your people to search his room.'

'What would we be looking for?'

'Anything that might tie Smit to Gul, it's quite simple.'

'OK, I shall instruct my security guys to carry that out.'

Pritchard wasted no time in calling Graham Roberts.

'I have some news.'

'I hope it's good news, Julian.'

'I am afraid it is not. The BND raided the Guls' place in Hamburg and neither Slade nor Walters were anywhere to be seen. Mustafa Gul was known to have been there before the raid was carried out, however he too was conspicuous by his absence.'

'Does the BND have a mole? Sounds like Gul was tipped off.'

'My thoughts entirely, Graham.'

'The good news for Slade is, that unlike the last time he was taken, when we were powerless to help, this time he was on an active Mi5 assignment, within the UK, we shall move heaven and earth to find him. Anyhow, without doubt, Gul has him and he may not survive. You know what to do Graham.'

'Yes, of course. By the way, I have some news on Quinten Proctor.'

'Go ahead, I hope we can nail him.'

'Well Julian, Proctor is a poof. Last Sunday, my men tailed him to a rather suspicious-looking bar in Soho. Proctor was wearing a pastel pink suit, a maroon shirt and one of those multi-coloured ties that the gay fraternity are all now favouring. As you can imagine, my men, Teddy and Merv were very reluctant to enter the bar, mainly because they were dressed in workman's clothes, donkey jackets included. Anyhow, forty-five minutes later Proctor left, hand in hand with a young boy, who, according to Teddy, was wearing a pair of see-through trousers. Apparently, his backside wobbled as they made their way into Leicester Square Underground. Together they entered a run-down building in the poorest part of Bethnal Green. Merv reported that Proctor was walking as though he had a roll of cling-film up his butt as he strode along Cambridge Heath Road.'

'Bloody hell. So, Proctor is a shirt lifter. I suppose it's no real surprise as most of the cabinet members are thought to be of the same ilk.'

'This is our opportunity to dispose of him, Julian.'

'Not with you, dear boy.'

'Oh, come on. Use your imagination, I thought you were the clever one.'

'I'm still not on the same hymn sheet.'

'Headlines will read, 'Junior Minister found dead in gay brothel, often frequented by other members of the house. '

'What a brilliant idea, Mr. Roberts. You should have been a policeman, keep me in the loop.'

Graham Roberts, fearing that time was of the essence if he was going to stave off the almost certain execution of his friend of nearly thirty years, dialled the number of a man listed as Albert on his mobile phone.

'Ah, Mr. Roberts, do you have something for me.?'

'Yes, I do, but it involves kids.'

'That's OK, as long as I don't have to kill any or change their nappies.'

'Of course not, it's more of a babysitting job.'

'That's good, give me the details.'

'Every weekday at 3.45 in the afternoon, a group of four, two boys and two girls leave Trinity Wood Private school and walk the half a mile or so to their mansion-like home on Hutton Mount, Brentwood. Your job is to take the girls, aged twelve and thirteen, to a safe hiding place. You will have to use chloroform as little girls scream a lot. You only have this afternoon for a dummy run. Tomorrow, you must do it for real. A man's life depends upon you being successful. I am sending you the photos of all four subjects, by email, right now. There can be no 'cockups, Albert.'

Slade, Roberts, and Pritchard had discussed, when Slade had first got the job with Azad Gul, as to what leverage, if any, they might be able to activate, should Slade ever be 'outed' as an undercover agent. The time to action their plan, had come. Azad Gul had two boys, aged eleven and thirteen. Mustafa Gul had two girls, twelve and thirteen. They all attended the prestigious private school, Trinity Wood, which stood proudly on the main road between Brentwood and Billericay, in Essex. Whilst Mustafa lived mainly in Hamburg, where he was a marked man, he believed in the UK's education system and therefore sent his two girls to school there, thinking they would not only obtain a good education, but they would also be much safer. Two of Roberts' men had been watching all four children for several weeks and whilst they were good at surveillance, they were not kidnappers.

Albert, Bobby, and Freddie Salisbury sat in a mark one, twelve-year-old, dark grey ford Mondeo. It was parked in a designated layby about two hundred yards from Trinity Wood School. The three brothers, once upon a time, the most feared of the many gangs that had ruled the East End's underworld, back in the day, were now no longer inflicting horrendous injuries upon their victims. Should that need to be done, they had the people to do it for them. Nowadays they ran their empire in a business-like fashion. Their reputation alone was normally enough to frighten their victims into parting with cash, cars or even property if the debt they were collecting was big enough. They, like many 'hard men' did not enjoy the frightening of children, however Roberts was a good client, and they all needed a holiday. It was a 'win-win' situation. The four kids passed the Mondeo without a second glance. When they were a hundred yards, or so, up the road, Bobby got out of the car and followed them. They crossed the busy A129 and entered the tree-lined, private, narrow road, that led to some of the most expensive housing in Essex. Sports, TV, and film stars occupied the houses of this select and desirable part of the world. The area was also home to some very nasty people, Azad Gul amongst them. Bobby trailed the four kids until they entered the double-sided drive of the massive house, that he presumed they all lived in. He walked past the house the youngsters were already inside. He noticed that there were no cars on the drive.

He clocked the name written on the face of what was once part of a rather large tree. It read Gulliver's, nice touch, thought Bobby. The youngest of the Salisbury brothers turned and walked back to the car.

The following day, the three men, plus a driver, known throughout the underworld as 'Stirling' sat in the same layby. This time their chosen vehicle was a Ford Galaxy, which had been stolen from Plaistow that very morning. The Galaxy boasted the normal five seats, plus two more, face-to-face, in the rear. The four scholars passed the people carrier, oblivious to its occupants. After the children had crossed the road and disappeared onto Hutton Mount, Stirling pulled away and followed. As they entered the private road that led up to Gulliver's, they drove past their prey, turned in the circle fifty yards after the drive of the house, drove back to the drive and stopped. The kids were unable to get through the narrow gap between the car and the hedge, they switched to the driver's side and as they did, Bobby and Freddie placed their hands over the mouths of the two girls. Their hands contained cotton wool that had been soaked in chloroform. The girls were lifted and laid between the two seats in the boot of the car. The whole thing took less than thirty seconds to perform. The two boys, seemingly mesmerized, did not react until the car had pulled away, turned right, and disappeared. The sons of Azad Gul ran to a neighbouring house and raised the alarm. One hour later, in no rush to attend the apparent abduction of the daughters of the cousin of one of the UK's most prominent criminals, the police arrived.

The stolen Ford Galaxy made its way through Brentwood town centre and entered the A12 at its junction with the M25. Thirty-five minutes later it came to a stop at an address in North Woolwich. The car was driven to the rear of an old Victorian house and parked in the already open garage. The girls, still out cold, were carried to the back door of the house and carefully lifted down into the cellar.

By now, Azad Gul and his wife, Sharon, a blonde beauty from Southend, and a former pole-dancer at a club in Basildon, were at home. Their two boys were playing, quite happily on their respective play-stations, oblivious to the mayhem that was going on around them. After the police had left his mansion, no doubt purchased from the proceeds of drug dealing, Azad Gul finally made the call that he had been dreading.

'Hi Azad, problem?'

'Yes. There is no way of making this easy for you to hear, Mustafa.'

'What is it that seems to be troubling you, my cousin.'

'Well, your girls were abducted on their way home from school today.'

'What the fuck, how can that happen?'

'All I know is what my boys have said. They told me that three men waited in a car outside my house and just lifted the girls from the street.'

'Why did they not take your boys as well, Azad?'

'I have no idea. Maybe they know you have the Mi5 agent.'

'Fuck me, why did no one collect them from school?'

'They always walk home, you already knew that, and you have never been worried.'

'Do you have any idea who is behind this?'

'No Mustafa, how could I? It could be anybody.'

'I will have to come over.'

'Don't think that is a good idea. You are a wanted man in the UK. Even if I get you here in one of the aircraft, undetected, the police will nab you within hours. Leave this with me, I will report as soon as I know anything.'

At 9.30 the following morning, Bobby Salisbury pulled into the yard of the Guls' warehouse in Southend. He already knew the make and licence plate of the Kurd's car, but it was not parked up. At 10.10 the black Range Rover, GUL 1, arrived. As Gul climbed out, he was met by Bobby.

'We have the girls.'

'And who the fuck, are you, old man?'

'It does not matter who I am. I know everything about you, and you know nothing of me.'

Gul reaching inside his leather jacket said,

'I should blow you away right now.'

'If you did that then your cousin would have two dead daughters.'

'So how much do you want, old man?'

'I don't want money, I just want Mr. Slade and Mr. Walters released and brought safely back to the UK.'

'I have no idea what you are talking about. Who is this Mr. Slade, Mr. Walters?'

Bobby walked away.

'Where the fuck do you think you are going?'

'I'm off. I have not got time to play your silly games.'

'Give me your number and I will call you later.'

'Don't work that way, you give me your number and I will call you tomorrow.'

Gul called out his number, Bobby plumbed it into his mobile, got into the Mondeo and was gone.

From his office, Azad called his cousin and explained what had just happened. Mustafa, now a lot more, hot-headed than his sedate cousin, aggressively asked,

'Who he is? He is a dead man. 'Just fucking find him, did you tail him when he left?

'You must calm down Mustafa. Like this you will achieve nothing.'

'I'm coming over. I will be using the plane that is bringing the gear tomorrow.'

'Please Mustafa, don't do that. They will take you and what then for your daughters?'

On Thursday, the 17th, February 2005, the sound of 'armed police' wafted through Gul's office door, one second later the door lay on the floor. Four large special op's men wrestled Gul to the ground. He was read his rights and marched out to the front-loading bay. Two-thirds of his large car park were occupied by all kinds of police vehicles. He saw Brian Dear and Don Rogers lying face down on the floor. Unbeknown to Azad Gul, seven of his depots, including the ones in Liverpool, Glasgow and Hull were subject to similar raids, all took place at the same time.

Twenty-three men at Southend, including Azad Gul, Don Rogers and Brian Dear were taken into custody. They were held, without charge, at seven locations around Essex. The raids had been ordered by Julian Pritchard. He had asked Commander David Skeels, James Reeves' successor at the helm of Special Branch to lead the operation. A further thirty-five men were held at the other locations, Bobby Keagan, Jamie Law, and Tony McDonald amongst them. They had just thirty-six hours to charge them with something and whilst they had hundreds of hours of video footage and thousands of photographs, there was no real evidence for them to use in court.

Azad Gul used the services of one of the UK's foremost Barristers whenever he was faced with criminal charges. Within twenty-four hours of being detained, he was let out. He was driven back home to Hutton by his moll. Using his wife's phone, he attempted to call his cousin in Germany. He tried several times, all to no avail, he simply heard the message, 'please try again later.'

Mustafa Gul was holed up in one of his safe houses, a log cabin deep inside the black forest. He had been driven there, together with Peter Slade and three heavies, immediately after he had received the tip-off from Dieter Smit. The cabin, centralised on the brow of a hill, within fifteen acres of dense forest, had been built as a retreat for Gul and his family, five years previously, although it had never been used as a family home. Under the cabin, not noticeable from the outside, was a large cellar. A door in the cellar opened into an underground tunnel, which, if required, could take anyone needing to escape, over a thousand metres from the cabin. In the five preceding years the tunnel had not been used. Unbeknown to Mustafa Gul the door to freedom had been left unlocked by the electricians that had recently fitted new lighting in the tunnel. Peter Slade, via the continued use of sedatives, was fast asleep in the cellar.

On Sunday 20th Feb 2005, at mid-day, Quinten Proctor strolled into the same Soho bar as the previous Sunday. This time his dress sense was not so flamboyant. An hour later, Teddy and Merv tailed him and his regular partner to the same shabby building, just off Cambridge Heath Road. Less than thirty minutes after arriving, the young man left alone. Merv moved quickly, entering the house via the door that the juvenile rent boy had left open. He found Proctor, naked and face down upon the bed, a bed that Merv clocked as not having seen a clean sheet for many a month. It seemed as if the date drug, administered by the departing gay boy, in return for five hundred smackers, had done its job. Taking three bungee ropes from his donkey jacket pocket, Merv slipped the shortest one around Proctor's neck, pulled it tight and then secured one hook to the other. He then dragged the limp body, which oozed a trickle of blood from the opening of its posterior, onto the landing at the top of the stairs. Taking the second, slightly longer bungee, he secured it around the one already cutting into the neck of the still-breathing, but limp victim. Proctor was then lifted-up and propped against the balustrade that prevented anyone from falling headfirst to the staircase below. One end of the third and final bungee was tied around the handrail and the hook was married up with the hook from the second bungee. The six-foot-six muscle man lifted the lifeless frame of Quinten Proctor and dropped him, headfirst. Merv never flinched when he heard the loud crack of his victim's neck snapping, some six feet below him. He was impressed at just how strong those bungee ropes were. Merv recorded the time of death as being, 14.45 on Sunday 20th, February 2005.

The headlines in most of Monday's newspapers read, **'Junior Home Office Minister commits suicide.'** He was found hanging, in a house in Bethnal Green, a locally well-known gay haunt. Thames House had leaked a report to the press on Friday 18^{th,} February, that Quinten Proctor had been accused of being the 'insider' for the UK's largest criminal drug gang. Julian Pritchard was never to mention anything about Proctor's death to anyone. Such was the way in which Mi5 worked.

By Monday, 21st, February, the two daughters of Mustafa Gul had been held in North Woolwich for six days. The girls were being looked after by Freddie Salisbury's daughter, Sadie. The girls were in no immediate danger. Knowing of Azad Gul's arrest, subsequent release, and possible surveillance, the three Salisbury brothers paid Don Rogers and his wife an unannounced visit. At 3.00am on Tuesday they rang the doorbell of a house located on a steep hill in South Benfleet. They were all armed. The Salisbury's had perfected their way of doing business. Freddie did the talking. He was softly spoken and very controlled. Albert and Bobby sat menacingly behind their brother when he began the conversation. They were fully prepared to use violence, should it be required. Freddie began.

'How long have you worked for Mr. Gul?'

'Why do I have to tell you?'

'Albert pulled a handgun from under his black camel-haired overcoat. A coat that had been popular amongst the old-time gangsters back in the sixties. Albert's coat was an original.'

'I will ask you one more time. How long?'

'Five years.'

'And how does Mr. Gul make so much money?'

'Import and Export.'

'Where do the drugs come from? Who supplies them?'

'Drugs, what drugs?'

'Now, now Mr. Rogers, don't treat us like idiots.'

Albert placed his gun down on the dining table.

'They arrive from Europe, Holland, Belgium, France, and Germany. But originally from Columbia and Afghanistan.'

'How do they end up in Southend?'

'We pick them up from various airstrips around the Southeast.'

'Where is Mr. Gul, right now?'

'As far as I know, he is at home.'

'How much do you have at the warehouse, at this moment?

'There is nothing, the old bill took everything away, last week.'

'Which airport handles the most?'

'North Weald, I think.'

'Is it still coming in?'

'As far as I know. The old bill did not touch the airstrips.

'OK, let me tell you what is going to happen.

'At 5.15, you, me and Albert are going to drive to North Weald, in your car.'

'Bobby will stay here, to keep your lovely wife company. That way, neither you nor her, will be able to talk to anyone. You OK with that?

'Do I have a choice?'

'No.'

At 6.05am, Don Rogers drove his red Audi A5 towards North Weald airstrip. Albert, gun drawn, sat in the back. Fifty-five minutes later, Rogers parked the car immediately outside the large, imposing doors that once welcomed World War Two fighters upon their return from battle with the Luftwaffe. The Salisbury brothers accompanied Rogers inside the warehouse that belonged to Gul Aviation. As the three men approached the portacabin that doubled as both the office and staff canteen, Jim 'Biggles' Snook, looked up from the bottom of his bottle-like lenses and said,

'Morning Don. Have not seen you this early for many a day.'

'You are right. Just showing our new Houdini and his mate where we are.'

Pointing at Freddie, Rogers continued.

'This one will be doing the pickups in future.'

'Is everything at Southend OK now, Don?

'Yep, all fine and dandy now, Biggles. I've come for the last five day's arrivals, should be about twenty-six kilos.'

'That's right Don. Can't pull the wool over your eyes, can we?' Bring the car in and we will load it for you.'

Rogers turned and walked back to get his car. Albert accompanied him. Freddie stayed put.

'So, you are the new Houdini, I wonder how long you will last?'

'Not long, but certainly a lot longer than you. On your own today then?'

'Until 8, the others start later than me.'

Rogers parked the car beside the pallet that contained 26 packages of pure cocaine and Biggles, under the watchful eye of Albert Salisbury, loaded them in the boot. With the two men sharing a joke, Albert took three paces forward and fired two shots. Both men hit the deck, blood oozing from the small round hole that each of them now had to the side of their heads.

Freddie walked into the office, ripped the hardware containing the CCTV from its leads, and threw it into the back of Don Rogers Audi A5. Both he and Albert buckled up and drove outside. Albert then went back and closed the large wooden doors. They then made their way back to South Benfleet. As they pulled up outside the Rogers family home, Bobby told Mrs. Rogers that she was still a fine figure of a woman. Slightly embarrassed, she replied,

'You're not so bad yourself.'

Bobby moved forward, as if to embrace her, he took the small pistol from his pocket and pumped two bullets into her heart. He had not gone for the headshot as he did not wish to spoil her good looks. The three men climbed into the Ford Mondeo, which was parked in an adjoining street, pulled alongside the Audi, transferred the cocaine and the CCTV player into its boot and then made their way back to North Woolwich. At current street value, uncut, the bounty in the boot was worth just over two million quid. Cut just once, the value increased to four million. The cocaine would be given to their eldest sons as the brothers just hated drugs.

Albert called Graham Roberts, the conversation was short and to the point.

'How much longer do we have to hold them?'

'Not sure Albert, we still have no word on our men.'

'OK, but we need to release them by Sunday, that's just six days away Graham.'

'I understand. I will get back to you as soon as I have some news.'

Mustafa Gul stepped down from the four-seater plane at 4.00am on Thursday 24^{th,} February, he had arrived at Little Baddow airstrip, just outside Chelmsford. The hire car, arranged by the manager of Gul Aviation, was ready for him to drive away. At 5.25 he pulled onto the drive of his cousin's house in

Hutton. At 6.40 the house was surrounded, and Mustafa Gul was taken away by officers from Chelmsford Police HQ, led by Superintendent Des Walker of Essex Police Special Op's unit. He was immediately charged with the illegal transportation of seven females into the UK and for enslaving the women for use as prostitutes at the apartment block in Westcliffe-on-Sea, Essex. He was also made aware of the fact that the German Police had issued a European Arrest Warrant, requesting his return to Germany to face twenty-seven separate charges, including murder and abduction. Azad Gul arranged for his brief to attend the subsequent interview, however on this occasion, evidence, supplied by the surveillance team working for Graham Roberts was strong enough to prevent Police Bail from being granted. Julian Pritchard was alerted of Mustafa Gul's arrest. Through the Chief Constable, Pritchard requested that they extract from Gul the whereabouts of Slade and Walters. He did not mention Gul's abducted daughters in the conversation.

In the Black Forest, Peter Slade was now fully coherent and had just been given some food and drink by one of the three 'minders' left behind by Mustafa Gul to ensure that Slade remained captive. As soon as the Kurdish jailer left Slade's lunch and returned upstairs from the cellar, Slade pushed down the handle of the door. To his utter amazement, the door opened, and he stepped into the tunnel and proceeded to walk, overhead lights came on, automatically, every, one hundred metres or so. After about three minutes, he was faced with a decision, he had reached a fork in the tunnel. His choice was, carry straight on or veer to the left, he chose straight on. Five minutes later daylight began to seep into the tunnel, as he walked on, the light became stronger. Suddenly he was at the end, the opening was secured from the outside world by fallen trees, branches, and leaves but he was able to slowly move enough of this undergrowth to enable him to squeeze through. Once he had, he found himself in an elevated position close to the top of a steep bank that sloped its way down to a small river below. He half-slid, half-rolled down the bank until he came to rest, just five-foot from the fast-running water. He followed the bank of the river until he came across a wooden, purpose-built footbridge. He crossed. He realised that he was on a public footpath and thirty minutes later he was clear of the forest and alongside a main road, signed as the 415. He decided to go left. There were hardly any vehicles on the single-lane road. In the distance he saw that there were road signs, on either side of the road. On his side he saw that he was just three km from the town of Lahr. On the other side of the road the sign read Kuhbach two km. He decided on Kuhbach, for no other reason than the fact that it was closer. He crossed the road at the point of a sharp bend, he must have forgot that he was not in the UK. He was facing the wrong way when the BMW hit him at 80 kmh.

Late on Friday afternoon, Mustafa Gul gave the full details of the whereabouts of Peter Slade. He informed Superintendent Des Walker that the other man was already dead when they opened the container in Hamburg. He would not, however, reveal what had happened to the body of Paul Walters. Gul had given this information after reassurances that Essex Police would do everything within their power to locate his two daughters. At that precise moment in time, the Police had no idea as to where the two girls were. The information given by Gul was relayed to Julian Pritchard, he in turn informed Graham Roberts. Pritchard, about to call his counterpart in Berlin, Wolfgang Moller, was saved that task as Moller was put through to the Mi5 boss at that very moment.

'I have some news in respect of Dieter Smit, Mr. Pritchard.'

'I too, have news for you Mr. Moller, regarding the whereabouts of Chief Superintendent Peter Slade.'

'You first, Mr. Moller.'

'We have found a mobile phone in a secret compartment within Smit's desk. It contains just six numbers, one of them is that of Mustafa Gul. The phone has been checked and I can confirm that Smit made two calls to Mustafa Gul around the time of our raid upon his premises. We also traced three bank accounts in Smit's name, he has over seven hundred thousand Euros saved up, all within the last three years. He could never have amassed such a sum from his salary as an Inspector. I have yet to decide Smit's fate. And your news, Mr. Pritchard?'

'We have Mustafa Gul in custody. He arrived in the UK yesterday, in search of his two daughters, who were mysteriously abducted from the street a week ago. At this stage we have no idea who is behind their abduction, but just to reassure you, the authorities here played no part in it. He has been charged with various offences and later I will get one of my staff to share that information with you. What is more important is that Gul has given us the address of a log cabin in the Black Forest, near to Kuhback as being the place where Peter Slade is being held. He assures us that Slade is unhurt, although the man that was with him, Paul Walters is said to be dead. I am texting you the address as soon as we finish this call. Please get back to me as soon as you have our man, by the way, he is guarded by three armed men.'

Graham Roberts phoned Albert Salisbury and informed him that, with a bit of luck, the girls could be released, possibly before Sunday.

Wolfgang Moller called the local Chief of Police in Kuhbach and informed him of the operation that he was setting up to free Peter Slade. Moller pointed out that the BND would take all responsibility for whatever the outcome of the raid upon the log cabin was going to be. Kuhback, was some eight hours away by road from Berlin. Moller arranged for a special services helicopter and six operatives. He asked Dieter Smit to accompany them. He then called Lieutenant Axel Koln, head of the special services and told him, I am sending my man, Dieter Smit. Please make sure that he does not return.

Under the cover of darkness, the chopper, six highly trained special services men and Dieter Smit landed in a clearing, around 7 km from their target. The remainder of their journey would be undertaken, on foot. With three men in position at the back and three, plus Smit at the front, the front door of the cabin was wired with explosives and detonated. Firing from inside the cabin was almost immediate. Two tear gas grenades were thrown into the cabin, shortly after, two of the Guls' most trusted men staggered through the opening that was once the front door. They died just seconds later, as did Inspector Dieter Smit, taken out in the crossfire by Lieutenant Axel Koln. The remaining gangster tried to escape via the rear of the cabin. He was gunned down and fell into the small lake that formed the boundary between the property and the dense forest beyond. Koln and one of his men silently made their way to the basement, expecting to find Peter Slade. The basement was empty. Koln tried the door, it opened, revealing the tunnel behind it. Koln shouted for two more of his men to join them. They walked the entire length of the tunnel, two men turned left at the fork, Koln and his colleague continued straight on. When they arrived at the opening, high up on the bank, Koln knew, from the recent disturbance of the undergrowth, that Chief Superintendent Peter Slade had escaped. He immediately reported his findings to Wolfgang Moller in Berlin. It was 7.00am on Saturday 26th, February in Germany and one hour earlier in the UK.

At home, Moller, on his laptop, and knowing the exact location of the tunnel exit, studied the map of the area of the black forest where he believed would be the most likely place for Slade to have resurfaced. He called the Chief of Police in Lahr and asked him to find out from all local stations if there had been any unusual happenings in the area within the last twenty-four hours. Three hours later, Chief Heinz Braemar informed Moller that there had been a hit-and-run on the 415 between Lahr and Kuhbach. Braemar added that the victim of the hit-and-run was carrying no identity but was believed to be in his early forties. He was now in the major trauma unit at Marien Hospital in Stuttgart and his condition is said to be critical. Moller asked Braemar to get a photograph of the unfortunate man and email it to him as soon as he possibly could. Peter Slade had reached the age of forty-one, just three weeks earlier.

At mid-day, Moller called Julian Pritchard and gave him a detailed report of the morning's events, adding that he was waiting for a photograph to be emailed to him. Pritchard thanked his German counterpart for all his cooperation and awaited receipt of the photo.

At 4.00pm, Moller forwarded to Pritchard, the photograph that had been sent to him by Braemar. Moller knew when he sent it on to Pritchard that it would be of no use as the head of the man lying in the critical care unit in Stuttgart, was completely swathed in bandages.

Graham Roberts took the call from Pritchard at 4.25pm. He and his family were holed up in the house at 38 Oban Street, Poplar. Roberts had taken them there as the Guls knew of his involvement in the investigation, headed by Peter Slade. He was traceable at the family home, and he believed that the Guls were more than capable of exacting their revenge upon his family.

'Graham, sorry to bother you at the weekend.'

'No problem, Julian. You have news?'

'Yes, but not good, I fear.'

Pritchard then went on to explain his conversations with Wolfgang Moller, at the end of which he asked Roberts as to how they were going to identify the man, close to death in Stuttgart.

'Well, when we were at school, Slade fell on a broken bottle and cut his left knee, he required several stitches. A few years ago, we played together in a charity football match, the old bill versus a team from the NHS, he showed me his knee, it still bore the scar left by the bottle.'

'It's worth a look, I'll relay this info to Moller in Berlin and get back to you soonest.'

'Before you go, Julian, how about Gul's daughters? We are supposed to release them tomorrow.'

'On the basis that I have no idea what you are talking about, I will leave that to you.'

Pritchard called Moller and asked him to arrange yet another photo, this time of the victim's left knee.

The following day, Sunday, Pritchard received five photographs of a person in a hospital bed. The 'unidentified patient,' was in a coma. His right arm and both legs were held in place by the traction that the hospital had to use to reset those limbs. All three limbs were encased in plaster. Any photograph of the left knee would be impossible until the patient was out of both traction and plaster. Everything about the accident, the location, and the time, together with the height and the age of the bedridden patient, pointed towards it being Peter Slade, however no one could be one hundred percent sure. They would have to wait, firstly to see the face and the knee and then to hear from the victim himself.

On Monday, Pritchard sent Pierce Nelson (Column) to visit Mustafa Gul, whom had been moved from Chelmsford to a high-security prison in Wiltshire. Column was to inform Gul that, thus far there had been no leads in respect of locating his daughters and until he gave more details of the whereabouts of

Paul Walters, it was likely that the police would take their time in trying to find them. To Column's surprise, Gul spilled the beans. Informing the man from Mi5 that the 'dead man' in the container had been taken to a slaughterhouse and was made into kebabs. Gul denied killing the man. Column offered no reply when asked by Gul to ensure that the police find his daughters.

This revelation by Mustafa Gul left both Pritchard and Roberts with a real problem. Walters' wife and three sons had reported him as a missing person. The local police in Plaistow, East London had not yet listed him thus, as he had a habit of disappearing whenever he had been involved in a crime. For now, both men would remain silent. Roberts had no way of knowing if Walters had shared with his wife the fact that he had met up with two old schoolmates recently.

With Peter Slade no longer heading up operation 'Daisy' both Julian Pritchard and Graham Roberts were in a quandary. There was no one that could be drafted in to continue the investigation into the most prominent of the drug gangs that were making millions throughout the UK and Europe. Whilst Mustafa Gul had been banged up in the UK, the distribution of drugs within Germany was taken over by associates of General Kos. Technically, the rise of Kos in Europe presented a much bigger problem than the Guls, as the General not only had the means to Import and control the distribution of drugs and arms he was also becoming a big player in the people smuggling business. His men, all trained killers, quickly eradicated those members of the Gul clan that refused to move over to his organisation.

James Reeves, at the request of Julian Pritchard, instructed the agents under his control, Asani and Topolov to turn their attention to the people that were now running the Guls' business in Germany.

In mid-March, with the man in the bed in Stuttgart still not identifiable, Pritchard made the decision to call a halt to every single surveillance that Roberts had undertaken on behalf of Slade. There was a great deal of sadness in both men's hearts that all the hard work, sacrifice, and sheer danger that Peter Slade had endured to bring to book those people that, through their total disregard for human life had inflicted so much suffering upon.

On Wednesday 2nd, March 2005, Graham Roberts called Albert Salisbury and asked him to release the daughters of Mustafa Gul. One hour later a black cab pulled up outside Limehouse Police Station and the two young ladies walked into the station and declared who they were. Mustafa Gul was informed of their safe release the following day.

Six weeks later, there was an explosion in a flat of the sixth floor of a high-rise block in Canning Town. The family of Paul Walters' were informed that he had met with his death in the explosion. The flat where he had met his death was a well-known 'crack house' his body was only identifiable by his teeth. The teeth in question had, unfortunately, been lost by the forensic lab that had examined them.

Jamie Law, Bobby Keagan, and Tony McDonald continued to be held on remand, awaiting trial on a total of seventy-nine combined charges. None of them would give evidence in respect of Azad Gul's part in their business. Gul remained free, albeit under constant surveillance, of which he was fully aware.

19 - THE LONG ROAD BACK

By mid-April 2005, Peter Slade had been in a coma, in a hospital bed in Stuttgart for nearly two months. Only once had he moved any muscle in his lifeless body, that was when the bandages were removed from his head. Julian Pritchard and Graham Roberts had arrived at his bedside just hours after they had been informed. Whilst he had undergone significant plastic surgery to his face, both of his visitors, the first for several weeks, were quite sure that the man they were looking at was indeed, Chief Superintendent Peter Slade. The scar to his knee was not visible, as skin, grafted from his backside had to be used in the rebuilding of his legs. When the two men left the hospital, they agreed, that for now, they would not reveal to anyone that they had seen Slade, alive. Albeit he was still in a coma. The Chief Medical Officer of the hospital had discussed with Pritchard and Roberts the possibility of moving the patient from Stuttgart to a specialist unit in the UK. They agreed to review that possibility in mid-May, with any decision being dependent upon Slade's progress.

With his friend out of the picture and Graham Roberts unable to investigate any further, as he was a 'private detective', operation 'Daisy' was, to all intents, 'dead in the water.' Julian Pritchard, reluctant to allow years of work to simply evaporate, asked James Reeves to talk to his successor at Special Branch, Commander David Skeels, with a view to keeping an eye on Azad Gul. Skeels agreed and he arranged surveillance on Gul's house and business. Three days into their watch, the operatives informed their Superintendent that Gul had not been seen entering or leaving either address. A raid by the 'proceeds of crime unit' at Gul's house, found it to be empty. Gul and his family had gone to ground.

Essex Police, investigating the triple murder of Don Rogers, his wife and Jim Snook were tipped off by a disgruntled employee of Gul Aviation, working at North Weald Airstrip, that Azad Gul, his wife, their two sons, and the daughters of Mustafa Gul, boarded the executive jet, belonging to Gul's company, the night before the murders took place, he was unable to give the police the jet's destination. Despite knowing the plane's identification, it had filed no flight plan, it had a range of two thousand miles and could be anywhere within Europe and possibly beyond. Commander Skeels was to ask the Chief Constable of Essex Police as to why Azad Gul was allowed, to keep his passport, whilst under investigation. In reply, Skeels was told that Gul's passport was being held at Chelmsford HQ and that he would not have required it anyway, as he was unlikely to have passed through any border controls.

With the Guls' UK distribution network effectively, 'closed down' and Birusk and Asti Gul not due for release until 2007, there was a huge gap in the marketplace. Several small gangs tried to fill the void however Kagan Kaptan was the rising star in the drug business. Using his knowledge and connections with the PKK in Kurdistan, he was soon to assume control. For some time, his people, having infiltrated the Guls' set-up, had been sending information back to him. Kaptan brought in the Albanian, Joseph 'Iron Man' Ardizzone as his number two and enforcer. Ardizzone had entered the UK as an illegal just under two years previously. He had been under the care of Nur Nazif at the North London Mosque. In his time in the UK, he had set up over four hundred car-wash outlets and employed nearly two thousand people, like himself, all illegals. Having disposed of all his own identity documents, he had taken the name of Joseph Ardizzone. Ardizzone had been a 'real-life' gangster in Los Angeles back in the 1930s. He was one of the first Albanians to be recognised in the USA as a 'don.' Through the car-wash business an enormous volume of drugs was being sold, all sourced by Kaptan and supplied by Ozturk Ozsoy, now the leader of the PKK in the immediate area of Kaptan's birthplace. Within weeks of Azad Gul fleeing the UK, Kaptan and Ardizzone had taken over the business of Gul Aviation. They did not require the Guls' distribution outlets, as they already had their own, however the established flight paths between Europe and the UK were a welcome addition to Kaptan's operation. As well as the importation of the drugs, the two men steadily increased the flow of illegals into the UK by adding some larger aircraft and increasing the arrivals, by the small boats that would land, in the dead of night, at many locations along the East Coast of the UK. Most of the poor souls that arrived in England, had been trafficked through the Petrov's' organisations in Bulgaria. All arrivals would claim asylum unless they were sent over to work in any of the businesses that the gang operated. Four London Solicitors worked full-time facilitating the applications of the newly arrived runaways, none of whom had the slightest idea that they would be put to work by one of the most feared gangs ever to operate in the UK.

By the end of May 2005, Peter Slade had shown no signs of improvement. Pritchard and Roberts decided that it might be best if he was brought back to the UK. On the 10th of June, Slade was flown by a specialist medical jet, from Stuttgart to Brice Norton Military Airbase and from there he was transferred to a Government Hospice facility in Wiltshire. He was not expected to ever regain consciousness and a decision would have to be made in respect of turning off his life support. The problem with that was that he had no known living relatives. Exactly who would decide his fate, was, at that time, difficult to know.

In the meantime, Alkan Asani, still working under the umbrella of James Reeves and Julian Pritchard, let it be known that Azad Gul and his family were living in a safe house, on the beachfront at Golden Sands, Bulgaria. The house belonged to Boyan Petrov. The arrangements had been brokered by General Kos. With Mustafa Gul being held in prison, in the UK, awaiting extradition to Hamburg, Azad had agreed that the General would temporarily take over control of the Gul business in Germany, in return, at some time in the future, the General would help the Guls eradicate Kagan Kaptan and his merry men.

On Monday 27th June 2005, Graham Roberts phoned his brother, Roy. He asked Roy, who had been looking after Peter Slade's house in Epping ever since Slade's ill-fated trip to Turkey, back in December 2003, if he could explain to Cheryl Smith that he would like to meet with her, as he had news about Slade's whereabouts. A short time later, Roy informed Graham that Cheryl was willing to meet with him at her house the following day. At 10.00am on the 28th of June, Graham Roberts rang Cheryl Smith's doorbell. Roberts immediately understood why his old schoolmate was so smitten by this lady. Sitting in her lounge, Roberts explained that Slade had been working on a project for HM Government, he was careful not to go into the details of the job. When he informed Cheryl of Slade's current situation, she broke down. Roberts allowed for a few minutes to pass and once the stunning forty-one-year-old had composed herself, he asked if she would like to visit her incapacitated, former lover, in hospital. Before she could answer, he let her know that Slade was still in a coma, some four months after his near-fatal accident in Germany. Cheryl did not hesitate with her answer,

'Of course, I would like to visit him.'

'OK then, we can go on Thursday, I will collect you at 9.00am.'

Whilst the UK side of operation 'Daisy' had been shut down, the European investigation, although no longer headed up by Peter Slade, was still 'live' and Alkan Asani and Borislav Topolov were still very much flat out with their investigations into the people that had been fingered at the meetings in Oban Street, Poplar E14. Utilising the list of private investigators given to them by Graham Roberts and in conjunction with the authorities in Germany, Holland, Belgium, Romania, Bulgaria, and Turkey, they had managed to arrange for all their prime targets to be monitored, around the clock. In Germany, Wolfgang Moller, head of the BND, had taken a deep interest in what was going on and he had alerted his counterparts in Holland and Belgium. All were willing to share the cost of the civilian sleuths as they were all aware of the risk of leaks within their own departments. This left Asani free to find out what intel he could, in both Bulgaria and Romania. Topolov was now very much entwined into the complex movements of the chief suspects in Turkey, Syria, and Jordan. Even with the demise of the UK investigation, overall, their workload was proving to be nigh impossible to maintain. What both men agreed upon was that General Kos and Boyan Petrov seemed to be at the heart of everything that was going on. It had only been a matter of a few months since they had met and discussed the operation with Peter Slade and Graham Roberts. They were both saddened by the news of what had happened to Slade and were fully aware that the UK no longer offered operational help to them. James Reeves informed Asani and Topolov that a meeting with Wolfgang Moller and Julian Pritchard had been agreed upon and that they would be required in Berlin on the 2nd of July.

At mid-day on Thursday 30th June, Cheryl Smith gripped Graham Roberts' arm as, together, they entered the room in the Hospice where Chief Superintendent Peter Slade lay. Whilst she had been prepared for what greeted her, she still wobbled as she approached Slade's bedside. She looked long and hard at the man that had held her tightly in his arms on many occasions. He looked different, facially. Wires were connected to all parts of his body and machines surrounded his bed. Her initial thoughts were to leave, to get away, it was all so painful for her. Roberts spoke some words of reassurance to her, he touched Slade's forehead and then said that he would wait outside for a short while. Cheryl Smith sat on a chair, positioned almost level with Slade's head. She leant over and kissed him, gently, on both cheeks and then held his hand. She then started a conversation with him, reminding him that they had missed their planned holiday together, in New Zealand, last winter. As she spoke, she thought that his hand had slightly tightened, around her own. She dismissed this as 'wishful thinking' but then, it happened again. She rose from her chair and positioned her face directly over his. She whispered,

'Peter, darling. Can you hear me?'

Did his eyelid just twitch? She said in her mind.

She squeezed his hand, he squeezed back.

'Graham, Graham, quick, come in here.'

Roberts entered the room. He immediately noticed that the heart monitor, which for months had been at a level that just defied death, was now pulsing up and down. He went back to the half-open door and called a nurse over, she came. She took Slade's wrist, placed her thumb on his neck, left the room and then returned with two doctors. Doctor Thacker quickly established that the patient was now no longer reliant upon the life support machine. Doctor Khan confirmed his colleague's diagnosis. Doctor Thacker turned to Cheryl Smith and said,

'I have no idea what you have done, but would you like to work here?'

'I just kissed his cheeks and held his hand, nothing more.'

'Then this man owes you his life, never let him forget that.'

Mrs. Smith and Roberts were asked to wait outside whilst the two doctors carefully removed wires and machines that were no longer required. Half an hour later they were allowed back in. Peter Slade was sat upright he was coherent but had no idea as to whom his two visitors were.

Cheryl lent over, to once again, kiss his cheeks. Cheeks that she thought were somewhat different to the ones that she had previously kissed.

Doctor Khan asked Slade,

'Do you know where you are and what happened to you?'

'No, I have no idea.'

'Do you know these two people?'

The mood in the room changed from the euphoria of Slade waking up, to the gloom that had descended when it was realised that he had suffered memory loss. The recent scans had showed no brain damage.

Doctor Thacker was the first to break the silence that had ensued after the announcement that the patient had no recollection of anything in his past. Walking over to shut the ward door, he returned and stood at the foot of the bed. Facing Slade, he said,

'Unfortunately, your loss of memory, which may only be temporary is not your only concern. Your spinal cord was severely damaged, probably when you hit the road upon landing. The report and x-rays that we received from Stuttgart show that your spine was crushed, they did the best they could to repair it, however this was done as part of saving your life at the time. Now that you are awake, we can take a further look at it and hopefully improve on what has already been done. I must tell you that at this moment in time you are paralysed from your waist, downwards. We will leave you with your visitors for a while. We shall be back later to discuss your longer-term treatment.'

Cheryl Smith burst into tears. She was comforted by Roberts, who himself was visibly shaken by the news that the doctor had just announced.

'Please, please do not worry, I shall overcome these problems. How long have I been here?'

A short question and answer session took place between Roberts and Slade.

'Your accident took place in Germany at the end of February, it is now the 2nd, July. You were moved from Stuttgart to this hospital just three weeks ago.

'Why was I in Germany?

'Well, Peter.'

'My name is Peter?'

'Yes, Peter Slade. You are an agent of Mi5.'

'What is Mi5?'

'To help you understand who you are, I am going to bring you all the recent files that you were working on. It will be a lot easier than me trying to explain. I am Graham Roberts, your, almost 'lifelong' friend. This is Cheryl Smith, your next-door neighbour and your almost partner. You know hundreds of people Peter and I am sure that many of them will want to visit you. Just leave that with me. I will come back tomorrow evening. I will bring you a mobile phone.'

Cheryl kissed Slade on his forehead. He knew not what to do, or how to react. Tears once again welled up in her eyes. She was looking at the man that meant everything to her, but now had to accept the fact that he no longer knew who she was, or how close they had once been. She decided, there and then that she was not going to let Peter Slade slip away from her.

In the car, during the two-hour journey back to Epping, Roberts and Cheryl discussed what they thought might be best for Slade's future. Roberts suggested that they should find out if Slade could be moved to a hospital closer to home. He would contact Slade's boss to see if this could be arranged. Cheryl confirmed that she would look after Peter, she would even convert her home to accommodate his needs, should he remain incapacitated.

After dropping Cheryl off, Roberts, still sat in his car, called Julian Pritchard, and explained the day's events. Pritchard sounded genuinely relieved that his star agent had woken from his slumber and was making something of a recovery, albeit the news of his paralysis was quite concerning. He was quick to agree to Roberts' suggestion that Slade be moved to a facility nearer to home. Promising Roberts that he would instruct Nigel Smalling to make the arrangements, he added that he would personally inform James Reeves of this good news.

The following day, Cheryl Smith threw her packed bag onto the backseat of her car and drove to Wiltshire. At mid-day she walked into the room where just yesterday she had seen Peter Slade wake up from four months of induced coma. Her heart slumped to her ankles when she saw that the bed that Peter had been laid in, was gone. As she turned, distraught and tearful, a nurse placed a comforting hand upon her shoulder and said,

'Do not worry, Mr. Slade is in theatre, undergoing corrective surgery to his spine.'

'How long will he be?'

'The operation is just about to begin. They estimate that it could take several hours.'

'OK, I need to go and find a hotel as I will be staying for a while.'

'You can stay here, in the hospital if you want to. There is a small room available, next door.'

'Oh, thank you. I will take you up on that.'

'There is a café on the ground floor, the food is not bad.'

Thanking the nurse for her help, Cheryl made her way to the Café and drank two strong coffees and managed a sandwich in between. Returning to the private ward, Cheryl sat in the chair beside the empty space, where the bed should have been. She read a magazine, had a nap, read a book, but mainly stared into space. Her thoughts only for the man that she knew she loved but had no idea of how he felt as just yesterday, he did not even know who she was. At a little after 7.30pm Peter Slade was wheeled back into the ward. At 8.15 he started to come around, as the effects of the anaesthetic began to wear off. Cheryl kissed him gently on the cheek. She asked him if he remembered her from yesterday.

'Yes, you were here with your husband, right?'

'No Peter, the man was Graham Roberts, not my husband but your lifelong friend.'

'Oh, I see. So, who are you then?'

'I am Cheryl Smith, your next-door neighbour and until you disappeared over two years ago, we were, what they call nowadays 'partners'.'

'I know that since your wife and children were murdered you have no living relatives. Both you and your wife's parents are deceased. You have no brothers or sisters and you have never mentioned to me the existence of Aunts, Uncles or Cousins. You seem to have no one, Peter, other than me.'

'My god, I was married and had kids, what happened to them?'

'Peter, I am going to let Graham Roberts explain all of that to you, he knows all the details. I am going to stay here with you until we can get you moved, nearer to home. I am now going to get some dinner you need to rest. When I return, I will be sleeping right next door.'

When Cheryl returned to the ward after finding a restaurant just ten minutes from the hospital, Slade was fast asleep.

Waking at 7.45 the following morning, Cheryl found that Slade was propped up and drinking tea. He informed his 'carer-to-be' that the doctors had been to see him and that he could not expect to know if there was any improvement in his mobility until at least a weeks-time. In the meantime, he would have to rest for at least five days. At 10.30 in walked Graham Roberts, he was dragging a medium-sized suitcase behind him. Roberts had been to his friend's house and had gathered up as much information as he could find. He moved a small table over to the bedside and began to place the contents of the suitcase upon it. There were photo albums, diaries, newspaper cuttings, and a book that had been put together by Sandra, his deceased wife. This contained a chronological map of his achievements and promotions within the Metropolitan Police Force. Cheryl left to get coffee for everyone.

'I am leaving all of this with you, Peter, in the hope that something jogs your memory.'

'What about my wife and children?'

'It's all there, Peter. Best left for you to see in private.'

'And my job? Is that the reason I am in here?'

'Tomorrow, James Reeves, your ex-commander will be here. All things appertaining to your recent activities will be brought by him.'

'How far am I away from my house?'

'You are a long way from home Peter, however as soon as you are well enough to be moved you will be transferred to a hospital that will be more convenient for everyone concerned.'

In a whispered voice, Slade asked Roberts,

'Who is the lady? How do I know her? She is bloody good-looking, is she not?

'Cheryl is the woman that you sought solace in after the death of your family. She cares about you Peter, and she is willing to devote her life to looking after you. Hopefully, at some time in the future, you will remember her, and me, you old 'bastard. '

Ten days later, and after visits by Julian Pritchard, James Reeves and much to everyone's surprise, even Nigel Smalling, none of whom Slade remembered, he was moved to a private hospital just outside Epping Town centre. The hospital boasted one of the UK's foremost spine specialists as an on-site consultant. Cheryl stayed with Slade throughout.

Mi5 agreed to pick up the tab for the alterations required for Slade's homecoming, albeit those alterations could only be made to his own house and not that of Cheryl Smith. Whilst in Epping, Slade was to undergo another seven operations on his spine, one of which involved re-aligning the nerve ends from his brain. Either of these operations could have killed him, however he was determined to go through with them all. Sadly, by the end of 2005, there was still no movement in his legs and despite reading everything about himself, he had no recollection of anyone, or anything post his accident.

In January 2006, Peter Slade was returned to his house in Epping and accepted that his life would be spent in either his electrically operated chair, or bed. With Slade's blessing, Cheryl sold her own house and moved in with him. She refused to accept that his life was meaningless and even shared the same bed as him. On their second night together, after helping him, with the assistance of the electric hoist, to get into bed, Cheryl's hand wandered to Slade's groin area. Within seconds he developed a sizeable hard, Cheryl was on him instantly. They now knew that they could have a sex life, even if it meant Slade 'laying back and thinking of England.'

A whole year elapsed, during which time Slade attended physiotherapy three times each week. His memory told him nothing of his life prior to him waking up in Wiltshire. Whilst he could not stand, his leg muscles were exercised by the staff, to stop them from becoming completely useless and he was given an upper body strengthening program. Visits by former colleagues became non-existent, only Graham Roberts maintained any interest in his friend's welfare. During the night of the first of January 2007, Slade had a dream. A dream so vivid that he fell from his bed. By the time that Cheryl had woken and ran to the other side, Peter Slade stood unaided. Cheryl gently sat him on the side of the bed, Slade stood again. He was to do this several times before declaring himself cured. It was 3.45am, nonetheless, Cheryl phoned Graham Roberts. At 4.30 on a cold and dark January morning the private detective pulled onto his lifelong friend's drive.

When he walked into Slade's living room, the Chief Superintendent was sat, not in his electric wheelchair, but on one side of a leather sofa.

'Miraculous,' was the first word out of Roberts' mouth, followed by, 'tell me what happened.'

Cheryl trotted off to make some strong coffee.

'Well Graham, it started with a dream, a dream so vivid that I thought it was actually happening.'

Slade waited until Cheryl returned before continuing. He was fully aware of the fact that what he was about to tell his schoolboy chum, she had not been privy to previously.

Cheryl returned. She placed three coffees and a plate of toast on the coffee table and then sat next to Slade, tightly holding his hand.

'The dream began with me lifting my head when a container door opened and allowed some light into an otherwise darkened space. Looking up, I saw the figure of Mustafa Gul stood over me. He uttered these words to another man that had entered the container with him.

'This one is dead.'

He was of course referring to Walters. I was shackled to the floor with chains and cable-ties. Gul grinned as he punched and kicked me. The two men left, returning later to untie me and bundle me into a van. We all arrived at a cabin in the woods. I was put into a cellar, unconscious. Later, when I was more alert, I escaped through a door that led into a long and narrow tunnel. I exited the tunnel at a steep bank and managed to get to a road that ran through the forest. I remember being hit as I crossed this road, after that I had no recollection of anything in my past. At this moment I can recall nothing in my life prior to being in the container. I have seen the face of Mustafa Gul from the photos that were in the files that you brought to my bedside, Graham. I apologise to both of you for not knowing who you are or what we may have done in the past. Maybe I can 'dream you' back into my life.'

'Well, it's great that you have recaptured at least some of your memory, Peter. There are specialists that can work with you that may be able to take you back in time. However, the best news currently is the fact that you have regained the use of your legs. At nine o'clock you should contact the hospital and arrange an appointment with the spine doctor. I am sure that they will be excited to hear from you.'

'If you are agreeable, I will come back here on Sunday and go through everything that I know about you, as this may help jog your memory.'

'You are so kind, Graham. I will treat you to lunch, Cheryl's paying.'

At ten past nine, Cheryl telephoned the hospital and spoke to Dr Thacker's secretary. She relayed the news.

'Dr Thacker is stood beside me would you like to tell him yourself?

'Yes, indeed.'

'Mrs. Smith, is Mr. Slade with you at present?'

'Yes, he is.'

'Can I speak to him?'

Cheryl handed the telephone to Slade.

'Hello, Doctor.'

'Mr. Slade, what great news. I will need to see you as a matter of urgency. My afternoon is free, can you come in, say around 2.30? You can tell me everything then. Please continue to use your wheelchair as you could inflict damage upon yourself if you try to walk before, I can examine you properly.'

'Yes, of course. We shall see you later. Thank you, Doctor.'

When Cheryl and Peter walked into Dr Thacker's room they were completely taken aback. There were at least a dozen other people, both sitting and standing. Dr Khan was amongst them.

'Well, Mr. Slade. You were already a celebrity here, now you have grown so much in statue that all these doctors asked to see you. We have tried to work out exactly why you have regained the use of the lower half of your body. In all honesty, not one of us believed that it was possible for you to do so. Firstly, we would like you to lie on the bed, face down, so that we can examine you. Dr Khan and I will help you out of the wheelchair and onto the bed.'

After everyone in the room had touched, prodded, lifted, and gently hit Slade's back, he was asked to turn over. The process was repeated. His blood pressure, heart rate and Stats were all taken, after which Dr Thacker concluded that his recovery was indeed, nothing short of a miracle.

'We need to send you for an MRI and some x-rays, after which you shall be brought back here.'

Slade was wheeled away in his chair, Cheryl followed behind.

Returning to Dr Thacker's room some ninety minutes later, the crowd had swelled to around twenty.

'Mr. Slade, it is remarkable. We have concluded that the fall, from your bed, has in some way repaired the alignment of your spine. Now we would like you to stand. We will help you at first and if we feel you are strong enough then you can do it all by yourself.'

Slade assisted by two doctors stood. He was asked to straighten up, he did. He was asked to sit, he did.

'Now try to stand unaided.'

He did that as well.

'Absolutely astounding.' Remarked Dr Khan. A round of applause followed.

'Mr. Slade, you will require intensive therapy for at least six months. Do not bend or get up from a chair too quickly. Our physio, Julie, who is stood shyly in the corner, will monitor your progress. I will need to see you again in ninety days-time. Unless Julie advises me otherwise. Your case will appear in the BMA journal, and I am sure that other specialists will want to meet with you.'

From all of us, we wish you well for the future and remember what I told you when we first met.

'You owe your life to this lady, look after her.'

When they left the hospital, Cheryl telephoned Graham Roberts and told him the good news. Roberts phoned James Reeves, he got in touch with Julian Pritchard and so on. Five days after his remarkable recovery, Peter Slade was the recipient of over two hundred greeting cards. Even the Salisbury brothers had wished him well, after all, without his abduction they would never have got their hands on two million pounds worth of cocaine.

Six weeks after his miraculous repair job, Slade received a letter on Government headed paper. Julian Pritchard had signed at the bottom of the page. Peter Slade had been 'officially' retired from duty. The whole of his police and Mi5 career had been taken into consideration when awarding him half a million pounds compensation for his injuries, sustained in the course of his work. He was also to receive his full pension, based on his twenty-seven years of distinguished service.

On the 30th of June 2007, having been discharged by Dr Thacker, Slade and Cheryl Smith embarked upon a six-month, around-the-world cruise. Slade's memory, other than the day that he was held captive in a container in Germany, had still not remembered anything prior to that enforced incarceration.

20 - KAGAN KAPTAN

In February 2007, Kagan Kaptan had returned to his homeland, a small village in the mountainous region that divides Turkey and Syria. Since his illegal arrival in England, back in 2003, he had successfully set up one of the largest networks of drug distribution ever to be seen in the UK. Kaptan, in just four years, had become one of the wealthiest Kurds ever to return to his roots. Ibrahim Kaptan, Kagan's young brother, had been left in charge of the ruthless gang that now controlled 60% of the UK's lucrative heroin and cocaine trade. The gang was based in one of the most unlikely of places, Fryening, near Ingatestone, in Essex.

Before he left, Kagan had warned his younger sibling that Birusk Gul was due to be released from jail after serving eight of a sixteen-year sentence for the manslaughter of two rival gang members in an East London Street back in 1999. The Guls and the Kaptan's, were from villages just a few miles apart in Turkish Kurdistan, however they were, and had always been bitter rivals. Birusk Gul would be looking to re-establish his family as the drug kings of the UK, Kagan was determined for that not to happen.

Having spent a few months in almost 'tourist' mode, visiting scores of family and friends all across Turkey, making sure that they all shared in his illegal gotten gains, word got through to Kagan, via a mutual friend in Istanbul, that Boyan Petrov would like to meet with him, the purpose of the meeting was to discuss the setting up of an alternative business, a business void of drugs and all of the risks that came with it, albeit operationally, it would be very similar to the cut-throat and dangerous world that both men had been involved with for the past few years. Petrov had guaranteed Kaptan's safety, the meeting was to take place in Varna on the first of June 2007. Kaptan would be allowed to take three 'minders' with him.

On the 25th of May 2007, Birusk Gul was released, on license, from Wakefield High Security Prison. On the 27th, May, Gul and twenty of his heavily armed gang members, arrived at a snooker hall in Brentwood, a stone's throw from Kaptan's twelve acres, of a heavily fortified operational base, which also served as his luxury residence. With no warning having been given, the Guls entered the snooker hall that Kaptan had purchased purely to allow his associates to have some leisure time, away from the laborious task of counting cash and cutting drugs. It took just minutes for Birusk Gul and his merry men to wipe out the seven unarmed heavies that Kaptan had left to look after his brother. Ibrahim Kaptan was dragged from a room at the rear of the building, where he was being given oral sex by a good-looking fifteen-year-old Filipino, he was laid, face down, fully naked, except for his socks, upon one of the full-size snooker tables. His arms were fed through the pockets at one end of the table and his flaying hands were tied with a bungee rope. His legs were spread apart as far as they could be. Taking the longest cue (the rest) from its rack, Gul forced the thickest end gently into Ibrahim's backside, he then laid the cue, still inserted into his rivals' buttocks, onto the soft green baize of the table and walked calmly down the room. He lifted Ibrahim's head upwards, forced open his mouth and pushed a red snooker ball inside. One of his men sealed the mouth with silver duct tape. Gul returned to the other end of the table, lifted the cue and forced it deep inside Ibrahim's body, he paused and then gave the cue another forceful shove, as he did so, the duct tape was removed from the mouth and seconds later the red snooker ball fell to the floor, when the end of the cue protruded from Ibrahim's mouth it was high five's and cheers from all of those in attendance. Gul took a piece of paper from his pocket and placed it under the black ball. Leaving all their weapons behind, Gul and sixteen of his men left the hall. The four men that had stood guard in the foyer joined them as they walked out into the street, they split into groups of four and met up, to celebrate, in London's East End, later that evening.

Three hours after the mayhem in the snooker hall and whilst sat outside a makeshift taverna, enjoying a glass of Turkey's finest red wine with one of the village elders, Kagan Kaptan received a call from Nur Nazif, the leader of the Aziziye Mosque in North London. Nur Nazif had given Kaptan safe refuge when he had first arrived in London and had been the 'go-between' in conversations and decisions with the Kurdish leaders back in their native country. Nazif informed Kaptan of the events that had taken place at his snooker hall. Kaptan gripped the half-full wine bottle that stood upright in front of him and hurled it at the ancient wall of the building that he was sat outside of. Composing himself, and speaking in his mother's tongue, Kaptan told Nazif that the death of his brother, cousins and friends could not pass without reprisals. Nazif told of the written message from Birusk Gul, left under the black snooker ball, it had been retrieved by one of his brother's gang members shortly after the massacre. The message had read,

'Now we are even, the Guls now run the business, you will suffer the same fate as your brother, should you choose to come after me.' The telephone call ended.

Five minutes later, Kaptan entered the house where he had been born and grew up in. He lifted a small stone from the floor in the corner of his bedroom and took out the satellite phone that had laid dormant for the best part of four years. He asked one of the many family members that drifted in and out of his house to charge up the phone. He would have to wait until the following morning before he could use this very safe way of communicating with others. At 8.00am on the 28th of May 2007, Kaptan called Mehmet Ozil, a friend since childhood. Mehmet was now the Chief of Police in Istanbul, and it was him that had set up the meeting with Boyan Petrov. Kaptan explained to his friend what had happened in the UK, asking him to contact Petrov and offer his apologies for not being able to make the meeting in three days-time. He then asked Turkey's most corrupt senior police officer if he could nominate some members of the underworld to carry out the execution of the entire Gul family, which according to Nazif, resided in the UK, Germany, the Netherlands, and Belgium. Mehmet Ozil asked Kaptan to leave that with him and that he would get back to him as soon as he could.

Kaptan could have summoned the elders from several local villages and put together a team that would have been more than willing to carry out his wishes, these men would 'die for the cause' however Kagan knew that should he take this action then it was almost certain that whatever plan they made to wipe out the Guls, the plan would almost certainly be shared with the elders of the villages just over the mountains, these villages were the birthplace of the Guls and whilst village elders were normally loyal and secretive, they could not help but to share their secrets. The plan, if effected close to Kaptan's birthplace would almost certainly be spread throughout the Kurdish Kingdom.

Just as the sun was setting that day, Kaptan answered his satellite phone, he already knew who would be at the other end. Mehmet Ozil informed his friend that it was just too dangerous to involve any Turks to carry out his wishes, instead he gave Kaptan the contact details of a man that could help, he did not give up the name of this man, he simply asked that when the man answered the call, he was to say,

'Oh, what a lovely day it is in Paris.'

Mehmet spoke no other words and the line went dead. Kaptan, normally a bold and decisive person, momentarily hesitated. Was he being set up by his lifelong friend? After all, Mehmet Ozil knew many members of the Gul family, had he been the right person to involve in this? Doubts now clouded his mind, what if he was being lured into a trap, what if Mehmet was in the pockets of the Guls. He now wished that he had not involved the Chief of Police, however he had, he could not undo that fact. Seconds later he called the number given to him by Mr. Ozil, in perfect English a voice pronounced,

'This is the General,' to whom am I speaking?

Whilst he felt rather silly at having to repeat the words given to him by Mehmet Ozil, he nonetheless found himself saying,

'Oh, what a lovely day it is in Paris.'

'Well, my friend, what is it that I can help you with?

'I would much prefer it if we could meet in person, General.'

'Of course, we should, you must come to my home. You should arrive at Tirana Airport in three days-time, you will be met and brought to me.'

Before Kaptan could utter another word, the General was no longer on the line.

Leaving the small, stone-built house, where he had been born twenty-five years before, Kaptan descended the hill that led to the office of the regional Kurdish Militia (PKK). When he opened the door and stepped inside, several men, nomadic in appearance, bowed and left. It seemed that everyone was in awe of him, he was, after all, the young man that had left to make a better life for himself and by doing so, he was able to provide his village with many things, that otherwise would not have been available to them. Kaptan was now alone with Ozturk Ozsoy, once the village elder and the man responsible for introducing Kaptan to Nur Nazif in London. Kaptan owed this man a lot and now he was once again about to ask for yet another favour. Ozsoy had moved up, he now controlled a large sway of the mountains on both sides of the border, he had over a thousand fighting Kurds at his disposal, together with unlimited arms, which consisted of, guns, rockets, tanks and even several planes, although most of the latter were grounded due to a lack of spare parts.

The two men greeted each other in the usual Kurdish manner, Ozsoy invited Kaptan to sit. A small wiry man, about eighty-plus years of age, served the strongest of Turkish coffee and left. Believing Ozsoy to be the most trustworthy of men, Kaptan told the story of the most recent of events that had taken place in London. At the end of his explanation, Ozsoy asked as to what he could do to help.

'I need a plane to take me to Tirana, I must land and pass through the Albanian Immigration and Customs as if I were a normal tourist,' replied Kaptan.

'And what is in it for the PKK?'

'I can get you the spare parts that you need for your broken aircraft.'

'And when do you wish to leave?'

'In two days-time,' a smiling Kaptan replied.

'OK, I will get you a detailed list of what we require for the planes.'

'And when will you return to the village?'

'I will not return the trip is one way only.' replied Kaptan.

The final words of this meeting were spoken by Ozsoy.

'OK, I wish you a safe journey. Please be at the Cizre Airstrip at 8.00am in two days' time. Your pilot will be the Albanian Gazmend Harizaj, he is the only person that can get you into Albania without questions being asked. May you achieve your aims, God be with you.'

Kaptan turned and left, he would never see his mentor again.

At 7.30am on the 1st of June 2007, Kaptan climbed into the armed Toyota pickup and sat beside one of his trusted cousins. Two men, in full camouflage uniforms sat on the open back, either side of the Russian-built anti-tank gun. It took just fifteen minutes to arrive at the small airstrip that the PKK had built, to all intents to aid them in their fight against the Turkish forces, it also existed to facilitate the arrival and distribution of drugs that emanated from Afghanistan, Pakistan, and Syria. A good quantity of those drugs would find their way into Europe and most of Kaptan's supply would pass through this single, grassed runway. At 7.55, Kaptan shook hands with Gazmend Harizaj, the pilot that looked more like 'Biggles' than an Albanian mercenary. The flight, flown at just 3,000 feet, took three hours, the alternative, commercial flight, which involved changing planes three times, would have taken just under twenty-four. After landing at Tirana International Airport, the small twin-engine Cessna veered to the right, away from the Terminal Building and came to a stop adjacent to the fire station that was void of any fire engines. Gazmend opened the door, and the unfolding steps came to rest upon a small area of tarmac. A battered old Mercedes pulled up just as Kaptan's feet hit the floor, the rear door of the car opened, and a man, in full military uniform invited him to get into the back seat. Kaptan was reluctant to do so, he could not speak Albanian, he bent down and spoke to the rear passenger in English, saying,

'I have to pass through the airport, I am being met by someone.'

To his surprise, the reply he received was in perfect English.

'I am Captain Hook, personal assistant to the General, I will take care of you until you are safely inside the complex.'

Kaptan held out his right hand, the captain held out his, he had no hand to shake, just a hook.

The captain laughed. Kaptan saluted Gazmend as the Merc sped down the runway, exited the airport through the already opened security gates and was, within minutes, speeding along a virtually deserted road.

Kaptan knew little of the General's abode, what he did know was that his complex straddled both sides of the Albanian/Kosovo border. Ozsoy had told him to expect to see something that was normally only available in fictional movies. After several minutes of silence, the worry of not being in charge, of his own destiny seemed to leave Kaptan, he turned to face the hook and asked,

'So how did you know when and how I would arrive in Tirana?'

Mr. Hook smiled as he replied,

'Well, my friend, there is nothing that General Kos does not know. If you were to go for a shit at ten o'clock tonight, then my General would be there to wipe your hairy 'arse'.'

The captain continued,

'You are known as the King of the Kurds, which is a whole lot better than being the King of the Turds, is it not? Both men laughed.

'And at such a young age. You are maybe twenty-five, twenty-six?'

"Twenty-six next month, answered a much more relaxed Kaptan.

After driving for around two hours, the Merc pulled off the road. Kaptan again became nervous he caressed the small handgun that nestled in a holster just under his armpit. The hook squeezed Kaptan's arm and said,

'No need to worry my friend, we stop only to get some refreshments.'

They came to a halt at a single petrol pump in a garage that looked as though it belonged to a film set from a 1940s Texas movie. The driver, whom the captain called Fido, mainly due to his 'dog-like' features and teeth, filled the tank, handed some money to a lifeless man sat on a chair, who may have died some years earlier, he then opened the coke-cola fridge and took out six bottles before returning to the driver's seat.

'If you need to take a leak, then you had better do it now,' said the captain.

Kaptan accepted the invitation, he got out of the car and shuffled himself to the rear. Just as he was undoing his flies, a shot whistled past his head.

'It's a fucking-ambush.' he thought. A split second later a helicopter flew past, a further second elapsed before two men fell into some bushes just 200 metres to Kaptan's left. The Turk, without even wetting the boot of the car, slid back beside the captain.

'Don't worry Mr. Kaptan, the helicopter is ours the dead men could be almost anyone.'

'How would they know that I would be in the car?'

'They would not know who you are, they just know that we make this trip many times, but only once have they managed to kill anyone. They attacked an envoy sent by Colonel Gaddafi when he was trying to buy arms from the General. Do not worry my friend, we will soon be home safe and sound.'

Twenty minutes later they were nearing the border town of Morine, had they continued, on the main road then they would have been stopped at the checkpoint, however the car took a right turn, onto an unmade road and supposedly crossed the border without seeing any sign to indicate this. At the end of this border evading road, they turned right, Kaptan noted the sign saying that the town of Vermica was just 8 km ahead. They never reached Vermica as they took another dusty, potholed road, this led them through a thick wooded area, then over a bridge that spanned a wide river after which Kaptan saw a twenty-foot-high wall that spread out, east and west, for as far as the eye could see. Concrete bunkers were set about every 100 metres in front of the wall, each bunker had a tank parked either side of it. They came to rest outside a pair of heavily fortified steel gates, decorated with camouflage paint and netting. Captain Hook picked up a 'walkie-talkie' pressed a button and spoke,

'Oh, what a lovely day it is in Paris.' Kaptan silently chuckled to himself.

'Welcome to Hotel California, Mr. Kaptan,' said the one-handed Captain. The gates opened and Fido drove the Merc slowly into what would later be described as 'the world's most secure complex.'

Looking out of the rear window of the car, Kaptan was mesmerized by what he was seeing. Either side of him was a vast open space, fully dressed and armed soldiers were carrying out drills. At least a hundred men to each unit, he could clearly see eight such units, at the front of each a drill Sergeant barked out orders. It was impossible for Kaptan to see exactly how many units in total there were. Captain Hook looked at Kaptan and asked,

'Impressive, yes? Well, you have seen nothing yet.'

The Merc stopped at another set of gates, replicas of those at the perimeter, they were attached to another high wall. Kaptan, keen to take in as much as he could, noted the CCTV cameras and the high sentry boxes that contained at least four armed soldiers each. The gates opened, as if by magic. The magnificent house was just about visible through a gap between two of the sixteen tanks that stood guard in front of the General's humble abode. As the car passed the fountain that was, without doubt, larger than Trafalgar Square, Kaptan could see a man of some considerable size, the man was dressed in white army attire, gold buttons and braid decorated the front and shoulders of his jacket, scores of medals hung from his left breast pocket and his hat was placed perfectly upon his head. He was, without doubt, not the cleaner.

The car came to a stop, a servant, dressed formally, stepped forward and opened the rear door, Kaptan stepped out, directly facing the General. The six-foot-six-inch man, looking as though he had just been auditioning for a Persil advert, clicked the heels of his highly polished black boots together, stood bolt upright and saluted his visitor.

'I am General Kos, you may call me General, welcome to Hotel California.'

Kaptan saluted back, smiling before he could say anything in reply. He smiled as he had seen the large replica of the Eagles Hotel California LP cover fixed to the pure white walls of the General's villa. Stepping into the reception area of the house, which he noted was larger than the whole of his house in the mountains of Kurdistan, Kaptan was offered a drink by one of the numerous Asian women that seemed to be crisscrossing this part of the house.

'OK, before we talk, I would like to show you around, my young friend.'

Kaptan followed the General. They passed through several, enormous rooms before arriving on a patio, a patio that was as large as a football pitch. Both men sat in the back of an electric golf cart and proceeded along a central avenue that was sheltered by trees on either side. Kaptan, although wealthy in his own right, was in awe of the surroundings. There were tennis courts, swimming pools, fountains, formal gardens, and seating areas for hundreds of people at the outside cinema. There were also several small villas contained within this, 'back garden.' Reaching the wall that retained the whole of the living quarters, there was yet another set of electronically controlled camouflaged gates. The cart moved slowly forward, into and out of a densely wooded area. What Kaptan saw was hard to believe. A vast valley was spread out in front of them. The valley was in fact half in Albania and half in Kosovo, although there were no markings whatsoever to indicate this. For as far as the naked eye could see there were rows and rows of timber-constructed barracks. There were tanks, helicopters, warplanes, armoured vehicles, army Jeeps and more men than Kaptan had ever seen in one place.

'Mr. Kaptan, I have four and a half thousand men here in total, they are all trained and ready to fight, anywhere in the World. I have over twelve hundred men fighting battles all around the globe, they are made up of over sixty nationalities, they are all mercenaries. They fight for governments, opponents of governments, illegal armies, dictatorships, drug lords, the mafia and anyone else that is willing to pay the price for their services. I can provide an entire fighting army, at a price, to anyone that needs it. I have made more money from selling these poor souls than I ever did from the smuggling of cigarettes, drugs, or arms, although I still dabble in those areas of death. Now we should return to the house, you can freshen up after your travels, we can then have dinner and talk. By the way, whilst you are my guest you have access to any of the beautiful women that may take your fancy, that is, except for the two ladies that you will see in a moment.'

Stepping back into the house, the General quickly disappeared, together with two stunning ladies that held onto each of his muscular arms. Kaptan followed the petite, dark-haired female that had earlier served him with a drink. She opened the door that led into a suite of rooms.

'This is your room. If you need anything else, just call 999 on the bedside telephone.'

She ran her tongue across her lips in a very suggestive manner as she left the room. Kaptan instinctively knew that he would be calling the police at some time in the not to, distant future.

Kaptan removed his dust-ridden clothes and entered the bathroom, he had seen bathrooms like this in magazines, he had once stayed in one of Dubai's so-called 'six-star hotels' but even that experience was surpassed by the sheer luxury of what now surrounded him. The shower cubicle was at least nine metres square, it had been configured in order that four people could share it. As he was alone, or so he thought, he did not bother to don one of the white cotton robes that hung neatly from solid gold hooks, neither did he wrap the towel around his midriff, when he had finished. Naked, he re-entered the bedroom, he noted that the thick velvet curtains on the far side of the room had been closed.

'Good room service', he thought.

In the semi-darkness, he sensed that he was not the only person in the room. Turning to his right, he saw the naked body of the woman that had shown him to his room, she was laid on her back, her legs slightly apart. Kaptan covered his manhood with both of his hands.

'Don't be shy Sir,' said the perfectly formed, slightly browned female. She beckoned him forward, he obeyed. Slightly lifting the top half of her body from the eight-foot-wide bed, she cupped Kaptan's balls with her tiny, soft hands, his reaction was immediate.

'Oh my god, such a big man,' she said.

Kaptan was oblivious as to what she had said, as her mouth closed around the tip his enormous penis. She was now sitting upright on the side of the bed, her mouth, and his penis in absolute alignment. As he began to moan, the moan that men do when they are about to make a deposit, she withdrew and laid, legs wide apart, on the bed. As Kaptan manoeuvred himself into position, gently spreading her legs wider, she whispered, in a voice that would have made a lot of men come there and then,

'Try not to hurt me, Sir.'

Whilst he was a murderer, many times over and had been responsible for hundreds of deaths via his drug distribution network, Kaptan was not void of feelings. Realising that his ten-inch, thick cock, could do this small, framed female some serious damage, he readjusted his position. Seconds later he was licking her fanny as if it were soft ice cream, she came within a minute. He turned her onto her front and dragged her carefully towards the edge of the bed and slightly lifted her arse, an arse he noted, that was as smooth as any that he had ever seen. He entered her from behind, his eruption was immediate.

Still naked, they lay side-by-side, his head on a pillow and hers on his firm, hairy chest. Kaptan began the conversation.

'So, what is your name and where do you come from.'

'My name is Imelda, I am from Cebu in the Philippines, I am twenty-one years old, Sir.'

'OK, I am Kagan Kaptan, I am from the mountains of Kurdistan, and I am twenty-six. I am also a very, bad man. Kaptan was surprised by Imelda's response.

'You cannot be a bad man, Sir, as you are a very gentle lover.'

Kagan smiled and said,

'Thank you, Imelda, but please believe me, I am bad.'

'So how did you manage to end up in the hills of Albania?'

Imelda, laughing, replied,

'The General brought me here, along with seven others from Cebu when he was recruiting men for his army, there are over five hundred girls here, from the Philippines, China, Thailand, Vietnam, Laos, and Cambodia. They are shared by the men in the barracks until it is time for those men to leave, none of them ever returns. I was lucky, I belonged to the General when I first came here, three years ago, but now the General has other, younger girls to keep him busy. He has allowed me to stay here, in the house and my duty is to look after visitors, like yourself.'

Kaptan looked, almost lovingly, into her big and wide brown eyes, and asked,

'Would you like to leave here?'

Imelda's eyes welled up, a tear ran slowly down her slightly dimpled cheeks and with a broken voice she whispered,

'The General will never let me leave Sir, he owns me, just like he owns all of the other girls here.'

There was a knock on the door, the voice behind it was the voice of General Kos, he bellowed,

'Have you finished my friend? Dinner will be served in ten minutes. Imelda, you are needed in the kitchen'. Imelda's reaction was immediate. She ran first to the bathroom, two minutes later she was dressed and heading towards the bedroom door.

'Thank you, Sir' she said, as she turned the doorknob and exited.

Kagan had no idea if she had heard his words as she departed, but what he had said, was,

'I will take you with me when I leave.'

Just three people were seated at the sixteen-place dining table when Kaptan took his seat. There was General Kos and two beautiful, young Asian ladies. These were the same ladies that, earlier had hung from the General's arms. This is 'Marilyn' named after the sexiest actress ever to fill the silver screen, and this is 'Diana' so called because my favourite singer is Ms. Ross. Imelda, whom you met earlier, is of course named after the former first lady of the Philippines, Mrs. Marcos. My Imelda has only two pairs of shoes, whereas her namesake had over three thousand. I hope that Imelda fulfilled all your needs, my friend. Kaptan sat and before his arse had settled firmly into the hard, wooden chair, Marilyn and Diana rose from their chairs, cupped their hands together, bowed and left.

'Now, Mr. Kaptan, I understand from our mutual friend in Turkey that you have some problems in the UK. What you should explain to me is, exactly how can I help you.'

Kaptan paused before replying, then, taking a swig of the expensive Whiskey that was to the right of his placemat, he said,

'General, I am sure that you already know what has happened to my family in the UK, they have been almost wiped out by the Guls. The Guls would like to take control of my business there, I cannot allow that to happen. It is a matter of honour I must avenge my brother's mutilation.' '

And you come to me to do what? my friend.'

'I come to you because our mutual friend told me that you could help.'

'Yes, of course I can help, I am General Kos, the most powerful man in Albania and Kosovo. There is just one problem, the Gul family have been good friends of mine for quite a long time. I protect all their drugs, arms, cigarettes and even fighters. If I am to give up that business, then you will have to offer me something big in return.'

Kaptan did not hesitate with his reply.

'If you help me eradicate those bastards, I will guarantee you all the heroin and cocaine that you want, at half the market price.'

'Well, Kaptan, you must want these Guls out of your hair pretty badly.'

'More than anything General, more than anything.'

Reaching over the table and gripping Kaptan's wrist, General Kos, lowering his tone, said,

'I like you, my friend, I like you a lot. You remind me of myself when I was your age. You can consider your request as done however it will take some careful planning, it will not happen overnight. Now, is there anything else that I can help you with?'

Retiring to armchairs in an adjoining room, where coffee and Port were already on the table, Kaptan, for the first time, was a little apprehensive when mentioning his other request.

'General, I would like to take Imelda from you, what do you say?'

Without flinching, Kos replied,

'Well, my friend, if you want her, then we will have to fight for her, she is one of my favourites.'

'How would we fight General?'

'With swords, at dawn, in the garden at the rear of the house.'

'This, you see, is traditional within my family.'

Kaptan, a man that had never ducked a fight in his lifetime, was visibly shaken, he told the General,

'I have never used a sword in my life, you will kill me, General.'

'Oh, don't worry young man, I will be blindfolded, just to make it fair.'

The General laughed out loud as soon as he had finished the sentence and then added,

'I am just kidding, if you wish to take Imelda, then you have my blessing.'

Kaptan held up his near-empty glass and thanked his host for his generosity. The General clinked his glass against that of his guest and said,

'Now you must do something for me. Today you were supposed to meet with Boyan Petrov in Varna, however you cancelled this meeting as you have come here to see me. I was also supposed to attend. We have rearranged this meeting, it will now take place in three days' time, you should come with me, we are to discuss some business that you may well be interested in. Whilst we are away, I will ask my contacts within the Albanian Government to get you and Imelda brand new identities. I will also arrange for you both to be smuggled into the UK as I know that you are a wanted man there. It will take some time for me to arrange for the right people to be in place to take out the Guls, not just in the UK, but also anywhere else that they may be hiding.'

General Kos called out for Imelda, when she arrived, he informed her that she now belonged to Kagan Kaptan, her smile filled the room.

Three days later, a plane load of spare parts, a gift from General Kos, arrived at Cizre Airstrip. Twenty minutes after arriving and with Ozturk Ozsoy and five of the PKK in attendance, the plane was blown to smithereens by two rockets launched from a passing fighter jet. No one survived.

21 - DUPED

On the 4th of June 2007, General Kos, and Kagan Kaptan boarded one of the many small jet planes that lined the tarmac runway that was situated in the Northwest of the complex. Kagan wondered why he had not been flown directly to this airstrip, instead of having to land in Tirana three days ago. The General answered Kagan's query without him having to ask.

'You are probably wondering why you did not land here when you arrived, the answer is simple. Only people that I know, and trust, have ever flown here directly. You are now amongst the few people that know the whereabouts of this landing strip, had you arrived here then I would have to have disposed of the pilot that brought you, as he would have known of its existence and whereabouts. You will see when we take off and circle around, just how heavily guarded my complex is. Kaptan, like everyone else that had ever visited General Kos, realised that he would be disposed of, should the two men ever fall out.'

The 800 km flight to Varna took a little over two hours. They landed at 2.00pm and were accompanied on the flight by twelve of the General's most elite soldiers. Waiting beside the runway, situated about a mile from the shores of the Black Sea, was Gregor Levski, once Nikolay Nikolov's executioner before the latter had retired. Levski was now number two in the Petrov clan, he was one of the few living people to have visited the General's complex as previously he was in attendance when the Mafia 'grass' Tommaso Buscetta and the Romanian Victor Bastovoi, were gunned down beside the General's runway. These murders foiled a plot by the dead men to take over the Petrov's' empire. After the traditional hugging and pecking of each other's cheeks, General Kos and Kagan Kaptan were invited to sit in the back of the burgundy Rolls Royce, that carried the number plates, SP 1 at the front, and BP 2 at the rear and whilst this may have been illegal, there was no one in Bulgaria that was going to issue a fine. Twenty minutes later the roller pulled up outside the Varna Viceroy Hotel, newly built by Boyan Petrov, at a cost of over Euros 300 million. Boyan Petrov, now aged 36, educated at Oxford and without doubt, Bulgaria's richest man, was stood, immaculately dressed, in the middle of the four large pillars that supported the grand entrance of the hotel.

Petrov, who had never met either of his visitors before, showed them into the reception area of his latest, and most expensive, piece of real estate. After giving them the grand tour of both the ground and mezzanine floors, he introduced his guests to the General Manager of the hotel. Petrov then asked the GM to take his guests to the two penthouse suites, just above the 23rd floor. As the threesome entered the 'express' lift, which would whiz them up to the top in seconds, Petrov asked his two guests to meet with him at 'Nutmegs' the five-star restaurant on the first floor, in one hour.

At 4.30pm, the three men sat at a six-seater round table, in the splendid restaurant that had been modelled on its namesake at the Hyatt Hotel in Singapore. Only the drinks and food waitresses were in attendance. General Kos congratulated Petrov on having built such a luxury hotel, asking as to whom exactly his clientele was going to be as most of the inhabitants of Bulgaria would not be able to afford to stay there. Petrov, not at all perturbed by the Kosovan's comments, replied that he was aiming to attract the rich and famous from all over Europe, especially now that the EU had accepted his native Country into European Union. In particular, he pointed out, was the attraction of the largest and swankiest casino in Bulgaria, which could not be found in any other former member of the old Eastern Bloc. The fact that gambling would only be available to those with either Euros or USD was a major factor in providing such a facility.

After the initial 'chit-chat' had finished, several glasses, bottles of wine, whiskey and brandy were placed upon the table. The conversation began in earnest. Raising his glass of Nuit-saint-George, Petrov simply said,

'To our future business gentlemen.'

General Kos, never one to beat about the bush, asked,

'Exactly why have you invited us to your wonderful establishment, Boyan?'

'Well General, Mr. Kaptan, since I returned from the UK, some 15 years ago, I have, wherever possible, tried to legitimise my business interests. Both my father and Nikolay Nikolov ran the empire with fists of iron, using intimidation and torture to get what they wanted. They nearly always succeeded, but along the way they made many enemies. I, on the other hand, have done what my father wanted me to do, that is, to use my education. I have gradually distanced myself from the drugs, arms, prostitution, extortion, and fraud businesses that were always enforced by violence. I am still involved, but from a distance. I sub-contract all those money-spinning rackets, leaving it to others to control the 'day-to-day' running of those dangerous aspects of my income. My concentration is on legit business, I have over 120 companies, registered in 48 different countries. Between them they can supply and deliver almost any commodity that my customers may require. Holding companies exist in various, tax havens around the world. I have powerful contacts in many foreign Governments, and I no longer need to threaten or blackmail any of them, as the money they derive from our dealings keeps them very loyal to me. This is something that both of you should consider, I would be more than happy to help you set something up.

'That is all quite interesting, Boyan, but I am sure you have not brought us here to give us a lesson in business etiquette, have you?' asked a slightly perplexed Kaptan.

Petrov outwardly smiled, inside he was thinking that the Kurd was chastising him. Petrov responded.

'Gentlemen, as you know, Bulgaria and Romania were welcomed into the arms of the EU on the 1st of January. For us in Bulgaria, this has opened-up so many opportunities. We are not yet a Schengen Area Member, this excludes Bulgarians and Romanians from visa-free entry into the other member countries of the EU, however it does not prevent people from the EU coming to and leaving both, of these countries. This has opened a good number of avenues for money-making schemes, one of which, I am sure you will be interested in. My International Trucking business operates in every single EU country. We also run our trucks into and out of, Turkey, Syria, Georgia, Iraq, Iran, and Afghanistan. We collaborate with partners in Morocco, Algeria, Libya, and Egypt via our office in Damascus. Kagan, you are well positioned in the mountains to help get the cargo from the Middle East countries into Bulgaria, for distribution to Europe. General, you have both the muscle and the logistics to ensure that our cargo always arrives at its destination. There are other people that I shall be introducing to this business, some of whom, I think you already know. However, I regard you two gentlemen to be of the utmost importance to its success, should you be interested?' Kaptan and the General looked at each other, both were puzzled by what they had just heard. Kaptan asked,

'So, what is the cargo Boyan, uranium?' The Bulgarian laughed.

'No, my friend, it is nothing so dangerous, it is people'.

'People' exclaimed an agitated General Kos.

'How are we to make money out of shipping people from one country to another?'

'Are you kidding General? I think you have been holed up in your complex for far too long.'

'General, people smuggling is the 'new' drug business.'

After finishing the last piece of his desert, Petrov continued,

'There are thousands, if not hundreds of thousands of refugees willing to pay everything, they have, to escape from poverty, war, slavery, prostitution, and a whole host of other life-threatening scenarios. Since it has been possible to enter 21 EU countries without being challenged at any border, we have managed to get over 8,000 of these poor souls out of Bulgaria and Romania and into the more, wealthy countries of the EU. France, Germany, Belgium, and the Netherlands are easy destinations and with the cooperation of our friends in these countries we can even get them into the UK, which is where 70% of them really want to be. We are only at the beginning, you two gentlemen have the chance to join with me, together we can set up the largest 'people smuggling' network in the World. What do you say?'

'I am interested', General Kos replied.

'Me too, but I have some pressing needs to take care of before I can be involved.' Said Kagan.

Petrov replied,

'Yes, I know of your problems with the Gul family, Kagan. I too have had dealings with them in the past. It would be better for all our sakes if they were permanently out of the picture, I will be cooperating with the General in this matter. Now let us all adjourn to the casino where we can have a drink and some fun. Tomorrow morning, we can discuss the finer details of my plan.'

Kaptan left his two future business partners after just an hour or so, he had never been a gambler and for the first time in his life, he was not interested in the beautiful Russian girls that were constantly trying to get his attention. His thoughts were for just two things, firstly Imelda and secondly, how would he get back into the UK? At 4.30am, he took a call on his mobile, it was his cousin Bora Kaptan, the son of his father's brother. Bora gave Kagan the bad news, Ozturk Ozsoy and five of his fighters were killed when the plane, arranged by General Kos, and carrying the spare parts for the PKK's broken fleet, had been attacked and demolished by a Russian-built, Turkish fighter jet, just seconds after it had arrived at Cizre Airstrip. Bora added that the jet bore no visible markings as they had all been painted out, but he was sure that it was once of the Turkish Airforce. His cousin's words faded from Kagan's mind as it flashed back to the day that he had first met with the General, there had been six such jets lined up alongside Turkish tanks, armoured vehicles, rocket launchers and various other military hardware, all had had their markings blacked-out. The General had beamed when telling him that his fighters had taken all of this from the Turks when they intervened in the Kosovan civil war back in 1999. Whilst Kagan was sad at hearing of the passing of Ozsoy, once his father's close friend, he was almost traumatized by the thought that General Kos may have been responsible for his death. He also wondered why the General had given up Imelda to him, so easily. Was he being 'set up' how would the actual Turkish Military had known about the plane carrying the spare parts? There had been hundreds of landings and take-offs from the PKK-controlled airstrip at Cizre, without incident. At 6.00am, Kagan picked up the phone beside his bed and rang the General's room.

'General, we have some problems, the plane that you sent to my homeland has been destroyed and the leader of the local PKK has died. I need to return to my home as soon as possible. The General extracted himself from the clutches of the two Russian blondes that had performed various sexual acts with him, just a couple of hours previously and asked Kaptan to meet him in the coffee shop on the ground floor in half an hour.'

Over the strongest of Expressos, Kaptan asked if it were possible for him to take the General's jet and fly directly to Mardin, as Mardin was the closest operational airport to Cizre, which was now out of commission.

'And what about me? How do I get back to my home Kagan? asked the General.

'I will be no more than two days General you have a good place to stay and several females to pass your time away with, what do you say?'

'OK, young man, but how about our meeting with Petrov later today?'

'It will have to wait until I return from the UK, General.'

The General called his pilot and asked him to 'ready the plane' for a 9.00am take off, destination, Mardin, Southern Turkey.

'Thank you General, I will ask Levski to arrange a car to drive me to the airstrip. Would you please offer my apologies to Mr. Petrov, and please stress that I am certainly interested in what we discussed yesterday.'

Kaptan had never let on that the jet that had killed Ozturk Oszoy was once of Turkish origin. As soon as Kaptan was out of earshot, the General called Captain Hook and asked him to arrange his collection from Varna by 1.00pm that day. As he hung up the call, Petrov walked into the coffee shop.

'Ah, Boyan, there have been some interesting developments overnight. This has meant the immediate departure of Kaptan, whilst I, myself will be leaving at 1.00pm.'

General Kos then updated Petrov on the events of the previous day, as told to him by Kaptan. Petrov, in turn, enlarged on his people smuggling business, asking that he update Kaptan once he returns from Kurdistan.

Kaptan arrived in Mardin at just before 11.00am. Cousin Bora collected him in an armoured carrier, several PKK soldiers followed in army jeeps. The funeral of Ozsoy would normally have been held on the day of his death, however it had been held over for a day in order that Kaptan could attend, such was his standing in the hills of Kurdistan. Arriving at the bottom of the stone-covered hill that led to both Kaptan's and the dead man's houses, the most successful man ever to have resided in this part of Kurdistan was unable to walk freely to his friend's house, due entirely to the number of people that had turned out to bid him farewell. Two guards fired several rounds into the air, the crowd dispersed, long enough for Kaptan to make it to the home of the man that had been both his father's and his grandfather's neighbour, for the best part of eighty years. Somehow Kaptan was able to get into the house of the now-dead, respected village elder. The Imam, knelt on an old Persian rug, with people squashed up all around him, was praying. Most of the gathered mourners were eating, the food was simple. It was flatbread, topped with ground beef, onion, and peppers. The only drink available was 'Ayran' a salty, yoghurt-like substance. Ozsoy's wife of sixty years, in time-honoured fashion, was wailing loudly, in the corner of the stone-clad room. Twenty minutes later, everyone in the room was on their knees, over seven hundred people that lined the streets outside prayed, this went on for three hours. Soon after, the body of Ozturk Ozsoy, having been cleaned, bathed, and wrapped in bed sheets, was carried, head high, through the ever-increasing throng of mourners. The noisy crowd hushed when reaching the small mosque that was centred in the middle of the village square. The body was placed on a high altar, the Imam started to pray, he prayed for ninety minutes, after which the body of the deceased was lifted from the altar by five close relatives, plus Kaptan. It was carried fifty yards to a graveyard, positioned, centuries ago, to overlook the mountains, that had been in place since time had begun. These were the mountains that Ozturk Ozsoy had seen, virtually every day of his life. The body was lowered into a concrete box which filled the six-foot deep grave. Two relatives climbed down and covered the box with three heavy pre-cut stones. After each mourner had dropped a handful of earth onto the top of the stone casket, the crowd began to disperse. Those closest to Ozsoy returned to his house. They were fed, again, they prayed, again. The last of the mourners left around twelve hours after they had arrived. Kaptan crossed the now, dark, and deserted street and entered the home of his birth, only cousin, Bora, was present.

'We need to talk, my cousin, but that can wait until later, for now, we both need some sleep.'

No sooner had Kaptan finished the sentence, he was fast asleep.

The following morning, Bora sat with his revered cousin, at a small table just outside the door of the house. This would be the first of three days of mourning for the inhabitants of the village. People, without speaking, nodded to Kaptan as they passed by. A silent queue of about two hundred people lined the slope that led to the graveyard. For the next few days these people, which included many armed members of the PKK, would offer their prayers to their fallen comrade. Kaptan was unable to concentrate with all that was going on outside, he asked Bora to go and find Ozsoy's successor as the head of the local PKK and anyone else that had witnessed the destruction of the plane carrying the spare parts. One hour later, Bora returned. With him was Altan Akar, temporary leader of the village and the local PKK and Ilkay Izzet, the man that had first spotted the jet as it descended from the mountains before unleashing two rockets into the stricken aircraft. Kaptan first spoke to Izzet, a veteran of the war in Serbia, he asked him to whom he thought the jet had belonged to. Izzet told Kagan that it was, without doubt, one of those that he himself had flown back in 1999, when Turkey was part of the NATO force, he added that all its markings were 'blacked-out' there were no visible signs of exactly whom it belonged to and that the attack was swift and without warning. Kaptan thanked his fellow Kurd for his information, gave him USD 200 and indicated that he was no longer required. Akar was already known to Kaptan, he was a distant relative of the Gul family, Kagan had had little or no contact with him, mainly because of who his relatives were. Akar would now be Kagan's 'go-between' replacing Ozsoy in the distribution of the drugs that came into Cizre on a regular basis. He would also be the 'linkman' with the PKK, as without the PKK's agreement, Kaptan's business would be dead in the water. Kaptan asked just one thing of Akar, he asked him to find out who was behind the assignation of Ozturk Ozsoy. Before he left, Kaptan handed Akar the satellite phone, that had, for many years, been held by Ozsoy.

After visiting and praying with Ozsoy's widow for two hours, Kaptan called the pilot that had brought him back home, he asked that the plane could be ready to leave, in one hour. At 5.00pm, they would be returning to the home of General Kos.

At 7.15pm, Captain Hook shook Kaptan's hand as he alighted the jet at the airstrip inside the General's complex. At 7.40 Kaptan was holding Imelda tightly in his arms. Over dinner, the General outlined to Kagan the plan that he had constructed for him and his wife-to-be, in respect of their imminent departure to the UK. Kaptan was a wanted man in the UK, he would not be able to simply arrive at Heathrow and conduct his business in the open. He would have to be 'smuggled' into England, as he had been, just over five years previously.

'Firstly, said the General, you will be flown the short journey from here to Sofia in Bulgaria. You will be met as soon as you leave the aircraft. Petrov's people will take care of your exit from the airport. You will then travel through Romania, in one of Petrov's trucks and onto Budapest in Hungary. You will have no problems at any of the borders. From Budapest you will have a journey of three days until you arrive in Belgium. There will be a small boat to take you to the East Coast of England, it will be a lot more comfortable than the last time you made such a journey. In the UK you will be met. Your brand-new identities will be ready for you soon, leaving you and Imelda to 'tie the knot.' You will both have my guaranteed safety. I will be in touch with you via one of my people once I get word that everything is well. After that, we shall deal with the Gul family. You will leave tomorrow afternoon, in the meantime, please feel free to treat my home as your home.'

As he and Imelda made their way back to their suite, Kaptan's mind was working overtime. As far as he could recollect, he had never mentioned to the General exactly when or how he had entered the UK five years ago. Ten minutes later, naked in bed with his petite new partner, Kaptan would soon forget about any suspicions he had towards General Kos. The following morning, taking the General at his word. He decided to treat the house as if it were his. He strolled to the end of the massive back garden. The gates dividing the house from the rest of the complex opened automatically for him and he stepped into the waiting golf cart. Kaptan had a purpose to his 'nose around.' He was not on a 'sight-seeing' trip, as such, he simply wanted to check out the armoury that the General had so proudly shown off a few days previously. Taking virtually the same route around the barracks and the vast training grounds, eventually he could see the articles of war that General Kos had so proudly shown off to him. Without making it obvious that he was looking, in case he was being watched by the CCTV, he could see that one of the six jets was no longer there. The five remaining fighting machines clearly had no visible markings, all had been blacked-out, with paint. Kagan was now nervous, he conjured up all kinds of scenarios in his mind, each one never had a happy ending for him, but what could he do? He was unable to simply walk out and go home. Was Imelda part of a sinister plot against him? He had no choice but to carry on with the General's plan, after all, why would he have taken the trouble to take him to meet with Petrov and then give up his jet to take him home and bring him back? The General could have taken him out and disposed of him within the confines of his complex and no one in the World would have known. For now, Kaptan would put his negative thoughts to one side.

Immediately after lunch, General Kos bid his guest and his former lover farewell, he did not travel in the car to the airstrip, which was about two km from the house. That duty fell to Captain Hook. And so, Kaptan's journey back to the UK, in search of his brother's killer(s) had begun. It took just 45 mins to arrive in Sofia. Kaptan expecting to touch down at Sofia International Airport, was a little surprised when he realised that this would not be the case. The plane arrived at a run-down, ex-military airstrip, which he estimated was to the Northeast of Bulgaria's capital. A couple of less than friendly-looking Bulgars met the plane. They had arrived in a battered old second world war jeep, this took Kaptan and Imelda just 400 km, across a deserted road, which divided the airport from a brand new-looking industrial estate. Around one hundred trucks, of all nationalities, were either backed onto the endless rows of warehouse doors or simply waited, in line, for a truck to depart, and thereby to take its turn to load. The jeep pulled up, alongside a completely solid, white-painted forty-foot trailer. The passenger in the jeep indicated that the newly arrived couple should follow him, they did. They climbed a narrow staircase and entered, through a solid steel door, into the warehouse. They were ushered into a large canteen, around eighty people sat at the tables or on the floor. They were men, women, and children. From their dress, Kaptan assumed that they were of many nationalities. Every five minutes or so, some of the people would be led out of the room and others would be brought in. After, what seemed like hours to Kaptan, a man, holding a clipboard, invited them out of the canteen and onto the loading bay of the warehouse. There were eight other people waiting. Two pallets of goods, some two metres in height had already been loaded, one woman and her child were led inside the trailer and told to stand against a pallet. Two bottles of water and a bag were handed to the woman. Another pallet was brought in by fork truck and was loaded in front of the mother and son. A man was led forward and asked to stand, he was also given water and a bag. He soon disappeared behind the next pallet to be loaded. This continued until all ten people had been loaded. All were ensconced, out of sight, behind pallets of vegetables.

Ten minutes later, the noise of the engine could be heard. As the truck made its way out of the industrial estate, each person would sit on the cold damp floor of the trailer, had they not done so then they could have been badly injured by the constant swaying of the trailer as it twisted and turned its way along the road. Not one person, except maybe Kaptan, had any idea of where they were going. Kaptan had listened carefully to the General when he had laid out their route to England. From memory he knew that they would be going through Romania, therefore Bucharest would possibly be their next stop. Kaptan had carefully concealed his mobile phone when everyone else had surrendered theirs in the canteen. He had not been pressurised into giving up his phone, which he had also turned off, to preserve the battery, he would use it only in an emergency. He had also noted from his expensive Rolex watch that the time was 4.00pm when they had left Sofia. At 1.00am the truck reversed and came to a stop. The cargo was unloaded, eventually revealing nine adults and one child. The child, still in the arms of its mother, seemed lifeless. She held the baby boy in her outstretched arms and cried. An armed member of the welcoming party came over to her, inspected her son and shook his head. Imelda tried to walk over, she was stopped by the armed man and then pushed back towards the others. The baby, with his mother now hysterical, was taken away. She would never see him again. Kaptan was now beginning to feel very uneasy, surely, as a friend of the General he would be treated differently to these other poor souls. Each of the nine adults that had exited the trailer from Sofia were given some pot noodles and a cake. They were each allowed to use the toilet. Seven others, who were already in the warehouse, were added to their party. Sixteen bewildered people, all looking for a new life, were led to an already loaded trailer and asked to climb a ladder and then crawl, along the top of the pallets and down to the front of the fully enclosed forty-foot box. At the front of the trailer, four cases of water and bags of food had been left on top of the first two pallets to have been loaded. The doors were locked, the engine started, and the truck rolled out into the darkness of suburban Bucharest.

Kaptan had managed to cut a hole in the fibre-glass roof, it was just large enough to poke his head through. According to his watch, it had taken eleven hours to reach their next stop, which from the amount of Hungarian registered trucks that were parked in the truck stop, was almost certainly somewhere close to Budapest. Four of the hitchhikers were called by name, all were females, they had to crawl along the top of the pallets but managed to get to the back of the truck. Four or five drivers chatted for about fifteen minutes, it did not go unnoticed by the Kurd that one of them was, without doubt, of Irish descent. The truck pulled out of the park and onto the highway. Kaptan next pushed his head through the top of the lorry when they arrived in Vienna. This time the back doors did not open. The tractor pulling the trailer was unhitched and replaced with another. Another driver took the wheel; however, it appeared that the Irishman climbed up into the passenger side of the cab. The twelve remaining stowaways had completely run out of food and there was precious little water left. They were all fatigued and on the point of collapse when the truck arrived, some eight hours after leaving Vienna. They were now in Frankfurt. The entire load was taken off and the twelve occupants were led into a converted container at the far end of the warehouse. A man, dressed as though he had just come out of Dunn's, approached Kaptan and Imelda. He spoke to them in Turkish, he turned, and they both followed him.

Once out of earshot of the others, the man offered the General's apologies for having made the two important people travel in such a manner. He led them into an office, they were given hot drinks and KFC. The man, who never once offered his name, informed Kaptan that he and Imelda would be driven, by car, to Antwerp, where they would be met by a fellow Kurd, he would take them, on a small boat, to England. This final part of the journey was familiar to Kaptan, he had arrived in England just over five years ago on a small dingy. His fellow escapee on that occasion, Adnan Mehmed had lost his life when swept overboard during the crossing of the North Sea. Just before 2.00am, and three days after leaving the complex of General Kos, the car carrying Kaptan and his intended bride, pulled up alongside a small jetty, just outside the port of Antwerp. For Kaptan, this was a Déjà vu moment. Out of the pitch-black darkness appeared a man, he greeted Kaptan in Kurdish, he was the same man that had landed the man from Cizre, in England previously. As before, the seafarer never offered up his name, although he was fully aware of exactly whom Kaptan was. The sailor led the cold and bedraggled couple to a small boat, which they all managed to board without a hitch, as the water in the small inlet was very calm. Imelda took Kaptan's hand and almost pulled him over in her haste to get him into the tiny cabin.

'Help yourself to coffee,' shouted the captain of the ship.

Ten minutes later, the two lovebirds were fast asleep in each other's arms. They were woken by the captain just as dawn was breaking along the East Coast of England. A few minutes later the boat was being pulled from the shallow water by a winch on the back of a converted truck until it rested itself upon a trailer that was half in, half out of the almost benign sea.

'Welcome, once again, to England my friend.'

These words were uttered, in Kurdish, by none other than Mehmet, the same Mehmet that had driven Kaptan to North London, where under an assumed name, he subsequently took control of the drug business in the UK, crossing swords with the Gul family in the process. The panic upon Kaptan's face was visible to see. Imelda asked,

'What's wrong Kagan?

'I cannot say at this moment, later I will explain.'

Climbing the large stone-laden bank of the beach, just north of Felixstowe, Mehmet invited Kaptan to take the front passenger seat of the powerful BMW 4x4. Imelda slid onto the back seat and was invisible from the outside, firstly due to her diminutive size and secondly as the rear windows were almost black.

'So, where are you taking us? Asked Kagan.

'To your safe house in Rayleigh.' Replied Mehmet.

'But first we will have some breakfast, I seem to remember that you enjoyed a 'full English' the last time we met.' Kaptan smiled,

Imelda asked what a full English was.

'You will see, very shortly my dear.' Said Mehmet.

Forty minutes later the BMW pulled off the A12 and found a parking space in the rear car park of the transport café. Kaptan noted that there were twenty or so trucks in the car park, he did not notice the dark blue Ford Mondeo that nestled between two large petrol tankers. Entering the café, Kagan and Imelda sat, backs towards the window that looked out onto the passing traffic of the A12. Mehmet walked to the counter and ordered three full English breakfasts and returned with three large mugs of tea, half of which he had managed to spill into the tray that he carried them on. With their stomachs full of England's finest, Mehmet indicated that they should be on their way. Mehmet held the door as Kagan passed. Imelda told them to carry on as she needed to use the washroom before they continued, on their journey to Rayleigh. The pretty Filipino turned and made her way to the other side of the café. Mehmet unlocked the car and he and Kagan entered the car together. Mehmet immediately locked the car from the inside. Kagan sensed a shuffling in the back, and as he turned, instinctively, to see who might be there, a single bullet entered his head. The last thing Kagan Kaptan ever saw, was the face of Birusk Gul.

Kaptan had been well and truly 'duped' by General Kos. He had no idea that Birusk Gul and General Kos had set the plan into motion as soon as Kaptan let it be known that he wished to get back to the UK. The General, a close ally of the Gul family for many years, had simply made it seem to Kagan that he wanted the Guls out of the way as much as he did. Kaptan had had his suspicions in respect of the General's sincerity in helping him, he should have acted upon those suspicions, it was now, of course, too late. Imelda was a willing party to the scheme to remove Kagan from the equation. She had been promised a new life in the UK, she would live in Kaptan's house in Rayleigh, that was until she had outgrown her use. Kaptan's mentor and lifelong family friend, Ozturk Ozsoy was in fact the brother-in-law of Osman Gul, however he never supported the family that he had married into and had helped Kaptan over many years. He did of course, pay the ultimate price for his betrayal of his own family. Altan Akar, the man that had replaced Ozsoy as head of the village and the local PKK, was in fact Birusk Gul's childhood friend. He would play an important role in the UK business that Gul and the General had just made their own.

Birusk Gul exited the BMW at the same time as Imelda exited the café. Imelda followed Kaptan's most bitter of rivals and together they opened the rear doors of the dark blue Mondeo and sat, side-by-side. There were two men in the front of the car. The driver asked Birusk,

'Where to boss?'

'To Rayleigh.'

The stolen BMW, with the head of Kagan Kaptan, looking backwards and wedged between the front seats was driven to a remote spot in Epping Forest. Mehmet smothered Kaptan's body in petrol before scattering the rest of the contents of the jerry can over the entire interior of the car. A half-full can of petrol was left in the boot. Mehmet doused a rag with petrol, stuffed it almost entirely into the opening of the petrol tank and set it alight. Mehmet was deep inside the forest when he heard the explosion. At a pre-arranged spot, in the car park of the High Beech Visitor Centre, Mehmet climbed into the passenger seat of a silver Mercedes and was driven back to Felixstowe, where fifteen minutes later he rested in the cabin of a large yacht, the name of which was 'Kos.'

Kaptan's body was burnt beyond recognition. The police concluded that the stealing and burning of a car, with a victim inside, was just another 'drug-related' execution. Within days, the General had despatched several of his top killers to take out the rest of the Kaptan crew. A similar operation was carried out in the mountains of Kurdistan, at the end of which, the Guls controlled five hundred square miles of the region around Kaptan's birthplace. Two weeks after his killing not a single member of Kagan's family remained alive, or so they thought.

22 - TAYSER MALIK

Not long after his brother, Leon, had been arrested, and incarcerated, Monzer Asmar had met with Tayser Malik, who for quite a while had been Leon's partner in crime on many lucrative smuggling deals. The two men had met at a function in Aleppo, Syria. The reception, involving some of Syria's elite, was hosted by Abu Najib, a cousin of the then vice President of Syria. It was discovered during this first meeting that Malik was a prolific user of Monzer's logistic company. Malik was moving hundreds of illegal shipments each month via Monzer's trucks, planes, and small boats. At the time of their first meeting, Monzer Asmar was not even aware of Malik's existence, let alone the fact that he was using his company to deliver vast quantities of arms, drugs and cigarettes to the Middle East, Turkey, Greece, and the Balkan countries. Monzer had decided to get out of the arms business after his brother was locked up for 363 years. The two men met, for a second time, in August 2007. Monzer made it quite clear that he was not interested in trading in arms, he was willing to consider drugs and cigarettes as he could transport those to places where Malik's network could not reach. Malik was quite interested in this proposal, although he was no longer dealing in drugs, having been forced into cigarette smuggling when the Taliban eradicated most of the Afghan poppy fields in the year 2000. The two men shook on a deal that would allow Malik to deliver boxed cigarettes to Monzer's distribution outlets in Damascus, Homs, Aleppo and Latakia. The building of a new warehouse complex at Daraa, in the South of Syria, which was also near to Nassib the birthplace of Tayser Malik, was almost complete and Malik would have use of it. This would enable him to supply neighbouring countries. Malik himself operated from Irbid in Jordan, where his personal protection was almost guaranteed by the Government Ministers that were in his pocket.

Tayser Malik had been born in Nassib, Syria in July of 1967, he was the youngest of the seven children that had been born to his father, Adel Abo Malik, and mother, Emarat. Before he was two months old, his two eldest brothers, aged 18 and 16 were killed in the uprising that saw Syria and their neighbours, Jordan, engage in a bitter conflict, named as 'black September.' The war between the two countries had been fought over Syria's support for the

Palestinians that had occupied the northern part of Jordan. The town of Nassib suffered from constant bombing, courtesy of the Royal Jordanian Air Force. In 1975 Malik's two sisters, at the ages of 14 and 11 were killed whilst visiting relatives in Daraa. The bus in which they were travelling was 'taken out' on the main road from Nassib by Israeli jets, in retaliation for Syrian and Egyptian attacks against Israel during the 'Yom Kippur War.' In 1980, to escape the constant border clashes between the Syrians and the Jordanians, Abel Ado Malik moved his family to the city of Hama, a large town in central Eastern Syria, far away from military incursions by any of Syria's neighbours. Abel was not to know, that from there, the 'Muslim Brotherhood' would look to overthrow President Hafez al-Assad. Hama had become, along with Aleppo and Homs, the strongholds of the Brotherhood's organisation. In February 1982, Government Military Forces attacked Hama, almost levelling it to the ground. Tayser Malik, six months shy of his 15th birthday, was away, in Latakia, pickpocketing merchant seamen, when his two remaining brothers, his father and mother, met their deaths when their makeshift mud and straw house was hit by a shell, fired from a tank, one of many that had stormed Hama during the night.

Young Malik was not to discover what had happened to his family until he returned to Hama some six weeks after their deaths. He had brought back enough money for his family to survive for at least six months. He now had the money however he no longer had any family. He decided to return to the town of his birth, Nassib, where he still had a few aunts, uncles, and cousins. His hate for the Syrian regime in Damascus totally consumed him. When he arrived at his uncle's house, a small, two-roomed building, situated down a side road on the edge of town, he realised just how far down the chain of wealth he really was. The house had no running water and no mains electric. It shared a small generator with an adjoining house, this was used sparingly, mainly to watch TV in the evenings or to heat just one room during the coldness of winter. If he were to wash, then Malik would have to do so in the nearby river, which flowed just north of the town. He shared duties with his cousins, fetching water from one of the wells that were just about within walking distance. The river dried up completely during the summer months, washing at the standpipe was the only option, other than smelling like a camel's arse. The town of Nassib offered little or no opportunity for Malik to earn money. His uncle, aunt and five cousins could not afford to keep him, Daraa City was very much controlled by the militia and Malik had no wish to spend any time there. One day, whilst leaving the market, where he would go every day to buy, and sometimes thieve, fresh food for his aunt, he noticed a bus that displayed its destination as being Irbid-Amman, both of which were in Jordan. Irbid was 40 km from Nassib and took about one hour by bus if indeed it made it there without breaking down.

Malik ran to the bus and asked the driver how much the fare was to Irbid, the driver told him it was eight Syrian Pounds, about one USD at the time, one way only, but as he was a child he should pay much less. Three days later, having told his uncle that he was looking for work in Daraa, Malik boarded the bus at 9.00am and handed the driver a small transistor radio that he had managed to secure whilst thieving in Latakia. Sitting on the running board to the right of the driver, he was able to ask many questions about Irbid. His heart missed several beats when they were stopped at the border. Two armed soldiers opened the rear door of the bus and took out two large wicker baskets, one contained fresh vegetables, the other was filled with fruit. Two empty baskets replaced the ones they had just removed. One soldier walked the length of the bus and signalled for the driver to go. The bus was not searched, and no one was asked to get off. Malik could only presume that the baskets of food were payment enough for the driver's unhindered entry into Jordan. As they approached the suburbs of Irbid, the young boy was impressed by both its size and just how modern it was, in comparison with towns and cities in Syria. His young mind wondered just how two countries, so close together, could be so different. As they pulled into the Bushra bus depot on Al-Hashmi Street, the driver informed his chatterbox of a passenger that there were four more depots before they reached the main bus terminus in the centre of the city. Malik asked,

'What time does the bus return to Nassib?

'Every two hours, the last one is at 6.00pm from the central bus station, and I shall be driving.'

'Thank you,' replied the streetwise, fourteen-year-old, boy, as he stepped down from the bus.

Malik had no clue as to where he would go, four days earlier he had never even known of the existence of Irbid, let alone what there was for him to do there. It was a little before 10.30 in the morning, he had the whole day to explore the delights of Irbid. He had no 'Dinar' the Jordanian currency since 1950, however he did have around USD 33.00, courtesy of a sailor that he had robbed in Latakia just before he returned home to Nassib. He soon found out that the mighty US currency could be used in Jordan, just as it could be in his homeland. The young boy's first stop when he set out to discover what Irbid had to offer, was a gas station. There were several customers in the small kiosk that sold limited amounts of food, chocolate, sweets, and things for vehicles. Malik was quietly relieved when he heard a conversation between two locals, they spoke Arabic, although with a slightly different dialect to his own. He picked up a sandwich, a chocolate bar and a coke and waited patiently until the man in front of him paid for his petrol. As the man turned, to leave the shop, Malik dropped his chocolate bar onto the floor. The man bent down to pick it up and with the skills of pickpocketing, honed, in Latakia, he lifted the money that was slightly visible, from his rear pocket. Handing over USD 2.00 to the cashier, he asked if he had a map of Irbid that he could buy. The cashier walked around the small counter, went over to where the engine oil was stacked and grabbed a folded-up map. He handed the map to Malik and said,

'Two dollars is enough.'

Malik smiled, turned and was back out onto the street. He turned left and walked 200 metres before he took from his pocket the money that had just come into his procession. He had managed to lift 85.00 dinar from the man in the garage.

Sat on a wall outside the Al Hamd Mosque, he tucked into his sandwich and chocolate bar. He then studied the map and found that there was a sizeable marketplace, along King Abdullah 11 Street, this would be his next destination. Twenty minutes later he arrived. The exterior of the market was made up of flower and fruit and veg sellers, these lined three streets of the massive square-shaped marketplace. They all operated from 'lock-up' kiosks that displayed most of their wares along the pavement. On the far side there were about thirty or so electrical shops. Malik had never seen so many TVs, Radios, Stereos, Fans, Aircon Units, Washing Machines, and other kitchen items in one place. In Nassib, Syria, there were just one or two shops that sold these goods, and they were almost all second-hand. Before he set out on his quest to find someone that was willing to give him a job, any job, he walked inside the market, the heat was intense, despite each stall or kiosk having at least two fans blowing air out into the aisles. He spent a good hour walking up and down every gangway, he concluded that there was nothing that could not be bought in this place. Before he exited on the far side of the market, he had managed to pick three pockets. He would never steal from there again. At 2.00pm, one by one, he asked each electrical shop if they had any jobs that they wanted doing. Some replies to him were courteous, some were darn right outrageous. At number twenty-two, the name of which was, Al Bakhit, Electronics Retail and Repair Shop, a man of about sixty years old, asked the young Syrian if he knew anything about fixing TVs or Radios. Malik was confident with his reply,

'Yes, of course I do.'

His answer was simply because he had repaired the radio that he had given to the bus driver earlier in the day.

'OK, then come in here and fix these. I am Al Bakhit, but everyone calls me Sparks.

The short frame of the fourteen-year-old had no problem in ducking under the counter flap and as he rose, on the other side, he informed Sparks that he was Tayser Malik, from Nassib.

'Have you run away from home young man? We get many absconders from Syria, but most of them are older than you.' Asked the short and podgy Jordanian.

'No, I am just looking for some work, I must help to support my family, but there is no work in Nassib.'

'OK, I understand, your country is in turmoil, I know that. See how you get on with these radios, I will pay you for each one that you can get to work'.

A beaming Malik simply replied,

'It's a deal Mr. Sparks.'

By 5.30pm, Malik had looked at four radios, two of which he had managed to fix. He informed Sparks that the other two were no good, but he would take them apart and keep the spares, for use in others.

'Now I must leave Mr. Sparks, I have to get the 6.00pm bus back to Nassib.'

'The bus terminus is a fifteen-minute walk, but if you walk through to the other side of the market you will see that the bus for Nassib stops right outside.'

'So, can I come back tomorrow, Mr. Sparks,'

'Yes, but we open at 6.00am.'

'But I cannot get here until 7.00 as the first bus from Nassib is at 6.00.'

'Then 7.00am it will be, my son, now you must go.'

Malik gave a slight wave to his new boss as he disappeared out of view. He was very tempted to pick another pocket on his way through the market, however he had decided it would be better not to do so, just in case he got caught, his new job would certainly be at an end if he did.

True to his word, the bus driver was the same one as he had given his radio to, nearly ten hours previously. Malik offered his fare, the driver declined. Eager to share his good fortune with someone, he chatted non-stop to the bus driver, until they reached Nassib marketplace.

'See you in the morning,' he said, as he left the bus.

Arriving at his aunt's house, five minutes later, he handed her twenty Dinar. Being as poor as anyone could be, she did not question her nephew as to where he had obtained the money. She would later exchange the Dinar for Syrian Pounds. After dinner, Malik walked to the river, took off all his clothes and bathed in the heat of the evening. He had arrived home with 142 Dinar more than he had left with.

Boarding the bus at 6.00am the following morning, the driver asked the young worker what he was going to do if he was to be challenged by the border guards. Explaining that whilst his bus was never searched by the guards that were on duty, almost every day, he could not be sure that this situation would last forever. The driver added,

'Would you like me to get you a Jordanian ID card? It will cost you fifty Dinar, you can pay me 1 Dinar every time you board the bus, until you have paid me back.'

Showing off, he pulled fifty Dinar from his pocket and gave it to the man that reminded him of his father. He would remain a man that Malik would never forget.

'Where did you get this from,' asked the boy's chauffeur.

'I am good at my job.'

The driver laughed; he made just twenty Dinar a week.

'You must get me a photograph of yourself,' he said.

Ten days later, the bus driver, who had informed Malik that his name was Omar Jamhour and that he had been born in Amman some 38 years since, but now lived in Irbid, where he had been a bus driver for 11 years, handed Malik his brand-new Jordanian ID card. He now had a double identity. In Jordan, if challenged, he would be known as Fahad Ensour. For many weeks, his days were a carbon copy of the day before. He became very efficient in the repairing of all things electrical, almost every day Sparks would send him to a customer's home address to repair their TV, toaster, kettle or aircon. Sparks gave him the strict instruction that on every fifth call he would tell the customer that his appliance was not repairable. Malik would then bring the 'unrepairable' item back to the shop on the Honda 50 motorbike that Sparks allowed him to ride. He would convince the client to come to the shop and purchase a new item and if they did then Al Bakhit would give them a 10% discount. The faulty product could then be repaired and sold on 'as good as new.' Malik would always get a good commission from these transactions. Not long after his 15th birthday, Sparks sent Malik to the home of a regular customer, a man always dressed in full Arab clothing. Upon arrival, the apprentice was shown into the house, he asked which appliance required his attention. The man, whom Malik would get to know as Tareq Mahmoud, informed the 15-year-old that he had nothing to repair, he was however, able to offer the cheeky young boy the opportunity to make a lot more money than he derived from repairing electrical items. Sitting in the backyard of the large house, away from the prying eyes, and ears, of the other occupants of the house, Tareq Mahmoud began the conversation.

'My boy, I have learnt of your story from Al Bakhit, and I admire what you are doing. I know that every day you arrive from Nassib with your radio, a radio that you play on the bus and that everyone enjoys. Every night you board the bus home with the same radio and that most of the passengers know you as the 'music boy'.'

Handing him a small, flat packet of white powder, Mahmoud continued.

'Could you conceal this in your radio for me and hand it to my brother in Nassib?

'Is it drugs?'

'Yes, my boy, I would not lie to you, it is,'

'I have given you 100 grams, take it tonight. My brother, Salah will collect it from you at 9.00pm.'

Upon his return to the shop, Sparks did not question his young assistant as to the outcome of his visit to the home of Tareq Mahmoud and Malik offered no explanation as to why he had returned having not conducted any electrical business with the Arab.

Every day for the next few weeks, Mahmoud would leave the same amount of powder at the shop, this would always be handed personally to Al Bakhit. The powder was always concealed in the bag of flat bread that Al Bakhit and Malik would consume for their lunch, around 11am. Also, in the bag was the twenty Dinar that Malik was getting for his part in the delivery of the drugs. One day Sparks informed Malik that he should once again pay Mr. Mahmoud a home visit. Mahmoud told Malik that he was pleased with him and that no one suspected him, a young lad, trying to support his family, of anything untoward and therefore he was going to increase the daily package to 500 grams. Without hesitation, Malik agreed, asking that the powder should be packed in five packs of 100 grams each, as that would be much easier for him to conceal. The following day, Mahmoud placed five bags, each containing 100 grams of heroin, into the bag of flatbread and left it with Sparks. Malik found an old radio cabinet, that he had saved in case it was needed one day, he took the body of the working radio that he carried each day, out of its much smaller case and cleverly fixed it into the much larger one and screwed the back on. The extra space that he had created within the casing of the enlarged radio meant that he could easily conceal up to 2 kgs of product. On the bus that evening, several of his regular travelling companions commented on their travelling companion's much larger radio. Malik was to receive one hundred dinars every time he handed over 500 grams of drugs to Salah Mahmoud. And so, Tayser Malik's entry into the world of smuggling had begun.

Malik was now earning over 3,000 Dinars a month. He could not bank this money. Mr. Sparks was converting the Dinar to USD for him on the black market. He was having to stash the notes into broken TVs, he would take out all the working parts and hide the money inside. The TVs would then be put onto the top shelves of the storeroom at the back of the shop. Fire was always his biggest fear. One day, Mahmoud failed to bring in the flatbread to Al Bakhit. Malik rode the Honda 50 to his house; he did not stop as he approached the gates as several police vehicles had surrounded the property. Subsequently the police came to the electrical repair shop, Malik panicked, wondering if he should 'leg it' but his nerve held firm. He watched, heartbroken, as Sparks was taken away. He was not even questioned. That evening he locked up the shop, boarded the bus, and went back to Nassib. At 9.00pm Salah Mahmoud arrived, as usual. Malik informed him of the events of that afternoon, he was never to see Salah again.

The following morning Malik boarded the bus at 6.00am, and whilst everyone on the bus knew of the events of the previous day, not a single person mentioned it. Opening the shop, Malik carried on trading as usual, albeit without Sparks there as company. He decided to look through the large pile of paperwork, that, somehow Al Bakhit just never got around to peruse. Halfway down the mountain of receipts, deposits, payments, and demands was an envelope, it was addressed to 'Tayser Malik, my young friend.' Whilst the letter inside was two pages long, Malik only absorbed the points that really mattered. Sparks had written, that as he had no one else, everything was left to him. This included the business and his house, the address of which was meaningless to him at that time. Malik was instructed to contact a solicitor in Irbid, this solicitor held his will and once his death had been confirmed Malik was to inherit everything. The letter included a short sentence from Tareq Mahmoud, requesting him to contact Amer Deeb at an address in Amman.

Days turned into weeks, during which time the young Syrian simply carried on with the business of repairing all kinds of electrical items. Two months after he had last seen Al Bakhit, he made the decision to meet with the solicitor in Irbid. He visited the offices of the old and bespectacled legal expert and informed him of Al Bakhit's disappearance. The solicitor told Malik that he was not surprised to learn of this news, adding that Al had amassed a small fortune, much, much more than a lowly electrical repair man should have had. He did confirm that Tayser Malik was Al's only beneficiary, however he had no proof or information that led him to believe that Al was no longer alive. The solicitor asked Malik to leave it for one week and then he should come back to see him again. Three days later, Malik took the bus to Amman and knocked on the door of Amer Deeb.

'What took you so long,' asked the smartly dressed Jordanian.

'Mahmoud has been gone for over two months I was beginning to think that something had happened to you.'

Sheepishly, Malik replied,

'I did not know what I should do, I was worried in case something bad was going to happen to me.'

Deeb, dressed in the finest of Arab clothing, smiled, before replying,

'You have no need to worry, my son. Mahmoud spoke very highly of you, telling me that you are a boy of the highest calibre. A boy that looks after others. I feel that I already know everything about you.'

With a sadness crossing his young face, Malik asked,

'Do you know where Mahmoud and Al Bakhit are right now.'

'I am afraid they have already met with their God.'

'My friends in the secret police told me they only lasted for two days after their arrests and that they never gave either of us up. They have both paid the price for their silence. We owe them our lives.'

With tears in his eyes, the youngster said,

'You mean they have been killed for just a few hundred grams of heroin?'

Pausing before replying, Deeb said,

'Oh, my dear boy. You have no idea, do you. There are many 'mules' like you, all controlled by our mutual dead friends. The hundreds of grams that you mention, were in fact hundreds of kilograms. At least thirty of your fellow Syrians were involved, everyone on your bus home each day was doing just as you were. The bus drivers, the border guards and many others are all on the payroll. The question now is, do you wish to continue? We would like you to, if you agree, then you will take over the role of Al Bakhit, after all, his business now belongs to you.'

Without thinking, Malik confirmed that he wished, more than anything, to carry on with what he had been doing, but wondered as to whom it was that was going to bring him the flatbread every day.

Deeb left the room and returned with an equally well-dressed Arab-looking man. He introduced the man with him as Farah Taha and told Malik that he would be bringing the flatbread to the shop in the future. To Malik, Farah Taha looked to be in his mid-twenties, he was tall, well-built, and sported a well-groomed black beard. He was a complete contrast to his much older predecessor, the late Tareq Mahmoud. Taha looked at Amer Deeb and asked as to the age of his soon-to-be partner in crime. In reply, Deeb said,

'He is nearly sixteen, but do not worry, he has the brains and presence of a twenty-five-year-old. I think you will get on well with each other.

'Taha will see you tomorrow young Malik and he will give you twenty bags. A new man will come to your house at 9.00pm, he will say,

'Good evening, do you have my apples.'

Please hand the twenty apples to him. The following day, Taha left the flatbread with Malik, later he would hand over the apples, this situation continued, unabated for several weeks. Malik was now making 12,000 dinar each month. He played music on the bus to and from Nassib every day. Only he had the knowledge that every other passenger on the bus was a mule for Deeb and Taha.

Al Bakhit's solicitor had sent a message to Malik, he had confirmed that his client had indeed, met with death, in the police station, whilst helping them with their enquiries. The message also informed him that he was the rightful heir to Al Bakhit's estate, however he would have to wait until he had placed a notice in a national newspaper, requesting that anyone who might have the right to any of the estate should come forward. Malik would have to wait for six months until Al Bakhit's wishes could be legally granted. Six months elapsed; Malik attended the offices of the solicitor. The solicitor read the will, it confirmed that Tayser Malik had, amongst other things, become the owner of a five-bedroomed house in one of Irbid's most sought-after neighbourhoods. The solicitor handed Malik two sets of keys, he explained that one set is for the house, and the other is for the Mercedes car. Malik had not been aware of the existence of the car. Before leaving the office, the solicitor handed over a small envelope. Written upon it were the words,

'Only to be opened by the son I never had, Tayser Malik.'

Tears filled his eyes as he opened the envelope. The folded piece of paper read,

'My dear boy, all my life I have saved. In the basement of the house, you will find just one wall that has been painted. Remove this wall. I wish you well in everything you do. Trust no one, other than Omar Jamhour, your bus driver. Goodbye my son, Sparks.'

Saying not a word to the solicitor, Malik refolded the piece of paper, placed it back inside the envelope and left. That night, he would not be returning to Nassib, he would be staying at his newly acquired house in Irbid.

Taking a taxi to the address given to him by the solicitor, Malik was completely taken aback upon arriving outside the six-foot high, walled frontage of the villa that stood on the corner of the street that served as a perimeter road to King Abdullah 11 Gardens, which contained both a zoo and a bird sanctuary. Hands shaking, he fumbled through the keys until he found the one that undid the padlock on the outside of the heavy steel gates. He proceeded to the front door. As he inserted the deadlock key, he felt a hand upon his shoulder, his heart missed several beats. Hesitantly he turned his head, his eyes met those of a tall, stunning-looking female, dressed as though she was going to the theatre or some well-to-do restaurant.

'Are you Tayser Malik?' she asked.

Before he could reply, she continued,

'I am Tamara, Al Bakhit's next-door neighbour. Al has told me all about you and he asked me to keep an eye on you, should you ever arrive here alone. I can show you around the house, you will want to know how everything works, I presume?'

Malik had gone from feeling nervous to then feeling completely at ease in the company of his charming neighbour. They entered the large hallway of the villa together. Tamara, in Malik's young eyes, was aged about 35, she showed him around, although he was not able to take in what was going on, as she seemed to be overwhelming him. He did notice that the place was enormous. The bathroom was larger than the whole of his aunt's house in Nassib.

'I have put some things in the fridge for you, but tonight I would like to invite you for dinner. I am on my own, except for my maid, so you have no need to worry about meeting anyone else.'

Her words disappeared from his still-growing brain. His concentration was upon her. Her figure, and everything else about her, was perfect, in every way. He had never had any interest in the opposite sex, he had been too busy just staying alive. Now his loins were reacting, in a way that he had never known before.

Together, they sat, in the warm air of the evening, in Tamara's back garden, the water in the swimming pool glistening in the fading sunlight. The maid brought out the dinner, the fish was unlike any that he had ever consumed before. Tamara lifted her glass of cold white wine and proposed a toast, to absent friends. Understanding the meaning of his host's words, he felt slightly uncomfortable as a single tear slid down the right side of his face. Taking the not-yet sixteen-year-old's hand, the perfectly formed female moved her chair nearer to his and whispered,

'It's OK to cry young man, I too have shed some tears for Al Bakhit, he was a perfect gentleman, but never my lover.'

'Now, would you like to take a swim?' She asked.

Before he could muster a reply, Tamara had stripped off her clothes and was stood as naked as the day she was born, in front of him. She gently undid the buttons of his white linen shirt and then slid her soft hand down the inside of his trousers. His erection was immediate. Letting go of his pulsating penis, she ran and dived headlong into the pool. As she came up from the bottom, she saw that her guest was still stood in the same position. She swam to the side of the pool, lifted her head out of the water and invited him to join her.

'But I cannot swim,' he replied.

'Don't worry, young man, it is not deep here.'

To hide his obvious embarrassment, he removed his sandals, but not his trousers. He ran to the pool and dropped, feet first into the water. When his feet hit the bottom of the pool, he was relieved to find that his head was still above the water line. Tamara disappeared, seconds later he realised that she was removing his trousers underwater. She surfaced, holding the trousers above her head as if they were a trophy. She swung them around, then let go of them, they landed near to the chair that she had been sitting on at dinner. Once again, the female, with a body that most men would have died for, disappeared. He groaned as she took his manhood and carefully slid it in and out of her mouth. Stopping at the all-important time, she surfaced, took the young man's hand, and led him towards the stainless-steel stairs at the end of the pool. She laid down on the warm, thick white towel that had been waiting patiently for her arrival. She spread her legs he did not wait for her invitation. He sunk his rock-hard manhood deep inside her, he came within seconds. Holding him tightly in her arms she asked,

'That was your first-time Tayser?'

'Yes.'

'I have never known anything like that before in my life.'

'Then tonight you should stay in my bed, I will show you things that you could never have imagined were possible.'

She kissed him gently on the lips and felt his erection swelling up against her body.

'We will save that for later, come, I can see that our desert is on the table.'

As she walked, naked, back to her chair, Malik, still hard, watched as her firm arse slowly edged away from him. Seconds later, he stood from a kneeling position, his erection still upright, as if it were a flagpole. Tamara beckoned him over,

'Come on, don't be shy, you are going to show me that many, many times in the future.'

After teasing him in the bath, they went to bed. It had been the fifteen-year-old Syrian's first-ever sexual encounter, the memory of it would stay with him for the rest of his life. Waking at 7.15am, Malik panicked when he realised that he was going to be late in opening the shop, he started to rush around. His lover calmed him down, pointing at a pile of clothes, laid neatly on the bed, she said,

'Here are some clothes, they once belonged to my late husband, I would like you to wear them.'

Putting on the shirt, trousers, and sandals, which happened to fit as if they had been made for him, he noted that the quality of the garments was far superior to anything that he had ever worn before.

'Thank you, can I get a taxi from around here?'

'There is no need Tayser, I will take you in your Mercedes, as I did for Al, almost every day.'

They drove for about twenty minutes and stopped, two blocks from the market.

'This is where you get out. Al always got out here. Nobody should learn of your inheritance, otherwise people will question you. I will be here at 6.00pm to take you home. Today I will be getting your house ready for you to live in. I have asked Al's maid to come back to serve you. Kissing him passionately on the lips, whilst cupping his balls with her soft hands, she ended by saying,

'See you tonight, young man.'

Arriving at Al Bakhit's electrical repair shop, a name that he would never change, Malik was admonished by three waiting customers, for making them wait in the hot, early morning sunshine. In his head he did not care about their complaints, he was rich, he had the most gorgeous of girlfriends, he could pick and choose when he should go to work, however he was still the same person as he was just a few days ago. He apologised for making the three, elderly men wait. He took their various appliances, gave them receipts, and then got to work, fixing the backlog of items that were due to be collected from him that day. At 11.00am Farah Tahar arrived with his lunch. Three pieces of flatbread, inside each of the three, large brown bags, expertly folded, and concealing a total of twenty small polythene bags, each containing 100 grams of the finest heroin. He took the radio that he carried to and from Nassib every day, opening the back of the radio, he realised that he had not delivered yesterday's consignment as he had not returned to Nassib. At lunchtime, he pulled down the shutter, picked up his radio, stuffed the twenty wraps that had been given to him earlier, into the pockets of his new trousers and then walked away from the market. He flagged down a cab and returned to his new home. He really did not know what he was going to do when he arrived. He had realised that a man, whose name he did not know, would have called at his aunt's house in Nassib asking for apples, no one would have known what to tell the man as only *he* knew of the arrangement with him. Tamara saw the taxi pull up. She called to Malik, inviting him in. He walked into the hall, placed his radio on a table and followed Tamara into her lounge. There, right in front of him, sat Amer Deeb.

'So, you are alive, my young friend. I had word from the apple man in Nassib that you did not return home last night, however the lovely Tamara has explained 'everything' so now there is no need to worry. Tonight, you must deliver two consignments of apples. Don't let me down.'

With that, Amer Deeb got up from his chair, kissed Tamara on the cheek and left the house. His driver pulled up directly outside the wrought iron gates and he was gone.

Bringing her young stud some tea, Tamara sat in the chair opposite him and told him that he must deliver the apples. She added that Deeb was not a man to be messed with. She would take him back to the market and he would take the bus after work and stay in Nassib that night. He agreed. He then asked as to what he was going to do every day from now on. Tamara replied,

'We must work out a plan, a plan that Amer Deeb should never know about. Tomorrow lunchtime I will collect you from the same place and we shall solve this problem.'

After seducing the now, much calmer young man, she drove him back to the dropping-off point and he continued his day as normal. That night Malik informed his aunt that he would not be home very much in the future as he had found work and a place to stay in Daraa City. At 9.00pm the apple man arrived, and Malik gave him two consignments. He then informed the apple man that his cousin Mohamad Malik would be handing over the apples in future. Taking his cousin to the river, Malik filled him in on what he was doing. Mohamad was excited, the following morning he would accompany his younger cousin on the journey to Irbid, he would learn how to fix electrical items, he would carry the large radio, to and from Nassib every day, he would hand over the drugs to Mr. Apple. For all of this, Mohamad would receive 100 Dinars per week. Malik did not, and would not, ever tell his cousin of anything else. Mohamad was grateful, he would never betray Tayser, not even under the threat of death.

The following morning the cousins boarded the bus. Mohamad, now in charge of the radio, played loud music. Tayser sat near to his friend and driver, Omar Jamhour. He explained to Omar that, for a short while, he would be taking Mohamad to and from Nassib every day. He handed Omar 200 Dinar and asked that he organise a Jordanian ID card for Mohamad, just as he had done for him nearly one year ago. In addition, he promised him 100 Dinar every week, just to keep an eye on his cousin. That evening, Tayser took Mohamad to the bus stop and made sure that he boarded the bus OK. He then walked to the spot where Tamara was waiting with his newly acquired Mercedes. After dinner they sat together in the sumptuous lounge of Tamara's house. Malik asked his lover, twenty years his senior, as to how she had become involved with Al Bakhit, Tareq Mahmoud and Amer Deeb. Tamara explained that Deeb, a Jordanian, and her late husband, Nur Jamal, an Afghan, were partners. She herself was Deeb's sister and she had met her husband-to-be when he had visited the family home in Amman. Nur Jamal was living in Kabul at the time and he and her brother had run several smuggling operations together. These operations involved supplying arms to Iran, Iraq and Syria, the arms had been sourced by a Pakistani by the name of Imran Hasni. They were transited from Karachi, through Pakistan and into Afghanistan. From there they would find their way into Iran, Iraq, and Syria. When Russia invaded Afghanistan in 1979 it became increasingly difficult to trade weapons in and out of the country. Jamal saw an opening in the drug trade. Several resistance groups, opposed to Russia's occupation of their country, began to grow opium, and would trade the refined, end-product, for arms. Jamal began to accept payment in opium instead of hard cash. The opium brought in four times more than payment in cash. My brother and my husband began an operation to supply heroin to Jordan, Syria and beyond. Today, Amer Deeb controls his own poppy-growing fields in Afghanistan. Tareq Mahmoud was a good friend of my brother, and it was he that found Al Bakhit, together they set up a network of over 400 mules, all young boys, like yourself. These mules took the product from Amman, Irbid and Kerak and into Syria, Israel, Egypt, Lebanon, and Turkey. In Irbid alone there are over thirty boys like you taking two kilograms of product into Syria, each day of the week. That is over 1800 kilos per month. The rewards are immense, but the business is dangerous. Tareq and Al have paid the price for their involvement, many others have suffered the same fate. My husband was taken from his house by the Jordanian Secret Police, he was tortured but he refused to give anyone up. He faced the firing squad, without any trial. My brother moved me from Amman and brought me here to Irbid. I looked after Al Bakhit and he looked after me, now he is gone. You have been chosen to replace Al and I will assume the role of Tareq Mahmoud. Now we should look after each other, if of course you wish to carry on in this business?'

'Of course, I do.' I have many ideas.'

'As I do, my dear boy, as I do.'

'Now let us go upstairs and make love.'

Tamara took Tayser's hand and led him into a night of passion.

The following morning Tayser mentioned the wall in the basement of Al's house. One hour later, he was busy demolishing it. By mid-afternoon he had broken through, only to be disappointed at what he had found. Stacked, floor to ceiling, wall to wall, were about eighty televisions. His initial thoughts were that Al Bakhit had simply played a joke upon him, that was until he threw a brick at one of the screens. The screen shattered, revealing tightly packed money, all of which was in USD. Just one TV contained over 20,000 USD. By the time he and Tamara had finished counting it, some two weeks later, he was one and a half million dollars to the good.

The day after the counting had finished, Tamara dropped Malik near to the market and waited. The millionaire walked to the lock-up shop and informed his cousin, Mohamad, that he would be away for a few days. He handed Mohamad 300 Dinar and walked back to the waiting Merc. Soon after Malik's departure, Farah Tahar delivered three bags of flatbread to the shop. Life carried on as normal. Malik climbed into the Mercedes. He had asked Tamara to take him to Amman, as he wished to have a discussion with her brother, Amer Deeb. Before pulling away Tamara told her young lover that it would not be wise to visit her brother just yet and that she would enlarge when they got back home.

Sat, in Malik's newly inherited Villa and having sent his maid to the market, Tamara began. As you know, my brother and my husband, Nur Jamal, were partners. They supplied vast quantities of arms to warring rebels. Nur bought some land in Afghanistan with the profits and began to grow his own poppies, this growing was quite legal as he could show documentation that his crop was being used in the legitimate pharmaceutical business, but of course he was cultivating heroin. Amer was not involved in this business, but he wanted to be. One day, around two years ago, Nur visited Amer in Amman. Amer made it clear to my husband that he wanted to be involved in the heroin business, my husband refused. He was later found, lying in the sand, vultures picking at his body, on the road to the airport. Before he died, he had signed over his land to Amer. Of course, I knew that my brother had killed my husband, but I could do nothing about it, other than to wait, knowing that my revenge is somewhere in the future. The killing did not stop there. Amer found out that Tareq Mahmoud and Al Bakhit were 'cutting' the heroin before giving it to the mules. This meant they were earning three to four times profit on every kilo. I have learnt that they were picked up by the secret police upon Amer's instruction, he paid a lot of money for them to be killed. Amer knows that I can do nothing to him, now he has put me in charge in Irbid and has asked that I make sure that you follow his every order. He would never kill me, but if you betray him then you will suffer the same fate as the others. If you do as I say, then you will be OK. It is not safe for you to visit Amer, you will receive your orders through me. I will never let anything happen to you. You have my word. One day Tayser, you will help me destroy my brother.

Life for Tayser Malik had changed beyond his wildest imagination. Together with Tamara Jamal and his relatives in Nassib, he expanded the distribution of heroin from Nassib, in the south of Syria to Damascus, Homs and even into Beirut in Lebanon. By 1989, his small electrical repair shop in Irbid was handling over 4000 kgs per month. Over sixty young men and three young females were now bringing electrical items to the shop, Tayser and his cousin, Mohamad, did not bother to repair them, they simply stashed the drugs inside and handed the items back the following day. Amer Deeb was more than happy, as he was able to provide more bulk shipments to Malik every week. The biggest problem for the partners in crime was what to do with the ever-increasing amount of cash. Both of their houses had steel doors fitted to their basements and the money, which by the beginning of 1989 totalled a staggering USD 17 million, was simply placed into old TVs, Radios and any other electrical item that had space inside, once its fittings had been removed. To expand the drug business, Malik opened an electrical repair shop in Nassib. He installed Mohamad's brother, Kamal, to run this operation. The shop, which Malik paid for in USD, had previously been a bank and therefore included two large vaults in the expansive basement, there were three stories of rooms above. Each day, four shabbily dressed men would enter the shop with tools and paint, two would slowly get on with converting the rooms into apartments whilst the other two would guard the basement with an array of weapons, supplied by Tamara Jamal, at their disposal. Kamal Malik was a lot smarter than

Mohamad and quickly set about employing his own mules to transport the drugs from Nassib to Aleppo. In Aleppo he opened a small computer repair shop, run by his sister. She was able to put together a small gang of couriers that would take the heroin into Turkey. They saturated the cities of Adana, Mersin, Antalya, and Izmir, each of which was situated on the Mediterranean Sea, ideal for supplying the ever-increasing foreign tourists. Systematically, almost all the cash was moved to the vaults in Nassib.

During 1989, Amer Deeb was beginning to have problems with supply. The soviets began to withdraw from Afghanistan, they had afforded Amer protection of his poppy growing fields in Helmand Province for many years, in return he supplied heroin to the high-ranking Russian officers, who in turn sold it to their troops. After the withdrawal of the soviet army, in late 1989, there was no one to police the huge poppy fields, that were, by then, producing over 4000 tons of the opium crop and, which unlike other crops, raw opium could be stored for long periods. Various factions of the Mujahideen began to take control of the poppy fields, they fought each other for the land. Amer Deeb began paying huge sums of money to the most powerful of the ancient nomadic tribes to protect his crop. He was forced to move his heroin refinery into northern Pakistan. Amer did a deal with one of Pakistan's most notorious smugglers, Imran Hasni to protect his interests. He and Imran had worked together on the smuggling of arms before Amer decided that he could make a lot more money from heroin.

Learning of her brother's problems and the fact that he had once again thrown his hat in with the Pakistani, Imran Hasni, Tamara discussed a plan with Tayser to eliminate her brother, Amer Deeb. She explained to Tayser that Imran had always had a crush on her, ever since they first met, in Amman in 1975. Imran, five years Tamara's senior, had asked Amer if he would consent to him marrying his sister, Amer had turned down his request as he did not want Tamara to be mixed up in his dangerous world. Now Tamara was willing to throw herself at Imran, just to get revenge against her brother. She got word to Imran, at his hideaway in Chagai, just inside the Pakistan border. She asked Imran to visit her at her home in Irbid, adding that she was lonely and remembered his fondness for her all those years ago. Imran already had three wives and two mistresses, another female in his harem would be a bonus, especially as Tamara was so good-looking. Imran Hasni, one of Pakistan's most wealthy criminals, flew in one of his private jets to Irbid. Tamara was there to greet his arrival. Their meeting took place in March 1990, Tamara was 42 years old. Imran knew nothing of Tamara's love for Tayser Malik. They spent 5 days together, Tayser, extremely jealous, returned to Nassib in order that he took no action against his Pakistani rival. Tamara made sure that it was she that did the seducing and once she was certain that Imran was hooked, she told him of how her brother had murdered her husband. At Tamara's suggestion Imran would invite Amer Deeb to Chagai, on the pretence that Nasim Akhundzada, the ultimate controller of the entire poppy-growing area of Helmand Province, would like to meet with him. Tamara told Imran that during the first night of Amer's stay at Imran's complex, a group of Taliban fighters would capture Amer and hold him for ransom. Tamara spoke these words as her hand was slowly moving up and down Imran's knob. Most men agree to a woman's request when in this submissive position. Imran was to be no exception. In early April, Amer Deeb took a commercial flight from Amman to Karachi. He crossed the tarmac and boarded a helicopter that belonged to the Pakistani Airforce, he sat behind the pilot, next to him was Imran Hasni. Flying just above the roof of the mountainous region that divides Helmand from the north of Pakistan and just five miles short of their destination a rocket-propelled grenade hit the helicopter flush on its nose. None of the three bodies on board were ever identified. The Taliban, at a cost to Tamara of a quarter of a million US Dollars, had undertaken the job. Tamara Jamal had taken her revenge and as her brother's only beneficiary, she was now in control of everything that he once ruled over.

After her brother's demise, Tamara was forced to move to Amman, she soon discovered that Amer had set up several companies and was laundering the drug money through the many suppliers that those companies dealt with. Tayser and Tamara, lovers for nearly eight years, were now only seeing each other sporadically. Having brokered a deal with the most feared of the Mujahideen factions that operated and controlled 95% of the poppy fields in Helmand Province, Tamara enjoyed almost uninterrupted freedom to refine and transport her goods into Amman. In total, over 1,000 people were employed by her 'legit' companies, 950 of them were involved in the heroin business.

With the withdrawal of the Russians, it was left to the Mujahideen to fight it out amongst themselves for control of Helmand and the surrounding area. 1994 saw the rise of the Taliban, they sent the Mujahideen running for the hills. Tamara had new partners. The Taliban loved heroin, they could grow, harvest, and refine poppy, however they had no means of distributing it outside of Afghanistan. In 1999 the world's single largest crop of poppies produced 5,000 tons of opium. In the year 2000, everything changed. Taliban leader, Mullah Mohammed declared the growing of poppies to be 'un-Islamic.' Farmers were murdered in their hundreds, crops were destroyed by fire, the result was that 99% of poppy growing in Taliban-controlled areas had been wiped out. Three-quarters of the World's supply of heroin simply disappeared, overnight. Tamara's operation ceased and with it Tayser's source of heroin came to an end. They had each amassed over USD 170 million, in cash, from their drug dealings.

In the hills on the Kosovo/Albania border, General Kos spent most of his time studying what was going on in the countries around him. He had known Amer Deeb personally and since his death, he had been keeping tabs on his sister, Tamara. He had found out about her rise to stardom in the heroin business and of her association with Tayser Malik. When the bottom fell out of poppy growing, he had contacted Tamara and asked for a meeting. Intrigued by the General's notoriety, she agreed to meet. In June 2001, the General, accompanied by a small army of soldiers, flew to Amman. He informed Tamara that he had come into possession of a large cache of Russian arms, left over after their hurried withdrawal from Afghanistan. He explained that her brother had arranged for the arms to be stored near Basrah in Iraq and now they were needed by the Taliban in Afghanistan. He pointed out to Tamara that she had established routes from Iraq, into Iran and then onto Afghanistan and Pakistan and that there could be more business in the future should she agree to his proposal to move the arms for him. In the meantime, Tayser Malik had gone into the illegal tobacco trade. Growing it in Jordan and selling it in Syria. This had become a massive business for Mr. Malik and his family. In the beginning he simply sold the 'raw' tobacco, by the truckload to people that knew what to do with it. Later he would create seven factories, all complete with 'state-of-the-art' cigarette machines, capable of churning out twelve hundred cigarettes a minute. He could print almost every brand of cigarette carton. Malik enhanced his profitability by adding all kinds of nasty substances to the tobacco leaf. From Syria he was able, via the logistics company belonging to Monzer Asmar, to distribute his illegal wares to Turkey, Greece, and the Balkan States. His main distribution point, in Daraa City was protected by his cousin, the head of the Political Security Division for the area.

When Tayser Malik and Monzer Asmar met, for the second time, in Aleppo in August 2008. Monzer suggested that his fellow Syrian might be interested in accompanying him to a meeting in Varna, Bulgaria, due to take place in just three weeks' time. When asked as to the agenda of the meeting, Monzer informed Malik that he himself did not know, however the meeting was to be hosted by Boyan Petrov and that he had been asked to find someone with distribution routes between Syria, Jordan, Iraq, and Iran. Malik, having such routes agreed to go.

23 - NEW BEGINNINGS

On the 3rd of January 2008, Peter Slade, and Cheryl Smith returned home after six months of cruising the world. The last six weeks of their voyage had been spent visiting the islands of the Caribbean and a cold and frosty, mid-winter arrival in Epping was not at all a pleasant homecoming for either of them.

By the third week of being back home, both were becoming bored. On the last day of January, a Thursday, Cheryl was to receive a phone call. It was from Viviane Downey, a former colleague at the forensic laboratory in London, where they had both worked for several years before Cheryl was forced to leave to care for her terminally ill husband. Ms. Downey, now the head honcho, offered Cheryl a job at the newly formed Institute of Forensic and Scientific Investigations, based in Harlow, Essex. Cheryl explained her current personal situation to Viviane, adding that she would discuss the offer with her partner and get back to her.

To her great surprise, Slade was one hundred percent in favour of Cheryl taking the job, confessing that he too, would search for something to do. They agreed that to stay as they were, was going to send them both 'stir crazy.' Day one of her new job, the first for over four years would be on Monday the eighteenth of February 2008. Returning home that evening, Cheryl explained to Peter that she had been given a position that was very, like that, held by Emilia Fox, in the successful TV series, Silent Witness, and that her work would take her to the 'scene of crimes' where she would look to find evidence that could be analysed back in the lab. She would be very much 'hands-on' and would liaise with various police forces around the UK. Peter was happy for her and whilst he had not yet found a position that suited him, he was spending his time going over the files that were given to him by Graham Roberts and James Reeves.

Whilst Slade was re-digesting the history of his previous investigations, nothing seemed to jog his memory. He could read about what he had done and whom he had investigated but he could not put himself back into the reality of it. He was intrigued by the likes of the Gul family, Jamie Law, Bobby Keagan, and Tony McDonald and how they seemingly controlled much of the UK drug distribution. He saw the faces of and read the profiles of his fellow undercover officers, Alkan Asani and Borislav Topolov. He knew that he had gone to school with Graham Roberts and Paul Walters. Roberts, he read, had been an integral part of his investigation, Walters on the other hand had met with his death in the container from where he was abducted and transported to Germany.

He was completely intrigued by the intel given by Asani and Topolov on the likes of the Petrov's, the Kaptan's, the Asmar brothers, General Kos, Tayser Malik and others, however one name was trying its best to enter that part of his brain that had long since forgotten it. That name was Sean Porter, formerly Michael O'Leary. His gut feeling was telling him that this, former member of the IRA was the lynch-pin in all of this, the problem was though, he was no longer an investigator, not for Special Branch nor Mi5, he had been 'retired' he had had no choice in the matter, he was just forty-four years old and he was left wondering exactly what it was that was going to fill the void left in his life.

During the first week of March, Slade was mentally chewing over the offer made to him by the UK arm of one of the world's largest security firms. If he accepted, he could be the top dog in their internal investigation unit, responsible to report only to the CEO, based in Los Angeles. He would have complete control in respect of looking into the corruption, that was rife within companies in that line of business. He would already have said yes to the offer, had it not been for the fact that he would be spending long periods of time away from home, he knew that he would miss Cheryl and that she would miss him too. Sat in his garden, enjoying his second 'cuppa' of the day, in the warmth of an early spring morning, having dropped his partner at her place of work in Harlow, his phone rang. The screen showed 'number withheld' he answered it anyway.

'Mr. Slade, how are you on this fine day?'

Just eighteen months previously, Slade would have instantly recognised the voice, but now, with no retentive memory for people from his past, he had to ask,

'Who is this?'

'Oh sorry, Peter. It's James, James Reeves. You have maybe read about me in your memoirs.'

'Ah, Mr. Reeves. I can only recognise voices that I have known since my recovery. What can I do for you?'

'I have learnt of a vacancy that you might well be interested in.

'Well, you have certainly called me at the right moment. I was on the point of accepting a position as head of security for a world-renowned company.'

'Put that on hold Peter. There is a much more interesting job in the offing.'

'Where and who with Mr. Reeves?'

'Firstly, Peter, let's dispense with the mister, I am James to you, there is no rank between us now.'

'There is to be a brand-new Government Agency, which is due to begin on the first of April. It will be called, the UK Border Agency and has been born out of the merger of the Border and Immigration Agency and the UK visas and detection functions of HMRC. They want someone to head-up the newly formed investigation section of the Immigration and Settlement Department. The job is right up your street Peter and it's yours if you want it. It is very much a desk job with the added perk of it being 'in the field' should you choose to join in. There is no tearing around from country to country and you would never be put into a position of danger. What do you say?'

'Who would my boss be?'

'Within the office, no one really. You would be under the 'Minister of State for Immigration' and given the life span of our Ministers, the incumbent of that position will be changing on a regular basis.

'So, who do I report to on a day-to-day basis?'

'It will ultimately be the CEO of the organisation, at present that role has not been filled. You will be free to appoint your own staff and operate freely. If the bods in Parliament do not like it, then you are sure to find out at some time.'

'Sounds too good to be true.'

'It's a good opportunity for you, it might allow you to conclude some unfinished business Peter and I am here to help, whenever I can. I still control some people, people you have read about but cannot remember.'

'Where will I be based.'

'In London Peter. It is a civilian role. Your title will be that of, Senior Director – Operations, Immigration and Settlement. I am told that your department will be responsible for policing the illegal entry of people into the UK. There will be a concerted effort, hand in hand with our EU friends to stem the ever-increasing stream of illegals landing on our shores. Your police pay out and pension are not affected.'

'I guess it's a yes then.'

'OK, I will make the call. Good luck Peter.'

'Thank you, James.'

As unlikely as it may seem, when Peter Slade entered the home office building on Marsham Street, SW2, he was not prepared for the events that followed. The UK Border Agency had been allocated two whole floors it was split into four divisions. Operations, Immigration and Settlement. International. Visas, and Law Enforcement. On the third floor, Slade saw that the entire left-hand side of the vast offices had been given over to, Law Enforcement, and the right-side, would-be home to Visas. Whilst the Agency was situated within the home office building, it was independent of their control, although ultimately the Home Secretary took responsibility for its actions. Taking the stairs to the fourth floor he found International to the left and his department, Operations, Immigration and Settlement was on the right. There was a door sporting a bright new brass plate, it read, Director – Operations, Immigration and Settlement. Slade entered. This was his office. It was plush. He sat his briefcase down upon the large oval-shaped oak desk and made his way to the door across the corridor. The brass plate read, Director – International. He knocked and entered.

'Hello old chap, you must be Slade?'

'I am Nicholas Pritchard, Nick' to my friends. Take a pew.'

Sitting opposite the Director of International, whom Slade judged to be no older than twenty-eight, the former undercover agent asked,

'So, where have you arrived here from, Nick?'

'Well, I studied at Eton and obtained a degree in politics five years ago. I then took a gap year, which turned out to be nearer to five. With the help of my father, whom you know very well Mr. Slade, I was able to work in various UK Embassies and Consulates, mainly in the Far East. When I returned my father informed me that there was to be a newly formed Border Agency, and here I am.'

Slade studied the man opposite him, a man at least sixteen years his junior, with no experience in running any kind of a department, let alone one of such national importance. Had the Home Secretary given this silver spoon upstart such an important job, based purely on the fact that he was the son of Julian Pritchard? Only time would tell, he thought.

'What do you know about the job? Have you been educated as to your role? It looks as though you have the same large pile of paperwork on your desk as I have on mine.'

'I met with the Home Secretary just a few evenings ago, my father knows her well. Her advice to me was to 'read up' as much as I could as to the objectives of this brand-new department. I was told that I should choose my staff from within the existing framework of the old regime. Apparently, the aim is to employ more staff at no less than one hundred and thirty-five countries around the world. The objective is to 'weed out' potential illegal visa-seeking individuals prior to them ever entering our shores.'

'So, you are the son of Julian? I have no memory of him, but I am aware that your father went out on a limb to help me during my recent troubles.'

'Well, Mr. Slade, we both have a lot of reading to get through. Perhaps we could have lunch, or dinner, sometime. My shout, of course.'

'Yes, indeed. I will look forward to that, Nick. By the way, it's Peter.'

Slade got up, crossed the hall, and entered his office. He sat in his plush soft-leather chair and realised, for the first time in many years, that he was maybe out of his depth. Shaking off his self-doubt, he needed a coffee before he got stuck into the thousands of pages that adorned the far side of his desk. He knew when he had entered the fourth floor that the reception area was not only void of any receptionist it also offered no facilities for the staff, this he thought, would have to change when he had some staff of his own. He had to descend to the ground floor before finding a coffee machine.

And so, Peter Slade, a former Chief Superintendent of Special Branch, a specialist undercover agent for Mi5 and a man that had nearly given his life for his country climbed eight sets of stairs and returned to his leather chair. Before pulling the top file from the first pile, of which there were five, in total, he wrote on the yellow stick-it pad in front of him, 'Urgent Coffee Machine.'

At 5.00pm, on the dot, Nicholas Pritchard stuck his head around the door and bid Slade goodnight. At 6.15, Slade locked his office door and took the stairs, he never returned them. He turned left out of the building and waited on the platform at St. James Park, with hundreds of others, for the underground train that would take him, firstly to Tower Hill, where he would change, five minutes later he would board a central line service at Liverpool Street, which would take him all the way through to Epping, at the very end of the central line.

When he eventually arrived home, just after eight, Cheryl placed a glass of red into his hand and declared that dinner would be ready in twenty minutes. Over dinner, the love of his life asked as to his day. Sighing a little, which was most unusual for him, Slade informed Cheryl that he found it difficult to believe that he, as well as Nicholas Pritchard, had been left to, ''very much fend for themselves.' Cheryl pointed out that this could be a good thing, as he would be free to do everything his way, there was no comparison to be made with predecessors as there were not any to compare with. Slade immediately felt better, she was right, a clean slate with which to build on was a whole lot better than having to clear up the mess left behind by others. He kissed her tenderly on the lips. They had an early night.

Day two of Slade's time in his new office was to take up where he had left off the previous day. He was to continue to troll through the stacks of paperwork that had been left for him to acclimatise himself with. He could never have known the extent of the massive task that lay ahead of him. He read an article written by the 'Minister of State for Borders and Immigration' which came under the control of the Home Office. This same MP also held the title of 'Minister of State for Revenue Protection at the Border' which fell under the guise of HM Treasury. The 'plan' as the report indicated, was to, 'secure our border, tackle border tax fraud, smuggling, and immigration crime.

All these intentions would be achieved by having 'stronger checks overseas' 'a powerful new force operating the frontline' and more effective checks in the UK. In addition, it was stated that 'there would be a large increase in the officers who work at our borders' and 'they would have new, stronger powers and be equipped with new technology.' Customs and Immigration would be combined at the frontline, to keep the country safe. Slade smiled to himself as he read, 'the public will notice that border controls are stronger.' 'They will see a primary checkpoint at passport control, and they will be quizzed about the documents they are presenting and the goods that they carry.'

In addition, he read an article about, 'Visas in the right places' which laid out that stringent checks would be made upon people applying for Visas abroad. Each application for a Visa to visit the UK would now be subject to the highest of scrutiny, to rule out the risk of individuals involved in crime or terrorism from ever landing on our shores. A new system of 'fingerprint Visas' had been introduced in 2007 and every visitor holding a Visa to enter the UK would have their fingerprint held on the Border Force database. By the end of 2007 over 2.5 million Visa applicants had been enrolled and 3,100 identity swappers had been apprehended. With the expansion of UK Border Force officers being stationed overseas, 210,000 people were prevented from boarding their flights during the last five years. The 'Advance Electronic Watch-List Checks' set up in 2002, had vetted 50 million passengers before they arrived in the UK and 1,700 'illegals' were arrested. Again, during the previous five years, over one million lorries were searched at EU Ports, by UK border officials and over 18,000 people were stopped from crossing the channel illegally.

Shortly after lunch, Slade's internal telephone rang.

'Peter, it's Nick Pritchard, are you free at 2.30?

'Yes, may I ask why?

'I will pop in to see you, there is someone who wishes to meet with you.'

'At 2.30 there was a single tap on Slade's door and in walked Nick Pritchard, the Home Secretary and one of her aides. Slade stood, and shook everyone's hand, asking them to be seated in the three chairs that had been lined up on the other side of his desk. Slade was sure that those chairs were not there prior to him going out for lunch. It was the Home Secretary that spoke first.

'Mr. Slade, I have heard so much about you. You are held in the highest of esteem by both Julian Pritchard and James Reeves and I would like to thank you personally for all that you have done to help keep our country safe and sound. Believe me when I say that your name is known in the very highest of places.'

'Thank you very much, Home Secretary. That means a lot to me.'

'Peter, may I call you that?

'Yes, of course, Home Secretary.'

'Officially, this meeting is recorded by my aide here. However, most of what I have to say will never see the light of day. For the past five years, we have been working towards setting up this brand-new Border Force department. We have identified a number, of countries, whereby we do not trust the authenticity of their passport security. In a nutshell, hundreds of thousands of passports are issued by eleven identified countries that we know for certain that corrupt officials are involved. We are increasing our staff in those countries to combat this. In the Caribbean and West Africa, we have undercover agents working in Government Offices to identify those responsible. By the end of this year, we are committed to delivering a Border Intelligence Service. This will serve to identify those responsible for arranging the trafficking of illegals and asylum seekers. I can report that the number of people entering the UK, illegally, as stated in the press, is merely the tip of the iceberg. Your role, Peter, will be to track down those responsible for the smuggling of those people into the UK and bring them to book. You will have access to our agents that are already working throughout the EU, the Middle East, Pakistan, and India. In the course of your work, you may well find that the journeys of those poor souls, trafficked for profit, emanate far beyond the places that I have just mentioned. You have a free hand, Peter. I have been informed that your expertise lies within this field of investigation. Of course, a lot of what you may have to do would never have been sanctioned by my office, I presume you understand the reasons behind that. Any questions?

'Who exactly will I be reporting to and who will give the green light in respect of specific operations?'

'The buck stops with me, Peter. You must do whatever you feel is right. My involvement will be purely on a 'need-to-know basis'.' Good day to you and good luck.

With his three visitors now gone, Slade took a few minutes to ponder. Had the Home Secretary just given him the green light to run his department anyway that he might choose? In the main office there were forty-two desks, each waiting to accommodate a new team member. Directly next door to his office was a smaller room, the brass plate on the door read, 'deputy director', he had forty-three vacancies to fill and at that precise moment he had no idea as to whom he would be appointing. Had this been a department of Special Branch then his task would have been that much easier. He would have been the 'Commander' he would have required a Chief Superintendent, two Superintendents, one Chief Inspector and two Inspectors. The rest of the team would have consisted of a few Sergeants with the balance being Constables. In this civilian role he had no clue as to how rank panned out. His priority, as far as the appointment of staff was concerned, was to find the right person to fill the role as his number two. He had someone in mind but was not sure if protocol allowed him to offer him the job.

For the next two weeks, Slade waded through the files. He came across several folders marked as 'classified. 'He did wonder if he should have received them. He installed a row of desks along the entire left-hand side of his large office. He meticulously laid out each file in order of how important he believed them to be. He then re-read all the files that Graham Roberts and Julian Pritchard had sent to him in the hope that the contents might allow him to recall the past. He made extensive notes from each file that he read and then crossed referenced them with information contained from within the files that once belonged to the now-defunct 'Border and Immigration Agency' (BIA) department.

One month into the task of collating everything that had been piled on his desk, he remained, with one exception, alone on the fourth floor of the home office building. The one exception was Nicholas Pritchard. In short conversations with his counterpart in the 'International' section of this newly formed organisation, Slade was aware that Nick had undertaken the exact same modus-operandi as he had. Both men were now ready to start putting bums onto the empty seats in their respective offices.

On Sunday 11th May 2008, Slade rang Graham Roberts. Roberts was aware of his friend's new role at the UK Border Agency. Slade, through the files that they were both working on prior to his abduction and subsequent accident, was fully versed in Roberts' role as a private investigator.

'Mr. Roberts, I have a proposition for you.'

'But I am a happily married man, Peter.'

'Oh, dam. I was certain that you would abscond with me.'

'Seriously though. I need to appoint a number two at the Agency.'

'No one springs to mind, Peter. Let me think about it.'

'It's you I want Graham. I know that you have your own commitments, however from reading the files of our recent venture, I cannot think of anyone else that might fit the bill. In fact, I cannot think of anyone else as I have forgotten everyone.'

'But I have several jobs on the go, currently Peter. It would not be possible for me to simply walk away from them.'

'Yes, I thought you might say that Graham. I have prepared a perfect compromise for you.'

'And what is that exactly?'

'You give me two days per week in the office. You will be paid as a consultant, no one else needs to know. I am sure that you have competent employees to cover for you. How many full-time staff do you have?

'I have eight salaried people on the payroll and a dozen or so that I give regular part-time work to.'

'OK, I will guarantee employment for any of the people that you choose to nominate. They will also be paid as consultants, the payments to be made directly to your company. You can retain those that you need to run your business whilst you are with me. As time goes by, your workload at the Border Force will increase, however we shall deal with that as and when it becomes applicable. What do you say?

'It's a big decision for me to have to make,' can I chew it over Peter?

'I need you now Graham. You see, you have not lost your memory and you were very much a part of operation 'Daisy.' In the files left on my desk, for me to study, I have seen the names of Boyan Petrov, General Kos, Tayser Malik and others. These same names appear in your resume of the prime suspects in the drug smuggling business. Alkan Asani and Borislav Topolov, both known to us as undercover Mi5 agents in the European investigation, also appear in home office files in connection with 'people smuggling.' In one classified file that I have read, it states that 9,000 illegals were stopped from travelling to the UK, in 2007, as a direct result of the newly installed 'exit checks.' In a paper in the same file, headed, 'for Home Secretaries eyes only' a junior minister has written that an estimated 85,000 people entered the UK undetected, with over sixty percent of them subsequently claiming asylum. It will be my job to get to the bottom of this and I can think of no one better placed to help me than you, Graham.'

'I will let you know by Tuesday.'

On Monday, 12th, May 2008, Slade sat opposite Nicholas Pritchard and began a discussion that he hoped would lead to them cooperating in their pursuit of the criminals that, in return for large sums of money, were arranging the transportation of many illegal immigrants from all corners of the globe. Both men agreed that 'official' government figures were simply fictional. When he left Pritchard's office, there was an agreement in place that on each Friday afternoon the two men would meet and update each other on any specific news that might help the other. In addition, they would share anything that might be deemed to be important, at any time. Slade, with one thousand times more experience than his young colleague, was pleased that the son of Julian Pritchard had agreed to his suggested cooperation, which, within government departments, was quite rare. The following day, Slade was elated when Graham Roberts informed him that he would accept the offer as being his number two, although, due to current commitments, he was unable to take his seat in the office next door until Monday 26th May. Roberts would be Slade's very first employee. He beamed when informing Cheryl later that evening. She was happy that 'her man' seemed to be getting his life back into gear.

With the knowledge that his former schoolboy friend would be joining him in just two weeks-time, Slade was determined to learn all that he could about the innermost workings of the Border Force and the future role that his department would play in the development of this newly formed organisation. He had also learnt from Nick Pritchard that a CEO was to be appointed within a matter of days. All four departments would be under the control of this man (or woman) which Slade presumed, would in some way curtail the way in which he chose to work, only time would tell. He was buoyed by the fact that Pritchard had the ear of the Home Secretary, so maybe the CEO would be of little consequence to him.

Reading through the paperwork that appeared on his desk every morning, although he had never seen anyone place it there, Slade read that the 'Borders, Citizenship and Immigration Act' was to be given 'Royal Assent' in July 2009, meaning that he and his three counterparts had just over a year to get everything in place. In a memo, each 'Head of Department' was encouraged to source their staff from the now-defunct UK Border Agency and that a total workforce of 23,500 would be spread over 130 Countries and needed to be in place by July 2009. For now, the existing workforce would be controlled by HMRC and the Director of Border Revenue. In the future, overseas staff would vet visa applications within the new guidelines being set out and operate intelligence networks, acting as the first layer of border control for the UK. All of this would fall under the control of Pritchard's department and Slade would need to glean a lot of information from the young, but astute man from across the corridor.

Slade began to learn the difference between 'People smuggling' and 'Human trafficking.' People Smuggling, he read, is the facilitation, transportation or illegal entry of a person, or persons across an international border, in violation of one or more countries' laws, either clandestinely or through deception, such as the fraudulent use of documents. The practice of people smuggling has seen a sharp rise in recent years. Unlike Human trafficking, people smuggling is consensual, an agreement between the customer and the smuggler and the most common reasons for the individual that wishes to be smuggled is, employment, economic opportunity, personal or familial betterment and escape from persecution, violence, or conflict. Slade was gobsmacked to learn that according to the last published figures, over 800,000 people had been smuggled across the Mediterranean and into Europe. They had emanated from a whole host of countries. It was thought that thousands of smuggling gangs operated along the most popular routes, many of these were 'family businesses' that each cooperated with the other, splitting the income at agreed rates. There was no known 'godfather' in the smuggling process, however there were people that could give advice to asylum seekers. Advice such as which EU country offered the best package of benefits. Two gangs that Slade came across quite often during his research were the 'Snakeheads' and the 'Coyotes.' The 'Snakeheads' were of Chinese origin and originally concentrated on smuggling people from Fujian Province into Hong Kong. Most of these 'illegals' took low-paid, labour-intensive work and all had to pay the local Triads to continue to stay there. In recent years, the 'Snakeheads' have expanded their operations 'Worldwide' and are responsible for a good percentage of the Chinese illegals that continue to flood into the USA and Western Europe. The 'Coyotes' operate their people smuggling business between Mexico and the USA, assisting hundreds of thousands of South Americans to enter the states via the extensive, and often unguarded border. In 2005 the Coyotes were estimated to have earnt over $7 billion. A similar figure was attributed to the gangs that smuggled people into the EU. In 2005, people smugglers charged from $4,000 for a simple 'cross border' transaction and up to $75,000 for a journey from China to either the USA or the EU. There was no intelligence on specific gangs operating people smuggling into the EU and then onto the UK. Slade would be tasked with establishing the identities of the more prominent players, he soon began to realise the massive task that lay ahead.

In an article, highlighted and left on his desk, Slade was to read all about Human trafficking and how it differed in comparison with the more consensual world of people smuggling. 'Human Trafficking' the report stated, 'is the trade of humans for the purpose of forced labour, sexual slavery, or commercial sexual exploitation for the trafficker or others.' Humans, he read, are trafficked to take part in forced marriages, the extraction of organs, forced labour, forced prostitution, for use as drug mules or simply as 'slaves.' In 2005, the International Labour Organisation (ILO) estimated that over $100 billion was earned as profit, by the gangs facilitating these crimes and that a total of 21 million people were trapped in 'modern-day slavery' worldwide. Human Trafficking was listed as the world's fastest-growing illegal activity. Under the heading, 'Bonded Labour' it was shown that individuals or families that take out loans, use their labour as a means of repaying the debt. Most times the loan is never repaid as the value of their labour is less than the loan, in these cases the victim works for nothing, forever. 'Forced Labour' is defined as being a situation whereby people are forced to work, against their will, under the threat of violence or some other form of punishment. Their freedom is restricted, and a degree of ownership is exerted. Forms of forced labour include domestic servitude, agricultural labour, sweatshop factory work, food service and begging. In some countries, over 50% of people working in the clothing, cocoa, coffee, cotton, and gold production are forced to do so. Over 210 million children worldwide are forced into work, either very lowly paid or not paid at all.

In a report generated by Colin Millburn a former employee of the previous Border Force, Slade learnt some stark facts about life as a people smuggler and their customers. Abu Hamada, himself a Syrian refugee, declared that he can earn upwards of £3 million per year, smuggling people across the Med from Egypt. He charges £700-£850 for a place on a boat for the short trip from Turkey to Greece. He helps Afghans flee from their homeland to Eastern Europe at a cost of £10,000 each. One Afghan, a prominent surgeon but under threat of death for treating the wrong people, fled Kabul at a cost of £30,000. During his journey, he was sent GPS coordinates, handed maps by nomads, and even met by cars at certain points along the route. Fraudulent work visas are available in several countries. One of the most disturbing chapters of Millburn's report was of a gang that operated in Libya. They were offering individuals in Eritrea, Syria, and Afghanistan a 'go now, pay later deal.' They were told that they could pay off their smuggling fees once they had found work in their chosen country. The reality was, that they were taken to Ajdabiya on the Libyan coast, held, and tortured until relatives paid a ransom and once the ransom was handed over the poor souls were released out onto the streets. People smuggling requires a host of specialist 'players' these include recruiters, transporters, hoteliers, facilitators, enforcers, organisers, and financiers. Some of the gangs are very streetwise, there are occasions when one of the migrants is given the key to the boat and he will drive it to a destination country and claim asylum along with his fellow passengers. The authorities find it difficult to charge the driver with smuggling as he himself has paid to be transported.

An Iranian national, himself a migrant, was landed in Italy by a gang. He studied every aspect of his journey and two years later he entered Egypt and set up his own gang. Millburn had found out via his sources that the Iranian, named Naz Uday, had arranged for over 10,000 people, of all nationalities to enter Italy. He had paid middlemen, sailing crews, shipowners, and the Italian police. To show that they were actively doing their job, the Italian police when capturing large volumes of illegals, would hold 15% of them and simply allow the other 85% to carry on with their journeys into Italy and beyond. Uday was said to have made over £4.5 million in 2006 alone.

In a separate, one-page report, Slade read that in 2004, 141 countries signed up to a new protocol in respect of 'people smuggling.' The emphasis was put on making the smuggling of people a crime, that the migrants themselves have committed a criminal act, however it was agreed that all-out action against the 'smugglers' was needed and not necessarily against the migrants, whose human rights should be maintained throughout, if detained.

A blue folder sat half on, half off, of Slade's packed desk. He picked it up before it fell to the ground. He had not intended to read it there and then, however when he saw the words, 'Human Misery – The Plight of the Sex

Slaves' written in large red felt tip pen, he opened it. What he read chilled him to his bones. This was the moment in time when he knew that he had to get to the bottom of what he had been hired to do. The file had been compiled by a network of Interpol Agents. The UK had chipped in with a team of four, former vice squad detectives that operated from the back of a KFC in Bermondsey, South London. The investigation, operational for the past four years, tells of a sadistic gang of Eastern Europeans that were preying on beautiful young girls, all were from the old Eastern Bloc countries. Various websites had been set up, to lure the unsuspecting females into the lucrative world of modelling. Sergiy Yakimov was the known leader of the gang and over one hundred and twenty gang members had been identified in fifteen EU countries. Yakimov himself lived in luxurious surroundings in the heart of Vienna. His most trusted men operated in Paris, Milan, London, Frankfurt, and Athens. To a lesser degree, agencies were doing business in Madrid, Nice, Amsterdam, Brussels, Stockholm, Geneva, and Dublin. The modus operandi was the same throughout. Slade was to learn of events that would sicken him to his core.

The websites, tailor-made for each country of origin, showed glamourous models and listed what each girl had achieved in her career. 'This could be you' was the common theme. Viewers of the sites were invited to submit their most personal details, along with a minimum of five photographs. One of which had to be posing in underwear or a bikini. If they were of interest, they would receive an email giving them further information on what to do next. No girl was ever rejected, such was the demand for their services.

In Bucharest, Romania. Helena, a seventeen-year-old single mum submitted her details and photographs to the online questionnaire of the website, 'Your World Awaits You. ' Three days later she was contacted and met by a handsome young Bulgarian man. He wined and dined her and was rewarded with sex at his penthouse apartment that overlooked the old quarter of Bucharest. Three days later the Bulgarian accompanied Helena to Vienna, where she was taken to the home of Yakimov. In a purpose-built studio, with swimming pool, sauna and games room, Helena was photographed. Over half of the photographs taken were of her totally nude body. Whilst she was enjoying dinner beside the pool, with her host, she was unaware that the photographs were being uploaded onto a 'dark web' site, only used by invited guests. At midnight two menacing-looking males arrived and took Helena. She was placed into the back seat of a Hummer and driven away. She was not frightened or worried as she had been drugged over a four-hour period. The Hummer arrived at the home of a well-known Austrian Government Official. He and three of his guests sexually abused Helena until the early hours of the morning. At 7.00am and still under the influence of what she had been given, she was thrown, half-naked into the back of a beaten-up old Renault van and driven to a shabby house in the South of the City. There she quickly became addicted and was forced to work as a sex slave. She would earn her captives around one thousand Euros per night. By the time she was twenty, she was a spent force and was discarded by the side of a disused railway siding. Yakimov alone was said to have made over one million Euros from this girl during the two and a half years that he used her as his slave. Yakimov continues his business, supposedly untouchable due to the protection afforded to him by those in power.

In Vilnius, Lithuania, schoolgirls Ruta and Nadia exit the school gates after a hard day of study. Ruta is holding a brochure for a local modelling agency. The brochure is one of many that were left at the school earlier in the day. Standing opposite the gates is Gino Rossi, a good-looking, well-dressed Italian man, aged just twenty-two. He approaches the girls and asks if they are interested in modelling. Ruta, a blonde-haired fourteen-year-old beauty, shyly smiles at the Italian and answers yes.

'Good, then come with me and I will take you to the agency.'

'But I must go home first otherwise my father will worry about me', says Nadia.

'Don't worry, we will not be long, just one hour, maybe.'

Gino forces himself in the middle of the two girls, they lock arms and skip, seemingly without a care, beside the dark-featured man from the Azuri.

Fifteen minutes later the girls were changing out of their school uniforms and into bra and knickers. Ruta was led from the changing room and asked to sit on a single chair in a completely white room. A few minutes later two men, each with cameras, arrived. Ruta was asked to remove her bra, she was reluctant.

'Oh, come on young lady. If you want to be a model you will have to do far worse things than that. Maybe you need a little something to make you less shy? A middle-aged woman entered the room, she carried a small plastic tray, which contained a plastic cup of water and two tablets.

'Take these, they will loosen you up a little and make you feel less nervous.'

Reluctantly, Ruta did as she was asked.

Thirty minutes later, she was led into another room and forty minutes after that she had sex with four very well-endowed men. All forty minutes of action were recorded on the video cam that stood at the end of the king-size waterbed.

In the meantime, Nadia had been led up to a room on the third floor, she went without question, having been told that she needed to be photographed in the natural light that the higher room afforded. When she was asked to completely disrobe, she refused. Like Ruta, she was offered two tablets, again she refused. To escape from the three hefty men that were in the room with her, she jumped out of the open window. Seconds later, she lay, motionless in a dirty courtyard below. The following day, Nadia's father reported her missing. She was never found, and no one was ever taken to task for her disappearance. Ruta was found two years later, in an alleyway on the East side of Berlin. She had overdosed, her body was battered from her head to her toes. She was just another victim of forced sex slavery, which increases year on year, unabated.

Four Bulgarian girls, all under the age of sixteen, arrive at Heathrow on a flight from Austria. Prior to meeting each other at the home of Sergiy Yakimov in Vienna, they had never met. Each girl had signed up to the modelling agency and had been driven, individually to Yakimov's residence. These girls were treated well whilst in Vienna and had been promised lucrative contracts for work in advertising, in London. All four girls travelled on fake documentation and those documents showed that they were all over the age of eighteen. They were greeted at the airport by Samantha Bloss, the one-time lover of Yakimov. She now played the role of being 'mother' to all new arrivals into the UK. A chauffeur-driven limo took them all to Shoreditch in the East end of London. They turned into an alleyway, the only light was a neon strip that read, 'Rosies Joint.' Bloss leads the girls through a fortified door, along a darkened hall, down two flights of stairs and into a large room containing eight bunk beds and dressing tables. Two men enter the room, Bloss leaves. The men begin to tear at the girl's clothes, ripping their tops and bras from them. All four cry, in despair. The men ogle them and then forcibly rape them, one by one. Another man enters the room and injects each girl. Within minutes they are all almost unconscious, laid stark naked upon their beds. After a few hours Andrei Berbatov enters the dormitory. The girls are woken, given coffee, and asked to put on the dressing gowns that lay on their respective beds. Berbatov, speaking very quietly, in their native tongue, calmly informs the frightened young females that they each owe the agency £10,000 but he asked them not to be worried as they will be able to work off their debt within a couple of years. He then informed the girls that each of them 'now belonged to him' and should they be tempted to escape, then, as he knew where they all lived in Bulgaria, their families would suffer. When eventually this sleazy back street brothel was shut down by a team of vice officers, there was no trace of the four, young Bulgarian girls.

There were forty-nine other reports on individuals that had been forced into slavery of the worst kind. Peter Slade was to read them all. When relaying his findings to Cheryl, he broke down. What he had read had made him even more determined to bring as many of these low-life criminals to book.

In his office the following day, he made a note. Firstly, he would seek out Colin Millburn, to find out if he were available to join his team. He would also investigate the status of the four men that had been holed up in the back of a

KFC in South London, as these were the kind of people that he wanted to join with him in pursuit of the ringleaders of these terrible crimes.

On Friday 23rd May 2008, Jonathan Dexter, a former Chief Investigator for the Criminal Ombudsman's office, was appointed as the CEO of the newly constructed Border Agency. He would sit on the second floor of the Home Office Building. It was unclear to Slade at this time, as to whether he would be reporting directly to this man, a man he had never heard of.

24 - THE TEAM

On Monday, 26th May 2008, Graham Roberts entered the reception area of the Home Office Building. Peter Slade was leaning against the counter, chatting to the rather young and attractive receptionist. As Roberts approached, Slade realised that another man was with his former classmate. Slade gestured for his long-time friend and his associate to be seated. A minute later Slade sat in the chair opposite the two men. He handed Roberts an identification badge and explained that he had already been vetted and pre-cleared, adding that he would have access to all but a few doors of the building. Before he could quiz Roberts as to the identity of the man that was with him, Slade felt the strangest of feelings beginning to swirl around inside his head. At the same time Roberts looked at his friend's puzzled face, pointed to the man sat next to him and said,

'Do you remember......... '

Whatever Roberts said next, Slade never heard it. A million images flashed through his brain at the speed of light and then stopped. It stopped at a point in his life when, as a young boy, he had nearly died. The man now sat next to Roberts was responsible for his 'near-death' experience. The images now in his head had slowed to near normal pace. He was fourteen and in the swimming baths, training for the upcoming school sports day. He was nearing the end of his fourth length when he was hit by a boy that had jumped from the high diving board, having ignored all attempts by those on the ground to stop him. The jumper had impacted Slade's head and he lie motionless on the bottom of the pool, at its deepest point. Mr. Thomas, the sports teacher and lifeguard for the day, was quickly into the pool and managed to get Slade to the surface. A crowd gathered around him, he was laid on his side, unconscious. A first aider was sought and found. A primitive form of CPR was carried out and Slade slowly recovered. When first opening his eyes, he was staring into the face of Rory 'Ringo' Starr. It was 'Ringo' that now sat by the side of Roberts. Although visibly shaken, Slade managed to string together the following few words,

'Have you come to finish me off, Ringo?'

Roberts, although concerned, was relieved that Slade had somehow remembered one of their former classmates. Roberts brought some cold water from the machine in reception and beckoned Slade to drink it. Slade began to come out of the haze that had engulfed him.

'I have brought Ringo with me as I think he may be an asset to the cause.'

'OK, let me get a visitor's badge for him, we can then go upstairs to my office.'

Five minutes later, all three men were sat in Slade's plush office.

'Now, what is it that Ringo can bring to the table, Graham?'

'Well, for the past three years he has worked for me as a tracker. When I wanted someone found, Ringo here, found them. Prior to that, he had been one of the most successful members of the SAS, taking part in thirty-six covert operations, none of which failed. Four years ago, aged forty, he was 'retired' from active field duty. They wanted him to train new recruits. He tried for a short while but missed the excitement of combat. We met, quite by accident, at an 'old boys' reunion and got talking. I needed someone to find people and Ringo here, needed people to find. He has a one hundred percent record. My idea is to give him a desk in the office, just for cosmetic reasons, however we can use him for what he is good at, that is, tracking down people that do not wish to be found.'

'What a splendid idea, Graham. I must say that I had not given any thought to such a role, but now that you have pointed it out, it's a no-brainer.'

Leaning over, Slade reached across and shook Ringo's hand.

'Welcome to the Immigration and Settlement department, Ringo. I would ask that you return to this office in two weeks, as there are procedures that must be met, I will leave it to Graham to obtain all the necessary information from you. Now you must please excuse us as we have a lot to get through today.'

Ringo hugged Roberts and left.

'Graham, I will show you to your office.'

The two men walked into the office next door. Roberts now sat behind the desk and Slade took the role of being the interviewee.

'As you can see Graham, I have left various files upon your desk. There are handwritten notes where applicable. Tomorrow we will be joined by Colin Millburn. He will operate from one of the private rooms within the main office. We will spend the whole day with him. We must glean from him as much as we can as to the workings of the Border Force. On Wednesday we will entertain four members of Interpol, we need not worry about lunch, as they will bring KFC with them.'

Roberts gave Slade an inquisitive look.

'Of course, you are not aware, are you? I have managed to get the Home Secretary, with the help of Nick Pritchard, whom I will introduce to you at lunch, to agree to the transfer of this small team from their home behind a

KFC in Bermondsey, to the more salubrious surroundings of the fourth floor of the home office building. These men, whose investigations you will read about, are just about the most experienced, and successful quartet of Immigration officers anywhere in the UK.'

'With these four, plus Millburn, the seven men that you are bringing, plus yourself, Ringo, and me, we will only have twenty-seven bums to place on seats. One of those will have to have equal status to Millburn, for protocol reasons and that person, plus the remaining twenty-six, will all have to be drawn from the now-defunct, Border Force department. On your desk you will find a short-list of a hundred or so names. I have chosen them from the thousands that were on offer. It will be your job to interview and select the successful candidates. I need them in place by the ninth of June, good luck.

'Before we join Nick for lunch, I may as well show you the main office.'

Slade pushed the double doors and the two men walked into a fully set-up office measuring some three thousand square feet. In one corner was an office, about half the size of Roberts.

'This will be Millburn's and the replica, in the other corner, will be for the new man of equal rank.'

'Are you OK with giving Ringo a desk in your office, after all he will be out, most of the time.'

'Yes, Peter. That will be fine.

'Now I will introduce you to Nick Pritchard, you know his father, and then we shall take lunch. And do not worry, Nick is paying.'

Before returning to their respective offices, Slade asked Roberts to read as much as he could of the report put together by the men from KFC. He had no need to inform his friend that what he would be reading he might find stressful. Roberts, a private investigator for over twenty-five years, had dealt with many cases of sexual violence, during his chosen career, he would not find anything in the file that he did not already know about.

Over lunch, during which young Pritchard seemed to get on swimmingly well with Roberts, the son of Julian let it be known that he was struggling to fill most of the positions within his department. Both of his elders offered their help, pointing out that they had access to many people that might fit the bill. Roberts even suggested that he could vouch for half a dozen investigators that had either worked for him or some of his competitors, all had experience in Immigration matters. Pritchard Jnr was quick to ask that Roberts contact them and arrange interviews. After lunch, and out of earshot of Pritchard, Slade queried as to why his friend had offered up six men to help Pritchard fill the seats within his empty office.

'Well, Peter. I figured that if we can place people in Pritchard's department, which covers International Investigations, then we have a ready-made chain of intel, without having to keep going to the boss, who, as you might imagine, may not be that forthcoming on the more sensitive information that we require.'

'That's exactly why I needed you here Graham. You have always been a little more devious than me.'

On the Central Line train from Liverpool Street to Epping that evening, Slade began to have flashbacks. As in the morning, a million images flashed through his brain. As the train was stopped at Loughton, one image stuck behind his eyes. It was that of the morning when his car had been blown to pieces, with his wife and two daughters inside. Slade slumped sideways a passenger pulled the emergency cord. Five minutes later a paramedic had him wired up to several portable machines. With the help of others, he was lifted from the train and laid on the platform. He began to come round, he explained recent events to the paramedic and the three, ambulance crew that had come to assist. Despite his protestations, he was persuaded to go to the nearby local hospital for checks. He rang Cheryl, telling her not to worry but he may need a ride home later. After three hours, in which time the A & E department had managed to track down his consultant, he was able to leave. The consultant had confirmed that the regaining of his memory had been triggered by the events of that morning and in all probability, he would regain full memory loss. None the worse for wear Slade was driven home by Cheryl and dropped off at Epping Station the next day.

At 10.00am the following morning, Roberts met Colin Milburn in the reception and led him up to the fourth floor and into Slade's office. Millburn looked to be aged about sixty, however from the information that Slade had on his desk, which included his career and full personal details, his date of birth was stated as June 1955, which made him just fifty-three. After the usual shaking of hands and exchange of coffee cups, that Roberts had nipped to the reception to get, Slade began.

'I see from your profile Mr. Millburn that before your ten years with the Border Force, you worked overseas, for the Foreign Office. Can you give us a brief resume of what you did and in which countries you operated from?'

'Yes, of course, Mr. Slade. And please call me Colin, and no, I never opened the batting for England.'

'For twelve years I worked as a liaison officer for various Embassies and Consulates, almost all were in Middle Eastern Countries. I was a kind of 'go-between' someone who obtains local gossip from diplomats and feeds anything important back to the Ambassador. I made a point of frequenting the clubs and bars where journalists liked to congregate. I would pick up all kinds of info, military, foreign policy, scandal and towards the end of my days overseas, it was the march of the poor sods that were, for one reason or another, forced to leave the land of their birth.'

'Was your research into the migration of the suppressed a voluntary thing or were you asked to do it by the Foreign Office', asked Roberts.

'It was very much orchestrated by the FCO, and I produced many reports in respect of the numbers of people that were fleeing their countries. I also gathered intelligence about the reasons why so many people seek to find a better life for themselves, elsewhere. Along the way, my journalistic friends gave me the heads-up on the names and whereabouts of the people smuggling gangs, this led me to begin my investigation into the human misery caused by 'trafficking' a much more sinister method of managing the future lives of those that will never break free from the debt that they incur when signing up for their journey to a new life.'

Slade picked up his phone and asked his newly installed receptionist to bring in three coffees. He then asked Millburn the following.

'If I were to get you the clearance, would you be willing to re-create your former role?'

'Depends on where it might be Mr. Slade.'

'From what we know now, albeit only from reading the masses of paperwork that was left for me to study, it appears that they are hundreds of smuggling routes from the Middle East and even further afield that require investigation and then eradication. When you finished Colin, where were the bulk of the illegals coming from?'

'There were so many Mr. Slade. Of the Middle East Countries, Iraq, Iran, Afghanistan, Syria, and Saudi Arabia were the most prominent. However, everything changes as soon as there is conflict. In Iraq it was the invasion in 2003 that led to the displacement of hundreds of thousands of people. In Libya, over half the population wished to escape the tyranny of Gaddafi. Iranians would give up everything to get out. Syrians, under the oppressor, Al Bashir think along similar lines. I identified sixteen Middle East and African countries whereby an endless stream of people, are constantly, on the march. If you add in the Chinese, Vietnamese, Indians, and Pakistanis that wish to escape to either the USA or Europe then you can arrive at a total of twenty-one million potential migrants every year. The problem is huge, and the money earned from arranged smuggling is mindboggling. In 2007, payments made by those contracting gangs to assist their escape was a staggering $150 billion. More and more gangs are turning away from drugs to get into the more lucrative and less dangerous trade of human smuggling and trafficking.'

'And where are the main consolidation points for the onward transportation of these people?'

'Without doubt, today it is Turkey, Bulgaria, Romania, and Hungary. In each of these countries the organised gangs operate unhindered, as they have the men on the take, at the very top of those Governments firmly in their pockets.'

'Would you be willing to give me three years of your life, and to be stationed in Turkey and Bulgaria?'

'If I thought it would help in bringing to book those bastards that bring so much misery to so many people and their families, then the answer is yes.'

'That is good to hear, Colin. I am going to seek approval from the FCO, either way, I am offering you a position in this department.'

'Well, Mr. Slade. I accept your offer. Something must be done about the continued proliferation of illegals into our country, otherwise our whole way of life, and security will be under threat.'

Slade and Roberts shook hands with Colin Millburn. Roberts escorted him back down to street level and returned to Slade's office.

'What do you think Graham?'

'We must have him on the team Peter. I think he will be an unbelievable asset.'

'I will ask Pritchard to arrange a meeting with both the Home and Foreign Secretaries, after all, if we can get the nod from the bigwigs, then Pritchard will benefit from having Millburn close to his Embassies in Turkey and Bulgaria. Of all no brainers Graham, this is top of the pile.'

On Wednesday at 11.00am the four men from KFC were shown into Slade's office by Jenny, the first of the many receptionists that he would hire during his time at the Border Force.

'Gentlemen, I have your files, photographs and personal details and these have been shared with my deputy, Graham Roberts.'

Roberts shook hands with all four. Jenny placed the coffee cups and the regulation plate of chocolate biscuits upon the boardroom table. Pritchard arrived he had been asked to sit in on the meeting as Slade believed it could be of some use to him.

Slade handed four files to Roberts. Prior to the meeting the two men had agreed that Slade would ask the questions and Roberts would make notes on the appropriate file. Slade, as would be expected, sat in the central position behind his solid oak desk. Roberts sat to his right and Pritchard to the left. The four men from the chicken shop formed a semi-circle around the other side of the desk. Slade invited the man on the far righthand side of the desk to begin.

'I am Fergus Hamilton, my friends, call me Fergie. I am forty-three years old and was born on the rough side of Glasgow. I was married at nineteen and widowed at twenty-four. My wife, a Singaporean, was the subject of a contract killing, although she was not the intended target. As a result of her murder, I joined the Glasgow Police Force and four years after serving as a uniformed bobbie I applied for undercover work. Aged thirty, I was drafted into 'special ops, ' and promoted to the rank of Sergeant. Three years later I became an Inspector and headed the surveillance team that was charged with looking into the people smuggling side of Jamie Law and his gang. Law was one of those arrested in the massive operation to bring down the UK's most prolific drug organisation, however when the head of the undercover operation was abducted the whole investigation began to fall apart. Law was released from custody and immediately resumed his criminal activities. I, myself, shot Law dead in an armed operation that took place at a small airstrip just outside Glasgow. My wife's death had been avenged as it was Law's gang that had mistakenly killed my wife. With nothing left to do in respect of bringing Law to book, I took up the offer from Interpol, to join with my three colleagues here and track down those responsible for the illegal importation and subsequent ill-treatment of those unfortunate enough to have paid large amounts of money to enter the UK. When my wife was knifed to death, in broad daylight, she had been wrongly targeted as a Chinese illegal that had recently escaped the clutches of one of Law's pimps.'

Slade had listened intently to the story offered up by Hamilton, his reply was short,

'I was the undercover officer that was abducted, Fergie. You have my deepest sympathy.'

By way of invitation to speak, Slade nodded to the man sat next to Fergie.

'I am Frederick Forsyth. I do not write books and I am not related to Bruce; therefore, I am unable to get anyone tickets for strictly come dancing. I prefer to be called 'Freddie.' I am forty-one. Unlike my three colleagues here, I have never worked in any section of the police force. After Grammar School and five years at Aston University, where I gained a degree in Politics and International Relationships, I failed to find a job in my chosen field. Desperate to contribute to my parents' household expenses, as it was, they, that had funded my education, I took a job in the civilian section of Interpol, working my way up the ladder to reach grade one level five years ago. For many years I have studied the various organisations that traffic people around the world. I have produced studies and given seminars in countries such as the USA, Canada, Singapore, Germany, and France. Two years ago, I was asked to join the UK team that liaises with similar set-ups, worldwide. Together with my three colleagues here, we have gathered reliable intelligence on both people smuggling and human trafficking. We have collated information from within fifty-seven countries and we can identify the most prolific of the gangs and the individuals that are responsible for the untold misery that is inflicted upon their victims and, in many cases, the victim's family. I am happy to work with you, Mr. Slade as firstly, I am aware of much of your background and secondly, it gets me away from fried chicken.

Picking up his telephone, Slade asked Jenny to arrange more coffee. Looking up at 'Freddie' Slade said,

'Thank you 'Freddie.' To have someone with your undoubted knowledge on the team will be like having Bobby Moore in the back four.'

Before Slade could invite interviewee number three to speak, Jenny arrived with the coffee. There was a brief interlude, which allowed those that needed to, to go to the toilet. Once everyone was settled back into their respective seating, Slade invited the man sat almost dead opposite him, to continue.

'I am Keith Martin, known to everyone as Bob. I am forty years old. I am what you may describe, as being a career policeman. I joined the met as a cadet when I was seventeen and two days after my twentieth birthday, I was assigned to Vine Street nick. Vine street, as you may well be aware, has a specialist vice crime set up, policing Soho and its surrounding area. Not surprisingly, we handed more cases of illegal prostitution, drug crime, living off immoral earnings and the like than most of London put together. In recent years I was working, 'plain clothes,' literally living the part of a pimp, in order that I could identify and take down the scum that derive luxurious livings from the poor souls that are forced to sell their bodies, with little or no financial return for themselves. During my work, I was able to uncover many of the individuals and gangs that run the lucrative business of selling girls, illegally landed in the UK, onto anyone that is willing to pay the price. Like Freddie, I too was asked to join the Interpol network. I never gave a second thought to my answer, which was of course yes. For two years we have unravelled a web that is so intricate, it is almost frightening. To be honest, although we can obtain information, we have no authority to act upon that info, therefore I for one, welcome the opportunity to work with you in the hope that together we can bring down those people at the core of all the suffering that is being caused by their complete contempt for human life.'

Looking at both Roberts and Pritchard before delivering his response, Slade replied,

'To have a man with your vast experience working with us will be a godsend, Bob. I have read your file several times, I am absolutely amazed at what you have uncovered in and around the Soho area. I, myself have worked extensively undercover, however some of your casefiles have left me quite drained. I thank you for attending today.'

'Gentlemen, we are left with just one introduction, that is from the man sat on the left-hand side of those gathered in front of my desk. This man is George Dixson, he needs no introduction to me. George is one of the most modest men ever to have been a Commander at New Scotland Yard. I am proud to offer you all a profile of his career.'

George Dixson shyly acknowledged Slade's brief introduction and inwardly hoped that he would not be too embarrassed by what was to follow.

'Commander George Dixson was my father's best friend. They attended the same school together and passed out from the police college at Hendon at the same time. It was at that point that the similarities between them both started to break apart. My father became a uniformed officer, reaching the rank of Inspector. He ran Plaistow police station for many years and retired with that rank. He never really harboured any aspirations beyond that. Commander Dixson and my father remained friends until my father passed, eight years ago. The Commander retired from the force in the year two thousand, aged sixty. Three years ago, he was asked, personally, by the Home Secretary, to head-up the small team that we all see sat before us today. I will not embarrass George by reading out his long list of achievements during his illustrious career. What I can say is, having George Dixson as part of our team is like having Pele, George Best and Maradona up front. I have held a private meeting with George, and he has accepted, not only his move to these offices but also the acceptance of his three KFC-eating colleagues.'

'Gentlemen, I welcome you all to the team. Graham Roberts is my deputy in all matters. Nick Pritchard runs a separate department here; however, the cross-sharing of information can only be of mutual benefit, I therefore encourage it. We operate a strict 'no rank' situation here, my door is always open to all of you. I hope you will all take advantage of that.'

'Unfortunately, I must now leave, as together with Mr. Pritchard I must attend a meeting with both the Home and Foreign secretaries. Roberts will brief you all from herein. Thank you.'

No sooner had Slade left when ex-Commander George Dixson asked if he may address those that had remained. Roberts was keen to get on with the matters in hand, however he was intrigued by what the more senior of the four new recruits might have to say.

'I imagine that Mr. Roberts here is fully aware of what I am about to say. For the benefit of the colleagues that I have worked with for the past three years, I feel that it might be of great benefit to learn a little about one of the UK's most decorated officers. Peter Slade has gone through hell in recent years. He has suffered the traumas of meeting with the top knobs in the IRA, having no idea if he would return home at the end of the numerous meetings that he attended on behalf of his country. His involvement with those people cost him his wife and two daughters. He was abducted and tortured whilst working undercover in Turkey but was able to recover from his ordeal and take up another dangerous mission. He was again captured by some extremally nasty people and suffered a near-death experience after breaking free from them. He spent months without any memory whatsoever and has only recently returned to anything like normality.

With tears welling up in his eyes, Dixson concluded his resume of Peter Slade.

'Gentlemen, we have an important job to do, not just for our country, but for Peter Slade personally. I know of no other officer that has given as much as he has, to help keep our country safe. We owe it to him to succeed, the problem of illegal immigration and the woe that it brings to those that are being used by the unscrupulous traders, operating in all parts of the globe, needs to be stopped. We should do our utmost to bring an end to this barbaric situation.'

The four men that had sat and listened to the ex-Commander's passionate words, clapped, as one.

Peter Slade and Nick Pritchard sat in the office of the home secretary. The Foreign secretary, together with his aide, was also in attendance. Slade outlined the details of seeking approval for the stationing of Colin Millburn within the British Embassies in both Istanbul and Sofia. Pritchard chipped in with a firm backing for Slade's request, adding that intelligence from these two countries would be a vital necessity if his own department, was going to be successful in reducing the flow of illegals into the UK. Slade was quick to point out that Commander Dixson and his team had agreed to work with him, making Millburn's presence in Turkey and Bulgaria an almost essential part of the operation.

Slade and Pritchard were asked to adjourn for a few minutes. Upon their return the home secretary confirmed that their request had been granted and that the decision would be reviewed every six-months, based on whether the positioning of Millburn was achieving any results. The Home Secretary stressed that this agreement was, at that moment in time, unofficial, and that no documentation would ever be produced. This, he added, was to keep the Governments of Turkey and Bulgaria from ever bleating about the UK's use of undercover agents in their respective countries.

Whilst Slade was over the moon at achieving his aims, he knew full well that it was only because of Pritchard's close affiliation to home secretary that he was able to get such an approval.

For the following three weeks Roberts, with the assistance of Colin Milburn, set about interviewing over fifty ex-border-force employees to fill the remaining twenty-six positions that were still available. By the 15th of June 2008, he had achieved his goal. All the successful applicants would start their new jobs on the first of August. Roger Barrington, a veteran of over thirty years within the immigration department and a man that was largely responsible for the establishment of the Border Force presence in France, Belgium and Holland was installed as the manager that would control and collate the day-to-day workload of the twenty-five newly recruited staff. The twenty-five consisted of seventeen men and eight females.

Colin Millburn arrived at the British Embassy in Sofia on the 15th of July 2008. Officially he was there to take control of the small team that vetted all applications in respect of the ever-growing number of Bulgarians that applied to live and work in the UK. Unofficially he was there to seek out the identities of the gangs and individuals that were trafficking people, of all nationalities to the EU/UK. Millburn's expertise was centred around the Middle East and Northern Africa, he had built up an impressive file of people that moved vast numbers of refugees from this area, the large majority of whom would end up in the hands of gangs that operated inside Bulgaria and Turkey. His network of informants, many of whom were gang members themselves, was spread far and wide. He already held information on the many traders in human misery that operated as far East as Pakistan, India, and Bangladesh. In the coming months he would divide his time between Sofia and Istanbul. At his disposal would be the contacts of the KFC team that now sat in the offices of Peter Slade in London.

On Monday the 4th, August 2008, the newly appointed former employees of the disbanded Border Force, plus the previous members of Graham Roberts private detective agency sat at their desks waiting for a briefing from Roger Barrington, who had occupied his own office, some three weeks earlier, and was now well-versed as far as the aims of this newly established department were concerned. Roberts would join the briefing, but only as an observer, filling in whenever he believed that some enlargement to Barrington's speech was required. Whilst they were to operate entirely outside of Barrington's control, the four members of the KFC team were asked to, sit-in on the briefing and to ask questions or to add detail should they feel it necessary. Peter Slade was initially introduced to everyone, he then sat in the shadows in the far corner of the room, making notes. The office of Colin Millburn, adjacent to that of Roger Barrington's, was of course, empty.

On the Friday of Slade's first fully operational week in charge of the department that had been set up by both the Home and Foreign Office to track down the perpetrators of the ever-increasing crime of people smuggling, he was to receive a surprise call from his former boss, Commander James Reeves.

'Peter, may I offer you my sincere best wishes in your new appointment. I hear that you have put together the best team for the job. I am sure that you will succeed, where others have failed.'

'Thank you, James. News obviously filters down, as it always has done.'

'I have some important information for you.'

'I am intrigued.'

'Yesterday I heard from Borislav Topolov, I presume he is now back in your memory banks?'

'Indeed, he is. I can now recall almost everything of my past. Including my meetings with Topolov and Alkan Asani. How come you are still in touch with Topolov?'

'I still maintain my position as the handler of five of our foreign undercover agents, Topolov and Asani included. We learnt a long time ago that it is much better to have handlers that are outside of departments such as Mi5 or Special Branch. This reduces the chances of there being a mole from within.'

'I understand James. What is the news that you have for me?'

'Topolov has an informant within Boyan Petrov's organisation. He reports that Petrov has set up a meeting with the main men from several countries. Ho does not yet have the actual date of that meeting, other than it will take place, in or near to Varna, later this month.'

'With all due respect James, Petrov is known to be a former arms and drug supplier, having channelled all the ill-gotten gains from his dealings, plus those of his deceased father, into legit business. Is he not Bulgaria's number one property baron?'

'Whilst that is correct Peter, in recent times Petrov has shown a keen interest in the people smuggling business and Topolov's contact seems to think that something big is about to happen. Of course, it may very well turn out to be a red herring, however as you now have your man in, Sofia I thought that it may be something that you wish to monitor?'

'How on earth do you know of my man in Sofia, James?'

'Peter, when one enjoys liquid lunches with the Home Secretary, all kinds of secrets are divulged.'

'Well, thank you for sharing this info with me James, I will of course follow it through.'

'You have a good man in Millburn, Peter. Make sure you protect him.'

'I will James, by the way, do you know what time I took a shit this morning?'

James Reeves laughed out loud before wishing Peter Slade all the best for the future.

Slade picked up his internal phone and asked Roberts and then ex-Commander George Dixson to join him. Having informed his two most senior colleagues of the telephone conversation that he had just had with James Reeves, he asked that neither of the two men should share this intelligence with anyone else, at least for the time being. Dixson now revealed some interesting news to the others.

'For some time, my KFC colleagues and I have been aware of a proposed 'cooperative' between the major criminal factions in and around the Eastern Bloc. We also have a snout within the Petrov set-up; however it has not been made clear as to the subject of this intended cooperation. I shall ask Freddie, as he handles Bulgaria, to get some updates. This way we can cross reference the intel. I shall not inform him of the telephone call that you have received, Peter. I will just ask him to make some enquiries.

'Good work George, let's meet again once we have a clearer picture of who will be attending the meeting and exactly what the agenda is going to be.'

Once his two colleagues had left his office, Slade took one of the secure, unlisted, mobile phones from his locked desk drawer and called Colin Millburn.

'Colin, how is Sofia?'

'It's hot, Mr. Slade, extremely hot.'

'I have some news for you. Mi5's undercover operative in Bulgaria has informed his boss of a pending meeting, to be held, we believe, in Varna, between Boyan Petrov and a whole host of 'dons' from foreign organisations.'

'So, Topolov has been in touch with James Reeves?'

'How, the fuck does everyone know about this?'

'Well, believe it or not, Topolov and I share the same snout within Petrov's inner circle.'

'So, you are aware of Topolov, Colin?'

'Of course, Mr. Slade.'

'Can you dispense with the Mr. Slade, Colin?'

'As you wish, Peter.'

'What is the news in respect of this meeting then?'

'Well, whilst neither I nor Topolov can confirm the actual attendees, we do know that Petrov's flagship hotel, the Viceroy, in Varna, has been subject to the most stringent of security procedures. No guests have checked in for nearly three weeks and over one hundred, armed members of Petrov's gang have closely guarded the complex during that time. Petrov himself has visited on a regular basis, however even our snout does not know when the meeting will take place.'

'Where are you with surveillance, Colin?'

'We have three teams working on this. One is monitoring Petrov's private airstrip another is staked out at Varna International Airport and the third is watching the Viceroy. We have face recognition cameras at all three locations, however not all may arrive by air therefore our main concentration will be at the hotel. We will be heavily reliant upon our mole's feedback.'

'You do realise that Topolov is involved in drugs and arms? He has no remit as far as our interest is concerned.'

'Yes, of course, but we have a good relationship and will share every piece of information that we gather. Topolov is certain that the agenda for the meeting is not purely in respect of drugs and arms. Peter, I think you may need to always keep your phone with you.'

'In fact, Colin, I will text you another number to contact me on. Good luck with what, you are doing, and stay safe.'

After returning the mobile to his drawer, Slade walked into Roberts' office and sat down, facing his lifelong friend.

'Lunch, Mr. Roberts?'

'Are you buying, Mr. Slade?'

'Of course, you know that I always get the bill when we go to the Pizza Hut.'

'At lunch, Slade updated Roberts on the events of the morning.'

'Why are you having this discussion with me in a Pizza Hut, Peter?'

'Because, our job is to watch people, catch people out. Who knows who may be watching us? Can you arrange a complete sweep of the offices, especially yours and mine, at the weekend?'

'Consider it done, Peter.'

'Now that we are potentially onto something big, please only call me on this number.'

Slade handed Roberts a yellow stick-it note.

On Wednesday, the 13th of August 2008, James Reeves received a call from Borislav Topolov. At almost the same time, Peter Slade answered his secure mobile to Colin Millburn. The content of both conversations was almost identical.

25 - THE MEETING

At 8.30am on Monday morning, Roberts and Slade met in Starbucks on the concourse of Liverpool Street Station. Roberts reported that their respective offices had been littered with bugs and listening devices and whilst he had had no time to check, it could be assumed that Millburn's office, currently used by Ringo, along with Barrington's would also be wired. Both men suspected Nick Pritchard as being behind this, what they could not agree on was whether Pritchard was the sole perpetrator of this act or if this had been requested and sanctioned by the Home Office. Roberts handed Slade a diagram that pinpointed exactly where each device could be found in his office, advising him to turn up his TV whenever he might be discussing something sensitive.

'Try not to use your desk telephones for sensitive calls Peter and use text whenever you are able to on your mobile. I will order some speech scramblers from my office, they are brilliant as they can convert whatever you say, into another language. Let us see how Mi5 cope with listening to you in Swahili.'

Slade found it ironic that the department (Mi5) that he had given so much to, was now monitoring his every move.

On the Friday of the same week, several of the main players involved in the deadly world of supplying arms and drugs to most of Europe and parts of the Middle East started to assemble at the Viceroy Hotel in Varna. Peter Slade answered his phone to his man in Bulgaria.

'Peter, I have some interesting news for you.'

'Go ahead Colin.'

'Thus far, the following have arrived at the Viceroy.'

'Monzer Asmar, Tayser Malik, Birusk Gul, Altan Akar, General Kos, Tamara Jamal, Sean Porter and just before I made this call, a man of Asian appearance checked in. This man is not known to us.'

'Thank you, Colin. I am aware of everyone except for Altan Akar, do you have any intel on him?'

'He is now the leader of the Kurdish rebels near to Cizre, he is the cousin of Birusk Gul, he has replaced Ozturk Oszoy, whom you may well remember?'

'OK, thanks. Please let me have some detail of the Asian man as soon as you can.'

'Do you know when the meeting will take place?'

'We think it will happen tomorrow, however the whole lot of them, including Boyan Petrov will be at the Ambassador nightclub tonight and our 'insider' will have a much better idea as to the timing and agenda of the meeting, once a few drinks have been consumed.'

Slade called James Reeves and informed him of the information that he had just received. Reeves confirmed that he had received similar info from Topolov. Both men agreed that something big must be going down as the assembled gathering was akin to being the premier division of the European gangster league. Both were also puzzled by the inclusion of the mystery Asian man.

Slade then asked Roberts to round up George Dixson and Roger 'Ken' Barrington and meet him in the Pizza Hut at 12.30pm.

Over large pepperonis and fries, Slade reconstructed the conversation that he had had with Millburn. He also informed his colleagues of the certainty that their every call from within the office was being listened to but soon they would have a device that would overcome that problem. After careful consideration, all four men agreed that Rory 'Ringo' Starr would need to be 'activated' and sent to Varna. He would liaise with both Millburn and Topolov.

Roberts, Dixson, and Barrington returned to their desks. Barrington wrote a note on a yellow sticker, walked into Ringo's office, and handed it to him. Written upon the sticker was the request from Slade that he should immediately go to the Pizza Hut.

'Ah, Ringo. Thanks for coming so quickly.'

'I would like you to go to Sofia tomorrow, you should book your own flight, at the flight centre, just around the corner, as the office is currently unsafe.'

'You will be met at the airport by someone from the Embassy. You will be given a diplomatic pass, a ticket on a flight to Varna and an unregistered phone. In Varna you will need to find and book yourself into the Promenade Hotel. This is as close to the Viceroy as you can get. You will be on your own. I am sorry but the fewer people that know of your arrival, the safer you will be. Tomorrow evening, at 7.00 you will wait at the bar of the Crazy Elephant, situated on the same Promenade. A man, whose name I do not yet know will identify himself to you as being, Harry Lime. Your response will be to say, 'The Third Man.' He will then talk, you will listen. On Sunday morning you will walk along the Promenade of Varna beach, and you will tell me of everything that was told to you the previous evening.'

'Good luck Ringo.'

Back in his office, Slade wrote a message to Roberts, outlining the instructions that he had given to their old schoolmate and former SAS man. He asked Roberts to call Dixson and Barrington into his office and let them read the message. He should then put the paper in his pocket and dispose of it, outside of the office.

Slade plucked his secure mobile from his drawer and walked slowly down to the main reception. He took a coffee from the machine and walked outside. From there he was safe to call James Reeves.

'Yes, Peter. What can I do for you?'

'I would like you to call Topolov and ask him to arrange for his man to meet with Ringo in the bar of the crazy elephant on Saturday evening at 7 o'clock. He must identify himself by saying the name Harry Lime. Ringo will reply with the words, The Third Man. Only then, should your man brief Ringo on everything that he knows about the meeting that is taking place at the Viceroy.'

'Consider it done, Peter. See you anon.'

Ringo arrived at Sofia Airport at 13.45 the following day. He was met at the 'crew and diplomats' area of Immigration where he was given his diplomatic pass and onward ticket to Varna. His connecting flight arrived in Varna at 16.05. He took a taxi to the Promenade Hotel, situated just two hundred yards from the Viceroy. At the reception he was given a small box, which he opened in the sanctuary of his room, that overlooked the seashore. The box contained a small handgun and a silencer. At 18.50 he walked into the 'crazy elephant' and sat on the middle of the five stalls that lined the front of the tatty-looking bamboo bar. Five minutes later two rough-looking blokes sat either side of him. Twenty yards away, a petite, good-looking blonde woman seemed to mumble each time she lifted her drink to her mouth. Ringo had seen this, many times before. He was certain that the woman was, 'wired.' What he did not know was to whom it was that she was speaking to. He waited, patiently, for some twenty minutes for one of the two men to utter the words Harry Lime after which he would reply, The Third Man. At 19.20, with neither man having mentioned the magic words, he stood, gripping his gun, tucked expertly into his waistband, and hidden from sight by the light-coloured jacket that he was wearing. He left ten Euros on the bar and walked out into the warm air of the evening.

The blonde watched as the other two men left, just seconds after Ringo had. She lifted her glass, and spoke into it, as if it were a microphone. She then followed the men out onto the street. Topolov, sat in his car, on the wrong side of the street, staring intently into his door mirror. Ringo passed by. The two men from the bar were fifty yards behind him. The blonde female was a similar distance away from them. As the two men reached the rear of his car the undercover Bulgarian stepped out and fired two, silenced shots, into the hearts of the pursuers of Rory Starr. The blonde female reached the car at the same time as Topolov fired it up. She got into the front passenger seat, and they drove slowly away. Ringo acknowledged the actions of his two saviours by touching his temple as they drove past him. He carried on walking. He passed the Viceroy and made his way to his hotel. In his room he lifted the phone and ordered some food from the menu that he had found inside the hotel directory. Fifteen minutes later there was a knock at his door. Holding his gun behind his back he slowly opened the door, keeping his foot close to the bottom, just in case there was any attempt by the visitor to storm into the room. When he was happy that no one was hiding under the trolley, he pulled back the door and allowed the waiter to push it into his room. Once inside, the waiter closed the door and removed the white towel that was dangling over his lower arm and hand, revealing the gun that he was holding.

'That was a close shave, was it not, Harry Lime.

'Why did you not show up in the bar?'

'I am Borislav Topolov. It was my informant that failed to show. Unfortunately, he did not make it. He was found with his throat cut earlier today. It is almost certain that one of Petrov's men did the deed. He must have revealed your meeting place, however he never told of the greeting that he would have said to you. That is the only reason you are still alive as had those men in the bar been able to identify you then you would have been killed there and then.'

'By the way, the two men that I killed were not Petrov's men. They had been brought in from Romania by Gregor Levski. Had they been local men they may well have recognised the girl that was looking out for you and the outcome may have been completely different.'

'Well, I owe you my life Borislav. And the girl too'

'Yes, she is Maria. Without her, you would be dead.'

'So, what do we do now? We no longer have ears and eyes on Petrov and what he is up to, do we?'

'But we do. You see, Maria is shooting for both sides. She is the girlfriend of Gregor Levski, Petrov's righthand man. She works undercover for Europol and deliberately met with Levski in the nightclub that Petrov gave to him. She is twenty-six years his junior. It was she that passed on information to Mikhail, my informant. We did it that way in order that Maria was not seen with me in public. Tonight, she is with Levski, Petrov and most of the arrivals. Tomorrow morning, she will update me about what went on at the meeting.

'My god, she is brave. Does she know what will happen to her, if caught?'

'Yes, she knows. Her parents were executed by the Petrov's ten years ago because they would not sell their land, along the seafront in Sunny Beach. When she was eighteen, she got herself to Paris and begged Europol to take her on as an agent. Four years ago, she returned to Varna and hung out in most of the gang's haunts, until she was noticed by Levski. She really wanted to hook

Petrov himself, however he is far too smart, he never has local girlfriends. Maria speaks French, English, and Italian as well as her local tongue. She is quite talented.'

'Please thank her for what she did for me.'

'I will, don't worry.'

'And you, Mr. Starr. You were once of the SAS, were you not?'

'Who has told you that Borislav?'

'Mr. Millburn has briefed me. You are a good friend of Mr. Slade, no less.'

'You know of Peter Slade?'

'Yes, we met a couple of times, in London. He is the bravest of the brave but is no longer required to be in the danger zone, I hear.'

'Correct, he has had more scrapes than a fifty-year-old woman.'

'Please be sure to give him my best when you return home, if of course, you do return home.'

'I certainly will Borislav.'

'Now I must go. Please leave the trolley outside when you have finished and do not worry about anything whilst you are in this hotel. It is very much a safe house, and almost everyone here is working for the same cause. Most of everything to the right of the Viceroy is owned, or controlled by Petrov, however this side is never touched by them. It is known as their 'Robin Hood' area as they first took it away from other, rival gangs and then gave it back to the people. Sleep tight, my friend. If you go for a walk in the morning, make sure you turn left, you will be safe. I will return as soon as I have news from Maria.'

The following morning, a Sunday, and after having breakfast, Ringo did indeed leave the hotel. He walked for nearly two hours, taking in the warmth of the late August sunshine, along the promenade, much of which was newly constructed. When he arrived back at the aptly named, 'Promenade Boutique Hotel' he was given an envelope by the pretty receptionist. Returning to his room, on the fifth floor, he opened the envelope and read the handwritten message that was inside. It read,

'There is a problem, you should wait until you see me before you call Peter Slade, The Third Man.'

With nothing much to do, other than to wait around for Topolov to return, Ringo undertook two more walks. He changed into tourist gear, shorts, t-shirt, and flip-flops. He did not take his gun. On the second of his strolls, he walked past the Viceroy Hotel. His years of training and operations had taught him to see things that less qualified people would not see. He clocked at least half a dozen, heavily armed men that were trying to hide behind the palm trees that lined the beach just across the road from the steps of the hotel. He saw three vans, each with blacked-out windows, parked in the road. Two were on the same side as the hotel, the other was on the beach side. They were at least eighty yards apart. Ringo was as certain as he could be that each van would contain armed men. As he passed the canopy that served as a shelter for guests to take cover from the hot sun or rain, whilst waiting for a taxi, bus, or private vehicle, he bent down and fiddled with his flip-flop, giving the impression to anyone that might be watching, that he was taking a stone from under his bare foot. He glanced to his left, he saw two men, armed with sub-machine guns, that were partially hidden by the bamboo plants that had been planted into large Cretan urns. Just inside the huge plate glass doors of the hotel, stood two men, each wearing camouflaged uniforms that were bedecked with almost every type of armoury that it was possible to carry on one's body. He recognised the style of the uniform as being that of the Kosovan army. Within a matter of a few seconds, he was on his way. No one had challenged him. Turning right at the next junction and then right again, put him at the rear of all the buildings that he had just passed, the Viceroy included. In the service yard of the hotel, he noticed five armour-plated army jeeps and a black Rolls Royce Corniche. He did not pass the Viceroy on his way back to his less salubrious residence.

Upon his return to his hotel, he had expected to see Topolov, or at least be given a note by the receptionist. Neither of these things happened. Ringo went upstairs, showered, and changed. On his way out he left a note with the young lady, asking that she hand it to Topolov, when he arrives. At 7.00pm he was sat, alone, in the bar of the crazy elephant. Three drinks and a burger later, in walked Borislav Topolov, it was 8.25pm. The Bulgarian sat at the small table. Ringo had chosen this area of the bar as it was away from everyone else, however the bar was not at all busy. The barman came over with two beers and placed them on the table.

'Are you OK, Borislav?' the barman asked.

'Sit down Dimitri, I have some bad news.'

Ringo gave Borislav a disapproving look.

'It's OK my friend; Dimitri is part of the team.'

'Maria failed to show up at our pre-arranged meeting place. I waited for over two hours.'

'Do you know where she is,' asked the barman.

'I do now Dimitri, she is in the morgue.'

'Do you know what happened,' enquired Ringo.

'Yes, she was dropped off a motorway bridge and hit by a juggernaut. Both Maria and the truck driver were killed'.

'How did you find this out?'

'Our police informant told me. I am unable to see her body as the morgue is being monitored by Levski's men.

'First, we lose Igor, our man on the inside, and now Maria. Levski must have made a connection between the two. Maria was supposed to meet me last night however she was asked to stay at the Viceroy and help with the entertaining of Petrov's guests. If they knew that Igor and Maria were passing out information their deaths were inevitable.'

Clutching Topolov's arm, as if to reassure him, Ringo asked,

'So now we have no one on the inside, where do we go from here?'

'We do have someone Ringo, we have Petrov's chauffeur. He is an Albanian, he was put in place by the General, to keep an eye on Boyan. We turned him when we let him know that General Kos had sold his two sisters to a pimp in Milan. They both died from heroin addiction. The Albanian, whose name I can never reveal, gives us some information, but not as much as we would like.'

Dimitri excused himself as his bar girl was outside smoking and two policemen were stood at the bar, waiting to be served.

'Does Boyan Petrov have a black Rolls Corniche, by any chance?'

'Yes, how do you know that?'

'Just a hunch, Borislav.'

'The problem we have with the chauffeur is that he is not allowed to go anywhere, other than the car. Petrov closes the dividing window between himself and the driver whenever he has a phone call or another passenger in the car. What the chauffer hears is quite limited.'

'Then we have to get the car wired.'

'How are we to do that? The car is left either at Petrov's home, at the back of the Viceroy or outside of anywhere that Petrov chooses to visit. He will be collected by a trusted colleague whenever the chauffeur is off duty or away for some reason.'

'Then you must arrange for something to be wrong with the car. Maybe the aircon breaks down. The chauffeur can take it to the dealer for it to be fixed and he could then get it to wherever you are able to arrange for it to be wired up. It takes only ten minutes to bug, a car these days.'

'OK. But I can only contact him by post. We write to each other, there is no safer way to communicate.'

'I will ask Millburn to sort out the bug and the receiver.'

'So Borislav, what can we do about the meeting? We now have no one on the inside. We know of all the people involved, except for the Asian guy, can we tail him, to see where he goes once the meeting has finished?'

'Yes, of course. We do know that he arrived in Varna from Sofia, but he could have begun his journey from almost anywhere.'

'Well, let's follow him all the way home and then take it from there, agreed?'

'Agreed, Ringo. I will put the wheels in motion.'

Ringo returned to the Promenade Hotel and reported to Peter Slade that he had nothing to report in respect of the meeting.

The next day, Boyan Petrov's invited guests began to leave the splendour of the Viceroy Hotel. Neither Ringo nor Topolov was any the wiser as to the agenda of the all-day meeting on Saturday. The Asian man was taken to Varna Airport in a taxi that belonged to one of Petrov's many companies. He was photographed checking in at the first-class desk of Bulgarian Airlines, his destination was Sofia. Upon arrival in the capital, he was tailed and was seen to enter an apartment situated on the edge of Kokolandia Park in the central district of Sofia, close to most of the Foreign Embassies.

On Monday morning he was seen walking, suited, and booted and carrying a briefcase. At precisely 8.30am he held a credit card-sized entry pass against the Perspex glass on the exterior wall of the Embassy of the Socialist Republic of Vietnam and entered the compound. Topolov's team had amassed over forty photographs of him. The photos had been run through Interpol's systems, but the man was not known to them. Topolov called into the Promenade and informed Ringo that the surveillance on the man that they now knew worked for the Vietnamese had drawn a blank.

Ringo was due to leave Varna that evening. In the presence of Topolov he called Slade and updated him. Slade asked Ringo to email a couple of the photos to him and then to take the flight to Sofia and to call him before he took the connection back to Heathrow. Slade called Millburn.

'Colin. Yes, Peter.'

'Do you hold records on the diplomats of our adversaries?'

'Of course, we do.'

'I am sending you some mug shots of someone we believe works for the Vietnamese. See if he can be identified.'

'No problem, Peter, give me a few minutes and I will get back to you.'

'Less than ten minutes after receiving the pictures, Millburn made the call.

'Peter, he has been identified as Vo Van Hiep. He is the first secretary at the Vietnamese Embassy. Our intel shows him as being as clean as a whistle. What is he up to?'

'That we do not yet know Colin. We do know however, that he has just attended a meeting at Petrov's hotel in Varna, along with some of the world's most notorious nasties. Do you have a file on Mr. Hiep and if so, can you get it to me?'

'It is going through to you as we speak. Do you want him monitored?'

'Topolov is on the case Colin, however it might be a good idea if the two of you can work together on this. Thanks for the help.'

'You are welcome, Peter. I will touch base with Topolov, usual channels for contact, Peter?'

'Yes, please Colin.'

Just over an hour later, Ringo called Slade from Sofia Airport.

'Any news, Peter?'

'Yes, indeed there is. Can you abort your connection and check in at one of the airport hotels and once I have digested the contents of a file that Millburn has sent to me, I will get back to you.'

'No problem Peter. I will await your call.'

As he sat nursing a beer in the lobby of the Hilton Airport Hotel, Ringo received the call from Slade, who himself was seated in the KFC just a few blocks from his office. With him were George Dixson, Ken Barrington, and Graham Roberts. Slade, since finding out that his office was 'bugged' had decided to include his three main men whenever he was to receive or make a call that would prove to be of importance to them all. He figured this would save him time in having to explain everything again to his most trusted colleagues.

'Hello Peter, do you have news?'

'Yes, I do, however it does not help us very much. I have read the file that we have on Vo Van Hiep. The Yanks have also chipped in with some Intel. Mr. Hiep arrived in Sofia on the 1st of April 1999, aged just thirty-one. He was very much a junior member of the Vietnamese Embassy staff. He has held posts in their Embassies in Bucharest, Moscow, Warsaw, and East Berlin. The bulk of his time has been spent in Bulgaria. The Americans monitored him for a while as they believed his constant moving around to be somewhat suspicious.'

'Just a moment Peter, the waiter is stood over me. It's OK now, he has gone.'

Slade continued.

'Now here is the interesting part. On New Year's Eve 2006, Hiep attended a party in the Grand Palace Hotel in Sofia. The Grand Palace is owned by Boyan Petrov. Our friends from across the pond video recorded the whole event and this video was part of the file that Millburn sent to me. Hiep is clearly seen being introduced to Petrov by the Bulgarian Ambassador, which is not exactly earth-shattering news by itself, however he has subsequently visited the Viceroy in Varna on four separate occasions. As we now know, he was present at the meeting that has just taken place.'

'That could just be a coincidence, Peter. Maybe his visit was planned a while ago and it simply clashed with the gathering. Petrov obviously trusts him, he would not know any of the other visitors, would he?'

'I would agree with you Ringo, except for one important revelation. He has met twice with none other than Sean Porter. We have the Yanks to thank for this info. Porter has twice visited the Vietnamese Embassy in Sofia. Vo Van

Hiep does not appear to be as squeaky clean as we might otherwise have thought.'

'What do you suggest then?'

'I would like you to stay in Sofia and shadow our Asian friend. Millburn will make sure that you receive whatever you need in the way of surveillance equipment and cash. We cannot, of course, give you any extra men on the ground as it would be dangerous to share what we are up to with anyone else.'

'I understand, Peter. I prefer to work alone anyway.'

Half an hour after Slade had returned to his desk, there was a knock on his door and in walked Bob Martin and George Dixson. Dixson started the conversation.

'Bob has dug up some interesting facts Peter, can we grab a coffee downstairs and discuss?'

The three men walked out into Marsham Street, turned left, and sat down at a table outside a coffee house in Great Peter Street.

'Must have been named after you Peter,' commented George Dixson.

'Most likely,' replied a smiling Peter Slade.

'I really must push Roberts in respect of the anti-listening devices. There is only so much coffee that one can consume in any given day. Over to you Bob.'

'With the help of our analyst, Freddie Forsyth, I have recently been working on the nationalities of the illegals that are most prevalent in and around the Soho area. It would appear, that since I left the job, there has been a sharp increase in the employment of Asian ladies, not just in London, but in other cities as well. Our colleagues, one floor down, have been busy conducting ad hoc raids on known, whore houses and sweatshops. This has revealed a large volume of Chinese, Philippine and Vietnamese women being trafficked into the UK. In addition, a good number of Vietnamese men have arrived here, illegally, with the sole purpose of the growing and supervision of weed. Only a few of those that have been arrested have been cooperative. However, all say that their journey from their respective homelands to the UK has involved transiting through Bulgaria.'

'With all due respect Bob, did we not already know most of this?'

'Yes and no, Mr. Slade.'

'Yes', to the fact that we were aware of the increase in trafficking, as opposed to that of smuggling. But 'no' to the routes that these people are now taking. There appears to be an ever-growing organisation behind what we are now seeing. Previously, many illegals simply set out and took their chances that they would arrive in Europe or the USA under their own steam. Now, it seems, those people with enough money, looking to better themselves in another country, seek out members of gangs that, for the right amount of dollars, can arrange their, 'door to door' delivery. The vast amount of these poor sods already had friends or relatives in the country of their chosen destination. They are given a guarantee by the gangs that they will be delivered to those friends or relatives, only to be put into forced slavery upon arrival. Of the illegals that have been detained and agreed to talk, all say that their escape from their respective countries was swift and very well organised.'

'So, there is very much a connection between the rise in illegals entering our shores and Bulgaria?'

'It appears to be so, Mr. Slade. There has also been a dramatic increase in the number of car-wash businesses that operate, both legally and outside of the law, here in the UK. Border Force raids on these businesses have shown a massive rise in the use of illegal workers from all parts of the globe. Border Force does submit figures to the National Statistics Office (NSO) but they never get published.'

'Good work, Bob, I would throw you a chocolate button if I had one.'

On Wednesday morning in Varna, at 7.00am, an envelope was slid under the front door of the flat provided to his chauffeur by Boyan Petrov. The note inside, read:

'Can you stop the aircon from working. Take the car to the dealer from where it was purchased and afterwards drive to, no 87, Atanas Hristov Street, off Vasil Levski Highway. They will be expecting you.'

Fifteen minutes later, the chauffeur left his flat on the old Honda motorcycle, provided to him as part of his job. Ten minutes later he arrived at the home of his boss. He punched in the code and the front gates slid apart. As he usually did, every morning, he parked the motorcycle under the bike shed at the side of the house, took a bunch of keys from his jacket, opened the oversized garage, and started the Roller. Before he drove from the garage, he reached down into the glove compartment and took out the leather-bound, Rolls Royce Handbook. He quickly found the page, headed, fuses, and located the 'fuse box' in the boot of the half, a million-dollar vehicle. He undid the protective cover of the fuse box and loosened the fuse that he had identified as being the one for the aircon. He then drove the car out of the garage and waited, engine running, for his employer to come out of his front door. At precisely 8.00am, Boyan exited his house. The chauffeur jumped from the driver's seat, hurried to the back door, and opened it for the man that he wished he could kill one day. When Petrov settled himself into the rear of his car, he drew back the dividing window and asked his driver to turn on the aircon.

'It seems to be broken, Sir. I have checked but cannot find the reason for it.'

'OK, after you drop me at the office you should go to the dealer and get them to fix it.'

'But you have a busy day today, with several appointments, how will you get to them?'

'No need to worry, Levski will take me. He was going with me anyway.'

'Shall I come back to the office when it is fixed?'

'You can call me I will then tell you where to go.'

'OK, boss.'

Thirty-five minutes after dropping Petrov off, the chauffeur drove onto the forecourt of the dealer that had sold his most expensive car to Bulgaria's most notorious of men.

The chauffeur explained the problem to the guys in the service bay. They immediately stopped what they were doing and all five of them peered into the boot of a car that collectively would have taken them an entire lifetimes salary to have bought.

'There is your problem. Just a loose fuse. Turn it on".

The chauffeur hit the aircon button on the dash and the motor sprang into life.

'Thanks, guys. I wished I had looked, would have saved me from coming here.'

Ten minutes later, the roller pulled up outside no 87, Atanas Hristov Street. The signage indicated that it was a computer repair shop. Two men, having seen the car arrive, came out. One of them opened the rear passenger door and in less than one minute, closed it again. The other man asked the driver for his mobile phone. The driver passed it to him and then followed the man into the shop. The phone was connected to a computer and three minutes later was given back to the driver.

'Whenever you want to record, just tap once on the app that I have just installed (poker-plus) and enter the code 0101. When you wish to playback the recording, enter the code, and follow the instructions. Should someone pick-up your phone and tap the app, all they will see is the ace of spades. Only by entering the code can they go any further. You can share conversations with other phones, but they will need to be 'synched.'

'And where is the receiver?'

'You, or anyone else will never find it. It is smaller than a pin head and it will not show up on any anti-bugging devices. Good luck, we hope your mission is successful.'

On Thursday morning, ten minutes after Vo Van Hiep had left for work, two men entered the rear of his luxury apartment block. They quickly gained access to the building, walked down to the basement, and shut down everything electrical, with the exception, of the service lift. In the plush reception area, the duty manager walked outside and called the maintenance company. Two men entered Hiep's apartment, on the fifth floor and within fifteen minutes had installed bugs into light fittings in the lounge, the bedroom, and the bathroom. As they exited the service lift, they reactivated the electrical boxes and left, quietly.

The following day, Friday 29th, August 2008, at precisely 8.00am, Boyan Petrov stepped into the back seat of his Rolls Corniche. One minute after setting off towards his office, he took a call. Before he closed the smoke glass window that would prevent his chauffeur from hearing the conversation, he was heard to say good morning to Mr. Hiep. As he stopped at the tail end of the queue that formed every morning before they could enter the underpass that took them under the motorway and towards the city, the chauffeur was able to activate the recently downloaded app. Petrov was oblivious to his drivers' actions.

Whilst Petrov was to stay in his office for the whole of the day, the chauffeur simply had to wait around as he could be summoned by his boss at any given time. At 4.30 in the afternoon, Petrov exited the eight-story office building, which was just one of the many buildings that he owned in the City of Varna. When they arrived home, Petrov informed his trusted driver that he was now finished for the day, adding that he would not require his services over the weekend as he had some business in Golden Sands. The chauffeur knew, from experience, that his boss would drive his expensive Porsche. Gregor Levski would accompany him and together they would spend the weekend partying with the several Russian beauties that have been installed into the seven million Euro apartment that overlooked the Back Sea.

The chauffeur, still not really understanding how the fuck he could listen to the conversation between Petrov and Mr. Hiep, decided to drive his fifty-cc motorcycle back to the computer repair shop that had both planted the bug in the Roller and installed the app onto his phone.

In the computer shop, the phone was connected to a laptop and in less than two minutes it was handed back to its owner.

'All done.' Said one of the two men in the shop.

'The puzzled driver asked, 'what now, do I take this somewhere else?'

'No need, we have downloaded whatever you have recorded and sent it over to the interested party.'

The driver did not know and did not want to know as to whom the recording had been sent to. He thanked the men in the shop and made his way to his small flat. Ten minutes after arriving home, the driver called General Kos, using the phone that was concealed behind the bath panel in his tiny washroom. He spent fifteen minutes updating the General on the events of the last five days.

In the British Embassy in Sofia, Millburn had listened intently to the conversation between Boyan Petrov and Vo Van Hiep. He immediately called

Ringo and informed him that the meeting that had taken place last weekend, was almost certainly in respect of the building of what could become the world's largest organised people trafficking operation. It appeared from the conversation that he had just listened to, that everyone that had attended the meeting would play an important role. At Petrov's suggestion, Hiep would be returning to Hanoi, Vietnam on Friday 5th, September. Millburn ended by saying that he would talk to Slade in respect of what action should be taken.

Slade and Millburn later agreed that Ringo should follow Hiep to Hanoi. Millburn had a contact in the consular section of the Vietnamese Embassy in Sofia, and he would ask him to sort out a thirty-day tourist visa, explaining that Rory Starr did not wish to travel on his diplomatic passport, as he simply wished to take a holiday. Had he used his diplomatic papers he would be monitored whilst in Vietnam. On Monday morning, Millburn would find out the routing that Hiep would take. He booked Ringo on the same flight(s). Ringo would travel economy, Hiep would be in business, however Millburn would ensure that both men's baggage would enter the carousel in Hanoi at the same time. This way Hiep would not disappear via the express channels that business class often afforded to its customers.

26 - THE INTEL

On the morning of Friday, the 29th of August 2008, Peter Slade, Graham Roberts, Fergie Hamilton, Freddie Forsyth, Bob Martin, George Dixson, and Ken Barrington sat around a large boardroom table in the conference room of a well-known hotel, just outside Harlow in Essex. James Reeves was present via a Skype connection and his face was clearly visible on the fifty-inch screen that was secured to a wall at the far end of the room. Reeves had asked Slade to include the soon to retire, head of Mi5, Julian Pritchard. Slade had resisted this request, from his former boss as he was almost certain that Nick Pritchard was batting for both sides and did not wish to run the risk that the contents of the meeting would soon be common knowledge around Whitehall. Reeves did not question his protégé as to the reasons for excluding Pritchard Snr.

At 8.50am, with the last of the coffee cups and empty biscuit plates having been cleared from the table, Slade gestured to the plain-clothed officer, stood next to the heavy wooden door. The officer left the room and stood, as a guard, on the outside. His remit was not to allow anyone to enter.

Slade spoke just one word, 'gentlemen' and the room became silent.

'Please turn off all mobile phones. You each have several files in front of you. Commander Reeves has the same at his disposal. Unfortunately, Colin Millburn is unable to join us, electronically. You will notice the recorder on the wall. This is being operated remotely by one of Roberts' many friends and it will be relayed to Millburn later. Millburn, in turn, will share whatever is necessary, with Ringo, Topolov and Asani. It is going to be a long day. We break for coffee at eleven and lunch at one. We have self-contained toilet facilities via the door behind me.'

'Most of what I am going to say, you will already be aware of. However, we are here to discuss and agree upon a way forward. Your input is welcome, without invitation, at any time.'

'Roberts will now update you with what we know of the events that took place in Varna, last weekend.'

There was a certain nervousness in Graham Roberts' voice when he began. He was used to being in meetings, but these were normally attended by the lower end of society, clients and their solicitors that had sought his services as a private investigator. He was now addressing some of the country's most prominent police and secret service personnel, this made him slightly uneasy, however he was amongst people that were now his friends and colleagues, he would soon shake off his nerves.

'In Varna, there was a meeting, hosted by Bulgaria's richest man, Boyan Petrov. In attendance were,

Monzer Asmar, a Syrian national, known arms, tobacco, and drug runner. Asmar owns, Trust Shipping and Forwarding, Syria's largest such company. They operate trucks, ships and planes throughout Europe and the Middle East.'

Tayser Malik, another Syrian who set-up a drug business in Jordan and subsequently branched out into the other lucrative, but illegal trade of tobacco and arms smuggling. Malik works hand in hand with Asmar, using his transportation to distribute his wares.

Tamara Jamal, the sister of Jordan's once most prolific arms dealer. She took over the reins after her brother's demise. She was the former lover of Malik and has good connections in Pakistan, Afghanistan, Iraq and beyond.

Birusk Gul, once Europe's most wanted drug baron and head of the Gul clan that originates from the dark crevices that exist within the mountains of Kurdistan. Gul was recently released after a seven-year stretch and has resumed his role as the head of the family. Since his release, several of his competitors have either met with violent deaths or simply disappeared. He works 'hand in hand' with Petrov.

Altan Akar has become the main man along the mountain tops that serve as a border between Turkey, Syria, and Afghanistan. Nothing moves in or out of Kurdistan without his approval. He has dealings with almost all the people that we are following.

General Kos, probably the most famous of all of those that we have profiled. We understand that it was the General that asked Petrov to set up the meeting in Varna. Kos has an entire army at his disposal. There are no boundaries to his empire, he has infiltrated every European country. He employs soldiers that fought with him during the Kosovan uprising and uses mercenaries from around the world. It is said that he could defeat the military might of several countries. Our intel suggests that he has grown tired of the arms and drugs business and has recently turned his attention to the safer trade of human trafficking.

Sean Porter, only a very few people know of him and today I share with you, what knowledge we have. Once known as Michael O'Leary, he was duped into helping the IRA and was captured by special forces. In return for information, he was given a new identity and moved to Spain. From there he found his way into Bulgaria and became friends with Petrov. He rediscovered his twin sons, who also run a European trucking business and has picked up from where he left off, prior to his capture. As far as the UK authorities are concerned, Porter, if recaptured, would be the icing on the cake.

Vo Van Hiep, we have only learnt of his existence and involvement within the last few days. We know that he is a Vietnamese national. He is a diplomat, based in Sofia, however he has been befriended by Boyan Petrov and there must be a good reason for this. Shortly after attending the meeting in Varna, Hiep was on the move and at this moment in time, he is in Hanoi. Ringo is tracking him.

As you all know, our colleague, Colin Millburn is now alternating between Sofia and Istanbul. He has extensive knowledge of the Balkans and is there to assist Ringo and the two undercover operatives that were put in place by Mi5 some time ago. We have a small network of anti-Petrov people in Varna, however two of them have met with their deaths in recent times. We also have someone that, from time to time, gets to know of the plans of General Kos, however the information out of the General's camp is sporadic and sometimes misleading.

Of course, there are hundreds, if not thousands of fringe players, but our interest will be concentrated on the people that I have highlighted here. We all know that the men at the top, invariably escape capture and subsequent punishment as nobody is ever willing to stand up in court and testify against them. We have the agreement from almost every country involved, that these people should be taken down. There is not much interest from anyone as far as holding fair and impartial trials are concerned.

You each have a comprehensive file on those that I have mentioned. We will now break for coffee, after which I will hand you over to Mr. Slade. Twenty minutes later, Slade rose from his chair.

'Thank you, Graham, for a well-informed resume of those that are of interest to us.'

'I believe that we should move forward by assigning each of you one or more particular people to monitor. I have drawn up the following –'

'George, would you take Asmar, Malik and Jamal. They operate in unison and are often seen together.'

'Fergie, can you track Gul. He spends most of his time in the UK, Germany, and the Netherlands.'

'Ken, it's the General for you. He hardly ever leaves his compound, he will be difficult, but I am sure you will find a way.'

'Bob, Porter will be right up your street. We know that he still likes the girls and is known to visit some of Petrov's red-light joints in Varna. With your experience in vice, you should be able to find him and see where he leads you.

'Asani is already keeping tabs on Alkar in the mountains.'

'Topolov is now very, close to some of Petrov's inner circle. Both men now report directly to me, and I shall share anything that I think may be relevant to your individual investigations. Millburn is assisting our two brave colleagues in Turkey and Bulgaria. In the files you will find his contact details. If you require his help, please use him.

'Freddie, no, I have not forgotten you. I would like you to go undercover in Germany. With your many friends within Interpol you should be able to find out who is responsible for the trafficking of people from there and into France, Belgium, and Holland. These poor souls succumb to the promise of a new life, only to find themselves as modern-day slaves. If we start at that part of the chain, we can then work backwards, hopefully finding the kingpins along the way.

'Ringo is now in Vietnam. A certain Vo Van Hiep is on his radar. We know little or nothing as to the involvement of the Asian gentleman, but knowing Ringo, as I do, it will not be long before we are informed of his every move.'

'Graham here will be collating everything at weekends. Not from his office though. He has his own little hideaway in the East End of London. Should you need help outside of our shores then Graham will point you in the right direction. He has a list of people that we can trust in almost every country that is involved in this operation.'

'We will now break for lunch. This is provided by the hotel, and we shall be in the company of others, so please, no reference to anything that we have discussed. Enjoy your lunch.'

After lunch there was a general discussion and mobiles with pre-plumbed numbers were distributed. Roberts had the final word, informing everyone that they should take their files home and not bring them to the office the following day. All questions appertaining to today's meeting should only be in writing and handed to me in my, office. There should be no verbal references, within the office, to any part of this operation. Slade's number two ended by saying that the next formal meeting would be at the end of November and that they would all be informed of the exact date and venue by text message.

On Monday, the 1st of September 2008, all seven men returned to their desks on the second floor of the Home Office in Marsham Street. There was an eerie silence amongst them. All communications were undertaken via various coloured stick-it notes. It did not take long for the other members of staff to pick up on this. By lunchtime everyone in the office was passing comments in this way. The silence was only broken when someone answered the telephone.

Roberts invited Freddie, Ken, Fergie, Bob, and George into his office at lunchtime and gave each of them a list of five local cafes and eateries. He explained that for this week they would meet at 1.00pm each day at one of the cafes. On Friday he would give them another five places in which to meet during the following week. They would update any intel they had gathered on their respective clients, and he would start to compile files that he would share with Slade at the end of each week. As the five men prepared to leave Roberts' office, he reminded them that they were not to share any information with Nick Pritchard or any of his staff.

The following morning Freddie handed Roberts a note informing him that he would be leaving for Frankfurt the very next day. At their lunchtime rendezvous, Roberts let everyone else know of Freddie's imminent departure. They all wished him well during the lunchtime briefing, which was held in a branch of Pret-a-Manger. Peter Slade then updated his team on Ringo's progress in Vietnam.

'Gentlemen, just over a week ago I received some intel from Millburn in respect of the mysterious Asian man. A short time ago our undercover operatives in Sofia managed to install listening devices into his apartment and he has been monitored ever since. He was visited by Gregor Levski, who as you know, is Petrov's righthand man. The two men flitted in and out of the apartment and most of their conversation took place on the balcony, however Milburn was able to glean the fact that Hiep was asked by Levski to return to Vietnam. Unfortunately, we do not know the reason for this. Millburn, via his network of informants, was able to get Hiep's flight details. Ringo has trailed Vo Van Hiep to Hanoi. The day after his arrival Hiep attended the Ministry of Foreign Affairs, which, for many years has been his employer. With the help of the British Business Group (BBG) which as you may know is affiliated to most of our Embassies around the globe, Ringo has secured the assistance of two Vietnamese nationals that very much have the UK's interest at heart. Ringo, or any of us for that matter, would stick out like a sore thumb if we were to follow Hiep around. Our Foreign Office has arranged for Ringo to occupy a desk at the BBG. He will, of course, be observed by the Vietnamese, therefore his movements will be limited, however he will be able to utilise the intel that the BBG have gathered on people of interest to us. What we have learnt thus far, is not earth-shattering, it is however interesting. Three days ago, Hiep was driven to the border town of Lao Cai and was seen crossing into the Chinese district of Hekou. He emerged two days later, accompanied by seven Chinese nationals. The Chinese were handed over to two men. Ringo's helpers decided to follow the group and let Hiep go his own way. They tracked the group until they arrived at the gates to the Port of Haiphong. The seven were handed over at the gates and escorted to a cargo ship, fortunately the ship was within sight of the gates, and they were able to get its name. We also have several photos of the men that boarded the vessel. Subsequent investigation has revealed the ship's itinerary, it will call at Saigon, Laem Chabang, Thailand, and Yangon in

Myanmar. There could be a perfectly reasonable explanation for Hiep's behaviour, however we feel that given his affiliation to Boyan Petrov in Bulgaria he could well be involved in people smuggling. I have held a meeting with the Foreign Secretary, and he has sanctioned the use of our people in both Thailand and Myanmar in order that we can monitor the group should they disembark in either of those countries. Hiep will be back on our radar once he returns to his job in Hanoi. Unfortunately, the Chinese authorities will not cooperate with us, we therefore have little chance of finding out the identities of the seven people that Hiep has helped to escape. Ringo will leave Vietnam when Hiep does.'

'Unless any of you have something to report, I will bid you goodbye until next week. Freddie, I wish you every success in Germany and please take good care of yourself.'

On Saturday, 6th, September 2008, Ringo informed Millburn that he was now back in Sofia, as was Vo Van Hiep. Millburn relayed this information to Peter Slade, who at that time was enjoying a long weekend, with his beloved Cheryl, at their hideaway home in Polperro.

On Monday, Sookchai Sirikul, a former Captain in the Thai Military but now very much working for British intelligence had reported to his handler at the BBG in Bangkok that the seven Chinese men that had boarded the ship in Haiphong had disembarked at the Port of Laem Chabang. They were then escorted to a large container ship, which will call at each of the major Northern European Ports. The handler confirmed to Graham Roberts, that photos, taken of the men as they crossed the Port, would be downloaded, and sent to him. When the call was over Roberts wrote down the following, Café Nero at 1.00pm, he then popped into the office of Ken Barrington and placed the note in front of him. Roberts then returned to his own room. Ken then called the others into his office and showed them the note.

At 1.00pm, Roberts, Barrington, Fergie, Bob Martin, and George Dixson sat at a corner table in Café Nero. Roberts connected Slade to the meeting electronically and relayed the contents of his earlier conversation with their colleague in Bangkok. Roberts added that he had obtained the sailing schedule of the ship in question and that it would call at Hamburg, Rotterdam, Antwerp, Le Havre, and Felixstowe. Arriving at Hamburg in twelve days' time and Felixstowe five days later. Slade then took the lead.

After apologising for not being present, in person, Slade continued -

'This is an opportunity that we cannot afford to pass us by. We have no idea as to which Port these people will be taken off at. We will require the absolute cooperation of our friends across the water. Ken, you are best placed to set this up as, due to your experience with our Border Force operations in France, Belgium, and Holland you have the necessary contacts. I shall talk to the

Foreign Secretary, in order, to get the green light. It should not require much manpower, possibly two men at each Port, to watch the group and should they disembark then a few additional people may be required to monitor them should they be taken elsewhere.'

Slade disappeared from the screen he was already late for lunch with Cheryl at The Blue Peter restaurant that overlooked the magnificent Polperro Harbour.

Roberts once again led the meeting.

'Ken, can you talk to your associates in Holland, Belgium, and France. I have no need to tell you what to ask for. Once Slade obtains permission from the Foreign Secretary, we will be good to go. I will ask Slade to make contact, with the main Immigration man in Germany and if it all pans out well, then we can ask Freddie to nip over to Hamburg to look after our interests. Fortunately, we have a bit of time to put everything in place.'

Ten days later the ship docked in Hamburg. Two senior customs officers had direct sight of the vessel from their vantage point in the cab of one of the huge cranes that pick up thirty-ton containers as if they were a small amazon parcel. Freddie sat, patiently, in the passenger seat of a Mercedes that was being driven by the Port of Hamburg's top Immigration officer. Fourteen hours later, the ship left. Destination Rotterdam. Four Customs officers had boarded and then left the ship. No one else stepped ashore.

In Rotterdam, it was a similar story. This time however, the Dutch sent a team of eight Customs staff onboard. Their remit was to undertake a thorough search of the vessel on the pretence that they were looking for contraband and illegals. This time, Ken Barrington was in attendance. Ken knew all the top Immigration people in Rotterdam, Antwerp, and Le Havre. It had been Ken Barrington that had set up the teams of UK Border Force officers that attempt to weed out any illegals, prior to them hiding themselves in the thousands of trucks that cross the Channel and North Sea every day of the week. Despite the extensive search, there was no sign of the seven Chinese stowaways.

John Stewart met Ken in Rotterdam and drove him the short distance to Antwerp. John Stewart was the head of the UK Border Force in Belgium and had known Ken for many years. The ship was due to arrive at the Port at 2.00am on the 21st of September. The darkness would make life a little more difficult when it came to identifying people, but they had all the relevant equipment, as did the team of six Customs and Immigration Officers that the Belgium authorities had put at their disposal.

At a little after 3.45am Ken was woken by John Stewart as he was napping beside him.

'I have just had the signal from the observation post. There is movement alongside.'

Barrington picked up his night vision goggles and momentarily froze.

'Fuck me, John. There are nine or ten blokes climbing into that transit and I am certain that one of them is wearing a uniform.'

Stewart was unable to acknowledge his friend's words as he was giving instructions to his team.

'Do not apprehend, just follow. Keep your distance, do not blow your cover. I will be at the rear.'

As the transit van approached the barrier at the dock gates, it was lifted. The van did not stop, it left the outside perimeter of the Port and entered the E17 expressway.

'It's an inside job, Ken. The customs are party to it.'

'It seems that way, John. As if our job was not difficult enough.'

Half an hour later the transit, clearly marked as a customs vehicle, took the ring road that circled Ghent and headed towards Ostend. A smaller, unmarked Citroen van followed, behind this was the Audi that belonged to Immigration and at the back was John Stewart's black, VW Passat. Its blue flashing lights were not operating.

A further forty minutes elapsed before the transit reached the dock gates of Ostend. It slowed to a stop and was then let inside. The convoy behind had driven into a lorry park in order not to be seen in the transit's rear-view mirror. Once the dark blue customs van, with its cargo of illegals was out of sight John Stewart assumed the lead and slowed as he approached the barrier. He flashed his lights once and the barrier was raised. Stewart was known to most of the security staff at both Antwerp and Ostend. The transit criss-crossed the labyrinth of roads inside the port. Stewart turned off his lights. The customs van came to a stop on the edge of a large marina. The marina was home to hundreds of boats, some big, no doubt costing millions, whilst others were small and old and did not look very seaworthy. Ken, John Stewart and the four other pursuers were able to park at the side of a building, out of sight of anyone from the transit van.

Stewart held his binoculars to his forehead and focused on the group of ten that were now on the floating pontoons that served the berthed boats.

'Well, I'll be, fucked exclaimed Stewart. It's Peter Volkmann's, he is one of my team.'

Ken looked at Stewart and asked,

'He is a Belgium national John?'

'No, he is Dutch, but he lives in Belgium. I would never have thought it possible Ken.'

'What are we going to do John?' asked Ken.

'It is your shout, Ken.'

As they were deliberating, one of the Immigration men intervened.

'If we are going to apprehend them then we have to do it now as they are boarding that orange dinghy.'

'Ken, we need a decision.'

'Let them go, they may well lead us to bigger fish. You will have to alert your coastguard and our own in the UK. Please tell them that this needs to be a covert operation, I don't want them spooked.'

'OK, Ken, no problem.'

Ten minutes later the dinghy left the safety of the marina, turned right, and headed towards the choppy waters of the North Sea. There were nine people on board.

Peter Volkmann's fired up the transit and made his way back to Antwerp. The decision not to apprehend him was made by Ken Barrington on the basis that the bent Customs officer may well lead them to other, more important targets.

Barrington telephoned Roberts and explained the day's events. Roberts said that he would firstly discuss what action needed to be taken with Slade and that he would get back to him as a matter of urgency.

Twenty-five minutes later Roberts called Barrington back and told him that a coast guard helicopter had been scrambled and that it would cover an area, from Dover in the South to Margate in the North of Kent. UK Border Force had suggested this stretch of coastline as being the most likely for an attempted landing as it offered the shortest crossing time from Ostend.

'Why are they not using a Border Force vessel?' asked Barrington.

'Well, believe it or not, Ken, the UK Border Force has only five patrol vessels, one of which is used to police the Med, one is constantly in dry dock for repairs, leaving just three to patrol our 7,000 miles of shoreline. Currently the closest vessel to the Kent coast is over eight hours away, hence the use of the chopper.'

Two hours later, there had been no word from the crew of the coast guard helicopter. This meant one of two things. The dinghy had taken a much longer routing, maybe heading for the Essex Coast, or something had happened to it. By mid-afternoon they had the answer. The Coast Guard had reported the sighting of a deflated, orange dinghy halfway between Ostend and Clacton-on-Sea. They had utilised their onboard infra-red imaging but had found no trace of life. Help from the Belgium lifeguard had been requested and they had despatched their state-of-the-art rescue ship to the area where the dinghy had been spotted.

Arriving at the scene, the crew of the Belgium lifeboat attached a line to the stricken dinghy and reported that three bodies, floating face down in the cold waters of the North Sea, had been recovered. No other bodies were within visible distance. Asked as to the identities of the deceased, Barrington and

Stewart were told that two were of Asian appearance, possibly Chinese, although no identification documents were found on either body. The other person was described, as being of Middle Eastern or Eastern European origin. A Bulgarian driving licence was found in his jean pocket, along with several thousand Euros.

Ken Barrington and John Stewart returned to Antwerp and sat in Stewart's office. Soon after a Skype conference call, involving both men, plus Peter Slade and Graham Roberts was taking place.

Barrington was the first to speak.

'I take full responsibility for these deaths. I could have stopped the dinghy from leaving Ostend.'

Slade gave his response.

'Slow down, Ken. No blame can be apportioned to you. The same applies to you, John. There were four Belgium officials with you, the decision to allow the departure of the illegals was theirs and they did nothing to stop it from happening. Both the dinghy and the bodies were found within Belgium territory and the initial findings are that they were hit by a large container ship, which would not have seen such a small object, even if directly within their line of vision.'

'A massive search is underway, five miles off the Flemish coast. The UK is not involved. This incident will be dealt with by the Belgium authorities, although they have agreed to share their findings with us. I have been informed that the Bulgarian, Veselin Kolov, whilst being a legal Immigrant, was wanted in Belgium and the Netherlands on a whole host of charges, including money laundering, pimping, extortion, and suspected murder charges. He will be of no great loss to society.'

'Whilst the death of these poor sods is distressing, there are some plus factors for us. We now know that Vo Van Hiep is part of the criminal trafficking operation and we have exposed the routing used. The fact that one of the dead men is Bulgarian, means, in all probability, that Petrov is somehow involved. We have exposed Peter Volkmann as being someone that can facilitate the onward passage of illegals from Belgium to the UK. With your agreement John, we should leave him in place. Although you will need to convince your colleagues in Antwerp to go along with that.'

'Ken, we should have a team meeting early next week in order, to ascertain exactly how we are going to use all the information that we have just gathered. John, thanks for all your efforts. You are doing a good job. I get regular updates as far as the number of, would be illegals that you and your team are able to prevent from entering the UK. It is a great pity that the French and Belgium authorities do not put in a little more effort to stop these people from endangering their lives whilst seeking shelter in our Country.'

After dinner, John Stewart drove Ken Barrington to Brussels, where he boarded the shuttle to London.

On Wednesday, the 24th of September 2008, Peter Slade, Graham Roberts, Ken Barrington, Fergus Hamilton, Bob Martin, and George Dixson sat around a large oak table in the basement of a London Bier Keller. They were the only customers, the entrance door having been locked by the manager, in return for several twenty-pound notes. Barrington gave a full resume on the events that had taken place in Belgium the previous week. There was a short break whilst the men from the Home Office sunk their teeth into the pork knuckle, cabbage and beetroot and then washed it down with litre glasses of Germany's finest wheat bier. After wiping the mess from their faces and allowing a sexy young Australian, posing as a German waitress, to clear the table, Slade took up the mantle where Barrington had left off.

'To update you all on what Ken has explained, six more bodies have been recovered from the North Sea. They were strewn across an area of some four hundred square miles. Two bodies were unidentifiable, from their features, however they were almost certainly Chinese, three others were, without doubt, Chinese and the remaining man was Bulgarian. All nine men aboard the dinghy have now been accounted for. The dinghy itself had been purchased from a specialist marine store, just a stone's throw from the marina from which it had set off. With the cooperation of Interpol, the Belgium Police sent photos of the five identifiable Chinese Nationals to Beijing and because of their wonderful system of keeping tabs on all its citizens, our communist buddies have been able to put names to the faces and have informed their families. All five emanated from Kunming, the capital of Yunnan Province. Kunming has a population of some six million. Fingerprints of the remaining two deceased Chinese have been sent and we await the outcome. Beijing has denied our request to interview the families.'

Roberts took over.

'So, what have we learnt from this, our first real operation? Well, we know that Vo Van Hiep is a trusted Vietnamese Diplomat. He has worked extensively in the Eastern Bloc and is now the number two in their Embassy in Sofia. We know that Hiep is in regular contact with Boyan Petrov and enjoys certain perks at the Bulgarian's expense. Hiep, himself has escorted Chinese nationals into Vietnam and arranged their passage to Europe, where they have been handed over to the Bulgarians. It is safe to assume that the people smuggling gang is being assisted by at least one, maybe more of the staff that work for the UK Border Force in Belgium. With the help of John Stewart in Antwerp we have left the known crooked operative in place, on the basis that he will eventually lead us to people further up the chain. We had previously known Ostend as a route used by illegals, however these mainly involved stowaways in the backs of trucks. We now know that crossings by boat are another option for those seeking to live their lives within our shores. Hiep has his apartment bugged and we have managed to get a listening device into Petrov's car. We have recordings of three conversations between Hiep and Petrov. We have unearthed a route that we were not previously aware of. We have, to presume that, many other, as, yet undiscovered routes also exist. Even this early into our investigations we would estimate that the official figures, given out by the UK Government, for the amount, of illegals entering each year, is only the tip of the iceberg. It could be up to ten times what is published. Millburn, Ken here, our two undercover operatives and Ringo will continue to work on this. In the meantime, Bob has some news to report.

'As you all know, I was assigned with the task of finding intel on Sean Porter formerly Michael O'Leary. Mr. Porter, as he became known, was given a new identity after brokering a deal with the UK Government back in the 70s. Whilst he was tailed by our friends at Mi5 for a long period of time, they managed to lose him and despite the fact that he is known to reside in Varna and visits both sides of the Irish border on a regular basis, the interest in him seems to now be non-existent. We are aware of his association with Boyan Petrov in Bulgaria and know from past intel that at least one of his twin sons is a frequent visitor to the Black Sea resorts controlled by Petrov. The twin's international trucking business has its tentacles spread throughout Europe and now reaches as far East as Bulgaria, Romania, and Albania, giving the smuggling of illicit wares and people an almost 'in-house' feeling. Last week I was having a beer with two of my old colleagues from vice and it was mentioned that in recent times several Bulgarians had been detained in connection with the ever-increasing trade of female human trafficking. According to my old mates, there is now an endless stream of young females, some as young as thirteen, that are being brought into the UK and forced to work as prostitutes. Historically these girls would have been put to work in and around the Soho area of London, well not any, more. They are initially brought to the West End and are then 'graded' depending on their age, looks and ability to speak English. Grade one girls are kept under the watch of the ruthless Eastern Bloc men that now control the large percentage of organised crime in our good Country. These girls are 'rented out' to businessmen of all nationalities, they can command up to two thousand pounds per day. The girls see none of this money. I believe that Sean Porter is deeply involved in the procurement, transiting, pimping and in some cases the early deaths of these poor unfortunate females.'

'Excuse me whilst I take a leak.'

Returning a few minutes later, Bob ordered another round from the bar and then took his seat.

'On a visit to Vine Street, the day after I met my old partners in crime, I was told that the Eastern Europeans and in particular, the Bulgarians, have become adept at assuming the identities of the dead. I was shown the file of a man, originally from a small town outside Sofia, that had assumed three different identities. It was explained to me that the police in Bulgaria inform certain members of Petrov's gang in the event of a death and providing the death is not public knowledge, it is covered up. The dead man's identity is only used if it can be ascertained that he has never held a passport or left the sanctuary of his homeland. Then, using corrupt officials within the passport issuing office, a 'first time' passport is issued using the photo of the person requiring a new identity. I understand that vagrants, drug users and rival gang members are murdered, simply to give someone a new identity.'

'Two days later, I returned to Vine Street, armed with the pictures that we have of Porter, taken in the late '90s, I was, allowed to view the files of the eighty-seven men that are currently on the vice squads radar as being involved in the various aspects of prostitution. I married up two photographs, different identities but very, similar photographs. I compared those photos with that of Porter from ten years ago. I am convinced that they are all the same man.'

Bob distributed the three photos and whilst his current colleagues were suffering from having 'beer goggles' they all agreed that there was, without doubt, a likeness.

'This man was only questioned by the vice squad. He was not detained. There is no record of either of the identities leaving the UK.'

'I believe that Sean Porter has assumed one or more new identities and that he travels to and from the UK as a passenger in his son's trucks. This way he is subject to the least scrutiny by Border Force. He also has the option of using one of the many illegal crossing routes that now exist between mainland Europe and the UK. The fact that he has met with Vo Van Hiep in the past would suggest that he is very much involved in human trafficking. By now, Porter may have yet another identity, he will not be easy to capture. At present a new system for identity fraud is being developed. This can detect the duplication of a photo that is used under another identity. It concentrates on the main features of the face, the eyes, mouth, nose, and ears. I am told that no two people on earth can have exact duplication of these four features. What this means is if Porter were to present himself to passport control, under a new identity then, within seconds the system would flag up the fact that his face had been used under another name, sometime in the past. Mindboggling, do you not think?'

It was now nearing 7.30pm. The meeting had lasted for over six hours. Slade suggested that they 'wrap it up' and head to their respective homes.

The following morning, with no real urgency to his day ahead, Slade picked up a file that had languished upon his desk for over two months. The file contained a debate, held in the House of Commons in July of that year. The debate was in respect of the growing concern amongst MPs, of the ever-increasing growth of Human trafficking. In his head, Slade conceded that he had not been trained in, or studied the plight of the millions of people that are subjected to the misery, enforced upon them by the many modern-day slave masters that would determine the future life of those that were moved around the world, purely for the financial gain of their masters.

Taking his time to read and digest exactly what had been discussed, Slade highlighted the following comments, observations, and facts.

Anthony Steen, the Conservative MP for Totnes in Devon was very much the leader of the debate. He paid reference, to the following –

'Having first visited Bulgaria and Romania in 2005, before their accession to the EU, I had no idea as to the abject poverty that these countries endured. I was not aware that fraud was 'a way of life' and that the judiciary and the police were amongst the most corrupt in the world. A 'Roma' community of some eight million disadvantaged people were living in conditions akin to that of the Middle Ages in Britain. Some 70 percent of people that live in small towns and villages are living on the breadline. Their only means of transport is a horse and cart. The horse shares the living accommodation and is sometimes killed, to be eaten by the family. Hundreds of thousands of children are sold by their fathers for the sole purpose of becoming slaves to their future Western European, masters. Others are taken away from their families to pay off debts that are owed to the organised criminal gangs. Prior to 2004, Human Trafficking, as we now know it, was unknown to the UK. Today, Human Trafficking is, financially, on a par with both drug and arms dealing and carries much less risk to the traffickers.

Official, published figures for 2007, revealed that 167 victims were discovered, 528 criminals were arrested, 822 premises were raided, 6,400 police reports were filed and £500,000 in cash was recovered. These figures were compiled from the statistics of the five major police forces in England. In fact, they cannot be trusted as a real guide to what exactly is going on. As an example, 35 children have gone missing without trace from South Wales alone. In the Plymouth area, 17 children have simply disappeared. They, like those in Wales, do not form part of the 'official' figures. The problem, in terms of numbers is maybe up to ten times of that reported. It would be of particular use if the Minister provided us with figures that incorporated those of all the various police forces and the UK Border Force. Of the 528 arrests in 2007 for trafficking, only 24 were successfully prosecuted and only 9 of those received custodial sentences. We have a situation whereby the police and CPS do not cooperate with the UK Border Agency.'

'I have tabled a motion, sent to every EU Government, requesting that there is a consolidated effort by all, to stamp out the proliferation of trafficking, before it becomes too large to tackle. By October of this year, we will have, hopefully set up parliamentary groups in Poland, Germany, Romania, Italy, and Holland. We will then attempt to do likewise in the rest of the EU.'

Andrew Dismore, the labour MP for Hendon, intervened.

'Whilst it is noted that the fight is being taken to Europe, it should be noted by the house that the majority of victims are trafficked from China and Thailand.'

In response, Mr. Steen replied,

'Whilst it is appreciated that a good number of souls are trafficked to our shores from the Far East, it is without doubt Europe that has the vast number of cases. During the world cup in 2006, our German friends trafficked an additional 40,000 prostitutes from the former iron curtain countries to facilitate the extra demand for sex.'

Peter Bone, Conservative MP for Wellingborough, thanked Mr. Sheen for his work on this project and his chairmanship of the all-party committee that is bringing Human Trafficking to the attention of the mainstream media. The trafficking of women and children into our country, to work as prostitutes is nothing more than modern-day slavery. The severity of this harrowing crime is recognised by all. In the press release of "Operation Pentameter 2" the Home Office commented that it is, 'one of the worst crimes threatening our society. Chief Constable Tim Brain, Gold Commander of Pentameter 2, stated that 'it is one of the most distressing aspects of serious and organised crime in this country. ' Tim Brain highlighted one of the crimes that his investigation uncovered.

A 14-year-old black girl from Kenya was brought into the UK by a middle-aged white man. The girl produced a passport with no name and no photo. She was still allowed into the country. She was taken to Liverpool, locked in a house, and forced to have sex with numerous men. Fortunately, she escaped and is now looked after by a charity. How many girls never get rescued and are simply locked into slavery for the rest of their lives or until they are no longer of any use to their masters?

Slade spent most of that day digesting the contents of the file. He drew two conclusions from what he had read. One, he was not happy that the UK Border Force was deemed to be a stand-alone operation, not colluding with other organisations, he was determined to change that. Two, he needed to get a copy of the Pentameter 2 findings. This, he learnt was the coming together of all 55 police forces to tackle the growing problem of Human trafficking. He made a note to set up a similar operation that would involve every aspect of the Border Force, both in the UK and overseas.

When he eventually turned out his office lights and closed the door, he finally realised what a mammoth task lay ahead of him.

27 - TURKISH DELIGHT

It was 8.30pm on the night of Friday the 3rd of October 2008 when Alkan Asani was introduced to and shook hands with Birusk Gul. The introduction took place at a table on the promenade outside the Koko pub and restaurant and was made by Altan Akar. Asani, working undercover for both James Reeves and Peter Slade had become friends with Akar after he had purposely bumped into his sister on the dancefloor of one of Istanbul's swankiest nightclubs. Azra (meaning Virgin in Turkish) had been sent to Istanbul by her brother, the newly installed commander of the Kurds in the mountainous region near to Cizre, to study. Had she stayed in the foothills near to her birthplace she would have been married off to some warlord from another tribe and in just a few years she would be well down the pecking list, as leaders in that part of the world take many wives.

Asani was a forty-eight-year-old Turk, he was rugged and handsome and had been born just 80 km to the west of Azra's hometown of Cizre. Azra was not the prettiest card in the deck, she was short and plump and at the age of twenty-five she would have considered Asani to be something of a catch. The undercover operative, although officially attached to Mi5, was giving all his time to a man that he idolized, Peter Slade. He had spun the yarn to both Azra and her brother that he was a commodity trader, at present dealing in the sale of coffee to the many Turkish buyers of that sought-after product. He had all the necessary documentation to back up his fictitious employment and had made sure that he was seen to be part of the coffee trading scene in Brazil, Columbia, and a few other South American countries. Millburn had his back and would keep him up to date with everything that he needed to know if questioned. Asani was always amazed by the efficiency of Mi5, they were able to provide him with identities and careers that suited the time and place, wherever he was operating from. Akar, a violent man, responsible for the deaths of hundreds of his enemies, seemed to like his sister's new boyfriend and was possibly a little lax, in so far as delving into his past was concerned. He openly boasted of his command of over two thousand-armed militia and would tell Asani of his drug, arms and people trafficking operations. Gul was at ease with the fact that he was sat with his cousin, Akar, and a man from the same area as him. It took only a few drinks before Akar brought up the subject of people smuggling.

Just as he began to tell Gul of the new opportunities that were emerging in the ever-increasing business of moving people from, oppressed nations, to more lucrative and safer countries, his sister arrived. All three men stood, Gul pecked Azra on each cheek, her brother simply nodded, but she and Asani embraced and shared a passionate kiss. Once more drinks were brought to the table, Akar carried on from where he had left off, unperturbed by the presence of his younger sibling.

'Birusk, as you learnt from the meeting in Varna, the business of buying, transporting, and selling drugs is becoming more dangerous by the day. I have since met with the General and Petrov separately and have been asked to meet with you in order, to lay down a plan, that within a few years will allow us all to leave behind the world of heroin, cocaine and all of the other substances that are now being sought by the proliferation of the many small-time gangsters that are looking to make a quick buck.'

Looking across the table at the two lovebirds, momentarily wondering if he should continue the conversation when there were people opposite him that he did not know, he skipped any doubts that he had, turned to face his cousin, and replied.

'Ever since the meeting at Petrov's place I have not been able to figure out how the vast sums of money that we make from drugs, can ever be replaced, let alone by the smuggling of a few destitute people from time to time.'

'My dear cousin, please let me explain. We are not interested in the poor people that are wishing to seek new lives in Europe. Our clients will be the more wealthy, professional citizens of the Middle Eastern and Asian Countries, some of them with vast fortunes. They will pay 'up-front' for the services that we will provide. It is estimated that up to five million people are looking to leave Syria, Afghanistan, Iran, Iraq, and Albania alone. Further afield the oppressed and financial migrants of Pakistan, India, Burma, Bangladesh, Thailand, Vietnam, and China are already on the move. It is not unusual for the wealthier amongst them to pay up to forty thousand Euros for the privilege of making the journey to the safety of Europe. At, the moment, there are no, real organised operations providing a 'door to door' service. Between us all we can offer this, the income is shared amongst us, the final amounts that we each receive will be based on what type of transportation we have provided.'

'What part will I be expected to play.'

'You have set up and operate your drug smuggling in Germany, Holland, Belgium, and the UK. We have no one within our cartel in France, this is open to you should you wish to take it. The sheer number of migrants that congregate in and around Calais are there for your exploitation. Only a few have the money to pay for their onward delivery to the UK, however you will be able to control them, put them to work until they pay off their debt to you.'

At this point, Azra excused herself, all three men stood and then sat back down when she had disappeared into the ladies, cloakroom.

Looking Altan Akar straight in the eyes, Asani shocked the king of the mountains with his words.

'I would like to ask your permission to let me have the hand of your sister.'

'You can have her hand, her foot, and her ample butt. I guess you have already taken her pussy?'

The three men laughed.

'But what do we know of you Mr. Asani, asked Birusk Gul.

'Well, I was born in Mardin, in 1960 and was taken to London by my parents when I was nine. My father was number two in the North London Mosque and my mother ran a clinic that helped young, Turkish mothers. As a teenager I sold drugs on the streets. When I was twenty, I was stabbed by a member of a rival gang. Asani showed the two men the large scar on the righthand side of his stomach. My father introduced me to the Imam and through his teachings I was led away from the world of drugs and into the life that I have now, that of buying and selling some of the world's most sought-after commodities. I now spend most of my time in and around the Middle East, I return to Europe on a regular basis and often visit South America. At present my interest is in Turkish coffee.'

Azra returned to the table, the three men stood and then they all sat, with the exception, of Akar, who remained standing. Tapping gently on the table, Akar looked down, smiled at his sister, and said -

'Asani has asked for your hand in marriage. I have given him my blessing. Are we to presume that an addition to the family is imminent?'

'No, no, no, my dear brother. As you know, my name means virgin, so how could I be pregnant?'

They laughed, as one.

Azra then took her husband-to-be by the hands, and they rose from their chairs together. They embraced and kissed each other.

'They are to be married' Akar announced to the crowded promenade.

A large cheer went up, glasses were raised, and a waiter delivered a bottle and four champagne glasses to the table. Azra was ecstatic, she had no idea that Asani was going to ask her brother for his blessing. She was blissfully unaware that Asani himself, was, until five minutes previously also void of any intentions in respect of becoming a husband.

He had acted on impulse, purely because this was his best chance of getting close to both Akar and Gul.

'So, when shall we plan for the big day, my sister? Asked Akar.

'I do not know I have only just found out myself that I am to be married.'

'The wedding will take place in Cizre my sister. It will be a very traditional Kurdish affair, with hundreds of guests and mountains of food and drink. What do you say, Asani?'

'Yes, it must be in your hometown if that is what Azra wants.'

'In fact, as you are an expert in coffee, I shall arrange for the wedding to be arranged around one of our most famous of ceremonies. Do you know of this Akar?'

'I do not think so, is it some, kind of ancient ritual?'

'Then you will find out. Your wife-to-be will be most interested in your reaction.'

Outwardly, Asani was smiling. Inside his nerves began to jangle. Cizre was so close to his birthplace. He would have to invite most of his family and many of them may have known that he had joined the police force in London. They may not know that he was now an undercover operative, working for one of the world's most famous secret services. Both of his parents were now deceased, but he had no way of knowing what they may have told uncles and aunties back home. He would have to visit Mardin, in order, to find out exactly what was known of him.

Later that evening, after having given Azra what she craved the most, sex, Asani informed her that he had to leave for London the following afternoon. Once Azra had left for work, as the PA of one of Turkey's most influential cabinet ministers, Asani met up with Colin Millburn. Millburn was in Istanbul to assist Asani; he would return to Sofia once he was needed by Boris Topolov. Asani handed Millburn his passport, the following day he would get it back. It would then include a departure and return stamp to cover the days that he would be away. Millburn also handed his colleague a mobile phone and explained that it contained just four saved numbers. The numbers were listed as, 'driver Istanbul, driver Ankara, driver Mersin and driver Mardin. Istanbul would answer 'kebab.' Ankara will reply 'lava bread.' Mersin would say 'Turkish delight' and you will hear Mardin say 'welcome home.' You are to reply 'coffee house' when hearing each greeting. You will then be picked up at a pre-arranged point. When your mission is over, you should throw this phone away.'

It was over 1600 km by road, from Istanbul to Mardin and would take, allowing for stops and handovers, some twenty hours. By air, it would have taken just two hours, however Asani would not have his passport, and air travel is traceable. There was no real alternative.

At 1.30pm on Sunday October the 5th, 2008, Asani called 'driver Istanbul' the recipient muttered the word, 'kebab' Asani replied, 'coffee house.' The driver responded with,

'Wait outside the middle door that leads into the Haydarpasa railway station. When I arrive, at 3.00pm, I will wind down the passenger window and light a cigarette. Please climb into the back seat.'

The line went dead.

At five minutes to three, Asani slowly cranked his head, from left to right and then back again. He perused the endless number of vehicles that were stopping to let people out before pulling away again. At 2.59 he noticed a black BMW had stopped, almost dead in line with where he was standing. The front passenger window slid down until it was encased in the door, a puff of smoke emanated from within. Asani did not hesitate, he strode purposely over to the waiting car, threw his hand luggage in front of him and then nestled into the rear seat. There was no greeting from the driver as the car pulled away from the station, turned left and then right. Seven minutes later they were on the E80 expressway, a road that would take them all the way to Ankara.

Asani opened the side pocket of his bag and pulled out a small brown paper bag. The bag contained two wraps, that he had purchased on his way to the station. He offered one of the wraps to his driver, who politely refused. In an accent that led Asani to believe that his chauffeur came from the same area of Turkey that he himself did, he was told that they would make a stop after two and a half hours. They would be able to take a leak and get some coffee and food. Asani took this opportunity to begin a conversation with the man that would be his companion for the next five hours or so.

'So, you are from somewhere near to Mardin?'

'I am from Cizre.'

Alarm bells sounded in Asani's head. Had he been set up? He reached over for his bag.

'There is no need to grab your gun, I am on your side. We have the same aims. Your next three drivers all come from Cizre. We have all suffered at the hands of the militia. We have all lost most of our family members to those bastards from the mountains.'

'How have you become involved in my particular problem?'

'I, myself and several others, work with a man that is very, close to your Mr. Millburn, when he wants our help, we are only too happy to provide it.'

'And what is your name?'

'You can call me Betty and I shall call you Al.'

'OK, I understand.'

'Maybe you know of our story, or maybe you don't. Either way, our people have always been under the control of the Kurds that rule in our part of the world. Until recently we were governed by Ozturk Oszoy. Oszoy was a fair man, unless you crossed him. He would let you come and go as you wished. He was killed in an attack at the airport and was replaced by Altan Akar. Akar is a tyrant and a lifelong friend of Birusk Gul, I am sure that you have heard of him?'

'Yes, I know of the Gul family and Akar is to become my brother-in-law. I was with both, of these men just yesterday evening.'

'You're fucking with me, right?'

'No, Betty, I am not. Last night I proposed to Azra, the sister of Akar. This was my way into the inner sanctum of the family and their associates.'

'And why would you be going to Mardin, may I ask.'

'Because I must make sure that none of my own family or friends are aware of my involvement in the taking down of these people. I am sure that Akar's people are going to check me out, that is why I am going to Mardin. If there is anyone still around that knows of my history, then I will have no choice other than to abandon the wedding and disappear into the night.'

At five minutes past eight on Sunday evening the BMW drew up in front of the mainline station in the middle of Ankara. Asani grabbed his bag, patted his driver on the shoulder and bid him farewell.

'Take care Al, I doubt we shall ever meet again.'

The BMW pulled away. Asani strode over to a small kiosk, situated on the exterior of the station, and purchased a triple expresso. He then opened the phone given to him by Millburn, noticing that the saved entry of 'driver Istanbul' had disappeared. He called one of the three remaining numbers, 'driver Ankara' before he could speak, he heard,

'I am lava bread. To whom am I speaking?'

'I am coffee house.'

'Please walk to the far end of the building and stop at the door signed number twelve. You will see a white, private taxi parked outside. Please climb into the back.'

Asani did as he had been instructed. One minute later he was sat in the rear seat of a Mercedes SUV.

The taxi pulled away from the concourse. Ten minutes later they were on the E90 road, a road that would take them all the way to Mersin on the Mediterranean coast.

When he saw the driver's eyes scanning him in the mirror Asani broke the silence.

'Do you have a name?' he asked.

'Yes, I am Bonnie. May I call you Clyde?'

'Why not.'

'If you open the box in front of your feet you will find some food and drink. Please help yourself.'

'How long before we arrive in Mersin.'

'It is 500 km and will take around five hours.'

'Would you mind if I grabbed some sleep.'

'Be my guest. I shall be stopping after three hours or so. If you are sleeping, I will not wake you.'

'OK, thanks, Bonnie.'

Asani did not wake during the scheduled stop. He was dropped off at Mersin station and the journey from there to Mardin railway terminus was undertaken, without hitch.

His collection from outside Mardin train station was a lot different from the three previous pick-ups. When he called 'driver Mardin' Asani noticed that this was the only number left on his phone. He had no clue as to how the other three listings had simply disappeared. The recipient of his call greeted him with the words, 'welcome home' and he responded with the words 'coffee house.' There was a long wait before a battered old Renault Laguna pulled up, the driver gesticulating that he should get into the back. The car drove for just a few moments before coming to a stop outside a barber's shop.

'Come, my friend, it is time that you had a shave.'

Asani felt the opening in his anus tighten. He grabbed his bag and pushed himself out of the rear door as his driver scanned the immediate area around them.

'Come, Alkan. Let me introduce you to some people that you have not seen for nearly forty years.'

They entered the barber shop.

'This is Mehmet Asani. He is the son of your father's brother. Your cousin, no less.'

Mehmet raised the cut-throat blade from the neck of his customer in tribute to his long-lost relative. He then wiped the foam from the face of his customer and invited him to leave, locking the door behind him.

'Over here is Otto. He is the husband of your father's sister. She is long since gone from this earth. Otto may be in his eighties, his body twisted and torn, however his mind is as sharp as a cut-throat. I do not believe that you will have any memory of these two family members?'

'And you, who are you?'

'I am your brother Alkan. A brother that you never met or knew existed. At the age of ten I left the family home and joined up with the rebels in the hills. You were born shortly after I left. I, like many children of my age, encouraged by our fathers, became a fighter against the Kurds. We have carried on with that fight for the whole of our lives.'

'But our parents never mentioned you to me.'

'When they left for the UK, I had not seen them for many years, they presumed I was dead. Had I come back to visit them their lives would have been in danger. I was relieved when they fled overseas as I knew they would be safe.'

'So, you are part of an operation to take down the Kurds?'

'Yes, there are one hundred and twenty-one of us. We count fourteen women amongst our members, but we do not allow anyone under the age of eighteen to join.'

'And do you know why I am here?'

'Of course. We know that you work for the British and of your association with the sister of Altan Akar, our sworn enemy.'

'You are still to tell me your name, my brother.'

'I am Bahadir, I share the same name as our father.'

'Are there any more relatives that I should be aware of?'

'None that are still living.'

'How about family friends? Any that may remember me from the past.'

'We do not think so, Alkan. Otto's wife has passed, and he has no one else. Mehmet has never married. We think he is gay, but he denies it. I married a girl from Mersin, and she is not aware of you. All in all, we think it is, quite safe, for you to be here. You will invite only us to your wedding.'

'You know about my wedding plan's then?'

'Of course, we do. Anything to do with the murderer that is Altan Akar is known to us. You are safe to mingle in the town. However, I suggest that you do not mention your close affiliation with Akar, otherwise you will not be leaving here.'

'Yes, I understand that.'

'You can stay at my humble dwelling and on Wednesday you will be taken back to Istanbul. Some of Akar's people have already been sniffing around, asking about you. But, other than us, there is no one that remembers you, which is very, good for your safety.'

The following morning, a Tuesday, Asani asked his newly discovered brother to drive him around the town. A town that he could only vaguely remember from his childhood. Mardin had a population of some 80,000 and its main claim to fame was the number of mosques. To Asani there seemed to be a mosque on every street corner.

After a couple of hours, which included a stop at Bahadir's favourite coffee shop, they came to a stop outside the gates of one of the World's oldest seats of worship, the Monastery of St. Ananias. Founded in the year 493AD and once the headquarters of the Syriac Orthodox Patriarch, until it relocated to Damascus. The site upon which the monastery had been built is said to have been a temple of worship as long ago as 2000BC.

As the Renault Laguna coughed and spluttered outside a set of massive wooden gates, four men pulled them inwards, after which the car drove slowly into a monumental courtyard. Asani asked himself how his brother had been afforded such access to this holy of all churches. The rear door of the car was opened by a man that looked as though he had died and then been resurrected four hundred years later. His clothes were reminiscent of those worn in biblical times.

Bahadir gestured for his brother to follow him and together they entered the 'outer hall' and quickly arrived at the spectacular, 'inner sanctum' of this building. A building that had taken over 100 years to erect. Hundreds of men knelt on prayer mats, so deep into the art of praying that not one of them noticed the brothers as they weaved their way through the maze of bodies before they disappeared into a darkened cavern on the far side of the prayer room.

There was a single door in the small space where they now found themselves. Two heavily armed men stood either side of the medieval-shaped door. One of the guards acknowledged Bahadir and tapped gently on the door, which opened from the inside. The two men entered. In each corner of the bare stone walled room stood more armed men. The room was noticeably high, the ceiling being at least fifteen feet above the floor. A man rose from behind a desk, a desk that had maybe been carved many centuries previously and greeted Bahadir.

'This is my brother, Alkan.'

'Alkan, may I introduce you to Sultan Kosen.'

'Alkan gasped; he had never seen a man so tall in his life. His quick estimation was that the man now looking down upon him was at least, if not more, than eight feet tall.

'Yes, I am tall, my friend. In fact, I am now the tallest man in the whole world. Some say that I am Mardin's most treasured asset. Please be seated.'

A tiny old lady entered the room and poured the strongest of Turkish Coffee into three small expresso cups and then left.

'Your brother has told of your forthcoming marriage to the sister of our enemy, Altan Akar. He has also mentioned your work for the British. I believe we have a common aim. The destruction of Akar and all of those that follow him. Nowadays the population of Mardin is fifty-percent Kurdish, only by eradicating the killers from the mountains will we, the Arabs, and rightful owners of this land, be able to once again, live in peace. Your involvement with these tyrants and the fact that it is your duty to help us, will result in one of the bloodiest defeats ever suffered by the murdering Kurds. I understand that you will return to Istanbul tomorrow. All we require from you is the date of the marriage. We are already aware of where it will take place. Now please go, in peace. The next time we meet will be a time of great celebration.'

Returning to the car, Alkan sat next to his brother in the front. Once outside the gates, he asked –

'So, what is the plan? Will I be in danger, on my wedding day? Will Azra be spared? I have, to know the details, Bahadir. Otherwise, I may not go through with it.'

'At this moment in time, my brother, I have no idea what the plan is. Only Sultan Kosen is aware of what will happen and thus far, he has not shared his thoughts with anyone. You must understand that within the monastery, there are many men that support Akar. To share operational plans with anyone would almost certainly lead to the death of everyone that worships within the walls of St. Ananias. I may not learn of what will happen until the day it takes place. Such is the mistrust within Kosen's head.'

That evening, Asani took dinner with his brother and his wife. Uncle Otto and Cousin Mehmet joined them. No word was spoken of the visit to the monastery. Asani concluded that Bahadir had not shared anything with his newly found relatives. In Asani's head it was much better that way. The fewer people that knew of the plot to take out Akar and his gang then the chances of it becoming public knowledge subsided. For now, Alkan Asani was happy to go along with it.

At 10.00am the following morning, Asani climbed into the back of his brother's car and was driven to Mardin station. He was collected soon afterwards by the same driver that had driven him from Mersin. The return relay, in reverse of his arrival, went like clockwork. He arrived back at Istanbul main railway station at 5.00am, on Thursday 9th, October 2008. Being aware of the fact, that the flight from London to Istanbul did not touch down until 1.00pm, he slowly made his way to the airport and at 1.50pm he called Azra and asked that she collect him. He had purposely made this arrangement with her, before leaving, in order, that if she were asked, she could confirm that she had picked him up from the airport. He had Millburn to thank for putting everything in place.

As she drove him back to her apartment in central Istanbul, Azra asked about his trip to London. Was it a success, whom did he meet, when would he be going again and maybe they could go there for their honeymoon, as she had never ever visited, the UK. Asani told her that most of his time had been spent in his employer's offices, in the heart of the city, they had put together a huge deal, a deal that would see over twenty-thousand tons of coffee beans being delivered to Turkey from Brazil and Columbia. Asani began to feel a little uneasy about Azra's line of questioning, she had never quizzed him about his work life before. Had her brother put her up to this? Was he being checked out prior to their intended marriage? All those thoughts disappeared from his head as soon as they stepped through the door of the apartment. Azra now had only one thing on her mind, sex, and she was very demanding. Asani slept like a baby until late into the following morning.

At 8.45am, Azra kissed her half-asleep fiancé on the lips and left for work. She walked for two blocks, in the early morning sunshine and then entered the building that housed her department, the Ministry of Trade. Azra was the PA of the Turkish Minister of Trade; she sat immediately outside of his office. He was thirty years her senior, however she had seduced him, and her brother had the video. It was their insurance against Azra ever losing her position within the upper echelon of Turkish society. It also guaranteed Altan Akar of having inside knowledge of what was going on within the Government.

The Minister bid Azra good morning at 9.25. Just before he entered the plush surroundings of his office, she commented,

'So, we are to receive a mountain of coffee soon.'

The Minister bent over her desk and whispered,

'Your brother is well informed my dear, he seems to know a lot of things before I do.'

Azra was happy and relieved. It seemed that her husband-to-be, really was a commodity trader and that he had just brokered the coffee deal. She could now confidently inform her brother that Asani was, whom he said he was, a poor boy from Mardin that had made his way to the top.

Asani would have reason to be grateful to Colin Millburn yet again. Millburn and the Turkish Minister of Trade had been good friends at King's College and had kept their friendship alive ever since. In return for a large amount, of Euros every year, the Minister fed Millburn certain information. On this occasion Millburn had asked him to go along with the coffee story in order, to protect his man in Turkey. The Minister had no idea as to the identity of this man or the fact that he had not only penetrated his secretary, he, had also gained the confidence of the Kurds, at the highest level.

At 8.00pm that evening, Asani, and his bride-in-waiting sat together in one of Istanbul's most renowned restaurants. Even before they had ordered their drinks, Azra, as excited as he had ever seen her, announced that they were to be married, in Cizre on Friday November 8th. She added that the ceremony will be 'traditional' and that he should put together a list of people that he wished to invite in order that her brother could approve such guests, in advance. The entire cost of the wedding will be met by her family and that there was just one condition, he must wear the centuries-old attire that befits such an occasion. Asani smiled lovingly as he held Azra's hand across the table. Returning home afterwards, Asani knew exactly what was in store for him. Even before he had removed his shoes, Azra was laid bare, upon the tiled floor of the living room.

Just before lunchtime on Saturday, Azra left the apartment to meet with her best friend for a day of 'wedding shopping.' Asani took a taxi to a small café about half a mile from the British Consulate. Millburn was already sat in the corner of the room, sipping from a cup that was no larger than a thimble. Asani updated his handler on recent events and then asked him to write down the following –

'The big day is set for Friday 5th, December, in Cizre, venue, yet unknown. '

Millburn was then given the name of Asani's newly found brother, and the address of the monastery in Mardin. Millburn looked at Asani with a puzzled brow.

'Yes, I know that is not the correct date, however the world's tallest man told me to add exactly one month to the actual date, just in case the note was intercepted.'

'OK, I got it. But do you know of the plans of our friends in Mardin?'

'No, I have no idea and I am not to be told anything until the morning of the wedding.'

'Are they guaranteeing your safety? How will you know what to do, where to go, or when they will strike?'

'I have been given no details at all. I can only presume that my long-lost brother will be watching over me. By the way, do you know of Sultan Kosen? He is only twenty-six and already in charge of the whole, fucking, lot of Kurdish rebels on the Turkish side of the mountains.'

'Yes, we know of him, however he is only a puppet a front man, it is your newly found brother that is running the show. Everything you saw during your time in Mardin was just a charade. We are not sure that Bahadir is, who he says he is. If he were, then why was he not up-front with you? There are many unanswered questions. Hopefully by the time you arrive in Cizre, we shall have the answers.'

Asani looked worried by Millburn's comments.

'Do not worry Alkan. We had your back the whole time you were in Mardin. Your, so-called brother, uncle and cousin have been on our radar for quite a while. We are aware of their plot to take out Akar and those that are closest to him. Your wedding will give them the opportunity that they have been waiting for. Our problem will not be their deaths, but exactly who will assume control afterwards.'

Millburn returned to the consulate and Asani to Azra's apartment, where he found his bride to be partying with several of her friends. As he made his way to the bathroom, to take a shower, his phone rang. The name of Altan Akar appeared on his screen, his heart missed several beats.

'Hello, my brother-in-law, tonight is your night. Birusk and I will pick you up at 7.00pm. You will enjoy an evening like none that have gone before. I must return home tomorrow and Birusk will go back to Germany, so tonight is our only opportunity to join with you to celebrate your last days of freedom.'

Asani really did not want to go out on a stag night with two of the world's most notorious criminals, however, a refusal would have aroused suspicions and he certainly did not want that either.

'OK, I will see you at seven. How should I dress?'

'Oh, nothing formal as you may well lose your clothes by the end of the night.'

At 6.55, Asani kissed, his now drunken fiancé lovingly on the lips and left her to enjoy the rest of her night with the few friends that remained.

He took the lift from the 23rd, floor of the apartment block. He then stepped out onto the concourse at the precise moment that the seven series BMW came to a halt beside him. A large, sinister-looking man appeared from behind one of the white pillars that held up the ornate canopy that covered the front of the block and opened the rear door of the car. Asani climbed in, as did the large man. On the other side of the car sat Altan Akar. Asani was trapped. He hated being in such a position. Birusk Gul sat in the front passenger seat. The driver was not someone that Asani had ever seen before. As the car drew away, Asani asked –

'Where are going?'

'Do not worry, we are going to drink coffee and then we will take it from there.'

On the second floor of the office block that stood opposite the apartment block, one of Millburn's operatives gave the order for the VW Golf, parked one hundred yards away, to follow the BMW. A small, bedraggled man, hidden in the darkness of an alleyway sent a text to Altan Akar, the text read –

'Dark Blue VW Golf up your rear.'

In the back of the BMW, the large sinister man held onto Asani whilst Akar relieved him of his wallet and mobile phone.

'What is your passcode?' Asked Akar.

Asani remained silent.

'I will ask you again, this will be the last time that I ask you.'

Asani did not respond.

'We have someone that can open your phone. You can save yourself a lot of pain by telling us.'

Within five seconds of not answering, Asani felt the sharp pain of a hypodermic needle as it entered his neck. His unconsciousness was immediate.

The BMW drove for a further fifty-five minutes until it reached Yardimci shipyard, situated to the south of central Istanbul. The BMW entered through the shipyard gates without being stopped. The Golf had come to a halt two hundred yards away and as it did, it was subjected to heavy machine gun fire. Both the occupants of the car were killed. An industrial-sized fork truck left the yard, picked up the Golf, took it back into the yard and dropped it into the deep water of the Marmara Sea.

Asani was carried from the BMW by two burly dockyard workers and taken into the hold of a merchant ship that was undergoing extensive repairs. He was shackled to the chains of an overhead crane and left, hanging limp and lifeless whilst Akar, Gul and their two helpers made their way to the living quarters of the ship. Ten minutes later another man arrived and within a matter of minutes he had unlocked Asani's phone. Akar examined Asani's wallet. He found various denominations of currency, GBPDS, Euros, USD, and Turkish Lira amongst them. There were several business cards, a packet of Durex and a photo of his sister, Azra. Akar found nothing incriminating. Checking the saved and recent part of his contacts he saw that most entries were simply of a one-word nature. In the saved part of the menu, he saw, 'Azra' 'Boris' 'Gurney' 'Millburn' 'Reeves' and 'Roberts' in recent calls there were many others, his own included. All recent communications by text and phone had been deleted. Akar randomly selected 'Millburn' from the list and sent a short text. It read –

'See you tomorrow, usual place at 10.30am.'

Millburn, sat having dinner with a few of his colleagues from the British Council, received the text almost instantly. He concluded that Asani was in trouble. He assumed this because whenever his undercover operative sent a text it would always be preceded by a three-digit, code number. There was no such number present. The system under which all the team worked was quite simple. The numbers 111 at the beginning of a message indicated that the contents were of no real importance, just idle banter. The numbers would escalate in importance until reaching 999, when it was deemed that the sender was in real and immediate danger.

Millburn excused himself from the table and legged it outside. He called his man in the offices opposite Azra's apartment and asked as to the status of the tail on Akar's car.

'We have lost contact, Sir. We have not heard anything for over one hour.'

Fuck me, where were they when they last reported?'

'Approaching the shipyard at Yardimci, one hour from the pick-up point.'

'Get some assets there straight away and report back when you have any news.'

'Yes Sir, we are on it.'

Millburn brought up the name 'Gurney' on his phone and pressed the button.

'Good evening, how is Istanbul at this time of year?'

'Sorry, Mr. Slade.' I have no time for chit-chat.

Millburn explained the events of the evening.

'He will be in the shipyard, that's for certain. I will make a call to my counterpart in Istanbul and ask for his assistance. Stand by Colin.'

'Of course, Mr. Slade.'

Less than five minutes later Millburn pressed the green button on his phone. He listened as Peter Slade said –

'There will be a team, led by Colonel Ozil, inside the shipyard within fifty minutes. He cannot risk using local people, due to the almost certain fact that everyone locally will be on Akar's payroll. You are to stay put. We cannot risk your identity becoming public knowledge. Let us hope that we are not too late.'

One hour and ten minutes later, Colonel Ozil had the unpleasant duty of informing Peter Slade that Alkan Asani had been found, still hanging from the crane, the entire contents of his body lay on the oily floor in front of him. He had been slit from neck to crotch. There were no witnesses. The on-duty sentry that occupied the windowless box at the entrance to the gates, had seen or heard nothing.

Slade informed Millburn. Millburn informed Boris Topolov in Sofia the following morning, a Saturday. It would not be until Monday that the rest of the team would learn of Asani's brutal ending.

Unbeknown to any of them at the time, the death of Alkan Asani had come about, as a direct result of having his identity revealed to the man that had sat in the barber's chair in Mardin when Bahadir Asani had introduced cousin Mehmet and Uncle Otto to him. The paying customer had informed his brother in Cizre of Asani's visit.

On Sunday, the 12th of October 2008, during prayer time at the Monastery of St. Ananias, in Mardin, a helicopter belonging to the Kurdish National Liberation Army, fired four rocket-propelled grenades into the middle of the temple. A small team of Akar's men quickly identified the shattered bodies of Bahadir, Mehmet, and Otto. Sultan Kosen was nowhere to be seen. He remains a double agent to this day. None of the dead men was related to Alkan Asani in any way whatsoever.

28 - REVISED STRATEGY

The day after receiving the distressing news, from Colonel Ozil, that Alkan Asani had met with an unthinkable death at the hands of Akar and Gul, Slade picked up the phone and rang his former mentor, ex-Commander James Reeves. They agreed to meet, at their usual watering hole, in Epping, Essex.

On his way back from the meeting, Slade took a call from Colin Millburn. Millburn informed his boss of the demise of the three men attending Sunday prayers in the ancient temple in Mardin. Slade now knew that he must act upon the advice given to him by Commander Reeves.

Back at home, Slade took one of the unregistered phones from his study desk, walked out into his garden, and called Graham Roberts. After updating his boyhood friend with the news of the last forty-eight hours, he asked Roberts to call each member of the team and inform them that there will be a meeting at 11am the following morning. The meeting place will be revealed to them by 9am and none of them is to go to the office beforehand. Roberts was also asked to get in touch with Millburn, who in turn should let Topolov know that he must be available to join the meeting via Skype. Slade returned to his study, poured himself a large brandy and settled back into his plush leather chair. There he remained until the early hours of Monday. By the time he retired, he had written an agenda for the meeting. A meeting that he would reflect upon later as being one of the most important that he had ever arranged during his many years in the job.

At 8.00am on Monday, the 13th of October 2008, Slade called Jill Griffin, the sister-in-law of his wife, Cheryl. He asked Jill to prepare the private function room at the rear of her upmarket bistro that sat proudly upon the high street in the prestigious village of Ongar. The bistro did not open on Mondays. Slade then called Roberts and asked him to arrange for a minibus to be outside Ongar Station at 10.45. He was then to call each member of the team and invite them to board the minibus. Half an hour later, Cheryl Slade drove her BMW Sports car to Ongar and parked it at the rear of the bistro and walked in via the back door. Slade then called Roberts back and asked him to meet him in Ongar at 10am, in order that he could prime his number two prior to the meeting.

At 9.55 Graham Roberts alighted the central line train that he had boarded at Stratford and walked out of the station. Waiting in the layby was the familiar sight of Peter Slade's top-of-the-range Mercedes. Roberts climbed in, beside a man who facially, looked to have the worries of the world upon his shoulders. Slade drove the 200 yards or so to the bistro and parked next to his wife's vehicle. Roberts greeted Cheryl, whom he had met many times previously and was introduced to Jill. The two men took seats at the large banqueting table. Jill brought coffee, biscuits and water and left the room. Slade opened his briefcase and handed Roberts several sheets of photocopied paperwork.

'Please read through these and offer any comments that you feel are relevant, Graham.'

As Roberts studied what had been given to him, Slade left the room.

Twenty minutes later, he returned. With him was a young, well-presented man.

'Graham this is Alan Griffin. He is Jill's son and held the rank of Chief Inspector before he was seconded by the newly formed UK Border Agency back in April. He comes highly recommended, by James Reeves, no less. Reeves had no idea that Griffin was a relative of mine, albeit on Cheryl's side of the family.'

'When did this all happen Peter?'

'Reeves made a call last night and this morning Griffin has joined the team.'

'And his position will be?'

'He will be my coordinator. I required someone young, clever, and affiliated to our line of work. Young Griffin here more than fits the bill. I will introduce him to everyone. He will sit in on the meeting, as an observer.'

Slade took a large pile of papers from his case and asked Griffin to distribute them. Placing them at each of the spaces that sported a cup and saucer.

By 10.50, Fergie Hamilton, Freddie Forsyth, Bob Martin, George Dixson, and Ken Barrington had each boarded the Addison Lee, shiny black, Mercedes Vito SUV that was parked in the exact same spot as Slade had occupied just one hour earlier. The driver was Kevin Roberts, Graham's brother. He was unknown to any of his passengers.

When the last of his passengers had settled into the rear of the minibus, Kevin Roberts closed the sliding side door and returned to the driver's seat. Turning to the five men in the rear, Kevin apologised before handing each man a thick, black balaclava. He asked that for security reasons they should place them over their heads. The balaclavas did not have eye holes. None of the five men questioned as to why they had been asked to wear such headgear. They all knew that the boss needed to keep the location of the meeting place to himself. The minibus pulled away, heading in the wrong direction. When it reached the junction with the A414 it turned left and then left again. They were now on a single track, country lane and whilst at least three of them were trained to observe, when blinded, they were all too busy exchanging stories, of their respective weekend trivialities, to have kept track of where they might be. None of them had a clue where they were when the bus came to a halt on the other side of the building that housed the bistro. Each man was carefully led from the bus. Once inside the meeting room, they were, allowed to remove their headgear.

Slade and Roberts greeted each of the new arrivals and Slade indicated to them as to where they should sit. The table held sixteen diners. Slade sat at the head, Roberts to his left. Fergie and Freddie sat with Roberts and Bob, George and Ken sat opposite.

'Gentlemen, I would like to introduce you all to Alan Griffin, once of Special Branch, lately of the UK Border Agency and now with us.'

Each man raised his coffee cup in recognition of the newest member of their team.

'Alan will sit in today, as an observer. Don't worry, I have not put him at the far end because of his BO.'

'Before we begin, there is coffee, tea, bites, and other stuff along the bar. Feel free to help yourself. Toilets are through the black doors behind me. Graham, would you fire up the magic box and welcome our holidaymakers.'

Roberts hit some keys on the laptop in front of him and the fifty-inch screen, visible to all, burst into life.

'Good morning, or should I say afternoon?'

The screen showed that Colin Millburn, who was still in Istanbul, and Boris Topolov, currently in Varna, were both still alive and well. Slade sombrely announced -

'Not all of you are aware of the events that took place in Turkey during the weekend. It is with deep sorrow that I must inform you of the death of our much-loved colleague, Alkan Asani.'

There were deep sighs from those that had no idea. Each man bowed his head.

'I will hand you over to Ken. Ken is the closest that we have to a religious man amongst us.'

Ken Barrington was totally unprepared for this. He stood. The others stood. Each man looked solemnly at the floor. Ken began -

'Our good friend and colleague, Alkan Asani has been taken from us. He, unlike most of us, had put his life in constant danger. He was aware of the consequences that may befall him and now they have. Whatever his religion was, we can only offer him our sincerest best wishes and hope that he finds solace wherever he is headed. We should observe one minute silence. May god, bless you, Alkan.'

After the silence, Ken received several acknowledgements from those around the table. Topolov, in tears, thanked him from Varna.

Slade was quick to lead his colleagues out of mourning.

'Now for the matters in hand.'

'As you know, we had a plan. That plan is now shredded. What we intended to do was just too dangerous. I have put certain individuals at risk, exposing them to torture and death. Alkan has paid the ultimate price; I accept full responsibility for his death. I am unwilling to ask any of you, that are in the field, to follow the old plan. What each of you has in front of you is a new agenda. One that will involve the cooperation and backup of some of the many organisations, that, from time to time, reach out to us. We are now going to call in the favours owed to us. Although, at this moment in time, none of them is aware of the requests that I shall be making.'

'You each have a wad of paper. I have prepared a blow-by-blow account of what your future role will be. We are here to discuss this. I do not mind comments or amendments to what I have outlined. You will all be exposed to a little more danger than you currently endure. Any of you are free, without hindrance, to refuse any of the tasks allocated to you. Your withdrawal will not, in any way affect your future within this or any other department. So, let us begin.'

Ken - 'I am taking you off the pursuit of General Kos. Your expertise in the Middle East leads me to believe that you are best suited to bring down Asmar, Malik and Jamal. I will be contacting the General Investigation Department (GID) in Amman with a view to releasing information that we, hold on the drugs, arms, and tobacco activities of those three reprobates. In return I will be asking for their complete cooperation in respect of their known people smuggling operations. I will ask that the GID touch base with their counterparts in Damascus with a view to them working together, in order, to expose the finer details of their operations in Syria. Ken, you will be based out of the Embassy in Amman, from where you will remotely monitor and liaise with the relevant people on the ground. I am not asking you to put yourself on the front line as there will be, a number, of others to undertake the more dangerous tasks that lie ahead. Any questions, Ken?'

'When will I go? How long will I be there? Whom do I liaise with?

'You will leave as soon as I have the agreement with the GID and the required clearance from those that are higher up the chain. I expect both to be a mere formality.'

'It is impossible for me to say how long you will be required to stay. You will arrive under an assumed identity, which Roberts will arrange. For your own safety and the secrecy of the operation, you should be prepared to stay within the confines of the Embassy.'

'Your contact here will be young Griffin. He will not conduct his business from within the office and he will deal only with those of you present in this room.'

Fergie - I know that you have been itching to get out into the field. Your itch is now scratched. You will go to Ankara. Your target will be Altan Akar. We would have liked you to be closer to the action, nearer to the mountains, however that would be far too dangerous. Next week I shall conduct conversations with the leader of the General Directorate of Security (GDS) they have strong links with us, here in the UK and are very, close to the Germans. GDS is part-funded by the Americans. You will have the same setup in Ankara as Ken will have in Amman. We shall also place one of our existing Mi5 personnel inside the Consulate in Istanbul. He will have direct links to you and will be under your control. The answers to the three questions, posed by Ken, will be the same for you.

Freddie - Your destination will be Frankfurt. The Federal Intelligence Service (BND) have a larger presence in Frankfurt than they do in Berlin. Not much in the way of people smuggling goes through the capital. Fortunately, I know the head of the BND personally. You will be incarcerated in their office in Frankfurt. Your target is of course, Birusk Gul. As you already know, Akar and Gul are related, they meet very often. You will need to know why and what their plans are.'

'Applicable to all three of you is the fact that all external operations will be conducted by the secret service that is in situ within your respective operational zone. By allowing the local operatives to carry out the painstaking and dangerous undercover work we will be making them happy, letting them feel important. Should there be any moles within their organisations then it will be for them to bear the brunt of any reprisals, as a result, of information leakage. I cannot stress enough that the loss of Asani has made me re-evaluate our whole structure. I do not wish to put any of you in a situation whereby the result will be the loss of your life.'

Bob - Your 100% concentration should be on Sean Porter. You will not be required to go anywhere outside of the UK. We know that Porter normally travels in and out via Heathrow or Dover. We now have facial recognition set up in, both, of these, arrival points. It is not failsafe as, yet, but it is improving all the time. Our recent intelligence suggests that Porter spends a lot of his time in the Soho area, which as we all know, is a place that you, yourself, are quite familiar with. Porter has provided hundreds of Asian girls to the clubs and pimps that operate in and around London. They are all illegal and have been put to work against their will. Many of them are drug-induced and consequently are not able to become reliable witnesses. Bob, you are to pick your own team. The corruptness that abounds within the vice squad makes it just too dangerous to use existing officers. You of all people understand that. You will liaise with George Dixson. He will be your confidant and will be, available to you, always.'

'Boris, whom I can see is watching intently from his hideaway in Varna, will continue, at his own request, in very much the same way as he has done all along. You will continue to bounce everything off Millburn, who will now devote all his time to events in Bulgaria in general and Boyan Petrov in particular.

'Gentlemen, I think I have covered everything. You should prepare yourselves for your forthcoming adventures. We shall reconvene in exactly two weeks from today, at a venue that I have yet to determine. None of you shall return to the offices. All queries can be channelled through Roberts. He will operate from a safe environment until our aims are achieved.'

Just as everyone began to talk amongst themselves, an uncertain voice at the far end of the table asked,

'How about Ringo, Mr Slade? You did not mention him.'

Of all the questions that his young protégé could have asked, this was possibly the most annoying.

Unbeknown to everyone in the room, with the exception, of Graham Roberts, Slade had purposely omitted their old school friend from despatches. No one else had seemed to notice the exclusion of the elusive man that they all knew operated on the wrong side of the legal fence. By bringing this up, Griffin had, opened a pandora's box. As one, the gathering looked at their boss.

Bowing his head, with tears welling in his eyes, Slade, in a voice as solemn as the Pope on a Sunday, said,

'In view of Asani's very recent demise, I did not want to tell you all, however we have not heard from Ringo since he was captured in Albania whilst following a convoy of illegals. His silence, which has lasted for some three weeks now, leads us to believe that he will never return to our protective bosom.'

Inwardly, Roberts breathed a sigh of relief. Of all the people in the room, only he and Slade were aware of the fact, that Ringo had, some six weeks previously, infiltrated the very heart of what General Kos referred to as, 'the largest private army in the world. '

Slade had got away with his bluff. The mood in the room had changed, from a buoyant one to that of a mournful and sad one. The others offered their condolences to both Slade and Roberts, having known that the three men once pulled on their cricket whites for the same school.

There was a consensus in the room that, given the recent death of Asani and now the disappearance of Ringo, Slade was, absolutely correct in wanting to protect his less combat-savvy colleagues from the dangers of working in the field. Their respect for their boss was to ratchet-up another notch.

After each man had been blindfolded and led back to the minibus and with only himself, Roberts and Griffin left in the room, Slade approached the latest addition to the team. However, before he could utter a word, Griffin mouthed,

'I am sorry Sir. It will never happen again.'

Slade was happy to leave it at that. He knew that the young man, destined to take over from him one day, had learnt his lesson.

That evening, at home, he kissed his beloved Cheryl goodnight and retired to his study with a large glass of brandy. From the bottom left-hand drawer of his ancient leather-topped desk, that was once his fathers and his fathers before, he took out an old-style Nokia phone, turned it on and checked for any new text messages. There were none. The last incoming message was five days old. It was from 'drummer boy, ' alias, Rory 'Ringo' Starr. Only Slade and Ringo communicated on this phone. All messages were incoming, Slade was not able to initiate or respond. Ringo was very much on his own and no-one, not even Roberts, was aware of Ringo's whereabouts or current situation.

It had been five weeks since Ringo had wandered into the Café XL bar in Prizren, Kosovo. Ringo knew, from his days as an active mercenary, that the XL was a favourite haunt of soldiers, both past and present and that many of them were just as he was, able to fight, for the right payday, for either side. On his very first visit to the bar, Ringo had struck up a relationship with the most striking of all the waitresses. She was known as Adrijana, and she was from Serbia. Adrijana, like all the female staff in this bar, not only served drinks but also offered sexual services, in exchange for money. Ringo initially sat by himself, when Adrijana brought over his beer, Ringo showed her the large open wound on his stomach. He had self-inflicted the cut a few days earlier.

'Where can I get this fixed?' He asked.

'I finish at midnight, come with me and I will see to it.'

Two passing soldiers, in full combat gear, had seen Ringo's wound and were keen to know how he had got it.

'Oh, I had a fight with an old enemy a few days ago. It was supposed to be a fistfight, but he was losing, and I did not see him take the knife from his boot.'

'And where is he now?'

'I left him lying by the side of the road after I had taken his van. He did not look too well after the bullet had entered his skull.'

The two soldiers sat. Adrijana brought more drinks.

'And how about you two? What are you up to?'

'We are part of the General's staff.'

'The General, who is the General?'

'You mean you do not know of Kos?'

'Oh, that General. Of, course I know of him. But why are you here, in Prizren?'

'Every month we get one weekend off. We are just 20 km from the border with Albania.'

'Where have you fought?'

'I think you mean, where haven't I fought.'

'And now, what are you doing?'

'I am looking for a new job, I have little money, but finding work in our kind of business is becoming harder and harder.'

'We can have a word with our Captain if you like. We have a recruitment office just outside the complex, we can put a word in for you.'

'Where do I go?'

'You just get to the border crossing at Morine-Vermice any morning before 6.00 and a transport vehicle will take you to Fort Knox. What is your name?'

'Sounds good. I am Jim Reagan.'

The three men exchanged handshakes before two heavily chested ladies came and took Ringo's new associates away.

At midnight, Adrijana arrived at Ringo's table. She had changed out of her working clothes. Ringo complimented her on her good looks. She was flattered. No one ever gave her compliments, all they normally wanted to do was to shove their unwashed penis into her and then, fuck off.

Outside, Adrijana climbed onto her battered old Vespa and beckoned for Ringo to sit at the back. Ten minutes later they arrived at a rickety old, wooden shack. Adrijana opened the unlocked door and Ringo followed her in. Within a minute the girl with the striking blonde hair was stark bollock naked.

'Come on then, don't be shy. I need some sleep, so shall we get started?'

'I am not here for that. I would like you to look at my wound.'

'You mean you do not want to fuck me? Are you gay?'

'No, I am not gay. I need somewhere to stay for a while. I will pay you.'

'I don't think so. I do not even know your name.'

'I am Jim Reagan, I am English. As you know, the English know how to treat women. Especially pretty ones, like you.'

'But I can earn money every night. One man will come back with me, and he is normally gone within one hour.'

'I will pay you whatever you earn each night, and I will treat you well.'

'Really, Jim? No one has ever looked after me. Are you sure?'

'Give it a try. If, after a few nights you do not like it, then I will leave. Deal?'

'OK, Jim. We have a deal. Take off your shirt, let me look at that cut.'

'It does not look that deep. I was a nurse in Serbia for three years. I treated many wounded men. What I am going to put on will sting a little, but it will clean the wound.'

After she had finished, she applied a bandage and then headed for the shower. She returned, still naked, with her hair tied back. Ringo felt a stirring in his loins.

'Do you mind if I use your shower now?'

'Of, course not but try not to get the bandage wet.'

Returning from the bathroom, he found that Adrijana was fast asleep. He climbed in beside her. His hard was immediate. She was simply feigning sleep. He placed his hand between her legs, she was wet. He entered her. They climaxed together. At 7.00am she placed coffee on the floor beside the bed. Jim knew that he had achieved the first part of his plan.

At 8.30am the morning after the meeting with his most trusted of people, Slade sat at his desk in the offices allocated to him in Marsham Street, SW2. At 9.05 he entered the main office and asked the staff to stop what they were doing. It did not take him long to inform the gathering, of around twenty-eight people, that as from that moment in time, none of them was required to carry on with their duties. He asked that should there be, any absentees would somebody please inform them of the situation. Slade added that each, and every one of them would receive six-months' salary and the highest of references, should any be required.

One man stood. He was Willie Mott. Ken Barrington had long suspected Mott of leaking information. The diminutive, scruffy, and bespectacled civil servant had been recommended by Nick Pritchard just a few weeks after Slade's initial recruitment drive. Pritchard, Slade's equal in rank, and leader of the international section of the UK Border Agency had long since dropped out of Slade's list of people that he could trust. Pritchard had the ear of the Home Secretary. Ken had been watching him and whilst they could not remove him from office, they now kept their distance. It had long since been agreed that Mott was Pritchard's eyes and ears within the department.

Mott spoke,

'Why Sir? Why are we all being laid off?'

'Because, Mr Mott, the powers that be are getting restless. We seem to be getting nowhere and we have lost two operatives in the process. We are being given a six-month sabbatical, although there is no certainty that we shall resume operations after this.'

Addressing the whole of the office staff, Slade continued,

'By way of a personal thank you, for all your efforts, I have booked a function room at the Café Royale for this Friday. I hope that you can all make it. Please inform those that are absent from this meeting. Please only remove your personal effects from the office. No files, mobile phones or other electronic devices that belong to her Majesty are to be removed. You will all be subject to a thorough search before leaving the building. This is not personal. The same protocol applies to me. I wish you all the very, best of luck and I look forward to seeing you all on Friday.'

As soon as Slade had left the room, Mott hit the keyboard of his desktop and attempted to send an email to Nick Pritchard. Ten seconds after sending his email he received the message 'unable to send, please check your connection. 'Mott was fucked. He had amassed a lot of intel. Intel that he wanted to send out to Nick Pritchard. He also wanted to know why the five senior men, all of whom reported directly to Slade, had not turned up for work that morning nor the previous day. He walked over to Barrington's office and turned the handle on the door. It was locked. The vertical blinds on the inside of the windows were half-open. He could see that the office had been cleared. Only a single telephone remained on Barrington's desk.

Whilst most of the office staff were either packing their stuff or chatting with each other, Mott left the office, walked the length of the hall, and proceeded to climb the stairs to the fourth floor. Slade caught a glimpse of his frame as he passed. He knew exactly where the grass was going.

Mott knocked and entered Pritchard's room. He explained what had happened one floor below. A few moments later, Pritchard left his office and legged it down to the third floor. He mouthed fuck it to himself as he saw the lift door close. Slade had left. Pritchard could not be seen to be chasing him in front of those gathered in the reception area of the building. He turned and headed towards Slade's office. He opened the door and went inside. He tried the drawers to the desk and those to the filing cabinets. Every one of them was empty. He returned to his own office. Mott had left. Pritchard unlocked his top left-hand drawer and picked up one of the burner phones. The Home Secretary denied all knowledge of the fact that Peter Slade's department had been shut down. Pritchard was not sure if what he had been told was true or not.

In the meantime, Slade was on the London Underground system, his destination being Bromley-by-Bow on the district line. From the station, carrying only his soft leather briefcase, he walked the one-and-a-half miles to Oban Street, Poplar. George Dixson, constantly monitoring the twelve screens that beamed CCTV images from every adjoining street, had seen the son of his one-time best friend emerge from Leven's Road. Dixson opened the door the instant that Slade had put his right foot firmly into the newly painted front porch. Roberts, Dixson, the new boy, Griffin, and Slade drank tea whilst they began to plot the downfall of their targets upon the whiteboard that surrounded three of the walls in the upstairs backroom.

At 5.30pm, having finalised their plan, Slade and Dixson returned to their respective homes. Roberts and Griffin stayed behind. Both would remain at this hideaway for the foreseeable future.

It was 9.30am on Wednesday 15th, October when ex-Commander James Reeves entered the Millbank branch of Café Nero. Peter Slade was already sat at a table on the far side of the eatery, two coffees were the only contents upon the shiny red finished surface.

'Peter, we have just one hour with the Foreign Secretary before he leaves for Brussels. We are dammed lucky to have even that amount of time. Over dinner last night I laid out our plans for rounding up the people that your team are after. He was very, supportive of the idea, especially the part whereby we are utilising the cooperation of our foreign partners. I am to be the liaison person between you and his office. Finish your coffee, my car is parked on a double yellow.' Together they left the café and climbed into the back of Reeves chauffeur-driven, top-of-the-range, black Jaguar.

At the Foreign and Commonwealth Office (FCO) the two men were quickly ushered into a lift and taken to the fourth floor. By the time the Foreign Secretary emerged from an adjoining room, fifteen of their allotted sixty minutes had already elapsed.

After going through the formalities of shaking hands and ordering coffee, the Foreign Secretary informed his visitors that he had already spoken with the PM and the plan, as laid bare by James Reeves, had been sanctioned by number ten. Looking directly at Slade, the Foreign Secretary said,

'Peter, I have no need to remind you that whilst your operation has the blessing of the PM, you are and will be on your own should it go tits up.

'I understand Sir.'

'Good. I have spoken to my counterparts in all the territories that James here has mentioned. All are keen to cooperate. As part of the deal, you will have to feed them some of the intelligence that you have gained from your previous experiences. I do not have to remind you that moles exist, even in the upper echelons of Governments, our own included. On that basis, only the PM, myself, James, and you are aware of this clandestine operation. The Home Secretary has not been briefed.'

The Foreign Secretary disappeared through a door in the far corner of the room. Reeves and Slade were shown out. Twenty minutes later Slade was dropped off at Liverpool Street Station, from where he made his way back to Epping.

Slade entered that hallway of his house at exactly, the same time as his wife Cheryl, was leaving the lounge. She saw that look on her husband's face, a look she had seen many times before.

'Are you OK Peter? Only you have that worried expression on your face.'

'I am fine darling, just under a bit of pressure at, the moment, that's all.'

Cheryl knew that she should not quiz him any further. From past, experience, she had learnt to leave him alone, until he was ready to tell her.

'I am making coffee. Would you like one Peter?'

'Yes, that would be nice, thank you.'

At 8.30 on the morning of Thursday 16th, October, Peter Slade entered Graham Roberts' safe house. George Dixson was already there, as was Alan Griffin. At 9.15 Slade was ensconced into the soundproof, bug-free downstairs room that was once known as the scullery of this Victorian property. Electronic equipment surrounded the small desk on three sides. Roberts' brother, Kevin, now running the private detective agency in Graham's longer-than-expected absence, had ensured that it was absolutely, safe to communicate with the outside world, without fear of being overheard by any would-be snoopers.

From his briefcase Slade produced several pages that had been given to him by the Foreign Secretary. He had been told that there were no copies. The paperwork contained the names, contact details and resumes of everyone that Slade had asked James Reeves to submit to the cabinet minister. On his desk there were seven mobile phones, each was of the old type. No apps or internet. Only calls and texts could be made from them.

Page 1 of the fourteen such pages contained the details of Colonel Ahmad Dahabi, the current Chief of Jordan's General Intelligence Directorate or GID as it was commonly referred to. Slade called the number as shown on the document. One of seven telephones rang in the office of the Colonel. The phone that rang was one that was seldom used, and the number was known to but a few of the top brass of Jordan's ruling party. On rare occasions, King Abdullah had been known to speak to the man that occupied the Colonel's chair.

'Dahabi.'

'Colonel, you do not know of me. I work for Mi5 in London. I am known simply as Gurney. I would like to talk to you about three people, Tayser Malik, Tamara Jamal and Monzer Asmar.

'I have had no briefing about you Gurney. It is most unusual for this number to be used without me having full knowledge of whom it is that is calling.'

'It must be this way, Colonel. On my side, only the highest of people in Government are aware of what I am about to discuss with you. That is of course, should you be willing to discuss. You can verify the authenticity of this call with your own PM.'

'I will do just that, however I am willing to listen to whatever you have to say, so please, carry on.'

'The three names I have mentioned to you are of great interest to us. We have monitored them for some considerable time, albeit by using people outside of official channels. Now we have changed track and are asking for your cooperation, in return we shall give up vast amounts of intel that we have gathered in respect of the drugs, arms and tobacco operations of these undesirables.'

'And what exactly is it that you want from us?'

'These people are big players in the illegal movement of people. These illegals are entering Jordan from Iran, Iraq, Afghanistan, Pakistan, India, and Bangladesh. The route into Jordan and then onward to Syria accounts for around fifty percent of all known illegal migrants that end up in mainland Europe and the UK. For us, this business is becoming bigger than the drug trade. It is costing the UK economy an enormous amount of money and is challenging our overstretched resources. In simple terms, we must stop this, at source.'

'I understand your concern, but as this does not really affect us, how can we help?'

'I will be sending one of my team to Amman. He will work directly with you, but you will never meet. Your PM has approved this. It is common knowledge that GID is the strongest of all such agencies in the Middle East and that you have the closest of cooperation with your near neighbours. You also share the strongest of relationships with the Americans, the Israelis and of course, our good selves.'

'OK, Gurney. You have sold the idea to me. In fact, my PM had already alerted me to the fact that I should expect this call. You will receive our utmost cooperation. When will your man be in position?'

'Within ten days. A telephone will be sent to your residence. Only our man will have the number. I thank you for your time, Colonel. You can get me on this number. Leave a text message if I am unavailable and I will get back to you soonest.'

Slade unlocked the door and climbed the stairs. He informed his three colleagues that the Colonel was onboard and asked that they make everything ready for the imminent departure of Ken Barrington to Amman. He asked Roberts to make, arrangements for a phone to be sent to the home of the Colonel and that the phone should originate, and be sent, from a local black-market dealer. It was to be delivered personally to the Colonel.

After a short break, Slade returned to the ground floor secure room and dialled a number on the second of the seven mobile phones.

In Ankara, Emre Fidan, a former Turkish Ambassador to the USA, pulled a small Ericson phone from his jacket pocket and simply said, hello.

'Mr Fidan, I am Gurney of Mi5 in London.'

'I have been expecting your call Mr Gurney. I have been briefed by my President.'

Emre Fidan, once ensconced in the Turkish Embassy on the edge of Central Park in New York, was these days, the Chief of the General Directorate of Security, (GDS) responsible for a vast array of policing, both civil and military. Under his rule, the prison population of Turkey had risen from 50,000 to 100,000 in just two years. Fidan was ruthless and in his short time in control, every facet of lawlessness had been strengthened. He had many security departments at his disposal. Two of them had been identified by Slade and his team as being of the utmost importance were they ever going to take down Altan Akar and his fellow Kurds. The GDS had a department known as the Ozel Tim. This was a tactical unit, made up of specialist operatives, they used special weapons and rapid deployment when taking down organised crime gangs. They also operated alongside German units, anywhere within Germany where there were high concentrations of Turkish Nationals. This, it was hoped, would lead them to Birusk Gul and his cohorts.

'Then, you will know that we are looking for your cooperation in the capture and detention of Altan Akar, his associates, and through your link with the German authorities the possible apprehension of Gul and his henchmen.'

'Please tell me how this is all going to work.'

'In essence, the plan is simple Mr Fidan. We will place an operative in Ankara. He will have direct contact with you. We shall divulge everything we have on those bastards in the mountains. All we ask for in return is the use of your team when it comes to eventually taking them down. We shall not operate covertly. You shall take the glory should we achieve our aims.'

'So, how do we communicate going forward?'

'A phone will be sent to your home. Just I and our man in Ankara will have access to it. We hope to be up and running within ten days. We are only interested in the people smuggling routes and the organised gangs that implement them within the borders of your country. We shall require around ten of your most talented, and trusted men.'

'I think we can accommodate your requests, as long as we have control, at all times.'

'You will Mr Fidan, you will. Thank you for your time and understanding.'

Slade once again climbed the stairs. He made four cups of tea in the kitchen before entering the room where Roberts, Dixson and Griffin had now almost fully covered one whole white-boarded wall with the operational plan for Amman.

'You will need to get cracking on the other wall. I have just got the green light from the head of the GDS in Ankara. Please prepare Fergie in the same way as you are doing for Ken. Do not forget, we need to pull Kidd's group in

Istanbul and get him prepared for Fergie's arrival. The Turks do not know of Kidd's involvement. Tomorrow I will touch base with the BND in Germany, in readiness for Freddie's arrival in Frankfurt. I will also have, an in-depth conversation with Bob Martin in respect of how we are going to handle Mr Porter. Tomorrow afternoon I have a conference call booked with Topolov and Millburn. No one has yet raised the name of Vo Van Hiep. In fact, I have left him out of the equation in the hope that he will turn up in Bulgaria as it is nigh impossible for us to get to him whilst he is in Vietnam.'

'Finally, tomorrow evening I shall be hosting the dinner for our staff at the Café Royale. Unfortunately, I cannot invite either of you or any of the others within our inner sanctum as I do not want any of you to be put into the line of fire that will undoubtedly shoot from the mouths of our former colleagues. I am sure that you all understand that.'

'Of course, Peter.' replied Roberts. Dixson nodded in acknowledgement. Griffin looked blank.

The next morning, Slade, picking up yet another of the unused mobile phones, called the German Federal Intelligence Service, better known as the BND. Slade had dealt with the BND in the past, he knew of the man that he was now seeking help from. What he also knew, was that the BND was the world's largest intelligence gathering organisation, with over three hundred locations around the world and six thousand, five hundred staff. Many of them were former military personnel, that were now attached to civil undercover operations. The BND was only answerable to the German Chancellor.

As you would expect, being German, Armin Ober, the Vice President of the BND had already been primed and was already armed with an untraceable, old-style Nokia phone.

'Good morning, Mr Ober.'

'Good morning, do I have your name?'

'I am Gurney, Mi5 are my employers.'

'That is not exactly true, is it Gurney? My understanding is that you are working on behalf of the UK Border Agency.'

'You are well informed, Sir.'

'As I must be. We Germans leave nothing to chance. I saw you three years ago Gurney. You were in a hospital bed in Stuttgart. You were oblivious to the fact that I had visited you. I have followed your path ever since. I must say, you have led a very, interesting life. I helped get you back to your homeland.

'Then I owe you a belated thank you, Mr Ober.'

'Well, although I know your real identity, you will be Gurney to everyone else.'

'Thank you.'

'We have waited a long time for this day, Gurney.'

'Not with you Mr Ober.'

'We also wish to solve the problems that people smuggling and trafficking are bringing to our country. I realised a long time ago that only through the cooperation of other, like-minded countries, would we be able to overcome the suffering that these poor unsuspecting migrants, must endure at the hands of the organised crime gangs, of which there are many. Like you, we are looking for ways to take down the whole chain. To simply bring about the arrest of those that operate within Germany, would not be enough as there are many others that would take their place. We must look to eradicate the entire organisation. My information is that you have a plan to do just that. On that basis we are with you, and you will have our full support.'

'Again, I must thank you Mr Ober. I am putting in place a group of people that stretches from Pakistan in the East, through the Middle East and well into Europe. I know of your personal involvement in the overthrow of the Kosovan Government and, also, that of your interest throughout the Balkans. You will be only too aware of the part that is played by Albania, Bulgaria, Rumania, and others in the organisation of the safe passage of illegal migrants that pass through those countries.'

'Indeed I am. We have a lot of intel on the leaders of the gangs that perpetrate the onward journeys of those people that are unfortunate enough to fall into the hands of these purveyors of human misery.'

'With your permission, Mr Ober, I would like to place one of my most trusted agents into your set-up in Frankfurt. He will not be giving any direct orders. He will assume the role of an 'advisor.' His information will come from us, here in London. It will be for you to decide if you would like to act upon what we can inform him of.'

'We are in, Gurney. Just let me know when we can expect to receive your man. We will make him very welcome, of that I can assure you.'

Slade entered the upstairs room and asked his colleagues to ready Freddie Forsyth for his vacation in Frankfurt. He outlined what Armin Ober had agreed and that they add the details of the BND to the empty whiteboard on the wall.

Returning to the secure downstairs room, Slade called Bob Martin and discussed the finer details of exactly how they were going to nail Sean Porter.

Prior to leaving for the Café Royale, Slade called Millburn, now back in the British Embassy in Sofia. Millburn invited Boris Topolov to join the newly established Skype link. A link that Roberts would delete and then re-establish when need be. Topolov did not reveal the exact location of where he was, however, it was assumed that he was in or around Varna. Which is where Boyan Petrov and those close to him, spend most of their time. At 7.30pm, Slade hosted a dinner for nineteen of his former employees. The dinner went by without hitch. It was noticeable that Willie Mott, Pritchard's snitch, was absent and whilst he was pleased that he did not have to face any questioning from the man that could have made his evening unpleasant, he knew that he had not seen or heard the last of him.

As he shook the hands of his, now redundant staff, as they filed, one by one, out into the chilly October Piccadilly night, Slade, trained as he was in such matters, could not help but notice the two men that stood in the shadows at the junction of Regents and Air Street.

With the last of his guests now gone, Slade turned left out of the Café Royale and headed towards the subway that would take him down to the London Underground. He was totally aware that the two men that he had spotted, were now following him.

29 - CAT & MOUSE

It was 11.20pm when Slade boarded the westbound Piccadilly line train. He entered through the single door at the end of the third carriage. The two newest members of his fan-club, whom he had now named as the two Ronnies, due to their physical resemblance to the world-famous comedians, had almost fell into the far end of the carriage. Slade stood, holding onto the upright pole at the end of a row of seats. His pursuers also stood, the small bespectacled, wanna-be spy with his back towards him, making it easy for Barker to have full sight of the man, that should be, according to Willie Mott, heading home to Epping, which, by now, they had realised was in the opposite direction.

Slade, of course, was already several episodes of the story in front of his trackers. As the train left the tunnel after leaving Gloucester Road, he took a phone from his jacket pocket and called Graham Roberts.

'I am being tailed.'

'What would you like me to do?'

'I am just pulling into Earl's Court. I will cross over and take the district line to Mile End. It will take around thirty-five minutes. I will need you to collect me. I will see you in Southern Grove, at the back of the station. Can you get Roy and a couple of heavies to collect Barker and Corbett? They need to be dropped off outside Pritchard's house. The address is in his file.'

'Consider it done.'

Slade made another call. This time his wife, Cheryl answered.

'Darling, pack a bag for three nights. In a few hours Roy Roberts, whom you have met previously, will pick you up and take you to Kings Cross. You are to visit your sister in York. I am not in any immediate danger but, right now I must disappear, simply to avoid being followed.'

Slade stepped onto the almost empty Upminster bound, district line train. The two Ronnies did likewise. All three men sat, albeit at opposite ends of the carriage.

Cheryl began to pack. Her phone rang. It was Graham Roberts.

'I just want to reassure you that there is nothing to worry about. There is no danger to you, or to Peter for that matter. We have everything under control. We are not involved in any life-threatening situations; we just need you to vacate the house for a short while. When Roy arrives, please give him a set of keys, he will look after things for you.'

'Thank you, Graham. I understand.'

It was a little after midnight when Slade climbed the stairs of Mile End station and came out onto the A11. He turned right and crossed Maplin Street. He then went right again, into Southern Grove. The comedy duo were fifty yards behind him. In the dimly lit street, he saw Roberts' Saab parked on the corner of Southern Grove and Hamlets Street. He purposely strode past the Saab and as he did, a black Mercedes van came to a halt a few yards behind him. The nearside door of the van opened, from the inside. Roy Roberts had left the driving seat of the van and in less than ten seconds both comedians were laying, face down, upon the cold steel floor. The Mercedes made its way back onto the A11 and headed west. Slade did an about-turn and climbed into the passenger seat of the Saab.

'Job well done, my friend.'

'Well, it certainly turned my evening into something worthwhile, Peter.'

It took just a few minutes for Corbett to confess that he and his partner were working under the orders of Willie Mott.

Thirty minutes after they had been lifted from the street, Slade's two followers had been given a strong sedative. Five minutes after that, the van turned into Kensington Square, the two men were left outside the three-million-pound abode of Nick Pritchard. Roy Roberts rang the bell, before calmly pulling away and heading, at a sedate pace, to collect Cheryl Slade from Epping.

Pritchard, with the small Mauser 1934 handgun, that his father had passed to him upon his death, held tightly in his right hand and hidden from view, opened the door of No.10 Kensington Square. There, beneath his feet, lay two unconscious males. Taking the miniature Motorola from the left-hand pocket of his expensive, paisley-printed dressing gown, he called Willie Mott.

'Are Little and Large anything to do with you, Mott?'

'Not with you Sir.'

'You know exactly what I am talking about. Now get yourself here and clean this up.'

Unknown to Pritchard, Mott was sat in his Ford Galaxy, on the other side of the square. Whilst the two Ronnies had been tracking Slade, Mott had been following the comedy duo. He waited fifteen minutes and then pulled up outside Pritchard's house. It was 3.20 on the morning of the 25th of October 2008. After a few minutes of face-slapping, Mott managed to rouse his two horizontal associates and get them into the car. Pritchard was upstairs, lovingly stroking the genitals of his young lover, Henry Winters.

Willie Mott, in his endeavours to impress his immediate boss, had fucked up badly. He had failed to secure any incriminating information about Slade during his time as Pritchard's mole, whilst he had been working inside the operation just one floor below and now Slade had disappeared into the night, with little chance of being found in the very, near future. Mott knew, from snippets of conversations with Nick Pritchard, that Slade was being fitted-up for something that had happened in his past, he just did not know exactly what it was that Pritchard was trying to nail him for.

At 5.11am, Slade, restless from a disturbed night, climbed out of the camp bed that Roberts had set up for him in the room adjacent to his 'bunker' in the downstairs of 38 Oban Street. He climbed the stairs, careful not to awaken his three comrades, sleeping, as they were in the luxury of the two upstairs bedrooms. He made himself some tea and returned to the small safe room. He took all seven of the mobile phones from the locked drawer of his tiny desk. Examining the screens of each phone, he saw the words,

'About to enter the inner sanctum.'

The message was from 'drummer boy' alias Rory Starr, alias Ringo and more recently, Jim Reagan.

These pre-agreed words meant that Ringo was close to getting himself entrenched into the circle of the people that were close to General Kos. How he had managed to achieve this, Slade really had no idea. What he did know, however, was that providing he remained undetected, Ringo could be the single most important person within the organisation that was charged with bringing to book the tyrants that prayed, upon the vulnerability of those poor souls that were willing to part with money, in order, to be given a new life, away from the hostilities of the countries of their birth. Slade also knew, that, should he be exposed, then Ringo, the boy that he and Roberts had spent most of their formative years with, would almost certainly be executed.

Thirty minutes after he had sent the text to Slade, Ringo had turned off the phone and pushed it into the slot that he had carefully cut into the mattress of the bed, the bed that he had now shared with Adrijana, for almost two months.

Ringo had waited for a whole month before returning to the Café XL bar. He had spent his time repairing Adrijan's humble abode and doing odd jobs for the local people that resided close by. Over the years he had become adept at several different languages and many people in this part of the world seemed to speak some English. Adrijana left at 2.00pm, every day, and returned a little after midnight. Ringo earnt only small amounts of money and was not able to give his landlady the amount that he had promised. For her part, Adrijana did not seem to care. In Ringo's eyes, she seemed to have fallen for him hook line and sinker. She added to her meagre wages by virtue of the tips that she received in return for the hand jobs that she gave to her sex-starved customers.

Entering the Café XL at 9.00pm on the fourth Saturday since his arrival, Ringo spotted the two soldiers that had befriended him, one month previously. He sat at a table a short distance from the men that he had earmarked as being useful to him. He waited patiently for them to spot him. As he had requested, Adrijana showed not the slightest interest in him.

'Hey, Jim.'

Said one of the men as he passed by on his way to the loo.

'Hi, how's it going, why, don't you go over and join Marko, by the way, I, am Stefan.'

Ringo picked up his beer and cigarettes, moved twenty yards to his left and gently tapped Marko on his left shoulder. Marko instinctively placed his hand inside his Serbian army jacket.

'Relax, my friend. Do you not remember me?'

'It's Jim is it not?'

'That's right. I just spoke to Stefan. He will be back in a minute.'

Marko raised his hand and beckoned Adrijana over.

'Do you remember this pretty girl, Jim? Just five minutes ago she jerked me off, outside.'

Ringo felt both jealous and embarrassed at the same time.

'Get us three more beers please and I think Stefan would like to try out your right hand soon.'

Stefan now sat dead opposite Ringo, asked,

'Did you sign up yet Jim? We have not seen you in the camp, but then there are over 3,500 of us there, so no real surprise that we have not seen you.'

'No, I have not been down to the border yet, but I would like to return with you two on Sunday night. If that is OK with you?' By the way, are you both Serbian?

'No Jim, we are from Skopje, Macedonia. We fought against the Serbs. The camp provides many different uniforms and we got these. You know, they even have American and British kits, but nobody wants to wear them as everyone likes to shoot at those bastards.

'So, will you take me with you on Sunday and do the introductions?'

'Of course, and if you are, who you say you are, then you will have no trouble in being accepted.'

'Thanks, guys, and what have you been up to lately?'

'Oh, we have been on a very, dangerous deployment Jim, escorting rag heads from Plovdiv, up through Sofia and into Romania. We leave them at Timisoara and then fly back to Plovdiv.'

Before Ringo could interject, Marko added,

'Yes, we are like babysitters. There is no fighting involved. It's dead easy Jim, we are escorting hundreds of frightened people at a time. We hand them over to the gipsies (Romanians) and our job is done.'

Ringo, careful not to quiz his new friends, simply replied,

'Sounds like I could handle that. I must go now, but can I meet you here tomorrow night?'

'Of, course Jim. And the beers will be on us, but you will have to pay Adrijana for her services.'

This comment alerted Ringo to the fact that his two new comrades had absolutely no idea that he was a lot more than an occasional hand job to the pretty young waitress.

Ringo returned to the shack. He did not acknowledge Adrijana as he left the cafe. He took a route that was not the norm as he was sure that the two Macedonians would be following him. They were not, he was slightly disappointed as he would have loved to have slit their throats. His main reason for wanting to exact such extreme punishment on Marko and Stefan was the fact that they were using his girlfriend for self-gratification. But then again, was he not doing exactly that?

On Sunday, after escorting Adrijana to the local church, he took her to lunch at the one-star restaurant that was situated inside the town's only Hotel. There he told her of his plan to join with Marko and Stefan when they left the Café in the early hours of Monday morning. She begged him not to go. She told him that she was in love with him and that she could not bear it if anything happened to him. He was quick to reassure her that he would not, for the foreseeable future, be taking part in any fighting. Immediately after lunch she left for work.

Ringo purposely arrived at the Café at midnight. He knew that his two new companions would not be leaving until around 4.00am. He did not want to drink himself to the point whereby he was incapable of making sober decisions. At 12.20am he saw Marko and Stefan enter the bar with two older women, he was pleased that Adrijana was not one of them.

Marko spotted him, sat all alone, with just a small amount of beer in his glass.

'Hey Jim, come and join us, have some fun. Soon we will leave.'

Ringo, feigning relief at seeing his fellow mercenaries, joined them at a table that seated six.

Marko grabbed Ringo's arm,

'This is Agnesa, her name means 'pure' but I can tell you, Jim, she does not live up to her name. This one is Elira 'the free one', but she is not free. She charges a King's ransom. They are both from Albania.'

Marko spotted Adrijana and called her over.

'Can you sit with my friend Jim? He is all alone.'

'No. I am sorry we are too busy for me to sit. Maybe later when it quietens down.'

For all of three hours, Jim sat whilst Marko and Stefan groped their elderly escorts, both of whom were well past their sell-by dates.

At 3.55am, a man that looked like a Mexican assassin approached the table.

'It's time.' Was all that he said.

Marko and Stefan produced wads of money from their pockets, laid it on the table, kissed their respective partners and left. Jim followed.

Outside, a bright yellow Dodge pickup truck, engine running, awaited their arrival. Marko and Stefan climbed into the seats behind the driver and Jim was left to sit next to El Bandido. Both Macedonians were unconscious by the time they had reached the edge of the small town. Half an hour later they stopped at the border gate of Morine-Vermice. It was 4.35am.

No one got out of the Dodge. Jim looked at the Mexican.

'It is the same every month. We arrive here. They sleep until the bus arrives at 6.00am. They get on the bus and then sleep again until they get to Fort Knox. They have no money left, they pay me on the way here, otherwise I would not take them back. So, we just wait. Try to get some shuteye.'

At six minutes past six in the morning, a Monday, the bus, an old Russian jalopy that had died several years since, chugged into view. The Mexican, shook both, of the backseat passengers. They got out of the Dodge and trundled, wearily, over to the bus and joined the queue of people that had been waiting at various places alongside the dirt track of a road. Marko and Stefan slumped into a seat near to the rear and Jim sat behind them. Nobody on the bus seemed to be coherent. It seemed to Ringo that everyone, apart from himself, was under the influence of alcohol or drugs. One bone-shaking hour of a ride later, the bus came to a halt at the gates of a complex, encircled by a metre thick, three metre high, brick wall.

Jim was astounded to see a building on the other side of the road that displayed a large sign, that read 'Recruitment Office of the Army of General Horatio Kos. '

'I thought they were pulling my leg.' was the thought passing through Ringo's, brain.

Marko and Stefan, now a little more alert after their power nap, accompanied Jim into the office. Around a dozen men, all in various military attire, were sitting around the perimeter of the room.

'Sergeant, this is Jim Reagan, a fighter of many battles. He would like to join with us.'

The sergeant, peering over the top of his square-framed glasses, took an A-4 clipboard from under the counter, attached two sheets of paper to it and handed it to Jim.

'Fill this in and give it back to me. Call the number on the back, in a weeks-time.'

'I do not have a mobile phone.'

'Then you will have to come back. We will then let you know if your application was successful.'

At that moment in time, Ringo had no idea that all unsuccessful applications ended in the death of the applicant.

The three men left the office and crossed the road.

Jim watched as Marko pressed his hand onto a glass pad that was inset into the exterior wall of the fortified complex. He looked up when he saw that one of the overhead cameras had sprung into life. In a large hut on the other side of the wall, a guard looked at the photo and details of the person on the outside. He was happy that the hand belonged to one of their own. A side gate opened, automatically, and Marko passed through the turnstile on the other side. Stefan then placed his hand on the pad before he also entered the barracks of the largest private army in the world, he turned to Jim and said,

'The bus will take you back to the border, but you will have to make your own way back from there. Good luck Jim. I hope to see you inside soon.'

Ringo arrived back at the shack too late to see Adrijana as she had already left for work.

During the first weekend of November 2008, Ken Barrington, Fergie Hamilton, and Freddie Forsyth were all safely settled into their respective new homes. Joe Worricker was already set up, waiting to assist Fergie in Turkey. Ken had been contacted and put in touch with Colonel Dahabi of GID. Likewise, Fergie had spoken with Emre Fidan of the GDS, and Freddie had had a conversation with Armin Ober, head of the BND. All three men awaited further instructions from the team in Oban Street. They were due to be briefed, by Roberts and Dixson on Monday the 3rd, November. However, an unexpected event took place at Heathrow that would delay the start of operations in Jordan, Turkey, and Germany.

It was a little after 7.00am when Slade took a call from Barry Bonner, the Chief Duty Officer of the UK Border Agency at Heathrow.

'Good morning, Sir. There is something you should be aware of.'

'Carry on, please.'

'A passenger, travelling under the name of Bob Tomlin, whom we know to be deceased, has just passed through our new biometric system.'

'Well, don't hold me in suspense Mr Tomlin, who is he?'

'Face recognition shows him to be Sean Porter. He has flagged up as being of interest to your department, Sir.'

'We are holding him for a document check.'

'How long would that normally take?'

'Around fifteen minutes.'

'Can you delay him for half an hour?'

'We can bang him up. He is travelling on a false passport.'

'I don't want him banged up. Give me ten minutes and I will get back to you.'

Slade legged it upstairs. Only George Dixson was in the ops room.

'George, who do we have at Heathrow, right now?'

'Bob Martin is there. He stays in one of the hospitality suites under the guise of being an Immigration operative, interested in people of concern.'

'Well, it's time he got out of bed as there is certainly someone of great interest there, right now. Get him on the blower, please George.'

'Bob Martin.'

'It's Slade, Bob.'

'Good morning, Sir. How can I help?'

'Your target is in the Immigration holding room, along with several others. In fifteen minutes, we will let him go. You know what to do.'

'Yes, of course, Sir, no worries.'

Slade called Barry Bonner.

'OK, let him go in fifteen minutes. Everything should then be in place. By the way, where has he arrived from?'

'Karachi, Sir.'

'Thank you, Mr Bonner. You have done a good job.'

'Anytime, Sir. Anytime.'

In the holding area, on the other side of passport control, Porter was handed his passport and advised that he was free to leave. This episode had not aroused any suspicion in the head of the former explosive's supplier to the republicans.

On the other side of the mirrored glass in the customs hall, stood Bob Martin. A full-length photograph of Porter, taken whilst he was awaiting the return of his passport, had already been downloaded and sent to the mobile phones of the six operatives under Bob Martin's control. Porter was allowed through Customs without hindrance. Martin followed, at a safe distance. Porter, with a single case, exited the main arrivals door, crossed to the far side of the pick-up area, and got into a dark grey, Ford Galaxy. The Galaxy pulled away, a white Ford Mondeo, driven by Phil Seater, tailed it. The four incumbents of the first-floor room in the house in Oban Street listened intently to the running commentary.

At J23 of the M25, where it meets with the A1, the white Mondeo dropped back. A silver Renault Megane, with John Lew at the wheel, took over. The driver of the Galaxy, Willie Mott seemed to be oblivious to the fact that he was being followed. The covert pursuit was maintained until the Galaxy turned off the M25 and took the A13 towards London. The Megane had been replaced by a cherry red, Ford Focus. Its pilot was the only female member of Bob Martin's team, Annette White. The Galaxy came to rest in Mona Street, Canning Town. Once the home of Porter in his younger days. Porter, suitcase in hand, approached the doorway of number 12. The door opened Porter stepped inside and shook the hand of his son, Mark McBride. The Galaxy pulled away.

At 7.00pm that evening, Porter left the house in Mona Street and walked to the station. He was unaware of the fact that he was being tailed. At 7.20 he stepped from the DLR train at Tower Gateway and two minutes later, walked into the Minories Bar. Sat in the far corner of the bar, in an enclosed seating area, was Nick Pritchard. John Lew entered a few minutes later and stood at the bar. He had no idea that the man that Porter was sat with was Nick Pritchard. He took the photo from his mobile phone as he pretended to talk into it. Seconds later the photo arrived with Bob Martin. Bob did know Pritchard. He was aghast. To think that Pritchard was colluding with Porter was beyond comprehension. Now he began to realise why Slade had taken the operation away from the office. He went outside and lit a cigarette. He did not smoke, but he knew that Slade had to be informed straight away. Carefully watching Pritchard and Porter, through the pub window, Lew called Bob Martin and explained what he had just witnessed. Slade, Griffin, Dixson, and Roberts were eating in the Robin Hood pub, close to Blackwall Tunnel when Dixson took the call. Immediately afterwards, he turned to Slade and said,

'Peter, Porter is currently sat with Pritchard in a pub close to the tower.'

'I knew it. From day one I have had a gut feeling about Mr Pritchard. We must act, quickly George.'

Leaving their unfinished food, the four men returned to Oban Street and sat together in the ops room.

Slade briefed his colleagues on the course of action that he was going to sanction. As one, they nodded in agreement.

'George, call Bob and ask him to make sure that his man sticks to Pritchard like glue.'

'How about Porter, Peter?'

'We know where he is, in fact he is holed up just one mile from where we are now sitting.'

'Graham, please touch base with Ken, Fergie and Freddie and apologise for not giving them our attention today. I shall speak with them tomorrow.'

Slade then descended to his small room downstairs and made the call.

'The target will arrive home later this evening. Make sure you are waiting for him. I am sending his mugshot, along with his address, now. Do it alone. Make it look like suicide. The payment will be left in your usual box at Paddington Station. When the job is done, and you are outside, bend down and tie your shoelaces. Do not call me back.'

Slade returned to the room above and simply said,

'Instructions have been given.'

They all knew what he meant.

In a side Street off Bermondsey High Road, the nephew of one of the UK's most notorious gangsters climbed into a BMW Sports car. Forty minutes later he parked directly outside the Vietnamese Embassy in Victoria Road, Kensington. He pulled the top part of his hoodie over his head, placed the syringe into its plastic holder and took the lock picking tools from his glove compartment. He then walked the half a mile or so to No.10, Kensington Square. Walking past the three-storey building, he saw no sign of life. He turned back and within a minute, he was stood in the hall. Only a small lamp, sat on a half-round table gave any light. He walked around the ground floor and then climbed the stairs to the first and second floors. He touched nothing. He noted that the bedroom of his intended victim was on the first floor. He took the stairs up to the second floor and sat in the armchair that faced out onto the square. It was 9.20pm.

At just after 11.00pm he heard the front door open and then shut. He realised that two people had returned. He was not expecting that. When the commotion of two drunken homosexuals had died down it became obvious to him that they had gone to bed. A long wait lay ahead of him. At 2.30am, he took off his shoes and walked silently down to the first floor. He was thankful for the plush carpets underfoot. The bedroom door was ajar. He pushed it just enough for him to have an uninterrupted view of the bed. Both men were out for the count. The light from the street showed that the youngest of the men was no older than seventeen. It seemed such a shame that he would not see his eighteenth birthday. From his long study of the photo that Slade had sent him, he was certain that his target was the one that was cuddling his young lover. On the bedside table, beside the half-empty whiskey glass, there was a gun, a Mauser. This was his lucky day. Without hesitation, he picked up the gun in his gloved right hand and fired one shot into the head of Nick Pritchard. Even before the gay young man had a chance to react the gun was forced into Pritchard's limp hand and placed firmly against the youngster's skull. The bullet was discharged immediately.

The assassin returned to the second floor and put on his shoes. He tied only the laces on his left foot. As he exited the front door, he bent down and tied the right shoe. He calmly walked back to his car and drove home. John Lew made the call to Bob Martin, who in turn passed on the news to George Dixson. At 3.10am, Graham Roberts opened his finest bottle of Port, and the four men drank to the demise of one horrible bastard, Nick Pritchard. It would be three days before the bodies were found, by a cleaner. The headlines read, 'Gay lovers in suicide pact. ' The story disappeared soon afterwards. Mi5 had done its job. Everyone was happy, except for Sean Porter. His inside man had bit the dust. He knew that he had to leave. He was completely unaware of the fact that he was subject to 24-hour surveillance. He would flee to Belfast, as a passenger, in one of his son's trucks.

On the day after the ending of Pritchard's life, Peter Slade held five long telephone conversations. He spoke to Ken Barrington in Amman. Fergie Hamilton in Ankara. Freddie Forsyth in Frankfurt. Colin Millburn in Sofia and Boris Topolov in Varna. He told each one of them that operation Asani was now live and that they were, at no time, to put themselves in the firing line.

It was 6.00pm when Slade was finally able to sit and talk to his three colleagues. They did not talk about Pritchard, that would be left for another time. What he ran past Dixson, Roberts and Griffin was exactly how were they going to deal with Porter. Roberts suggested that it would serve them best if he could be tailed back to Pakistan and then monitored by the locals, to see where that led to. Griffin announced that he would like that job. Slade shook his head in disagreement. In protest Griffin replied,

'But I am young, unattached and in need of some adventure.'

'OK, I will ask Commander Reeves to talk to the Foreign Secretary. He can then ask his counterpart in Islamabad if they will cooperate. I will do this first thing in the morning. You should prepare yourself Alan as you may have to leave at the drop of a hat.'

'Yes, Mr Slade. I will leave now and then return with everything I need.'

By late afternoon of the following day, Slade had touched base with Pakistan's Federal Investigation Agency (FIA) and its head of operations, a Mr Syed Ali. An agreement was reached, whereby Griffin could operate from within the British High Commission in Karachi. Sean Porter was not mentioned by name. Slade only indicated that his interest was in bringing down the gangs that arranged the trafficking of large numbers of illegal immigrants through Pakistan, enroute to Europe.

Roberts was asked by Slade to urgently seek a diplomatic visa and airline ticket for Griffin. He would leave whether Porter had returned or not.

Slade got hold of Bob Martin and emphasised to him that Porter could not be lost and that he needed to know his every move.

The following day, Ringo walked into the recruitment office close to the borders of Kosovo and Albania. He approached the desk. Before he could utter a word, the Sergeant said,

'Ah, Reagan. You have certainly done your fair share of combat, had you been in a bona-fide army you would no doubt have a string of medals across your chest. You have been accepted into the General's family, although I must warn you, there are several thousand members. Can you go to the machine in the corner and place your hand, flat, upon the glass?'

Jim Reagan did exactly as he was instructed and then returned to the counter.

'Here is your ID, you may be asked to show this on many occasions. You are now ready to enter Fort Knox. Your previous exploits afford you the rank of Captain. There are twenty-one others with that rank. The General has been informed of your past record and he may wish to seek you out. There again, knowing Kos, he might just put a bullet into you. Your existence here is really, just on a day-to-day basis. Just cross the road and place your hand upon the glass plate on the wall. Welcome to the madhouse.'

Ringo had undertaken tasks that had brought him to the point of death on several occasions. He viewed his arrival at the camp of General Kos as being a simple adventure. He would find out in the coming weeks whether that assumption was correct. What he did know, for sure, was that the CV that had been compiled for him by George Dixson, had, without doubt been responsible for his seamless entry into the world's most dangerous army barracks. He had memorised every single detail that had been written about him. He fully expected to be quizzed as to its authenticity.

Now inside the complex, he was saluted by everyone he first met. He was given three sets of fatigues. All were those of the rank of a Captain. A golf cart took him from the stores, up a hill, down a dip and then straight for about half a mile. He came to a stop on a tarmac square, surrounded on three sides by well-built, wooden huts. His driver, a corporal, left his seat and saluted. Picking up the uniforms and boots, the corporal asked that General Kos' newest Captain follow him. They stepped up from the tarmac and onto the raised entrance to the hut. The corporal opened the door and allowed Captain Jim Reagan to enter first. Laid on the bed in the left-hand corner was a very, large man. He stood and held out his hand. Reagan shook it.

'I am Captain Valeri Popov, once a Colonel in the Bulgarian National Guard, but nowadays a lowly Captain that watches life, go by, without much action.'

'I am..........'

'We know who you are Reagan, your notoriety proceeds you.'

'I had no idea that I was famous, Captain.'

'You are English, you have fought everywhere in the world. You have commanded within the SAS. Did you not think that would get you noticed?'

'Well, all of that is in the past. I am here just to do a job and take the money. Just like you, no doubt.'

Sean Porter exited a car in the yard of McBride's trucking and warehousing business adjacent to Haydock Park racecourse. It was a little after 5.30pm on Friday the 7th of November 2008. Porter climbed onto the step of a DAF truck and entered the passenger seat. The driver, Patsy O'Hagan, acknowledged his arrival with a nod. He had been told that his job was to get his hitchhiker to Belfast, no questions asked. He would do exactly as he had been told. John Lew, driven by his colleague, Stephen Lazelle, had followed the car, with Mack McBride at the wheel, from Canning Town. He was certain that he had not been compromised. Lew did not enter the yard. Lazelle had parked up 100 yards further down the road and then walked back until he was close enough to get a good view as the truck left the yard and turned left, towards him. He snapped several times on his phone and immediately sent the pictures to Bob Martin. Less than a minute later Martin sent the pictures onto Graham Roberts. Roberts picked up his phone and called Neil McCleod, an old friend and now head of operations at Birkenhead Port.

'Neil, can you do me a favour?'

'Depends upon what it is Graham.'

Giving over the registration of the truck, Roberts asked,

'I just need to know what crossing this vehicle is booked on.'

McCleod tapped his keyboard and replied,

'This evening's sailing. Leaves at 21.45.'

'Many thanks, Neil. I owe you one.'

'Any time Graham, take care.'

Roberts brought up Stena Line on his computer and booked one ticket, to collect prior to departure, for Stephen Lazelle. He then called Brendan Brady at the Northern Ireland Security Services and asked that he arrange for the collection of Lazelle from Belfast Port at around 5.45am the following morning and that he should let him know the make, colour, and registration of the car. Roberts gave Brady the reg number of the truck and asked that it be identified when rolling off the ferry and then be followed to its, final, destination. Brady agreed to all the requests.

Having firstly identified Porter, keeping him, within vision, all the time, Lazelle then spent the next eight hours gazing out at a dark grey, choppy Irish sea. Only the occasional light of a passing ship broke up what would otherwise have been the most tedious of journeys.

Just after 6.00am Lazelle was sat beside a man that gave his name, simply as Brian.

'We have to follow the McBride truck when it leaves the Port.'

'OK, no problem. Should be a piece of cake.'

Several trucks, all pulling forty-foot trailers behind them, passed the dark blue fiesta, in which sat Brian and Stephen Lazelle. Brian spotted the McBride truck in his mirror and alerted his passenger. Lazelle could see that there was a driver and a passenger, although the passenger was slumped against the heavily misted-up window.

'OK, shall we go, Brian?'

The fiesta filed into the line of trucks. It was three trailers back from the target. By the time they reached the third roundabout the other trucks had taken alternative routes, the fiesta was now directly behind the McBride vehicle.

In the meantime, seven other McBride trucks had left the ship. Porter was the passenger in the fourth of them. The truck pulled into a service station just outside Belfast Ferry Terminal. Porter got into a black Range Rover and was driven the five miles to George Best International Airport. One hour later, travelling under the name of Vincent McBride, he boarded a flight to Manchester. George Best Airport offered no biometric checks. From Manchester Porter flew to Amsterdam and then on to Karachi. He exited the airport in Karachi and took a taxi to the Pearl Continental Hotel in the City Centre.

By mid-morning on Saturday, Bob Martin informed George Dixson that Porter had been lost. Slade vented his anger upon Martin, one of his senior team members. Martin, in turn reprimanded John Lew and Stephen Lazelle. Spooks, Roberts' dog, who had come to stay at Oban Street, for the weekend, did not escape Slade's wrath. He received a sharp kick up the rear and cowered in the corner for most of the day afterwards.

Griffin, primed and ready for action, in Pakistan, was informed of the fact that Porter had escaped through the net and that, at that time, they had no idea as to his whereabouts.

Once recomposed, Slade held an informal meeting with Roberts and Dixson. He conceded that, whilst glaring errors had been made by those responsible for tailing Porter, he also acknowledged that Porter himself was a master of escapism. He had spent the best part of his life on the run. He was now sixty-four years old and had learnt to be one step ahead of the game. Between them, they concluded that it was most likely that he had returned to Pakistan, where he felt safe. They also agreed that he had not travelled using the passport that had been produced upon entry to the UK several days previously. Dixson was given the task of asking the relevant authorities in Pakistan to release the names of all passenger arrivals, from, European Airports, to Karachi during the period of Saturday the 8th and Sunday the 9th of November. This request was to be made, by George Dixson first thing on Monday the 10th November.

30 - THE STITCH UP

Five days after his entry into Fort Knox, Captain Jim Reagan was summoned to meet with the General himself. His roommate, another Captain, by the name of, Valeri Popov, drove him, in a golf cart, on the one-mile journey from his barracks to the Generals Villa, the likes of which Reagan had never seen before. They entered the grounds of Hotel California. Tanks adorned the massive square that fronted the building. Two men stood on the flagstone area immediately in front of the covered outer room of this magnificent villa.

For the previous four days, Reagan had spent almost all his time at the side of Popov, whose task it was to acclimatise the most recent of the General's Captains to the procedures and daily workings of the platoon that would soon be under Reagan's control. Until now there had been no mention of drugs, arms or people smuggling and Reagan was not about to trip himself up by asking.

'Captain Reagan, welcome to the General's humble abode. I am Captain Hook.'

Jim Reagan had already clocked the fact that Hook's right hand was missing.

'This, my friend, is General Kos.'

The General, a striking specimen of a man, standing six-foot-six tall and weighing at least one hundred and ten kilos, did not step forward. He simply retreated inside the Villa. In a terracotta floor-tiled holding room, situated prior to entering the main part of the Villa, Kos beckoned for Reagan to sit. At this point, Popov snapped his heels together and retreated. He mounted the golf cart and was gone. Reagan was now on his own. Alone with one of the world's most notorious renegades and his righthand man. Or, as Reagan chuckled to himself, his left-hand man. A beautiful Asian-looking girl entered the room. She placed cups, coffee and tea upon the hand-carved wooden table that was surrounded, on three sides by luxurious leather, two-seater sofas.

'Please sit Captain.' The words were spoken by Hook. Kos had not yet uttered a word.

'Thank you, Captain Hook.'

Regan wondered if there had ever been a Monty Python sketch involving two Captains and a General.

His thoughts were cut short by the General's first words –

'So, you are one of the world's greatest fighters, Reagan.'

'I would not say that General. I have just always had good men by my side.'

'Why do you come to my army?'

'I have heard that you are involved in many battles, and I have little money these days.'

'But your own Government are fighting wars with their American friends, why not join them?'

'I am too old General. I am in my mid-forties. I would not get a battle posting.'

'Well, I have read your file. I see that you were part of the SAS that took Stevan Modric in 1998. Captain Hook was in Zlatibor at the time. Tell me what happened.'

Without hesitation, Regan responded.

'Oh, you mean, operation ensue?'

'Yes, we do.' Replied Captain Hook.

'There were four of us. I was chosen as I spoke fluent Serbian, as did my three comrades. The US had identified Modric as being holed up in a cabin in the woods. We entered the cabin, there was no resistance. We bound and gagged our target, loaded him into our vehicle and drove to the Drina River. We drugged him and put him into an inflatable and crossed the water. We carried him for two miles, he was then put into a Bosnian chopper and flown to Tuzla, where he was formally charged with war crimes. This was one of the few operations that was leaked to the press. This was done in order that the Serbs knew they had nowhere to hide.'

The General looked at Hook, Hook nodded in acknowledgement.

The General then spoke to Reagan in his native tongue, Serbian.

Regan responded, without hesitation. The General was impressed.

'And how about the night of the 16th, June 2003? Tell us about that Captain.'

'Yes. This was a joint operation between G Squadron of the SAS and B Squadron, Delta Force. We were tasked with capturing, Lieutenant-General Abid Hamid Mahmud, number four in the command of Saddam Hussien. We conducted a helicopter and ground assault upon his base in Tikrit. There were no casualties, on either side.'

Again, Kos looked to Hook for a response.

'I was there Reagan. I was fighting for the Iraqis. I witnessed the whole thing. A brilliant job. You have my respect.'

General Kos stood and indicated that Captain Reagan should follow him.

'We shall take dinner together Captain Reagan. Tomorrow you will accompany Popov on a much less dangerous mission than you are used to.'

After dinner, Reagan asked if he was free to walk back to his barracks. In reply, the General said,

'You my friend, are free to walk anywhere you like.'

It had not gone unnoticed by Reagan that CCTV cameras were visible throughout the compound.

At 5.00am the following morning, Popov dropped an AK-47 onto Reagan's chest as he lay in bed.

'Come, my friend. Today is your first payday.'

Twenty minutes later, a dark green army jeep took the two Captains to a square about two miles from their billet. On the square were twenty-two, fully armed soldiers. There were two Sergeants, two corporals and eighteen privates. Three choppers straddled the edge of the square.

Popov addressed the men.

'This is Captain Jim Reagan. Known to you all as Sir. He has fought more battles alone, than all of you put together. You will follow his orders, always.'

Three groups of eight men climbed into the waiting choppers. The flight from the complex to a point just East of Plovdiv, Bulgaria, took one hour and twenty minutes. They landed, one by one, inside a heavily fortified ancient fort. Each chopper was refuelled and left shortly afterwards. Inside the fort there were hundreds of men, women, and children. All were civilians.

As they sat, at the edge of the hot and dusty courtyard, drinking coffee. Regan asked Popov a question, a question that he already knew the answer to.

'Who are all of these people?'

Popov smiled, before replying –

'They are our wages, Jim. When the sun goes down today, we shall escort them to the border with Romania and hand them over to our gypsy friends.'

At 5.30pm, with the sun disappearing into the horizon and with a distinct chill in the air, 150 immigrants were lined up, facing the large wooden gates, that when opened would allow them access to the next part of their journey. Reagan and Popov were at the front of the well, organised queue. At intervals, on either side of the column there was a Sergeant, followed by nine privates, followed by a corporal. All carried rucksacks as large as their own torsos. Four donkeys carried several large saddle bags each.

'How long is the march?' Asked Reagan.

'Normally about three days.'

'How about stragglers?'

'If they are too weak, they are helped by their friends. If they die, then the vultures have a feast.'

During the first hours of the trek, Popov would continually stop and wait for the whole line to pass him by. He would then make his way back to the front. This gave Reagan the chance to strike up some conversations. It took him only a short while to realise that there were several nationalities amongst those looking for their freedom in the West. Regan was well-versed in Arab languages. At first, he was careful only to make passing remarks to those that were closest to him. At midnight and after six hours of non-stop walking, they finally rested. This gave Reagan the chance to remark to his fellow Captain that there were, Pakistanis, Afghans, Iranians, Iraqis, Syrians, and Turks among the people that they were escorting to the Romanian border.

'What happens to them when we hand them over?'

Regan was careful not to make his questioning seem official in any way. His quizzing was interspersed with humour.

'As far as I know, they are loaded onto trucks at Ruse, offloaded near Bucharest and then reloaded and transported to Budapest. From there they are distributed throughout Europe.'

'How many make it?'

'About eighty percent make it to Romania, after that I do not know, but nobody cares, as they have already paid.'

Reagan decided to suspend his questioning. He would have plenty of opportunities to continue. He did not want Popov to become suspicious of him.

After one hour's rest, the march continued. The only light was that which came from the moon. It was a clear night, and the terrain was mainly flat, which would be the case until they reached the foothills of the Balkans.

A Pakistani, man, was now at the head of the file, Popov was busy talking to one of the Sergeants at the rear. This, together with the cover of darkness, gave Reagan the opportunity to strike up a conversation. The Pakistani spoke good English.

'So, where have you come from?'

'I am from Lahore.'

'When did you leave.'

'What is the date now?'

'It is November 21st, 2008.'

'I left my home on the 19th of August.'

'You mean you have been on the road for over three months?'

'Yes, it must be if it is now November.'

'Have you walked the whole time?'

'No, after my family paid the money, a man came to my house and took me, in a car, all the way to Karachi. I believed I would be flown, from there, to Europe. I did not care where I ended up.'

'What happened when you arrived in Karachi?'

'I was held in a warehouse for about ten days. There were lots of other people. Not just my fellow countrymen, but others, from India, Burma, Vietnam, Cambodia, there were many from China.'

'Do you know how much your family paid?'

'I believe my uncle handed over about ten thousand US Dollars. We had to pay in dollars.'

'Where is your next destination?'

'I do not know. None of us know. We just keep walking. We have nothing, other than the clothes we have on our backs. We are given one small bottle of water each day and we eat in the morning and at 4.00pm.'

Reagan, realising that Popov was now almost within hearing distance ceased his conversation.

As Captain Popov drew level with him, Reagan asked -

'Have you ever encountered any problems when on these marches?

'No, never. Nobody would dare mess with the General, Mr Reagan.'

'You are free to transfer these people whenever you like, then?'

'Yes, four times each month there is a march. Today we have 150, other times we can have as many as 300. It depends very much on how many our friends can send to us.'

'So, why are there so many men at the barracks if only this amount is required for the job?'

'I think you are slipping my friend. There are up to 40 different routes. Some begin in Bulgaria, some in Romania and Albania, others in Greece, Macedonia, Belarus and even from the Ukraine. We do not ever go East. The Turks look after everything from as far away as China. We take care of everyone that is delivered to Bulgaria. Over 1,500 of the Generals men are needed just to control that. The whole thing is massive. I am told it is much more rewarding than doing drugs, or arms and with much less risk.'

Reagan did not ask any more at this time, however he quietly worked out in his head that if the 150 illegals on this march had all paid USD10,000 then a total of USD1.5 million would have changed hands. That equates to USD6 million per month and if that same income was derived from all 40 routes, then it was feasible to assume that over USD240 million could be amassed each and every month of the year.

Back in London, Willie Mott was still upset by the death of his boss, Nick Pritchard. He was certain that Peter Slade was involved in the demise of a man that he not only admired but was also in love with. Mott obtained a file on Slade that included all his past activities. He was now trying, to make contact, with a certain, Billy Gardner, once a Chief Superintendent under Slade when he ran Special Operations from New Scotland Yard.

On Monday 10th, November 2008, George Dixson, following protocol, had asked the International Division of the UK Border Agency, once Nick Pritchard's department, to formally request the release of the names of all arrivals into Pakistan from European Airports. Some ten days later Dixson still awaited a response.

Ken Barrington had now been in Amman for two weeks and was in daily contact with Colonel Dahibi. He had already given over a substantial amount of information that had been gathered from the previous operations of Peter Slade and his team. That information was mainly in respect of the drugs, arms, and tobacco dealings of Monzer Asmar, Tayser Malik and Tamara Jamal. It had been agreed that Dahabi would not act until it was certain that the whole of the people smuggling network within Syria, Jordan, Afghanistan, and Pakistan could be taken down. To arrest the three on non-smuggling charges would simply leave it open for others to take over.

Fergie Hamilton in Ankara, and his assistant, Joe Worricker in Istanbul had already begun trading information with Emre Fidan and the GDS. It had been revealed to Hamilton that Birusk Gul and Altan Akar were meeting, on a regular basis in Mardin and that the two had flown, by private jet, to Varna in Bulgaria. Topolov had reported that they were now frequently meeting up with Boyan Petrov. Fidan was keen to apprehend both Gul and Akar on drug-related charges. Hamilton convinced him to hold fire until the whole operation could be melted into one, which, if played out correctly could bring the world's largest and most organised people smuggling operation tumbling down. Fidan had agreed to Hamilton's request. At least for the time being.

Freddie Forsyth, in Frankfurt, was having similar problems with Armin Ober at the BND. The information given to Ober from the files that Slade had compiled when pursuing Gul and his family members during the previous investigation was more than enough to apprehend both the family and a considerable drug-running empire. Forsyth convinced Ober to hold fire until all sections of their current investigation were in place. There was a view, shared by Forsyth and the others that should any of their cooperatives, act, unilaterally, then operation 'Asani' could be dead in the water. Timing was of the essence. It would only take one, over-eager commander, acting alone, to bring the whole thing crashing down. Forsyth put in a request that Slade should speak to his counterparts and convince them to wait until they were all singing off the same hymn sheet.

Millburn, in Sofia, had reported that Vo Van Hiep was seen to have checked into Petrov's Hotel in Varna.

On the 22nd of November the Pakistani Immigration Services finally released the inbound passenger manifests for the period that had been requested. There were hundreds of pages. Three days after receipt of the logs,

Griffin discovered that a certain Vincent McBride had arrived in Karachi via a domestic flight from Islamabad. Griffin, having previously read everything that he could find in respect of Sean Porter, had remembered that Porter had spawned twin sons. The sons had taken their mother's name after having been abandoned by their father.

Griffin then asked Mr Syed Ali, head of the FIA in Islamabad to arrange the release of any CCTV from both Islamabad and Karachi Airports that might be applicable to spotting McBride at the times that he would most likely be picked up by the cameras.

Two days after receipt of the CCTV records, Porter: aka McBride could clearly be seen exiting Karachi Airport and getting into a white Mercedes taxi.

Having released this information to Mr Ali, it was confirmed to Griffin, within twenty-four hours, that McBride had been dropped off at the Pearl Continental Hotel. Before Griffin could send the formal request for surveillance, Ali confirmed that McBride was being watched 24/7 and that 'they' would not lose him.

Peter Slade, constantly collating every snippet of information, with the help of both George Dixson and Graham Roberts, was convinced that they were on track to bring down the largest people smuggling operation in the world. He just had to make sure that none of the people that had agreed to take part in this operation, would attempt to go it alone and consequently, fuck it up for everyone concerned. Of all the worries that he had at that time, one stuck out, like a sore thumb, over all the rest.

He had not heard from Ringo for over a month, and he had no way of either contacting or rescuing him from imminent danger. He needed to know what his position was. Had he managed to infiltrate the Generals inner sanctum as he had mentioned in his last, short message? And if so, what had he learnt? The General was potentially the major player in the people smuggling business, without his participation all the others would be struggling to move their prey from the war-torn and deprived countries from which they evolved. Without news from Ringo, he would be gambling, as to the success of operation 'Asani.
'

By the end of November, Captain Jim Reagan had just finished his third tour of duty. He had, together with Captain Valeri Popov successfully moved over 550 destitute souls from Plovdiv, in central Bulgaria to its border with Romania. Not a shot had been fired in anger, however seventeen of those that had paid a King's ransom for the privilege of being herded, like sheep, across several hostile countries, had perished along the way. On his return to camp, Reagan was informed by Captain Hook that he would be leading the next convoy, without the help of Popov as he, would be tackling a different route.

Popov left on that same day to lead yet another column of people, from Plovdiv to Ruse.

On Saturday, 29th, November, Captain Jim Reagan boarded the bus outside Fort Knox and arrived at the border gate fifty minutes later. Reagan clocked the bright yellow dodge pickup that belonged to the Mexican, strode over to it and threw his backpack onto the back seat.

'Home James.'

Thirty minutes later, at 6.45am to be precise, the dodge came to a half outside Café XL. Reagan paid the small, leathery-skinned sombrero-wearing driver and took a seat just outside the door of the building. A waitress came over and took his breakfast order. He had never frequented the Café at this time of day and therefore, he knew no one and no one knew him, or so he thought.

After devouring the best food that he had consumed for nearly a month, he hitched the rucksack onto his back and set out on the two-mile journey to the home of his lover, Adrijana.

Upon opening the door to the shack, that he had done his best to repair, he was not greeted by the outstretched arms of the woman that had confessed to loving him, instead she held aloft a mobile phone and asked –

'Who, have you been messaging Jim?'

Those were to be the last words that Captain Jim Reagan, alias Ringo, ever heard.

From behind him, a single shot penetrated the back of his skull. He died instantly.

'Good work, Adrijana. The General will be very, pleased.'

The words were spoken by Captain Hook.

Ringo could have had no idea that Adrijana was Hook's girlfriend and that she had lured others into her sinister web of deceit. The outcome had always been the same as Captain Jim Reagan's. Death.

Hook took the phone from the trembling Adrijana and left. Three men entered, gathered up Regan's lifeless body and bundled it onto the open back of a bright yellow dodge. The Mexican sang loudly as he disappeared along a dirt track of a road. Stopping after a mile, he backed the dodge up against an open wooden fence and dragged the body until it fell into the filth and mud that made up the pigpen. Within seconds, several wild boars feasted, noisily, upon their own breakfast.

Hook walked into the living area of the Villa and sat next to the General. He turned on the phone, revealing the last text message to have been sent. It read -

'About to enter the inner sanctum. '

'So, whoever our friend was working for, they would expect to receive another message. Would you agree Hook?'

'Without doubt, my General.'

'Then let us not disappoint them.'

The General, not being that good with communications, asked his number one Captain to send the following –

'Nothing to report, all quiet here. Having dinner with the General. '

'That should satisfy their expectations, whomever they are.'

In Oban Street, Slade immediately hit the button on the phone. He read the message and then legged it upstairs as fast as he could.

'We have a problem. Ringo is in trouble.'

'How do you know, Peter?' Asked a concerned Graham Roberts.

'Well, encrypted into this phone are three numbers. These must be input before sending a message. To show that it is bona-fide. The numbers do not show on the sender's device however they show on mine and this time they are not there. Someone has Ringo's phone.'

'Where is he, Peter?'

'His last message, which included the three digits, indicated that he had managed to get himself entrenched into the compound of General Kos. If they have his phone, then we can assume that he is no longer with us.'

'What can we do Peter?'

'That is the problem. We can do nothing. This was a clandestine operation. Ringo, as you know, preferred to work alone. This is a major setback for operation Asani. I need time to gather my thoughts, please excuse me for a while.'

Slade returned to the secure downstairs room, sat at his schoolboy-sized desk, and buried his head into his hands. His thoughts were all about the fact that he had been responsible for the death, of yet another of his schoolboy friends. This time it had been made decidedly worse by the fact that he was not one hundred percent certain of Ringo's demise and even if he were, how had it happened, where did it happen and would he, or anyone else for that matter, ever be able to mourn his death, or to know where his body lay. Without his knowledge, things would turn decidedly worse for Peter Slade before the day ended.

In a basement bar in the Earls Court area of London, Willie Mott sat patiently waiting for his date to arrive. At ten minutes past seven in the evening, Billy Gardner, Chief Superintendent when under the command of Peter Slade, walked into the bar.

Mott stood and shook Gardner's hand. Gardner knew instinctively that the young man was Gay. Taking a file from his soft leather briefcase, Mott invited the ex, Scotland Yard man to peruse it. Peruse it he did.

'Well.' Asked Mott.

'It's all true. Our man was not only bent, he, was responsible for the death of that young Sergeant.'

'So, tell me, in your own words what really happened.'

'Slade was my boss, he projected an aura of being completely squeaky clean, however he was on the take. A major crime lord was paying him not to investigate him. They came up with the idea of framing someone to take the can for several unsolved crimes. Slade found a small-time petty crook that he would set up to take the fall. He assigned a newly promoted female Sergeant, to work undercover. The fall guy, the one you have a photo of in your file, was Oliver Bailey, known as dodger on the streets. Slade encouraged the officer to seduce him and extract all kinds of confessions from him. These taped confessions were then edited and made to sound authentic. Bailey sussed out what was happening and murdered the young copper. Slade was dragged over the coals and then disappeared for a while, but no action was ever taken against him. Fuck knows what happened to him.'

'I will tell you what happened to him, he arranges the murder of anyone that crosses him. He is alive and well and working at the highest level and, with your help, I intend to take him down.'

The following morning, Mott sat in an upmarket bistro in Chelsea. His companion was Terry Wheeler, a gay junior minister within the Home Office. The two had enjoyed several evenings of pleasure together. Mott outlined the conversation that he had had with Billy Gardner the previous evening and asked that Wheeler share this discussion with the Home Secretary. On Monday morning, the 1st of December 2008, Wheeler relayed the story to the first private secretary of the Home Secretary. It would take another ten days before the Home Secretary was made aware of it.

With Ringo now off-line, Slade decided that he must act fast. His worry was that General Kos could alert others within the organisation to the fact that a mole could possibly have exposed their operation. For the next two days Slade discussed with Dixson and Roberts the options that were available, in order, to initiate the actions that must be taken if they were to have any chance of taking out the main players before they were able to change tactics. Any strike must be coordinated with his counterparts in each of the countries that were cooperating with them. As he pondered his next move, Slade took a call from Colin Millburn in Sofia.

'Peter, I have some news. Topolov has informed me that one of Monzer Asmar's trucks has been found abandoned on the bridge that straddles the Danube at the point where it crosses the Bulgarian-Romanian border. Asmar has a large warehousing complex in the Eastern Industrial Zone alongside the

Port. There were 76 dead bodies inside the trailer, made up of several nationalities.'

'Well, I suppose this is not the first time this has happened. How did Topolov get this information?'

'That is the interesting part of the news. A man claiming to be Captain Valeri Popov has handed himself in to the American Embassy in Bucharest. He claims to have been working with a Captain Jim Reagan, an Englishman. The only Englishman he has ever known to be working with General Kos.'

It was at this point that Slade informed Millburn of the situation surrounding Ringo.

'You must get to Bucharest Colin. You have, to interview this man. I will clear this with the Yanks. Do not forget to take a photo of Ringo with you. Treat this man as a friendly. Can you be there by tomorrow?'

'Yes, I can drive there.'

'Good man. Be careful Colin.'

'Indeed, I will, Peter.'

On Wednesday, the 4th of December, Slade made contact, with each of his overseas team. This time he telephoned from the upstairs, operations room in Oban Street. He wanted to ensure that both Dixson and Roberts were up to date with events, as they happened, as he had no time in which to brief them later in the day.

Separately, he spoke to Griffin in Karachi, Barrington in Amman, Hamilton in Ankara, whom he asked should share the conversation with Joe Worricker in Istanbul. Finally, he jointly spoke to Millburn and Topolov in Bulgaria. He had informed them all of Ringo's disappearance and that, based on that information he felt that all targets should be hit within the next ten days. He asked each man to share his intentions with the heads of the various Government bodies that were assisting them and that, should any of them have a problem, they were free to call him directly. He thought long and hard before deciding not to include Bob Martin in the loop. Martin was ultimately responsible for losing the surveillance on Sean porter. In his head, Slade could not understand how one of the very, best undercover operatives ever to work in vice had lost his man. In his gut, he simply had a feeling that something was amiss. Martin had resumed his role at Heathrow and Slade was content to leave him there.

The following morning, Millburn arrived at the American Embassy in Bucharest. He presented himself at the window that fronted the street in sector 1 of the Romanian Capital. He simply gave his name and showed his passport, normally all that was required, in order, to gain entry, if pre-cleared. There was a problem, Millburn's name did not appear on the computer screen of the American that was on the other side of the glass.

'Sorry, Sir. Your name does not show on our list for today.'

Millburn stepped back from the window. Another visitor took his place. He walked to the junction, his own, British Embassy was within his sight. Out of anyone's earshot, he called Charlie Tucker, a lifelong associate and currently deputy Ambassador.

'Charlie, I have a problem.'

'Something you would like me to fix, old chap?'

'Yes, very much so.'

Millburn then explained why he was there and whom he wished to meet with. Ten minutes later, Tucker left the British Embassy and shook his old friend's hand. Together they approached the window of the US Embassy. Tucker held aloft his diplomatic passport and beckoned for Millburn to do the same. The turnstile was released and both men entered the compound. Inside the building. Tucker's counterpart, Tom Huddlestone, was waiting in the hallway.

'How can I help, Charlie?'

'Mr Millburn here should have a pre-clearance to meet with and interview a 'walk-in'.'

'Well, we have received a request, from London, however clearance has not yet been granted.'

'Can you make it happen, Tom? It is of the utmost urgency.'

'The problem Charlie, is that the Ambassador is out of station and will not be back until tomorrow afternoon.'

'Then, my dear friend, you will have to exert your authority, in his absence. You do have that authority, do you not.'

'I do indeed, however the CIA wish to be the first to question the subject, which makes it extremely difficult for me to grant you your wish.'

'Many lives may depend on us getting access to this man, Tom.'

'In that case I will see what I can do. Can you wait in the holding room? I will return shortly.'

One hour later, after having made several calls to Washington DC, Huddlestone returned.

'Gentlemen, please follow me.'

The three men entered a room, the interior of which was grey. A medium-sized steel desk sat in the middle of the room. Four grey, plastic chairs surrounded it. A single, armed guard stood, bolt upright in one corner of the room. Huddlestone gestured to him, and he left. Sat at the table, dressed in the uniform of a Serbian soldier was Valeri Popov.

Millburn, Tucker and Huddlestone joined the captain the table.

'I am Colin Millburn, attached to the British Embassy in Sofia. This is Charlie Tucker, stationed here in Bucharest and to my left is Tom Huddlestone, deputy US Ambassador, here in Bucharest. I would like to talk to you about someone of interest to us.'

'If you are referring to General Horatio Kos, then go ahead. I know much about him.'

'Actually. It is not the General that we wish to discuss with you, at least not at this moment in time.'

'Who then?'

Millburn opened the blue manila file and removed five A5-size photographs. One by one he placed them on, the otherwise empty desk.

'Are you familiar with any of these faces?'

'These four I do not know of. But this one, I do know. It is Captain Jim Reagan. A most revered fighter and someone that I have recently had the pleasure to have met.'

'Where have you met him, Valeri?'

'I have known him for a little over a month. We led a group together.'

'A group?'

'Yes, a large group of illegals. We escorted them through Bulgaria and handed them over at the border.'

'And from whom do you take your orders?'

'From the General of course. But then you already know this.'

'Why have you decided to turn up here, in the US Embassy?'

'Because it would be unsafe for me to have turned to the Bulgarian, Romanian or any other of the corrupt Governments in this part of the world.'

'And where is Jim Reagan now?'

'I left him at the barracks. He made his way back to Prizren, Kosovo. He was due two days R & R. I did my next tour of duty and decided to call it a day when I realised that all our cargo was dead.'

'Dead, Valeri?'

'Yes. 76 poor souls. They were locked into a sealed refrigerated truck in the yard of Trust Forwarding in Ruse. One of our men, stationed in Ruse told me before I was due to return to Plovdiv. I boarded the truck and drove it to the Romanian side of the bridge. Which is where I left it, knowing that it would cause maximum grief to the authorities, and more importantly, the General. I flagged down a small van, at gunpoint and drove the 80 km to Bucharest. Since I have been here, I have seen the story being broadcast on all the news stations.'

'You have indeed caused quite a stir, Valeri. We would like to transfer you to the British Embassy, however before that can happen the Americans may wish to quiz you on other matters.'

'I understand. I have no allegiance to either of you. I do not agree with what the General is doing these days. He used to be a fighter, like me. Now he is a babysitter, killing innocent people. I just wanted out. One last thing, Reagan told me of his love for a girl named Adrijana in Prizren. She is known to almost everyone at the barracks. They would all have liked to have been her lover. She is in fact the lover of Captain Hook, the General's most trusted soldier.'

'OK. We must leave now. My superiors will sort out the protocol for your transfer, it may take some time. Depending on the American's interest in you. Goodbye, for now, Valeri.'

'Yes, goodbye Mr Millburn.'

Millburn returned, with Huddlestone, to the British Embassy. He then, made contact, with Slade in London and briefed him accordingly.

From the briefing, Slade, Dixson, and Roberts deduced that Ringo had fallen into a trap. A trap spawned out of lust. He would neither be the first or the last to have succumbed to the charms of a pretty woman.

One week after learning of Ringo's disappearance, Slade decided that it would be folly to wait much longer to finalise operation Asani. He knew that he would not be able to bring down the General, holed up as he was, in the most secure place on earth. However, Topolov had reported that Boyan Petrov had not been seen for days and his capture, or demise, was an integral part of the operation. Elsewhere, everything was in place.

On the 11th of December, at his morning briefing with the Home Secretary, Terry Wheeler finally brought to her attention the summary of events that had been given to him by Willie Mott. As soon as she heard the name, Peter Slade, the Home Secretary gave her underling her full attention. Slade had managed to outwit Nick Pritchard time and time again. Pritchard had been given the job at the UK Border Agency simply to monitor Slade's progress in bringing down the major players in the illegal movement of people into the UK. The Home Secretary was certain that Slade had arranged Pritchard's murder, albeit the official word was that he had taken his own life.

'Where is Slade now?' She asked Wheeler.

'That is the problem, Home Secretary. We do not know.'

'OK, on your way out, send in Smales.'

Kevin Smales was the Home Secretary's press secretary. He entered the room. The Home Secretary put her finger to her lips and beckoned Smales to follow her.

On the roof of the building in Marsham Street, the same building that both Pritchard and Slade had occupied, she asked Smales the following –

'Do you still have the ear of the cronies that run the nationals? And if so, can we get the front pages tomorrow?

'It's a yes to both questions, Home Secretary.'

'Take this file and compile a story that will almost certainly bring our man out into the open.'

'Consider it done, Home Secretary.'

The following morning, George Dixson was the first of the three men into the kitchen of 38 Oban Street. He lifted the two newspapers from the coconut mat that was placed on top of the hallway carpet and fell back against the wall.

'Fuck' me, he whispered to himself. The headlines read –

'Top Cop behind Irene Wastell's death.' The sub-headlines went on –

'Peter Slade used young officer as honeytrap in the framing of petty crook, Oliver Bailey.'

'Slade remains on active duty but has gone to ground.'

Dixson made the tea and waited upstairs until Slade and Roberts emerged from their nests.

Peter Slade, a man of the highest repute, who had risked life and limb for his country on many occasions was absolutely shattered by what he was reading. Looking at the others, Slade announced -

'I am handing myself in.'

He called James Reeves.

'Commander, have you seen the papers?'

'Yes, I have Peter. I know there is no truth in this. They want you, that is all there is to it. The Home Secretary has asked me to find you and bring you in.'

'Thank you, James. Can you arrange a brief for me? Let me know where and when and I shall be there.'

Dixson, in full agreement with Slade's decision, asked –

'How about the operation, Peter?'

'Let me clear this up and then we shall resume. Just delay until Petrov shows up.'

'OK. That is a good enough reason.'

At 3.00pm that afternoon, Slade, and Reeves entered the London Wall offices of the UK's foremost solicitors.

Rupert Thwaites, the most senior partner and one time University chum of James Reeves asked Slade a direct question.

'Is there any truth in the allegations?'

'No, none, at all.'

'Then I shall ask for a meeting with the powers that be before they can get up a head of steam.'

'That's it? Asked Slade.

'Yes, Mr Slade. I needed to ask you the question, face-to-face as it were. I now know where to go.'

'So, what happens next?'

'Today is Friday. I shall arrange a meeting for Monday. Are you available?'

'Yes, of course.'

'Then, I shall be in contact. And do not worry, Peter. We shall take them to the cleaners.'

Early on Monday morning, Slade received confirmation from Topolov that Petrov had re-emerged. He had been seen stepping ashore from his super yacht in Varna Harbour.

Slade told Dixson and Roberts -

'This will have to wait until I return. I am meeting with the Home Secretary and the head of New Scotland Yard at mid-day.'

At noon on Monday 15th December 2008, Peter Slade, his brief, Rupert Thwaites, James Reeves, Terry Wheeler, on behalf of the Home Secretary and Carol Webb, the new head of Special Branch, sat in one of the meeting rooms at 2 Marsham Street. Carol Webb read out the allegations against Slade and reminded him that he need not answer any of the questions.

Rupert Thwaites, speaking on Slade's behalf denied all the allegations and asked as to whom had made them. That information was not forthcoming.

Carol Webb made a brief statement, in which she confirmed that at the time of Irene Wastell's death a thorough investigation had been launched and at least two informants had implicated Slade. Slade himself went undercover whilst the investigation was in full swing. He came close to death during his time in Germany and received commendations for his work. The file was slipped to the bottom of the pile. Only now, with yet another informant have we decided to re-investigate his part in the operation that saw an innocent man charged with offences that he did not commit. This falsehood led to the death of the young female police sergeant. We have absolute grounds to charge Peter Slade with complicity in the murder of his former colleague. We shall not charge him today, however after discussions with the Home Secretary, Peter Slade will be suspended from all duties at the UK Border Agency, with immediate effect and until further notice.

Looking across at Slade, she continued –

'Mr Slade, are you able to tell us who is running your current operation in your absence?'

'George Dixson.'

'You are to have no further contact with Mr Dixson, I hope that is clear Mr Slade?'

'Absolutely.'

'Are you able to give me the contact details for Mr Dixson.'

Slade lent across and whispered into the ear of his brief. Rupert Thwaites nodded. Slade gave the mobile number of George Dixson. Terry Wheeler responded –

'In view of your twenty-seven years of service and the fact that you have cooperated today it has been decided that you will not be charged with any offence until this case has been reviewed. You are to have no further input into events at the Border Agency. We shall be asking everyone involved to stand down. It is not clear, at this moment in time if the department will ever be reinstated. Thank you all for your time.'

Outside in the street, Slade asked Thwaites as to what he should do now.

'Go home, put your feet up and do not be tempted to contact any of your colleagues. They are expecting you to do just that. It will not be good, going forward, for you to do so.'

After Thwaites had left, James Reeves told Slade that he would talk to Roberts. Officially Roberts was not working for the Border Agency. Reeves added that he would also find out exactly who it was that has brought this matter to the attention of the Home Secretary. The two men shook hands and went their separate ways.

On the train home to Epping, Slade called his wife, Cheryl and asked her to come back from York. He did not enlarge on what had happened to him earlier in the day.

It was late afternoon when George Dixson took the call from Jonathan Dexter, the CEO of the entire Border Agency and a man that Peter Slade had very, little to do with.

'I was taken aback when I heard the news about Slade and even more shocked to have learnt that he had detached himself and his whole team away from Marsham House. As you can imagine the egg is still trickling down my cheeks. I must now inform you, that you have all been stood down Mr Dixson. Peter Slade has been suspended and your operation is, as of now, officially closed. Would, you kindly convey this message to everyone else. We are, of course aware as to whom they are. Individually you will all be reassigned to other departments, not necessarily within the Border Agency. I will be in touch in due course.'

George Dixson descended the stairs and entered the secure room at the back of 38 Oban Street. He opened the drawers of the desk, took out seven mobile phones, placed them into a small carrier bag and returned to the ops room. He then laid each phone upon his desk, turning them face down. This revealed a place name, written in white tip-ex, by Peter Slade.

He picked up the phone marked Berlin and hit the button.

'Good evening, Gurney.'

'It is not Gurney, I am afraid. Gurney has been reassigned. I am George Dixson, and I must inform you that operation Asani no longer exists.'

'How can I possibly know that what you are telling me is true?'

'I am calling from the secure phone that has only been used between you, Mr Ober, and Gurney. If you are unsure of my authenticity, then you are free to check with our Home Secretary. Other than that, on behalf of Gurney and his team, I thank you for all your cooperation.'

Dixson then used the phone marked, Jordan and repeated his previous message to Colonel Dahibi.

A similar call was made to Emre Fidan in Ankara and to Syed Ali of the FIA in Islamabad.

With Roberts' help, he then called Millburn, Hamilton, Forsyth, Martin, Barrington, Griffin and Topolov. He asked Hamilton to let Joe Worricker, in Istanbul know. Each one of them was totally shocked at what they were hearing. It was explained to them that it would not be advisable to discuss matters on the telephone and that they should all return to the UK and then make contact, with Roberts, once here.

Cheryl Slade returned home from her sisters in York. Her husband, whilst careful not to give her any information that might make her worry, did inform her of his suspension and that he did not think that he would be reinstated.

One by one, the team returned to the UK. Each one of them had been red flagged and were picked up at their point of entry. Soon after they were contacted by the office of Jonathan Dexter and given a time and date for them to attend a debriefing interview at Marsham House. All of them made contact, with Graham Roberts and were waiting for him to advise as to when they would all meet up.

In the meantime, James Reeves had let Roberts know that Willie Mott, once of Pritchard's team and Billy Gardner, formerly an underling of Slade's, had colluded, in an attempt, to discredit Slade. This collusion had led to the situation that now ensued.

Over a period of ten days, each member of the team was to sit face-to-face with Jonathan Dexter. The outcome of those meetings was that –

George Dixson – Aged 68 and taken out of retirement, by the Home Secretary, three years ago was asked to slip back into his gardening. He was reminded that he was still subject to the official oath.

Ken Barrington – Aged 56 and once the top man in the Border Agency on the other side of the Channel, was asked to stay on, as a consultant in the Immigration Department. He would be stationed in Rotterdam. He agreed.

Colin Millburn – Aged 53. For many years, an expert in people smuggling in the Balkans, with over 30 years of service in various Government Departments, including Special Branch, Mi5 and the Immigration Services, was asked to take early retirement, on full civil servant's pension. Three months later he was offered and accepted a role in statistics on the Middle East Section of the Overseas Visa Authority.

Fergus Hamilton – Aged 43 was responsible for the lawful shooting of Glasgow gangster, Jamie Law. He was drafted into Interpol prior to becoming part of Slade's team. He was offered the position of Chief Inspector in the Serious Organised Crime Agency (SOCA) and five years later became the number two in the newly formed NCA.

Frederick Forsyth – Aged 41. Prior to joining Slade's team, he was assigned to the UK arm of Interpol, responsible for the monitoring and capture of known European people traffickers. He had spent his whole career in that arm of the law. It was only fitting that he was offered Slade's job, albeit with much less authority. Early in 2009 Forsyth became the head of the Immigration and Settlement Department.

Keith Martin – Aged 40 was formerly attached to the Vice Squad at London's Vine Street station in Soho. Dexter was particularly keen to retain Martin's services. He asked him if he would be willing to return to Vine Street, as an undercover operative, reporting, not to the station Commander, but to Forsyth at the Border Agency. When he asked as to his rank, he was told that he would hold no rank, however his paygrade would be that of a Chief Superintendent. He shook Dexter's hand and resumed work one week later.

Alan Griffin – Aged 28 was the son of one of ex-Commander Reeves oldest friends and by sheer coincidence, Slade's nephew, by marriage. He was being primed to eventually take over from Peter Slade. He had been educated at Cambridge and was highly intelligent. He already boasted ten-years-service. Some of which had been with Special Branch. Dexter asked Griffin to work alongside Forsyth, as his number two. He made it clear to the young man that one day, he would assume control of the department that was fast becoming of special importance to the UK Government. For Griffin, this was a no-brainer.

Borislav Topolov – Aged 36 and one of former Commander, James Reeves, most trusted undercover foreign agents, was asked by Dexter if he would join the team of the newly appointed Freddie Forsyth. Officially, Topolov was not employed by anyone, he had worked as a freelance operative for Reeves and almost all his time had been spent in Bulgaria, gathering information on Petrov and his criminal dealings. However, Dexter, after conversations with both Reeves and Millburn, was, of the opinion that the Bulgarian would be a great asset to the new team. Topolov agreed to work with Forsyth and was asked to stay in the UK until meetings, to discuss strategy, going forward, were held.

Dexter spent several days, collating the information that he had heard from each of the men that he had debriefed. He needed to find out exactly what action, if any, the heads of the various foreign agencies had taken. He held a more senior position than Slade and would therefore be a name that his overseas counterparts would be aware of, albeit he had never had any direct dealings with them. In the brief period that he had been at the helm of the UK Border Agency, there was no doubt that the number of people entering the UK, illegally, had increased to an unacceptable level. On the advice of the

Foreign Secretary, Slade had been allowed to do his own thing without having to consult with him. He now had to reign in this situation and would make Forsyth aware of the fact that he was answerable to him.

Unlike Slade, whom Dexter saw as being something of a maverick, he would not pick up an unregistered mobile phone and speak, randomly to people. He was old school, educated at Eton. He followed protocol to the letter. He was forty-eight and it had taken him twenty-five years to reach the position that he now held. He would do everything by the book, including reporting to his immediate boss, the Home Secretary.

He dictated four letters to his secretary and had her fax them to the recipients. He did not yet trust the electronic world of emails. The letters were sent to, Colonel Dahabi in Amman. Emre Fidan in Ankara. Armin Ober in Berlin and Syed Ali in Islamabad. The replies that he received were nothing less than he had expected. Basically, he was told that once they were asked to stand down in respect of their cooperation with Gurney, they did just that. The pursuit of their targets would carry on, based on the drugs and arms dealing information they had been given. Each reply insinuated that such matters were now of an internal nature and therefore, did not involve the sharing of the outcomes with the UK.

On Monday, the 5th of January 2009, Barrington, Hamilton, Forsyth, Martin, Griffin and Topolov sat in the meeting room of Jonathan Dexter, on the 2nd floor of the Home Office Building in Marsham Street. Also, in attendance was, Terry Wheeler, on behalf of the Home Secretary and Diane Myers. Myers, 43 was introduced as being an expert coordinator within the Immigration Services and that she had her hand on the real figures in respect of just how many people were entering our shores.

Exactly one month after his meeting at the offices of his solicitors, Peter Slade took a call from Rupert Thwaites.

'Peter, are you able to get to my office, tomorrow?'

'Yes, of course. What is the news?'

'Best left until we meet, Peter.'

At 2.00pm the following day, Slade was sat with Rupert Thwaites. No one else was in attendance.

'On my desk, Peter, are several documents, delivered to me yesterday. It is for you to decide what it is that you would like to do.'

'That will depend on the content.'

'Basically, after discussions between the Home Office and your former employers, the Metropolitan Police. It has been decided, that in everyone's best interest, yours included. You should offer your immediate resignation.'

'But I have done nothing wrong. I did not instruct Irene Wastell to seduce Bailey, in, an attempt to frame him for wrongdoings. Therefore, I cannot be blamed for her murder.'

'That is as it may be Peter. If the nationals had not run the story, then, in all probability, we would not be sat here today. However, in order, to make all of this disappear, you are the unfortunate scapegoat. They have agreed to pay you the full thirty-year pension, even though you accumulated just twenty-seven years of service. You will be given a certificate of exemplary service. You can appeal however, it would be messy, Peter. Very messy.'

Slade took a pen from the top pocket of his jacket and signed the four documents that lay in front of him. There ended the twenty-seven years that he had given to his Queen and Country.

'What happens now? Slade asked Thwaites.

'Well, we sue two of the more prominent daily groups. With what you have been given by the Met, it will only be a matter of how much we can squeeze out of them.'

Immediately after he stepped out into the street, Slade called Graham Roberts and gave him the news.

'Bastards. You gave them your life, and this is how you are treated. No one is safe, Peter.'

Roberts made a call. He called the same South London gangster that his lifelong friend had used to do away with Nick Pritchard. Two days later, Willie Mott, a man, the size of a jockey, was eased over the 11th, floor balcony of his flat at Canary Wharf. There were no witnesses. After discovering that Mott was being blackmailed and had virtually no money in his bank account, the inquiry into his death set the verdict as 'suicide whilst the balance of his mind was disturbed.

Eight months after taking out a lawsuit against two of the UK's most prominent daily newspapers, Slade was awarded a substantial financial payout in respect of the false allegations that had been made against him. In the interim, he had taken a position as head of security for the world's largest gold trader.

31 - A NEW BROOM

On the 12th of January 2009, one week after his first briefing, Freddie Forsyth was summoned to the second-floor offices of Jonathan Dexter. Freddie smiled, inwardly, when he spotted the brass plaque on Dexter's door, it read, 'Jonathan Dexter, CEO, UK Border Agency & Immigration Enforcement' he smiled outwardly when he sat down and peered directly at the horizontal triangular, black onyx oblong that sat at the very edge of the 'well past its sell by date' dilapidated oak desk. The words, etched in gold, on the plaque were 'Jon Dexter, CEO, UKBA & IE.' Someone had cocked up, thought the man that had been given the unenvious task of filling Peter Slade's shoes.

Dexter, a smartly dressed, well-spoken man of 45 years of age, had arrived in the job after impressing as an investigator for the criminal ombudsman's office. He was, and would remain to be, a very formal and upright member of Her Majesty's civil service. Graham Roberts had investigated Dexter's background, on behalf of Peter Slade. Roberts had reported that whilst there was a department entitled 'criminal ombudsman' nobody seemed to know exactly what its responsibilities were. It had been concluded that Dexter was very much the snout of the Home Secretary and as time went by Forsyth's suspicions were enhanced by the fact that Terry Wheeler and Diane Myers, both of whom were very close to the Home Secretary, were almost always at any meeting that he attended at the behest of the man with two plaques.

'Forsyth, thanks for coming. I have asked you here so that you can cosy-up to Wheeler and Myers, they have the ear of the Home Sec, and unlike before, we are required to keep her in the loop, always. Together we must formulate a plan. The amount of illegals entering our shores is now way beyond anything that is acceptable.

Dexter handed the floor to Terry Wheeler.

'Thank you, Mr. Dexter. There is one thing that we learnt from Mr. Slade's time here, and that is that the number of people entering the UK illegally, whether by trafficking gangs or under their own steam, is up to twelve times more than is officially reported. If this is allowed to carry on, then, by the year 2020 there will be up to three million that are seeking asylum or that will have simply disappeared into the black economy, which is increasing at a rate of knots. Your predecessor, Mr. Forsyth, believed that he could bring down the major players in the well-run trafficking operations by 'taking them out' and to this end he was colluding with his counterparts in several countries. I can tell you, Mr. Forsyth, that this would never have worked as at least three of the people that were cooperating with Mr. Slade were in fact batting for the other side. Our colleagues at the FCO are currently working with their equivalents in Pakistan, Turkey, and Jordon to remove those corrupt officials from their posts. Our Foreign Secretary gave a lot of his time to Mr. Slade. This time around your department will have no access to him, all your work and findings will have to be shared with the Home Office. I shall be available for weekly briefings, either here, in Mr. Dexter's office, or in my own, on the third floor. Ms. Myers has agreed to be transferred to your department, you will find her knowledge and expertise to be of invaluable help to you. Kindly make a desk and communications available for her by the end of this month.

Wheeler, a razor-thin, six-foot-three specimen of a man, nodded to both Dexter and Myers, shook Forsyth's hand, and left the room.

'Will that be all, Mr. Dexter? 'Asked Forsyth.

'Yes, I think that just about covers it. You will need to bring a detailed operational plan and any needs that you may have, with you at the next meeting. Thank you, Mr. Forsyth. '

Freddie rose from his chair and touched hands with Diane Myers. The sensation that he felt from that simple, gentle touch was unlike any that he had ever felt before. Ms. Myers smiled and looked deep into the eyes of the man that would, in a few weeks' time, be her new boss. Forsyth nodded, formally towards Dexter and left.

'I sensed a little bit of chemistry between you and Forsyth, Diane.

'Well, if I am to do what is being asked of me, then I suppose there has to be, Jonathan.'

'Quite right, shall I see you this evening? '

'Indeed, you will. Yours or mine? '

'Oh mine. I have already instructed cook to make your favourite dinner. '

'See you at 7.30, then. '

Diane Myers, even at the age of 43 was a fine-looking woman. She had the figure of a nineteen-year-old and the features of someone at least 15 years younger. She had no doubts as to her ability to entice Freddie Forsyth into her web.

Officially, Graham Roberts did not figure in the plans of Jonathan Dexter. Forsyth, on the other hand, had realised that the lifelong friend of Peter Slade was probably going to be his most important asset. On the morning of Tuesday, 13th January 2009, Freddie Forsyth peered into the small glass dot that had been inserted into the door of number 38 Oban Street, Poplar. In the upstairs backroom, Graham Roberts stared into one of the eight screens that made up his CCTV security, he saw the face that belonged to the man that he had begun to trust more than any of the others that were previously members of Slade's team. Roberts pushed a button on his computer and the front door opened. Roberts met Freddie at the bottom of the staircase and invited him into the secure room at the back of the ground floor of the house. Freddie was blissfully unaware of the fact that within this room one of the most sophisticated, currently available, invisible scanning devices was fully operational 24/7. The device would pick up any type of listening or electronic equipment that might be carried upon a person's body. Roberts sat behind the small desk in a room that had once been the sanctuary of his friend, Peter Slade. Without Freddie's knowledge, Roberts was looking at Freddie's body image. He could see a mobile phone. It was currently switched off and was not emitting any signals. There was also a key fob. The message on his screen confirmed that it was of no concern.

'Shall we go upstairs, Freddie? It is much more comfortable up there. '

'Yes, of course, Graham. '

'Please go up, I'll put the kettle on. '

Freddie made his way upstairs. Roberts monitored him on the screen. Freddie did not nose around, he simply sat on one of the plush swivel chairs and waited patiently for his tea to arrive.

'I have asked you here Freddie after having a long conversation with Peter. I have known him for most of my life and I would bet my house on the fact that he was fitted-up by the people at the Home Office. Time will prove me to be right. What are your comments?

'I agree wholeheartedly Graham. Of course, I cannot claim to know Peter as well as you do, however I do not think for one minute that he could carry out the actions of the charges that were levied against him. '

'I am so pleased to hear you say those words, Freddie. You see, Peter has a very close association with the Foreign Office but his reluctance to share his investigation with the Home Office has basically ended his career. James Reeves has stepped down and Peter has been asked to fill his shoes, albeit covertly. We have heard that Millburn has been put out to graze, however the FCO will be able to bring him back and put him somewhere in the Middle East. '

'How about your own position Graham? '

'Well, I will carry on. My role will be much more concentrated than it was previously. I will be more of the middleman, between you and Peter. Griffin, as one of Peter's relatives, will be able to play a part as suspicion will not be aroused by regular meetings between the two of them.

'And payment? How will you be paid, Graham? '

'The FCO will pay a sizeable amount to Millburn. He in turn, via non-traceable accounts, will pay both Peter and me. It has all been worked out, we only require your approval. '

'I'm in Graham. Next week we have a meeting of the entire department. Wheeler from the Home Office will be there, as will Diane Myers. Can you do one thing for me, Graham? Could you do some digging on Ms. Myers, I have a gut feeling about her. She has already made a play for me. '

'Consider it done, Freddie. Now I presume that you must get to work. I will be in touch. '

'Thanks for the tea, Graham. See you anon, as they say. '

It was the following Tuesday, January 20th, 2009, that the first 'planning and operational' meeting was held in the offices of Freddie Forsyth. Jonathan Dexter was absent, however both Terry Wheeler and Diane Myers did attend. Wheeler had no real input into events, his job was to simply liaise with Dexter, who in turn would formulate a report, which they would then jointly present to the Home Secretary. Myers on the other hand was able to play a part, as she herself would be joining Freddie's team at the end of the month.

Also, in the room were, Ken Barrington, Fergie Hamilton, Bob Martin, Alan Griffin, and Boris Topolov. Freddie introduced Wheeler and Myers to the others. He then addressed his colleagues as follows –

'As you are all aware, I have been given the task of carrying on where we left off, albeit our procedures will be a lot different than before, and this department will be under the strict leadership of Mr. Dexter, who in turn will be reporting to the Home Secretary via Mr. Wheeler. Ms. Myers will be bringing a wealth of information to us. She has, for some considerable time, concentrated on the facts and figures surrounding the arrival into the UK of hundreds of thousands of individuals and families, that have, in the main entered our shores illegally. She will assume her role at the end of this month. '

As one, the gathered ensemble nodded towards the pretty, petite figure that sat two places along from Freddie.

'With regard to everyone's position, it is as Dexter has already advised you all and I am I agreement. For everyone's benefit I shall enlarge. '

'Ken, with the approval of the FCO, you will take up a role in Rotterdam as you have some considerable experience in dealing with our continental friends. As before, your jurisdiction will include the Netherlands, Belgium, and France. '

'Bob, you will return to Vine Steet as an undercover operative. You will have no title; however, your pay grade will be that of a Chief Inspector. Your task will be to infiltrate the sharp end of the trafficking gangs. You will be armed, and you will have to access and return your weapon to the station in the normal way. '

'Fergie, you will be based here in the office. You will be responsible for collating all worthwhile information and presenting it to me. Your role is now different to that offered to you previously. '

'Boris, except for Ken in Rotterdam, we have no authority to place operatives outside of our shores. I am going to ask you to work from Dover. This is a different role from that Dexter discussed with you previously. The Port Authority will provide you with an office and any assistance that you may require. You will be able to sit in at any interviews involving trafficking suspects. Should our position change later, I will have no hesitation in sending you back to the Balkans. '

'Griffin will be my number two. You are all free to bounce any concerns that you may have off his very broad shoulders. He will relay to me anything that he feels I should know. '

'As you are all aware, George Dixson and Colin Millburn have both been put out to pasture, although either, or both, of them could be brought back to assist if needed. The decisions were not made by me, and I have wished them well on everybody's behalf. My door is open wide to any of you that may wish to discuss matters in private. I thank you all for your attention. '

That evening Freddie received a call, on a secure phone, from his former boss, Peter Slade.

'Freddie, I have news of Valeri Popov. The yanks decided not to hand him over to us. They have fully debriefed him and now have him holed up somewhere in the US, awaiting a new identity. He has apparently been very helpful to them in respect of certain military operations in and around Kosovo. Before they send him off to enjoy his new life in Florida, they have given us unrestricted access as they know he could be very helpful to us in our fight against the traffickers. '

'Whilst that seems to be very good news Peter, neither of us can simply get on a plane, swan into the white house and conduct an interview. '

'Of course, not Freddie. That is why I have asked Roberts to go. '

'But Roberts is not officially part of the team, part of any team for that matter. '

'I agree, however he is very well-known to certain people at the Pentagon, having worked closely with them in the past. His visit has been sanctioned and I doubt very much that Mi5 has any interest in him. '

'OK, then let him go. '

'He is already on his way. For security purposes he will liaise with me. He and his wife will arrive in Miami tomorrow. Arrangements are being made for the meeting to take place at the convention centre which is holding a seminar on international law enforcement. He will not be out of place and special agents will be everywhere. '

'OK, thanks, Peter. I await your further news. '

On Thursday, the 22nd of January 2009, Graham Roberts, and his wife Vivian arrived at Miami Airport. The following morning, after breakfast, which was taken in the swish dining area of the Fontainebleau five-star hotel, situated right on the white sandy beach that runs the entire length of the small island that house's the Miami Beach Convention Centre, Roberts kissed his wife of thirty-five years on the lips and climbed into the rear of a grey, grand Cherokee Jeep. Roberts had surprised his wife when informing her that he was attending the seminar, he surprised her even more when asking if she would like to tag along. At a little after 10.00am he was dropped off directly outside the main doors of a building that hosted seminars, conventions, trade shows and leisure events throughout the year. Less than thirty seconds after having his pre-printed badge zapped by the laser gun that was being held by a pretty, young girl of Chinese origin, Roberts was approached by a small, fat, balding middle-aged man who nearly shook his arm out of its socket.

'Graham, Graham, it's so nice to see you again, after all these years. 'Said the slightly perspiring tubby American.

'Follow me. '

As instructed, Roberts strode purposefully behind his old friend. A friend that he had never seen before.

They stepped onto a well-populated escalator, which climbed up to a mezzanine floor that housed scores of eateries, bars, and private meeting rooms. As they approached a door marked M2001, a very well-proportioned, suited and booted all-American male opened it. The small man carried on walking. His job was done. When the door closed behind him Roberts was frisked by a uniformed clad security man. With the frisk done another door opened and a man that looked as though he had gone thirty rounds with Mike Tyson beckoned their guest in. Roberts was asked to step into a glass cubicle, the doors closed, and a green circular laser scanned the whole of his body. He was clean. He stepped out of the transparent tube and stepped through a third door. In this room there was a desk and two chairs. On the desk there was a writing pad, a pen, a large jug of water, two glasses and a pair of headphones. A voice, that appeared to be coming out of the wood-panelled wall, simply said,

'Please be seated. '

Roberts sat. Seconds later, a man, clad in camouflage walked into the room. He had arrived via a section of the wall that opened from the other side, there was no handle.

'Please be seated. '

'This interview will be video recorded, and a copy will be available later today. A code to access the recording will be sent to your phone two hours after you have left the room. Anything you write down will be left here. You will leave here with nothing other than what you arrived with. ‘

Roberts scanned the room before addressing the man now sat opposite him.

‘So, you must be Valeri Popov. ‘

Captain Popov stood and saluted in acknowledgement.

‘Yes, indeed I am. And you are? ‘

‘I am Graham Roberts, a freelance investigator, connected to, but not employed by the UK security services. ‘

‘And what can I do for you Mr. Roberts? ‘

‘It is understood, from our American friends that you undertook some missions with one of our own. That man, known to you as Captain Jim Reagan was in fact working undercover with us. He was Rory Starr, better known to us as ‘Ringo. ‘You identified him to our Mr. Millburn whilst you were in the American Embassy in Bucharest. ‘

‘Yes, a fine brave man, Captain Reagan. ‘

‘We have reason to believe that he is no longer with us. I know from your debriefing with the yanks that you were not with him when he returned to Prizren. You also said that Ringo had a girlfriend named Adrijana, who in fact was the lover of Captain Hook, General Kos' righthand man. Is that correct? ‘

‘Yes, that is so, Mr. Roberts. ‘

‘We need to get access to the girl, Mr. Popov. Can you help with that? ‘

‘It can be done, Mr. Roberts but it would be dangerous, very dangerous and should not involve anyone, locally. As no one can be trusted. ‘

‘Do you have an exact location for Adrijana? ‘

‘Yes, I do. I, and many others have enjoyed her company at a small shack just outside Prizren.‘

The TV screen, fixed to the wall on the left-hand side of where Roberts sat suddenly sprang into life. Both men turned their heads. The screen showed the city of Prizren, Kosovo. The operator zoomed in to show Prizren in more detail.

‘You need to find the bar. It’s called ‘Café XL’ it is on Vatra Shqiptare.‘

Café XL came up on the screen almost as soon as Popov had mentioned it.

‘From there you need to head South until you can see the junction of Anton Cetta and At Gjergi Fishta Adrijana’s shack is the very last one on the righthand side. At the back there is a well, everyone on the street draws their drinking water from that well. ‘

The screen went back to being black.

‘What can you tell me about General Kos and his set-up, Mr. Popov. ‘

‘As much as you want to know, I guess. ‘

For the next two hours Roberts quizzed the ex-Serbian fighter about his time with the General. He was particularly interested in the regular visits that he made from his base to Varna in Bulgaria.

At just before 1.00pm, Roberts thanked the Serbian for his cooperation. He stood and offered his hand to the man that had fought so bravely for his country. Popov, in true military fashion, saluted, turned, and disappeared through the wall.

At 2.00pm, Graham Roberts was laid on a sunbed beside his wife, sipping an ice-cold Bud.

'How was your meeting, Darling? '

'Oh, you know, boring old stuff, boring old people. '

'Do you have to go back tomorrow? '

'No, I have achieved what I came here for. I have purchased some great new surveillance gear. It will be shipped to the UK in six weeks' time. '

At 3.00pm, Roberts excused himself, returned to his room and opened his laptop. He entered the code that was sat on his phone, inserted a USB device into the computer and downloaded the video recording onto it. He then encrypted the video and sent it to Peter Slade. Slade, sat at his desktop in his harbourside cottage in Polpero, sat through the entire three hours of the interview, making written notes as he did so. The clock in Slade's lounge had just struck 11.00pm when he picked up his mobile phone and called Martin Shore, the Foreign Secretary's personal assistant and once Slade's number two during his high-flying days at special branch.

'Mr. Shore, how the devil, are you? '

'I am fine, Peter. Do you have news for me? '

'Yes, I do. Our target has been located. The coordinates are on the secure portal that Roberts set up for us. We want the target to be alive and well so please do not send in a gung-ho team. '

'I understand Peter. I have earmarked an old friend of yours to be the commander of the mission. '

'Oh, I am intrigued as to who that might be. '

'Well, cast your memory back to our school days and try to remember that little bastard that blew up the chemistry lab. '

'I am with you Martin, surely at his age he cannot still be actively leading some of our finest. '

'He is indeed my friend. He now has more gongs than anyone else in the entire history of the SAS. '

'It's hard to believe that someone that was such a wimp in his younger days could now be the most decorated military man in the entire UK forces. '

'Well, he's your man and he is sure to do a good job. I will give you the nod when everything is in place, and you will be able to watch events in real-time via Roberts' wonderful technology. '

'I will update the Foreign Sec, who, by the way is completely on board with this. '

'Thanks, Martin. We must have that beer one day. '

'Indeed, we must. '

At midnight the following day, Slade received a text message, it read –

'Go to the portal. '

Slade lifted the lid of his laptop and typed the forty-one-digit code into the topmost line of the screen. Almost immediately he could see that the wearer of the night vision goggles was hurriedly making his way through a maze of dense undergrowth. He was seeing exactly what the soldier was seeing. After ten minutes or so the terrain became open, the trees disappeared. The soldier was following a well-trod path that had been etched out in the otherwise long and dry grass. He then re-entered another wooded area before it opened to reveal two buildings. The buildings were positioned either side of a dead-end road. The coordinates, which were shown on the bottom right of the screen matched those that he had given to Martin Shore just over twenty-four hours earlier. For a split-second Slade panicked. He recalled that he had told Shore that the building in question was the last one, on the righthand side, however the soldiers were approaching the road from the other end, which meant that the building would be on the left. He need not have worried, as less than thirty seconds later, four of the six men from the UK's special forces had entered the correct building. One minute later the four men and a captive were back in the woods. Slade had seen and heard gunfire from within the building. He had no idea why. Without warning his screen was blank.

At 3.30am on the morning of Saturday the 24th of January 2009, Slade, who had been waiting for the call, wished Martin Shore good morning.

'We have the target. We took down one other. Identifiable by a hook at the end of his right arm. The target will arrive at a secure location within the UK tomorrow afternoon. '

'Thank you, Martin. And thank our old friend for a job well done. '

'When will you require access to the captive? '

'Monday, pm, if that is OK. I will have Roberts with me. '

'That's fine Peter. You will need to go back onto the computer at midnight tomorrow. The holding address will appear for just five minutes. '

'Well noted. Now get some well-deserved sleep. '

Graham Roberts and his wife, Vivian touched down at Heathrow on the evening of Sunday 25th January. Slade had driven from Polperro during the night, in order, to meet them. At midnight Slade accessed the web page and saw that the captive, Adrijana, was being held at RAF Brise Norton, just West of Oxford and close to the A40.

At 10.30 the following morning Slade and Roberts showed their passports to the armed guard stood at the gates of one of the UK's most important Air Bases. The guard took the documents, entered a building to the side of the gate and then returned with what looked like a credit card machine. With the machine the guard drew circles around each of the visitors' faces. A voice from inside the building spoke into the guard's earpiece. Both men were cleared to enter. Following the given instructions, they drove around the inner perimeter of the base and then followed the signs that read 'high-security area.' They were waved into a specific parking area. A man in full combat uniform approached the car. Slade and Roberts exited the vehicle. The soldier saluted and said –

'Well, fuck me, it's been a long time since I saw your ugly boats. '

Roberts was the first to recognise him.

'Good God, Stephen Lazell. It must be forty years. '

'It certainly is, and you two are still stuck together, like glue. '

All three men were laughing as they entered the completely black building.

'Let me introduce you to Air Chief Marshal, Henderson. '

Lazell knocked firmly upon Henderson's door and was immediately welcomed in.

'Dickie, these are the bastards that I have been telling you about. Slade here, is well-known for all the wrong reasons. Roberts, whilst never in the military has served his country well, albeit from a slightly shady background. '

Henderson stood and shook the hands of both of his visitors and asked if they would like a drink. From an adjoining door Martin Shore appeared.

'Is it a school reunion? ' asked Roberts.

All five men laughed.

As they drank tea, the Air Chief Marshal looked towards Slade and said –

'Your young lady is in a room just down the hall. You have Commander Stephen Lazell to thank for her safe capture. '

Slade responded,

'We would thank him, however he has never apologised for destroying the school lab, for which I took the blame. Seriously though, it was a wonderful job. I watched it all from the comfort of my study. '

'I must tell you that only one of you will be allowed to interview the detainee, protocol, you know. '

'Understood, Air Chief Marshal, It, will be me. 'Replied Peter Slade.

Slade entered the room where Adrijana was sat. The two guards stood diagonally in opposite corners both left. Roberts, Shore, and Lazell watched, via CCTV in an adjoining room. Henderson remained in his office.

'I am Peter Slade of British Intelligence. You, I understand are known as Adrijana. '

The good-looking Serbian female remained silent.

'You know my friend, 'Ringo' who was known to you as Captain Reagan, is that correct? '

There was no response.

In the concealed room Shore and Lazell looked at each other and then asked Roberts –

'Ringo, not our Ringo surely? '

'Yes, I am afraid so. Rory Starr, set up by that young lady and killed by her lover, Captain Hook. '

'Captain Hook. Is he the bastard that we took out two nights ago? '

'Yes, he was. '

'Had I known I would have made him suffer a little before putting his lights out. And the girl? '

'The girl set Ringo up. According to intel from a defector, she did this more than once. '

'Let me have ten minutes with her, she will soon open her mouth. '

'We can't do that Stephen. The rules of the jungle cannot be used in these situations. '

'So, who were the hook and the girl working for? '

'Someone very close to your heart, I think. General Horatio Kos. '

'Well, fuck me. I'd like to take that bastard out. '

'You and twenty thousand others I should think. '

The three men turned their attention back to the room next door.

'Well, if you are not going to cooperate then we shall return you to Pritzen, where you will no doubt be charged with the murder of Captain Hook. '

'OK. But before I talk, I want to know what you intend to do with me, afterwards. '

'That is not my decision, however I will recommend that you are given a new identity and allowed to make a life here, in the UK. '

'Then I will tell you, my story. '

'I was born in the South of Serbia in 1983. In 1998, during the conflict, my whole family was wiped out. My father and two brothers were tortured in front of me, and my mum was raped, many times, before they cut her throat. I was fifteen years old. I was put into a detention camp near to the border with Albania. Every week Captain Hook would come to the camp and select girls for the General. I was sent to the General's complex, and he chose me as one of his playthings. Most of the girls at the camp were given to the soldiers and many of them died. For two years I lived at the General's villa. I was one of seven girls that the General kept. He called me Monday as I would only share his bed on that day. I was allowed to walk in the gardens but never allowed out of the complex. Although I was imprisoned, my life was many times better than most of the other girls. When I became eighteen the General discarded me. He told me that I was too old. I was to be transferred to the camp barracks, to be shared amongst the soldiers. Captain Hook asked the General if he could take me and the General agreed. Hook took me to Prizren and gave me a home, but in return I had to make friends with new recruits. I would meet these men at the bar, the XL Café, where I had to work, and take them back to my home. My job was to find out where the men had come from and to report anything they said, or did, back to Hook. As many as twenty men have met their deaths at the house where I lived. Some were killed by me, but most by the captain. '

Slade intervened.

'Why did you never try to escape? '

'There were two reasons. Firstly, every person in the neighbourhood worked for the General. Hook told me that I would not get past the first checkpoint before I was gunned down. '

'And the second reason? '

'Just after Hook took me away from the complex, I found that I was pregnant. The baby belonged to the General and it was a boy. Hook informed Kos and I was made to give birth in the hospital inside the complex. Two days after the birth, my baby was taken away from me and has been brought up by someone else. Every Monday I am allowed to see him; he is nearly eight now, but he does not know that I am his mama. Now you may understand why I had to stay with Hook. Can you get my son for me? '

'Unfortunately, it will not be possible for us to get you your son. Please tell me what you know about Captain Reagan. '

'Jim was not like any of the other soldiers that I took back home. He was kind, he never threatened me or hurt me, but I had my job to do. I really loved him and did not want to betray him but when I found his phone hidden inside the mattress, I knew that I had to inform Hook. It was Hook that shot Jim, he asked me to do it, but I could not. '

'And his body, where did they take him? '

'The taxi man, the Mexican, took him away. Just like he had done many times before. '

'And they buried him where? '

Now crying profusely, Adrijana sobbingly replied –

'They fed him to the pigs. Hook always laughed when he told me that the little pink smelly porkies were having a feast. '

'What do you know about the General. Does he ever leave his compound? '

'When I lived at the villa he was always going away. You know he has his own helicopters and planes. Recently Hook told me that nowadays he goes to just one place, Varna in Bulgaria. He has a Russian girlfriend there. One time he brought her to the bar, but he normally takes her to the best restaurants in Prizren, his favourite is the Konak Kafe Nargile, which is very close to the bridge. He took me and the other girls there on special occasions. When he goes there, he always takes several guards with him. '

'Thank you, Adrijana, you have been most helpful. '

'What will happen to me now? '

'I believe that you will be held here as some other people will want to question you. After that you will be given a new identity and a place to live. Even I am not told where that will be. You do know that you can never return to Kosovo as you most certainly will be killed. '

'Yes, I understand. But I will miss my son so much. '

'Take care of yourself, and just so you know, Jim was one of my oldest friends. '

Slade left Adrijana and stepped into the adjoining room. He knew exactly what Stephen Lazell was going to say.

'We must take out this General Kos, Peter. '

'Of course, we do Stephen. '

'We now have a lead on him. I have already looked up the Konak restaurant on the drone photos. It will be a piece of cake. When can we go? '

'You are getting ahead of yourself. I have no authorisation to enact such an operation. '

'Who does then? '

'The Foreign Secretary and even he will need the PM's approval. '

'Well, let's get it done. Are you going to allow this bastard to get away Scot free? '

'It must be meticulously planned, and it cannot be us that does the deed. We would have a major diplomatic row on our hands if our troops were to undertake such an operation on foreign soil. '

Fuck diplomacy Peter. I can obtain Russian choppers, hardware, and even the right uniforms. It has been done before and it can be done again. '

'Shore here will have to run this past the Foreign Sec. I do know that Kos has been the subject of discussion in the past and his demise would be a godsend for thousands of refugees. '

As they drove back to Essex, leaving Shore and Lazell to mull over old times, Roberts' curiosity got the better of him.

'Peter, just how does a disgraced top cop get to carry on with his life at the highest level? '

'It's easy Graham. All the people at the top know of my innocence. James Reeves had a certain amount of scandal attached to him however he was able to operate, answerable only to the Foreign Sec for all those years. Within the force they were happy to have got someone for the death of Irene Wastell. It cleans up their act and makes the public think that no one is untouchable. If I had really done what I have been accused of you and I would not be sitting together right now. Reeves told me a long time ago that I would be his successor and if I can do the job, even half as well as he did, then I would have achieved more than I ever thought was possible. '

'I presume that none of what has just happened is for anyone else's ear's? '

'Absolutely Graham, not even Dexter will know of these events. '

'By the way Peter, I have done some digging on Diane Myers, at the request of Freddie and it appears that she is not as she would appear to be. '

'Any enlargement to add to that statement, Graham? '

'Well, she turns out to have been an undercover operative, working for a specialist unit that investigates people in the highest of positions. She has the ear of the Foreign Sec and does not need to run all her findings through Wheeler. She has already got into Dexter's Y-Fronts, and Freddie may well be her next target, the good thing is that he is fully prepared for her. '

'Think you should let Freddie know, Graham. '

'Indeed, I will. I'll be in touch. '

Roberts exited the car. Vivian opened the front door as he strode towards it. She gave Slade a wave and was gone.

32 - FREDDIE'S PROGRESS

Two days after Slade and Roberts had interviewed Adrijana at Brise Norton, Slade called his long-time friend and former colleague, Colin Millburn. Whilst Millburn was no longer in the employment of HM finest, he had stated that if ever he was required, he was available.

'Hello Colin, what are you up to? '

'Doing a bit of gardening Peter, how about yourself? '

'Well, as you know my old mate, one can never really retire from the business that we gave most of our lives to. '

'So, what do you want me to do for you, Peter? '

'Very presumptuous Colin. '

'I know you too well Mr. Slade. You would not call me to wish me happy birthday, would you? '

'You can read me like a book, Colin. '

'Indeed, I can Peter. '

'Do you have contacts in Kosovo, in particular Prizren? '

'Do you really need to ask me that? As you know the Balkans and its neighbours are my specialities. '

'Yes, no need to be smug about it. '

'What's on your mind then? '

'We have a particular interest in a target that resides on the Albanian-Kosovo border. Recent intel suggests that he frequents a restaurant in Prizren. We need to place someone inside the restaurant to monitor the frequency of his visits, who he dines with and, if possible, the security that accompanies him. '

'OK, understood. You have no need to tell me who the target is. I will need all the other details though. Please send them over on my secure fax line. That seems to be the only electronic device that is safe from scamming these days. '

'Will do Colin. Enjoy your garden. '

At 2pm on Monday the 2nd of February 2009, Freddie Forsyth, the man that had assumed Peter Slade's role as the operational head of department, sat with his team in his private office. Boris Topolov had been summoned from Dover and Diane Myers was attending her very first meeting since her transfer to Forsyth's department. She had however, spent a few hours with her new boss earlier in the day, when she had outlined to Forsyth just how much worse the numbers were in comparison to those that were made available to the British public. At 12.55, just before she left for lunch, she made her move. Looking Forsyth straight in the eye, she asked him if he were free to have dinner the following evening. Forsyth was, of course, expecting her to entice him in some way. He readily agreed. They would meet at the Argentinian steak house, Gaucho's, in Piccadilly at 7.00pm. That evening, Freddie would inform his wife that he would not be home on Tuesday night.

As a result of the meeting the previous day, Topolov was asked to fly to Paris and then make his way to the woods that bordered the Port of Calais. The woods, the successor to the Sangatte camp that had been destroyed by the French Minister of the Interior, Nicolas Sarkozy, was considered by the Foreign Office to be where the largest concentration of migrants was gathered. Topolov's brief was to get himself ensconced into the camp on the basis that he had been trafficked from his native country of Bulgaria. Myers had made it clear to the whole of the team that Romania was the source of the largest percentage of transiting migrants and as Topolov spoke very good Romanian, he was the ideal choice for the job. He was told not to put himself in danger, he would carry no weapons, no papers and only a little money. To cement the fact that he was like everyone else, he would have to try to escape via one of the many lorries that crossed the channel every day. If he were caught whilst still on French soil, he was to return to the camp. Should he manage to get to England and was then detained, he would ask the authorities to contact Stephen Browne at the FCO and inform him that they had 'The Bulgarian 'in custody. Stephen Browne would then arrange for his release, and he would return to Calais.

Freddie Forsyth was already seated when Diane Myers entered Gaucho's restaurant. Whilst he believed that this meeting was not going to have a physical end to it, he could not help but notice as to just how sexy this lady really was. He stood as Diane approached the table. They embraced and pecked each other on the cheek. Freddie had already ordered the wine, a £155.00 bottle of Malbec that one could easily find on Tesco's finest shelf, for just £12.99. Freddie did not linger in letting his date know that she was playing two roles.

'So, Diane, you are here at the behest of Dexter. On the other hand, you are firmly in the camp of the Foreign Secretary and all your findings are filtered through Martin Shore. Am I on the right track? '

'You are very well informed. How long have you known? '

'From the moment that I ran a check on you. '

'Oh, and who undertook that check for you, Freddie? '

'Of course, I am unable to disclose the source. '

'If you knew this, why did you agree to meet with me tonight? '

'Because Diane, I believe that we are batting for the same side. My boss is Dexter. I do not trust him. You are in bed with him, so to speak and will therefore be privy to his innermost secrets. Am I correct? '

At that point, a waiter stood over the couple with a large wooden serving board that contained a dozen steaks. The waiter carefully explained the differences between each piece of meat. Strangely they both chose the same cut.

'I will now take a calculated risk, Freddie. I am working for Slade, your former boss. '

Freddie leaned back in his chair, picked up the expensive bottle of red and filled both glasses.

'You did not know, did you? '

Freddie did not know whether to bluff his way through or come clean. He chose the latter.

'I had no idea. As far as I was aware, Peter had been banished to live out his life by the seaside, albeit on a very handsome pay-out package.'

'Well Freddie, Mr. Slade said that you would be surprised when I told you. '

'He was quite right, I am, extremely surprised. On the other hand, you could be leading me up the garden path as this could simply be a ruse by Dexter to draw me out. '

'Rest assured Freddie, it's bona-fide, call Slade if you want. He said you might think that I was double-dealing. '

A trolley arrived. Two perfectly formed Argentinian steaks were put in front of them. A selection of Sainsbury's 'taste the difference 'vegetables were placed into the middle of the table and an array of condiments were presented to them.

'Would Sir or Madam like another drink? '

'Another bottle of Malbec, please 'Replied Diane.

For the next two hours the couple discussed exactly how they were going to carry out a deception that would be able to fool everyone around them. They agreed that she would only give over to Wheeler info that would be of little importance. He would keep her in the loop on matters that might be of interest to Slade. They had one common concern, neither of them trusted the Home Secretary.

At 10.40pm Freddie asked for the bill. He tried to hide his astonishment when reading the bottom line. £626.00 was the damage. Apparently even the smallest cut of Argentinian fillet cost £95.00 each. The vegetables, off the shelf price £4.99 had weighed in at £44.00.

'We are in the wrong business. ' Said Freddie as they walked towards the exit.

'Where are you staying, Freddie? If indeed you are? '

'I am at the Thistle, near to the Tower. And you? '

'Oh, I live in Kensington, with Toby. '

'Toby is your partner, husband? '

'No, no, no, Toby is my Dog. A Labrador. '

At Piccadilly station the couple parted.

At 11.45 there was a faint tap upon the door of room 314 of the Thistle Hotel. As Freddie opened the door, clad only in his boxers, Diane Myers opened the front of her coat. She was wearing nothing underneath.

They awoke at 7.35 the following morning, kissed and got ready for work. By 8.30 they were at their desks in their respective offices. They were never to spend another night together. In the office there were no awkward moments. After work Freddie returned home to his wife and Diane to her golden Labrador, named Toby.

In the woods, just north of Calais, Topolov was sat around a campfire with several other non-French nationals. They were cooking food that had been stolen from one of the town's supermarkets. Topolov was using his native tongue to converse with two other Bulgarians. He was able to listen to conversations that were being made in English however he never let on that he could understand anything that was said. One man introduced himself as Anton, a Romanian. Topolov was able to talk to him. He told the Bulgarian that he had paid Euros 3,000 to a member of a notorious Bucharest gang that specialised in the trafficking of people. He had left the Romanian capital five months earlier and had made twenty attempts to cross the channel into England. He added that every single person in this camp, and others close to Calais, were intent on getting into the UK. Topolov asked him as to why it was so important for them to get to England as surely, they were safe in France. Anton had smiled when replying, telling Topolov that the UK was known around the World as being the land of handouts. A country where anyone claiming political asylum would be looked after. From this point onwards, Topolov would watch Anton very carefully. In the coming weeks he would learn a lot from this man.

At the end of the first week of February 2009, Freddie received a call from Bob Martin. On Saturday morning, together with Alan Griffin, they met, at a diner, alongside the A1 in Hertfordshire. After the formalities of talking about the demise of their previous operation, Martin was asked why he had summoned his colleagues to a meeting. Freddie and Griffin listened intently as Martin explained.

'I got to know of a joint investigation by the Immigration Services and the Met to take down a brothel in Hadley Wood, near to Cheshunt. The brothel is controlled by the Romanians and up to thirty girls, all from, in and around

Bucharest, are working there. I have been staking out the address, a large mansion, that changed hands for three million just two years ago. The registered owner of the property is Nadia Oarza, she is the sister of the currently serving Romanian Foreign Minister. Her husband is Constantin Oarza, acknowledged as the overall boss of the Romanian Mafia. He currently resides in Mexico.

Griffin intervened.

'All very nice Bob, but what bearing does this have on our task? '

'If you let me finish, Alan, you will find out. '

'There is one girl that commutes between Hadley Wood and various supermarkets. She drives a very expensive BMW. She seems to shop, almost daily, seemingly to provide food and other goods to the girls that never leave the house. I have clocked up to 150 blokes entering the house over a four-hour period. I deliberately bumped into her in Sainsbury's. She is not the prettiest banana in the bunch, so I asked her out. She agreed. We are due to meet at a restaurant in Cuffley, a short drive from the house. We will meet on Tuesday evening. I just wanted to run this past you and ask if there is anything that you feel that I should be asking her. '

This time, it was Freddie that spoke –

'Well, Bob, you do seem to have unearthed something that we can get our teeth into. The fact that both the Romanian Foreign Minister and the leader of one of the World's most prominent crime families are involved, would seem to be somewhat significant. Alan and I will give this some serious thought. I will get back to you by Monday evening. '

In the car park of the diner, the three men said their goodbyes. Griffin and Freddie arranged to meet up on Sunday evening, at a pub in Saffron Walden, which was of equal distance for each of them to drive.

Over dinner the two men compiled a list of questions that Bob should put to the girl without her becoming suspicious. Over after-dinner brandies, Griffin looked at his boss and said –

Fuck it, Freddie. Why don't we just let Bob play it his way. He knows what he is doing, he has far more experience than either of us in these matters. '

'You are right Alan. Let him play it as a first date. Asking only the questions that one would ask a lady in those circumstances. If it takes more dates to draw her out, then so be it. I will talk to Bob tomorrow. I am sure he will be more comfortable with this idea. '

On Monday evening, Freddie relayed his agreement with Griffin to Martin. Martin breathed a sigh of relief, saying that he was more than happy to handle things in this way.

'Just one thing Bob. In case this turns out to be you that is being set up, someone will be watching your back. '

'I would expect nothing less, Freddie. I will get back to you soonest. '

At 7.25 pm on Tuesday the 10th, Feb, Bob Martin pulled up in the rear carpark of a Mediterranean Restaurant in Cuffley. The carpark was sparsely populated, Martin found a space away from the other cars. He sat for a few minutes, observing his surroundings, before he exited the vehicle. As he made his way to the high street, he saw the long legs of his date as they swung out of her BMW. Good timing, he thought to himself. He was also happy with the fact that there appeared to be no one else around. He did however spot the two men that were sat in the rear of the black London taxi that was parked in a layby outside of the Tesco Express Store. Politely taking the girl by the arm, he led her into the restaurant.

After being seated right by the window, which Martin had requested when booking, the waiter handed each of their guests a menu and asked what drinks they would like. Martin nodded to the girl, who now appeared to look a whole lot prettier than when he had first seen her.

'I will have a glass of Chardonnay, please. '

'Same for me. In fact, fetch us a bottle. '

As the waiter strode towards the bar, Martin looked directly at the black-haired, blue-eyed girl and said –

'I do not even know your name. And by the way, you look very attractive tonight. '

'My name is Maia Radakanu, and I am from Constanza, on the Black Sea coast of Romania. '

'Ah, I know of it, Maia. I went there on holiday when I was just nineteen. '

'And your name is? '

'I am Bob Murray, and I am from East London. I am a surveyor, working on a possible development just down the road in Cheshunt. '

'And you Maia? What is it that you do? '

'I am the personal assistant of the Romanian Ambassador in London. This week I am off as I have just moved to this area. '

'Wow, Maia. You are indeed a high-flyer. '

At the very moment that Bob Martin was entertaining the controller of an illicit sex-house in Hadley Wood, Boris Topolov was one of eleven people being unloaded from the back of a forty-foot trailer bound for Dover. After being quizzed by UK Customs, he and his ten would-be escapees were let go. Not one of them carried any paperwork. Topolov returned, unaccompanied, to the woods on the edge of Calais.

By 10.00pm Martin could sense that his dining companion was becoming a little edgy.

'I am sorry Bob, but I must go now. I have a lot to do. '

'No problem, Maia, I understand. Can we do this again? '

'Shall we meet here on Friday evening, I like it here, Bob. '

'Yes, I would like that. Can I have your mobile number? '

'I am sorry Bob, but I do not have a mobile right now. '

'That's OK, shall we say same time, same place on Friday then? '

'Yes, thank you, Bob, now I really must go. '

'OK, you go. I will get the bill. '

Maia stepped out into the chilly evening air. As she hit the button on her key fob a black London taxi drew alongside her. Within seconds she was in the back. One of the two men took her keys from her, exited the taxi, and climbed into her pristine white beamer. Forty minutes later the taxi pulled into the concealed yard at the rear of Vine Street Police Station. The BMW was parked on the third floor of the multi-storey carpark in Duke Street and its occupant went home for the night.

At 8.00am the following morning the keeper of the brothel in the upmarket area of Hadley Wood was taken from her overnight cell and placed into an interview room. At 8.10 Bob Martin walked into the room and placed two Starbuck's coffee cups onto the steel table. Freddie Forsyth and Alan Griffin stood behind a one-way, smoked glass window, that had vision of both occupants of the interview room. In addition, they could clearly hear every spoken word.

'I hope you take sugar, Maia? '

Through tears, Maia replied –

'So, you are a policeman, Bob? '

'Yes, I am, and I would like to think that you are going to help us, Maia. '

It was a little after 9.15 in the morning when Topolov sat, around the campfire, with Anton and a few others. Anton began a conversation, in Romanian, with Topolov.

'So, my friend. You have experienced your first taste of failure. '

Topolov looked at Anton as if he had no idea as to what he was talking about.

'You were caught and sent back, were you not? '

'Yes, but I will try again and again until I am successful. '

'There is another way, you know. '

'How? '

'I can get you on a dinghy and you will land safely on an English beach. It will cost you money, but you will be met by our people and taken somewhere where you can work until you pay back what you owe to us. Are you interested Boris? '

'What kind of work will I have to do? '

'That is up to you. If you have a trade, maybe a plumber, carpenter, bricklayer or similar then my friends will find you work, with a good salary and you will pay back just a little each week. '

'Why do you ask me, Anton? Some of these guys have been here for months and have tried to cross many, many times. Why don't you give them the chance? '

'Boris, you are different to these people. You are educated, they are mainly illiterate and have no real future. I think you can be trusted to pay us back if we help you. '

It was at this point that Topolov knew that Anton had never been trafficked here. He had not paid Euros 3,000 to any gang member. He was, without doubt a member of the organised crime gang that duped unsuspecting illegal migrants into agreeing to take the costly shortcut to the UK.

In the Vine Street interview room, Bob Martin asked Maia, who had so easily been lured into his clutches, the following question –

'So, Maia, you are working at the Romanian Embassy? Exactly where is the Embassy and what route do you take to work each day? '

Maia gripped the Starbucks cardboard coffee cup, spilling some of its contents onto the steel tabletop.

'Of course, you already know Bob, that I do not work at the Embassy. '

'Then tell me how you came to England, how long you have been here and who are your contacts in Romania. '

'If I tell you all of this then I am to be killed. '

'If we send you back to Constanza then I am sure that the same fate awaits you there. If you cooperate then we can protect you, the choice is yours Maia. By the way, do you know Nadia Oarza? '

'OK, I will tell you my story, but you must promise to protect me, forever. '

'It's a deal, Maia. '

'Five years ago, I was working as a lap dancer in one of Constanza's upmarket clubs. I was just twenty-one. One night, as I was rubbing my fanny into the face of a very ugly and overweight Russian man, a flannel was put over my mouth, I remember nothing else until I woke up in a hotel room. Ten minutes later the woman that I now know of as being Nadia Oarza sat by my bed and offered me a cigarette. She asked me if I would like to go to the UK. Of course, I replied that I would. I was not allowed to go back to see my family. Nadia told me that I would be leaving on a flight to London the following day. I was given a passport which included a work permit. She told me that if I were asked, I was on my way to work at the Romanian Embassy. At Heathrow I was met by a Romanian guy, whose name I would never know. He took my passport from me and then drove me to Soho. I was made to work, as a 'whore,' for one year. After one year I was taken to a big house. I still do not know where it was. There was only one way in and out of this house and there were always two men guarding the door. There was CCTV in every room. There were eleven other girls. When one of them left, another would appear. The clients were much better than those in Soho and I would receive tips from them. I was allowed to keep the tips. I worked for twelve hours every day and during that time I would have sex with twelve men. Everything was recorded and downloaded onto the web, which was controlled in Romania. Two years ago, I was taken to the house in Hadley Wood. Soon after Nadia came to see me. She told me that I would no longer have to have sex with men that I did not know. She told me that I would be the housekeeper, responsible for all the girls that were working there. For the first time I was allowed to go out. I did everything around the house, but I was not allowed to collect the money. Two men, that sat in the reception all the time took the money from the clients before they were allowed to see the girls. There are fifteen working rooms and one big place where the girls can sleep when not working. Sometimes one of the two men would talk to me, he would tell me about Nadia and that her husband was the head of the Romanian Mafia and that I should never dare to escape otherwise I would be cut into tiny pieces and fed to the pigs. Every week I am given one thousand pounds, in cash. I must run the house with this money. The girls also give me money to buy special things for them. Every week I can save about three hundred pounds, but now I have nothing. '

'Do you know where Nadia spends most of her time Maia? '

'She is mostly in Bucharest but also visits her husband in Mexico. One of the men that guard the house is very handsome. He and Nadia spend a lot of time together when she is here. He tells me many things about her. '

'What kind of things does he tell you? '

'That she does not love her husband anymore. He has many senoritas in Mexico, but she will never leave him because she likes her lifestyle too much. I was told that Constantin Oarza can fly in and out of Romania whenever he likes. His brother-in-law, Nadia's brother, is the Foreign Secretary of Romania. It is Nadia who controls the flow of workers into the UK. Her husband runs a similar operation from Mexico into the USA. '

'Do you know where Nadia is right now? '

'She was here, in the UK just two days ago. The guard that I told you about, Darius, left to meet her and hand over the money. '

'Do you have any idea where they might be staying? '

'Of course, Darius always boasts about his nights in the arms of his lover in one of the most splendid places that he has ever been to. '

'And just where might that splendid place be? '

'The Savoy, of course. Nadia always stays at the Savoy. '

In the room next door, Griffin called Graham Roberts. He explained the situation and asked that he keep Fergie Hamilton in the loop.

Martin thanked Maia for her cooperation, adding that they should take a break. Maia was taken back to the holding cell. Martin joined Forsyth and Griffin in the room next door.

'Shall we go and grab a pie and a pint. 'Asked Martin.

'Good idea, but let's keep it clean, Bob. '

The three men left Vine Street, crossed Piccadilly, and walked for three minutes before entering the Three Crowns in Jermyn Street.

Griffin got the drinks in whilst his two colleagues found a table in the far corner of the bar.

Martin was the first to talk.

'So, what do we do now? '

Forsyth responded to his question.

'Well, the good news is that it is Nadia Oarza that is running things and not her old man, tucked safely away in Mexico. We should leave him out of the equation and concentrate all our efforts upon his wife. '

Martin intervened -

'And how about Maia, do we charge her and if so, with what? '

'We must do exactly what you promised her Bob. We must give her a new identity and ship her off to Sunderland, or some other exotic-sounding place. Of course, her lifestyle will change beyond comprehension, but at least she will be free. '

'And do we involve Dexter in all this Freddie. '

'Oh, fuck no. We must keep this far away from Dexter and the Home Secretary.'

'But will this not require home office approval? '

'Well, strictly speaking, yes. However, Slade can arrange this, it's a minor detail. '

As soon as Griffin had uttered these words, he knew he was in trouble.

'What has Slade got to do with this. ' Asked a startled Forsyth.

Griffin spent the next twenty minutes explaining the situation surrounding their ex-boss. Freddie was not at all happy however just as he was about to reprimand his two underlings for withholding all of this from him, Bob's mobile rang.

Bob listened, intently. His two colleagues guessed that it was Roberts on the other end of the line. All they heard Bob say, in reply, was –

'No, no. Nowhere near Vine Street. Put her under, blindfold her and take her to your place. We will be there later. By the way, any resistance? '

'None at all, given the position we found them in it was impossible for them to react. What do we do about the man? '

'Call your mates at Vine Street, explain that he is an illegal and possibly involved in trafficking and ask that they hold him for 36 hours. That will give us enough time to decide what to do with him. '

Bob laughed just before hanging up.

'Well Bob, don't keep it to yourself. What was so funny? '

'When they entered the room, Nadia was tied, hands and feet to the four-poster. She had a cornetto inserted into her love box and Darius was busy eating it. '

All three men laughed and then high-fived each other.

Together they took the tube to Bromley-by-Bow and then walked for twenty-five minutes. Just prior to reaching the door of number 38 Oban Street, Bob nipped into the corner shop and purchased a cornetto.

Nearly three weeks after they last spoke, Colin Millburn sent a fax to Peter Slade, the fax read –

'Xherdan and Kida Vula have been working at the café for two weeks now. They are a husband-and-wife team that have a particular reason to loathe a certain military man. They reported yesterday that the target has been for dinner on consecutive Tuesdays. When they dine, they bring two extras with them, both are additional waiters. Two sentries are posted outside the entrance, at street level and a further two guard the door into the reception area. In addition, a very big man always stands in the kitchen. The target arrives in a black Mercedes with a blonde Russian girl. They sit at the back; the windows are blacked-out. There is a driver and an armed passenger, he wears the military uniform of the Kosovan Army. At the bridge there is a camouflaged Jeep, containing four men. Excluding the target and the girl there are eleven minders in total. It is believed that all of them are armed.

Slade pondered and then made a call.

'Martin Shore at your service Peter. '

'We need to meet Martin. The sooner the better. '

'Shall we say, 6.00pm tomorrow at the old school playground? '

'Yes, that would be fine. See you then. '

Bob Martin, Forsyth, and Griffin were let into the hallway of Roberts' hideaway in Poplar. Roberts shook each man by the hand and led them down the hall, through the small kitchen and into the secure room at the back. Nadia, still groggy from her enforced inhaling of chloroform was slumped in a chesterfield armchair that once belonged to Ronnie Corbet. Peter Slade had spent most of his time in this chair when ensconced in his lifelong friend's safehouse.

Roberts dangled a small phial of smelling salts under the Romanian's nose, and she began to regain some of her senses.

Griffin came in with a tray of coffees that he had poured from the pot that was always on the stove. As he offered the girl a cup, Bob Martin intervened and poked the sharp end of the cornetto into her mouth.

'Would you rather I shove it somewhere else? ' He asked.

The girl opened her hands as if to say that she did not understand anything that was being said to her.

Forsyth took control of the room.

'If you want to play the 'I do not understand card' then we are going to be here for a very long time and your night-time accommodation is not very pleasant. In fact, it's as far away removed from the Savoy as it possibly could be. '

Roberts, Martin, and Griffin left the very cramped room and climbed the stairs, where they watched and listened via the CCTV.

Forsyth very calmly questioned the girl that had surely been responsible for hundreds of her fellow natives ending up as sex slaves, drug addicts and criminals. Diane Myers, through her work on illicit Immigration had previously told him that there were potentially thousands of trafficked girls that had simply disappeared. Most were thought to have been dead.

For four hours Nadia remained silent although she did smile at many of her interrogator's questions and accusations.

At 7.30pm, Forsyth asked Nadia to follow him. He led her into the kitchen and through a door that opened onto the backyard. At the rear of the house there was a brick-built Victorian toilet. Its original door had been replaced with a solid steel version. The only light was that from the kitchen window, it was enough to show that the toilet and its wooden cupboard-like surround, had been removed. In its place there was an armchair. On the armchair there were two blankets. The old steel cistern, with its long dangling chain was still fixed to the back wall, high above where many people had previously sat to empty both their bowels and bladder.

Nadia resisted Forsyth's invitation to go inside, he gently nudged her. She spoke, for the first time –

'I'm not fucking, going in there. '

'Oh, yes you are. '

Forsyth manhandled her into the cubicle, closed the door and locked the two deadbolts. Inside it was pitch black. Nadia began to shout, scream, and bang on the door, all to no avail as the ex-toilet had long since been soundproofed.

Calling from the foot of the stairs, Forsyth invited his three colleagues to join him for dinner. The four men jumped into Roberts' car and headed for Penny fields, where ten minutes later they climbed the concrete steps that led into a dilapidated Chinese restaurant.

'Don't worry gents, the place is crap, but the food is superb. '

With their bellies full, Roberts dropped Forsyth, Griffin, and Martin off at Mile End station and then made his way back to Oban Street. He neither checked the backyard or gave his Romanian captive a single thought as he climbed into bed.

33 - A RIGHT RESULT

It was a little after 6.00pm, on Friday the 13th, February 2009, when Peter Slade entered, what was once his old school playground. It had long since been turned into a public open space. As he approached the wooden bench that had remained in place for over sixty years, having originally been put in position in remembrance of Mr. Joseph Jetter, a man that had been the school's headmaster for some thirty years. The bench now displayed four brass plaques, one of which paid tribute to the headmaster of Slade's years at the school. Mr. George Wilks. It was Mr. Wilk's influence, and contacts, that had led to so many of his pupils becoming entwined into the world of Policing and Espionage.

Whilst he knew that he was meeting with Martin Shore, the PA of the Foreign Secretary, Slade was surprised to see that he was accompanied by Commander Stephen Lazell, a man that Slade had met just the previous week, for the first time in over forty years. Shore and Lazell both stood and held out their hands.

'We meet again Stephen. '

'I have asked Stephen to join us, Peter, I hope you don't mind? Ultimately the contents of our meeting were to be relayed to him, after all, it is Stephen that will be heading the operation. '

'It's no problem at all, Martin. In fact, it now seems like a very good idea. '

'It's a little chilly tonight, shall we walk down to the Bridge House? '

'Yes, of course. '

As the three men made their way, on foot, to the pub where they had taken their first-ever drink after leaving school, they reminisced about the old days. Lazell remarked that they could never had imagined that in 2009 they would be discussing matters of national importance.

'How proud old Wilko would have been of us, remarked Peter Slade.

The Bridge House is a busy place on Fridays and the threesome had to wait until people left before they could find a table to sit at. Once settled, with food ordered, it was Martin Shore that opened the dialogue.

'Stephen and I have had several conversations during the last week Peter. The info that you have given to us in respect of the target's movements has been very helpful. Stephen will now offer you his well-thought-out plan. '

'I have been in touch with a man that I met in Kosovo over twenty years ago. He was a Sergeant back then. He could have risen to the very top of his Country's military elite however he chose not to. He is a man that has more knowledge and experience of covert operations than anyone I have ever met. He was part of my team during the conflict at the end of the eighties. I would trust him with my life. '

'When would you be ready to implement the operation? Enquired Slade.

'We will wait for Xherdan's next report. If it transpires that the General dines at the restaurant next Tuesday then I will set the wheels in motion for the following Tuesday, the 24th. Providing, of course that a booking is made in the normal way. '

'And will you be there yourself Stephen? Or leading from afar? '

'You bet your butt that I will be present. We have Ringo's horrific death to avenge, and I wish to carry that out personally. '

'Personnel Stephen? '

'Myself and five of my top men. The Sergeant and six of his, thirteen in total. '

'How about the husband and wife? '

'They will make their escape via the back door of the kitchen. This part has already been rehearsed. '

'I would love to be there. ' Said Slade.

'You can almost be there, Peter. Martin here is arranging for a satellite link to be established in order, that the Foreign Sec can watch. I can arrange for a link to be available that Roberts can access. '

'That would be good. '

Shore addressed Slade.

'Before we part there is another matter that I need your help with Peter. '

Slade looked quizzically into Shore's eyes.

'Jonathan Dexter could be a problem. How much does he know? '

'As far as I am aware, he knows nothing of the events of recent days. Myers is still stalking him. She only drip feeds him snippets, but nothing to do with the Romanians or the operation that we are discussing now. '

'Well, the Foreign Sec wants him to know that Nadia Oarza has disappeared. No other details are to be revealed to him. '

Slade frowned at his old schoolmate. Lazell was more vocal.

'Do we have Nadia Oarza? '

'Classified, my old friend. '

'Classified my arse. I have twice been given the task of eradicating her old man and twice he had been tipped off. What I would give to turn out his lights. '

'One operation at a time Stephen, one at a time. '

Slade interjected –

'I can get Myers to drop Nadia's disappearance into her bed talk. '

'That's good Peter. The sooner the better. '

On Saturday morning, at 8.30, Roberts unlocked the reinforced steel door that had held Nadia Oarza captive for just over twelve hours.

'I need the bathroom. '

Roberts led her into the kitchen and showed her the door to the downstairs toilet. A few minutes later she came out. Roberts invited her into his small, but secure room.

'Would you like some coffee and a piece of toast maybe? '

Nadia nodded in acknowledgement.

'What is going to happen to me? '

'Well, the consensus is that you are to be drugged, taken to Soho, and put to work. Your future will be very much the same as the hundreds of poor souls that you have given a similar fate to. '

'This is the UK; you do not work like that. '

'Oh, my dear. In special circumstances we waive certain protocols. You are without doubt a special circumstance and given the heartache that you and your fellow comrades have inflicted upon so many, innocent, young women, we do indeed 'work like that.'

'And if I tell you stuff, what can you do for me? '

'That will depend upon exactly what it is that you have to tell. '

Roberts picked up a mobile and called Forsyth.

'How soon can you get here? '

'In about one hour. '

'OK, see you then. '

Forsyth immediately phoned Griffin. The two men arrived in Oban Street at a little after 10.00am.

In Epping, Peter Slade called Diane Myers and filled her in on the previous night's conversation, asking that she inform Dexter of Nadia's disappearance. Myers confirmed her understanding. Fifteen minutes later Cheryl Slade drove her husband to a local golf course. She would return early evening and they would enjoy dinner together in the plush clubhouse restaurant.

At 1.00am, under the cover of darkness, and having agreed with the Romanian, Anton, to take the dinghy route to the UK, in return for £3,000, which would have to be paid back from any earnings he was able to make, Topolov and ten other migrants waded into the sea that gently rolled into the small inlet five miles west of the Port of Calais. All ten men were helped into the black rubber dinghy by two Romanians. Not one of the escapees was provided with a life jacket.

The outboard motor, operated by one of the migrants, chugged into operation upon the third time of asking. On top of the sixty-foot-high cliffs that overlooked the English Channel, stood three French policemen. Topolov clocked them when one of them lit up a cigarette. These men, thought the Bulgarian, were there to stop the continual flood of migrants from leaving France. As history would one day tell, the French were more than willing to turn a blind eye to what was going on.

At the time that Peter Slade was teeing off from the first green, the dinghy reached the coast of England. Two men walked out into the shallow water of the Kent coast at a point between Dover and Folkestone. Both men spoke Romanian. Exhausted, cold, and soaked through, the eleven reluctant sailors struggled to walk across the large, pebbled beach. Once off the beach they were assembled into a tight group. One of the Romanians made a call, a few minutes later a long-wheeled base, dark blue, Citroen van could be seen driving towards them on the dirt track of a road. Topolov memorised the number plate. The eleven men were ushered into the back and made to sit on the floor. One Romanian joined the driver in the front whilst the other sat in the back, up against the doors. Each illegal was given a small bottle of water, which they gratefully accepted. What they really needed was a cup of hot, strong tea.

Most of the migrants, having not slept at all during the choppy crossing, were now happily snoozing away, oblivious to the fate that awaited them. Topolov, whilst feigning sleep, was wide awake to everything that was going on around him. There was no division between the driver and the rear of the vehicle, Topolov was able to listen to the conversations between the three Romanians. He heard that five men were to be dropped off at an abattoir on the outskirts of Lenham in Kent. Four more were to leave the van at a farm near to Sittingbourne. Topolov and the only other remaining immigrant, an Afghan, who spoke no English at all, left the back of the van inside a massive warehouse. At that time Topolov had no idea at all as to his whereabouts. The two men were shown into a canteen at the back of the warehouse and were given food and drink. Four other men, all presumed by Topolov to be fellow illegals were seated together at one of the five tables.

At 2.00pm the six men were ushered out of the canteen and asked to board a black transit van that was parked inside the warehouse. This van had seats. Again, Topolov made a mental note of the van's registration. Topolov and the Afghan sat in the rear. Ten minutes later the van came to a halt alongside a cold store that held fish. The six men were invited to alight and moments later they were climbing from the quayside and onto the deck of a small fishing vessel.

Within five minutes the vessel chugged its way into the open water of the river Medway before entering the mouth of the Thames. Some forty minutes later, the foul-smelling boat arrived at the Grain Battery, a granite-built tower that projected itself upwards from the riverbed. Topolov and his five fellow migrants were ushered into a small black dinghy that was hidden just out of sight under the cavernous lower part of the tower. In the dinghy were six table tennis bats. The skipper of the fishing boat gestured that his discharged human cargo should head towards the light that had just flashed several times. Ten minutes later, the Bulgarian undercover operative and five others had arrived on the Isle of Grain. The six migrants, accompanied by two men that Topolov believed to be of Romanian descent, marched along the coastal path for about half a mile before they turned onto a dirt road. Ten minutes later they were assembled inside the barn of a long-since abandoned farm.

At 6.00pm a khaki-coloured Jeep Cherokee pulled up outside of the splintered wooden doors of the barn. Topolov, trained as he was, in the art of observation clocked the licence plate. The driver of the Jeep entered the barn and spoke, in Romanian, to one of the two men that were guarding the migrants. Topolov heard the name of Anton mentioned. He now knew for certain that he was in the middle of a carefully organised, international trafficking operation. The driver returned to the Jeep and brought back eight bags of KFC. Five minutes later he drove off into the now-dark Kent countryside.

Griffin, Forsyth, and Roberts had spent the whole of the day quizzing Nadia Oarza. What she had revealed to them was way beyond anything that they might have expected to hear from her. As the wife of Romania's number one criminal and the sister of her country's Foreign Secretary, she was indeed a catch, a catch that no one could have envisaged just two days previously.

It was around 6.30pm when Roberts called his brother and asked him to find a safe house for a few days. At 7.15, Nadia, once again sedated, was laid onto the back seat of Roy Roberts' black Mercedes SUV and driven away. Even the three occupiers of 38 Oban Street had no idea as to where she was being taken.

For the next four hours, the three men listened intently to the recording of Nadia's interview. Forsyth noted down everything that was of interest. At 10.30pm, Griffin called Bob Martin and asked him to come to Oban Street at 9.00am the following morning.

Just prior to Nadia being taken away, Diane Myers had slipped into the shower of her Kensington flat just a few minutes after Jonathan Dexter had slipped out of her. When she returned to the bedroom, her boss had opened the bottle of expensive red that he had brought with him a few hours earlier.

Draped in a large bath towel, hair still wet, Myers took a sip of the wine before snuggling up to Dexter on the bed.

'So, what's new Diane. '

'Oh, nothing that exciting. Usual stuff, keeping Forsyth in the loop with facts and figures. '

'Must be very boring for you? '

'Yes, however I did hear a whisper that a Romanian girl had been lifted from the street. The boys were whispering about it for most of yesterday '.

'Which girl, do you have a name? '

'I think it is Nadia Oarza, the name means nothing to me. '

Myers was watching the face of her lover intently. She could sense that Dexter was uneasy at hearing the name of Nadia Oarza.

Without a word, Dexter climbed off the bed and headed for the shower. When he had finished, he returned to the bedroom, dressed, knocked back a whole glass of wine and then announced that he must leave immediately.

Myers did not question him; she knew that the mention of the Romanian's name had ruffled his feathers. As Dexter headed for the hallway, she followed him to the door and gently kissed him on the lips. This would prove to be the last time that she ever did so.

As soon as he was inside his car, Dexter took out a mobile phone from the glove box and turned it on. He had received several messages, all were from the same person, his gay assistant, Terry Wheeler. Each message read the same -

'Please call as soon as you can. '

Dexter called.

'I thought you would want to know Jonathan, the Home Secretary has been informed that Nadia Oarza, the sister of Ilie Gheorghiu, the Romanian Foreign Secretary, has been abducted, by persons unknown at this time, however, there has been a leak that Peter Slade is somehow involved. The Romanian Ambassador was informed, and Ilie Gheorghiu is rumoured to be on his way to London. '

On the afternoon of Sunday 15th February 2009, Stephen Lazell and five of his finest men touched down at Skopje International Airport, North Macedonia. All six men were dressed as businessmen and were met at the airport by a representative from the Gold Hotel, a three-star establishment on the fringe of the city centre. The six men, each carrying one small suitcase, climbed into the clapped-out Datsun minivan and half an hour later they were stood in the reception of a hotel that Lazell deemed to have been awarded two stars too many.

At a little after 6.00pm, a small tour bus arrived at the front of the hotel and Lazell and his team boarded it.

Fifteen minutes later the bus came to a halt in a deserted tree-lined street just off Cevtan Dimov, one of the main arteries serving the city. Almost immediately an ambulance pulled alongside. Lazell and his men were invited to board the ambulance. Thirty minutes later the ambulance arrived at the rear of the Re-Medika Hospital on the far side of Gazi-Baba Park. Waiting at the door was Sergeant Ivan Dogani. Lazell was the first to climb out of the bus, he and Dogani embraced as if they were long-lost lovers. Lazell then introduced his five men to the Sergeant before they all entered the building.

'A hospital Ivan? '

'Yes, why not, a perfect disguise, would you not agree? '

'Well, it's probably the last place I would think of looking for you. '

'You see, the front of the hospital is operating normally, but only treats minor injuries. This part can only be accessed from the back. It is the perfect base for our operations. Our CCTV observes every person and vehicle that enters the grounds. '

'But surely your men, arriving in combat uniform would attract a lot of attention? '

'No one, not even I, are allowed to enter or leave in anything other than clothing that a medical man would wear. Hence my white coat Stephen. We have a large ambulance that reverses up to the laundry room doors. We load everything we need into the ambulance and only prepare ourselves just prior to the operation that we are going to. '

'Ingenious Ivan, ingenious. '

'On Tuesday morning, at 5.00am, the same tour bus will collect you from your hotel. You are to dress as you are now. You will be met, enroute, by the same ambulance and brought here. Only then will you learn of the rest of the plan. It truly is good to see you again Stephen. Until Tuesday then. '

The six men boarded the ambulance, they then transferred to the tour bus, which took them around the city. They took in lunch at a restaurant that overlooked the Vardar River and arrived back at the Gold Hotel mid-afternoon. To anyone observing, they would seem like any other group of visitors that were in Skopje for a conference. It just so happened that Skopje was hosting an International Trade Fair at the Matka Exhibition Centre on the shores of Lake Matka. Martin Shore had made sure that all six men had official invitations to attend, all under assumed names.

It was pitch black, cold, and raining heavily when the black transit van pulled up outside the barn where six migrants and their two guards had spent the night. It was just after 5.00am on Monday morning. Just half an hour later the six weary men were unloaded from the van and asked to join half a bus load of what Topolov presumed to be people in a similar position to him and his fellow travellers. Each of them was given overalls, boots, and high-viz jackets. At five minutes to six the bus entered, unchallenged, the Kent Port of Thames Port. At a building signed-up as being Kent Stevedoring and Port Services, they were offloaded. Around twenty men sauntered off in various directions. Topolov and his five other new arrivals were taken into the building and shown into a dimly lit room. A few minutes later a very large and imposing man entered. He was Romanian. When he spoke, the four men that Topolov and the Afghan had first set eyes upon in the canteen of the warehouse, somewhere in Kent fully understood what he was saying. Topolov also understood, however he acted as though he had no idea as to what was being said. The Afghan was totally oblivious to what was going on. Looking at Topolov, the large Romanian asked if he understood English, again the Bulgarian remained blank. All six men were led from the building and told to follow another man. After fifteen minutes of walking past endless rows of shipping containers they came to a halt on the edge of a brand-new quay. At least forty men were already at work. Topolov knew from what the fat bloke had said that they were preparing the quayside for the erection of three giant cranes, that would, one day be loading and unloading containers onto massive container ships. Trained, as he was, Topolov scanned the area. His initial thoughts were that there were at least four people on guard. They were there to simply prevent anyone from absconding. Another man, whom Topolov immediately identified as being of Albanian descent, assigned each of the new arrivals to a different crew. The leader of the crew that Topolov joined pointed at a fork truck and gestured in a way that was asking him if he could drive it. Topolov nodded, jumped up into the driver's seat, started the diesel-powered machine and drove forward, then backwards. He lifted the forks into the air and then pointed them towards the ground and then into the air, as if he were waving to someone. The crew leader clapped. Topolov had his job. The Afghan was not so lucky, his role was to be that of a labourer.

At 8.30am, on Monday the 16th of Feb, the ancient Datsun noisily ticked over on the road outside the hotel, eagerly awaiting the arrival of its six smartly dressed passengers. One hour later the visitors showed their passes to the pretty girl at the door of the hall and the visiting businessmen spent the next three hours walking the aisles of the less-than-impressive exhibition. At each stand they were asked for a business card. Only one of them had a card. It read, Ray Puxley head of procurement, British Chamber of Commerce. It showed no address, however the telephone number was bona-fide and was manned by a civil servant, sat at a desk somewhere in Whitehall.

In London, one hour after Lazell and his team had entered the exhibition hall, Jonathan Dexter entered the Romanian Embassy at Palace Green, W8. He was unaware of the fact that he was being watched by the controller of the surveillance room that had operated from Admiralty Arch for the past three years. The controller picked up a phone and informed Freddie Forsyth of the fact that Dexter had just entered the Embassy. Earlier it had been confirmed that Ilie Gheorghiu, the Romanian Foreign Secretary, and brother of the detained Nadia Oarza, had arrived at Heathrow, unannounced, the previous evening. Forsyth called Martin Shore and gave him the news.

Bob Martin, now armed with several pages of information, that he had collected from Griffin in Oban Street, had returned to his base in Vine Street, where he was met by Chief Superintendent Reginald Smith, second in command at the Serious Organised Crime Agency (SOCA). For the next three hours they discussed the information that had been gleaned from Nadia Oarza.

One hour after Dexter had been seen entering the Romanian Embassy, the Ambassador had sent a note to the British Home Secretary asking if they were aware of Nadia's disappearance and if so, did they know where she was. The reply from the Home Secretary's office was that they were unaware of anyone by the name of Nadia Oarza having ever entered the UK. Dexter left the Embassy one hour after arriving. He was tailed to Gatwick Airport and was prevented from boarding a flight to Bucharest.

As he drove around the quayside, Topolov studied the poor souls that were being forced to work in the freezing cold, wet conditions. Even at break time they were not allowed to go anywhere. Hot drinks and meagre food rations were brought to the site, and no one was allowed more than ten minutes to devour what they had been given. There was just one portable loo, and it was disgusting. When men simply needed to pee one of the guards would accompany them to the back of a container. Topolov knew how he would be making his escape later that day.

At 5.00pm, exactly one hour before work would stop for the day, Boris Topolov drove the fork truck to towards the guard that was positioned the furthest away from the others. He stopped and indicated to the man that he needed to take a leak. The two men walked past two stacks of containers before disappearing out of sight. Topolov garrotted the guard with the copper cable that he had managed to pick up, undetected, from the pile of rubble that had grown larger by the hour. Within ten minutes, the undercover Bulgarian had secured himself on top of the back axle of a loaded container truck. The truck pulled away almost immediately. Twenty minutes later the truck pulled into the Texaco garage in Watling Street, alongside the A2. Topolov dropped to the ground and crawled out on the opposite side to where the driver was filling up. As far as he knew, he was not noticed by anyone. He walked into the garage shop and spent five minutes perusing. He had no money, no cards, no phone. He was still wearing his overalls and high-viz jacket but did not look out of place. He knew exactly what he was going to do. He walked from the shop and ambled over to an empty pump. Looking towards a young lady who was filling her red fiesta, he exclaimed –

'Someone has stolen my car did you see anyone? '

'No, I did not notice. What car was it? '

'A silver BMW, 5 series. I left my keys in it as well as my wallet and phone. '

'No, sorry. I did not notice it. '

'Could I borrow your mobile, luv? '

'Yes, of course. Are you going to ring the police? '

'Yes. '

The young lady handed Topolov her phone. He did not dial 999.

'Hello, Graham. '

'Boris, where are you? Still in France? '

Topolov started to move away from the girl.

'Sorry, luv, bad signal. '

The girl, realising that she was causing a queue for the pump, walked into the shop to pay for her petrol. This gave Topolov the chance to briefly explain to Roberts what had happened and where he was.

'Wait there. I should be with you within ninety minutes. '

Topolov handed the phone to the girl when she returned from the shop and thanked her for her help.

Another motorist, who had heard the tail end of Topolov's woes, had returned from the shop with a large coffee and a sausage roll, which he handed to the stranded Bulgarian.

'Can I drop you somewhere? '

'Thank you very much. However, my friend will be here shortly, and I must wait for the police. '

Graham Roberts pulled into the garage at 7.40pm. As he thawed out on the journey back to Poplar, Topolov gave his driver a blow-by-blow account of the events of the last week. When he had finished, Roberts looked over at him and said –

'You need to write a book one day. '

Prior to arriving back at 38 Oban Street, Roberts stopped to buy fish and chips for them both.

Topolov, void of any real sleep for days, woke up at 8.45. An hour later Forsyth arrived and debriefed one of the most gifted undercover people that he was ever to meet.

Shortly after breakfast at the Gold Hotel in Skopje, Stephen Lazell and his five colleagues checked out and boarded the Datsun. They were taken to and dropped off at the airport. To all intents they were on their way back to the UK. One hour later they were picked up at the arrivals point by a Ford Galaxy SUV. The switch over to the ambulance was seamless and at 2.30pm on

Tuesday the 17th, February they pulled up outside the rear entrance of the Re-Medika Hospital. They were met by a man wearing the green uniform of a surgeon. They followed him into a room that they had not been shown on their previous visit. The room was enormous and was occupied by six men plus Sergeant Ivan Dogani.

'We meet again my friend. '

'Indeed, we do Sergeant. '

Lazell and his men looked intently around the room. They saw pile upon pile of uniforms and military hardware.

'You can try on the uniforms until you are comfortable with them. You can choose your weapons from those that you see all around you. When you are happy with what you have you should load them into the ambulance. We should be ready to leave by 4.30.'

At 4.28 the doors of the ambulance were shut. At 4.30 eleven men boarded the tour bus that was parked outside the rear door. One of the General's men took the wheel. The ambulance was driven by yet another of the General's men and one other occupied the passenger seat.

They drove for less than thirty minutes and then entered a seemingly disused airfield, situated Northwest of the City. Apart from the chopper, which was parked out of sight behind a large hanger that had its best days behind it, there was nothing else to suggest that this was once an operational airbase.

Within minutes the ambulance was unloaded and five minutes later, the Chinook Helicopter, twin rotors whirring overhead was heading towards the clouds.

'Where did you get the chopper from Ivan? '

'Spoils of war, Stephen. That is all you need to know. '

By road, it would have taken over two hours to arrive in Prizren. The helicopter ride would take only twenty minutes and would not be subjected to any security enroute. During the short journey each man put on their respective uniforms, all of which were Russian, they also checked their individual armoury. The chopper came down in a clearing in a heavily wooded area, just east of the small town of Dojnice, Kosovo. The time was 5.55pm. They were 5 km from their intended target.

Sergeant Ivan Dogani scanned the tree line, some 200 metres away. He saw one flash of light. He gestured towards Lazell. All thirteen men made their way towards the source of the light. As they approached the opening that had been cut into the woods, they could see three black vans. Each had its own driver. Silently, Dogani and four of his men climbed into the first van via the sliding side door. Lazell and three of his elite former special forces team did likewise at the second van and two men from each squad occupied the third vehicle. At precisely 6.15 in the evening, the three vans followed the outer perimeter of the woods, using an unmade road. They left the woods and turned, one by one, with a minute interval between them, onto the R115, a road that would link them directly to the bridge where the Kafe Nargile could be found. Each driver had been given separate instructions by Xherdan Vula as to where they should park.

At 6.40pm and still five minutes away from the bridge, Dogani received a text from Xherdan, it read –

'Starters have been ordered. '

This message was confirmation that General Kos was already at the Kafe Nargile.

During his debriefing with Forsyth, Topolov had given his boss the details of the three vehicles that had been used by the gang that had collected and dropped off several of the illegals. He added that five men were dropped off between the beach in Kent and what he believed to be an animal slaughterhouse. Four more trafficked men were taken from the van at a farm, not far from his own drop-off point. He informed Forsyth that the boat that took him and the others to the Isle of Grain, was from the putrid smell, without doubt a fishing vessel. In Thames Port they had all arrived at the offices of the Kent Stevedoring and Port Services. Almost all the gang members were of Romanian extract.

Armed with this information, which had been gleaned from Topolov whilst sat in the comfort of Roberts' safe house, Forsyth called Griffin and asked him to speak to one of his old mates at the Kent special ops in Ashford. Less than thirty minutes later Chief Inspector Alan White confirmed to Griffin that all three vehicles that had been seen by Topolov were registered to the same person, a certain individual by the name of Richard Weeks. White added that Weeks was a known drug Importer and was married to a Romanian, Ana Weeks, formerly known as Ana Albu. Ana had arrived in the UK as an illegal but had claimed asylum and then married Weeks. She had known associations within organised crime. Kent police had been watching them for some time but had never been able to pin anything on either of them. Griffin asked the Chief Inspector to trace the vehicles by means of recent ANPR sightings. White had been one step ahead, confirming that this had already been done. He also confirmed that none of the vehicles was kept at their registered addresses. Griffin asked his one-time colleague to assemble a team, tail the vehicles and stand by. He also mentioned that he would be requesting the participation of an outsourced chopper.

It was now 6.55pm in Prizren. The large man that always stood in the kitchen of the Café Nargile whenever General Kos was dining there, stepped out of the back door to take a cigarette. Kida Vula, Xherdans wife joined him. Kida had been flirting with the overweight Kosovan each time that he was there to watch over the rear of the building. Kida backed him up against the white-painted wall and slowly unzipped the flies of the trousers that clung tightly to his huge stomach. She then slipped her hand inside. His erection was instant. He closed his eyes in anticipation of what might follow. He was never to open them again. At the very moment that Kida clasped her tiny hand around the big man's penis he was to receive one shot to his temple. Not even Kida had heard the assassin before he fired the fatal shot. The killer, one of Sergeant Ivan Dogani's best, dressed entirely in a uniform that once was the property of the Russian military, beckoned Kida back into the kitchen. Less than two minutes later, one of the two men, that were dressed as waiters, was asked by Kos to go into the kitchen and fetch some olive oil for the Russian girl's salad. He was never to return to the table. The beautiful blonde, the current favourite of one of the world's most ruthless men was not happy with the fact that she was having to wait for her dressing. Kos despatched the second of his 'waiters' to the kitchen. From behind the inward opening door the specialist soldier closed his left hand tightly around the guard's mouth whilst slitting his throat with his right. Both dead waiters were dragged across the tiled kitchen floor and laid outside, next to the fat man.

Whilst all of this was going down inside the restaurant, two well-endowed hookers had distracted the two men whose job it was to guard the entrance to the restaurant. As they flirted, unbeknown to them, Stephen Lazell and his Sergeant, a martial arts expert had dropped from the roof of the single storey building and were now behind them. Their fixation upon the girls in front of them meant that they did not see, or hear the two men that, would, in a matter of seconds, end both of their lives.

Just as the two men hit the ground, a walkie-talkie burst into life. Sergeant Wilson picked it up, pressed the transmit button and said –

'They won't be home tonight. '

Lazell and Sergeant Mike Wilson made their way, unopposed to the entrance of the restaurant. At this moment, Lazell hit the button that connected his video camera to the screen in the secure room at 38 Oban Street. Roberts, Forsyth, Griffin and Todorov watched as events in Prizren unfolded. Simultaneously, just above them on the bridge, Ivan Dogani and his number two snuffed out the lives of the driver of the Mercedes and his armed passenger. Further along the one-way bridge a phosphagen grenade was dropped into the window of a camouflaged army jeep. Before any of the four occupants could react, an explosion ripped it apart. No one survived.

From the villa inside the vast complex that belonged to General Kos, Captain Adolf Bajram, the successor to the recently killed Captain Hook, was summoning twenty of his finest fighters. Ten minutes later they left, armed to the teeth, in one troop-carrying armoured truck.

Commander Stephen Lazell and Sergeant Mike Wilson stood at the table where General Kos and his Russian girlfriend were sat. Xherdan and Kida Vula came from the kitchen, they both nodded to Lazell as they passed him and left through the front door. Outside, only Dogani and his next in command remained. Nine other Russian uniformed men had left the scene.

The Russian girl began to scream. Mike Wilson put paid to that with one chop of his hand into her perfectly formed neck. Lazell sensed that Kos was ready for the fight but before the man that was responsible for thousands of deaths could raise the handgun up from under the table, Lazell put two bullets into him, one in each shoulder. Lazell, who had been stood directly in the General's eye line now moved behind him. 'This is for Ringo 'were to be the final words that General Horatio Kos would ever hear.

The occupants of 38 Oban Street, clapped, as one.

Lazell and Wilson left the restaurant, turned right, away from the bridge, jogged down a narrow alleyway, turned left and then right and jumped into the already open side door of the van that had brought them to the place that was now a macabre scene, containing thirteen dead bodies.

Whilst they were on their way back to the woods, to be reunited with their chopper, the troop-laden truck, under the command of Captain Bajram was hit from both sides by RPGs just as they crossed through the border gate at Morine-Vermice. The gate divided Albania and Kosovo. A yellow, dodge pickup truck containing a Mexican taxi driver was hit in the crossfire, he died instantly.

By 9.45 that evening, Sergeant Ivan Dogani, Commander Stephen Lazell, and the men under their joint command were safely resting in the large room at the rear of the hospital. The following morning six businessmen boarded a twelve-seater minibus and were taken to Skopje International Airport. After their arrival at Gatwick in the early hours of Wednesday the 18th, February 2009, the men went their own separate ways. They were never to meet, as a group again. Their operation was never publicised. General Kos and his men were scooped up by the Kosovan Secret Police and their bodies were disposed of. Their demise never became public knowledge. Soon after, the complex in the hills that divided Albania and Kosovo was razed to the ground and seven years later it would become a national park, with the barracks that once were home to thousands of mercenaries, becoming log cabins for visiting families.

At almost the same time as Lazell and his men were in the air, on their way back home, Chief Superintendent Reginald Smith, Bob Martin, Martin Shore, and Peter Slade focused their eyes on the bank of sixteen screens that made up an entire wall in the covert offices of SOCA. At street level the premises, in Sackville Street, London W1 portrayed that of an antique book dealer. Once through the door that divided the shop from the rest of the building, there was a state-of-the-art, high-tech labyrinth of rooms that housed some of the best surveillance equipment outside of GCHQ. The four men had gathered to witness the well-organised raids on the thirteen addresses that Nadia Oarza had given up, in return for her own safety.

Essex Police, under the command of Superintendent Peter Robinson, was primed and ready for entry into the four properties within their jurisdiction. Hertford Constabulary had a similar number of properties to bring down, including the prestigious address in Hadley Wood. Chief Superintendent Paul Dowse was in overall charge. In Kent, three large houses in the Chatham, Rochester and Sittingbourne area were to be raided. In charge was a Chief Inspector that would one day become infamous for being on the other side of the law. The remaining two illegal brothels were to be found in the troublesome area of Green Lanes in North London. Bob Martin's former colleague within the vice squad, and now its commander, Paul Philips was to be the first man through any of the doors that were about to be taken off their hinges.

At 5.00am on Wednesday 18th, February 2009, the individual leaders of each operation gave the order for the teams under their control to gain entry, by force, or otherwise, to the thirteen targeted addresses. In Essex, the raids were upon large properties in Clacton, Basildon, Grays, and Southend. The location of the properties in Hertford were Stevenage, Welwyn Garden City and St. Albans. Technically, Hadley Wood was within the jurisdiction of the Met, however it had been agreed that given the geography it would, on this occasion come under the control of Hertford.

As was customary in these types of police raids, a verbal request to open the door was given. In all thirteen cases no time was allowed for any of the occupants to get to the door in time to carry out the request. Eleven, fortified front doors were smashed down. Two were impenetrable and entry was gained via the weaker, back doors. By lunchtime, thirty-seven arrests had been made and 143 girls and women had been detained. There was just one failure. The team led by Chief Inspector Gary Wright of Kent police had reported that there were no occupants of the house in Sittingbourne that he and his team of three officers gained entry to. In the control room in Sackville Street, it had not gone unnoticed by Chief Superintendent Reginald Smith that the live feed from the Sittingbourne raid had gone down just prior to the knock on the door. It would take several days to interview each of the arrested men. It would take many weeks to interview the 143 sex workers that were caught up in one of the largest raids of its type ever carried out in the UK.

In the meantime, in Kent, Chief Inspector Alan White, in charge of the operation to monitor the movement of three vehicles, together with what the known criminal, Richard Weeks and his Romanian wife, Ana Albu were up to, had reported to Alan Griffin, that the collection of illegals from the Isle of

Grain and their subsequent distribution to various places in Kent was very much a daily routine. Griffin reported all of this to Freddie Forsyth. Forsyth, already preoccupied with the events of the past few days asked his number two to take control of the situation and to use Boris Topolov as his backup man. On Saturday morning, Griffin and Topolov arrived at the second-floor offices of the Kent Police Special Operations Unit. They spent the whole day with CI Alan White and Superintendent Paul Beasley from the Border Force based in Dover. Together they put together a plan that would be acted upon the following day.

At 5.00am on Sunday 22nd of February it was blowing a blizzard on the Isle of Grain. From a rooftop vantage point inside the Isle of Grain Power Station, Sergeant Harry Webb trained his powerful night vision binoculars onto a point where the river's Thames and Medway met. Through the heavy snow he could just make out a small vessel that had just arrived at the Grain Tower Battery, some 900 metres out into the estuary. Webb, a lifelong Kent resident, knew from his childhood learning that the battery, built as long ago as 1855 as a first defence against a French invasion, was nowadays privately owned. Low tide reveals a causeway that can be walked upon, enabling the battery to be reached on foot. On this morning, the tide was already in retreat and soon after he witnessed the arrival, onto the muddy beach, of six people, none of whom were wearing a life jacket. He then saw a light, swinging to and throw through the snow. The six followed the man with the torch, they headed North, towards the coastal path. A path, that Harry Webb knew like the back of his hand. The Sergeant radioed to CI Alan White –

'They are here, Guv. Six have landed. Two more are with them. '

Webb climbed down from his vantage point and headed towards his car, parked just inside the power station. He already knew the route that the migrants would be taking.

Sticking closely behind the two men that had met them on the beach, and with the belief that they would all soon be given food, drink, warm clothing and later, a place to live with all the benefits that the UK so generously hands out to its uninvited guests, the six migrants willingly followed behind. After a mile or so of marching along the shoreline, now being covered by snow, they turned left, taking a narrow pathway that in turn led onto a one-track, tarmac road. A few minutes later they boarded a dark blue Citroen van through its back doors. The van had been ready and waiting in the car park of Grain Beach. The Citroen, with its eight passengers onboard, pulled out of the car park and onto the B2001, a road that would take them to the BP refinery and onto the A228. Topolov watched intently on the screen fixed to a wall in the special ops room in Ashford. The pictures were beamed from a helicopter that had been loaned to the police by a well-known communications company.

Thankfully the weather improved the further inland the van drove. At the roundabout, Harry Webb, driving his wife's twelve-year-old Fiesta, dropped out. An unmarked Range Rover, containing four armed police took over the pursuit, albeit a few vehicles back from the target. The van turned onto the A289 which would lead it onto the M2, heading South. At the junction with the A229 it turned off and was then enroute to the M20. At this point, CI Alan White instructed three, armed and marked units to stand by at the service station where the A229 meets the M20. Soon after, the target vehicle took the slip road from the M20 onto the A20, heading towards Lenham. The abattoir at Lenham was already being watched, however much to everyone's surprise the van continued along the A20, passing the abattoir. Fifteen minutes later, at Charing, it turned right onto an unmarked lane, passed under a railway arch, and came to a halt outside the padlocked gates of another abattoir. A few minutes later, a hunch-backed man came out of one of the many portacabins that were dotted around the premises and unlocked the gates. The van drove inside. Three of the migrants were taken from the van and led away. Alan White radioed for two of the vehicles that were at Lenham to move down the A20 and take up a position close by. The pictures from the helicopter showed the van leaving Charing and heading back along the A20 towards the M20. At a distance, the Range Rover followed. Turning off the M20, the van took the A249 towards Sittingbourne, where it turned left, arriving at a large farm on the outskirts of Bobbing. White had called forward two more units and as the three remaining migrants were offloaded, White calmly spoke the words –

'Go, go, go. '

Simultaneously, police raids took place at Sheerness Docks, Thames Port, two Abattoirs, the farm just outside Sittingbourne and the home address of Richard Weeks and his wife Ana. Griffin and Todorov were only able to watch the events from the farm as the chopper, was directly over that property.

A total of 17, armed police units, 22 Border Force officers, 5 police dogs and a helicopter took place in the raid. 15 people were arrested and detained. 9 were cautioned, pending further enquiries. 87 illegals, none of whom had any identifying paperwork, were taken to a holding centre near Folkestone for processing. At the home of Mr and Mrs Weeks over one million pounds in cash, as well as 30 kgs of class A drugs were found.

A meeting took place on the 25th & 26th of February at Marsham Street. In attendance were, Martin Shore, on behalf of the Foreign Secretary, Peter Slade, Alan Griffin, Boris Topolov, Freddie Forsyth, Diane Myers, Bob Martin, and Chief Superintendent Reginald Smith (SOCA).

Martin Shore addressed the meeting –

'Gentlemen, I am honoured to be among you. Your combined efforts, over many months and years have resulted in the most successful result that has ever been achieved by those that strive to eradicate the trafficking and illegal entry into our country of migrants from all parts of the globe. The Foreign Secretary has asked me to state that whilst we sympathise with those people that attempt to gain entry to the UK without going through the legal channels, we have a duty to our citizens to ensure that wherever possible we will hunt down and deal with the criminals that choose to profit from the plight of those that give up their place of birth and considerable amounts of money to live amongst us. '

As you are all aware, last week we sanctioned three operations, one of which was outside our own jurisdiction, nonetheless, we solved a particular problem, with the help of some of our friends in the Balkans. A certain General, his immediate chain of command and their entire operation was taken down. Our own man, Commander Stephen Lazell, who unfortunately could not be here today, led a team that joined forces with Sergeant Ivan Dogani and inflicted irreparable harm upon the people responsible for trafficking tens of thousands of migrants to the UK and mainland Europe. For this, Commander Lazell and Sergeant Wilson are to be commended. It is with sadness however, that last night I received word from my counterpart in Macedonia, that Sergeant Ivan Dogani and five of his men were killed by an IED whilst enroute to another confrontation in Albania. We have sent condolences to his family. I should also mention, and thank, the husband-and-wife team that, without whose help the operation could not have gone ahead. Again, through the proper channels our sincere thanks have been offered.

In an operation first identified by Bob Martin, spearheaded by Chief Superintendent Reginald Smith and in conjunction with the police forces of Essex, Hertfordshire, Kent and the Met several properties were raided, 37 arrests were made, with more expected to follow. 143 girls, put to work as sex slaves by those we have arrested were detained awaiting formal identification. No decisions can be made in respect of their futures until we know who they are and from where they originated.

Nadia Oarza, a Romanian, with no legal right to be in the UK, has been identified as the ringleader and she is currently being detained for her own safety. She will face trial at some time in the future. Access to thirteen properties was gained, all of which are owned in the name of Nadia Oarza. Over six million pounds were recovered from the various addresses. The CPS are, at this moment drawing up documents, under the proceeds of crime laws, to seize the properties, money and all other assets that are in the name of Ms. Oarza and anyone else that has been detained as a direct result of this operation. It is thought that the Romanian Foreign Secretary, Oarza's brother, is heavily involved in the trafficking business. Unfortunately, there is not much we can do to implicate him. Orza's husband is regarded to be Romania's number one gangster. He resides in Mexico and is currently, out of our reach. Another unfortunate part of this operation is that it has identified one of our own as being involved. Inspector Gary Wright is known to have tipped off the occupants of a house in Sittingbourne prior to it being raided by him and three other officers. One of those officers has come clean and revealed that all four of them were taking money for turning a blind eye. Whilst we have a Sergeant and two Constables in custody, Wright is thought to have fled to Tenerife. Steps are being taken for him to be returned.

The third operation that I am extremely happy to report upon, took place last Sunday. In a joint effort undertaken by Kent Police, led by Chief Inspector Alan White, and with the participation of the UK Border Force, headed by Superintendent Paul Beasley and some of the people present here, a sizeable trafficking operation was brought to its knees. 15 were arrested and have subsequently been charged. 87 migrants, none of whom have had the opportunity to claim asylum are being held. Whilst we believe this to have been a good result, it is only the tip of the iceberg. We have eyes on 47 similar trafficking groups, and I shall be pushing both the Foreign and Home Secretaries to put a lot more resources into bringing them down.

In the months that followed that monumental week, accolades and commendations flowed like beer from a tap.

Peter Slade, still only 45 years of age, with money to burn, rented out his house in Upminster to his wife's nephew, Alan Griffin and took the job offered to him previously. They relocated to Dubai.

Freddie Forsyth, now 50, retired as number one in the specialist Border Force department. He and his wife emigrated to Portugal.

Alan Griffin, aged just 29, took over Forsyth's role in June. The position of Home Secretary had changed hands and Griffin had been convinced that the new incumbent, unlike the previous one, was hell-bent on cleaning up the trafficking problem.

Bob Martin (40) was headhunted by Chief Superintendent Reginal Smith and agreed to join SOCA as the controller of their drug and trafficking division.

Boris Topolov, at 36, was transferred to the British Embassy in Sofia. He would be Griffin's 'eyes and ears' in the Balkans, universally accepted as being the hub for all European migrants.

Diane Myers, still only 43, was instilled as Griffin's number 2. She would be responsible for liaising with the private secretaries of the Foreign and Home office.

Graham Roberts (45) would still be in the loop, when required.

Fergus Hamilton (44) initially wanted to quit; however, Griffin convinced him to stay and take over Myers statistical role. He agreed, stating that it was his desire to retire in six years' time, when he reached 50.

Colin Millburn, now 54, was lured out of retirement and took a position in Bucharest. He was to operate from the British Embassy and would 'babysit' Topolov.

For his part in the highly successful events of that week in February 09, Superintendent Peter Robinson of Essex Police was promoted to Chief Superintendent. Paul Philips, commander of the vice squad received a commendation. Chief Superintendent Paul Dowse of Hertford Police took early retirement. Sergeant Harry Webb, who had risked his life when undertaking the initial surveillance of the trafficking gang, was promoted to Inspector.

Chief Inspector Alan White was promoted to the rank of Superintendent and was asked to set up a small unit in Dover. He is to report directly to Alan Griffin.

Jonathan Dexter was sent down for 15 years under the official secrets act.

Terry Wheeler was removed from his job at the Home Office and was last seen frequenting the gay bars in and around Patpong 3, in Bangkok.

Maia Radakanu (26) the Romanian girl that had befriended Bob Martin and subsequently told him everything about the house in Hadley Wood and its controller, Nadia Oarza, was relocated to a safe house in Durham.

Nadia Oarza (32) despite believing that she would be given preferential treatment for spilling the beans on the whole sordid operation, got 21 years for a whole host of charges. After her sentence had been served, she would be returned to Romania.

Richard Weeks received a life sentence for drug, trafficking, extortion, and money laundering charges. The judge told him that he would serve a minimum of 25 years.

Ana Weeks was given 12 years for aiding and abetting her husband, and an additional five for living off immoral earnings.

The French Police, having been tipped off, tracked down the man in the woods, Anton Balan. They found him, covered over with leaves. His throat had been cut.

Printed in Great Britain
by Amazon

22359310R00270